SAS

STORIES OF HEROES VII

PETER CAVE
PETER CORRIGAN
SHAUN CLARKE

BLITZ EDITIONS

This edition published in 1996

Published by Blitz Editions
an imprint of Bookmart Limited
Registered Number 2372865
Trading at Bookmart Limited
Desford Road, Enderby
Leicester, LE9 5AD

ISBN 1 85605356 3

Typeset by Hewer Text Composition Services, Edinburgh
Printed in Great Britain by Cox and Wyman Limited, Reading

SOLDIER T: SAS

WAR ON THE STREETS

Peter Cave

1

Lieutenant-Colonel Barney Davies, 22 SAS Training Wing, cruised slowly down the Strand and the Mall, then turned into Horse Guards Road. It was not the first time he had been summoned to a Downing Street conference, and he'd learned a few of the wrinkles over the years. Finding a parking space was the first trick. You had to know where to look.

Finding his objective, he slid the BMW into a parking bay, climbed out and loaded the meter to its maximum. These things had a nasty habit of stretching out for much longer than anticipated. What might start as a preliminary briefing session could well develop into a protracted discussion, or even a full-scale planning operation. Failing to take precautions could prove expensive.

He turned away from the parking meter and, glancing up to where he knew the nearest security video camera was hidden, treated it to a lingering smile. Every little helped. If they knew he was coming it might just cut down the number of security checks he'd have to be stopped for. Picking his way between the buildings, he ducked into the little labyrinth of covered walkways which would bring him to the back of Downing Street and ultimately to the rear security entrance of Number 10.

In fact Davies was stopped only twice, although he suspected he had identified at least two other plain-clothes men, who had allowed him to pass unchallenged. He preferred to assume that this was due to his face having become familiar, rather than security becoming sloppy. There could be no let-up in London's fight against terrorism.

The final checkpoint, however, was very thorough. Davies waited patiently as the doorman checked his security pass, radioed in his details and paused to await clearance. Finally, he was inside the building and climbing the stairs to Conference Room B.

He pushed open the panelled double doors and stepped into the room, casting his eyes about for any familiar faces. It was always a psychological advantage to re-establish any personal links, however tenuous, Davies had always found. It gave you that little extra clout, should you find yourself out on a limb.

Of the five people already in the room, Davies recognized only two: Michael Wynne-Tilsley, one of the top-echelon parliamentary secretaries, and David Grieves from the 'green slime'. Davies decided not to bother with Wynne-Tilsley, other than to give him a brief nod. On the single occasion he had had any dealings with the man before, Davies had found him to be a close-lipped, somewhat arrogant little bastard, and far too protective of his job to give out any useful information. He would be better off having a preliminary word with Grieves. The man might be MI6, but he would probably respect Davies's grade five security clearance enough to give him at least an inkling of what the meeting was about. And forewarned was forearmed. Davies hated going into things blinkered, let alone blind.

He sauntered over to the man, smiling and holding out his hand. 'David, how are you?'

Grieves accepted the proffered hand a trifle warily. 'Don't even ask,' he warned, though there was the ghost of a smile on his lips.

Davies grinned sheepishly. 'Come on, David, you're here and I'm here, so somebody's got to be thinking of a joint operation.'

Grieves conceded the point with a vague shrug.

Davies pushed his tactical advantage. 'So where in this benighted little world are we going to get our feet wet now?' he asked. 'First guess: central Africa.'

Grieves smiled. 'Wrong,' he said curtly. 'A bit closer to home and that's all I'm telling you until the Home Secretary opens the briefing.'

It was scant information, but it was enough to tell Davies two things. First, if the Home Secretary rather than the Foreign Secretary was involved, then it was a sure bet that it was a purely internal matter. Second, Grieves's guardedness suggested that he had been called to another one of those 'This Meeting Never Happened' meetings. It was useful information to have. Briefings conducted on a strictly need-to-know basis were invariably the stickiest.

Wisely, Davies decided not to press the military intelligence man any further. He looked around the room, trying to guess at the identities of the other three occupants. The youngest man looked pretty bland and faceless, and Davies took him to be a minor civil servant of some kind. The other two were a different breed. Both in their late forties or early fifties, they had the unmistakable stamp of those used to exercising authority. The senior of the pair was tantalizingly familiar. Davies felt sure that he ought to recognize the man, quite possibly from exposure in the media. But for the moment, it just would not come.

Grieves followed the direction of his gaze. 'I take it you recognize McMillan,' he muttered.

It clicked, finally. Alistair McMillan, Commissioner, Metropolitan Police. Davies must have seen the man's picture a dozen times over the past few years. Seeing him out of uniform had thrown him off track.

'And his colleague?' he asked.

'Commander John Franks, Drugs Squad,' Grieves volunteered. 'Now you know almost as much as I do.'

'But not for much longer, I hope,' Davies observed. The Home Secretary had just entered the conference room, flanked by two more parliamentary secretaries. Davies recognized Adrian Bendle from the Foreign Office, and wondered what his presence signified.

The Home Secretary wasted little time. He moved to the octagonal walnut conference table, laying down his papers, and nodding around the room in general greeting. 'Well, gentlemen, shall we get down to business?' he suggested as soon as he was seated. He glanced over at Wynne-Tilsley as everyone took their seats. 'Perhaps you'd like to make the formal introductions and we can get started.'

Introductions over, the Home Secretary looked at them all gravely. 'I suppose I don't really need to remind you that this meeting is strictly confidential and unofficial?'

Davies smiled to himself, momentarily. Just as he had suspected, it was one of those. That accounted for the absence of an official recorder in the room. Pulling his face straight again, he joined in the general nods of assent around the table.

'Good,' the Home Secretary said, and nodded with satisfaction. He glanced aside at the young parliamentary secretary who had accompanied him. 'Perhaps if you could close the curtains, we can take a look at what we're up against.'

The young man rose, crossed the conference room and pulled the thick velvet curtains. Pressing a remote-control panel he held in his hand, he switched on the large-screen video monitor in the far corner of the room.

As the screen flickered into life, the Home Secretary continued. 'Most of you will probably have seen most of these items on the news over the past few months. However, it will be useful to view them all again in context, so that we can all see the exact nature of the enemy.'

He fell silent as the first of a series of European news reports began.

Davies recognized the first one at once. It was the abduction of the Italian wine millionaire Salvo Frescatini in Milan, some three months previously. The report, cobbled together from amateur video footage, police reconstructions and television news clips, covered the kidnapping, in broad daylight, the subsequent ransom demands of the abductors and the final shoot-out when the Italian police tracked the gang down. It was a bloody encounter which had left eight police officers dead and a score of innocent bystanders wounded. The film ended with a shot of the hostage as the police had finally found him – his trussed body cut to shreds by over two dozen 9mm armour-piercing slugs from Franchi sub-machine-guns. The kidnappers had been armed like a combat assault team, and were both remarkably professional in their methods and utterly ruthless.

The sequence ended, the venue switching to Germany and more scenes of murderous violence. Angry right-wing mobs razing the hostels of immigrant workers to the ground, desecrated Jewish cemeteries and clips of half a dozen racist murders.

A student riot at the Sorbonne in Paris came next, with graphic images of French riot police lying in pools of their own blood after protest placards had given way to clubs, machetes and handguns.

The screen suddenly went blank. Daylight flooded into the conference room once more as the curtains were drawn back. The Home Secretary studied everyone at the table for a few seconds.

'France . . . Italy . . . Germany,' he muttered finally. 'The whole of Europe seems to be suddenly exploding into extremes of violence. Our fears, gentlemen, are that it may be about to happen here.'

There was a long, somewhat shocked silence in the room, finally broken by Adrian Bendle. 'Perhaps I could take up the story from here, Home Secretary?' the Foreign Office man suggested.

The Home Secretary agreed with a curt nod, sitting

back in his chair. Bendle took centre stage, standing and leaning over the table.

'As you're probably aware, gentlemen, we now work in fairly close co-operation with most of the EC authorities,' he announced. 'Quite apart from our strengthened links with Interpol, we also liaise with government departments, undercover operations and security organizations. Through these and other channels, we have pieced together some highly unpleasant conclusions over the past few months.' He paused for a while, taking a breath. 'Now the violent scenes you have just witnessed would appear, at face value, to be isolated incidents, in different countries and for different reasons – but not, apparently, connected. Unfortunately, there *is* a connection, and it is disquieting, to say the least.' There was another, much longer pause before Bendle took up the story again.

'In every single one of the preceding incidents, there is a common factor,' he went on. 'In those few cases where the authorities were able to arrest survivors – but more commonly from post-mortems carried out on the corpses – all the participants in these violent clashes were found to have high concentrations of a new drug in their systems. It is our belief, and one echoed by our European counterparts, that this is highly significant.'

Commissioner McMillan interrupted. 'When you say a *new* drug, what exactly are we talking about?'

Bendle glanced over at Grieves. 'Perhaps you're better briefed to explain to the commissioner,' he suggested.

Grieves climbed to his feet. 'What we appear to be

dealing with here is a synthetic "designer" drug of a type previously unknown to us,' he explained. 'Whilst it is similar in many ways to the currently popular Ecstasy, it also seems to incorporate some of the characteristics, and the effects, of certain of the opiate narcotics and some hallucinogens. A deliberately created chemical cocktail, in fact, which is tailor-made and targeted at the youth market. Initial tests suggest that it is cheap and fairly simple to manufacture in massive quantities, and its limited distribution thus far could only be a sampling operation. If our theories are correct, this stuff could be due to literally flood on to the streets of Europe – and this country is unlikely to prove an exception.'

'And the connection with extremes of violence?' Commander Franks put in.

'At present, circumstantial,' Grieves admitted. 'But from what we know already, one of the main effects of this drug is to make the user feel invulnerable, free from all normal moral restraints and totally unafraid of the consequences of illegal or immoral action. Whether it actually raises natural aggression levels, we're not sure, because we're still conducting tests. But what our boffins say quite categorically is that the use of this drug most definitely gives the user an *excuse* for violence – and for a lot of these young thugs today, that's all they need.'

The Home Secretary took over again. 'There are other, and equally disquieting factors,' he pointed out. 'Not the least of which is the appalling growth of radical right-wing movements and factions which seem to be popping up all over Europe at the moment.

Many, if not all, of the incidents you have just seen would appear to be inspired by such ethology. The obvious conclusion is both inescapable and terrifying.' He broke off, glancing back to Grieves again. 'Perhaps you could explain our current thinking on this, Mr Grieves.'

Grieves nodded. 'In everything we have seen so far, two particularly alarming factors stand out. One is the degree of organization involved, and the second is the degree and sophistication of the weaponry these people are getting hold of. We're not talking about kids with Stanley knives and the odd handgun here, gentlemen. We're dealing with machine-pistols, sub-machine-guns, pump-action shotguns – even grenades.'

Commissioner McMillan interrupted. He sounded dubious. 'You make it sound as though we're dealing with terrorists, not tearaways.'

Grieves's face was set and grim as he responded. 'That may well be the case, sir,' he said flatly. 'We have reasonable grounds for suspecting that a new type of terrorist organization is building in Europe, perhaps loosely allied to the radical right. If we're right, they are creating a structure of small, highly mobile and active cells which may or may not have a single overriding control organization at this time.'

Commissioner McMillan was silently thoughtful for a few moments, digesting this information and its implications. Finally he sighed deeply. 'So what you're telling us, in effect, is that a unified structure could come into being at any time? That we face the possibility of an entirely new terrorist force on the rampage in our towns and cities?'

The Home Secretary took it up from there. 'That is *exactly* what we fear,' he said sombrely. 'And we believe that conventional police forces may be totally inadequate and ill-prepared to deal with such a threat.' He paused, eyeing everyone around the table in turn. 'Which is why I invited Lieutenant-Colonel Davies of the SAS to this briefing today,' he added, quietly.

There was a stunned silence as the implications of this statement sank in. Of the group, no one was more surprised than Barney Davies, but it was he who found his voice first.

'Excuse me, Home Secretary, but are you saying you want to put the SAS out there on the streets? In our own towns and cities?' he asked somewhat incredulously.

The man gave a faint shrug. 'We did it in Belfast, when it became necessary,' he pointed out. He looked at Davies with a faint smile. 'And it's not as if your chaps were *complete* strangers to urban operations.'

Davies conceded the point, but with reservations. 'With respect, sir, an embassy siege is one thing. Putting a full anti-terrorist unit into day-to-day operation is quite another.' He paused briefly. 'I assume that's the sort of thing you had in mind?'

The Home Secretary shrugged again. 'Yes and no,' he muttered, rather evasively. 'Although personally I had seen it more in terms of a collaboration between the SAS and the conventional police forces. A joint operation, as it were.'

Davies held back, thinking about his response. Finally he looked directly at the Home Secretary, shaking his head doubtfully. 'Again with respect, sir, but you are aware of the rules. The SAS does not work with civilians.'

The Home Secretary met his eyes with a cool, even gaze. 'I think you're rather stretching a point there, Lieutenant-Colonel Davies. I would hardly call the police civilians.' He thought for a second, digging for further ammunition. 'Besides, the SAS Training Wing works with various types of civil as well as military groups all over the world, so why not on home ground? Think of it more in those terms if it makes you feel better. A training exercise, helping to create a new counter-terrorist force.'

The man was on dicey ground, and he knew it, Davies thought. Nevertheless, his own position was not exactly crystal-clear, either. They were both dealing with a very grey area indeed. For the moment, he decided to play along with things as they stood.

'And how would the police feel about such a combined operation?' he asked.

McMillan spoke up. 'We have discussed similar ideas in principle, in the past, of course. But obviously, this has come as just as much of a surprise to me as it has to you.' He paused for thought. 'But at this moment, my gut feeling is that we could probably work something out.'

The Home Secretary rose to his feet. He looked rather relieved, Davies thought. 'Well, gentlemen, I'll leave you all to think it through and come up with some concrete proposals,' he said, collecting up his papers from the table.

'Just one more thing, Home Secretary,' Davies called out, unwilling to let the man escape quite so easily. 'We'll have full approval from the relevant departments on this one, I take it?'

The man smiled cannily. He was not going to be tempted to stick his head directly into the noose. 'Grudging approval, yes,' he conceded. 'But of course you won't be able to count on anyone with any real authority to bail you out if you come unstuck.'

It was more or less what Davies had expected. He returned the knowing smile. 'So we're on our own,' he said. It was a statement, not a question.

'Aren't you always?' the Home Secretary shot back.

It wasn't a question that Davies had any answer for. He was silent as the politician left the conference room, followed by his aides. There was only himself, Commissioner McMillan, Commander Franks and David Grieves left around the table. No one said anything for a long time.

Finally, Franks cleared his throat. 'Well, it would seem to me that the first thing you are going to need is a good, straight cop who knows the drug scene at street level,' he said thoughtfully. 'No disrespect intended, but it really is foreign territory out there.'

It made sense, Davies thought, taking no offence. Franks was right – the theatre of operations would be something completely new and unfamiliar to his men, and they didn't have any maps. They would need a guide.

'Someone with a bit of initiative, who can think for himself,' Davies insisted. 'I don't want some order-taker.'

Franks nodded understandingly. 'I'll find you such a man,' he promised.

2

The blue Porsche screamed round the corner into the narrow mews entrance at a dangerous angle, clipping the kerb with a squeal of tortured rubber and wrenching the rear wheel up on to the narrow pavement. Bouncing back down on to the cobbled street, the car slewed erratically a couple of times before straightening up and slowing down, finally coming to a halt outside one of the terraced cottages. Like everything else in this part of south-west London, the house was small but expensive.

Glynis Jefferson glanced sideways out of the car window, looking at the number on the house to check the address. There was no real need. The sounds of rave music and general merriment issuing from the house showed that the party was still in full swing, even at three-thirty in the morning. Relief showed on the girl's strained face as she opened the car door and stepped out.

Her knees felt weak, buckling under her. She leaned against the side of the car for support, trying to control the violent shudders which shook her whole body in irregular and involuntary spasms. It was a warm night, yet she was shivering. Her young face, though undeniably attractive, was taut and lined with tension, ageing her beyond her years. Her eyes were wide, apparently vacant, yet betraying some inner disturbance, like a helpless animal in pain.

She pulled herself together with an effort and dragged herself up the three stone steps to the front of the mews cottage. She rang the bell, fidgeting impatiently as she waited for someone to answer it.

The door was finally opened in a blast of sound by a young man in his early thirties. Glynis did not recognize him; nor did it matter. Names were not important to her.

Nigel Moxley-Farrer lolled against the door jamb, appraising the young blonde on his doorstep. His eyes were glassy, the pupils dilated. He was either drunk, or stoned – probably both. An inane, vacant grin on his face showed that he approved of his attractive young vistor.

'Well hello, darling. Come to join the bash? You're too gorgeous to need an invitation. Just come on in.' He lurched backwards, inviting her into the house.

Glynis shook her head. 'I'm not partying. I'm just looking for Charlie.'

Despite his befuddled brain, Nigel's face was instantly suspicious. His eyes narrowed. 'Charlie? Charlie who?'

Glynis shuddered again. Her voice was edgy and irritable. 'Aw, come on, man. Don't piss me about.' She paused briefly. 'Look, I was at Annabel's tonight. A guy called David told me I could score here tonight.'

So it was out in the open; no need for any further pretence. They both knew exactly what Charlie she was looking for. C for Charlie – the code word for cocaine among the Sloane Ranger set.

Still grinning, Nigel shook his head. 'You're too

late, darling. Charlie's been and gone.' He spread his hands in an expansive gesture, giggling stupidly. 'Hey, can't you tell?'

Another violent spasm racked Glynis's body. A look of despair crept over her face. 'Oh, Jesus!' she groaned. She looked up at Nigel again, her eyes pleading. 'Come on, somebody's got to be still holding, surely? The money's no problem, OK?'

Nigel shook his head again. 'Not a single snort left in the place. We all did our thing a couple of hours ago.' He reached out, grasping her by the arm. 'But don't let that bother your pretty head, darling. We've still got plenty of booze left. Why don't you just come in and get chateaued instead?'

Glynis shook free of his grip with a sudden, violent jerk. The sheer intensity of her reaction wiped the grin from Nigel's face for a second. He stared down at her more carefully, noting the perspiration starting to show through her make-up, the nervous twitching of little muscles in her face.

'It's really that bad, huh?'

Glynis nodded dumbly. She looked totally dejected and pathetic. Nigel looked at her dubiously for a while, finally coming to some sort of a decision.

'Look, I'll tell you what I'll do. Got a pen and paper?'

Glynis nodded again, this time with a flash of hope on her face. She rummaged in her handbag and fished out a ballpoint pen and an old clothing store receipt.

Nigel took them from her trembling fingers. Holding the scrap of paper against the door-frame, he began to scribble.

'Look, this guy is strictly down-market, and he charges way over the odds on street prices . . . but he can usually come across, know what I mean?'

The girl nodded gratefully. 'Yeah. And thanks.'

She turned to go back down the steps. Nigel called after her. 'Hey, look, don't forget to tell him Nigel M sent you. It puts me in line for a favour, know what I mean?'

Glynis didn't answer. Nigel remained in the doorway for a few moments, watching her as she climbed into the Porsche and backed hurriedly out of the narrow street. A slim female hand descended on his shoulder, and a pair of red lips which smelled strongly of gin nuzzled his ear.

'Hey, come on, Nigel. You're missing the party.'

Nigel turned away from the door, finally.

'Who was it – gatecrashers?' his companion asked.

Nigel shook his head. 'No, just some junkie bird chasing Charlie. I sent her to Greek Tony.'

His girlfriend pulled an expression of distaste. 'Ugh, that slimeball? She must have been pretty desperate.'

Nigel nodded. 'Yes, I think she was,' he muttered.

Detective Sergeant Paul Carney sat at his desk, sifting through a growing pile of paperwork. Several empty plastic cups from the coffee machine and an ashtray filled with cigarette stubs testified to a long, all-night session. There was a light tap on his office door, and Detective Chief Inspector Manners let himself in without waiting for an invitation. There was a faintly chiding look on his face as he confronted Carney.

'Didn't see your name on the night-duty roster, Paul,' he observed pointedly.

Carney shrugged. 'Just catching up on some more of this fucking paperwork, when I ought to be out there on the streets. Bringing this week's little tally up to date.'

Manners clucked his teeth sympathetically. 'Bad, huh?'

Carney let out a short, bitter laugh. 'You tell me how bad is bad. In the last four days we've snatched five and a half kilos of coke at Heathrow alone. That means a minimum of twenty-five kilos got through. This morning we pulled a stiff off an Air India flight. Two hundred grand's worth of pure heroin in his guts, packed in condoms. One of 'em burst during the flight. What you might call an instant high.'

'Jeezus, I thought those things were supposed to *stop* accidents,' Manners said.

'Not funny, Harry,' Carney muttered. 'Christ, we're under fucking siege here. Provincial airports, the ferries, commercial shipping, private boats and planes, bloody amateurs bringing back ten kilos of hash from their Club 18–30 holidays on Corfu. And we haven't got a fucking clue yet what's going to come flooding in through the Channel Tunnel. There's shit coming at us from all sides, Harry – and we're being buried under it.'

'We . . . or you, Paul?' Manners asked gently.

Carney shrugged. 'Does it matter? Caring goes with the job.'

Manners conceded the point – with reservations. 'Caring, maybe. Getting too personally involved, no.

You're getting in too deep, Paul. Maybe it's time to think about a transfer out of drugs division for a while.'

Carney blew a fuse. 'Dammit, Harry, I don't want a bloody transfer. What I want is to get this job *done*. I want every dealer, every distributor, every small-time school-gate pusher out of business, off the streets, and in the nick.'

'That isn't going to happen, and you know it.'

Carney nodded his head resignedly. 'Yeah. So meanwhile I'm supposed to just tot up the casualties without getting uptight – is that it?' He paused, calming down a little. 'I suppose you know we've got a batch of contaminated smack out on the streets in the SW area?'

Manners shook his head. 'No, I didn't,' he admitted. 'How bad is it?'

'Bad bad,' Carney muttered. 'Two kids dead already and one more in a coma on a life-support system. That's just the tip of the iceberg. We don't know yet how much more of the stuff is out there, or how widely it's already been distributed. And on top of that, there's this new synthetic shit which has started to come in from Europe. Early reports say that it's really bad medicine.'

Manners smiled sympathetically. 'OK, Paul, I'll get you what extra help I can,' he promised. 'Meanwhile, you go home and get some sleep, eh?'

Carney grinned cynically. 'We don't need help, my friend – we need a bloody army. That's a fucking war out there on the streets.'

'Yeah,' Manners said, and shrugged. There was

nothing he could say or do which would make the slightest amount of difference. He turned back towards the door.

'Oh, by the way,' Carney called after him. 'You think I get too personally involved. You want to know why?'

Manners paused, his hand on the door-knob.

'The kid on the life-support system,' Carney went on. 'His name's Keith. He's fifteen. His parents live in my street.'

Glynis Jefferson studied the row of sordid-looking tenements through the windscreen of the Porsche with a distinct feeling of unease. This was definitely *not* Sloane Ranger country. This was ghettoland. Under normal circumstances, she would have jammed the car into gear and driven away as fast as she could. But tonight she was not in control; all normal considerations were driven out of her mind by her desperate craving. She checked the address on the slip of paper, identifying the block in question. Glancing nervously about her, she stepped out of the car and walked up to the front door. Rows of bells and small cards identified the building as divided into numerous bedsitters and flatlets.

The door was slightly ajar. Cautiously, Glynis pushed it open, wrinkling her nose in disgust at the stench of filth and squalor which wafted out. She stepped gingerly over the threshold into a dark, dingy and filthy hallway, littered with junk mail and other debris. For a moment her instincts screamed out at her to turn back, run away. But then the shudders shook her body again, a pain like a twisting knife shrieked through her guts. She walked down the hallway past a row of grimy doors, most with bars or metal grilles over the glazed top half.

She stopped at the fifth one and knocked urgently. There was a long pause before the door opened a few inches and a pair of shifty eyes inspected her through the crack. Obviously they liked what they saw. The door opened fully to reveal Tony Sofrides, grubby and unshaven, with dark, oiled hair hanging down to his shoulders in greasy, matted strands. He was wearing only a soiled T-shirt and a pair of equally filthy underpants. His eyes ran up and down Glynis's body as though she were a prime carcass hanging in a meat warehouse.

'Well, you're a bit out of your patch, aren't you, princess?' he drawled, noting her expensive night-club apparel. 'What's the matter? Lost our way to the Hunt Ball, have we?'

Glynis thrust the piece of paper under his nose. 'Nigel M sent me. I need to score.'

Sofrides snatched the paper out of her hand, scanning it with suspicious, furtive eyes. 'Did he now? Presumptuous little bastard, ain't he? So what did he tell you?'

'That you were a reliable supplier. I need Charlie. You holding?'

Sofrides leered at her, revealing a row of yellowed teeth. 'I'm always holding, baby,' he boasted. 'Regular little mister candy-man to those who know how to treat me right.' He stepped back from the door, inviting her to enter. 'Come on in, sweetheart.'

Glynis hesitated, despite her urgent craving.

Sofrides shrugged. 'Look, you wanna score or not? I don't do business in hallways and I ain't got time to fart about. Now you either come in or you fuck off. Your choice.'

Glynis made her choice. Reluctantly she stepped into the sordid bedsit, glancing around at the filth and mess in disgust as Sofrides closed the door behind her.

Catching the look on her face, Sofrides glared at her. 'No, darling, it ain't your daddy's country house in Essex, but it's where I live. So don't turn your pretty little nose up, OK?'

Glynis rummaged in her handbag and pulled out a thin wad of notes. 'Look, can we get this over with? I just want a couple of hits to tide me over, but I'll take more if you want to make a bigger deal.'

Sofrides glanced at the money contemptuously, returning his eyes to her body. 'Actually, darling, I'm not exactly strapped for cash right now,' he said. He paused, jerking his head over to the grimy, unmade bed in the corner of the room. 'But I am a little short on company, if you know what I mean. Wanna deal?'

Glynis shuddered – but this time it was mental revulsion rather than the desperate need of her drug-addicted body. 'No thanks,' she spat out, turning towards the door.

Sofrides jumped across the room, cutting off her retreat. 'Wise up, kid,' he said, grinning wickedly. 'It's four in the morning and I'm your last chance. Do you really think you can hold out for much longer?' He raised his hand, extending one finger and running it slowly across her lips, down her throat and into the cleavage of her breasts. 'Now, are we going to play or not?'

3

The sex was quick, violent and sordid. Afterwards Glynis felt dirty all over, and it wasn't just the accumulated sweat and grime clinging to the grey bedsheets. Thankful that it was over, at least, she dressed hurriedly as Sofrides lay back on his pillow, grinning with post-coital pleasure.

Glynis glared at him, undisguised loathing in her eyes. 'Right, you've been paid in full. Now what about my score?'

Sofrides leered at her. 'I got bad news for you, princess. Apart from having me tonight, you're right out of luck. Ain't a snort of coke in the place.'

It took several seconds for the words to sink into Glynis's mind. When it finally did, her first reactions were of shock and sheer panic, quickly followed by a wave of pure hatred. 'You lousy little bastard,' she screamed. 'You told me you were holding.'

She hurled herself across the room in a blaze of fury, her arms flailing wildly. Sofrides uncoiled from the bed like a snake, warding off the attack by grasping her by the wrist and twisting her arm savagely. Drawing back his free hand, he smashed her across one side of her face and backhanded her on the other. He pushed her to the floor, where she lay sobbing.

The dealer looked down at her without pity. He crossed slowly to a chest of drawers, opened it and pulled out a flat tobacco tin, which he tossed on to the bed. 'I got some smack, that's all. Take it or leave it.'

Glynis crawled to her feet, shaking and in pain both from the violence of his attack and her appalling craving. Uncertainly, she moved towards the bed and opened the tin. She stared dumbly at the loaded hypodermic syringe it contained.

'Well, come on, darling. I ain't got all night,' Sofrides challenged her, seeing her hesitation. He moved up beside her, taking out the syringe and thrusting it into her hand. 'Shoot up and get out, before I change my mind.'

Glynis stared at the syringe in horrified fascination. Her face was a mixture of desperation, fear and bewilderment. She glanced up at Sofrides, her eyes almost pleading.

His lips curled into a scornful sneer as he identified her problem. 'You little silver-plated spoon-sniffers. You've never shot up before, have you?'

Glynis could only nod.

'Here, I'll show you,' Sofrides said. He clenched his fist, pumping his forearm up and down half a dozen times. He pointed to his slightly throbbing vein. 'Just there, see? Just stick the needle in and push the plunger. That's all there is to it.'

Awkwardly, Glynis copied his movements, holding the syringe clumsily in a trembling hand, almost at arm's length. Fumbling and shaky, she pushed the gleaming point of the needle towards her arm.

Sofrides looked away, letting out a little snort of disgust. 'Oh Christ! Go in the bloody bathroom and do it, will you?'

Still unsure, Glynis slunk into the poky bathroom and closed the door behind her. Sofrides threw himself back on the bed, propped himself up with a pillow and lit a cigarette. He plumed smoke up at the ceiling, grinning. He felt very pleased with himself.

The cigarette had burned down to a stub before he thought about the girl again. After crushing it out in the ashtray he pushed himself off the bed and strode to the bathroom door, rapping on it with the back of his hand. 'What the hell are you doing in there?' he demanded irritably. There was no answer.

He tried the door handle. It was unlocked. Sofrides pushed the door open to find Glynis sitting stiffly on the toilet, her head lolling back against the pipe from the cistern. The empty hypodermic dangled loosely from her fingers at arm's length. Her face was ghostly white, her eyes wide and staring and her body twitching convulsively and obscenely.

Sofrides looked at her without sympathy. 'Feel rough, huh? Don't worry. A couple of minutes and you'll be high as a kite.' He reached down to seize her by the elbow, and hauled her roughly to her feet. The empty syringe dropped from her fingers, shattering on the tiled floor.

'Come on, I want you out of here,' Sofrides told the girl curtly, as he tried to drag her out of the bathroom.

Glynis took a couple of shuffling steps and stopped, her legs sagging beneath her. She would have collapsed to the floor but for the dealer's grip on her arm. He pushed her back against the bathroom wall, propping her up. There was the first trace of concern on his face as he noted her wildly rolling eyes, the tremors which rocked her body and the shallowness of her breathing. Even as he watched, Glynis seemed to be torn by a convulsion of pain which caused her body to jackknife and made her clutch at her abdomen with her free hand. She let out one long, shuddering groan and went limp, before sliding down the wall to sit on the floor like a puppet whose strings have just been cut.

'Oh shit!' Sofrides spat out in anger – but it was fear that registered on his face. He dropped to his knees, staring into the girl's wide, but unseeing eyes. They were completely still now, and her body was totally motionless. Panic rising in him, Sofrides snatched up her wrist, feeling for the faintest hint of a pulse. There was nothing.

Sofrides pushed himself to his feet and stood there shaking for a few seconds, his brain racing. He turned towards the telephone, thinking briefly about calling an ambulance but rejecting the idea almost immediately. The girl's face was already puffy and showing signs of bruising where he had struck her. He remembered the bite marks he had put in the soft flesh of her breasts during their brief sexual encounter. With his criminal record, reporting the girl's death was tantamount to placing himself on a manslaughter charge at the very least.

He tried to think, as he paced round the small bedsitter several times, trying not to look at the girl's lifeless form slumped just inside the bathroom door. He crossed to the room's single window and stared out into the dark and deserted street.

There was only one choice, he realized finally. Somehow, he had to get the girl's body into his car without being seen. After that it would be easy. London had hundreds of backstreets and alleyways where the body of a drug addict, drunk or vagrant turned up every so often. With nothing to connect the girl to him, she would be just another statistic.

His mind made up, as quietly as he could Sofrides began to drag Glynis's body towards the door.

Paul Carney tidied up the paperwork on his desk and switched off the Anglepoise lamp. Rising, he crossed to the door and switched off the main light, plunging his office into darkness. Locking the door, he strode across the deserted main office towards the outer reception area.

The desk sergeant looked up at him, grinning, as he walked past. 'Barbados for our hols this year, is it, Mr Carney? Or a world cruise, with all this overtime you've been putting in?'

Carney smiled at the man wearily. 'Oh yeah, at least,' he muttered. 'Goodnight, Sergeant.'

The man nodded. 'Goodnight, sir.'

Carney walked out into the night air, taking a deep breath before heading for the rear car park. On reaching his Ford Sierra, he climbed in and drove slowly to the main gates. He was exhausted, yet in no hurry to get home. Or at least back to the Islington flat, Carney reminded himself, thinking about it. It had ceased to be a home when Linda had walked out, over six months earlier. She'd even taken the dog.

The roads were almost deserted. Carney cruised

past the rows of darkened office buildings for a couple of miles before turning off into the residential back-streets around Canonbury. He passed a small row of shops, some with their windows still lit or showing dim security lights in their rear storage areas.

The grey Volvo took him by surprise, shooting out from a small side road only yards ahead of him. Carney stamped on the brakes instinctively, allowing the car to complete its left turn and accelerate away from him with a squeal of rubber on tarmac.

Crazy bastard, Carney thought, reacting as a fellow road-user. Then the copper in him took over, asking the obvious question. What could be so damned urgent, at four-thirty in the morning? He stamped down on the accelerator, making it his business to find out.

Carney caught up with the Volvo at the next set of traffic lights. He pulled across the vehicle's front wing and leapt out of his own car. He wrenched the driver's side door of the Volvo open.

'All right, you bloody moron. What the hell do you think you're playing at?' he growled, before he had even seen who was sitting at the wheel. There was a long, thoughtful pause as he recognized the driver.

'Well, well, well,' Carney said slowly. 'If it isn't Tony the Greek. And what particular form of nastiness are you up to tonight, you little scumbag?'

Sofrides looked up at him with a fearful expression, cursing the cruel vagaries of fate which had thrown Detective Sergeant Paul Carney across his path this night of all nights. They'd had run-ins before – almost every one of them to his cost.

'I ain't done nothing, honest, Mr Carney,' Sofrides whined, desperately trying to bluff it out.

Carney grinned cynically. 'You don't have to do anything, Tony. Just being in the vicinity constitutes major environmental pollution.' He held the door back, jerking his head. 'Out.'

Reluctantly, Sofrides climbed out of the car, still protesting his innocence. 'I'm clean, Mr Carney – honest.'

Carney shook his head. 'You wouldn't be clean if you bathed in bleach and gargled with insecticide,' he grunted. He paused, staring at the young man thoughtfully. There was something wrong, something out of character. Sofrides was not displaying his usual arrogance. He looked frightened, guilty.

'What's wrong with you tonight, Tony?' Carney demanded. 'Where's all the usual backchat, the bull-shit? You're scared, Tony – and that makes me very suspicious indeed.'

Increasingly desperate, Sofrides tried to force a smile on to his face. 'I told you, I ain't done nothing. I just don't feel so good, that's all. Must have been something I ate.'

It wasn't going to wash. Carney was convinced he was on to something now. He peered at Sofrides's face more closely.

'I do have to admit that you don't look so good,' he muttered. 'In fact, Tony, you look as sick as the proverbial parrot.' He paused momentarily. 'Know what I think, Tony? I think you've just made a collection and I've caught you bang to rights. I think you're carrying a major consignment of naughties, that's what I think. The question is: what, and where?'

Carney suddenly seized Sofrides by the arm, forcing it up around his back in a savage half nelson. He frogmarched him over to his own car, opened it and pulled a pair of handcuffs out of the glove compartment. Snapping the cuffs around the young man's wrist, he pushed him back to the Volvo, wound down the window a few inches and clipped the other bracelet to the door-frame.

'So let's take a little look-see, shall we,' he suggested, returning to his own vehicle for just long enough to grab a powerful torch.

The Volvo seemed clean, much to Carney's disappointment. Sofrides watched him search thoroughly beneath and behind the seats, in the glove compartment and underneath the dashboard.

'See, I told you I ain't done nothing. So how about letting me go, Mr Carney?' Sofrides suggested hopefully.

Carney shook his head. 'We've only just got started, Tony. It'd be a pity to break the party up this early now, wouldn't it?' He straightened up from searching the interior of the car. 'Right, let's take a little look in the boot.'

A fresh glimmer of panic crossed Sofrides's eyes. 'Look, tell you what. Suppose I make you a deal?' he blurted out.

Carney sounded unimpressed. 'Oh yes, and what sort of deal would that be, Tony?'

Sofrides snatched at his slim remaining chance eagerly. 'I know a couple of new crack houses which

have just opened up. I can give you names . . . places
. . . times.'

Carney grinned wickedly at him. 'But you'll do that
anyway, once I get you nailed,' he pointed out. 'You'll
sing your little black heart out just as soon as you see
the inside of the slammer. You'll have to do a bit
better than that, Tony.'

Sofrides was really desperate now, clutching at
straws. 'How about if I set someone up for you –
someone big?' he suggested. 'I'm only a little fish, Mr
Carney – you know that.'

Carney paused, tempted. 'And who might you have
in mind?' he asked.

Sofrides picked a name at random. 'How about
Jack Mottram? He deals in ten Ks at a time.'

Carney sighed wearily. The little bastard was trying
to wind him up, he thought. 'Jack Mottram wouldn't
piss on you if your arse was on fire,' he said scath-
ingly. 'Now stop jerking my chain, all right?' He
pulled the key to the handcuffs from his pocket,
releasing them from the Volvo door. He grabbed
Sofrides by the scruff of the neck, dragging him
round to the back of the car and nodding down at
the boot.

'Right, just so we don't hear any little whinges
about planted evidence,' he muttered. 'Open it up
and we'll take a little look in Pandora's box.'

For a moment, Sofrides was tempted to try to
struggle free and run for it. As if sensing this, Carney
tightened his grip. 'Don't even think about it, Tony.
I could outrun a little lardball like you in twenty
yards flat. Besides, you might have a little accident

resisting arrest, and we wouldn't want that to happen, would we?'

Sofrides sagged, realizing he was beaten. His heart pounded in his chest as Carney turned the key and opened the boot, then shone the torch inside.

Carney was not prepared for the sight which greeted his eyes, and he was visibly shaken. It was revulsion, quickly followed by a wave of rage, which washed over him as the beam illuminated the girl's contorted body, her sightless eyes staring up at him out of her pale, bruised face.

'Jesus,' Carney muttered, with a long, deep sigh. His body quivered with shock and anger.

The desperate urge to run washed over Sofrides again at that moment. Not really thinking clearly, he twisted his body to break free from Carney's grip and jerked up one knee at his groin.

Carney's reactions were fast, but not quite fast enough to avoid contact altogether. Twisting his body, he winced with pain as Sofrides's savage blow connected with the side of his hip bone. That, on top of his grisly discovery, was enough to make Carney snap. His mind exploded in a red mist of pain and rage. Suddenly, everything came out – his tiredness, his frustration with the job, his total loathing of little low-lifes like Sofrides. He raised the heavy torch and smashed it against the side of the dealer's head, shattering the glass. Sofrides screamed in agony as Carney drove a full-blooded punch deep into his solar plexus and then cuffed him across the ear as he began to double up in agony. Several more blows followed as the policeman went berserk, venting the full force of his frustration in a few moments of blind, senseless violence. Finally he pushed Sofrides over the lip of the boot until he was half lying across the girl's body, and brought the heavy lid crashing down.

There was a last, agonized scream from Sofrides, then silence.

Mentally drained and utterly exhausted, Carney fell back against the side of the car, breathing heavily and cursing himself under his breath. Sanity had begun to return now, and he knew he'd gone too far.

There was no smile of greeting on the desk sergeant's face as Carney strolled into the station later that morning. 'Excuse me, sir, but the DCI asked me to tell you to report to his office as soon as you came in.'

Carney nodded. He had been expecting it. 'Thanks, Sergeant.' He headed straight for Manners's office and tapped lightly on the glass door.

'Come.' The man's tone was curt and peremptory. He stared grimly at Carney as he walked in. 'Sit down, Carney,' he snapped, pointing to a chair.

Carney did as he was told, his heart sinking. Harry Manners's use of his surname had given him a pretty good clue as to the severity of the dressing down he was about to receive. He looked across at his superior with what he hoped was a suitably contrite expression on his face.

There was a moment of strained silence before Manners spoke. 'Tony Sofrides is in the Royal Northern Hospital,' he announced flatly. 'He has two skull fractures, a broken arm, ruptured spleen and three cracked ribs.'

Carney could not resist the only defence he had. 'Christ, sir, did you see that girl?'

Manners nodded. 'I saw them both.' He paused for a moment, sighing heavily. 'Goddammit, man, what the hell got into you? Don't you realize you could have killed him?'

Carney hung his head, although there was a spark of defiance left. 'So what should I have done? Slapped his wrists and told him he'd been a naughty boy? Look, Harry, I know I blew my stack, and I'm sorry.'

Manners was shaking his head doubtfully. 'I don't think that's going to be enough – not this time.'

Carney realized for the first time that he was looking suspension, possibly dismissal, in the face. He could only presume upon their years together as colleagues, and as friends. 'Aw, come on, Harry. You can cover for me on this one, surely. There's a dozen shades of whitewash. Resisting arrest, assaulting a police officer, injured while trying to escape . . .' He tailed off, studying his superior's face.

Manners shook his head again. 'I'm not sure I can – and what's more to the point, I'm not sure that I should,' he said. 'The bottom line is that you had a chance to make a righteous arrest and you blew it. Not only that, but you beat the shit out of the suspect as well. That's bad policework, and we both know it. It was sloppy, it was excessive – and it was dangerous.' He paused, sighing. 'And it's not the first time.'

There was a pleading look in Carney's eyes. 'Oh Christ, Harry. Don't throw that crap at me as well.

35

Three isolated incidents, spread over fifteen years in the force. I've been a damn good copper, and you know it.'

Manners nodded regretfully. 'Yes, you have been a good copper, Paul. But you've got a touch of the vigilante in you, and that makes you a risk. One that I don't think I can afford to take any more.'

There it was, out in the open at last. Carney sighed heavily. 'So, what happens now? Are you going to suspend me? Or would you prefer me to do the honourable thing, and resign? Hand over my card and go the way of all ex-coppers and take a job as a private security guard?'

Manners fidgeted awkwardly. He was not finding his task at all pleasant. 'That's not your style, Paul — and we both know it.'

'Then what?' Carney demanded. 'Is there any kind of choice?'

Manners looked uncertain. He shrugged faintly. 'I don't know . . . there might be,' he murmured.

Carney snatched at the thin straw of hope. 'Well what is it, for Christ's sake?'

Manners looked apologetic. 'Sorry, Paul, but I can't tell you anything more at the moment. It's just something which has filtered down from the boys upstairs. I'd have to look into it more closely, and it might take a bit of time.'

'And meanwhile?' Carney asked.

'Meanwhile you take a rest, on my direct recommendation,' Manners said firmly. 'You're suffering from stress. Overwork, the sheer frustration of the job, you and Linda splitting up. Let's just call it a period of enforced leave for the time being, shall we?'

4

Maybe it wasn't such a crazy idea after all, Davies thought, on the drive back to Hereford. He'd spent the remainder of the previous day and most of the evening hammering out the bones of a workable scheme with Commander Franks and Commissioner McMillan, and they had made surprising progress.

What had particularly impressed him had been both men's total commitment to the job, and their willingness to be flexible. While he had not been given a total *carte blanche*, most of his ideas and suggestions had been listened to and given serious consideration. By the end of the day, they were all more or less in agreement as to the general size and structure of the unit they would create, and had a good idea of the sort of personnel who would make it up.

This factor alone had allowed Davies to take some vital first steps. After leaving the two policemen, he had checked into the Intercontinental Hotel and spent the rest of the night making a series of telephone calls. Most of the key personnel who would help set up the new force were already either on recall to active duty, or about to receive transfer orders. For obvious reasons, SAS officers with experience on the streets of Northern Ireland had been high on the list, along with individuals with particular skills or interests which might be required for such an unusual operation.

Now he was on his way back to Stirling Lines to

start the tricky process of recruiting his foot soldiers, leaving Commander Franks to fulfil his promise to provide a nucleus of hand-picked police officers. It now seemed more than feasible that together they could merge the two interests and peculiar skills into a single, if somewhat hybrid, task force which could transpose the disciplines and tactics of a military force into a civil environment.

Only one thing had changed from the Home Secretary's initial briefing. For try as he might, Davies had been unable to share the man's conviction that the job could be seen as an operation for the SAS Training Wing. It had become increasingly clear to him that the task was in fact almost tailor-made for the Counter Revolutionary Warfare Wing. In many respects, the CRW team had already been doing that very job for a number of years. Davies intended to place the day-to-day operations of the new unit under their jurisdiction at the earliest opportunity and then duck out, remaining available solely as a liaison officer between SAS commanders and the Home Office should such contact prove necessary. That was the theory, anyway. But first came the people, for a unit was only a collection of individuals moulded to a common purpose. And finding the right individuals was crucial.

It would take a very special kind of young man to do the job properly, Davies was well aware. And young they would have to be, if Grieves's theories were correct and their enemy was deliberately targeting the youth culture. Infiltration might well prove their best weapon, at least in the early days, which effectively ruled out anybody over the age of twenty-five. But they would also need to be sufficiently mature and stable enough to cope with the pressures and possibly the temptations they might be exposed to. They needed to be resourceful as well as tough, disciplined yet independent thinkers.

Davies nodded to himself thoughtfully as he pulled off the M4 at the junction which would bring him into the north-east suburbs of Hereford. Yes indeed – a very special breed of young man, for sure!

The white Escort shot through the red light and came screaming out of the side road into the main flow of traffic along Oxford Street. A collision was inevitable. The driver of the mail van stamped on his brakes and attempted to swerve, but was unable to avoid clipping the offside front wing of the Escort and spinning it round in a half-circle. The car bounced up the kerb, scattering terrified pedestrians in all directions, glanced off a bus stop and finally came to a halt half on and half off the pavement, facing the oncoming traffic. The squeal of brakes and the heavy thumps of a multi-vehicle pile-up continued for a full fifteen seconds. It was a nasty one. The shunts finally stopped, and there was a blessed few moments of silence before a concerto of angry car horns began to blare out.

Constable John Beavis slapped his forehead with the flat of his hand and let out a weary groan. It was only his second week of traffic duty and something like this had to happen. Even worse, he'd been due to go off duty in less than fifteen minutes and his daughter's school sports day started at twelve-thirty. He'd promised to be there to cheer her on in the three-legged race. He began to walk towards the long snake of crashed vehicles, counting them gloomily. This little mess looked like it would take a couple of hours to sort out.

He hurried past the line of irate drivers, ignoring the dozens of shouted complaints and curses which were hurled in his direction. The sight of a uniform seemed to give them all a scapegoat, someone to blame. Finally reaching the end of the line, he approached the white Escort which had started it all and peered in through the closed passenger window.

There were two occupants, both young. A male driver and a blonde female. Both sat rigidly in their seats, gazing fixedly straight ahead of them through the windscreen.

Constable Beavis rapped on the passenger door with his knuckles. There was no reaction from inside the car. The couple continued to stare blankly ahead, ignoring him. He banged the window again, more angrily. Neither occupant even glanced sideways. It was as if they were both totally oblivious of what was going on around them.

Beavis felt his anger rising. They were probably both dead-drunk, he thought, and it made his blood boil. It was a miracle that no one had been seriously injured, let alone killed. As he wrenched open the car door the girl turned to face him slowly, like a video replayed in slow motion. Her face was blank, utterly devoid of expression. Beavis felt the hairs on the back of his neck prickle slightly as he stared into her eyes.

They were wide open, but vacuous, almost dead. Like two small green mirrors, they seemed to reflect back at him. Beavis noted the dilated pupils, the strange facial immobility, and came to a revised decision. Not drunk, worse than that. They were both stoned on drugs, blasted out of their minds, the pair of them.

His anger reached a peak and he thrust his hand into the car, grasping the girl by the arm. He wanted to pull her out, shake her, slap some life and some sense into her pretty, but stupid little face.

The girl's lips curled slowly into a scornful smile, which was almost a snarl. 'Fuck off, pig,' she hissed, with sudden and surprising vehemence. Then, sucking up phlegm from her throat, she spat full in his face.

The young man also came to life. As Beavis staggered back, clawing at his face and trying to clear the sticky spittle from his eyes, he reached forward to the car's dashboard locker, opened it and reached inside. His hand came out again holding a 9mm Smith & Wesson 39 series automatic pistol. With cool deliberation, he leaned across his passenger and brought the pistol up, taking careful aim. Then, with an insane little giggle, he shot the policeman straight through the forehead, between the eyes.

The youth lowered the gun again and unhurriedly opened the driver's side door. He climbed out, dragging his girlfriend behind him. Hand in hand, they crossed the paralysed road to the far pavement and began to stroll casually in the direction of Marble Arch, firing shots indiscriminately into the crowds of panicking shoppers.

*　　*　　*

Two hours later, Commissioner McMillan had a full report on his desk. He read it gloomily, digesting the horrific facts. The constable had died instantly, of course. Of the four subsequent victims, one young woman had been dead on arrival at hospital and an older woman was on life support and not expected to make it. The two other bullet wounds were serious, but not critical. The Escort, stolen two days earlier in West Hampstead, had contained several bundles of right-wing pamphlets and propaganda material, along with a Czech-built Skorpion machine-pistol in the boot. The couple had eventually disappeared, unchallenged, into the underground system. By now, they could be anywhere.

McMillan finished reading the report with a heavy, sinking feeling in the pit of his stomach. All the pieces seemed to fit the pattern. Pushing the document across his desk, he sighed heavily. So it had started already, he reflected bitterly. He'd been hoping they'd have a little more time.

5

Sergeant Andrew Winston took a careful and calculated look at the pot on the table before flicking his eyes over his hand again. It was not an easy call. Seventy-five quid in the pot, a fiver to stay in the game and he was holding a queen flush. Winston hesitated, feeling vulnerable. Three-card brag wasn't really his game; he was more of a poker man. He'd only allowed himself to be suckered in out of boredom.

'Come on, Andrew,' Andy Collins taunted him from across the table. 'Put up or fold up. Or are you chicken?'

Winston never got a chance to answer the challenge. A strange hand plucked the three cards from his hand, dropping them face down on the table.

'He's not chicken – he's just sensible.'

Winston whirled round, ready to jump to his feet and ready for a fight. Interfering with a man's gambling hand was serious business. He recognized Lieutenant-Colonel Davies at once, instantly relaxing. His face broke into a surprised grin. 'Hello, boss. What a coincidence, seeing you in this boozer.'

Davies shook his head. 'Not really. I was looking for you.'

Winston was still puzzled. 'How did you know I'd be here?'

Davies smiled. 'I didn't. But I've already been to just about every other pub in Hereford.' He nodded at the cards. 'Pick up your money. I need to talk to you.'

Winston looked uncertainly at the two players remaining in the game.

'Don't even worry about it,' Davies assured him. 'Collins wasn't your real threat, except he'd have kept you both in the game longer and cost you more money. Pretty Boy's the danger. My guess is that he's holding a run – or better.'

It was a prediction which was about to be put to the test. Emboldened by the fantasy that he had bluffed Winston out of the game, Collins dropped his jack flush triumphantly. 'See you, Pretty. Got you, I reckon.'

Pretty Boy Parrit shot him a scornful glance. 'You got to be fucking joking, my old son.' Slowly, deliberately, he laid out the king, queen and ace of spades and reached for the ashtray full of money.

Collins's face dropped. 'You spawny bastard. I thought you were bluffing.'

Pretty Boy grinned wickedly. 'Who dares wins,' he joked, scooping up the pot.

Impressed, Winston looked up at Davies. 'How did you know?'

Davies shrugged. 'Probably from playing a damned sight more games in the spider than you've had hot dinners. And from knowing men, being able to read faces.' It was an expression of quiet confidence, rather than a boast.

Winston pushed himself to his feet. 'But what if you'd been wrong?' he asked.

Davies grinned. 'I'd have paid you myself,' he said

– and Winston had no doubts at all that the man was perfectly sincere.

'So, what did you want to talk to me about, boss?' Winston asked, after Davies had bought fresh pints and led the way to an empty table. Davies took a sip of his bitter, eyeing Winston over the top of the glass. 'Something's coming up,' he said flatly. 'And I want you in on it.' He paused for a few moments, savouring his beer. Finally, when the glass was half empty, he launched into a slightly edited account of the events of the past two days.

Winston listened carefully until Davies had completely finished. There was a slightly ironic smile on his face when he finally spoke. 'Excuse me for pointing it out, boss, but aren't you forgetting something rather important.'

Davies looked puzzled. 'What?'

Winston laughed. 'For Christ's sake, you're looking at it. Or are you getting colour-blind in your old age? I'm black, in case you hadn't noticed.'

Davies stared at the big Barbadian's grinning features with a perfectly straight face. 'Fuck me – are you?' he said, in mock surprise.

Both men shared the joke for a few moments, before Winston spoke again. His face was more serious now. 'No, seriously though, boss. If we're really talking about mixing with a bunch of these crazy fascist bastards, having me around ain't going to help much, is it?'

It was Davies's turn to be serious now. He felt a little awkward, knowing that he had to step on sensitive ground. 'Maybe *you're* forgetting something,

Andrew,' he pointed out. 'Like it or not, the fact is that a high proportion of London's drug abuse occurs within the black community,' he went on, almost apologetically. 'You'll be able to get to places, gain the confidence of people who wouldn't give us poor honky bastards a chance.'

Winston conceded the point with a nod. 'Yeah, you're right there, boss. I hadn't thought of that.'

There was a moment of thoughtful silence. 'Well, what do you think?' Davies asked eventually. 'Do you want in?'

Winston didn't really need to think about it. He was normally a mild, easy-going man who never made a big thing out of race, and he was well aware that some of his more militant brethren would probably refer to him disparagingly as a white nigger for doing the job he did. But he had a quiet, but unshakeable pride – both as a man and as a black man. All extremes of bigotry offended his sense of decency and humanity. As he would sometimes say, if pressed on the matter: 'We all bleed the same colour.'

He looked Davies in the eyes, nodding his head firmly. 'I'm in,' he muttered. 'All the way.'

'Good.' Davies raised what was left of his pint by way of a toast. 'I'm calling a briefing in the Kremlin for 0900 hours on Thursday. Meanwhile, I'd like you to come up with a few names, if you can. You're closer to ground level than I am these days.'

'Who have we got so far?' Winston wanted to know.

There seemed no reason to withhold the information, Davies thought. He felt totally confident that he could count on the man's discretion. 'I've already called in Major Anderson from Belfast. And Captains Blake and Feeney will be at the meeting,' he said. 'With you on board, that should take care of the officer level. What we need now is a couple of dozen young but reliable troopers with plenty of recent experience in the Killing House. If we're putting combat-armed men out on the streets, they're going to need bloody fast reactions.'

Winston nodded in agreement. Davies was right about the last point. Knowing the difference between friend and foe was preferable in combat, but not absolutely crucial. Mistakes could, and did, happen – a death by 'friendly fire' was an unfortunate but accepted risk that every trooper took. If it happened, there would probably be an enquiry, but not a major scandal. The same could not be said for a mistake being made among the civilian population. One innocent person shot by mistake, and at least seven different flavours of shit would hit the fan.

That was where the 'Killing House' came into its own. Officially known as the SAS Close Quarter Battle building, it created remarkably lifelike situations in which mock battles could take place – often demanding lightning-fast reactions and split-second judgement by the combatants. At any moment they might be confronted by a dummy or pop-up target which could be anything from a terrorist with an Armalite to a blind man wielding his stick. Hesitate and you were dead, losing valuable points. Shoot too hastily and you risked being sent back to basic training, or worse. More than one SAS hopeful had been RTU'd purely on poor performance in the Killing House.

'You'll also be needing at least four specialist snipers, of course,' Winston added.

Davies nodded. 'And a couple of men with Bomb Squad training, and at least two good demo men,' he confirmed. 'But the fundamental requirement is going to be youth, which will probably mean a fairly high proportion of probationers. That's why sheer quality is so vital on this one. We won't have any leeway for any guesswork, or don't-knows. Every unit boss will have to have absolute and implicit trust in every single man under his command.'

Winston thought about it for a few seconds, finally whistling through his teeth. 'That's a pretty tall order, boss.'

Davies nodded at him. 'I know – a shitty job with a lot of responsibility. That's why I'm asking you for your personal recommendations.'

'Well, thanks, boss,' Winston muttered, grinning ruefully. Being put on the spot like that was something of a backhanded compliment. He nodded discreetly over towards the table where the card game was still in progress. 'Off the cuff, I'd say that Pretty Boy would be a rather good contender. He seems like a real laid-back bastard at times, but he's got the reactions of a bloody mongoose.'

Davies cast a brief glance in the man's direction. 'Any specials?' he wanted to know.

Winston nodded. 'Explosives and demolition. That man can blow a hole in a building wall without rattling the windows.'

It was a wild exaggeration, but Davies knew what he meant. 'Age?' he asked.

Winston shrugged. 'Twenty-eight, but he looks younger. And his accuracy scores on the range are impressive.' Winston broke off to grin. 'Despite his nickname, he's not just a pretty face.'

It was time for a more direct and important question, and Davies asked it. 'Would you want him covering your back?'

There was not a second of hesitation. 'Rather him than a hundred others,' Winston stated unequivocally.

Davies took the personal recommendation at face value. 'All right, bring him in,' he said quietly. He drained his beer and pushed himself to his feet, adding: 'Well, I'll leave you to go and lose some more money.'

Winston looked at him sheepishly, then grinned. 'Your confidence in me is totally underwhelming, boss.'

6

Paul Carney's telephone rang. It was by far the most exciting thing that had happened to him in two days. He virtually jumped across the flat to snatch it up.

'Paul?' The voice on the other end of the phone was hesitant, almost apologetic.

And so it ought to be, Carney thought, recognizing the caller as DCI Manners. The man had, after all, virtually suspended him. His response was somewhat less than enthusiastic. 'Yeah?' he grunted. 'What is it?'

There was a long sigh on the other end of the line as Manners got the message. It was more or less the reaction he had been expecting. 'Look, Paul, about that special job I mentioned to you,' he muttered, finally. 'They want to see you.'

'They? Who's they?' Carney asked guardedly.

'Sorry, Paul, but I can't tell you that,' Manners apologized. 'But there are a couple of Special Branch officers on their way round to your flat now. I'm sure they will explain everything to you.'

Eagerness, and the air of mystery, had already raised Carney to a pitch of anticipation. A sense of frustration was not far behind.

'Special Branch?' Carney queried irritably. 'For Christ's sake, Harry, what's going on here?'

'Sorry, but that's all I can tell you for the minute,' Manners said flatly. He had only the sketchiest idea of what was going on himself, and he'd been pressed to secrecy. Whatever the full facts were, they were well above the level of a mere Detective Chief Inspector. Even as a friend, there was nothing he could tell his colleague on that score. There was, however, something he *could* say, and he needed to say it.

'There's one other good piece of news I think you ought to know,' Manners went on after a brief pause. 'You know that batch of contaminated heroin you were worried about? The stuff that killed the girl?'

Carney jumped on it immediately. 'Yeah. What about it?'

'We've pulled it in – hopefully the whole lot,' Manners told him. 'And you were right – it was real bad shit. Adulterated up to seventy per cent and cut with bleaching powder, among other things. Lethal.'

Carney let out a sigh of relief. 'Yeah, thanks, Harry. That is good news. How did you get on to it?'

'Sofrides talked,' Manners told him. 'He led us straight to his supplier. A callous little bastard out for a quick profit and damn the consequences.' He was silent for a while. 'Just thought you'd like to know, that's all.'

'Yeah, thanks.' Carney felt equally awkward, not sure what to say to his boss. The line was silent for a long time.

'Well, good luck – whatever happens,' Manners said finally, and hung up.

Carney slipped the receiver back into its cradle and began to pace about the flat, trying to figure out what was going on. He did not have to wait very long. Less than three minutes after the call from Manners, there was a light but firm knock on the door.

There were two men standing in the hallway as Carney opened up. They both looked businesslike and efficient. They were unsmiling.

'Paul Carney?' one of them asked.

Carney nodded. The two men exchanged a brief glance and took the admission as an invitation to enter. They stepped across the threshold, the second man closing the door behind him.

Minutes later, Carney was in the visitors' car, being driven south to New Scotland Yard.

McMillan gestured to a vacant chair at the table. 'Please sit down, Carney. Would you care for a drink?'

Carney felt himself tense up, both physically and mentally. Was this the opening move in some sort of test? he found himself wondering. Coppers weren't supposed to drink on duty. So did they want to see if he lived by the book?

He forced himself to relax, rationalizing the situation. All this secrecy was making him paranoid, he decided. The offer was probably an innocent and genuine one. Besides, he wasn't officially on duty any more, and he could certainly do with a drink. He nodded, finally. 'Yes, thank you, sir. A Scotch would be fine.'

The commissioner allowed the faintest smile to cross his face. So Carney was a man, and not just some order-following drone. Carney noticed the smile, realized that he *had* been tested, and could only assume that he had passed.

McMillan stood up, opened a filing cabinet and pulled out of a bottle of Glenfiddich and a chunky tumbler. He splashed a healthy measure into the glass and carried it over to Carney before resuming his place at the table. He looked at Carney thoughtfully for a while. 'Well, no doubt you've been wondering what all this is about,' he said at last.

Carney allowed himself a small grin. 'You could say that, sir.'

Commander Franks consulted a slim dossier on the desk in front of him. He studied its contents for a few seconds before looking up at Carney. 'Your superior says you're a tough cop, Carney,' he said. 'You know the streets and you know your enemy.'

Carney shrugged. 'I just handle my job, sir.'

Franks nodded. 'But unfortunately you can't always handle your temper,' he pointed out. It was a statement of fact, not quite an accusation, but Carney was immediately defensive.

'I just hate drugs. And I hate the villains who are pushing them to our kids,' he said with feeling.

'As do we all,' Franks observed. 'But our job places certain restrictions upon us. We have to work to specific rules, standards of behaviour which are acceptable to society. You went over the top, Carney – and you know it.'

It was an open rebuke now, inviting some sort of apology. Carney bowed his head slightly. 'Yes, sir, I'm aware of that. And I'm sorry.' He did not attempt to justify his actions in any way.

It seemed to satisfy Franks, who merely nodded to himself and glanced across at McMillan, passing some unspoken message. The commissioner leaned across the table, resting his elbows on it and forming a steeple with his fingers. 'Right, gentlemen,' he announced in a businesslike tone. 'Let's get down to it, shall we?'

For the next forty-five minutes Carney faced an almost non-stop barrage of questions. Some seemed totally irrelevant, and a few were of such a highly personal nature that he found himself becoming irritated by what he thought were unwarranted intrusions into his private life. As the session drew to an end, however, he began to realize that the three men in that room now knew just about everything there was to know about Paul Carney the policeman and Paul Carney the man. His opinions, his personality, his strengths – and his weaknesses. It was a rather disconcerting feeling.

Finally McMillan glanced at each of his colleagues in turn, inviting further questions. There were none. He turned his attention back to Carney.

'Let's get to business, then. It would appear that you need a job, Mr Carney. We have one for you, if you want it. A very special job, I might add.' He paused. 'Are you interested?'

Carney was guarded. 'I suppose that would have to depend on what the job was,' he said.

'Ah,' McMillan sighed thoughtfully. 'Now that gives me something of a problem. Basically, I cannot give you any details about the job until you agree to take it. You will also be required to take a grade three security oath.'

Carney was flabbergasted – and it showed on his face. He gaped at McMillan for several seconds before finally finding his voice. 'With respect, sir, that's crazy. How can I agree to a job without knowing what it is? It might not suit me. I might not suit it. I couldn't be a pen-pusher, buried behind some pile of papers, for a start.'

McMillan smiled faintly. 'I appreciate your candidness, Mr Carney,' he murmured. 'But I can and do assure you that far from being desk-bound, you'd be out there fighting crime. In the very front line, so to speak.' He paused briefly. 'But that's all I *can* tell you at this point. It's now completely down to you. We can proceed no further without your agreement.'

Carney's head was spinning. In desperation, he looked over at Commander Franks. 'If I turn this down, sir, what are the chances of my being returned to normal duty?'

Franks shook his head slowly. 'None,' he said, bluntly. 'The very qualities which make you attractive to us also preclude your continued service in the conventional police force.'

The finality of this statement was enough to push Carney over the edge. He made his decision on impulse as much as anything. 'All right, so let's say I'm in,' he muttered, still slightly dubious.

McMillan nodded gravely and signalled to Grieves, who produced an official-looking document from his pocket and slid it over the table towards Carney. 'Read and sign this,' he said curtly.

Carney scanned it quickly, eager to find some clue as to what he was letting himself in for, but the document itself told him virtually nothing. Finally he looked up at Grieves again, who silently handed him a fountain pen. Hesitating for just a moment, Carney read the security oath aloud and signed the paper. McMillan and Franks added their own signatures as witnesses and Grieves returned the document to his pocket. It was done.

'Right. Now we can tell you what we have in mind,' McMillan said. He began to launch into a detailed account of the plans formulated thus far.

7

'I'll tell you right away that I have some serious reservations about this whole concept,' Barney Davies said candidly. 'But I agreed to treat it as a workable idea, and you're the man they've sent me. So if we can work something out, we will.'

Carney tried to think of a suitable rejoinder, and failed completely. An opening speech like that was a hard act to follow. And he was already feeling a little out of his depth anyway.

He'd been ordered to report to Lieutenant-Colonel Davies at SAS HQ in Hereford, and that's what he'd done. Merely passing through the gate guard had been like walking into the lion's den. Like most civilians, Carney had only a sketchy picture of the SAS and how they worked. Fact was thin on the ground, and the man in the street could only form his own mental image from the fiction and the legend. And that legend was of a special breed of super-heroes, just one step removed from Captain Marvel or Superman.

'I'll try to keep that in mind, sir,' he managed to blurt out eventually.

Davies smiled. 'Lesson one,' he said. 'We don't place a great deal of emphasis on rank in the SAS. A man is respected for what he is, what he can do, rather than the extra bits of material sewn on to his uniform. In your case, as you're basically an outsider, and a largely unknown quantity, you'll be just another trooper. So don't expect any deference from the rest of the men you'll be working with. To them, you'll be just another probationer.' Davies paused, his tone softening a shade. 'And you don't have to call me "sir", by the way. "Boss" is perfectly acceptable.'

Davies flipped quickly through the file which Commander Franks had faxed to him. 'So you think you're tough,' he muttered, without condescension.

Carney bristled slightly. 'I don't think anything,' he protested. 'But I can look after myself, if that's what you mean.'

Davies nodded, looking faintly pleased. 'Good. You don't allow yourself to be put down too easily. But don't get any inflated ideas. Keep in mind that any one of my men could probably fold you up, stick a stamp on you and stuff you in the second-class post before you even knew what was happening.'

Carney took this somewhat colourful piece of information at face value. It was delivered not as a boast but as a hard fact – and he found himself believing it.

'I assume Commissioner McMillan has already briefed you as to the general theory?' Davies went on.

Carney nodded. 'You want me to advise a special task force. Basically point you in the right direction.'

Davies nodded again. 'In a nutshell, yes. But you'll be more than just an adviser, more like a seeing-eye dog. We're going to need a man on the ground. Someone who knows the right people and the right places.'

'Or the wrong people and the wrong places,' Carney suggested.

Davies found this mildly amusing, and smiled. 'Whatever.' He was thoughtful for a while. 'Of course, in an ideal world you should never be required to get involved in a combat situation. However, we don't live in an ideal world. There may be times when you find yourself up front. What have you done in the way of weapons training?'

Carney gave a faint shrug. 'Standard police training. Revolver and some sniper rifle practice.'

Davies consulted Carney's file again. 'Not bad scores,' he observed, in a matter-of-fact tone. It was the nearest thing to a compliment he had given out so far. He made a note on the file. 'But we'll check it out in a minute.' He eyed Carney up and down like a piece of meat. 'When was your last physical?'

Carney had to think about it. 'I'm not sure,' he admitted. 'Probably about five or six months ago.'

Davies made another note. 'We'll have to do something about that, as well.' He looked at Carney appraisingly. 'You look reasonably fit. Do much in the way of training, working out?'

Carney shrugged. 'Just regular health club stuff, once or maybe twice a week. Weights, bike machine, a couple of miles on the rolling road.'

'Sports? Pastimes?' Davies asked.

Carney smiled ruefully. 'Don't get a lot of time these days. I used to climb a bit, and I was junior squash champion at school.' He studied Davies's eyes carefully, noting that the SAS man was unimpressed. 'Actually, all this raises something I wanted to talk to you about,' he said.

Davies raised one eyebrow. 'Which is?'

Carney paused for a second, framing his thoughts. 'Look, I have a pretty fair idea of the sort of men I'm going to have to work with,' he started out. 'And I'm prepared for the fact that there's quite likely to be a certain amount of resentment – me being an outsider and all.'

Davies made no attempt to deny it. There would have been no point. However, it was good that Carney appeared to have a realistic viewpoint. He eyed him thoughtfully. 'So what's the point you're trying to make?'

Carney took the bull by the horns. 'If I'm to stand any chance of gaining the men's respect, I know I'm going to have to earn it,' he said quietly. 'That's why I'd like to get involved at ground level, if it's at all possible. What are the chances of my joining some of the men in basic training?'

Davies was impressed – both with the man's accurate assessment of the situation and with with his bottle. He smiled thinly. 'Have you got the faintest idea of what you might be talking yourself into?' he asked.

Carney was perfectly truthful. 'No,' he admitted. 'But I'd still like to give it a go.'

Davies's smile broadened. 'Look, it's fairly obvious that, like most members of the general public, you have a somewhat simplistic view of how we operate,' he said, without sounding patronizing. 'It's not a question of "six weeks basic training and you're in the SAS". All our volunteers are already highly trained soldiers. Our selection training is short, brutal and perhaps the most intensive in the world – but it doesn't just stop there. Basically, an SAS soldier never stops training from the day he joins the Regiment to the day he leaves. It's an ongoing thing.'

Carney digested all this information stoically. 'All right, I concede that I'm not prime material to start with. But I'd like to get some time in with the men.'

Davies was more and more convinced that Franks had sent him the right man, but he wasn't giving anything away. He merely nodded faintly. 'OK, I'll see what can be arranged,' he promised as he rose to his feet. 'But right now, let's get you down to the range and see what you can do.'

He ushered Carney out of the room and along a long corridor, eventually stopping by a steel-shuttered door. Producing a security key from his pocket, Davies unlocked the heavy door and swung it open, revealing a flight of concrete steps which led down into the basement. As the door opened, a barrage of loud noise echoed up the stairs. It took Carney a few seconds to identify it as the sounds of gunfire in an enclosed space. He followed Davies down the stairs and through another security door, finally stepping into the vast underground indoor firing range.

The sudden appearance of Lieutenant-Colonel Davies seemed to act as some sort of signal. The half a dozen or so troopers using the target range discharged their weapons quickly, put them down and walked away. Davies led the way over to a shooting booth next to the armourer's office, summoning the man with a click of his fingers.

The armourer stepped over smartly, slipped a fresh clip into a handgun and laid the weapon down.

'What have you used in the past?' Davies asked, glancing at Carney.

'Standard-issue army Webley .38 revolver,' Carney told him.

Davies nodded, picking up the semi-automatic in front of him. 'We tend to use these,' he explained. 'The Browning 9mm High Power handgun. They've been around for a good few years now, but we find they do the job.' He picked the gun up and thrust it into Carney's hand.

Carney weighed the weapon, assessing its feel. It was somewhat lighter than the heavy pistols he was used to, yet oddly it felt somehow more solid, more real. Instinct told him that this was not a gun which had been designed, or ever intended for, making holes in paper targets. This was a weapon expressly created to kill people.

Davies quickly ran through the weapon's operation, finishing with basic safety instructions. 'You've got eight shots in that magazine,' he said, 'although normally it'll hold up to thirteen. Don't put it down, or point it away from the target area, until you've emptied it.'

Carney moved into the firing position, spreading his feet slightly and balancing his body. Holding the gun in the approved two-handed grip, he squinted down the sights towards the black silhouette at the end of the range.

'Carry on,' Davies muttered.

Carney squeezed gently on the trigger, loosing off the first three rounds before checking the target. All three shots were high – the semi-automatic had a greater kick than he was accustomed to. Lowering his aim to compensate, he tightened his grip and fired off three more rounds. They were better – both body hits. He put the final two slugs smack in the middle of the target's blank black face and laid the gun down again.

'Not bad,' Davies said, with grudging approval, as the armourer slid over and inserted a fresh clip into the magazine. 'But don't be too obsessed with going for head shots. The traditional "double tap" through the forehead isn't quite as fashionable now as it used to be.'

Carney looked at him in some surprise. 'I thought a guaranteed kill was the object of the exercise?' he said.

Davies nodded. 'Oh, it is. Basic SAS philosophy is that you don't point a gun at someone unless you fully intend to kill him. But there can be other factors.'

Carney was intrigued. 'Such as?'

Davies shrugged. 'Suppose we were dealing with a hostage situation, involving armed terrorists,' he suggested. 'The prime consideration would be to neutralize the gunmen before they could do any harm and to protect the hostages as much as possible. Think about it, Carney – a head is a small target, and the human body is a bigger one. Accurate, sustained fire to the body is going to put your man down just as efficiently, but with less loose bullets flying about the place.' He paused, nodding down at the the gun in front of Carney. 'That's why the Browning is a good weapon. It has real stopping power.'

There was a sudden crash from behind them as the

inner steel door was kicked open. It was followed, almost immediately, by the roar of an angry voice. 'I warned you, Davies – you bastard!'

Carney whirled round, to take in the burly figure of the soldier who had just burst into the underground range. His eyes were blazing cold rage, and his mouth was contorted into a mask of fury. They were looks that could kill – and the L1A1 self-loading rifle that he carried slung at his hip gave him the capacity to do exactly that.

'I told you what would happen if you turned down my transfer,' the man raged on, moving purposefully towards Davies. 'Now I'm going to kill you, you bastard.'

Out of the corner of his eyes, Carney was aware of the armourer trying to edge towards the arsenal. The movement was also noted by the armed intruder, who barked out a warning: 'Don't even fucking think about it.' He advanced upon them inexorably, his finger curled lazily around the trigger of the rifle.

Perhaps foolishly, the armourer made a quick and desperate grab for a gun. The rifle bucked twice in the soldier's grip. The armourer let out a brief cry of pain as the two shots cracked out, then began to sink to his knees, clutching his hand to his belly.

Carney's guts churned over. He had no doubt now that he was going to die. It was so stupid, so pointless, that he felt a seething, blinding anger more than anything else. It was this, and a sense of desperation, which made him act instinctively, without thinking.

He pivoted on the balls of his feet with grace which would not have disgraced a Russian ballet dancer. In one smooth movement, he snatched up the loaded Browning and dropped to the floor, rolling away from Davies and bringing the gun up into position.

The sudden action took the soldier unawares. He had not been prepared for the intervention of a civilian. In the fraction of a second it took him to recognize the threat, and to swing the rifle in its direction, Carney had fired off three shots. The soldier stopped dead in his tracks, the rifle dropping from his hands. Then, soundlessly, he collapsed to the floor.

Carney was trembling all over. He found it hard to catch his breath. The jolt of adrenalin which had surged through his system had put his mind and body into overdrive. He could not think clearly, other than register the fact that he had just killed a man. Wide-eyed and questioning, he could only gape at Davies's face as though the man could offer him some sort of an explanation.

None was offered. Davies's face was impassive, composed. He seemed perfectly calm, as though nothing out of the ordinary had happened. Carney's brain reeled. It was as if the man had no emotions at all, nerves of absolute steel.

Then Davies began to smile, to Carney's further astonishment.

'Good, you have no compunction about killing in a crisis situation,' he murmured with quiet satisfaction. 'Quite a few people won't, you know – even when their lives are directly threatened. They tend to freeze up – until it's too late.'

Carney could understand none of it. Still bemused

with shock, he tore his eyes away from Davies's face to the soldier on the floor.

The man was scrambling to his feet now, a broad smile on his black face. The armourer, too, had miraculously recovered and was once again standing calmly beside the gun store.

'Blanks, of course,' Davies said casually. 'Just a little test, you understand. You passed, by the way.'

Carney felt like hitting him. Instead he forced himself to breathe slowly and deeply until he started to feel reasonably normal again. His victim was standing beside him now.

'Mr Carney, meet Sergeant Andrew Winston,' Davies said by way of introduction. 'You'll be working quite closely with him. Winston writes poetry and kills people – and does them both very well indeed.'

Winston extended a hand. 'Hi,' he said.

Carney had no choice but to take it. He received a warm, hearty handshake. 'You were fast,' the big Barbadian complimented him. 'Bloody fast, as it happens.'

'I said you'd be working closely together. I don't expect you to fall in love with each other,' Davies said mockingly. He clapped his hands together, rubbing them in a gesture of satisfaction. 'Well, gentlemen, now that's all over, perhaps we should retire to the Paludrine Club for a drink.'

8

Three weeks later, Paul Carney was a much fitter, wiser man, and bore a deep and lasting respect for the men of 22 SAS, along with a fierce pride in his involvement with them.

True to his word, Lieutenant-Colonel Davies had cleared it for him to train alongside his military colleagues. The first few days had been sheer hell, the next two weeks worse, but Carney had come out of the experience with a whole new perspective on things. He now knew that it was possible to push the human body, and the human spirit, to the limits of pain and beyond the boundaries of endurance. And he was beginning, slowly, to understand the almost mystical sense of group pride and loyalty which bound together the men of the finest combat regiment in the world.

His initial fears about his acceptance by the rest of the men had been proved right. For the first few days he had simply been ignored. And when that had ceased to be a feasible proposition he had been treated with guarded suspicion, even hostility. Then came the jokes at his expense, the insults and the humiliation, culminating in a series of cruel practical jokes, many of them bordering on the savage. For days after the ragging finally ceased, Carney found it difficult to readjust himself to the taste of tea which had not been enhanced with the flavour of piss.

But he'd stuck through it all, with dogged deter-
mination. He'd learned to survive a twenty-mile
route march across rugged hill country with a 24-lb
bergen strapped to his back. He'd faced extreme
weakness from near-starvation and learned how to
appease his hunger by eating raw slugs and snails
and the roots of certain wild plants and grasses.
But most of all, and perhaps most importantly, he'd
learned the strange exultation of knowing himself
to be a survivor against adversity and a rare breed
of man. A strong individual – and yet an even
stronger member of a team, a unit. Carney felt
he had been granted a great privilege afforded to
few men.

He had won the men's respect, if not yet their full
acceptance. That would take time; perhaps it might
never fully occur. It didn't really matter. What did
matter was that the team had been formed, and it
worked: a quartet of four-man patrol units, forming
a full troop, which would serve as the sharp end
of the operation. With intelligence backup and a
further eight troopers on standby, they were all set
up and ready to go. Davies had already granted them
their autonomy, as he had always intended. Having
fulfilled his original brief, he no longer had an active
role to play, and the SAS had little use or regard for
padding.

There remained only a final briefing, and their first
assignment. That, as it happened, was closer than
anyone yet suspected.

They were all assembled in the Kremlin, the SAS
Operations Planning and Intelligence cell at Stirling

Lines. Major Mike Anderson, recalled from under-
cover work in Northern Ireland, had been assigned
Troopers Phil 'Jumbo' Jackson, Eddie Mentieth and
Pete Delaney. All were recently badged, having com-
pleted their fourteen weeks of Continuation Training
only two months earlier. The second unit, headed by
Captain Barry 'Butch' Blake, also consisted of three
probationers and was the stuff of an 'Englishman,
Irishman and Scotsman' joke, cockney Mike Peters,
Jimmy Phelan and Ian 'Aberdeen' Angus.

Captain Brian Feeney's unit was complemented
by another mixed bag, with the mercurial blend of
Scouser Ted Brennon, Cornishman Miles Tremathon
and the sole Welshman of the troop, Hugh Thomas.
The 'North–South' split of the group was largely held
in check by Hugh, who had already earned himself
the nickname of the Lethal Leek, from his prowess
in CQB, close-quarter battle.

Officially Carney was not attached to any particular unit, his role being somewhat vaguely defined as
adviser to all four. Yet he found it almost impossible
not to associate himself with Andrew Winston, with
whom he had established a strange bond which was
not quite friendship, not quite trust. Backed up
with Pretty Boy Parrit, the unit was brought up
to full strength by the addition of young troopers
Terry Marks and Tony Tofield, the pair of them
known throughout the Regiment as Tweedledum
and Tweedledee, from their habit of staying close
together. A few years older than most of the others,
Winston had picked them mainly because he knew
and trusted them implicitly, both of them having

accompanied him on a particularly hazardous mission in the mountains of Kazakhstan, in the former Soviet Union, several months previously.

The assembled men waited for David Grieves, the man from the 'green slime', to give them a briefing update and final clearance to go into operation. After that, they would largely be on their own, and the meeting would open out into a 'Chinese Parliament' in which every man, regardless of rank, was free to have his say.

Grieves arrived and took the rostrum, facing them squarely. 'Gentlemen, we now have a name for our enemy,' he announced, a trifle melodramatically. 'The drug goes under the street name of Nirvana.' He paused, a thin and rueful smile on his lips. 'For those of you not clued up on oriental religions and mysticism, it's a word which Buddhists use to describe a state of supreme inner peace. Particularly ironic, since this drug has the exact opposite effect.'

'You mean like a bloody laxative?' Ted Brennon shouted out, raising a guffaw of laughter from the rest of the men.

Major Anderson shot him a withering glance. Until Grieves had finished, he was still nominally in charge by virtue of rank. Bullshit from the men would only be tolerated once the Chinese Parliament was under way.

Grieves took the brief interruption in his stride. 'With what limited tests our forensic scientists have been able to conduct, it is estimated that the use of this drug raises natural aggression levels by between fifty and sixty per cent,' he went on. 'In other words, anyone under the influence of this substance is at least one and a half times more likely to commit an act of violence, even sadism. Of course, this rough guide becomes somewhat meaningless if the user happens to be of a violent nature to start with. Even worse, we don't yet know what the build-up factor is likely to be. Continued use may well raise these aggression levels on an exponential, and possibly permanent, scale.'

Carney put up his hand, attracting Grieves's attention. 'Form and administration?' he asked.

Grieves knew exactly what he meant. 'Currently we believe it is being produced as a pill, the active chemicals contained within an inert and largely harmless base compound. However, because the drug works in incredibly low dosages, and has a high absorption factor in humans, it may also occur in microdot form.'

Carney accepted the information stoically, although from his point of view it was probably the worst possible scenario. Pills were the most popular form of drug-taking with thrill-seeking kids, especially the very young. Current drugs such as Ecstasy had made massive inroads into new markets by virtue of the fact that they appealed to a whole new generation of kids who might balk at injecting themselves or inhaling crack. Pills and microdots had a perceived image of being 'clean', even fashionable.

There was another negative factor. Given quite moderate production facilities, pills were quick and easy to manufacture and simple to distribute. And tracing that distribution network would be more difficult, since the established and fairly well-known chain of needle-users was virtually useless.

As Carney pondered on these problems Grieves continued his briefing.

'We're pretty sure that the drug originated in Germany, and the initial distribution through mainland Europe was controlled from there,' he went on. 'However, that is no longer the case. Production facilities are now beginning to pop up all over the place.' Grieves paused for some time before coming to the main point of his address.

'And here's the good news, gentlemen,' he announced finally. 'We are pretty sure we have already identified one of these factories operating from a disused farm in Norfolk. Busting that factory will be your first assignment.'

Grieves stepped back from the rostrum, indicating that he had said what he wanted to say. The meeting was now open.

Major Anderson climbed to his feet. 'But surely that should be a job for the conventional police forces?' he queried. 'Isn't sending us in rather like taking a sledgehammer to crack a walnut?'

Grieves shook his head grimly. 'The German police, fully armed, tried a similar operation just over two weeks ago,' he said. 'They lost five men. We don't want to take that sort of risk, and besides, it gives you an early chance to try yourselves out. Hopefully, it will also serve as a warning to these bastards that we're not going to take the soft approach. It may be a slim hope, but if we could frighten them off before they get really established in the UK, we might save ourselves a whole lot of trouble.'

'So basically what we're talking about here is sending one load of psychotic bastards in after another load of psychotic bastards?' Pretty Boy observed facetiously.

The comment evinced a wave of groans and protest.

'You speak for yourself, Pretty Boy,' Aberdeen Angus shouted out. 'I'm as sane as the next man.'

This claim was hotly disputed by most of the other troopers, several of them pointing out the fact that he was, in fact, sitting next to the lethal Leek, who was widely known to be as barmy as a bedbug. The Welshman's predictable arguments of self-defence were in turn rubbished by various accusations of sheep-shagging and other unsavoury practices in the Black Mountains.

Major Anderson let the men enjoy their few moments of good-natured ragging. It was something of a tradition, if not standard SAS procedure, to indulge in a bullshit session after a briefing. Rising from his chair, he strolled over to Carney, who was sitting beside Winston.

'Look, you're the nearest we've got to an expert on drugs abuse,' he muttered. 'Why the hell should kids want to dose themselves up on something which is going to drive them crazy. That's what I fail to understand.'

Carney could only shrug. It was a question he'd been asked many times before, and he still didn't have an adequate answer.

'Why not?' he asked. 'They've been doing equally stupid things for years. Shooting shit into their veins which they know to be addictive and physically destructive. Popping amphetamines which turn brain tissue into something resembling gruyère cheese. Deliberately tripping out into the world of nightmares and insanity.' He paused, letting it sink in. 'So why not this new drug? Something which raises violence into a near-ecstatic experience would seem almost a natural for some of these kids. It's the ultimate trip for the nineties. Just look at a bunch of football hooligans on the rampage.'

Anderson stared at him piercingly. 'You're a cynical bastard, aren't you?' he observed.

Carney merely smiled bitterly. 'Let's put it this way, Major. You've fought on your battlegrounds; I've fought on mine.'

There wasn't much to offer in the way of a rejoinder, Anderson thought, remembering nights on patrol in the Shankill Road. Nodding faintly, he turned away and made his way over to Grieves for further information on the location of the suspected drugs factory.

Carney turned to Winston. 'So, what's my position on this one?' he asked.

The Barbadian grinned at him. 'Your position is that you don't have one,' he said firmly. 'This little jaunt will be strictly down to us death or glory boys.'

Carney nodded. It was exactly the answer he had been expecting, but he still looked disappointed.

'Hey, listen, you've still got an important job to do,' Winston reminded him. 'Out there on the streets, that's where the real battle's going to be fought.

You're our eyes and ears out there. We're still going to need information on the distribution network for this stuff.'

The little speech made Carney feel better, as it was intended to do. Winston was right. He *did* have a job to do – and he fully intended to do it to the best of his ability.

9

'I don't know about you, boss, but I feel a right prat,' Pretty Boy complained bitterly. Known as something of a snappy dresser when he was in mufti, he was currently clad in khaki shorts, thick brown socks, heavy walking boots, a padded blue checked shirt and carrying on his back a bright blue and yellow rucksack which boasted the legend 'Hiker's Friend'.

Winston, similarly dressed, looked at him with a vaguely peeved expression. 'Stop bloody moaning and just enjoy yourself,' he said. 'We're just a couple of country-loving ramblers out for a nice quiet stroll. What could be better than a leisurely stroll in the open air on a nice day like today?'

Pretty Boy grunted, unconvinced. 'Well, I think we look like a couple of bloody poofs,' he muttered. 'Fancy holding hands to make it a bit more convincing?' Changing his trudging walk into a mincing gait, he sidled up to Winston's side, slipped his index finger into the man's huge palm and tickled it.

Winston shrugged him away with an exaggerated gesture. 'Fuck off,' he growled good-naturedly. 'Otherwise I'll start believing all those rumours about you that float round the shower rooms.'

Pretty Boy laughed, moving away again and falling into normal step beside the big sergeant. They continued walking up the rutted lane, which curved around to the right of a cluster of derelict barns about a hundred yards ahead of them.

'Right, now keep your eyes peeled,' Winston hissed, suddenly becoming very serious. 'According to my information, the farm's just around that bend, between the outbuildings. And look casual, for Christ's sake. It's a ten-to-one shot they'll have someone on lookout, and they're bound to be suspicious of strangers, even at a distance.'

Pretty Boy nodded, now equally businesslike. 'You got it, boss,' he said quietly.

The abrupt change in dialogue betrayed the true nature of their mission. Far from being on an innocent ramble in the country, they were carrying out a vital reconnaissance of the suspected farmhouse, which had now been under intensive surveillance for three days. The SAS rarely jumped into anything without extremely careful preparation – and this mission would be no different. Detailed information as to the position and structure of the main building and outbuildings was of supreme importance, as was any information which could be gathered about personnel, guards and possible defensive positions. Although Major Anderson had established a concealed observation post on the far side of the farm, and conducted round-the-clock surveillance using high-powered zoom cameras and night-sight binoculars, this was the closest anyone had yet ventured to the buildings themselves. Aerial reconnaissance had furnished valuable plans of the general layout of the farm, but Winston and Pretty Boy needed a good view from ground level. They were hoping to pick up information on any vehicles which might be parked out of sight among the barns and out-buildings, besides checking out the lane as a possible attack point.

They were less than sixty yards from the nearest barn when Winston tensed suddenly, his keen ears picking up the low growl of engines in low gear grinding up the lane some way behind them.

Pretty Boy had heard them too. He cast a quick look over his shoulder. 'They ain't in sight yet, boss,' he said hurriedly. 'What do we do – dive for cover?'

Winston stopped, considering the suggestion in a flash. His eyes darted from side to side, taking in the limitations of the open terrain around them. Short of hiding in a narrow rain culvert on one side of the lane, there was no decent cover to speak of.

'Forget it,' he hissed. 'Just keep walking. Whoever it is may have bumped us already, and it would look fucking suspicious if we suddenly disappeared, wouldn't it?' He began to move again, deliberately slowing his pace as the sound of the approaching vehicles drew nearer.

There were two, his keen instincts told him. A fairly small 4WD vehicle such as a Landrover or a Shogun, and a much heavier lorry. He hissed aside at Pretty Boy. 'Right, discreet surveillance as they go past. 'I'll concentrate on the car, you check out the truck.' He broke step momentarily to let Pretty Boy move a foot or so in front of him, so that they would both have clear and unobstructed side vision. The vehicles were right on their heels now, less than thirty yards from the turn-off to the farm buildings.

They stepped to the side of the lane, waiting to let the vehicles go past.

The smaller vehicle was in fact a Jeep Cherokee. Winston eyed it covertly as it rolled past him, counting its occupants. Driver and passenger in the front, one more man sat on the back seat.

The lorry which followed it was older, and probably a four-tonner, Winston estimated. He looked away from it, letting Pretty Boy fulfil his side of the deal. The lorry's brake lights flashed on almost as soon as it had ground past.

'Bingo,' Pretty Boy breathed. Up to that point neither of them had been sure whether the two vehicles had any connection with the farm at all. But now they were definitely slowing, preparing to turn in between the buildings.

Winston and Pretty Boy started walking again, moving towards the far entrance as the lorry's tailgate disappeared from view. Both cast quick but penetrating glances between the cluster of outbuildings as they strode casually past and continued up the lane. Neither spoke for nearly a minute, until they were out in open countryside again.

Suddenly Winston stopped, on the pretext of retying his boot laces. Kneeling down, he cast a wary eye back towards the farm to check everything before rising to his feet again and glancing questioningly at Pretty Boy.

'Well? What do you think?'

Pretty Boy looked at him dubiously. 'I think we could have a problem,' he said. 'That lorry was empty.'

'You sure?' Winston asked.

Pretty Boy nodded emphatically. 'I checked the underframe and the wheel clearance as she went by. She was riding high. That truck was unladen, I'd swear it.'

'Shit.' Winston vented his frustration in the single, explosive curse. The implications were obvious. Lorries served one of two purposes. They either delivered things, or they carried them away. And if it was arriving empty, it was a pretty sure bet that it wouldn't be leaving in the same condition.

'Looks like they're getting ready to ship a consignment out,' Pretty Boy observed. 'Guess we're going to have to change our plans, eh, boss?'

Winston nodded. 'And bloody fast,' he added. 'We'd better get back to the RV pronto.'

'At a standard rambler's pace?' Pretty Boy asked sarcastically.

Winston glared at him. 'What do you think? We backtrack until we're out of sight of that farmhouse and then we run like fuck.'

Which is exactly what they did.

The rendezvous point and main base had been set up in a small copse on the blind side of a hill which overlooked the farm. Offering good cover for the men and supplies, it was an excellent vantage-point, and would have been ideal for a sneak attack at night. In broad daylight, however, it was next to useless. Having left the cover of the trees, anyone trying to approach the farm down the side of the bare, grassy hill would be in clear view all the way.

Inside the operations-control lorry, Major Anderson listened to Winston's report, accepting the unwelcome news with a worried frown. Besides screwing his plans up, it also gave him a tough decision to make. It was all a question of timing. How soon would the drug manufacturers make their move? he wondered.

It was a question Winston had already considered. 'Well, can we afford to wait for nightfall as we'd planned?' he asked.

Anderson shrugged. 'Who the hell knows?' He was silent for a long time, pondering over the problem and trying to weigh up all the possibilities and their consequences. It was a complex issue, and one he really wished he didn't have to decide upon so hastily. His original plan, to insert his men under cover of darkness and achieve a quick surprise attack, had been basically simple.

More for his own benefit than anything else, he voiced the alternatives. 'If we wait, then we run the risk of them getting that lorry loaded and out. Then there'll be another batch of this stuff hitting the streets. If we go in too early, we lose any element of surprise and we risk taking losses.' Anderson paused, looking at Winston. 'Any suggestions?'

'Only one,' Winston murmured. 'Suppose we just back off and wait to intercept the lorry well away from the farm? Then we can attack the HQ later, as per the original plan.'

Anderson shook his head. 'Two main problems. Firstly, there's still the chance that the green slime have this all wrong and there's really nothing particularly sinister going on at that farm. We shoot up a vehicle and perhaps kill a couple of civilians doing nothing more than shipping a few sacks of horse shit and we'll have really blown it for ourselves. Number two, even if they are what we think they are, there's a strong possibility they'll have some sort of radio link between the lorry and the base. First sign of trouble and all the birds will have flown the nest. We'd have no chance of rounding them all up in open countryside like this.'

'So what it boils down to is either we play safe and risk letting them get the drugs out, or we go in early and risk ourselves?'

Major Anderson nodded, a wry smile on his face. 'No choice at all really, is it?' he said. He looked up at Winston. 'How soon can you have your unit ready to go?'

The question didn't really need any consideration. The two Tweedles were currently manning the observation post less than quarter of a mile away. A simple recall over the radio and they could be on their way back to base. Then it would be simply a question of getting to the armoury lorry and tooling up.

'Twenty minutes,' Winston said confidently. 'Fifteen if you're in a hurry.'

Anderson smiled. 'Oh, I think we might stretch to half an hour,' he said generously.

He pulled out the aerial reconnaissance map and spread it out. 'Our best chance is to split into two forces and RV again here,' he said, jabbing his finger down at the spot Winston and Pretty Boy had just left. 'I'll take Captain Feeney and his men and skirt around the far side of this hill to approach the farm from the opposite direction. You'll join up with Butch Blake and make the most discreet approach you can along that lane.' He looked up questioningly. 'What sort of cover are you going to have?'

'There's a flood ditch which seems to run all along the side,' Winston told him. 'We can use that.'

'Good,' Anderson said, looking relieved. 'That means we should all be able to get at least as far as the farm outbuildings without being bumped. After that it's anyone's guess.' He paused, studying Winston and Pretty Boy intently. 'I don't need to stress to either of you that we are dealing with civilians here, and we're in a very sticky and unusual situation. We do not open fire unless fired upon. However, if and when that happens, then strict CRW rules apply. All targets are to be neutralized unless they surrender unambiguously.'

'Got you, boss,' Winston muttered. 'It'll be as clean as our friends down there want it to be.'

Anderson nodded. 'Right.' He traced his finger over the map and into the cluster of outbuildings, finally locating the main farmhouse. 'Once we break cover of these buildings we'll be totally exposed and only a direct frontal attack will be open to us. One unit apiece will take the front, back and sides of the farmhouse and we'll go in together, after achieving our priority aim of disabling that lorry. I'm taking in an M72 anti-tank weapon. If we are under fire at that point I'll blow out the front wall of the building to facilitate entry.' He looked up from the map. 'All clear?'

'As a virgin's piss, boss,' Pretty Boy said, grinning. 'Not that I ever met one, of course.'

Anderson seemed as satisfied as he could be with the hastily changed plans. 'Right,' he said, checking his watch before looking at Winston. 'Recall your men, get kitted up and join up with Captain Blake. We'll RV at exactly 1730 hours.'

Winston grinned. 'Just when they'll be having their tea,' he said sarcastically. 'Won't that be a pleasant surprise for them?'

He turned to leave, ushering Pretty Boy ahead of him.

'Oh, by the way,' Anderson called after them, having an afterthought. 'You two *will* get changed into something a bit more suitable, won't you? You look like a couple of pooftahs dressed like that.'

Pretty Boy turned on him, a sheepish grin on his face. 'We'll be dressed in our Sunday best, boss,' he promised.

Anderson smiled back. 'No you won't,' he insisted. 'You'll be wearing Noddy suits and respirators. If that *is* a drug factory down there we don't know what kinds of chemicals and stuff are likely to be floating around if the bullets start to fly.'

10

Paul Carney heard the faint sound of music coming from the inside of his flat as he reached the top of the stairs, and was instantly on the alert. He crept up to the door and slipped the key into the lock as silently as he could. Taking a deep breath, he flung the door open and threw himself into the room, tensed for potential trouble.

Linda sat on the sofa, sipping at a gin and tonic and listening to the stereo unit. She looked up quickly as he burst in, at first in alarm and then in relieved amusement.

'Who were you expecting? The Mafia?'

Carney sighed. 'What are you doing here?' he demanded.

Linda shrugged. 'Well, I must admit that I hadn't expected a rapturous welcome,' she observed. 'But I am still your wife, and I still have a key.' She paused, forcing a thin smile. 'I thought it was time we talked, Paul.'

Carney sighed again. 'We *did* talk,' he reminded her. 'And we decided it was best if you left for a while. Gave me the time I needed to think things over.'

'It's already been nearly seven months,' Linda pointed out. 'And where the hell have you been for the past three weeks? You've left your job, you've not been answering the phone and all Harry Manners would tell me is that you'd had some sort of transfer and couldn't go into details.'

'I've been away,' Carney said simply. There wasn't much else he could tell her, under the restrictions of his security oath.

Linda accepted it at face value, given no other choice. 'Well, are you ready to talk about us yet? See if there's any chance of patching up our marriage?' She looked like a helpless child. 'For Christ's sake, Paul, I still love you. I made a stupid mistake, and I'm sorry. It was a one-night stand and I'll never do it again. I know now what I could lose – what I may already have lost.'

Carney's face was an agony of indecision. Part of him wanted to rush towards her, sweep her up in his arms and kiss her, tell her that he forgave her. But the other part, the deep, inner part which was still hurting, fought against the impulse, reminding him that he just did not have the capacity to forgive. It was more than wounded male ego, more than stupid pride. It was a fundamental part of his being, so powerful and inflexible that it was one of his greatest strengths – and his greatest weakness.

He stared at his wife hopelessly. 'I still need time, Linda. You have to give me some space.'

'For what? Meditation on a mountain top?' Linda demanded, her desperation lending a shrill edge to her voice. 'Do you have to purify yourself before you can even consider forgiving me? For God's sake, Paul, you're forty-three years of age and you haven't yet learned to forgive the world for not being perfect.'

Carney looked defensive. 'It's not like that,' he muttered.

'So what is it like? Are you afraid that some of my dirt is going to rub off on to that nice shiny suit of armour you wear?'

Carney spread his hands in a gesture of impotence. 'Look, I've got a lot of other things on my mind right now. My new job — it's important.'

Linda nodded sadly, reading the implicit message between the lines. 'And I'm not, I suppose?' She finished her drink, rose to her feet and set the empty glass down on the mantelpiece. She looked at him miserably for several moments, waiting for him to say something to stop her leaving. But he was silent.

Finally, Linda gave in, accepting the inevitable. 'All right, love, you go and saddle up Rosinante and ride off to the windmills. But Sancho Panza quits. I'll see a solicitor next week.' She took a key from her handbag and placed it next to the empty glass before walking to the door. 'Goodbye, Paul.'

Carney stood mutely, watching her go. He wanted to say something to her, but nothing would come. Linda closed the door behind her and he was alone. He heard her soft footsteps fade away down the stairs. In sheer frustration, he crossed the lounge and slammed his fist against the wall. It didn't make him feel any better.

He picked up the telephone and dialled Harry Manners's number. 'Harry? It's me, Paul. Listen, what's the latest on Sofrides?'

Manners was guarded. 'What's your interest, Paul?'

'Purely professional,' Carney assured him. 'Basically, is he in or out?'

Manners paused on the other end of the line, still unsure of Carney's motives. But he'd been ordered to afford the man every assistance, so he didn't have much choice in the matter. 'All right, Sofrides is still in the hospital,' he admitted finally. 'But he should be discharged in the next day or so. After that, he walks.'

'Jesus Christ!' Carney found it impossible to control his anger and sense of frustration.

There was no hint of apology in Manners's voice. 'You didn't leave us much choice, Paul. Sofrides claims that the girl turned up at his flat already stoned and just keeled over. He says he was taking the girl to hospital when you stopped him, but you never gave him a chance to explain.'

Carney snorted derisively. 'Taking her to hospital? In the bloody *boot*? Come off it, Harry. You believe that crap?'

'I don't – but a jury might,' Manners said. 'It's just not worth bringing a prosecution. A good brief, and he'll get off scot-free. The little bastard might even bung in a claim for aggravated assault as well.' The man paused. 'Which brings me back to my original question – what's your interest in him now? Any further contact might be construed as police harassment.'

'I just need to talk to him, that's all,' Carney said reassuringly. 'I won't even raise my voice at the little scumbag, I promise. It's just that Sofrides shouldn't have been handling smack in the first place. He's always been strictly a nose-candy man in the past. Which could suggest he's branching out into new areas – and if he is, he may well have heard some whispers on this new drug. It's a long shot, but it could be worth following up.'

It seemed like a reasonable explanation, and Manners accepted it, albeit grudgingly. 'OK, I'll grant you clearance to see him,' he conceded. 'But just watch yourself, that's all.'

'Yeah. I'll be a regular boy scout,' Carney promised, and hung up.

Tony Sofrides looked up from his hospital bed apprehensively as Carney strolled into the ward. He reached hurriedly for the emergency button dangling above his bandaged head.

Carney strode across the room and snatched it out of the youth's hand before he had a chance to use it. 'You won't need that, Tony,' he said, grinning savagely. 'Just a nice friendly little chat.'

The look of fright on Sofrides's face faded away, to be replaced with one of arrogance. He realized that Carney had probably been warned not to even touch him. 'Yeah? Brought me some grapes then, have you, copper?'

Carney smiled. 'Better than that, Tony. I'm bringing you a chance of staying alive – at a price.'

Sofrides looked alarmed again. 'What are you bloody talking about?'

Carney shrugged and spread his hands. 'Oh, it's quite simple really. You offered me a deal – remember? To set up someone like Jack Mottram for me?'

'Get stuffed, Carney,' Sofrides blustered. 'All deals are off. My brief says I walk this one, no sweat. You fucking blew it.'

Carney refused to be rattled, keeping a chilling smile on his face. 'You might find it rather difficult to walk – with both your kneecaps missing,' he pointed out. 'Jack's a bad lad. He doesn't like grasses very much.'

Sofrides grinned defiantly. 'Yeah, well, I ain't gonna grass, am I? There's no bloody percentage in it for me now, is there?'

Carney sighed heavily. It was obvious that the dealer didn't quite get the picture, so he decided to spell it out for him. 'Now, *you* know that . . . and *I* know that. But Jack Mottram doesn't know it. And when a heavy hand descends on his collar, and a friendly little voice informs him that a certain little Greek put the word out, you're not going to be a very good life-insurance prospect, Tony.'

The brief flicker of fear which crossed Sofrides's face was quickly snuffed out by a look of bravado. Coppers – even undercover drugs coppers – didn't do certain things. There was a certain amount of understanding between the police and the criminal fraternity. A code of practice.

Sofrides sneered. 'You wouldn't fit up someone like Jack Mottram, and we both know it,' he said confidently.

Carney flashed his cool smile again. He had an ace up his sleeve now. He was no longer bound by his previous limitations. 'Oh, did I forget to tell you,

Tony? We just changed the rules,' he said in a quiet but utterly menacing tone. 'Like you said earlier, all deals are off, and so are the gloves.'

'You're bluffing, you bastard,' Sofrides said, but he didn't sound quite so convinced.

'So call it,' Carney suggested casually, turning as if to leave. 'Get smart for the first time in your miserable little life, Tony. I'm offering you the best deal you're likely to get.'

It seemed to swing the balance. Sofrides called after him as Carney moved towards the door. 'OK, so what do you want to know?'

Carney smiled to himself before turning round again. When he did so, his face was composed and serious. 'Nirvana, Tony? Ever heard of it?'

A slightly puzzled look flitted across the Greek's face. 'Yeah, I've heard about it,' he admitted. 'Ain't never come across it yet, though. It's pretty new.'

Carney took this at face value. 'But if you *did* want to get hold of it, where would you go?' he asked.

The puzzled look returned. 'What's the big deal with that stuff? It's only pill-poppers' rubbish, from the whispers I've heard. I mean, like it ain't heavy shit or anything. Wouldn't have thought it was even in your league, Carney.'

It was interesting information, Carney thought. 'So that's the word out on the streets, is it?' he queried. 'That Nirvana is just a low-grade buzz?'

Sofrides shrugged. 'Something like that. Club stuff – know what I mean? Not the sort of gear any serious dealer gets involved with.'

'But there must be some sort of distribution network,' Carney pointed out. 'Somebody's got to be handling it in bulk.'

Sofrides shook his head. 'Well, if there is, then I don't know anything about it – and that's the truth.'

Knowing Sofrides for a lying little toerag, Carney was quite surprised to find that in this case he believed him. He tried another tack. 'You said it's on the club scene. Give me the name of a couple.'

A crafty look spread over Sofrides's face. Something told him he was going to get off light. 'And if I do, you'll back off?' he asked.

Carney nodded. 'That's the deal,' he confirmed.

Sofrides thought about it for a second, before giving a faint shrug. 'OK, but there's only one place I've heard of. Norma Jean's, down Kilburn way.' He looked up at Carney, a flash of his old arrogance returning. 'Now, how about you fucking off and leaving me in peace?'

Carney grinned, turning towards the door. 'Sure, Tony. And I'll give your love to Jack Mottram when I see him.'

He walked out of the ward without turning round to see the look of fear that had returned to the young man's face.

11

Two hundred yards from the farm's outbuildings, Winston lay on his belly in the mud of the culvert, for once in his life actually glad to be wearing the protective NBC suit. Immediately behind him, Pretty Boy and the two Tweedles had also come to a halt, waiting for Major Anderson and Captain Feeney to complete the longer journey around the far side of the farmhouse.

Winston checked his watch, then wriggled over on to his side, holding his Heckler & Koch MP5 sub-machine-gun clear of the mud. He raised his head just enough to see over the prone figure of Pretty Boy and identify Butch Blake and his men, some fifty yards behind them. He held up three fingers, receiving a brief thumbs up from Butch in return. Three more minutes and they would complete their approach, hopefully just as Anderson reached his own destination.

Pretty Boy pulled himself up over Winston's legs, lifting his S-6 respirator away from his face and grinning. 'We're going to look pretty stupid if there's nothing but a bunch of carrot-crunchers in there, aren't we?' he whispered.

Beneath his own mask, Winston smiled to himself, knowing exactly what the man meant. Suited up and armed to the teeth as they were, they represented a lethal, full-scale attack force which would strike terror into the hearts of even the most hardened terrorist group. If the green slime had got it wrong, and they burst in on a group of perfectly innocent yokels, there were likely to be deaths from heart attacks without a single shot being fired.

And an attack force they most certainly were. In addition to guns and knives, each man carried six grenades clipped to his belt webbing. Three 'flash-bang' stun grenades and three of the conventional fragmentation type. Their sheer fire-power was awesome; in addition to the standard Browning HP handguns in their belt pouches, every trooper carried a devastating MP5, with the single exception of Tweedledum, who had chosen to arm himself with a Remington 870 pump-action shotgun.

Winston checked his watch again, as the seconds to RV time ticked away. Finally he rolled back on to his belly and began to wriggle along the culvert in the direction of the farm buildings once more. If Major Anderson's estimation had been correct, the combined assault should start exactly on schedule. A few moments later, he had the satisfaction of seeing a faint flash of something dark moving against the green of the open countryside on the far side of the farm entrance. It could only be Anderson and the rest of the force. Using the contours of the land, he had managed to get the main body of his men to within fifty yards of the outbuildings. They were almost ready to attack.

Winston strained his eyes, picking out individual troopers and the deployment of the two units. One man – it looked like Jumbo Jackson – had dropped behind to set up a heavy machine-gun to provide rear covering fire. The rest were making their way stealthily towards the farm entrance, using the massive bulk of one of the disused barns to hide their approach from the farmhouse itself. Provided there were no lookouts in the outbuildings, the trap should be sprung in a matter of moments.

It proved to be a vain hope. As Anderson led his men clear of their last ground cover, Winston heard the sharp, staccato bark of an Uzi machine-pistol. He saw one of the troopers throw his MP5 into the air as he was hit. He fell, rolled over, and lay still.

'Fuck it!' Winston growled under his breath. Their chance of a surprise attack was gone, and there was no longer any doubt that they were facing an armed and dangerous enemy. The sound of the Uzi had now been supplemented by the individual crack of at least two handguns, and Anderson and his men were caught in a very open and vulnerable position. The only choice now left open to them was a frontal rush assault, counting on Winston and Butch to come in behind them. Winston jumped to his feet, clambering out of the ditch into the lane. 'Shake out,' he yelled at the top of his voice, and broke into a zigzagging run towards the outbuildings.

Anderson had bolted straight for the protection of the old barn at the first sound of gunfire. Now, pressed against its reassuringly thick wall, he and the rest of the men who had made it had at least temporary protection, although they were effectively pinned down. Glancing back over his tracks, he counted two black, unmoving shapes lying in the grass. Quickly checking his companions sheltering against the barn wall, he identified them as Trooper Eddie Mentieth and Captain Feeney. Both good men, he thought, bitterly – although they were all good men. Anderson looked back again over the fields to where Jumbo had finished setting up the general-purpose machine-gun behind the partial cover of a small, grassy hummock. Knowing exactly what his comrades needed, he began to lay down a blanket of short-burst fire over their heads towards the farmhouse.

It was time to move, Anderson thought. Butch and Winston could only be a matter of a few seconds behind them now, and the longer they stayed where they were, the more vulnerable their position would become. It was impossible at that point to get an accurate fix on the position of the Uzi, and if the gunman chose to move his vantage-point, it was possible that he could get a direct line of fire upon them. Pinned against the walls of the barn, they'd be like little tin ducks on a fairground shooting range. Anderson edged his way along to the end of the barn wall and took a lightning glance around the corner. Beyond a rectangular block of concrete pigsties, there was a clear view to the farmhouse, some two hundred yards away down a slight slope.

Anderson pressed himself back against the wall, gesturing to the other men to bunch up behind him. He began to unstrap the M72 anti-tank weapon from his back as he barked out orders.

'Right, on my signal you'll make a direct assault on the farmhouse. Winston and Butch will be coming in behind you. Move in fast, zigzagging as much as possible. When you're down low enough to be clear of the rocket trail, I'll blast out the front wall and come down after you.'

Anderson spoke with a little more assurance than he actually felt. The M72 was essentially a fairly close-range weapon. Although a skilled operator could hope to hit a static target up to 300 metres away, there was no guarantee of success, and no second chance. It was a strictly one-shot weapon, firing a single 66mm rocket by conventional optical sight. Once fired, the entire system was thrown away – burned out and useless.

He pulled off the protective caps at either end of the launcher tube, extending it into firing readiness and causing the pop-up sights to click into place. Hauling it on to his right shoulder like a bazooka, Anderson wrapped his finger gently around the trigger switch. He was ready.

'OK, go!' he barked out, flattening himself against the wall as the rest of the men rushed past him and out into the open. He counted slowly to five, giving them time to get lower down the sloping approach to the farmhouse before throwing himself round the corner of the barn.

Just one shot. He had to make it good! Anderson squinted down the M72's sights, fixing them on a spot between the front door of the farmhouse and a small ground-floor window. It seemed the logical target point, since the wall would be structurally weakest around the door frame, and the window was the most likely position of any gunmen inside the building. Holding his breath, he steadied the firing tube against the corner of the wall and squeezed the trigger.

He had already tossed the spent launcher aside and pulled his MP5 up into a businesslike position before the streaming rocket trail completed its slightly erratic smoke-trail course towards the farmhouse. After setting the weapon for three-round bursts, he launched himself in pursuit of his men.

The rocket exploded with a dull roar which echoed off the surrounding hills, drowning out the sounds of gunfire for a few seconds. When the dust and falling debris had cleared, a hole the size of a small saloon car had been blown in the front wall of the farmhouse. Anderson bounded down the slope towards the rest of his men, who had taken temporary cover behind the low concrete walls of the derelict pigsties. He dropped to his stomach beside the Lethal Leek, straining to identify the continuing sounds of gunfire. Up on the hill, Jumbo was still laying down a blanket of five-second bursts with the GPMG, more for psychological effect than with any chance of doing real damage. Aiming as he was over the heads of his own colleagues, Jumbo was taking no chances and deliberately firing high, most of the heavy 7.62mm slugs merely stripping slates off the roof of the farmhouse. In the lulls between the bursts, there was only the sporadic crack of perhaps three or four handguns, one of which seemed to be coming from an upstairs window of the farmhouse. The crackle of the Uzi could not be heard. Perhaps the gunman was already dead, Anderson thought. If not, he was either changing the clip or had run out of ammunition completely.

Seconds later, the machine-pistol opened up again, slugs stripping off small chips of concrete above his head.

'The bastard's moved,' the Lethal Leek observed. 'My guess is that he's over there.' He jerked the barrel of his Heckler & Koch MP5 in the direction of an old stable block to the right of the farmhouse.

Anderson accepted this assessment moodily. If the Welshman was right, it was bad news for all of them. Not only were he and his men pinned down, but the gunman would have a direct line of fire into the open courtyard between the farmhouse and the outbuilding through which Winston and Butch's units would have to make their approach. It gave the man a tactical advantage out of all proportion to his true fire-power.

But for now, Anderson had his own problems. Basically, he was stuck in a fairly safe but useless position from which he could neither advance nor retreat without snatching the initiative. He nudged the Lethal Leek in the ribs, nodding up towards the left upstairs window of the farmhouse.

'Let's take these bastards out one at a time,' he suggested. 'I'll draw his fire and you give him everything you've got.'

The Lethal Leek nodded. 'Got you, boss.' Setting his MP5 on full automatic fire, he waited for Anderson's move.

It was not long in coming. Anderson tensed himself, then rolled out of the cover of the pigsties, firing his own weapon towards the upstairs window as he did so.

The ploy worked. Three bullets smacked into the ground in his wake, as the gunman behind the window went for his first clear target. It was a calculated gamble, Anderson counting on the assumption that a handgun would be fairly inaccurate at that range. Two more shots followed, and Anderson heard the slugs whistle harmlessly over his head.

'Take him,' he hissed over at the Welshman, as he continued to draw fire from the window by spraying the top left-hand corner of the farmhouse until his magazine was empty.

The Lethal Leek sprang to his feet from behind the cover of the pigsties, his own MP5 bucking in his hands as he loosed off another full clip of thirty 9mm slugs. What was left of the glass in the window exploded into a crystalline shower of tiny shards, the surrounding frame shattering into a splintered mess. There was no returning fire. The Lethal Leek grinned over at Anderson as he rolled back into cover.

'I reckon we taught him the error of his ways, boss,' he observed, discarding the empty magazine and slotting in another.

Anderson nodded, looking around to identify the positions of his remaining men. Ted Brennon and the big Cornishman, Miles Tremathon, were crouched together some fifteen feet to his left. Only the muzzle of an MP5 poking over the concrete lip of the sties identified Pete Delaney on the adjacent side of the rectangular structure. To join them, he would have to make a skirting run around the back, but his cover was good.

Again Anderson listened to the sounds of gunfire. Just two automatic pistols remaining, he gauged – one of them on the ground floor of the farmhouse and the other coming from somewhere outside, judging by the sharper, echoless report. The Uzi was still firing in staccato bursts, but no bullets were flying their way. Anderson could only assume that the gunman had now turned his attention to the second attack force of Winston and Butch and their men.

The Uzi would have to be their problem, Anderson realized. Right now he probably had his best chance to make the final assault on the farmhouse. Two handguns would be no match for five MP5s. He glanced aside at the Lethal Leek, and then at Miles and Ted. 'OK, let's shake out,' he yelled. 'We're going in.'

Leaping to his feet, he began to run down the slope towards the farmhouse, firing three-round bursts into the gaping hole in the building's wall.

Winston, the two Tweedles and Pretty Boy remained crouched behind the cover of the outbuilding furthest from the farmhouse, where they had gone to ground immediately on bursting through the farm entrance. On the opposite side of the entrance drive, Butch, Mike Peters, Aberdeen Angus and Jimmy Phelan were similarly placed behind an old and rusting baling machine, waiting for Anderson to make his main assault.

It had seemed the only sensible course of action,

given their single choice of a closer approach and the defensive position of the farmhouse itself. Even though their enemy appeared to have strictly limited fire-power, the SAS men's only access to the farmhouse was across a wide, open courtyard in which they would all be sitting targets. The lorry, parked in the middle of it and facing them, might offer a safe halfway house, but only after Anderson had neutralized any threat from the farmhouse itself. By staying put, they were at least effectively blocking off any escape route and were poised to sweep in behind Anderson in a quick and clean mopping-up operation.

A renewed burst of firing from the quintet of MP5s announced that this final assault was in fact at last under way. Winston glanced over to Butch, who nodded back at him. As Anderson and his men broke from the cover of the sties and started their final run towards the farmhouse, the eight troopers launched themselves out into the drive and began a zigzagging run towards the lorry.

The Uzi chattered angrily at them. From the corner of his eye, Winston saw Jimmy Phelan twist awkwardly in mid stride, give a little yell of pain and go down, blood gushing from a thigh wound. Acting instinctively, Winston dropped on to his belly and rolled sideways to the fallen trooper as his companions continued their run towards the lorry and drew away the fire from the Uzi. He rolled Jimmy on to his back, then hastily stripped off the man's belt webbing and tightened it around his thigh above the wound to create a makeshift tourniquet. There was little else he could do. Rolling Jimmy gently back on to his belly again, Winston thrust his MP5 into his hands and patted him on the back. 'You can still give us covering fire,' he muttered to the injured trooper, preparing to scramble back to his feet and make a run for the lorry.

He held himself in check, suddenly realizing that he had given himself an unexpected tactical advantage. In the few seconds it had taken him to see to Jimmy, not a single shot had been fired in their direction. The gunman was now totally obsessed with the nearer threat of the main body of the men, now almost at the lorry. Winston's mind raced, plotting through the implications with computer-like efficiency.

The Uzi had to be positioned somewhere ahead of him, covering the vehicle. Somewhere high, Winston figured. He raised his eyes, scanning the buildings surrounding the courtyard and using his keen ears at the same time to pinpoint the source of the chattering machine-pistol.

In the old stable block to the right of the farmhouse, a small, square hole looked down over the rest of the farm buildings. It had probably once been a hayloft, Winston thought. Now it was a handy little nest for a gunman. He dropped his eyes back to the rest of the men, who had all made it to the comparative safety of the lorry. He watched Tweedledum blast out the nearside tyres with a couple of shells from the Remington, then put another couple of rounds through the radiator for good measure before joining his companions in a huddle behind the sagging vehicle.

They were now all almost directly below the hayloft, and although they were protected from its direct line of fire, their presence rather ruled out Winston's initial thought of lobbing a hand-grenade into it. The square baling hatch presented a small target, and should the grenade fail to find it, it could easily bounce off the wall and roll towards the lorry. There had to be another way to take out the Uzi, Winston thought frantically.

A slow, delicious grin spread over his black face as it came to him. An old hayloft would probably still have a fair amount of hay inside it. Even if it was empty, the wooden structure would be as dry as a tinder-box. Such a scenario offered distinct possibilities.

Still lying prone, and moving very slowly and cautiously, he released the magazine catch on his Heckler & Koch and slipped out the empty box.

They had originally all been prepared for an attack in the dark, and their armoury had reflected this probability with typical SAS efficiency and attention to detail. Winston reached down to his spare ammunition belt and, having selected a fresh thirty-round box magazine, locked it into position.

Sometimes, when making an attack in pitch darkness, it became imperative to let your fellow-troopers know your exact position. Equally, it was often extremely helpful to pinpoint a blind target, or gain a quick visual signal as to your accuracy. A short burst of tracer achieved both these objects, speedily and efficiently. And a fresh magazine of one-in-five tracer was exactly what Winston had just loaded into his MP5. Each white-hot magnesium flare would serve equally well as an incendiary device, he knew.

Jumping to his feet, Winston aimed the MP5 at the hayloft and emptied the entire magazine into it before dropping to the ground again. As he changed back to regular ammunition, he had the satisfaction of seeing the first wisps of light-coloured smoke begin to drift out of the small hatchway. Even as he watched, the smoke darkened and turned into a small but thickening cloud. It was already billowing out as the first licking flames appeared around the edges of the hatch.

The Uzi ceased firing as the flames built up quickly, reinforcing Winston's supposition that the hayloft still contained a large amount of hay or other highly combustible material. Winston climbed to his feet again and began running towards the lorry, still keeping a watchful eye on the hayloft and his finger on the trigger.

The gunman appeared, framed in the square hatchway and illuminated by the growing inferno behind him. He had little choice but to jump for his life. Given the thirty-foot drop, he might just have survived as a permanent cripple, but Aberdeen Angus saved him the pain and inconvenience. A five-second burst took the man as he fell, ensuring that he was dead before he hit the ground.

Winston completed his run to the lorry. Butch clapped him on the shoulder as he arrived. 'Smart idea,' he said warmly.

Winston grinned. 'I have a burning desire to succeed in life,' he retorted. Then, his face clouding, he glanced across at Tweedledee. 'Listen, Jimmy's been hit back there. Go and do what you can for him, will you?'

'Sure, boss.' Tweedledee didn't hesitate, setting out for the injured trooper at a loping run and pulling emergency field-dressings from his belt pouches as he moved.

'Right, let's join the boss,' Butch suggested, nodding his head towards the farmhouse. Anderson and his men had surrounded it now, and the last automatic pistol had ceased firing, its owner either dead, dispirited or out of ammo. It didn't really matter either way. From now on, it looked like a simple clean-up operation.

Anderson himself was edging along the front wall of the farmhouse, a stun grenade ready in his hand with its pin already pulled. Reaching the jagged edge of the gaping hole left by the M72 rocket, he lobbed it almost casually into the interior of the building.

Before the rolling echoes of the explosion had finished bouncing off the surrounding hills, Anderson was in through the gap, closely followed by the Lethal Leek and the rest of his men. Winston, Butch, Pretty Boy and Tweedledum were only seconds behind them, leaving Mike Peters and Aberdeen Angus to guard the crippled lorry and cut off any escape bids.

The ground floor of the farmhouse had been almost completely gutted, with interior walls knocked down, and ceiling joists inserted, to make way for a small-scale manufacturing set-up. Vats of chemical compounds, mixing drums and a pill-making machine took up most of what must have been the kitchen and living-room. The place appeared to be deserted, apart from the dead body of a single gunman slumped under a window.

Anderson pointed towards the stairs with the barrel of his MP5. 'Go and secure upstairs,' he snapped at Miles and the Lethal Leek. He looked over at Winston. 'We'll cover this floor. You sweep the storage area.'

Nodding a brief acknowledgement, Winston moved towards a clutter of crates and cardboard boxes on the far side of the makeshift laboratory. As he approached, there was the slightest sign of movement from one of the piles of boxes. Winston's finger flexed against the trigger of his Heckler & Koch. The piled boxes jumped into the air, flying apart to reveal a flash of white clothing as someone dived sideways for safety.

'Surrender now,' Winston screamed. 'You have one chance and five seconds.' He held the MP5 trained on the last estimated position of the hiding figure.

It was an offer not to be refused. A man, wearing a white laboratory coat, rose slowly from behind the scattered boxes. His hands were empty, but his eyes were full of hate. Regarding Winston with a cold, vicious stare, he spat something out in German.

'What did he say?' Winston barked to Pretty Boy, who was standing immediately behind him. Apart from his other talents, the trooper spoke five European languages with varying degrees of fluency.

'He called you a shit-eating nigger,' Pretty Boy informed him unemotionally. 'Not very polite, is he?'

Winston resisted the urge to make his own reply in fluent Heckler & Koch. The man was obviously a chemist who had been overseeing the drug production. He might have some rather useful information to pass on, so it made sense to keep him alive. At least, that was the idea.

The chemist tensed his body suddenly, jerking his right arm stiffly into the air. It was a serious mistake. The SAS were honed to split-second precision in terrorist or hostage situations. The rules were clear and unequivocal. Surrender had to be total and unambiguous. Any sudden or violent movement could only be interpreted as a potential threat, and immediately neutralized.

The Remington in Tweedledum's hands boomed out, the full charge of shot taking the chemist full in the chest at less than twelve feet. The man's immaculate white coat flowered into a wild, abstract crimson pattern, and the force of the close-range blast lifted him several inches into the air and threw his body across the jumble of boxes. Afterwards there was a sudden and complete silence.

Finally Tweedledum spoke. 'Sorry, did I do the wrong thing?' he asked.

Winston turned on him slowly, a rueful smile on his face. It was impossible to criticize the young trooper in any way. The death of their apparently sole surviving witness was regrettable, but Tweedledum had followed orders to the letter. Winston told him so, putting the soldier's mind at ease.

'What the fuck was he *doing*?' Tweedledum demanded, after a slight pause.

Winston smiled thinly again. 'He was about to give us an old-fashioned Nazi salute,' he murmured. 'You're too young to remember.'

Tweedledum gave a short, nervous laugh. 'Jesus, Sarge, what are we taking on here?'

Winston shrugged. 'I haven't got the faintest idea, Trooper,' he admitted. 'Nobody tells us a fucking thing.'

12

Norma Jean's nightclub was in a basement, directly under a large block of semi-derelict warehouses. Advertised only by a street-level entrance and a neon representation of the young Marilyn Monroe, the place had a scruffy, almost sordid look about it. From deep in its bowels, the pounding, repetitive beat of techno music echoed up into the darkened streets.

It was difficult to see the club's appeal, Carney thought, yet it was obvious that it was a highly popular venue. From a concealed position across the street, he'd been watching the place for over an hour, noting the steady stream of customers, some of them dressed in party finery as though they were going to the Lord Mayor's banquet. The clientele appeared to be predominantly white, and exclusively young.

What Carney failed to appreciate was that it was the generally unsavoury appearance of the place that gave it its greatest appeal – the direct result of a calculated approach to both design and marketing. It was geared almost exclusively to the 'rave' crowd. The deliberately planned downbeat image created the illusion of spontaneity, an almost temporary, makeshift meeting place in which the thrill of a somehow illicit party could be savoured. The incessant mind-numbing music, along with alcohol and designer drugs, did the rest.

Carney moved out from his hiding place and crossed the street for a closer look.

'What you think you're hanging about for, grandad?' said a coarse, aggressive voice from the doorway of the club.

Carney looked up into the cold, disdainful eyes of the burly bouncer who had just stepped provocatively into his path. He made a tentative move as if to sidestep the man, but the bouncer shifted his position, adopting a direct challenge.

'You deaf, grandad?' he said.

Carney stood his ground, eyeing the bouncer up and down carefully. He was young – no more than twenty-two, Carney estimated – and powerfully built, with a barrel-like chest, broad shoulders and a thick, bull-like neck which supported a stubble-covered blonde head. The standard doorman's outfit of dinner jacket, white dress shirt and black bow tie looked totally incongruous on the man, who might have looked more appropriately dressed in a rancid bearskin. He stood just over six feet tall, and probably weighed in around fifteen stone. Most likely a boxer, Carney reflected – and probably not a very good one either. The sort who was too slow and too stupid for defensive manoeuvring and relied purely on his bulk and a heavy punch. All the same, not someone to be easily pushed out of the way, and Carney didn't try. He didn't much care for the epithet 'grandad', but he kept his cool.

Carney nodded towards the club entrance. 'Thought I might take a look-see,' he said. 'I'm a music-lover,' he added sarcastically.

The bouncer snarled contemptuously. 'Fuck off. You some sort of pervert of something?'

He took a step back and pushed up the right sleeve of his tuxedo a few inches. In the faint glow of the neon lights Carney noted with a vague sense of unease the ugly symbol of the swastika tattooed on his wrist. It was there again – the connection between Nirvana and right-wing extremism – and it threw him for a few seconds. Recovering himself, he ran through a hastily improvised plan of action and decided it might just work.

Forcing an easy smile, Carney nodded at the tattoo. 'Well, at least you've got sense enough to be a member of the Brotherhood,' he said in a friendly tone. 'And here was I thinking you were just an ugly, dumb ape with nothing but highly compressed pig shit between your ears.'

This took several seconds to sink in. When it finally did so, the burly bouncer let out a strangled bellow of rage and drew back his ham-like fist.

Carney was ready for him. His few weeks of training with the SAS had added a few extra tricks to his repertoire. He avoided the pile-driving punch easily, pivoting on the balls of his feet and stepping neatly around the bouncer's side. He drove a short, stabbing knuckle punch into the area of one kidney, then spun round and delivered a toe kick to the other. Balancing himself again, Carney slammed his knee into the base of the man's spinal column.

The bouncer let out a bestial grunt, his huge frame arching backwards in agony. Carney's left arm coiled around his neck and windpipe from behind, choking off his air supply. A rabbit punch to the back of the thick neck delivered the *coup de grâce*. The man went limp in Carney's grip, and began to crumple to the pavement.

He was stunned and winded – but not unconscious. He stared up at his conqueror with dumb incomprehension in his dull eyes. Carney merely grinned at him. 'I really ought to kick your teeth in,' he said casually. 'But I'll let you off as you're one of us – even if you are in need of some serious combat training. Any one of my boys could take you apart and reassemble you as a woman in five seconds flat.'

'Your boys?' the bouncer croaked helplessly, taking the bait.

Carney nodded. 'Sons of the Swastika,' he said, picking the first name that popped into his head. He could only hope it sounded sufficiently fanatical and outrageous to be plausible. 'We take our politics seriously.'

He was acutely aware that he was on borrowed time. Several revellers arriving at the club had already witnessed the brief battle and had run inside to raise the alarm. It could only be a matter of seconds before other heavies started to pour out on to the street. Carney had time for just one parting shot.

'Maybe I'll bring a few of my lads round one night, just to suss out the recruitment prospects,' he told the still-helpless youth. 'Only next time you see me, I'll be expecting a little more respect.'

It was time to make a discreet exit. Carney managed to stroll in what he imagined to be a casual and unhurried manner as far as the first street corner, then turned into it and began to run for his life. He had already disappeared into the shadows by the time a twelve-strong gang of louts had raced out of the club and reached the corner.

Finally deciding that he was safe from pursuit, Carney slowed to a walk again and began to retrace his steps to where he had parked his car. He had one more call to make.

The Tunnel Club was more geared to Carney's age-group, if not his moral outlook on life. The late-night drinking den was predominantly frequented by the criminal fraternity, with a smattering of resting actors – although it was not unknown to a few undercover cops, Carney among them.

This time the doorman greeted Carney guardedly but with grudging respect. 'Evening, Mr Carney. Official, is it?'

Carney shook his head. 'Relax, Danny. Just a purely social call. Frankie Conran in tonight?'

Danny grinned. 'Does a pigeon shit?'

Carney took this, correctly, as an affirmation. He slid past Danny and through the tiny reception area to the long, dimly lit bar beyond.

Conran was propped up on a tall stool at the far end of the bar, chatting up a blonde former starlet who was now past her ascendancy. Carney had seen her most recently in a TV commercial for toothpaste. Tellingly, she had just started playing the mother in ads.

'Evening, Frankie,' Carney said in a friendly enough tone, seating himself beside the man. 'Drink?'

Conran looked up without smiling. His greeting was neither friendly nor wary. It was merely one of acceptance. They were not friends, yet not enemies, even though they were technically on opposite sides of the fence. Conran was basically a crook, and Carney knew it, even if the man did hide many of his more nefarious activities under the cover of a legitimate computer information service. But he hated drugs, and in this respect if nothing else he had been Carney's ally in the past. His own daughter had got caught up in the heavy drugs scene some three years earlier, and it had been primarily Carney's influence which had got her off a major charge and on to a methadone treatment scheme which eventually cured her addiction. It was a favour owed. Conran's relationship with Carney was now a strange and fragile one, walking a tightrope across the uneasy hinterland between crime and the law. Yet it was a liaison which was not all that uncommon between the two worlds. In many ways, it sometimes served both sides.

'Slumming it, are you, Carney?' Conran asked. He jerked his head towards the blonde. 'This is Pauline Ferris, the actress.'

Carney nodded. 'Yeah. Hello. Great teeth.'

Turning to the barman, Carney ordered himself a beer.

'I take it this is not a chance encounter?' Conran queried.

Carney smiled. 'You're uncommonly sharp tonight, Frankie. A word in your shell-like would be appreciated. Could we have a minute in private?'

Conran didn't look too upset about being torn away from his potential conquest. He hadn't really entertained great hopes of scoring anyway. He turned towards the actress, draping his arm briefly about her shoulders in a gesture of ownership. 'Look, sweetheart, I'll be back in about five minutes. OK?'

The woman shrugged. 'Don't hurry on my account.'

Conran stood up, picked up his drink from the bar and carried it across to an empty table at the back of the smoky room. Carney stayed at the bar for long enough to order himself an expensive beer and strolled across to join him.

'So, what are you after?' Conran asked as he sat down. 'I'm not in the grassing business, as well you know.'

'Sure,' Carney agreed. He took a sip of his beer. 'How's Dorothy, by the way?'

Conran brightened visibly at the mention of his daughter's name. 'She's fine,' he said enthusiastically. 'Still on the straight and narrow, thank God. She's got a new job with a travel firm now. Doing pretty well.'

'I'm glad to hear it,' Carney told him. The sentiment was genuine, even if he had brought the subject up as a rather unsubtle reminder.

Conran had not missed the point. He sighed heavily. 'All right, Carney – I still owe you. Now what is it you want to know?'

Carney paused to take another swig of beer. 'Have you still got that Eurolink computer set-up?' he asked.

Conran nodded. 'Too right,' he replied. 'Best little

idea I had in years, that was. Instead of just supplying info on British companies, I now cover almost the entire commercial and industrial network of the EU. Punters are queuing up on both sides of the Channel to use the facility.'

Carney smiled knowingly. 'And no doubt it comes in useful for the odd bit of industrial espionage?'

Conran shot him a reproving stare. 'Information technology, Carney,' he corrected. 'The business of the future – and all perfectly legit.'

Carney was unconvinced, but he shrugged it off. 'Yeah, well, right now I could do with a bit of information technology myself.

'You got it,' Conran said generously. 'Give me some details of what you want.'

Carney paused for a few moments, refining his earlier vague thoughts on the subject. He wasn't sure how much he ought to reveal, and eventually decided on the bare minimum. 'All right, there's a new drug hitting the streets, originates from Germany,' he said. 'From what we know so far, it's probably hallucinogenic and possibly a derivative of LSD. If that's so, then it's almost certainly based on ergotamine tartrate and was probably developed as a side-product of legitimate pharmaceutical research. What I need is a scan of European pharmaceutical companies known to have conducted any such research during the past two to three years. Obviously Germany's the place to concentrate on, but it wouldn't do any harm to take in Switzerland, Austria and possibly Italy. Also, it would be handy to know of any companies or organizations currently importing sizeable quantities of ergotamine tartrate into this country.' He stared Conran in the eye. 'Well? Do you think you can help me?'

Conran was thoughtful. 'This new drug,' he said eventually. 'Bad shit, is it?'

Carney nodded emphatically. 'Real bad shit,' he confirmed.

It was enough to swing the balance. 'I'll see what I can do,' Conran promised him. 'It might take a day or two.'

'Thanks, Frankie,' Carney said gratefully. 'Give me a buzz if you get anything, will you? On my home number. I'm not at the office any more.'

Conran raised one eyebrow quizzically. 'Don't tell me Mr Straight has finally fallen out with the boys in blue?'

Carney grinned secretively. 'No, I'm still firmly on the side of law and order, Frankie. Let's just say I'm running more with the boys in brown these days.' He did not elaborate, and Conran didn't push it. Their relationship had certain limits, which neither of them would ever exceed.

Carney glanced over towards the bar. The actress was just getting to her feet and preparing to leave with a muscular, good-looking young blond man who looked as though he had just come from a work-out at the local health club.

'Sorry, Frankie,' Carney said. 'But it looks as though the tooth fairy just scored herself a toy boy.'

Conran shrugged. 'What the hell,' he muttered philosophically. 'The wife wouldn't have liked her, anyway.' He glanced down at Carney's almost finished pint. 'Fancy a bit of serious drinking?'

Carney thought about it for just a moment. After the unpleasantness with Linda earlier in the day, any company was better than none, he decided.

'My round, I think,' he said, before picking up his glass and draining it.

13

It was post-mortem time in the Kremlin briefing room. A chance for the men to discuss the success or failure of the previous day's operation and to hold a Chinese Parliament about their next moves.

Making a realistic assessment of the farmhouse raid was a tricky call, Major Anderson had already decided. It could be deemed a success in one respect only – they had seized nearly a hundred kilos of the finished drug and destroyed the remaining chemical stocks along with all the manufacturing equipment. Other than that, they had achieved virtually nothing. They had no leads to follow, and virtually no idea of where to look next; or indeed who or what to look for. In effect, they were still at square one.

It was a bit like catching a lizard by the tail, Anderson reflected. The reptile's defence systems simply snapped off the trapped appendage and sealed the damaged area, and the creature scuttled away to grow a new one. It was more than just frustrating, he thought bitterly. What made it particularly galling was the fact that they had lost men – apparently pointlessly. Thanks largely to Winston's emergency medical treatment, Trooper Phelan would make it to fight another day, but Captain Feeney and Trooper Eddie Mentieth had failed to beat the clock. That made it personal, raised the stakes. It was no longer just a mission, could no longer be viewed with professional detachment. The men of 22 SAS were at war now – but where was the bloody enemy?

That Anderson's pessimistic views were shared by most of his colleagues was evident from the subdued atmosphere in the room. There was none of the usual bluster and bravado, the macabre but understandable boasts of a clean kill or a particularly close brush with death. No sick jokes, no good-natured piss-taking, no sense of elation among the survivors of yet another encounter with danger. It was as if every man present somehow sensed that he was out of his natural element, thrown into a strange and confusing situation in which the usual rules simply didn't apply.

It was probably because most of them were so young and so recently badged, Anderson decided. The requirements of their mission, and the nature of the personnel needed had forced that limitation upon them, and it had its drawbacks. Virtually none of the men had the faintest idea what it was like to face a hidden, civilian enemy. Besides himself, there were only two other troopers who had seen a tour of duty in Northern Ireland.

Anderson understood, of course – only too well. Two years of nights and days on the streets of Belfast had taught him to come to terms with the fears and uncertainties of not knowing, minute to minute, who and where your enemy actually was.

The fifteen-year-old kid on the street corner. Was it a packet of cigarettes he was just pulling from his bomber-jacket pocket – or was it a hand-grenade? The pretty girl with the smiling green eyes and the soft, lilting voice. Was she inviting you into her bed – or to an ambush where you'd be forced to your knees and shot through the back of the head?

The next car coming down the road towards the security checkpoint. Friend or foe? Was it carrying joyriding kids or armed killers?

That little glint of silver in the green country lanes of Derry. Was it the sunlight glinting off a stretch of cattle fencing – or was it a trip-wire connected up to the land-mine now only yards ahead?

So many unknowns, so many life-or-death decisions. Every day. Every hour. Every minute. The youngsters couldn't be expected to know the answers. They didn't even know the questions.

Sergeant Andrew Winston had his own set of questions to occupy his mind, and the possible answers were terrifying. Paul Carney had called him first thing that morning, passing on his discovery of yet another direct connection between the extreme right and the drug Nirvana. So soon after his own experience with the German scientist at the farmhouse, Winston found it all infinitely depressing.

How could it all start to happen again? he asked himself with a sense of disbelief. Just half a century after the holocaust which had ravaged the world and extinguished the lives of at least fifty million human beings, the madness was abroad once more. A student of modern history, and a humanitarian despite his profession, Winston carried the figures in his head. Twenty million Russians, twelve million Germans, six million Poles, six million Jews, half a million French, six hundred thousand Americans, four hundred and fifty thousand British had perished in Europe alone – all because of a single insane belief that some races were inferior to others.

How could it happen again? The question repeated itself in his brain. Was it just that people had short memories, or was the need to hate programmed into the human psyche?

As ever, there were no answers, or none that made any kind of sense. And more than anyone else, a man with black skin needed those answers.

Winston's concentration was jolted suddenly back to the present, as Major Anderson rose to his feet to open the meeting.

'It goes without saying that every trooper did his job and I'm proud of you all,' Anderson announced, starting on a positive note even though he had nothing encouraging to back it up with. 'But for the moment, at least, it's now going to be a question of waiting to see what the green slime, or our own OPI, can come up with next.' Anderson paused, looking hopefully out over the heads of the seated men. 'Unless, that is, any one of you has any useful suggestions.'

Captain Butch Blake rose to his feet. 'I assume that someone is checking out the lorry's registration?' he put in.

Anderson nodded. 'The police are running checks,' he confirmed. 'But the general feeling is that it'll turn out to be stolen, or at least fitted with false plates.'

It was time for Winston to pass on his information. He stood up, clearing his throat. 'Actually, boss, we don't all have to sit around twiddling our thumbs altogether,' he said. 'Paul Carney called me this morning with a possible new lead. He's found a London club where the drug is rumoured to be available – and, once again, there are strong indications of a link with ultra-right-wing organizations.'

It sounded promising. Anderson accepted the information gratefully. 'So what's your suggestion?' he asked.

'Carney's, actually,' Winston admitted. 'He thought we ought to send a few of our younger lads in to make contact – see what they could dig up.'

Anderson nodded thoughtfully, considering the suggestion. 'Good idea,' he admitted. 'Can I leave it to you to set something up?'

'Sure thing, boss,' Winston agreed. He paused briefly, then added: 'I also have one idea of my own. It might be a good idea to compile a list of all the known right-wing organizations and splinter groups currently in existence. It would give us another line of enquiry to be working on.'

Anderson smiled without condescension. 'OPI are already way ahead of you on that one,' he told Winston. He produced a sheet of paper from his pocket and unfolded it. 'Take your pick from this little lot. National Front Party, National Rights Movement, Britain First, National Socialist Alliance, Freedom from European Federalism, Aryan Association, White Tigers, Socialist Union Group.' Anderson broke off to draw a breath. 'Oh yes, and something called the Thule Society, whatever that is.'

Winston frowned heavily. 'I might be able to shed a little light on that one, if you're interested,' he offered.

Anderson nodded. 'Go ahead. All information is useful information,' he said.

Winston shrugged. 'Well, I'm not sure about that,' he admitted. 'But it might give you a clearer idea of the sort of nutters we could be dealing with.' He paused, putting the facts together in his head before launching into a brief history of the Thule Society.

'The original legend of Thule goes back to the mists of Nordic mythology. It was supposed to be the island centre of a vastly superior race of super-beings, which was destroyed in some great natural disaster – much like the Atlantis legend. However, around 1920, an Austrian named Dietrich Eckhardt dredged this legend up from the past and took it one stage further. Tying it in with a few other conveniently similar myths, he came up with the theory that not all the supermen of Thule had actually perished with the destruction of their island home. Some, he claimed, had survived to disguise themselves as ordinary, mortal men, and had remained hidden through thousands of years, biding their time and waiting for a mysterious new messiah figure who would lead them to greatness again. At that point, they would conquer the world, exterminate the false and inferior species of mankind and bring about a new super-race.

'Eckhardt formed a secret society, which he called

the Thule Society, and gathered a few fanatical followers around him who dedicated themselves to magical ceremonies, blood sacrifices and other mumbo-jumbo which was supposed to call this messiah into being.'

Winston paused for breath, and Anderson took advantage of the break to interrupt. 'This is all very interesting,' he muttered. 'But what does a nutcase and a load of mystical claptrap have to do with a bunch of neo-Nazis?'

Winston smiled bitterly. 'Only that one of the Thule Society's earliest converts was a young army corporal named Adolf Hitler,' he announced. 'Eckhardt took it upon himself to groom Hitler as his natural successor. He was initiated into secret rituals and blood oaths which apparently involved human sacrifice on quite a large scale. By the time Eckhardt died in 1923, he had left behind a nucleus of believers who included Hitler, Hess and a man called Karl Haushofer. It was Haushofer who took an ancient magical symbol for the sun – the swastika – turned it on its side and created the emblem for the National Socialist Party. The rest, as they say, is history. Several quite level-headed historians have suggested that Hitler's extermination of six million Jews and three-quarters of a million gypsies was no more than his own continuing blood sacrifice to the supermen of Thule.'

Winston finished his little speech. There was a slightly uncomfortable silence for a while. Finally Pretty Boy spoke up, a note of awe in his voice.

'Jeezus, Sarge, I didn't know you were into all this mythology stuff.'

Winston smiled faintly, tapping the side of his nose. 'Know your enemy,' he answered. The smile broadened into a grin. 'Anyway, back to more important matters. Fancy a spot of London nightclubbing?'

Pretty Boy did not look overenthusiastic. 'Depends on who my dancing partner's going to be,' he said dubiously.

'I thought you might take Mike Peters along for the ride,' Winston told him. 'He's young, and another Londoner. You should both blend in fairly well. With a bit of luck, you might both even get your leg over.'

Pretty Boy still wasn't quite convinced. 'What's the deal?'

Winston shrugged. 'Decent hotel room for a couple of nights ... hundred and fifty quid spending money.'

Pretty Boy considered it. 'Separate hotel rooms?' he queried. 'That bastard snores.'

Winston nodded. 'Separate rooms,' he confirmed.

Pretty Boy's face brightened. 'Throw in an extra issue of condoms and you've got yourself a volunteer,' he said.

Winston laughed sardonically. 'Sometimes, Trooper Parrit, your unselfish and unswerving dedication to duty makes me weep with pride.'

14

Over the next two days Paul Carney received three phone calls. The first was from Winston, telling him that he, Pretty Boy and Mike Peters would be in London for the Wednesday evening.

That was the good news.

The bad news came from David Grieves. 'We appear to have stirred up the shit,' were his opening words. He proceeded to fill Carney in on the unpleasant details.

Less than forty-eight hours after the SAS raid on the farmhouse, there had been an instinctive, knee-jerk and violent reaction from the people behind the drugs factory – in the form of a message telephoned direct to the newsroom of the BBC. The enemy had announced themselves.

'As we suspected, it's ultra-right-wing radicals,' Grieves explained. 'This particular bunch of nasties call themselves Second Holocaust. They're threatening violent retribution for our interference in their little operation. My guess is that we hurt them, and now they're going to hit back.'

Carney digested the information gloomily. 'What's the threat?' he asked Grieves.

'They plan to bomb a pub,' the man from military intelligence said flatly. 'It will be a place belonging to the Consolidated Breweries group, and it will only be a warning. More pubs in the same chain will continue to be attacked until they cough up a ransom of £300,000.'

Carney sucked in his breath. 'Jesus Christ,' he sighed heavily. 'Any chance it's just a bluff?'

Grieves did not sound too hopeful. 'They never bluffed in mainland Europe,' he pointed out. 'Anyway, we should know soon enough.'

Carney's brain was racing. 'How many pubs in the Consolidated group?' he asked.

'One hundred and eighty in the Greater London area, another seventy-three in the Home Counties. A total of well over a thousand nationwide,' Grieves informed him. 'Absolutely no chance of any effective preventative measures, I'm afraid. We'd need the entire bloody army.' He paused briefly. 'I've passed the information to Hereford, of course, but there's not much any of us can do except sit and wait. The bastards appear to have us by the balls.'

It was a sobering, and probably quite accurate, assessment, Carney thought. 'Why the sudden change of tactic?' he asked.

'Again, only a personal guess,' Grieves replied. 'But the way I see it, they were probably counting on the street value of that drug consignment to keep the wheels oiled. Deprived of it, they've got to find a source of emergency funding – and quick. That's probably why they've picked a large company and gone for a comparatively small ransom demand. Chances are they'll want to pay up quickly, and under the counter, no matter what the authorities advise them, or order them, to do. Company blackmail like this isn't without precedent. It's been going on for years, and it doesn't always get made public.'

It wasn't a point Carney was prepared to argue with. He'd heard of enough comparable cases to know that Grieves was right. All sorts of scams had been pulled, with varying degrees of success, over the years. Poisoned food in supermarket chains, factory-floor sabotage, computer frauds. Often it was cheaper for the companies to pay up quietly and discreetly than to risk loss of both business and standing. Even the banks deliberately hushed up the true extent of credit-card fraud, simply writing it off in the loss column of their accounts each year.

Grieves appeared to have said his piece. 'Anyway, I just thought I'd bring you up to date,' he finished, somewhat lamely. 'I'll be in touch again if there are any new developments.'

'Yeah, thanks,' Carney said, and hung up. As Grieves had already said, there was nothing left to do except sit and wait.

He did not have to wait very long. The first pub bombing was the lead story on the BBC's *Nine O'Clock News*. It was an early report, but it seemed that they had got off comparatively lightly, with only one death and seven minor injuries.

Carney wondered if the Miller's Arms, on the fringes of Notting Hill, had been a deliberate rather than a random choice. Situated where it was, the pub had a high proportion of West Indian customers. The actual bombing was a crude and simple operation, although devastatingly effective. A standard hand-grenade, fixed to the inside of the toilet door with some sticky parcel tape, a few drawing-pins and a piece of string. As the door was pushed open, the pin of the grenade was pulled – and the simple mechanics of the crude booby-trap were activated inexorably. The poor bastard who had picked the wrong moment to go for a piss never stood a chance.

The rest of the crowded pub's clientele were luckier. The toilets were situated well away from the main bar, and an outer door shielded the interior of the pub from the force of the blast. The majority of the minor injuries were from flying glass.

The brief news item ended. Carney noted that there had been no mention of the ransom demand, or the threat to bomb other pubs. He wondered if Grieves had managed to arrange a hasty D-notice on that particular aspect of the business. It was more than probable. Media censorship was not quite as dead as many people fondly imagined.

The telephone shrilled. Carney thumbed the remote control, switching off the television, and walked across the lounge to answer his third call.

It was Frankie Conran. As promised, he was calling Carney with an update on his computer scan.

'So, what have you got for me, Frankie?' Carney asked hopefully.

'Not a great deal, I'm afraid,' Conran admitted. 'In fact, almost nothing on the drugs research front. It appears there has been virtually no new commercial research into new hallucinogens going on anywhere in Europe over the past five years.'

'I don't believe it,' Carney said flatly.

Conran was in full agreement. 'I don't believe it either,' he said. 'That's why I said it *appears* that way. Or perhaps is meant to appear.'

'Security clamp-down?' Carney asked.

'Looks like it,' Conran replied. 'The very lack of information available suggests a fairly widespread security net over the whole subject. The other possibility, of course, is that whatever research *has* been going on has been under government rather than private control.'

Carney sighed, unable to conceal his disappointment. 'Well, thanks for trying, anyway.' He was about to put the phone down when Conran spoke again.

'Hey, hold on a minute. I said I didn't have much. I didn't say I had nothing at all.' He paused for a while. 'Like I said, nothing showed up about recent research, or on official databases, so I decided to dig back a bit and hack into a few places I probably shouldn't.'

'And?' Carney pushed, ignoring the illegality of the act Conran had just admitted to.

'Something turned up which you might find interesting,' Conran went on. 'It sort of spun off from my suspicion of government-funded research and gave me a name. So I did a bit of checking back and found what might be a minor can of worms. Also, it's more than possible that this 'new' drug of yours isn't so new after all.'

Carney was intrigued, and suddenly enthusiastic again. 'Hold on while I get a pen and paper.' Returning to the phone, he said: 'Right, so what have you got?'

'You want everything?' Conran asked. 'There's a load of details and stuff in here which might not even be relevant.'

Carney nodded. 'Give me the lot,' he confirmed. 'I can sort out what is or isn't important later.'

There was a faint hiss of indrawn breath at the other end of the phone as Conran prepared himself. After a moment, he began to read from the notes he had prepared.

'The name is Dietrich Kleiner. Born in Munich in 1918. Entered the University of Bonn in 1936 to study organic chemistry and apparently got heavily involved with campus politics almost immediately. He joined the Hitler Youth in the same year, and was a fully active Nazi Party member by late 1939. By this time he had already published a couple of scientific papers about the effects of chemical contamination on the human system, and was reckoned to be something of a whizz-kid by his contemporaries. During the war years, he was almost certainly working for the Nazis – probaby on potential chemical or biological warfare projects. His name popped up again at the Nuremberg war crimes trials; he was accused of conducting experiments on Jewish internees in Buchenwald. He was found guilty and sentenced to ten years' imprisonment. He was released early, in 1951, and settled in Austria. It seems he lectured at the University of Vienna during the period 1953–57 in what was then the new science of biochemistry. In 1959 he returned to Germany, where he took up a research position with a major pharmaceutical company and stayed with them for ten years. Most of his work at that time was with LSD and the new synthetic offshoot MDA.'

Conran paused. 'That's alphamethyl-3, 4-methylene, by the way. See what I mean about a load of extraneous details?'

Carney brushed the digression aside impatiently. 'I told you – just give me everything you've got.'

'OK.' Conran paused only to draw another deep breath. 'So, that takes Kleiner up to the early 1970s,' he continued. 'He then moved to a smaller company, called Fleisch-Müller Pharmaceuticals, where he was probably involved in similar work. And here's where it starts to get interesting. In 1973 Fleisch-Müller attracted the interest of the East German authorities with the development of some new drug which apparently had distinct military potential. But that's where the trail seems to come to an end. A pretty solid security curtain drops down after that.'

It was starting to come together, Carney thought. A drug which raised natural aggression levels would have fairly obvious warfare applications. The East Germans would probably have been acting purely as brokers for their puppet-masters, the Soviets. At that time the Cold War was still very much a reality.

'Anything at all on Kleiner after that?' he asked.

'Nothing at all,' Conran replied. 'He just disappears from the face of the earth. The assumption, of course, must be that he went over the Wall.'

That was the one bit which refused to make any kind of sense, Carney realized. Why would a dyed-in-the-wool fascist want to go to work for a left-wing regime? Unless, of course, he had been given no choice in the matter.

'Anyway, that's it as far as Kleiner is concerned,' Conran continued. 'He could well be dead by now. But there's just one little postscript to the story which might interest you. Three years ago, Fleisch-Müller Pharmaceuticals ran into some financial troubles. They were bought up and asset-stripped – including the purchase of all the patents they held at the time – by a financial consortium. The actual purchasing company was German, but the parent concern is British – Trans-Europe Holdings PLC, the chairman of which is none other than Cecil Hargreaves.'

The name rang vague bells in Carney's head, but he had to think about it for a while.

'Hargreaves – wasn't he the guy who launched that "British or Bust" campaign back in the mid-eighties?' he said finally.

Conran chuckled. 'The very same. A real nationalist nutcase. Right-wing as they come. Interesting, eh?'

It was indeed. Very interesting, Carney reflected. The saga seemed to have come full circle, and the timing was just about right. It coincided perfectly with the first outbreaks of violence in Europe, and it placed Dietrich Kleiner's formula in the hands of a rich, powerful man known to have extreme right-wing sympathies.

Whether or not it would lead anywhere from there was something else again.

15

By the time Winston, Pretty Boy and Mike Peters arrived at Carney's flat on Wednesday evening, the second pub bombing had taken place as threatened. Another Consolidated Breweries outlet, the Prince Albert, situated in the heart of the City, just off Bishopsgate, was frequented mostly by business executives, office workers and secretaries. The attack had taken place at six o'clock in the evening, in broad daylight, and when the pub was filled to capacity with people having a quick drink after work.

It was cold-blooded carnage. At least a dozen commuters would not catch their evening trains home to the suburbs that night, or ever again.

Again, an ordinary hand-grenade had been used – but there was a difference. No crude booby-trap this time, the bomb had been fired directly from a launcher through the pub's street window from a passing car. It was another chilling reminder of what sophisticated modern weaponry these people seemed to be able to get their hands on.

And the ransom demand had gone up – from three hundred to four hundred thousand. Another message to the BBC newsroom warned that it would rise a further hundred thousand each day until the ransom was paid in full.

Winston sprawled out on Carney's sofa as Pretty Boy and Peters carried a succession of large cardboard boxes up from the Range Rover they had driven from Hereford. Carney viewed the mounting pile of boxes dubiously. His flat was rapidly beginning to look like a storage depot.

'Travelling light, I see,' he said to Winston.

The big Barbadian shrugged. 'We needed an equipment cache in London,' he explained casually. 'Didn't think you'd mind.

'Equipment?' Carney raised one eyebrow querulously. To confirm his sudden suspicion, he walked over to the nearest box and opened it, peering in at its contents. His first impression had been wrong, he realized. His flat was not being turned into a storage depot – it was being turned into an arsenal. He took a quick look at the contents of a couple more boxes, hardly believing the sheer amount of weaponry the SAS men had brought with them. Guns, grenades, spare ammunition. There was even what looked to Carney's untrained eye like some sort of rocket-launcher.

He looked over at Winston in disbelief. 'Jesus Christ! Are you expecting a bloody siege or something?'

Winston looked a bit more serious now. 'We need a place where we can tool up quickly, and on the spot,' he explained. 'As this isn't exactly the sort of luggage you can leave in a locker at Waterloo Station, and we can't all walk round the streets of London looking like extras from a Rambo movie, we thought your place was ideal.'

Carney conceded the point grudgingly. 'It's gonna give me a hell of a lot of explaining to do when the vicar pops in for tea,' he muttered, smiling ruefully.

Pretty Boy had just carried in the last box. He glanced at Winston. 'Where do you want the plastic explosive, boss?' he asked casually.

Winston was equally laid-back. 'Just dump it down anywhere for the time being,' he said.

Pretty Boy took the command at face value, doing exactly that. He dropped the heavy box to the floor with a thump which brought Carney's heart up into the back of his throat. 'Relax,' he said, grinning, seeing the man's obvious discomfort. 'This stuff's safe as houses until you stick a detonator into it.'

Carney remained unconvinced. He took another incredulous look at the armoury which had been deposited on his living-room floor. 'What do you need all this stuff for?' he demanded. 'There's only three of you, for Christ's sake.'

Winston gave a friendly laugh. 'Hell, man, it's not just for us – it's for the whole unit,' he said. 'Sorry, didn't I make that clear?'

Carney suddenly felt rather stupid. 'No, I don't think you mentioned it,' he said sheepishly, shaking his head.

Winston's face took on a serious look. 'Anyway, from the way things are shaping up, we might need it,' he pointed out. 'We don't know what sort of stuff we're going to come up against. I suppose you've heard that the bastards used a grenade-launcher in the latest attack?'

Carney nodded grimly. 'Yeah, I heard,' he said.

'What other nasty little tricks are they likely to have up their sleeves?'

Mike Peters shot him a reassuring grin. 'Nothing we can't match,' he boasted. 'We have a few little aces of our own.' He reached down to one of the boxes, drawing out a short, squat sub-machine-gun which looked as efficient and deadly as it was compact. 'These little beauties, for starters. Ain't they gorgeous?'

It was hardly an adjective which Carney would have used. The gun was a coldly efficient killing machine, nothing more.

'What the hell is it?' he asked, not recognizing the gun.

'Specially modified Heckler & Koch MP5K,' Peters told him. 'Designed expressly for counter-terrorist work. So short you can hide it in the glove compartment of a car – or even under your arm, if need be. Basically, you can take one of these little babies anywhere.'

'But not into a bloody disco, I hope,' Carney said warily. He had just had an apocalyptic vision of the two young men strolling into Norma Jean's looking like Delta Force Three.

'No, unfortunately not,' Peters agreed. He looked, and sounded, quite disappointed. A second later, his face brightened. Peeling back his jacket, he exposed the Browning 9mm High Power handgun tucked neatly into a specially designed armpit holster. 'Just gonna have to rely on the old peashooter instead.'

Winston, who up to this point had seemed completely laid-back, showed the first sign of authority. 'No bloody way, Trooper,' he said in a quiet but firm voice. 'You can forget any ideas about taking hard-ware into a crowded public place. This is supposed to be just a recce mission – remember?'

Peters's look of dismay was immediately echoed by Pretty Boy, who went one stage further by vocalizing his concern. 'Jeezus, boss, you ain't gonna strip us clean?'

The look on the young man's face was almost one of anguish, Carney thought, failing to understand the reluctance of all SAS troopers to go into any situation without some sort of a weapon, even if it was only a knife. It was a regimental tradition which had become almost a superstition.

But tradition or superstition, in this case Winston was adamant. 'No guns,' he repeated flatly. He uncoiled himself from Carney's sofa and crossed to another of the unopened boxes. 'However, you won't be quite as innocent as a pair of choirboys,' he added, drawing out from the box a pair of oblong black plastic devices slightly larger than a TV remote control. 'You'll be carrying Scorpion electronic stun-ners, for emergency use only.'

Carney was fascinated. He held out his hand to Winston, hoping for a closer look at one of the gadg-ets. Winston handed him one, and Carney studied it closely. It did indeed look like a remote control, except that the numbered buttons were missing. There were only three main touch controls, plus a small rocker switch mounted on the side. There was also a translucent, ridged plastic panel at one end, which reminded Carney of the electronic flash unit of a camera. But the most distinctive feature of the otherwise bland black box was the pair of pointed, shiny metal prongs which protruded from its end like horns.

'What is it, exactly?' Carney asked.

Winston grinned. 'It's basically an upgraded version of an anti-mugging device they've been marketing in the United States for some time. Illegal in this country, of course, although there has been some talk of issuing them to the police. Actually, we've been waiting for a chance to field-test them.'

Carney had heard of such devices, although he had never actually seen one before. 'Do they work?' he asked.

Winston nodded emphatically. 'Oh, they work all right. Fully charged up, this little beast will deliver an electric jolt of between forty and fifty thousand volts. That's enough to stun, or partially paralyse, the average person for at least forty-five seconds.'

'Can they kill?' Carney wanted to know.

Winston shrugged. 'Under certain circumstances, yes,' he admitted. 'That's one of the main reasons why they're still banned in this country. Anyone with a weak heart, for instance, or an epileptic, would be at risk. And of course they'd be absolutely lethal to anyone wearing a pacemaker.'

Carney hefted the Scorpion in his hand experimentally. 'I suppose the general idea is, you stab your victim with the metal prongs and then zap him?'

Winston nodded. 'That's the basic procedure,' he agreed. 'Although this particular model has a couple of rather handy little extra features. For a start, it'll fire a pressurized-gas-powered metal dart on a wire, up to a distance of five metres. So you can disable an attacker before he actually gets close enough to touch you.' He pointed out the plastic panel. 'And there's also a high-intensity flash unit as an alternative defence mechanism. It'll give either a single bright flash or a pulsing strobe effect. Either will effectively blind anyone for several seconds if it goes off directly in their eyes. Particularly effective in the dark, of course.'

Winston paused. 'Here, I'll show you.' He thumbed the rocker switch on the side. The gadget began to emit a faint electrical hum as its capacitors charged up. Suddenly, without warning, Winston thrust the machine towards Carney's face and discharged it.

The world suddenly exploded into an incandescent white fireball, turning quickly to pitch-darkness in which a negative image of Winston stood like a life-sized snowman. Then the black faded too, to be replaced by a red, swirling haze in which dark blotches danced like a swarm of demented butterflies.

Carney was completely and utterly disoriented. He felt off balance, frightened and vulnerable. The sound of Winston talking to him came through like a voice from the other side of the grave. 'Right now you're totally helpless,' Winston was saying. 'I could do just about anything to you that I wanted.'

Not in a mood to argue, Carney screwed his eyes shut and shook his head, trying to clear his brain and his vision. The first took no more than a few seconds. It was almost a full minute before he could see normally once more. He glared at Winston. 'I asked you how the bloody thing worked, for Christ's sake. I wasn't expecting a personal demonstration.'

Winston was unrepentant. 'Count that as your first instruction lesson,' he said. 'If you ever have to use one of these things, make sure you blink or look the other way.' He paused, grinning. 'Now, anything else you'd like to know?'

Carney grinned. 'I suddenly seem to have lost all sense of curiosity,' he said. His eyesight had recovered sufficiently to allow him to glance at his watch. It was nearly ten p.m. 'Probably time to make a move,' he suggested.

Winston nodded, and jerked his thumb down at the boxes of hardware on the floor. 'Let's just get this little lot stowed away somewhere and we'll get moving.' He looked up at Carney. 'Got any suggestions?'

Carney could only shrug. 'Put it anywhere you can find room for it,' he said, becoming almost as blasé about the armaments as his colleagues. 'Only I'd probably sleep a bit better if you didn't stash it under my bed.'

16

Following Carney's instructions, Winston pulled the Range Rover into the kerb about two hundred yards short of the entrance to Norma Jean's. He switched off the engine and lights, then turned to Peters and Pretty Boy in the back seats.

'Right, you've each got your brief. Go in with a high profile, put yourselves about a bit. You're a couple of likely lads who like to live high and aren't averse to a spot of bother. Find out what you can, do your jobs and don't enjoy yourselves too much.' He paused, allowing a faint grin to creep over his face. 'Oh, and if either of you should find yourselves waking up in a strange bedroom in the morning, remember we RV at Carney's flat at exactly 1000 hours.'

'And what are you going to be doing while we're struggling not to enjoy ourselves, boss?' Pretty Boy asked.

Winston smiled. 'Oh, the usual high-society hob-nobbing and social whirl. Carney and I are going to pay an unscheduled visit to the rich and powerful Mr Hargreaves.'

'Well, give him our love, boss,' Peters said, reaching for the door handle. He jumped down to the pavement, quickly followed by Pretty Boy. They began to walk up the street towards the nightclub.

Winston did not start the Range Rover again immediately. He fished under his seat, eventually pulling out a Browning HP and a shoulder holster, which he dropped in Carney's lap. 'Here, put this on before I forget.'

Carney looked at the gun, and then up at Winston's serious face, in surprise. 'I thought you said no hardware?'

Winston nodded thoughtfully, his face still serious. 'Yeah. But *we're* not going dancing, are we?'

Winston eased the Range Rover down the long, tree-lined drive which led to Cecil Hargreaves's private estate in an exclusive area of Borehamwood.

'Impressive, huh?' he said to Carney, with a brief sideways glance.

Carney said nothing, studying the mansion-like building beyond the high metal gates at the end of the drive. It looked like some latter-day fortress, the house itself standing some hundred yards behind a sturdy ten-foot wall, topped by a further eighteen inches of razor wire, probably electrified. Hargreaves was obviously a man who did not care for unexpected vistors.

Winston slowed down, pulling up just short of the gates. 'What now?' he asked.

It was a good question. Carney thought about it, as he took a good look around at the other security devices protecting the house and grounds. The place was sealed off as tightly as any high-security facility. That their approach to the gates had already been monitored was in little doubt. Carney had noted the rows of partially concealed floodlights between the trees all the way up the drive, and was sure he had also spotted at least four video scanners mounted high up in their branches. The presence of two wide-angle TV cameras set on top of the massive gatepost supports seemed to confirm this. Studying them more carefully, Carney figured they were probably part of a highly sophisticated, multi-function security system set for full-colour visual and infra-red scanning. They were fully motorized for a 180-degree sweep and vertical tracking, and their field of vision left no blind areas. Tiny red LED indicators showed that they were active. It would be impossible to approach the gates without coming under close surveillance.

Turning to Winston, Carney finally answered his question. 'The way I see it, we really don't have much choice,' he pointed out. 'Basically, we knock on the door and ask if Cecil can come out to play.'

He opened the Range Rover door and stepped out. Almost immediately, a bright spotlight snapped on, bathing him in its illumination. Probably activated by body temperature, Carney thought. Hargreaves had obviously cut no corners with his security arrangements. He waited for Winston to climb out and join him before walking cautiously up to the gates.

There was no need to ring the bell set into the right-hand gatepost. A gruff voice grated out from a small speaker mounted just above it.

'Who are you, and what do you want? Unexpected visitors aren't welcome here.'

Carney drew his ID card from his pocket, holding it up towards the video scanner above his head. 'Police. We'd like to speak to Mr Hargreaves.'

There was a moment's hesitation before the speaker

grille squawked again. 'Got a warrant? If not, fuck off and come back when you have.' The intercom system gave a loud click and fell silent.

'Well, I guess that gives us our answer,' Winston observed laconically. 'Our Cecil isn't the fun-loving type.'

'Yeah.' Carney shrugged carelessly and turned back towards the Range Rover. 'Well, I suppose we might as well go home.' He began to walk back towards the car.

Winston ran after him, catching up and about to say something. Carney silenced him with a warning flash of his eyes. He climbed back into the Range Rover and closed the doors before speaking in a low whisper. 'I thought the gate area might be bugged for sound as well as visual.'

'So, what are you thinking?' Winston whispered back.

Carney sucked at his teeth. 'I'm thinking that if Hargreaves won't come out, then we're going to have to go in,' he said. 'The question is – how? That place is sewn up tighter than Fort Knox.'

Winston grinned roguishly. 'There's always a weak spot,' he said. 'We've just got to find it. If we can't, we'll just have to make one.' He started the engine and did a three-point turn in the drive, which was suddenly plunged into darkness again behind them as the security floodlights cut out.

It was almost like a signal for the furtive whispering to stop. Carney relaxed visibly, adopting his normal voice. 'Seems to me that all we have to do is get in there,' he pointed out. 'Once we're in, what the hell can the man do? Whoever is on guard duty already thinks we're cops, and he'll probably report straight to Hargreaves. No matter what he's actually mixed up in, to all intents and purposes he's a respectable and fairly public figure. He couldn't risk any violence on his own home patch.'

It made sense, Winston realized. Slipping the Range Rover into gear, he set off back down the drive, glancing at Carney. 'Let's take a little scenic tour of the rest of the estate, shall we?'

Pretty Boy nodded at the pint glass in Peters's hand, a slightly scornful look on his face. 'The boss said high living,' he pointed out, shouting above the din of the disco music. 'And you're slurping down pints of bitter like a bloody navvy.' He waved his own can of expensive Japanese lager in the air. 'You got to have a bit of class these days.'

Peters was unimpressed. 'All these fancy designer beers taste weak as virgin's piss to me.'

Pretty Boy looked smug and superior. 'You're just not with it, mate. Out of touch.'

Peters shrugged and took another long draught of his beer. 'Who the fuck cares?' He jerked his head towards Pretty Boy's drink. 'Anyway, what does it taste like?'

Pretty Boy grinned. 'Like a virgin's bloody piss,' he admitted. 'And these plonkers pay the equivalent of about four quid a pint for it.'

The bar area was on a mezzanine level mounted above the crowded dance floor. Pretty Boy looked down over the twitching and jerking mass, screwing up his eyes against the glare of the flashing disco lights and pulsing laser beams. 'Anyway, we were told to make contact,' he reminded Peters. 'See anything you fancy making contact with?'

Peters swept his eyes over the floor, finally picking out a willowy blonde girl dancing with a slightly plump redhead. 'How about those two?' he suggested. 'Don't think much of yours, though.'

Pretty Boy gave the two girls a cursory glance, finally shrugging philosophically. 'The blonde looks fine to me, my old son. Let's go for it.' Leaving the half-finished can of beer on the bar, he began to stride purposefully towards the stairs leading down to the dance floor. Peters followed him, grinning awkwardly. He'd been conned again. But what the hell? It was only a job, after all.

Winston was wrong about the weak spot in Hargreaves's security system, and he was man enough to admit it. After a third futile sweep of the estate's perimeter walls, he was about ready to concede defeat. 'Short of parachuting in, I'd say we were buggered,' he said flatly. 'And as we're a bit short on air support right now, I don't have much to offer in the suggestions department.'

But Carney wasn't really listening. He was thinking. The germ of a wildly improbable idea was just beginning to sprout in his mind. A faint, almost secretive smile began to spread across his face. It was just so bloody crazy, it might just work, for Christ's sake!

Winston couldn't help but notice the expression on Carney's face. 'You got a plan,' he asked, in surprise.

Carney nodded thoughtfully. 'Maybe "plan" is rather too strong a word,' he admitted. 'But I do have an idea, which is a start.'

Winston was intrigued. 'Well, are you planning to share it?'

Carney did not answer him directly. 'You know the old saying – that a chain is only as strong as its weakest link?' he said. 'Well, maybe that works the other way round, as well.'

Winston was totally confused, and it showed on his face.

Carney grinned. 'Perhaps the best place to create a weakness is at the strongest point,' he went on. 'Use the very strength of the system against itself.'

Winston was now completely lost, and admitted it. 'I haven't the faintest idea what you're talking about,' he told Carney.

It was time for an explanation, Carney realized, the final scheme only just having come together fully in his head.

'The main gate,' he said. 'It's where they must think their system is absolutely foolproof. All we have to do is convince them that it isn't.'

Slowly and carefully, Carney began to spell out his idea in greater detail. Dubious at first, Winston nevertheless found himself increasingly impressed. He wasn't a man who gave his respect easily – especially to a civvy. But Paul Carney was earning it – and quickly.

The blonde and the redhead had turned out to be a double disaster, on all fronts. Close up, the blonde had about as much sexual allure as the bouncers and the plump redhead's face sprouted acne like midnight in a mushroom patch.

More importantly, neither of them wanted to talk. All attempts to start a conversation were met with the same blank, glassy-eyed stare and the cow-like cud-chewing of gum. It was fairly clear that all the two girls wanted to do was to dance – or at least continue to move, zombie-like, to the non-stop pounding bass. After ten minutes in which both Peters and Pretty Boy had failed to elicit the first names of their new companions, it had become glaringly obvious that their value as an information source was absolute zero.

Exchanging a quick and meaningful glance, the two troopers cut out in mid-number, leaving the two girls still gyrating on the dance floor. Two other young men stepped in to take their place without a break in the beat.

Pretty Boy headed back to the bar.

'Well, that was a bloody waste of time,' he said irritably, then ordered himself another can of lager.

Peters nodded in agreement. 'Maybe we're going about this the wrong way,' he said. 'Trying to pick up a pair of birds together ain't gonna get us anywhere.'

'So what do you reckon?' Pretty Boy asked.

Peters grinned wickedly, nodding over to a table overlooking the dance floor where a reasonably attractive brunette sat with a rough-looking man, looking slightly bored. 'How about stirring the shit up a bit?' he suggested. 'I'll be here for backup if you get into any bother.'

Pretty Boy flashed him a contemptuous but good-natured sneer. 'You patronizing little bastard.' He took another deep swig of his beer.

'Dutch courage?' Peters taunted him. 'Or are you just waiting for me to make the first move?'

Pretty Boy's eyes glittered. 'No, I was waiting for you to place your bet,' he said. 'Fifty quid says I can pull it off in one.'

Peters rose to the challenge. 'You're on.'

Pretty Boy grinned triumphantly. 'Right, now watch a master in action – and eat your fuckin' heart out,' he declared, striding off towards the couple at the table.

The young man eyed Pretty Boy with guarded hostility as he hovered provocatively above the table, openly ogling the brunette. 'What the hell do you want?' he rasped.

Pretty Boy smiled disarmingly. 'I want to finish my beer,' he said casually. 'Then I can ask this gorgeous young lady to dance with me.' He was watching the girl's green eyes like a hawk, reading her reactions. For the moment, they showed just the faintest flicker of amusement. It was enough!

The young man's face registered only incredulity at the brazenness of Pretty Boy's challenge – for challenge it most certainly was. At once, primal, instinctive forces came into play.

The girl's companion glared up at Pretty Boy. 'She's with me,' he growled. 'And she stays that way. Now fuck off – unless you're looking for trouble.'

It was crunch time. Pretty Boy knew the rules of

the game, and stuck to them. With casual, deliberate menace, he drained the last drop of lager from his can and proceeded to crush it slowly in his fist into a mangled ball of metal before setting it down on the table top. It was one of Pretty Boy's favourite party pieces, and rarely failed to impress – even though it involved technique as much as brute strength.

'Trouble?' he enquired innocently, with a quiet, confident smile on his face. 'No, I don't want any trouble, man. I've already got all the trouble I can handle.'

He looked into the girl's eyes again, finding the glitter of excitement and admiration he had been seeking. 'Now, how about that dance?' he said softly, reaching out to take the girl's hand as she rose from her chair.

Peters watched the little scene play out to its conclusion, a grudging smile on his face. Confident that the girl's former companion was not going to make a move, he turned back towards the bar, mentally shrugging off his fifty quid. There were usually compensations in life, he thought to himself philosophically, as his eyes fell on the pert little table waitress who had just approached the bar beside him.

'This place is pretty deadly, ain't it?' he murmured, with a knowing grin. 'How does a guy get a bit of a buzz around here?'

The waitress looked at him with a slightly mocking smile. 'Depends what you're looking for,' she said, a trifle warily.

Peters shook his head, still grinning. 'Nah. It depends on what's available,' he corrected her.

The girl smiled more openly. They understood one another.

17

Everything hinged on the field and range of the body-heat scanner. Carney was counting on the fact that it was a ninety-degree fixed beam, covering the area of the drive directly in front of the gates. If he was right, they should be able to approach the gates by creeping round the outside of the perimeter walls without triggering off the floodlights. If he was wrong, then the plan ground to an abrupt halt right there.

The theory was about to be put to the test. His back flattened against the wall, Carney was no more than two feet from the high brick pillar of the left-hand gatepost, the charging Scorpion stunner humming faintly in his hand. He edged a few inches nearer and froze, his eyes fixed on the tiny red eye of the video scanner as it slowly panned from side to side, monitoring and recording everything in its wide field of vision. It was a field of vision which ended with the massive bulk of the gatepost itself! And since that protruded out a good eight inches from the main wall, that left a small blind area which was protected from the camera's prying eye.

Carney smiled to himself, realizing that Winston had been right after all. There *was* always a weak spot – or at least a tiny flaw which could be exploited. Still with a watchful eye on the camera, he slid further along the wall until he was safely tucked into the safety zone. On the other side of the driveway,

Winston had taken up a similar position, and so far the floodlights had not come on. It was looking hopeful.

He glanced down at the Scorpion in his hand, checking that it was in single-flash mode. Satisfied that it was, and that it was fully charged, he raised the device above his head at arm's length in preparation.

Timing was crucial. Carney bided his time, allowing the video camera to make two complete sweeps and gauging the time it took to complete its full 180-degree pan. The entire cycle took exactly twenty-five seconds. Tensing himself, he watched the camera complete its scan in his direction, stop for a fraction of a second and then begin to swing back towards the centre of the drive.

He moved quickly out of the protective lee behind the gatepost, pointing the flash unit directly at the camera lens and firing it off. In the momentary glare, he could just pick out the bulky shape of Winston, copying his move with utter precision. A second flash exploded into the lens of the right-hand camera.

The plan was essentially simple. Somehow they had to convince whoever was monitoring the security scanners that the system was malfunctioning. The glaring discharge of the light guns would appear on the monitor screens inside the mansion house as a sudden and inexplicable burst of static — first one camera, then the other. One or two such occurrences might be dismissed as nothing more than a temporary fault. A continuing series could well suggest a complete system breakdown.

The camera, still on remote control, began to swing

back in Carney's direction. The Scorpion units had a recharge time of at least twenty seconds, which left very little leeway. Holding his breath and muttering a silent prayer, he pressed the firing button as the camera completed its return traverse. Their luck was holding; the Scorpion fired again, exactly on cue.

Winston set off his second discharge seconds later. Carney glanced up at the nearest camera hopefully. The red operating light was still on, the smooth traversing motion unbroken. He initiated the sequence twice more.

Carney's heart jumped as the panning camera stopped suddenly, in mid-sweep. The tiny red light flickered out. As he had hoped, whoever was monitoring the scanning system was shutting it down temporarily, perhaps hoping that it would reset itself automatically.

It was time to move. There was no way of knowing how long the camera would remain switched off. Carney could only assume that the entire security system was linked together, and there was no independent backup. Ducking out from behind the cover of the gatepost, he dashed into the centre of the drive in front of the tall wrought-iron gates as Winston ran out to meet him.

Swiftly Winston uncoiled the length of nylon rope he had brought from the back of the Range Rover. With a heavy tyre lever tied to one end, it was a hastily improvised grapple. Swinging it in his hands, Winston threw it up over the gate, where it lodged securely in position behind a couple of the ornamental spikes on top. Giving it one quick tug by way of a test, Winston began to shin up the front of the gate, flipping himself over the top to slide down the vertical bars on the inside. Carney was a matter of a few seconds behind him. They were inside the grounds.

'Come on, this way,' Winston hissed. Breaking into a loping run, he headed across the large lawn towards the side of the house. The silence was suddenly shattered by a loud bark, which echoed through the darkness towards them. Carney felt his heart sink. He hadn't even thought about guard dogs. Straining his eyes towards the house, and the sound of the barking animal, he was just able to pick out the vague shape of a huge German shepherd bounding across the grass towards them.

'Leave this to me,' Winston hissed, pushing Carney out of the way behind him. He bent to a crouch, directly confronting the charging dog. Just as the animal reached the end of its attack run, and launched itself into the air at his face, Winston flexed his knees, springing up to his full height. His arms snaked out, grasping the dog's front legs and wrenching them savagely apart with all his strength. There was a horrible sound of splintering bone and tearing sinew. The dog let out a single brief and bloodcurdling yelp of agony and dropped dead at Winston's feet, bright fresh blood frothing from its mouth.

Winston backed away, his huge frame shaking with anger and revulsion. 'Shit,' he cursed under his breath, with real feeling. 'I love dogs.'

Carney looked down aghast at the dead animal. 'What the hell did you do?' he whispered.

Winston regarded him glumly. 'Design fault,' he

muttered. 'They've been bred for shape – long, lean body and big chest. It's caused a certain degree of malformation in the internal skeletal structure. Ribcage is set too far forward. Put sudden and heavy strain on the front shoulders and it splinters inwards, puncturing the heart.' He looked up at Carney, giving a thin, bitter smile. 'It works on Dobermanns, too. It's Rottweilers that are the tricky ones – you have to punch them directly under the snout before they get their teeth into you.'

Carney wrinkled his nose in distaste. 'Thanks for the crash course in advanced dog handling,' he murmured. 'Now let's get the hell out of the open before they send an RSPCA hit man after us.'

It was a savage joke, but underlined a very real danger. The dog's frantic barking must have alerted someone, and it could only be a matter of moments now before its sudden disappearance, coupled with the apparent failure of the security cameras, caused that someone to put two and two together. Judging from the scope of Hargreaves's security measures so far, it was a pretty fair bet that he would also have armed bodyguards as a backup. Carney's original hypothesis – that Hargreaves would not want to risk violence in his own grounds – was no longer quite so secure. The unavoidable killing of the dog had changed things. The security guards now had an excuse for direct retaliation, and if they were feeling jumpy, they might well shoot first and ask questions later. Standing out there in the middle of the lawn, they presented a tempting target.

Similar thoughts had already occurred to Winston.

Poised on the balls of his feet, he shot Carney a brief, querulous glance. 'Where?' he hissed.

Carney shrugged, realizing that they had little choice other than to revert to the original plan. They had to make contact with Hargreaves direct, trusting that he would react as Carney had assumed. He nodded towards the house, where lights had begun to snap on in several of the ground-floor rooms. 'I guess we go for the front door,' he suggested. 'I think someone's expecting us.'

Breaking into a run, both men headed for the front of the house. The massive door was already opening.

Standard heavy, Carney thought, as he eyed the formidable bulk of the man framed in the stone porch. All brawn and very little brain, and trained to follow very specific orders. Without such orders, he was not a threat.

The man looked at Carney and Winston with a surly expression. 'Persistent bastards, aren't you?' He jabbed a thick finger in Carney's chest. 'I told you once to fuck off. Now I'm telling you again – and take the razor with you.'

The racial slur brought a frown to Winston's face. He recognized the criminal rhyming slang – razor-blade, spade. 'Now that's not very polite,' he said sombrely. 'And I get very angry when people aren't polite. Now you just trot back indoors like you've been trained to do and give your boss a message that we want to see him.'

The heavy's countenance darkened. He turned on Winston, his ugly face creasing up into a snarl. 'Uppity bastard,' he spat out. 'Maybe I'd better teach you a lesson.'

His right hand dived behind the lapel of his jacket, reaching for the Mauser holstered under his shoulder. His movements were fast – but no match for the highly tuned reactions of an SAS trooper. Winston's own hand snaked to his right-hand pocket, flashing out again with the Scorpion stunner firmly in his grip. In one smooth movement, he jabbed the pointed prongs of the device through the thin material of the man's shirt and pressed the discharge button.

The big man stiffened. Almost simultaneously there was a muffled explosion and the smell of cordite. The heavy crumpled to the floor.

Winston cursed for the second time that night. 'Fuck it,' he said wearily. 'That wasn't supposed to happen.'

Carney understood only too well what had gone wrong. The man must have reached the butt of his gun at the very second Winston had used the stunner. With his finger already wrapped around the trigger, he had been ready to draw as the charge hit him. Muscular reflex had done the rest. The jolt had travelled down his arm to his hand, contracting the muscles. Still trapped inside the confines of the holster, and at point-blank range, an exploding .32 slug carried a hell of a punch. The heavy had a hole the size of a fist blown in his side.

The echoes of the gunshot had hardly died away before Carney and Winston heard the click of two revolver hammers being cocked immediately behind them.

'Freeze right there, or you're both dead,' came a harsh voice, utterly chilling in its sincerity.

Carney spread his hands out slowly from his side, palms upward. Winston dropped the stunner, adopting a similar stance. Carney winced slightly as a gun barrel was jammed viciously into his ribs. A well-trained hand frisked him quickly and efficiently, drawing the Browning HP from its hiding place. The rest of the contents of his pockets quickly followed. Winston was not treated so leniently. A vicious kick in the back of his knee sent him sprawling to the ground with a dull groan of pain. A heavy boot slammed down on the back of his neck, pinning him there.

It was a strange and unbelievably tense little tableau which seemed to last for ever. Frozen like a dummy, Carney fully expected to feel the searing pain of a bullet tearing through his back at any second. Finally, through the half-open front door, he saw the figure of a man step out into the hallway of the house.

It had to be Hargreaves, Carney figured. The man was in his late fifties, but in superb physical condition for his age. His face, sun-tanned and healthy-looking, was surmounted by a leonine mane of silvery-grey hair, immaculately styled. Clad in a scarlet and gold Japanese robe of pure silk, he looked like the living epitome of wealth and power. Incongruously, there was a thin smile on his face, although it was possible to detect a seething anger just behind it.

'Bring them in,' the man snapped.

Carney lurched forward as the gun jabbed painfully into his ribcage again. The second bodyguard removed his foot from Winston's neck, urging him back to his feet with a couple of kicks in the side.

The party stepped forward over the body of the doorman and entered the house. The man was not yet dead, but no one made any move to help him. It was only a matter of a few moments, and he was well beyond any miracle of medicine or surgery.

'You do seem uncommonly anxious to see me,' the man said to Carney, confirming that he was indeed Hargreaves. 'Although telephoning for an appointment would have been so much less messy.' He paused to glance dispassionately at the dying man sprawled over his front porch. 'And good help is *so* difficult to find these days.'

For just a second, a look of concern showed through the mask of the fixed smile. 'I take it you've killed the dog as well?'

Winston nodded. 'I'm sorry about the dog,' he said quietly, meaning it.

Hargreaves ignored him, still directing himself to Carney. 'I shall quite miss the vicious beast,' he murmured, sounding almost affectionate for the merest fraction of a second. As though embarrassed by any sign of human weakness, his mood changed abruptly. 'Bring them to my study,' he snapped curtly to the two bodyguards, turning away and walking down the long hallway towards the rear of the house.

Once in his study, Hargreaves seated himself behind a huge, green-leather-topped desk. 'Make sure they're both completely clean,' he told his bodyguards. 'And then leave us. One of you had better wait outside the door, just in case.'

Carney and Winston had no choice but to submit to a second and completely thorough frisking, during which the contents of their pockets were dumped unceremoniously on Hargreaves's desk. Their two Brownings, with the ammunition clips removed, were laid down last of all.

Hargreaves seemed satisfied. He dismissed the two bodyguards with a curt nod of his head. As they left the room, he picked up Carney's ID card and glanced at it briefly before looking up at him curiously.

'An official police warrant card,' he mused, also picking up one of the handguns and studying it. 'But this is hardly standard police issue.' He paused, thoughtfully. 'Exactly who are you working for, Mr Carney?'

Carney said nothing. It seemed to be an answer in itself for Hargreaves, who nodded knowingly. 'Ah,' he murmured, as if everything had suddenly been made clear to him. 'Quite obviously there's no point in my picking up the phone and making a top-level complaint about the pair of you breaking into my home.' He sat back in his swivel chair, the fixed smile returning to his face. 'So what can I do for you?' he asked.

'Nirvana,' Carney said abruptly, seeing no reason to beat about the bush. 'Know anything about it?' He was watching the man's eyes like a hawk, searching for the faintest trace of a reaction, but there was nothing. The man was as cool as ice.

Hargreaves merely smiled wistfully. 'Yes, a state of inner peace,' he mused. 'Alas, not something that a businessman finds much of these days.'

'Cut the crap, Hargreaves,' Winston snapped testily. 'You know exactly what we're talking about.'

The Barbadian provoked a reaction where Carney had failed. For the briefest instant a look of vicious loathing blazed in Hargreaves's eyes.

Carney noted it with a faint sense of satisfaction. The man's racial hatred was strong enough to make it a weakness. It might be possible to play upon it.

But not for the moment. Hargreaves recovered his icy composure, looking at Winston with the innocence of a child. 'I haven't the faintest idea what you mean.'

They were getting nowhere, Carney realized. The verbal fencing could go on all night unless they established a position of strength. Perhaps it was time to throw a few cards on the table and see how they fell.

'Then let me spell it out for you,' Carney said quietly. 'Nirvana – the street name for a new drug which gives the user a sense of well-being and at the same time increases aggresion. A drug very similar in fact to one developed by a certain Dietrich Kleiner while he was working for Fleisch-Müller Pharmaceuticals in Germany. A drug for which one of your subsidiary companies bought up the patent and formula just three years ago. And now that drug is on the streets, and people are getting killed.' Carney took a long, meaningful pause. 'I'd say that puts you in a rather vulnerable position – as an accessory to murder – wouldn't you?'

Hargreaves was silent for a long time. His eyes, although betraying little, were thoughtful as his mind raced through all the implications and possibilities.

Finally he smiled. 'An extremely tenuous connection, I'm sure you'll agree,' he pointed out. 'I control dozens of companies, but I don't have – couldn't possibly have – a day-to-day say in what they do, or what they buy and sell. No, I think you'll have to do a lot better than that, Mr Carney.'

It was the answer Carney had expected, and he conceded the point. 'All right. Let's look for some other connections then, shall we? Dietrich Kleiner was a Nazi. The drug has now fallen into the hands of a new bunch of neo-fascists. Your own personal links with the extreme right might not stand too close a scrutiny – if someone took the trouble to dig deep enough.'

Hargreaves didn't look quite so sure of himself any more. He was beginning to get a little rattled, Carney thought. He pushed his advantage.

'If we know this much already, you can bet your life we can find out more,' he stressed. 'And, as I think you've already worked out for yourself, we're not restricted to conventional procedures. If we dug up a connection between you and a militant neo-Nazi group, the picture might look a little different, don't you think?' Carney paused for effect. 'Second Holocaust, for instance?'

He was rewarded by a momentary flash of fear in Hargreaves's eyes.

'So you've heard of them?' he asked, seizing on it.

Hargreaves nodded faintly. 'Yes, I've heard of them. They're nasty – and they're dangerous.' All the man's bravado and confidence was melting away fast now. He looked up at Carney with a slightly helpless expression which was almost a plea. 'Look, they're absolutely nothing to do with me, you've got to believe me.'

'Then what are you afraid of?' Carney challenged him. That the man was afraid of something was no longer in doubt.

Hargreaves took a deep breath. 'Look, I've never made any great secret of my political beliefs,' he said finally. 'But I'm merely a nationalist. I'm not a Nazi.'

'There's a difference?' Winston put in sarcastically.

Hargreaves ignored him, continuing to direct himself to Carney. 'Look, you're a policeman, you must see what's happening to our society. We've allowed the very fabric of this nation to go rotten, its people trodden down and demoralized. Our very sovereignty is threatened by an increasingly federalistic Europe. Criminals freely roam the streets and get suspended sentences if they are caught at all. Children commit the most brutal murders. We have three million native Britons out of work, yet immigrants continue to pour into this small and overcrowded island home of ours . . .'

Winston cut the party political broadcast short with a bitter laugh. 'I wondered how long it would take to get round to that,' he observed. Repatriation's the answer, right? Pack us all into banana boats and ship us back to the coconut groves?'

For the first time, Hargreaves confronted him directly, an ingratiating smile on his face. 'Believe me, I have nothing personal against you people,' he whined. 'It's not your fault. It was our own spineless left-wing liberals who brought you into the country after the war to do all the dirty, low-paid jobs that nobody else wanted. It was a mistake. No one had taken into account your breeding capacity.'

For his own sake, as well as Winston's, Carney did not want to hear any more. He felt sickened. Hargreaves's 'you people' had said it all. He slammed his fist down on the man's desk. 'I'll repeat my earlier question,' he barked. 'What are you afraid of? Second Holocaust worries you – why?'

Hargreaves's eyes flickered nervously. He let out a long, deep sigh. 'I made the drug formula available to certain parties without knowing the connection,' he admitted finally, in a small, weak voice. 'It was a mistake, an error of judgement, and I regret it now.' The pleading look crept into his eyes again. 'But that's the sum total of my involvement, believe me. As I said, these people are dangerous – as I now know to my own cost.'

'Your cost? How?' Carney demanded, seizing on the admission.

The businessman managed a thin, bitter smile. 'You surprise me, Carney,' he muttered. 'If you could dig out Dietrich Kleiner's name, I would have thought you would have done your other homework more carefully.' He paused briefly, before dropping his final bombshell. 'Didn't you realize that Consolidated Breweries was one of the companies in the Trans-Europe Holdings group?'

There was a long, stunned silence, broken finally by the sound of Winston whistling through his teeth. 'Talk about biting the hand that feeds you,' he observed sardonically.

Hargreaves looked at the two men warily, his eyes glittering with a mixture of hope and cunning. 'So it occurs to me that we might be able to make some sort of a deal,' he suggested. 'Perhaps we are in a position to help one another.'

Winston's face was a picture of revulsion. 'Jesus Christ, I'd as soon hand-feed a fucking rattlesnake,' he muttered, even though the realization that they didn't have much choice had already dawned on him.

Carney was rather more philosophical. 'What do you suggest?' he asked calmly.

Hargreaves looked relieved. Rather *too* relieved, Carney thought. As though he had expected more opposition. The man clearly had more to hide than he was letting on.

'There are a couple of things which might help you,' Hargreaves said eventually. 'First of all, there's a big rally coming off in the very near future. It will ostensibly be the official National Rights Party, but members of all the fringe organizations are bound to be there, including Second Holocaust. I can give you names, contacts.'

'And the second thing?' Carney prompted.

Hargreaves looked nervous again. 'I've already decided to pay the ransom,' he muttered after a moment's hesitation. 'Moves to make contact and arrange the details have already been initiated. Suppose I were to arrange for you to make the delivery?'

Carney thought about the offer at some length. 'So what do you get out of all this?' he asked gravely.

Hargreaves shrugged. 'I stay clean,' he said simply. 'You make no more enquiries into my political affiliations or business connections. I would also need your reassurance that the ransom money would be handed over straight and with no tricks. The money will be genuine, and I want the transaction to go smoothly. Consolidated Breweries cannot afford a prolonged siege.'

Winston was shaking his head. 'No way,' he said flatly. 'We're out to stop these bastards, not help finance them.' He paused, staring Hargreaves in the eyes. 'Now here's the deal as I see it. You help us, and we'll back off from you personally. But we handle the ransom hand-over our way, or not at all.'

Fear flashed in Hargreaves's eyes. 'But they'll kill me if they think I've double-crossed them,' he pleaded.

There was no trace of pity on Winston's face. 'Then you'll just have to keep your head down until we've done our job, won't you?'

Hargreaves's face revealed an agony of indecision as he contemplated all the frightening possibilities. Finally he caved in with a hopeless sigh.

'All right, we'll do it your way. I'll get out of the

country for a while, move to one of our operations in Germany. I have friends there.'

Winston's face creased into a scornful grin. 'Yeah, I bet you fucking have.'

18

The morning meeting had been convened in Carney's flat, as planned. It was time for the group to pool their knowledge thus far and to plan future moves.

Winston looked at the two young troopers expectantly. 'Well? Get anything?'

Pretty Boy grinned ruefully. 'Only a quick wank,' he volunteered. 'It was the wrong time of the month for a deep-penetration mission.'

Winston glared at him, letting him know that he was out of order. There were times to let bullshit and banter go unchallenged, but this was not one of them. 'Any more cracks like that and I'll deep-penetrate your arse with the business end of an M16,' he threatened.

'You're all promises, boss,' Pretty Boy shot back at him, but then fell silent, suitably chastened.

Winston glanced at Peters. 'Well? Anything we can use?'

Peters nodded. 'Maybe,' he said. 'I managed to get chatting with a bird who works at the place regularly, and I picked up a few pieces of information that could be useful.'

'Such as?' Winston prompted.

'Nirvana's usually available, at about fifteen quid a throw,' Peters told him. 'Only the word is that it happens to be in rather short supply at the moment and the two guys that deal regularly haven't been around for a couple of days.'

Winston smiled to himself. 'Surprise, surprise,' he murmured. 'So we did manage to throw a spanner in the works.'

Peters didn't look too enthusiastic. 'Yeah, well, don't get too carried away, boss. The girl seemed pretty confident there would be another batch on the streets in a day or so.' He paused, to shrug briefly. 'It could be that we only dented their distribution network a little bit.'

It was more or less what Carney had anticipated, so he wasn't too disappointed. It was unrealistic to expect them to keep all their eggs in one basket. 'No idea of the source of this new supply, I suppose?' he wanted to know.

Peters shook his head. 'Nothing, sorry. It seemed to be pushing my luck to ask too many questions on first contact. But I think she trusts me, if I ever need to get back to her.'

Carney could only nod in agreement. The young trooper seemed to have an instinctive understanding of the situation. Undercover contacts could only be built up slowly, through mutual trust.

Winston had returned his attention to Pretty Boy. 'What about the bully-boy brigade? Anything on that front?'

Pretty Boy looked vaguely optimistic. 'Could be,' he said guardedly. 'Cheryl, the bird I scored, seems to go for the hard-man type. I think it turns her on. Anyway, I sort of gave her the impression I was a bit of a Jack-the-Lad and enjoyed the odd bit of

Paki-bashing for kicks. She didn't give me anything definite, but she did drop a few vague hints that some of the guys who use the club make a few quid on the side hiring out their fists from time to time. It sounded like some sort of rent-a-riot set-up.'

Winston glanced across at Carney. 'Sound like anything you've come across before?' he asked.

Carney nodded grimly. 'All too bloody familiar,' he said. 'Amateur yobbos come a lot cheaper than professional thugs. It's not unusual for some of the more militant groups to go recruiting round the pubs before a big street rally or a demo.'

'Actually, boss,' Pretty Boy cut in, 'it occurred to me that we might set up a little demo of our own – with your help, of course.'

It was obvious that the young trooper had some kind of idea. As ever, Winston was willing to listen to it. 'Explain,' he said.

'I've arranged to meet this bird again tonight,' Pretty Boy told him. 'Like I said, she seems to be heavily into the aggro bit. I thought we might be able to put on a little show for her benefit.' He paused, looking at Winston with an awkward, rather sheepish grin.

It was this look, rather than what had already been said, that put Winston on his guard. 'What exactly did you have in mind?' he asked warily.

Pretty Boy adopted a more serious expression. 'I thought it might be possible to set up some sort of confrontation – between you and me,' he explained. 'I do you over, proving to Cheryl what an evil, nigger-hating bastard I am.'

Peters, who had been listening to all this with increasing amusement, could not resist putting in his two pennyworth. 'Christ Almighty, Pretty Boy,' he said dismissively. 'This has got to be your richest stroke yet. You get to beat the shit out of poor old Sarge so you can impress some shit-brained bird?'

Winston, however, was giving the idea serious consideration. He finally nodded his head thoughtfully. 'Yes, it might work,' he mused.

Pretty Boy looked awkward again. 'The only real problem is that it would be hard to fake,' he pointed out. 'In order to make it look totally convincing, I'd have to come in really hard. You could get hurt.'

Winston smiled knowingly. 'Yes, that thought had already occurred to me,' he said. He was thoughtful for a few more seconds. 'I could always wear a certain amount of hidden body protection, and we can rehearse a few stunts which will look convincing,' he added at last. 'Just as long as you're bloody careful where you put the boot in.' He considered it for a few seconds more, then finally made up his mind. 'OK, let's pencil that one in for a go – as long as we get time.'

The matter was decided. It was time to move on to more important business. Winston brought the two troopers up to date with their encounter with Cecil Hargreaves and his unexpected willingness to co-operate with them.

'So, basically, it's now down to Second Holocaust,' he summed up, finally. 'Consolidated Breweries are going to pay the ransom once the arrangements have been made, and we play the delivery boys.

Depending, of course, on getting final approval from official channels through Lieutenant-Colonel Davies and all the backup we're likely to need.'

Pretty Boy voiced the doubt which had occurred to all of them. 'How far can we trust this Hargreaves bastard?' he wanted to know.

Winston was brutally frank. 'About as far as I'd trust you with a teenage virgin,' he admitted. 'But then it wouldn't appear to be in the man's best interest to dump on us. He's got too much to lose.' He paused, and shrugged philosophically. 'On the face of it, this could give us our best chance yet of tackling these bastards face to face, putting them under some real pressure.'

'How do you see it?' Carney asked.

Winston smiled grimly. 'If we can hit them on two fronts – choke off their drugs and extortion funds as we move in closer to their actual membership structure – something's got to give. We've got a couple of new angles now – maybe it's time to pull out all the stops and really put the squeeze on. Let the bastards know we're coming.'

'And then what?' Carney asked bluntly. 'We don't really know exactly how desperate, or ruthless, these jokers are likely to get.'

Winston nodded glumly. 'That's why I'm going to have to talk to Barney Davies,' he admitted. 'Basically, I think it's high time the bright sparks who dreamt up this little caper in the first place decide exactly how far they want, or are prepared, to go.'

19

The answer, when it finally came, was the unequivocal 'All the way'. On Lieutenant-Colonel Davies's direct orders, the entire force had been put on a state of alert and was ready to move at a moment's notice. The men of 22 SAS were ready to go to war and more than spoiling for a fight. Everyone had been expecting a quick and early breakthrough with the raid on the farmhouse drug factory. When that had turned into a non-event, it had left behind a deep sense of frustration. Now, at last, there was a sense of purpose again. Two new names had been added to the plaque on the base of the regimental clock at Stirling Lines and the legendary camaraderie of the SAS demanded vengeance – just as soon as the enemy chose to show itself.

Winston's London unit had been supplemented by Ted Brennon, Miles Tremathon and Hugh Thomas, the Lethal Leek. The transfer of personnel served two purposes, strengthening Winston's ability to cover any possible leads arising from their current contacts and giving the three troopers a new boss following the death of Captain Feeney. Perhaps more importantly, it also ensured that there was a reasonably sized strike force ready and on the spot should the rumoured fascist rally take place at short notice. It left Major Anderson and the main force free to respond to any new information from intelligence sources as well as primed to back up the ransom hand-over, once the details had been finalized.

Carney's little flat had now become a temporary barracks room as well as an arsenal, with Carney himself feeling increasingly out of place. He had been able to relate to Winston, and had managed to get along fairly well with Pretty Boy and Peters. Outnumbered six to one, and acutely aware of the age gap between himself and the young troopers, he was beginning to feel like the proverbial spare prick at a wedding.

He managed to convey these vague feelings of uneasiness in a rare quiet moment alone with Winston, as the troopers took over his bedroom to play cards.

Winston listened patiently as Carney expressed his misgivings. Finally, his face registered a sympathetic smile. 'But that's not all, is it?' he said knowingly.

Carney shook his head, impressed by the big Barbadian's capacity for sympathy and understanding. 'No, that's not all.'

Winston was thoughtful for a while. 'Look, what you're really worried about is that you're about to be frozen out,' he said, hitting the nail squarely on the head. 'You're afraid there isn't going to be any part for you to play if things start really popping. Am I right?'

Carney nodded miserably. 'And you're not going to assure me otherwise, are you?' he said, making it a statement rather than a question. He looked Winston squarely in the eye, waiting for the man's response.

It was a look of regret, confirming Carney's worst fears. Winston shook his head slowly. 'No,' he said flatly. 'I can't tell you anything different.' He paused, racking his brains for something to say which might conceivably soften the blow. In the end there seemed little more he could say than to remind Carney of something he should have realized all along. 'You were told at the start that you'd be kept out of combat situations wherever possible,' he said gently. 'Nothing's changed from that.'

Carney let out a short, bitter laugh. 'Goddammit, a hell of a lot's change. I got involved, for a start.'

Winston fell silent. He could only feel sorry for the man. Carney had been given a rare insight into a different world, a different way of life which was almost impossible for the average outsider to even contemplate, let alone understand. He had received a taste of what it could mean to be SAS, to be part of a uniquely close, almost mystical brotherhood who lived and shared danger and companionship on a completely different level from most other men. To have been that close and yet so far, Winston reflected. Yes, he could only feel sorry for Carney, with his sense of impotence and frustration.

He offered him the only comfort he could. 'Look at it this way, Paul,' he said, using Carney's first name for the first time since they had met. 'This thing isn't over yet – not by a long way.'

As if right on cue to confirm this statement, Carney's telephone shrilled. He jumped up, crossing the lounge to snatch it up. It was Hargreaves, and he sounded edgy. Carney flipped on the tape recorder Winston had wired into his telephone.

'Is everything arranged?' Carney asked.

There was a faint catch in the other man's voice as he answered. 'They're prepared to go ahead – but there's a problem,' he said shakily.

'What sort of problem?' Carney demanded, trying to hide his sudden concern.

'They've taken out a little insurance policy,' Hargreaves told him. 'There's another bomb, in another pub. But this one's different – it's already in place, and fitted with a timing device. We'll only get the exact location and instructions for defusing it if the ransom hand-over goes without a hitch.'

'Damn.' Carney's mind raced, trying to see ways round the unexpected complication. 'When and where is the money due to be handed over?' he demanded.

'That's the only part we don't know yet,' Hargreaves told him. 'The method of transfer has already been arranged. The money is packed in a red Samsonite suitcase which is ready and waiting for collection at the reception desk of the Courtland Hotel in Knightsbridge. The actual hand-over will be tomorrow. Details will be announced in the personal columns of the *Evening Standard* this evening. It will take the form of a message to Gloria from Stanley, giving a time and meeting place.'

Carney ran the plans through his head quickly, looking for anything which didn't sound right, or could possibly go wrong. There were a dozen such things, he realized – but the basic scheme seemed workable enough.

'All right, so how do we collect the money?' he asked.

'The hotel manager is expecting someone by the name of Gilmour,' Hargreaves told him. 'He will hand over the case on request at exactly nine o'clock this evening.'

Faint warning bells rang in Carney's head. He didn't like the idea of being pinned down to a precise time. 'Why not until nine?' he asked suspiciously.

'Because that's when he comes on duty,' Hargreaves said. 'And only he can authorize the handing over of the suitcase. That's *my* little insurance policy – against someone making a sneak pick-up.'

'And what else?' Carney asked brusquely. There was something the man hadn't told him, he was sure.

There was a short pause as Hargreaves thought about things. 'All right, there is one more little detail,' he admitted at last. 'By nine o'clock I'll be on a flight to Bonn. 'I need to feel sure that I am safe and out of here if anything goes wrong.'

It all made sense, Carney decided, although his suspicions were far from allayed. But there was not much more he could do about it. For the moment at least, Hargreaves was calling the shots. He dropped the receiver back into its cradle and rewound the tape recorder for Winston to check the conversation.

'Well?' he asked, after Winston had played the tape through a couple of times.

The Barbadian looked dubious. 'I don't trust that bastard,' he said candidly. 'And something smells.'

Carney shared his sentiments exactly. 'Seems to me we're the only ones without a safety net here,' he observed. 'The point is, what the hell can we do about it?'

Winston was thoughtful for a while. 'I think we need to modify our plans slightly,' he said at last.

As promised, the brief coded message in the personal columns of the *Evening Standard* gave precise instructions:

'Gloria – See you by the bandstand in Green Park at midday – Stanley.'

Later editions of the paper, and the evening television news, carried no stories of further bombings. On the face of it, Second Holocaust appeared to be keeping their word.

20

'Well, how do I look?' Winston asked, parading himself like a model on a catwalk.

Pretty Boy, Carney and the Lethal Leek scrutinized him from all angles, taking in his general appearance. There was no doubt that he looked slightly odd to those who knew him well and were used to his huge, muscular but lean frame. Now, with several rolls of crêpe bandage bound around his ribcage, a bullet-proof vest under his shirt and a padded, heavy-duty sports jockstrap protecting his groin area, he looked strangely swollen and misshapen.

Pretty Boy delivered the consensus of opinion. 'Well, you look a bit like a sumo wrestler who's been on a diet, boss, but I guess you'll do.'

Winston glanced at Carney, inviting a second, more critical assessment. Carney shrugged faintly. 'What the hell?' he said. 'You're not going to be under a spotlight and no one's going to be looking at you that closely. I don't see any problem.' He paused, giving Winston a reassuring grin. 'Besides, this is showbusiness.'

Winston seemed satisfied. He turned to Pretty Boy. 'Right, now remember those moves we rehearsed, and don't throw anything unexpected at me.'

Pretty Boy nodded, now completely serious. 'By the book, boss,' he vowed.

Winston checked his watch. It was nearly eight

o'clock. They had exactly half an hour to get Pretty Boy to his date and set up the fake fight and a further half an hour's leeway to arrange the pick-up of the ransom money. There was just enough time for one last run-through of the arrangements.

'OK, let's just make sure that everyone knows his job,' Winston said. 'Trooper Peters goes directly to the nightclub to follow up his own contacts and wait for Pretty Boy and his girlfriend. That gives us a homing pigeon if Pretty Boy has any info by the time he gets to the club.' Winston nodded at Hugh Thomas. 'The Leek stays here with Carney. They're our relay station and emergency backup unit. Anyone with any information can pass it back here for forwarding to Major Anderson at Stirling Lines if deemed necessary. That also goes for anyone hitting unexpected trouble.'

Winston paused to take a breath, then turned to Ted Brennon and Miles Tremathon. 'You two will shadow me discreetly until the fight is over. Just in case any other young thugs decide to join in the attack, you'll be around in the background to make sure I don't get seriously hurt. As soon as it's over, and you know I'm safe, you make the pick-up at the Courtland Hotel and bring the money straight back here.' Winston finished his little speech and eyed each man in turn. 'Any questions?'

There were none. Winston had spelled everything out in clear, logical terms. Each of them had his specific orders to follow.

'Right, let's do it,' he said firmly. 'It's showtime.'

* * *

Winston was already installed in the pub as Pretty Boy walked in with the girl. He sat alone at a table near the door, sipping at his beer and ignoring the rest of the customers, especially the big Cornishman Tremathon and the wiry little Scouser Brennon, sitting up at the bar on stools.

He did not, however, ignore Pretty Boy's date, casting a frankly admiring gaze over her shapely young body as her escort ushered her through the door. It was a prearranged move, but Winston enjoyed it anyway. Cheryl Taylor was quite a looker, he had to admit. Perhaps just a shade top-heavy in the tit department for his personal taste, and a bit too wide in the hips – but a body definitely designed for comfort rather than speed. Her face was pretty enough, and shown off to its best advantage by a curly mass of naturally blonde hair. It was only the corners of her generous mouth, turned down in an apparently permanent pout, and the cold precision in her blue eyes, which lent her a hard, almost sluttish appearance.

But certainly not a woman any man would want to kick out of his bed, Winston decided. The delicious irony of the situation brought a smile to his face. He was going to get beaten up to improve Pretty Boy's chances of getting the girl into bed in the first place. Ogling her as he was, his smile passed for a lecherous leer, which did not go unnoticed.

Cheryl was used to the hungry looks of men – black or white. As usual, she took it as a compliment. Not so Pretty Boy, responding as programmed.

'Is that black bastard blimping you?' he growled.

Cheryl shrugged it off. 'Let the bastard dream,' she murmured casually. 'Before he goes home to his big fat momma.' She looked away from Winston, casting her eyes around the uncrowded pub for more sops to her vanity. Brennon and Tremathon obliged, both running approving eyes up and down the girl's shapely legs and body.

Pretty Boy led her to the bar and ordered drinks. When they arrived he paid and they made their way to an empty table at the rear of the pub, Pretty Boy all the while casting baleful looks in Winston's direction.

'Why so jumpy?' Cheryl asked, aware that Pretty Boy seemed upset by the black man's presence. 'You're not the jealous type, are you?'

'Bloody right I am,' Pretty Boy said vehemently. 'And I don't like the way that nigger looked at you.'

Discreetly, he scanned the girl's eyes, noting the faint glimmer of excitement which crossed them momentarily. She liked being a catalyst, he told himself. She'd encourage, even welcome violent jealousy, though she wouldn't push it.

'Did you hear about the surfer who found a drowned nigger on the beach?' he asked the girl in a loud voice. 'He skinned the fucker and made a new wetsuit.'

Winston deliberately ignored the vicious joke. It was sicker than most and just happened to be one that he hadn't heard before. He found himself wondering idly whether it had already done the rounds back at Stirling Lines. Or whether Pretty Boy had ever told it before under other circumstances. For personal reasons, he preferred to think not.

Cheryl giggled nervously, reaching across the table to clutch at Pretty Boy's arm. 'Shush – he'll hear you,' she hissed under her breath.

He shrugged with affected bravado. 'I don't give a shit if he does,' he boasted loudly. 'Gutless bastard won't have the bottle to do anything about it. Only time they'll fight at all is when they're at least three to one.'

Cheryl was suddenly aware that the focus of attention had shifted from herself. 'Anyway, forget about him,' she said, clutching Pretty Boy's arm again possessively. 'Where are you going to take me tonight?'

Pretty Boy shrugged. 'I thought we'd have a couple of drinks and go on to the club,' he suggested. 'Maybe score a little buzz – you know?'

Cheryl pouted sexily, eyeing him over the top of her glass of Diamond White. 'And I thought you might be wanting to score something else tonight,' she teased him, openly provocative. 'My little problem – it's finished now.'

Pretty Boy grinned widely. 'Even better, darling,' he said as he laid his hand over hers and squeezed it.

Winston glanced at his watch. They were running short of time. He made a big show of finishing his drink, finally pushing himself to his feet. He allowed his eyes to linger on Cheryl's body again, a slightly mocking smile on his face, before moving towards the door.

Pretty Boy's face was taut with anger. 'He did it again, the cheeky bastard,' he spat out. 'That black shit gave you the eye.'

Cheryl could sense something was about to break,

and she wasn't sure that it suited her purpose for the moment. The time for trouble was later, when her date had had a chance to spend a bit of money on her, show her a good time. She most definitely did not fancy going round with some dishevelled and possibly beaten-up wreck of a guy for the rest of the evening. She smiled disarmingly. 'I didn't see anything,' she lied. 'Maybe you were just imagining it.'

'No bloody way,' Pretty Boy told her angrily. 'That bastard looked you over as if you were something hanging up in a butcher's window – and I'm not going to let him get away with it. That's one jumped-up nigger who needs teaching a lesson.'

Pretty Boy threw the rest of his drink down his throat, glaring over at the door through which Winston had just exited. He jumped to his feet, looking down at Cheryl. 'I'm going after that sonofabitch,' he told her. 'He needs a bloody good kicking. You want to wait here until I come back?'

Cheryl sighed resignedly, thinking it through quickly. It was obvious that she wasn't going to get the attention she demanded until this little game was over. In the meantime, she might as well get a little vicarious excitement, she thought. Just in case the evening was going to turn out a complete washout on other fronts. She ran through various worst-case scenarios in her calculating little brain. If Pretty Boy came out the worse for wear from the encounter, she could always dump him. That still left her choices. She could go to the club on her own, confident that there would be another man with money in his pocket and a prick in his pants. There always was. On the other hand, she could come back to the bar and finish her drink. She had already noticed the two hunky guys propped up at the bar as she came in with Pretty Boy. So what if one of them sounded like a yokel and the other spoke with a Liverpool accent you could cut with a knife? They were both beefy men – and both interested. Cheryl had seen the looks they had given her earlier. They were interested all right.

She pushed her half-finished drink to the centre of the table, standing up to join Pretty Boy, who was clearly itching to get after the departed black man.

'I'll come with you,' she told him. 'But just watch yourself, OK?'

Pretty Boy sneered at her. 'I can take that bastard with one hand tied behind my back,' he said with total confidence.

Pulling the girl by the hand, he headed for the door, looking out on to the darkened street. Winston had crossed the road, and was just about to turn down a narrow alley between some shops. It was all part of the plan, and Winston's insurance. The fight would look more convincing in the dark, and the more private it was, the better.

'Come on,' Pretty Boy said, dragging the girl across the road. Reaching the far pavement, he paused, rooted around in his pocket and pulled out a bicycle chain.

Cheryl looked at the weapon with a certain awe, her eyes glinting. 'You really come prepared for bother, don't you?' she said, unaware that all the props for the little charade had been bought only that afternoon.

Pretty Boy shook his head. 'Not prepared – looking,' he said thickly. 'I fucking hate those black bastards.' He coiled the chain around his hand, leaving a loop of eight or nine inches hanging loose. Telling Cheryl to stay behind, he ran into the dark alley in pursuit of his quarry.

Winston was walking unhurriedly past rows of dustbins and empty cardboard boxes. He stopped suddenly, turning round warily at the sound of running footsteps. For a moment it seemed that he would turn again and run, but he stood his ground.

Pretty Boy stopped and sized up the situation. Cheryl stood at the end of the alley, watching Pretty Boy as he started to move forward again cautiously until he was within six feet of the big man. He swung the chain menacingly from his wrist.

'I want a word with you, nigger,' he hissed.

Winston's white teeth flashed in the dim light as he grinned back defiantly. 'You'd better run on home, white boy,' he sneered. 'Before you get more than you bargained for.'

Pretty Boy flexed the chain in his hand, edging a few steps nearer. 'I didn't like the way you looked at my girl,' he growled.

Winston grinned again, but moved back cautiously against the partial protection of the wall. 'Maybe you'd better ask her how she feels about it,' he challenged. 'Looked to me like she was the sort of bitch who liked her meat on the dark side.'

'Bastard,' Pretty Boy roared, apparently stung by the slur. He ran forward, wielding the chain above his head and swinging it in a vicious arc at the black man's head. For a horrible second he thought he had misjudged the distance and was going to catch Winston's face with the end of the chain – a mistake which would almost certainly have smashed the man's jawbone. He needn't have worried. With lightning-fast reactions, Winston ducked, twisting his body away so that the heavy chain merely smashed into the wall, sending chips of broken brick flying in all directions. Jumping back, Winston's hand flashed under his jacket, emerging with a wicked-looking eight-inch commando knife in his grip.

It was Pretty Boy's turn to jump backwards, assuming a more defensive position. He poised himself on the balls of his feet, facing his opponent and allowing the chain to uncoil from his wrist to its full length. Knowing that Cheryl couldn't see his face, he flashed Winston a quick, knowing smile. They were now in a position they had shared a dozen times before – albeit under the controlled conditions of the close-quarter combat gym back at Stirling Lines. Two superbly trained warriors, with both fighting and defensive skills honed to a degree of precision which was almost an art form. From here on, it was pure choreography.

Winston leapt forward, his knife arm fully extended. With a vicious slicing motion, he made a feinting stab at Pretty Boy's belly. As though he had springs built into his feet, Pretty Boy jumped backwards a good three feet, landing on his toes. Extending his own arm, he began to whirl the chain in front of him like a propeller.

The next moves had been painstakingly rehearsed

for much of the afternoon. Appearing to make an error of judgement, Winston tried another feinting lunge at Pretty Boy's guts, holding the knife at arm's length. The whirling chain connected solidly with the heavy metal blade, sending it spinning away out of his grasp. It clattered to the floor of the alley several yards away in the darkness.

'Got you now, you nigger bastard,' Pretty Boy screamed, for Cheryl's benefit. He moved in towards his now defenceless victim, slashing the chain in a criss-cross pattern at Winston's padded chest and drawing a series of convincing grunts of pain from the black man's lips.

It was time to go down, Winston realized. He backed away from Pretty Boy's attack, losing his footing on the rough cobbled ground and falling backwards. He collapsed on to his back, absorbing some of the shock by rolling sideways.

Pretty Boy moved in for the kill. Make it look good, Winston had urged him when they had plotted out the fight. Caught up in his role, although hardly enjoying it, Pretty Boy stepped towards his fallen opponent and swung his right foot viciously towards the man's ribs, only turning his foot at the last moment so that the side rather than the point of his boot made contact.

With all the flair of a professional actor, Winston screamed in agony, writhing on the ground as though badly hurt. Pretty Boy continued to rain kicks into his chest, grunting with the sheer exertion of his efforts.

Satisfied that her man now had the situation firmly under control, Cheryl began to walk down the alley towards them, as they knew she would.

'She's coming. Time for the big scene,' Winston hissed.

Sneaking his hand quickly into his jacket pocket, he pulled out the two capsules of imitation blood which he had purchased in Soho earlier that day. He sliced them open with his thumbnail and squirted the red over his head and face. In the dim light, it looked more than convincing. Winston lay still now, apparently unconscious. Pretty Boy stepped back from his battered, blood-stained victim as Cheryl approached. She looked down at the black man's crumpled body without compassion.

It was time for the *coup de grâce*, Pretty Boy decided. He stepped forward again, drawing back his right leg and aiming one final, vicious kick at Winston's ribs. Inch-perfect, the heavy front of Pretty Boy's boot slammed against the two thin slats of wood which Winston had carefully taped against his ribcage. Muffled by the layers of crêpe bandage and his jacket, the sharp crack which they gave out provided a more than passable imitation of snapping bone.

Pretty Boy stepped back, glancing aside at the girl with a look of savage joy on his face. 'That taught the bastard,' he said, triumphantly, between heavy gasps for breath.

Cheryl's eyes were dancing with fire. Her face was flushed, her red lips slack and slightly apart. She too was breathing heavily, erratically. She looked like a woman on the point of orgasm, Pretty Boy thought – and the realization both excited him and repulsed him at the same time. For the merest fraction of a second, he felt like taking her right then, against the wall of the alley. He fought the momentary impulse, instead marshalling his thoughts. There was a job to do, and it wasn't over yet. The entire, violent charade had been for a greater purpose than just a quick and animal-like knee-trembler.

Controlling himself, Pretty Boy moved away from Winston's prone form, pushing the girl ahead of him. 'Come on, we'd better get out of here,' he grunted, whirling the bicycle chain above his head and flinging it away into the darkness.

Cheryl pressed herself against him, wrapping her arm around his waist. Pretty Boy could feel her body heat surging into his flesh in pulsing, orgasmic waves. Temptation rose in him again, stronger this time.

But the girl's next words were as effective a passion-killer as any icy shower. 'You really showed that piece of black trash,' she told him, her tone at the same time cold and appreciative. 'You should have killed the bastard.'

21

The Lethal Leek was bored. He rummaged through Carney's tape and CD selection for the fourth time that night, still failing to find anything that appealed to him. Unusually for a Welshman, his tastes did not run to opera or classical music, and what few pop albums Carney did possess were years out of date.

He picked up the TV remote control and flicked through the channels without finding anything which took his interest. 'You should have satellite,' he complained to Carney rather peevishly. 'There'd be some sport on, then.'

Carney said nothing. He'd given up trying to converse with the Welshman at least an hour earlier, when it became apparent that there was absolutely no point of contact between them. Hugh Thomas had joined the army straight from school, serving three years with the Welsh Guards before transferring to the SAS. It was the only world he had ever known, and it seriously limited both his field of experience and conversation. Rugby Union, and the many different ways of killing a person with one's bare hands, were just about it.

The Welshman stared morosely at his watch. 'Reckon the boss should be limping his way back home about now,' he said. 'Looks like patching him up will be about the only excitement we're going to get tonight.'

It was not what Carney wanted to hear. He was still in a state of mild depression following his earlier talk with Winston, and the last thing he needed was more gloom and despondency. Reminded by the Lethal Leek's reference to the time, he wondered idly how Ted Brennon and Miles Tremathon were getting on with the pick-up and how it must feel to cart nearly half a million pounds in banknotes halfway across London.

There was a knock on the door. Caught in a day-dream, Carney wasn't concentrating. His usual sense of caution went to the winds. Without thinking, he crossed the room and opened the door, half expecting to see Winston's black face grinning at him.

He was wrong – on all counts. The face which greeted him was white – deathly white – and it belonged to Cecil Hargreaves. And he most certainly wasn't grinning. Carney had only a fraction of a second to recognize the look of fear on the man's features before two other, even more disconcerting factors registered. One was the pair of nasty-looking heavies who stood immediately behind him, and the second was that both were wielding sawn-off shotguns. After that, everything happened in a blur.

The two gunmen burst into the flat, pushing Hargreaves ahead of them. As the nearest one covered Carney, his companion leapt across the room towards the Lethal Leek, who was already clawing inside his jacket for his shoulder-holstered Browning.

'Don't even think about it,' the second heavy barked warningly. In the split second in which the Welshman froze with indecision, he had stepped forward and smashed the twin barrels of the shotgun against the side of his head. The SAS man collapsed soundlessly, out cold. Even as he fell to the floor, the gunman was rushing past him to search the other rooms of the flat. He returned quickly, nodding reassuringly at his companion. 'It's clean,' he called out, in what seemed an unnecessarily loud voice.

From outside in the hallway, a fourth man stepped into the flat and closed the door quietly behind him.

Carney appraised this new visitor carefully. He was different from his companions, physically tall but lacking the brutish bulk of the professional bodyguard or thug. His clothes were well cut and chosen with some taste, and his cool grey eyes were alert and analytical, betraying a keen intelligence. There was also something about the way the two gunmen acted almost deferentially towards him which told Carney he was a man of some authority, if not a leader.

The two thugs were merely true to type. The first, the one who had so efficiently disposed of the Lethal Leek, was muscular and powerful, with a square-jawed, bullet-shaped head atop a thick, stubby neck. His companion was shorter and heavier, and seemed ill at ease, even nervous.

Hargreaves was starting to blubber apologetically, his former composure completely shattered by obvious terror. 'They picked me up at the airport . . . I had no choice but to tell them,' he blurted out. 'They'd have killed me.'

Carney regarded the man with a contemptuous, pitying sneer. 'You bloody fool,' he said coldly. 'They're going to have to kill you anyway.'

The grey-eyed man turned to Carney, a faint but chilling smile on his face. 'Ah, you're a realist, Mr Carney,' he murmured. 'I do so admire a man who can see things in a pragmatic light. Perhaps that means that you'll be sensible enough to co-operate with us.'

Carney glared at him. 'Who the hell are you?'

The man's eyes narrowed thoughtfully for a moment, then he shrugged his shoulders in a careless gesture. 'Since it really isn't going to matter too much to you, I don't see why I shouldn't tell you,' he said quietly. 'My name is David Scott. But perhaps more to the point, who – or what – are you?'

Carney held the man in an eyeball-to-eyeball confrontation. 'You appear to already know my name,' he pointed out.

Scott allowed himself a thin smile. 'Oh yes, I know your name, Mr Carney,' he conceded. 'Our mutual friend Mr Hargreaves was most helpful with what limited information he had at his disposal. However, he was less forthcoming on specifics. He apparently seems to imagine that you're part of some special unit, or task force of some kind.' Scott paused, to emphasize what he was about to say. 'The thing is, Carney, I don't care a great deal for mere speculation. I like to *know* things.'

Carney grinned defiantly. 'Life must get terribly frustrating for you,' he said, with mock sympathy.

Scott was not amused. He clucked his teeth irritably. 'Oh dear, I do hope you're not going to be tiresome, Mr Carney,' he chided. 'It gets so messy.'

He nodded over at the shorter of the gunmen.

'Roger, please show Mr Carney what we do with people who cause us problems.'

Carney tensed as the thug turned towards him, giggling inanely. Seeing the mad gleam in the man's eyes, he was forced to revise his earlier opinion. He had taken his excitable and awkward manner for nervousness. But he'd been wrong. Roger suffered not from insecurity but from serious mental instability. The man was a nutcase, probably a psychopath.

Scott rolled his grey eyes heavenwards. It was the look of an employer seriously considering dismissing an underling for total incompetence. 'No, Roger, don't damage Mr Carney just yet. He may still be useful to us.' He glanced sideways at Hargreaves, who had sunk down on to the sofa. 'I think Mr Hargreaves will suffice as a demonstration model for the moment. I don't believe we've yet pointed out to him the penalties for trying to double-cross us.'

As the heavy stepped towards the quaking businessman, Scott flashed Carney a chilling smile. 'Observe the artistry of a craftsman at his work, Mr Carney,' he cooed.

Repulsed and yet fascinated, Carney watched the thug launch into a savage and ferocious attack on the defenceless man, using the butt and barrels of the shotgun on every part of his head and body. In seconds, Hargreaves's face was a mask of blood and his body reduced to a crumpled, quivering heap. The beating continued with sadistic precision until finally he passed into merciful unconsciousness.

Scott had watched it all with cold detachment. His face was devoid of expression when he finally looked back at Carney. 'Now, back to business,' he said calmly. 'I need to know exactly what sort of unit you are working with, its approximate strength and the full scope of its brief.'

Despite what had happened to Hargreaves, Carney dared to be defiant. Some little inner voice told him that compliance with Scott would not save him from a beating – or worse. On the contrary, it might even hasten it. The best he could do was to play for time, and Scott himself was the key to that. The man was basically an educated bully. He revelled in showing off his power and he enjoyed the sensation of engendering fear. He was also an egotist, Carney figured, inordinately proud of himself and boastful to the point of vanity.

'Who we are is not really important to you,' Carney said firmly. 'What matters is that we're strong enough to stop you.'

He tensed himself, waiting for the signal which would set Scott's gorilla upon him, but it didn't come. Instead, Scott merely chuckled, as though he found Carney an amusing diversion to be savoured.

'Stop us, Mr Carney? Oh no, you won't do that. At best you might slow down, even slightly hamper, the growth of our operation in this country. But our strength in mainland Europe is already something too powerful to be stopped. We can only grow, spread – control. The time is right, you see, Mr Carney. History is on our side. The world has been waiting for us.'

Carney could only stare at the man in blank incomprehension. That an apparently educated and civilized man could still believe in such an old and insane dream was incredible in itself. What made it totally lunatic was the fact that the man appeared to regard himself as some sort of a messiah. He resisted the impulse to laugh openly in Scott's face. For the moment he was winning precious extra minutes of life. It would be stupid to throw that small advantage away by openly antagonizing him.

He nodded down at Hargreaves. 'Your former colleague already outlined what he thought was wrong with society,' he pointed out. 'So what's your prescription for the malady?'

Scott's eyes searched Carney's warily, seeking the faintest trace of derision. 'Are you being flippant, Mr Carney? I do hope not.'

Carney was straight-faced. 'Actually I'm quite serious. I'm a copper, after all. There are a few things about the System I'd like to change myself.'

Scott nodded thoughtfully. 'Yes, I'm sure there are,' he said. 'But somehow I don't quite see you as a potential convert.' He paused. 'However, my "prescription", as you put it, is basically quite simple. We tear a rotten society apart from the inside and then reshape it into a new order. With the help of our drug, we have the ability to turn the dregs of the younger generation into a ragged, undisciplined yet reasonably effective army of destruction. And what they destroy, we shall be in a position to rebuild, using all the hidden wealth and power which has been buried in Europe and this country for over half a century.'

Carney was unable to resist a note of sarcasm creeping into his voice. 'So the revolution starts tomorrow, does it?' he asked.

Scott smiled thinly. 'There's no great hurry, Mr Carney. The tide of history has taught us patience, and now that tide is flowing in our favour. You have only to look at the trend of European politics over the last few years. A new kind of radical federalism is already with us.'

Suddenly Carney did not feel quite so confident. It was easy to dismiss a madman with a mad dream, comforting to believe that the forces of rationality and right would always prevail. But there was a frightening plausibility in Scott's argument – a germ of truth. With a sickening feeling in his gut, Carney realized that the man was in part right.

Perhaps Carney's face betrayed the fact that Scott had got through to him. For whatever reason, it seemed the man had tired of talking. The Lethal Leek was recovering consciousness. Groggily, he began to pull himself to his feet. Bullet-head let him rise, eventually prodding him with the business end of his shotgun until he collapsed on to the sofa beside the still-unconscious Hargreaves.

Scott eyed the latter dispassionately for a few seconds before turning back to Carney. 'Now, the answer to my question,' he snapped. He reached into his coat pocket, drew out a 9mm Beretta pistol and methodically screwed a fresh silencer on to the end of the barrel. He flashed Carney one of his ice-cold smiles. 'In the interests of saving time, I have decided not to have you beaten up, Mr Carney,' he announced. 'It occurs to me that you are probably the sort of man who would take a lot of unnecessary punishment before talking, and we are starting to run behind schedule. We have a rendezvous with some of your colleagues at the Courtland Hotel, I believe.'

Carney sneaked a quick glance at the clock on the mantelpiece. It was nearly ten to nine. 'I think you're going to be too late,' he pointed out. 'You've just cost yourselves four hundred thousand quid.'

Scott seemed unperturbed as he cocked the Beretta and aimed it deliberately at the Lethal Leek's head. 'As a matter of fact, it is your friends who will be too late,' he said calmly. 'And you now have exactly ten seconds to tell me the precise nature of your special task force before your companion here dies.'

The Lethal Leek glared up at Scott defiantly. 'Don't tell 'em a fucking thing,' he hissed. 'Let the bastards find out the hard way.'

Carney's eyes were hypnotized by Scott's finger, flexed against the trigger of the pistol. His mind raced as the precious seconds ticked away. It was not just the Welshman's life at stake here, he realized. He now knew that Tremathon and Brennon were walking straight into a trap. There was also the terrifying possibility that Scott and his cronies would search the flat after they had killed the Welshman and himself. It was unthinkable that the cache of sophisticated weaponry concealed there should fall into the hands of such fanatics. Out of panic, and sheer desperation, a wild bluff was born.

'All right, I'll tell you,' Carney blurted out. 'Seeing as how you'll be finding out in another couple of minutes anyway.'

The Beretta wavered, momentarily, in Scott's hand. Carney dared to hope that he had at least cast doubts into the man's mind. Finally, Scott lowered the gun. 'Explain yourself, Mr Carney.'

Carney faced him squarely. 'As you have worked out for yourselves, we are part of a special SWAT team,' he lied. 'And of course we have more than adequate backup.' Carney paused, forcing a look of confidence on to his face which he didn't really feel. 'Did it not occur to you that we would have some sort of fail-safe procedure?' he said calmly. He nodded over towards the telephone. 'My orders are to call in to base every thirty minutes as long as the situation is green. Your unexpected arrival postponed one of those calls.' Carney feigned a triumphant smirk. 'So you see we are in a much stronger position than you imagined. At this very minute this building is being surrounded by trained snipers. You'll never get out alive.'

Doubt flickered across Scott's face. His eyes bored into Carney's, seeking the faintest sign of weakness and finding none.

'You're bluffing,' he hissed, but there was uncertainty in his tone.

Carney grinned – genuinely this time. He had the man rattled, and it was time to press the advantage. 'You're not a stupid man, Scott,' he said quietly. 'Misguided, perhaps, but not stupid. You *know* I'm not bluffing. Why else do you think I was so eager to hear you talk about your insane little plans? Did you really imagine I wanted to hear all the drivel from your sick and twisted little mind? I needed time, Scott – time that you and your pet animals just ran out of.'

Carney was chancing his luck now, and he knew

it. He had no idea how far the man could be pushed, especially in front of his thugs, but it was essential that he made his play as convincing as possible. And insulting a man holding a gun seemed as good a way as any of reinforcing a bluff, even if it was highly dangerous.

The Lethal Leek had caught on to Carney's little ploy now, and added his own fuel to the smouldering fire. 'Looks like we got a great chance here to check out our response times,' he muttered. 'The next couple of minutes should be interesting.'

It was the final touch which pushed Scott over the edge, from uncertainty into panic. His eyes showing open fear now, he snapped his fingers at Bullet-head. 'Check the windows and the landing outside,' he barked.

The man hastened to obey, striding across the flat to peer through the curtains into the dark street below. 'I can't see nothing,' he growled, turning away to cross the room again and check outside the door. 'It looks all clear to me.'

For a fraction of a second, the smile returned to Scott's face, but it was cosmetic, masking the worry beneath it. He stared at Carney again, an unspoken question in his eyes, but the policeman's face was bland, giving away nothing.

Finally, Scott seemed to come to a decision. 'So we both lose, Mr Carney,' he said resignedly. 'A pity.'

Scott backed away towards the door, still holding the pistol. Carney's stomach felt like an ice-pack resting on top of his bowels. A single bullet through his brain – or the blast of a twelve-bore into his guts? He wondered, momentarily and fancifully, if any one form of death was preferable to another. One popular fallacy, however, was dispelled once and for all. Facing extinction, his past life did not flash before him like a video on fast forward. On the contrary, every remaining millisecond seemed to grate past with agonizing slowness, like a series of freeze frames.

Suddenly Scott was gone, followed closely by Bullet-head. The Giggler remained – a sort of rear guard, covering the room with the shotgun as he too began to back slowly towards the door.

Carney's eyes were rooted on the two deadly circles made by the barrels of the shotgun. The Giggler was framed in the doorway now, one foot already in the passage outside. Now was the time, Carney thought, wondering if he would see or hear anything before a cone of lethal lead pellets tore his body to shreds.

Then the shotgun dipped towards the floor. The Giggler moved fully back into the outer hallway, fumbling for something in his pocket. Carney heard a faint metallic click, the sound of something heavy thudding on to the carpeted floor of the flat and the door slamming, quickly followed by running foot-steps.

His eyes flashed to the floor, identifying the hand-grenade before it stopped rolling. So he'd been wrong, he thought bitterly. Death came in three choices, not two.

The Lethal Leek had seen the grenade too, and his

brain raced into overdrive. Conventional Mills bomb, army issue. Probably a standard seven-second fuse, once the pin had been pulled and the spring-catch released.

Seven seconds . . .

It was not just his superb training which spurred the Welshman into lightning action. It was a fury born of desperation, an instinct for survival which went beyond normal human reaction.

'Dive,' he screamed to Carney, already springing to his feet and clawing at the inert body of Hargreaves on the sofa beside him. The man was a dead weight, and it took an almost superhuman effort to pull him from his slumped position. But pull him upright the Lethal Leek did, using the inertia of the man's moving body to throw him forwards and downwards to the floor, his belly pressed over the grenade. Swivelling on his toes, he launched himself in a long, low dive over the back of the sofa.

A split second before he hit the floor, the Lethal Leek heard the dull 'whoomph' of the exploding bomb. The pressure shock made his ears pop, and rocked the interior of the flat, but Hargreaves's soft body absorbed the main force of the blast, along with the deadly shards of flying shrapnel.

It was a full thirty seconds before the Welshman hauled himself to his feet, his head throbbing. He looked first at Carney, lying face down in the far corner of the room where he had dived for cover. The man was moving, he thought, with a sense of relief. He staggered across to Carney as he pushed himself up on to his elbows, reaching down to grasp his arm and steady him as he began to crawl groggily to his knees and then to his feet.

The Lethal Leek was too bloody ugly to be an angel, Carney thought, his mind still dazed by the blast. That meant he was still alive. He found it almost impossible to take in, and scanned his own body with disbelief. Apart from the fact that his ears felt as though they were plugged with wet concrete and a whole gang of navvies were using pneumatic drills on the inside of his skull, he appeared to be undamaged. Eventually Carney stood upright on shaky legs, propping himself up against the padded arm of the sofa.

A dim memory of the last few seconds returned. He looked across the floor to where the shattered, shapeless and bloody form of what had once been Cecil Hargreaves was completely ruining five hundred quid's worth of fitted beige carpet. He had to fight the impulse to retch, as nausea rose in his throat to join the throbbing in his head. It felt like the grand-daddy of all hangovers.

The Lethal Leek grinned at him. 'Sorry about the hasty redecoration job,' he muttered as he ran his eyes over the blood-splattered walls and ceiling. 'I hope red's one of your favourite colours.'

Some sort of thanks were called for, Carney thought. 'Christ, how did you move so bloody fast?' he asked. He nodded down at the remains of Hargreaves. 'But for you, we'd both be like him. I guess I owe you my life.'

The Welshman shrugged. 'Actually, you weren't the first person in my thoughts at the time,' he admitted with a grin.

It seemed to put things in the right perspective, somehow, Carney realized. His admiration for the men of the SAS moved one step closer to hero worship.

The Lethal Leek was already moving towards the telephone. He snatched up the receiver and held it to his ear, but it was dead, its delicate internal parts rendered useless by the explosion.

'Shit,' he growled, dropping the useless instrument to the floor. He looked across at Carney, his face taut with the sudden urgency of the situation. 'I've got to get to a bloody phone and report in to Major Anderson. From the sound of things, Ted and Miles could be walking straight into a bloody ambush.'

Carney's mind jerked back to reality. He thought quickly. 'Turn left outside . . . the next street corner,' he snapped. 'There's a payphone there.'

The Welshman dived into the bedroom, emerging again with an MP5K in his hand. He turned again towards the door. 'Look, I'm going to call in and then head straight for the hotel myself. They might need all the help they can get.'

Carney managed a thin smile. 'And leave me all alone to explain this lot to the bloody neighbours?' he muttered. 'I'm coming with you.'

The Lethal Leek looked dubious. 'Aren't we supposed to keep you out of possible combat situations?'

Carney laughed openly, quickly surveying the shattered flat and the body of Hargreaves once more. 'What the fuck would you call this, then?' he asked.

The Lethal Leek did not have time to argue. And Carney did appear to have a point.

22

Winston sat in the bar of the Courtland Hotel, where he'd checked into a second-floor room some half an hour earlier. Although he didn't know it at that point, his initial mistrust of the man Hargreaves had been well founded, and the contingency plans he had initiated were about to be put to the test.

With apparent disinterest, he let his eyes rove casually around the bar and into the lobby beyond, surveying his fellow guests and customers. Two faces were more than familiar to him, but he did not acknowledge them. Together as ever, Tweedledum and Tweedledee shared a small table by the bar's front window, in a position from which they had a clear view of the hotel's double swing doors and the street. The two bulky carrier bags which nestled beneath the table ostensibly contained nothing more than the results of a day's shopping in the capital. Only they, and Winston, knew differently.

At Winston's insistence on backup, the pair had been flown down from Hereford in one of the Italian-designed Agusta A-109 helicopters maintained by the Army Air Corps' S Detachment permanently based at Stirling Lines. Landed at City Airport helipad, and quickly transferred to the hotel by taxi, they had been there by the time Winston had taken a few small but essential pieces of luggage up to his room.

212

Of Miles Tremathon and Ted Brennon, there was still no sign. Winston glanced anxiously at the clock on the wall of the lobby. It was seven minutes past nine. With a slight feeling of annoyance, he wondered what was holding them up.

In fact, it was the canny and close-handed nature of the Cornishman which had held the pair up. Compared with a true son of the red soil, a Scotsman was a veritable profligate, as anyone who had ever waited for someone else to buy the next round in a Penzance pub knew only too well.

Unused to what he considered to be 'fancy' city prices, Tremathon had taken it into his head to quibble about the cost of taxi fares with a cockney cabby even though they were already running three minutes behind schedule. The resultant prolonged argument had not resulted in any cash reduction but the Cornishman would forever after claim – with some justification – that it had saved his life.

For in the lobby of the Courtland Hotel, other eyes besides Winston's were watching the clock and becoming very nervous indeed.

Daniel Jefferies was good at following orders, even passing them on to others, but none too inventive when it came to making his own decisions. It was this essential character flaw, as much as anything else, that had led him to Second Holocaust in the first place. Shielded within the protective shell of an organization which cloaked itself in secret power and violence, even the weakest of men could feel an illusion of strength. Now, faced with an unexpected situation, Jefferies was helpless again. He needed instructions. Reaching for the mobile phone in his pocket, he punched out a number. The call was answered almost immediately.

'Something's wrong, boss,' Jefferies said nervously. 'No one's shown. What do we do?'

On the other end of the phone, David Scott sat suddenly upright in the rear seat of his Lexus, a look of worry on his face. He leaned forward, hissing to Bullet-head in the driving seat. 'How long before we get to the hotel?'

Bullet-head shrugged. 'Dunno, boss. With this traffic, maybe five, maybe ten minutes.'

Scott gave vent to a muffled curse. As he had told Carney earlier, he didn't care for uncertainties and he liked it even less when things went wrong. His original plans had been simple, direct – and intended to kill two birds with one stone. Jefferies and his two other henchmen planted in the Courtland Hotel had been instructed to watch out for whoever came to pick up the ransom payment, track them, kill them and snatch the case. Quick, clean and efficient, the scheme should have achieved the dual object of securing the money while neutralizing more of the opposition. The failure of that opposition to turn up was more of an irritation than a problem.

Scott ran swiftly through his immediate priorities. The money was of supreme importance. Without that, he would be forced to go cap in hand back to his superiors, who disliked abrupt changes of plan even more than he did. Even worse, any suggestion of incompetence was punished – quickly and decisively.

So the money first, Scott thought. He would have

to take any other problems as they came. He returned his attention to the car phone.

'So, what do you think?' Jefferies was asking, more than a little nervous himself. The penalties for failure permeated right down through the structure of the organization. The buck always stopped at the last guy in the line.

Scott forced himself to sound calm. 'Just make the pick-up yourself and then get the hell out of there. After that, just follow instructions as planned. You shouldn't encounter any problems.'

Scott was wrong. He hadn't counted Sergeant Andrew Winston into the equation.

Winston eyed the man using the mobile phone with the faintest glimmer of suspicion. Not that there was anything unusual about the act in itself, he thought. Mobiles were everywhere – the current craze among the yuppie set, the serious business community and the poseurs. Yet a couple of things didn't seem quite right. The man was standing less than ten feet from the hotel's own bank of courtesy phones, which offered some degree of privacy and comfort with stools and a soundproof Perspex hood. Yet he chose to make his call standing in the middle of a crowded lobby. To Winston's mind, that suggested an unusual degree of urgency, even panic. His keen senses alerted, he studied the man more carefully.

There was no doubt about it – the man was nervous. Winston could tell from his body language alone, even though he was too far away for him to see his face clearly. Slowly the SAS man raised his hand to the top of his head, pretending to scratch at his wiry black thatch. It was a subtle, prearranged signal to the two Tweedles. Confident that they were now watching him, Winston made a discreet but perfectly clear gesture with his index finger, directing their attention towards Jefferies, then rose to his feet and crossed the bar towards the lobby area.

Replacing the mobile phone in his pocket, Jefferies signalled his own backup team with a faint nod in their direction. It was a gesture other men might have missed, but Winston was already looking out for it. Instinct had alerted him to the man's suspicious behaviour, but it was pure logic which told him that Jefferies was unlikely to be working alone. Following the man's eyeline, Winston rapidly identified his two cronies, who had been lurking around the hotel brochure racks, pretending to check out sightseeing trips. They were both young, and seemed somehow ill at ease in their smart suits, as though they would have been more comfortable in jeans. The same was true of the way both men clutched their black attaché cases. It was an awkward, nervous grip, not the relaxed hold of someone used to carrying such an item. Winston suspected that each case contained something far more deadly than boardroom documents.

Suddenly he no longer suspected. He *knew* – with that sixth sense for trouble which had been programmed into him by a lifetime of training. He changed direction, skirting around the edge of the lobby towards the far end of the reception desk as the two men began to move towards Jefferies.

Back in the bar, Tweedledum picked up Winston's

sudden wariness. He'd worked close to the big Barbadian enough times to know every little nuance of
his body language. It was something approaching
telepathy. He nudged Tweedledee gently in the ribs.
'Something's about to pop,' he murmured.

His companion merely nodded silently. Moving
in complete unison, like twin parts of a well-oiled
machine, both men began to reach down slowly and
with apparent casualness to the carrier bags secreted
beneath the table.

Like the flywheel of some giant engine gradually
building up power, events began to move now with
increasing speed and inevitability, generating their
own momentum.

Shadowed by his two colleagues, Jefferies moved
towards the reception area, attracting the attention
of the young girl behind the desk. She slid over with
a polite smile, listening to him attentively. Seconds
later, she beckoned to the manager, who stepped over
to join them. After a few seconds of conversation, the
man nodded, withdrawing a bunch of keys from his
pocket and bending down behind the desk. Rising
again, he placed a red Samsonite suitcase on the
counter.

Tweedledum and Tweedledee had their respective
carrier bags on their laps now, the masking pieces
of fancy wrapping paper inside peeled back to reveal
the ready and waiting MP5Ks. They stared intently
across at the little tableau unfolding at the reception
desk, and checked Winston's relative position. He was
now edging his way round the far wall of the lobby,
towards the front door.

'It's looking a little messy at the moment,' Tweedledee whispered anxiously.

Tweedledum nodded, knowing exactly what his partner meant. There were at least a dozen people milling about in the lobby, creating a wall of innocent potential victims between them and their target. He glanced sideways towards the front door, nudging Tweedledee to make him follow his eyes. Tweedledee nodded, attuned to his buddy's thoughts. The doorway and the vestibule were clear, giving them a safe and direct line of fire should it become necessary.

Winston had already considered the problem, and was also taking up a safe position. He unbuttoned his jacket casually, giving him immediate access to the Browning under his shoulder. He watched Jefferies like a hawk as the man picked up the suitcase from the reception desk and turned towards the door.

It was looking good, he thought, with a certain amount of relief. The vestibule was the trap area. Once Jefferies and his men were within ten feet of the door, he could take them with a minimum of dramatics. The Tweedles were there to keep things clean. It should be simple, effective, and quick enough to avoid any panic.

Jefferies walked towards the hotel entrance, feeling increasingly relaxed. His earlier fears of a trap were beginning to recede now, as it seemed the pick-up had been smooth and uncomplicated. He felt sure that any interception would have occurred the moment the suitcase appeared on the reception desk. He'd been looking out carefully, but had seen no sign of a reaction anywhere in the lobby. With increasing confidence in every step, and secure in the knowledge that Dennings and McKinley were right on his heels, he strode towards the swing doors.

These opened inwards at that precise moment, as Tremathon and Brennon chose to make their belated and exceedingly ill-timed entrance, to be confronted by the sight of a man carrying a red Samsonite suitcase hurrying towards them.

Jefferies froze in his tracks, instantly alerted by the two men's immediate reaction. The look of panic which flashed across his face was in turn a clear signal to the two troopers, triggering in them a gut response. The situation was now taking on a life of its own, heading towards a crisis with terrible inevitability.

Watching the sudden drama explode before his eyes, knowing what was about to happen and utterly powerless to do anything about it, Winston felt frustration rise like a solid lump in his throat. His eyes flashed to the two henchmen, who were both snapping open their attaché cases and drawing out what Winston immediately recognized as a pair of Czech-built Skorpion machine-pistols, their folding metal stocks clipped down over the front of their stubby barrels.

They were all perhaps split seconds away from a civilian catastrophe, Winston thought. Each of the 7.65mm weapons boasted the short-burst capacity of a full sub-machine-gun. If the gunmen opened fire in the middle of the crowded lobby, it would be a slaughter.

There was nothing he could do to help Brennon and Tremathon. Their only protection lay in the fact that Jefferies was temporarily caught smack in the middle of the line of fire between them and his own men. Tweedledum and Tweedledee were equally hampered by the number of innocent bystanders clustered around the two gunmen. Winston made the only move he could.

The Browning leapt into his hand. Raising it above his head, Winston fired two shots into the ceiling. 'Everybody hit the floor,' he screamed out at the top of his voice, racing for the cover of a drinks machine positioned between the two lift doors.

There was a moment of stunned silence as Winston's pre-emptive move took effect. With superb reflexes, Brennon and Tremathon took advantage of their brief and precious respite to throw themselves back out through the heavy glass swing doors, drawing their own handguns and taking up defensive positions.

Then panic erupted. The lobby was suddenly a mob of frightened, screaming people, some throwing themselves to the floor as Winston had commanded, some turning to run for the nearest protection they could find.

Jefferies dropped the red suitcase to the floor, diving into his coat to pull out a heavy Colt automatic. He grabbed the arm of the woman standing nearest to him and pulled her to his side, wrapping his left arm around her neck. Pulling her in front of him like a human shield, he held the Colt against the side of her cheek. His eyes darted around the lobby and beyond, searching out the opposition.

Pressed against the side of the drinks machine,

Winston mouthed a silent prayer to a God he only half believed in. The situation was still critical, still potentially explosive, but miraculously no shots other than his own had yet been fired. If everyone kept their heads, they might all get through the next few crucial minutes without casualties.

Jefferies' two gunmen had now begun to herd a small bunch of terrified people into a group, covering them with the Skorpions. The boss had his own hostage, and could take his chances. It was every man for himself.

'Holy shit. What the fuck do we do now?' Tweedledee hissed under his breath. He cradled the MP5K impotently on his knees under the cover of the bar table, knowing that it was useless in the present circumstances. There was no way they could open fire while the gunmen held hostages, yet the two men themselves presented clear targets. It was a nasty position to be in.

Tweedledum gazed fearfully over at Winston. 'More to the point, what about the boss?' he whispered back, realizing that Winston was in the most vulnerable position of all. His brain raced into overdrive, seeking a way out. A series of tiny, winking lights to Winston's right suddenly attracted his attention. It was the lift indicator. Someone was descending to the ground floor, or the lift was returning on automatic, he realized, and in that second a wild idea sprang into his mind.

There was only seconds to put it into operation. He kicked Tweedledee's legs under the table, getting his instant and full attention. 'The second that lift door by the boss opens, get ready to bug out and create a diversion,' he hissed.

Tweedledee's eyes flashed a question. 'Bug out where?'

His partner gave a thin smile. There's only one way out,' he said jerking his head slightly to indicate the window behind them. You've seen 'em do it in the movies.'

The lift indicator had sunk to the bottom light. The doors began to hiss open. Putting their faith completely in Winston's uncanny reaction time, the two Tweedles threw themselves to their feet, grabbed up their chairs and made a dive for the window. Tweedledum had just time to scream a single clue to Winston as they both crashed through the glass and into the street outside.

'Going up, boss.'

Winston had already heard the faint hiss of the lift doors, but his first thought had been only of another innocent bystander bursting unexpectedly into an already volatile situation. The sudden and unexpected commotion over in the bar, and Tweedledum's hastily shouted message, poured into his calculator of a brain like an information overload. It was only pure instinct which enabled him to process it in time.

The young girl stepping out of the lift didn't even have time to react to the sight of armed gunmen rounding up hostages. Winston's huge body crashed into her, knocking her backwards through the open mouth of the lift door. Winston threw himself in behind her, pressing against the side of the lift cage and punching the top floor and emergency-close buttons simultaneously. A single shot from Jefferies' Colt slammed harmlessly into the back wall of the lift as the doors began to slide to.

The lift began to move upwards. Winston bent to the floor and hauled the badly winded but otherwise unhurt girl to her feet. She stared at the gun in his hand in terror, her mouth dropping open in preparation for a scream.

Winston knew he had only a few precious seconds, as the Courtland Hotel was only five stories high. He clamped his huge hand over the girl's mouth, speaking quietly but insistently.

'Listen, you've just got to believe me but I'm one of the good guys,' he told her. 'When this lift stops I want you to get out, find the first available fire alarm and set it off. Then make for the emergency fire escape as fast as you can and get out of here.' He took his hand from the girl's mouth, smiling at her. 'Now, have you got that?'

The girl nodded, uncertainly. The lift stopped with a faint jolt and the doors began to open. Winston pushed the still frightened girl gently towards the landing, flashing her another smile. 'Please trust me, and do it,' he said quickly, before ducking back into the lift and stabbing at the button for the second floor.

The shrill, insistent sound of the hotel's fire warning system was already filling the corridors as Winston reached the door of his room. He smiled to himself with grim satisfaction, reassured that at least the bulk of the residents and staff would shortly be on their way to safety. Letting himself into the room, he rushed across to the bed, reached underneath it and drew out the single holdall he had brought with him. The radiophone was tucked away beneath a small pile of spare magazines for the Heckler & Koch. He snatched it up and punched out Major Anderson's priority number. His call was answered almost immediately.

Winston's opening message was terse and to the point, covering the basics. 'Major? It's Winston. We have a hostage situation at the Courtland. Three gunmen that I know of – two Skorpions and one handgun. I'm on the inside, and I'll do what I can.'

Anderson digested the information rapidly. 'Estimate of hostages?' he asked.

'Probably around twenty,' Winston told him. 'Hopefully the majority of the guests are evacuating right now via the emergency fire escapes.'

'Situation?' Anderson's questions were the basic ones, part of the standard operating procedure for dealing with all types of siege or hostage situations. SOPs served a valuable and well-defined purpose in SAS tactics, providing a speedy and comprehensive checklist of the various factors involved. They helped commanders to collect vital information which would assist them in making an early assessment of each individual situation and planning a successful rescue.

'At the moment, the ground floor – lobby and bar areas,' Winston reported. 'But they could move. It's too open and too vulnerable. My guess is that they'll probably lock the main doors and move the hostages to a more secure area. The kitchens might be a good bet.'

Winston broke off and took a few seconds to consider his own position. 'Anyway, I'm getting set to bug out,' he told Anderson when he spoke again. 'They know I'm loose and one of them will probably come looking for me. I've got four men on the outside and I can probably be of greatest use with them.'

'I agree,' Anderson said. 'You can count on backup within the hour. I'll have Lieutenant-Colonel Davies get official clearance and set up a command cell at the local police station. Sit tight until we establish communication and see if they have any demands.'

'And if shooting starts in the meantime?' Winston asked.

'ERP,' Anderson replied curtly. It was the answer Winston had expected. Once the first hostage got killed, standard operating procedures went by the board and the emergency rescue plan swung into operation. It usually meant a direct frontal assault, in which casualties could be high. It was not a preferred option, but it usually worked, and it underpinned the basic beliefs of most government and security agencies around the world. There was no giving in to terrorism. Only swift and complete retribution.

'One last thing,' Winston said. 'My guess is that these bastards are still counting on their pub bomb as a negotiating factor. Are we in a position to neutralize that threat at this time?'

'About fifteen seconds after you sign off and get the hell out of there,' Anderson assured him. 'We finally got to use the boys in blue.'

Winston nodded with satisfaction. He cut off the transmission, tucking the instrument safely away in his belt. Returning his attention to the holdall, he began selecting his weaponry.

23

True to his last word to Winston, Major Anderson's first call was to Commissioner McMillan.

'Sir, I think it advisable that we initiate the emergency procedure that we discussed earlier at this time,' he said simply.

There was no argument. 'I'll see to it at once,' McMillan said, replacing the receiver in its cradle for just long enough to break off the connection. Lifting it again, he keyed the number for the direct line to the special operations room at Scotland Yard and passed on the order.

It was a large-scale operation, but it had been well rehearsed and carefully prepared. On McMillan's command, a standby team of twenty secretaries and switchboard operators manned a prepared bank of telephones which had been cleared of all other incoming and outgoing calls. Each operator had a typewritten list of numbers to call. The entire operation had been timed to take exactly twelve minutes. At the end of that time every Consolidated Breweries pub in the Greater London area would have been warned, evacuated and placed under police guard at a safe distance.

It was the first fully joint operation between the SAS and the police. It had taken a massive mobilization of manpower, but it would work. Consolidated

Breweries might lose another pub, but there would be no loss of life.

Tremathon and Brennon were still crouched in a defensive position on the outside of the hotel doors, discreetly watching the developing situation inside the lobby through the plate glass. Most of the hostages had now been lined up in a sort of human wall between the vestibule and the three gunmen, who had now taken up position behind the reception desk, each with two hostages held at gunpoint. For the moment, it was a stand-off situation in which neither side could do anything except wait.

'Hello, what have we got here?' came a familiar voice from behind Tremathon's back. 'A couple of pervy peeping Toms, from the look of it.'

The Cornishman whirled to confront Tweedledum and Tweedledee, both grinning and still shaking splinters of glass out of their hair. Apart from a few slashes in their clothing, they both appeared undamaged.

'Where the hell did you two come from?' he asked in surprise.

Tweedledee grinned. 'We used the emergency exit,' he said. His face became more serious. 'Did the boss make it out of there OK?'

Brennon nodded. 'He suddenly made a dive for the lift and then he was gone,' he said, much to Tweedledee's obvious relief. 'So far no one's gone after him. I think they're still too busy trying to figure out what to do. Something tells me our friends in there aren't all that used to this sort of thing.' He broke off, to nod at the MP5Ks the two Tweedles were toting. 'Well, thank God somebody thought to bring some heavy artillery,' he muttered. 'All Miles and I have are our Brownings and one spare clip apiece.'

Tweedledum was taking a quick look in through the door at the line of hostages. 'Not that anything's much use to us at the moment,' he observed glumly. 'Fucking Gazza couldn't sneak a shot past that defensive wall.'

'So, what do we do?' Brennon asked. It was a good question, to which nobody had a good answer.

Tweedledum shrugged. 'I guess we can only wait,' he suggested feebly. 'It depends on what the boss is doing in there, and whatever else is going on. At a pinch, I'd say that all hell's going to break loose any time now.'

It was a pretty safe bet, since it was obvious that something had to happen soon. The hotel fire alarm was still clanging shrilly, as neither Jefferies nor his men had yet thought to shut it off. The noise had already attracted a crowd of sensation-seekers, who were congregating at a safe distance on the other side of the road. Their numbers were being swelled by evacuees from the hotel, who were pouring out of the emergency exits at the rear of the building and coming round in desperate need of information or reassurance. The emergency services must already be on their way. Tweedledum wished the boss was there to take charge of things. He was dressed in mufti, carrying no identification or papers and without any form of authorization. Trying to explain to the police what he was doing carrying a sub-machine-gun around the streets of central London was not a task he was relishing.

As if to reinforce these misgivings, the first faint sounds of approaching sirens and fire-engine bells could be heard in the distance.

The situation seemed reasonably stable for the moment, Jefferies thought. He had absolutely no idea of what was going on outside, or what steps the authorities might be taking. But for now there was no direct threat, and the large number of hostages would appear to be keeping them safe from attack. His only immediate worry was the armed black man who had escaped from the lobby. Jefferies had no doubt that it was he who had set off the fire alarm, and that he was probably still somewhere in the hotel. Who he was, and what he could possibly do, were completely unknown factors.

The initial panic of the hostages had started to subside now, as the stronger of them came to terms with their fate and the more nervous elements merely cowered into submission. Screaming had given way to quiet sobbing and a dull buzz of anxious conversation as the confused hostages hopelessly quizzed each other in half a dozen languages. In any case most of it was completely swamped by the continued noise of the fire alarm.

His own initial tendency to panic had been controlled by more direct means. At the first opportunity Jefferies had popped a small white pill into his mouth and swallowed it. As always, the drug absorbed rapidly into the bloodstream and hit the brain, producing an illusory feeling of calm and well-being. Other effects would follow later, he knew, but for the moment Nirvana made him feel rational and in control of the situation. Control was power. Power was control. The two fed on each other like a snake chewing its way up its own tail.

Jefferies dragged his female hostage in the direction of the hotel manager, waving his Colt under the man's nose. 'Can you shut this damned alarm off?' he demanded.

The man nodded. 'There's a master control underneath the desk.'

'Then do it,' Jefferies snapped. 'And no bloody tricks.'

The manager moved nervously along the desk, doing what he was told. The abrupt shut-down of the alarm also served to stun the hostages into momentary silence. A deathly hush fell over the lobby.

Jefferies took advantage of the brief respite to pull out his mobile phone. He pushed his hostage roughly aside, waving the gun at her. 'You just stay right there,' he told her. 'I'll be watching you.' Retreating to a quiet corner, he punched out David Scott's mobile number.

Scott received the unwelcome news with a sinking feeling in the pit of his stomach, his initial flare of anger at Jefferies' stupidity quickly swamped by concerns for his own highly vulnerable position.

Much of the apparent confidence he had exuded to Carney earlier in the evening had been mere bluster. In truth, Scott knew only too well that Second

Holocaust's UK operation was still embryonic, still lacking the cohesive organizational structure of its European counterparts. Slow but insidious growth was the essential nature of the entire movement. Essentially a cellular development, it depended on the creation of large numbers of small, largely independent units which served mainly as recruitment centres and drug distribution networks. Given the nature of the recruits, and the effects of Nirvana, spin-offs into other forms of criminal activity were virtually inevitable, with the result that each cell was more or less self-funding. Growing dependency upon the drug ensured a loyal following and created a strong inducement to recruit further members in return for free supplies.

In the past this underground structure had been one of the movement's greatest strengths, allowing it to grow and spread almost unnoticed by the authorities. Like a fungus, it spread its filaments underground until individual groups became large enough and powerful enough to overlap, merge and become part of the greater, more unified organization. It had worked in Germany, it had worked in Italy and it was showing every sign of working in France.

But something had gone wrong in Britain. They'd been picked up and identified too early, and they'd been attacked with unusual tenacity. The loss of the drug factory in Norfolk could in itself perhaps have been written off as just a temporary set-back, but it was being followed up with a combination of intelligence and direct action which suggested a concerted and sophisticated counter-force.

It was almost as if they were being coerced into coming out into the open, Scott thought to himself. Someone, somewhere, appeared to have an instinctive knowledge of how the organization functioned, and how best to attack it.

And now this fiasco at the Courtland Hotel, Scott reflected bitterly. He should have known better than to entrust such a delicate mission to a poor fool like Jefferies. A direct confrontation on this scale was the last thing they needed, and its timing could not have been more disastrous. The massive London right-wing rally, and the invaluable propaganda and recruitment opportunities it would present, was now only days away. Representatives and delegates of a dozen political movements were already converging on the capital, along with section chiefs of many of the European chapters of Second Holocaust. It was a time to be showing strength, not weakness.

As his car approached the Courtland Hotel, Scott leaned forward to Bullet-head. 'Just drive past slowly,' he snapped. 'Then take the first turning and find somewhere quiet to park. I must think this thing through.'

Scott stared out through the tinted side windows of the Lexus as it cruised past the hotel entrance, noting the four armed troopers still crouching in the doorway. Looking ahead through the windscreen again, he saw the flashing blue lights of the first of a small fleet of police cars converging on the hotel from the opposite direction and frowned heavily. The whole area would soon be swarming with cops. It would not be a healthy place to be, especially with two sawn-off shotguns and a brace of hand-grenades in the car.

It was time for a hasty change of plan. Scott tapped Bullet-head lightly on the shoulder. 'Forget that last instruction,' he muttered. 'Keep driving for another mile before you turn off.'

He sat back in his seat as the car began to gather speed again, forcing himself to relax and try to think things through in a logical manner. The significance of the two sub-machine-guns had not escaped him. Hardly police issue, they were almost certainly army weapons, Scott realized – which tended to override his earlier theory that his persecutors were merely a special police unit of some kind. It would also help to explain the devastatingly successful raid on the farmhouse, which appeared to have been carried out with military precision.

Taking this assumption one stage further, Scott applied it to the current situation at the hotel. If some branch of the military *were* involved, then they had all the fire-power and manpower at their disposal to turn it into a completely hopeless situation in which there could only be one possible outcome. The unfortunate incident would quickly turn into a full-scale siege which would end in either total surrender or a bloodbath. Either way, it seemed depressingly obvious that Second Holocaust could only come out of it as the losers – and would be clearly seen to be so. The possible consequences were frightening.

It was the single word 'siege' which finally gave Scott the clue that brought it all together in his head in a series of vivid and dramatic mental images.

Princes Gate, the Iranian Embassy, 1980. And a group of men who had created a piece of history, a modern legend.

With a final, sickening certainty, Scott knew who his enemy was, and his shoulders slumped in resignation. A particularly cruel fate had pitched him against no less an adversary than the SAS. His despair was complete now, as a lifetime of grandiose dreams started popping away in his mind's eye like so many insignificant little puffs of smoke.

24

The first police car slewed to a halt outside the hotel entrance. This was the tricky bit, Tweedledum realized. He lowered the Heckler & Koch gently to the pavement, then stepped towards the car slowly and cautiously with his hands held above his head and smiling as reassuringly as he could.

The cop in the passenger seat was only a kid, he thought, seeing the young man's frightened face staring at him through the closed window. He was probably pissing his pants, the poor little bastard. One minute cruising along in his nice comfortable patrol car ogling the tarts and kerb-crawlers and the next confronted by a bunch of dangerous-looking nutters with sub-machine-guns. The main thing was that neither the kid nor his partner should panic. Still holding his hands up in an attitude of surrender, he stopped at the side of the car and waited for a reaction.

Apparently beginning to realize that the armed men offered no immediate threat, the young cop wound down the window and peered out nervously. In the driver's seat, his partner kept the engine running and his hand on the gear lever.

'What the hell's going on?' the cop wanted to know, in a slightly shaky voice.

It was a fair enough question, Tweedledum thought. He was about to launch into an explanation when

Winston appeared from nowhere, gently nudging him to one side and taking control of the situation. 'I'll handle this, Trooper,' he said firmly.

Tweedledum grinned with relief. 'Good to see you, boss,' he said. 'I wasn't sure you could make it.'

Winston flashed him a grateful smile. 'Thanks to you,' he replied. 'That was good thinking.' He turned his attention back to the two cops in the car, who were now looking even more confused and wary.

'Have you had any briefing from base for this operation?' he demanded.

The first policeman shook his head. 'We were pulled off routine patrol in response to a fire call,' he explained. 'It was only a couple of seconds ago they told us there was some sort of a situation developing down here. I think there's about four other units on their way.' He paused, then repeated his earlier question. 'So what the hell *is* going on?'

Winston put it as succinctly as he could. 'There is an armed terrorist situation inside this hotel. They have a large number of hostages. I'm Sergeant Andrew Winston, of 22 SAS, and these are my men. I take it neither of you are armed?'

The cop shook his head again.

'Right, then I suggest you pull out of this immediate area,' Winston told him. 'And start clearing people off the streets as fast as you can. We're going to need room to move and there could be a lot of gunplay.'

Both policemen looked unsure. Winston understood that it was difficult for them to trust him. In their position he would have felt exactly the same. Nevertheless he needed to convince them quickly.

The sooner the area was cleared, the better. He spoke again, this time more forcefully. 'Look, right this minute my superiors will be contacting yours,' he explained. 'Complete authorization from the very top to let us get on with our job should be approved in the next few minutes. In the meantime you could be doing a lot to make sure that no innocent people get hurt.'

The two cops were almost convinced, Winston thought, but suddenly it didn't matter any more. Three more police cars appeared from the other end of the street, escorting a pair of fire engines. One of the cars pulled up beside the first. A uniformed sergeant jumped out, hurrying over and banging on the driver's side window. 'You two get your arses out of here,' he barked. 'I want this entire area cordoned off for a quarter of a mile in every direction.' He turned his attention to Winston. 'You Winston?'

The Barbadian nodded. 'Have you been fully briefed?' he asked.

It was the police sergeant's turn to nod agreement. 'Our orders are to hand control over to you until your immediate commanding officer gets here. We're to assist you in any way we can. Just tell us what you want us to do.'

Winston glanced to one side as the first police car began to move away. 'Looks like you're already doing it,' he observed. 'Just get everybody out of the area and keep them away.' He paused, looking at the fire engines and their baffled crews. 'And get those vehicles out of here. There isn't any fire and they'll only cause additional confusion.'

'You've got it,' the sergeant said. He eyed Winston curiously, a shadow of doubt remaining on his face. 'Look, Sergeant, this is the real thing, isn't it?' he asked. 'I mean, it's not a combined forces or civil defence drill or anything like that?'

Winston's face was grim as he shook his head and said: 'No, this is the real thing, all right. Real terrorists, real guns and real hostages.'

'Shit,' the sergeant hissed. It wasn't the answer he'd really wanted to hear.

Daniel Jefferies was a frightened man. It was now nearly ten minutes since he had called Scott for instructions and he still hadn't received a reply. Had the man abandoned him, left him to sort out the mess for himself? If so, what was he supposed to do? His men were getting edgy, having received no clear instructions themselves. How were they likely to react if this stalemate continued to drag on indefinitely? And the hostages – how much longer could they be expected to remain comparatively docile?

So many questions, buzzing around inside his head like a swarm of angry flies. Questions that he didn't have answers for, problems which demanded decisions he was unable to make. And that was only inside the hotel. What the authorities might be planning or doing on the outside created a whole new set of imponderables. Jefferies had seen the flashing blue lights of several police cars through the glass swing doors, and he was uncomfortably aware that the doors themselves remained under armed guard. But what was actually *happening*?

In desperation, Jefferies popped another Nirvana pill, in the vain hope that the drug could somehow fill the cold, empty void he seemed to feel in his head and in his guts.

Scott felt a strange sort of calm descending on him. Perhaps it was resignation, yet it didn't feel like it. It was an odd sensation, which actually seemed to be filling him with a new sense of purpose and confidence.

Actually knowing who the enemy was, and realizing the total hopelessness of the situation, had at first brought nothing but despair. Yet, perversely, that realization also narrowed the choice of options, serving to focus and concentrate his attention. When there was no hope at all, worrying about it seemed both pointless and irrelevant.

And the situation at the Courtland Hotel was most definitely hopeless, Scott knew. There could be no possible doubt about that. Jefferies and his two thugs could not possibly win against the might of the SAS under any circumstances. Whether the siege lasted an hour, a day or even longer, the hotel would eventually be stormed and they would be killed or captured. So Jefferies still had a choice. He could surrender or die.

Scott had little doubt about which option the man, left to his own devices, would choose. He doubted very much if Jefferies actually had the bottle to hold out once he understood the true nature of his situation. In fact, Scott was slightly surprised that he had had the guts to take hostages in the first place.

He could only think that it had been a panic reaction rather than a planned and considered move.

The question that Scott had to deal with was which option would best serve him and the organization. Jefferies and his two gunmen didn't even enter into the equation. They were totally expendable, irrelevant, cannon-fodder – as were the rest of the street louts and bully boys which Second Holocaust used to further its ends. But even cannon-fodder had its uses, as every warmonger since Attila the Hun had known only too well. And perhaps every movement needed its martyrs, Scott reflected.

An idea was beginning to gell in his head. While he still retained a strong element of control over the outcome of the situation, perhaps he ought to be using it. Once the SAS made their move, it would be lost for ever. But just for the moment, Scott was still the puppet-master who held the strings. Jefferies and his men would still jump to his commands, and could force the next moves in the game.

To order them to surrender seemed pointless, achieving nothing except failure in the eyes of the world. They would be exposed as impotent and weak, having neither the guts nor the ability to back up their tough talk. Better a blaze of brief glory in which they could be seen to be crushed by a ruthless and vastly superior force. The spark of political freedom and thought extinguished by the mindless mechanics of authority.

There was one major flaw in this scenario, however – the essential weakness of Jefferies. Scott somehow doubted that he would have the guts required to follow orders if told to make a stand, turn the siege into a fight. He would need to be given some incentive – something even stronger than the fear of punishment for failure. A chance to believe that there was some hope, that he was not alone.

Scott smiled to himself, aware that he had exactly what was needed at his fingertips. All over the city, the gangs of thugs and rowdies were already on standby for the rally. Scott would simply call some of them out a little early. He grabbed his mobile phone and started to make a series of calls. Afterwards he got back to Jefferies. The man sounded panicky. A few more minutes and it might have been too late.

'What's happening? What's going on out there?' Jefferies asked in a tremulous voice.

Scott's tone was calm and reassuring. 'It's going to be all right,' he said. 'I've already taken steps to get you out of there safely. Now all you have to do is to sit tight, stay calm and wait for further instructions. No one's going to start shooting until they open up communications and see what demands you are going to make. We've just got to make sure that we have a few extra negotiating points.'

Scott broke off the connection before the man could start asking too many awkward questions. For the moment, just the promise of help would have to be enough to keep him quiet.

25

Seated at the bar in Norma Jean's, Pretty Boy noticed the small group of yobbos heading towards his table and tensed himself for trouble. He recognized only two of the gang, but it was enough to start warning bells ringing faintly in the back of his mind. One of the group was the young man who had been with Cheryl the previous night, before he had bluffed him off. It looked as though he had recruited a few of his mates, along with the big ape Pretty Boy recognized as the bouncer who usually stood outside the club.

'I think your boyfriend could be coming to claim you back,' Pretty Boy said to the girl sitting opposite him. 'Jealous type, is he?'

Cheryl glanced up as the gang approached. She looked back at Pretty Boy, smiling. 'Forget it,' she said. 'Johnny's OK about that. I've already squared him. Besides, Max, the bouncer, won't have any trouble inside the club.'

She seemed pretty confident, Pretty Boy thought. Even so, he remained on his guard as the group reached the table and stopped. He looked up stony-faced, eyeing the former boyfriend in a direct challenge.

There was no trace of animosity on Johnny's face. For the moment, he simply appeared to be weighing up the SAS man.

'Cheryl here reckons you're a bit tasty in a fight,' he said matter-of-factly. 'Is that right?'

Pretty Boy maintained full eye contact as he shrugged with deliberate casualness. 'I can handle myself,' he said flatly. 'If I *have* to,' he added, with heavy emphasis. He paused for a couple of seconds to let that sink in. 'Well, do I have to?' he asked finally.

Johnny grinned, returning the shrug. 'That's up to you,' he said easily. 'Just thought you might fancy a bit of excitement, that's all. And make yourself a few quid, if you're interested.'

Pretty Boy wasn't quite sure where the conversation was headed. It seemed best to just play along for a while. 'I'm always interested,' he murmured guardedly, his face still giving nothing away. 'It depends on the deal.'

Johnny thought about this for a while and at last nodded. 'Fair enough,' he conceded. 'OK, I'll level with you. A friend of ours needs a little street demo set up real quick and we could do with all the bodies we can get hold of. Show stuff – know what I mean? Bit of rioting, bit of aggro, maybe loot a couple of shops – that sort of thing. Couple of hours, that's all. And there's fifty quid in it for you, no questions asked. A bit more if you get busted, or get hurt.' Johnny paused, looking at Pretty Boy questioningly. 'Well? What do you reckon?'

Caught on the hop, Pretty Boy was forced to do some pretty fast thinking. Nothing had been said that in any way suggested a link with either the drug distribution network or Second Holocaust. All he had actually been invited to join appeared to be a street riot, as a hired thug. He reminded himself that his orders were to infiltrate the bully-boy network and find out everything he could. Johnny's offer was surely his best chance yet of doing exactly that.

It was a tricky call, but on balance Pretty Boy was very tempted to let it pass. The immediate problem was how to extricate himself from the situation without spoiling his future chances, or appearing to chicken out. The girl seemed his best bet. Perhaps he could use her as an excuse.

He glanced across the table at Cheryl. 'Well, how do you feel about it?' he asked. 'It'd hardly be that nice quiet romantic night I had in mind, would it?'

Pretty Boy had been hoping for backup, but it wasn't forthcoming. Cheryl's eyes were sparkling. 'What the hell?' she said recklessly. 'It could be a blast.' She smiled across the table at him, a suggestive, sexy pout tugging at the corners of her lips. 'Besides, I could always lick your wounds for you afterwards.'

Johnny appeared to be getting anxious. It was obvious that there was some urgency in the situation, and it put Pretty Boy under even more unwanted pressure.

'Well?' Johnny repeated. 'You coming or not? We've got to get across to this fucking hotel in Knightsbridge.'

Pretty Boy had already more or less resigned himself to the situation, but this final piece of information was the clincher, he realized with a shock. He had no idea what the possible connection could be, but it was just too much to be pure coincidence. His eyes darted briefly towards Peters, seated some fifteen feet away at the bar. As he had expected, the man had been monitoring the situation discreetly, ever since the group had first approached Pretty Boy's table.

Pretty Boy looked up at Johnny. 'OK, I'm in,' he said decisively. 'But I've got to take a piss first.' Without giving anyone a chance to object, he rose from the table and headed off towards the toilets, counting on Peters to read the situation correctly and follow him. Out of the corner of his eye, he had the satisfaction of seeing his colleague begin to slide off his stool.

Pretty Boy was waiting for him just inside the toilets.

'What the fuck's going on?' Peters hissed, clearly concerned. 'You got trouble?'

Pretty Boy shook his head. 'Not that sort of trouble.' He explained the situation as briefly as possible. 'I haven't got the faintest idea what's actually going down,' he admitted finally. 'But you'd better make sure somebody knows about it.'

'Damn right,' Peters said. 'Leave it to me.' He clapped Pretty Boy on the shoulder. 'Look – you watch out for yourself, OK? Those bastards look like they could be mean.'

Pretty Boy grinned. 'So can I,' he said quickly.

The police had done their job with remarkable efficiency, Winston thought. The immediate environs of the Courtland Hotel had been cleared and cordoned off in a matter of minutes and the surrounding area sealed off with hastily conscripted reinforcements. The command control post had been set up at Knightsbridge police station and was now fully operational and backed up with two well-equipped mobile communications and relay vans on site. Winston now had a direct telephone link to the main switchboard of the hotel, which had itself been isolated to cut off any other incoming or outgoing calls. Also at his disposal were a PA system and a pair of broadcasting loudspeaker vehicles capable of blasting out a couple of hundred watts of sound. The idea of bombarding siege locations with ear-splitting music was currently popular in the USA, but Winston was not convinced of its effectiveness. To his way of thinking, it could have an equally debilitating effect on the hostages as well as the terrorists – and a tense, nervy hostage could be a recipe for disaster. Besides, he and his men would also be affected, even wearing ear protection, and he preferred to work with a clear head.

Perhaps twenty minutes had now passed since his initial call to Major Anderson, and the situation inside the hotel remained stable and outwardly calm. It was time to check in again.

'So, what's the picture?' Anderson wanted to know. He sounded alert, but not worried.

Winston told him. 'Nothing much has changed. They haven't even moved from the lobby. We could go straight in through the windows at any time. Do you want a candid personal assessment?'

'Which is?' Anderson asked.

'These guys are strictly amateurs,' Winston said confidently. 'I think they just panicked and now they haven't the faintest idea what to do. My guess is that by now they're probably primed for a little friendly suggestion.'

Anderson thought it over for a few seconds, then said: 'Yes, you could well be right. I suppose there's no harm in giving it a try. I assume you have communication set up?'

'Interior and exterior,' Winston confirmed.

'All right, give it a try,' Anderson told him. 'Offer them the chance to give themselves up, or at least release some of the hostages as proof of good intent. They'll probably try to use the pub bomb as a bargaining point, but it might not be a good idea to let them know we have at least partially neutralized that threat. Feeling they still have an edge might well make them feel more secure, and we don't want them getting too edgy. If there's the faintest chance of ending this thing quickly and cleanly, we might as well go for it.'

'And if not?' Winston wanted to know.

'Captain Blake and his men are already well on their way in another Agusta,' Anderson said. The police have already arranged for one of their own choppers to intercept them and guide them in. They're also trying to pick up detailed plans of the hotel in case you have to storm it. They've identified the architect and they're trying to contact him. If they can get hold of the plans they'll be delivered directly to you as soon as possible.' Major Anderson paused. 'Oh yes, and the Lethal Leek's also on his way to join you, but he might have Carney with him. I want him kept well away from the action, is that clear?'

'You got it, boss,' Winston assured him.

'Right, anything else you need to know?'

Winston shook his head. 'No, I think that about covers it for now. I'll be back to you after I've spoken to our friends.' A sudden afterthought struck him. 'Oh, what's the ETA on Butch Blake and the Third Cavalry?'

'About another thirty minutes,' Anderson said. 'And then as long as it takes to find the nearest drop zone. We're not sure yet if the hotel has a flat roof or not.'

Winston tucked the radiophone back in his belt and headed for the nearest communications van. He'd try the discreet approach first, through the conventional telephone lines. It would cause less panic than having messages blaring out over the PA system, and it was more personal. If his theories were right, the three gunmen should be about ready to listen to the calm, reassuring voice of reason. With a bit of luck, they might even be ready to take up the first sensible offer of a quick and clean way to end this thing. There was only one way to find out.

26

In the oppressive silence of the lobby, the sudden and unexpected buzzing of the reception desk switchboard made everybody jump, not least Jefferies. Unable to identify the nature or the source of the sound immediately, he sprang in the direction of the manager, waving the Colt menacingly in his face.

'What's that?' he hissed, aggressive yet edgy at the same time. The overdose of Nirvana coursing through his system was already producing erratic responses, causing violent and unpredictable mood swings. Although it gave him anger as a motivating force, it could not eradicate his basic cowardice and sense of insecurity, which in turn increased his sense of rage and frustration. He was in a highly volatile state of mind.

The manager indicated the switchboard behind him with a shaking finger. 'Incoming call,' he croaked through dry lips.

Jefferies thought quickly. It could just be a routine enquiry, although it seemed far more likely that it would be the first attempt by the authorities to establish contact. He was mildly surprised that they had not attempted to communicate before now. It was certainly not from David Scott, who would undoubtedly have used his mobile. Faced with direct confrontation for the first time, Jefferies was suddenly and uncomfortably aware that he had not even the faintest idea of how to handle the unfamiliar situation. He didn't even know what he was supposed to ask for.

He toyed with the idea of simply ignoring the call. Let the bastards sweat it out for a bit, he thought. Let them come crawling when they got worried enough. But this feeling of defiance faded quickly in the cold light of reality. It all boiled down to a question of who was sweating the most. Neither Dennings nor McKinley had said anything directly to him since the siege began, but he had caught enough of their nervous, uncertain glances to know that the two gunmen were as unsure of themselves as he was. Jefferies was not at all sure how much pressure either man could take, or how far they were prepared to go. They were both thugs, and he had no doubts that each of them had killed in the past. But whether or not they would be prepared to open fire on a crowd of innocent hostages was another matter.

The switchboard was still buzzing and the frightened manager was looking at him with nervous, questioning eyes. Jefferies made a snap decision.

'Answer it,' he barked.

His hands trembling violently, the manager stepped over to flip the incoming call through the nearest desk phone and picked it up. 'Good afternoon, Courtland Hotel,' he grated out, from pure force of habit.

Winston listened to the faltering, shaky voice on the other end of the line and made his own instinctive judgement. It didn't belong to one of the gunmen, he was sure. He kept his voice deliberately low and reassuring. 'Who am I speaking to?' he asked guardedly.

'I'm the manager,' the man stuttered. 'Can I help you?'

Winston's voice exuded calm confidence. 'Now listen to me,' he murmured gently but insistently. 'Just relax and try to stay calm. We're going to get you all out of there safely. Now let me speak to whoever seems to be in control in there.'

It was an unfortunate choice of phrase for someone in a state of mind like that of Jefferies, who had been eavesdropping the brief conversation. Flaring up with anger again, he snatched the telephone from the manager's hand. 'Not *seems* to be in control, you bastard,' he spat aggressively into the mouthpiece. 'I *am* in fucking control – and don't any of you pigs out there forget it.'

The response was totally different from what he had expected, and it threw him.

'I'm going to terminate this conversation,' Winston told him in a calm, deliberate tone. 'I'll call back in ten minutes when you may be prepared to talk more reasonably.'

Winston hung up the phone abruptly, sitting back to reflect on the brief but highly illuminating exchange. Though little had been said, it had actually told him a great deal, and established a definite psychological advantage in his favour. He now had a much more detailed mental profile of the man holding the hostages. He was impetuous, which meant he was nervy; he was aggressive, which invariably suggested underlying fear; and he was egocentric, a stance almost certainly masking insecurity. Every one of these weaknesses could be used as a potent weapon against the man, and in fact Winston had already fired the first shot. Cutting the conversation off had been exactly the right thing to do, Winston thought confidently. Like a spoilt child throwing a violent tantrum, the very last thing Jefferies was expecting was to be ignored. Winston's reaction would confuse, hurt and ultimately weaken the man even more. It had also clearly indicated who actually held the trump card. Who controlled the communication also controlled the negotiations.

All in all, Winston felt quite satisfied with the results of his first contact. No harm had been done, and a position of strength had been established. Two other small clues had been gleaned from the man's use of the term 'pigs'. He probably hated authority figures and was obviously under the impression that he was only up against the conventional police force. Winston made a mental note not to disillusion him on that score too early in the game. As long as he was expecting normal police tactics, he would be totally unprepared for any of the peculiar little tricks the SAS kept up their sleeves. In a crisis, that could prove a very welcome advantage.

Paul Carney's keen nose for trouble was already picking up a strong whiff that all was not as it was supposed to be. The nearer the taxi got to the hotel, the stronger the feeling became. He stared out of the taxi at the growing number of young rowdies on the streets.

'Odd,' he said under his breath, more to himself than anyone else, but the Lethal Leek picked up on it.

'What's up?' he asked. He too had noticed the groups of prowling youths, but unfamiliar with the capital, had assumed it to be normal.

Carney glanced at his watch, checking his earlier supposition. 'All these kids on the streets,' he murmured. 'Something's up. It's far too early for the pubs to be turning out.'

The Welshman failed to understand Carney's concern. 'Doesn't look all that different to Cardiff on a Saturday night to me,' he replied with a faint shrug.

But Carney was unconvinced. It wasn't just the sheer numbers of kids, or the fact that they all appeared to be headed in the same general direction. There was something else – something indefinable about the way the individual groups had an almost uncanny sameness about them. Something about the swaggering, openly aggressive manner in which they walked, the odd suggestion of some common purpose. For some reason Carney found himself reminded of columns of soldier ants, or perhaps lemmings preparing to swarm.

He glanced at the Lethal Leek and shook his head. 'No, there's something in the air, something going on. I can almost taste it. Trouble's brewing, but I can't figure out why.'

The Lethal Leek didn't feel disposed to argue the point. Carney knew his patch, and he knew his job. The boss seemed to trust and respect him, and that was enough for the Welshman.

'So what do you reckon?' he asked, quite prepared to act on any suggestion Carney might make.

Carney leaned forward to the taxi driver. 'Pull in to the kerb for a minute, will you?' he asked.

The man did as he was instructed. Carney turned back to the Welshman. 'Look, you go ahead and join up with Winston at the hotel,' he suggested. 'I'm getting out to see if I can figure out what's going on.'

The Lethal Leek was slightly dubious. 'You sure you want to go out there on your own?' he asked. He had started to pick up some of Carney's bad vibes, and the faintest trace of menace in the air. Many of the smaller groups of youths had already started to form sizeable gangs, and their demeanour seemed to be hardening from mere truculence into a more open challenge. 'Maybe I ought to come with you,' he added.

Carney shook his head. 'No, Winston probably needs you more than I do. And don't worry – I'll keep my head down.' He opened the door and was stepping out when he turned back, a faint grin on his face. 'Why so concerned, anyway? I'd have thought you'd be relieved you don't have to explain my unwanted presence to Winston.'

The Welshman smiled back. 'Shit, Carney, of course I'm concerned,' he said. 'You're almost one of us.'

Carney jumped out and slammed the cab door behind him, feeling his face warm with a flush of embarrassment.

Or perhaps it was just pride, he told himself.

*   *   *

255

At the front of a small convoy of three vehicles from the nightclub, Pretty Boy sat on the back seat of a customized Shogun, slightly crushed between Cheryl and the huge frame of Max. Up at the front, Johnny was driving, flanked by the tall, gangly Scouser they called Spider. For a yobbo, Johnny drove a pretty flash set of wheels, Pretty Boy thought. He wondered where he got his money from.

They had already started to pass several smaller groups of rowdies patrolling the streets, all converging on the Knightsbridge area. Johnny seemed heartened by the sight. He half turned towards the back of the car, grinning broadly. 'Looks like we've got a pretty good turnout,' he observed. 'Should be one hell of a night.'

It was time to ask a few questions, Pretty Boy decided. Apparently casual, he said: 'What is all this in aid of, anyway?'

Johnny shrugged evasively. 'Favour for a favour – know what I mean? And no questions asked,' he added pointedly.

Pretty Boy took the hint. Still no wiser, he fell silent as they continued to cruise towards their destination. At last Johnny brought the Shogun to a halt and switched off the engine. 'Right, this is as far as I want to take the motor,' he announced. 'No point in risking getting it all smashed up with the others.' He looked through the front windscreen up the road ahead, to where gangs appeared to be bunching up into more of a mob. Turning back to the rear of the vehicle, he grinned again. 'Besides, we'll let some of those other suckers take the initial heat from the fuzz. Time we get there, they'll have their hands full.'

He delved into his pocket, pulling out a small, flat tin and flipping it open. Picking out a small white pill, he popped it into his mouth and then offered the tin to his passengers. 'Anyone need a little hit to keep their bottle up?'

Max and Cheryl dived towards the proffered pills gratefully, helping themselves. Johnny waved the tin in Pretty Boy's direction.

'Nirvana?' Pretty Boy asked.

Johnny looked slightly surprised. 'Sure. What else?'

Pretty Boy shrugged, picking out a single pill. 'Someone told me this stuff was in short supply just now,' he said coolly.

Johnny grinned. 'Only to those who don't know the right people,' he boasted. 'You got to be one of the chosen few.' His eyes narrowed slightly as he studied Pretty Boy with the faintest trace of suspicion. 'You're a curious bastard, aren't you?'

Pretty Boy turned it into a joke, grinning stupidly. 'Yeah,' he agreed. 'It never made me any fucking smarter, through.'

Johnny smiled, apparently satisfied, but Pretty Boy had already made a mental note not to underestimate the young man again. Perhaps his boast about knowing the right people had been just bluster, but suddenly Pretty Boy doubted it. It was now more than possible that Johnny was a little higher up the organizational structure than Pretty Boy had first suspected. If so, he might well be a very useful source of information when it came to tearing it down.

Certainly it would not pay to arouse his suspicions. Pretty Boy made a great play of popping the pill into his mouth and swallowing it. Conjuring tricks had never been one of his specialities, but he did the best job he could of palming the pill and dropping it discreetly to the floor of the car, where he trapped it beneath his foot. Fairly confident that no one had noticed, he waited a few seconds before carefully pushing it out of sight under the front passenger seat.

The rest of the cars had pulled up behind the Shogun. Johnny opened the driver's door, jumped out, ran round to the second car and opened the boot. He began to pull out a selection of stout wooden batons, baseball bats and metal bars, handing them out to the other members of the gang like an official armourer.

Pretty Boy watched the scene with mounting disquiet. This was more than just a street demo, he realized grimly. This was a war party.

Bullet-head completed his second sweep around the area immediately outside the police roadblocks. He pulled the Lexus in to the side of the road and stopped, then turned to Scott. 'Seen everything you want to see, boss?'

Scott nodded. 'Yes, let's go home.' He settled back into the car's plush upholstery as it slid away again, feeling vaguely comforted by the results of his efforts. His hastily convened mob was building up nicely, perhaps even better than he had hoped. There were probably well over two hundred young thugs out on the streets already, and the smell of trouble alone would be enough to attract others. Once the rioting started in earnest, the rabble would become a wild, undisciplined but quite formidable army. The police presence he had so far observed would be totally unable to restrain them. Even if the mob achieved nothing else, they would provide an extremely effective diversion. After that, Jefferies and his two gunmen would have to make their own chances, although Scott was still willing to offer his personal advice.

He picked up his mobile phone and tapped out the man's mobile number.

'Right, everything is in place,' Scott told him. 'There's a mob out on the streets who will be converging on the hotel within the next half hour or so. They have instructions to keep the police occupied while you make a break for it.' Scott lowered his voice to a whisper. 'Are McKinley and Dennings anywhere near you right now?'

'No,' Jefferies answered, puzzled. 'Why?'

Scott resumed his normal voice. 'Then listen carefully,' he said. 'Your best chance will be to use them as live bait. When the mob storm the hotel, send all the hostages out through the front door and instruct Dennings and McKinley to follow them out, prepared to fire if there's any opposition. There should be enough panic and confusion to let you make your own escape from the rear of the hotel or by the fire escape. Got that?'

'Yeah, sure,' Jefferies said, but his tone did not match the words. 'You really think this is going to work?' he added.

'Trust me,' Scott assured him, lying through his teeth. 'It will work. Just make sure you grab the money and get clear of that hotel while the police still have their hands full. Lie low somewhere for a couple of days and don't attempt to contact me. I'll get in touch with you when things quieten down.'

Scott signed off, knowing that he had done everything he could without getting himself directly involved. He didn't believe for a second that Jefferies had a snow-ball's chance in hell of getting away. But there was nothing else to lose, he told himself philosophically. If the million-to-one shot *did* come off, and Jefferies got clear, then he would at least have some temporary funds and the chance to fight another day. If not, he would be on the first available flight to Frankfurt, where he'd have to take his own chances with his superiors. His time would come again, he promised himself. One way or another.

The taxi carrying the Lethal Leek stopped at the outer perimeter of the orange plastic tapes which the police had strung across the road to cordon it off. One of the four uniformed officers hurried over to the cab, waving his arms in a clear gesture for the driver to pull back and turn around.

'I'm sorry, but this area is sealed off,' he started to explain, falling abruptly silent as the Welshman opened the cab door and climbed out.

'I'm with the SAS,' the Lethal Leek said. 'Where's my CO?'

The policeman nodded at the Heckler & Koch in the other man's hands with a faint smile on his face.

'Well, I didn't think you were with the bloody boy scouts, sir,' he said deferentially. He jerked his thumb up the road. 'And the rest of your Rambo brigade is up by the hotel.'

'Thanks,' the Lethal Leek said. He paid the cabby and ducked under the tape in search of Winston.

27

Winston had already waited the full ten minutes, and was in no great hurry to communicate with the gunmen inside the hotel again, figuring that any delay could only work in his favour. So the unexpected arrival of the Lethal Leek, and the necessary exchange of information between them, meant that at least quarter of an hour had elapsed since the last contact by the time he finally got back to the communications van.

The telephone was answered immediately this time. Winston recognized Jefferies' voice, although he still didn't know the man's name. He didn't sound quite so arrogant, but he appeared to be less nervous than before. Winston was surprised. He had fully expected the man to be showing signs of caving in, yet he seemed to have gained, rather than lost, confidence.

'Well, are we ready to discuss this thing sensibly yet?' Winston asked in a calm and reasonable tone.

Jefferies was noncommittal. 'Depends on what you have to say,' he countered. 'But there will be no release of hostages, under any circumstances.'

The very definiteness of the statement was another surprise. Winston had the unnerving feeling that he had lost the initiative somehow, and couldn't figure out why.

The answer came suddenly, in a flash of intuition, and Winston cursed himself for his oversight. The mobile phone! The man had his own means of communication with the outside world, and had probably been using it. And somehow, in the last fifteen minutes, he must have been given a new source of hope, which suggested that some sort of rescue plan was already in operation!

Winston was thrown, but it was imperative that he did not let Jefferies know it. He forced himself to keep talking, even though his mind was racing along new paths, dealing with a whole new set of variables.

'Perhaps you'd better tell me exactly what it is that you want,' he said. 'Then we can start negotiating.'

Jefferies giggled insanely. 'What I want is for you pigs to fuck off before people start getting killed,' he said. 'But we both know that isn't going to happen, don't we?'

The man sounded drunk. Or more likely drugged up to his eyeballs. Knowing the effects of Nirvana, and the man's sudden and unprovoked reference to killings, to Winston it was another new and disturbing factor.

It was time for a change of tack. 'There's no need for anyone to get killed,' Winston said gently, accepting that he was now on the defensive. 'We can stop this thing right now. You can walk out of there any time you choose.'

A snort of derision came over the line. 'You think I want to walk out of here and straight into a prison cell?' Jefferies snarled. 'Think again, pig. When I do any walking, it'll be straight to freedom.'

'And we both know *that* isn't going to happen,' Winston said flatly, echoing the man's earlier comment. It seemed vital to find some way of denting his new-found sense of confidence. 'There are only two ways out of that hotel. In custody, or in a box. The choice is yours.'

Winston paused, giving the statement time to sink in before he played his last card. 'Oh, and there's one other thing,' he added. 'This will be the last communication over the telephone. From now on we will be using the PA system, which means that your two chums will be able to hear everything as well. You're going to have to be pretty confident that you can count on them to back you up when the crunch comes. How far do you think you can trust either of them?'

There was no immediate reply. No smart answer, no show of bravado. Winston felt a faint, inner glow of satisfaction, knowing that the silence showed he had rattled the man again, exposed his insecurity.

Jefferies was more than just rattled. A sudden feeling of panic had suddenly swept over him again. He needed Dennings and McKinley for Scott's plan to work. Without their continued allegiance and support, he had no chance at all. And the bloody pig was right – if it came down to a direct choice of surrender or death, there was only the one sensible option for either of them. As it stood, they faced only a minimal prison term for armed assault – three years at the most. Would either of them be willing to risk life by killing hostages? It was unlikely, Jefferies figured. If he only had the guts to face the same option himself, he knew what he would want to choose.

But he was not free to make that choice. The cold, all-powerful and irrational fear which lurked deep within him made it impossible. Jefferies could never even consider any sort of a prison term, and it had nothing to do with any sense of claustrophobia. It was something worse, something he had carried inside him since childhood.

Jefferies shuddered as the old memories came flooding back. He had been just seven years old, a normal, happy, outgoing child. Bright, good-looking, wanting to learn and willing to trust. And who would such a child trust if not the teacher he admired most?

But that trust had been so cruelly abused. What the innocent child had taken for professional interest had concealed a different, more insidious motive.

The sexual attack had not been serious, but it had instilled a deep-seated hatred of homosexuals in the child which had grown into an irrational fear and loathing in his teenage years. He had passed through puberty in the constant fear that he was somehow marked as a target for queers. It was this all-consuming hatred of a minority group which had led him towards extreme-right-wing politics in the first place. Now, as an adult, it was stronger than ever.

He was young, and still considered good-looking. He had heard horrible, stomach-churning stories of what happened to attractive young men in prison. Rape, sex slavery, infection with AIDS. It was unthinkable. Jefferies would rather die than face a single day behind bars.

Winston's voice came over the line again, snapping him back to the present.

'Well?' the man was saying. 'What are you going to do?'

Jefferies fought against his panic, racking his brains in desperation. The promised mob could only be minutes away now. Somehow, he had to play for time.

'All right,' he blurted out, 'suppose I were to show you I was willing to negotiate? What do you want?'

Winston was quite taken aback by the sudden and dramatic change of mood. He had obviously struck a raw nerve – but how? Why? Perhaps it was just a side-effect of the drug. Whatever the reason, he had to act on it, follow it up.

'Release half of the hostages immediately,' he said flatly. 'Then we'll talk some more.'

'No.' Jefferies' voice rose to a scream. He needed the hostages just as much as he needed the two gunmen. In desperation he tried to think of anything else he could use as a bargaining point.

'Look, suppose I give you the location of the pub bomb?' he finally suggested. 'It's not set to go off until midday tomorrow. I can tell you where it is, and how to defuse it. You could save dozens of lives.' Jefferies paused, his voice taking on a slightly pleading tone. 'That would be a gesture of good faith, wouldn't it?'

Winston took a couple of seconds to consider the offer. It meant nothing in terms of saving lives, since that threat had already been dealt with. But Jefferies didn't know that, and the fact that he was willing to make any concession was in itself a breakthrough. In virtually every hostage or siege situation, opening the first negotiations was the hardest step to make. After that, there might be the chance of real progress.

'O,K, it will do as a start,' Winston conceded. 'Give me the details.'

'The bomb is inside the fruit machine in the lounge bar of the Bull & Bush in Camden Town,' Jefferies told him. 'It is not fitted with any anti-handling devices. You simply have to disconnect the timer to deactivate it.'

Winston wondered briefly how they had managed to place a bomb inside a one-armed bandit, but decided not to press it for now. He made a mental note to make sure all the staff of the machine leasing company were questioned later.

'You realize we're going to have to check this out?' he said.

'Yes, of course.' The man sounded relieved, Winston decided, and wondered why.

In fact, there were many things the SAS man was wondering about, and he needed time to think it all through.

'I'll get back to you,' Winston said curtly, and hung up.

Stepping out of the communications van, he saw the Lethal Leek running towards him. The Welshman looked worried.

'I think we got more trouble, boss,' he said, pointing up the street away from the hotel.

Winston followed his eyeline, through the cleared area and beyond the line of the police cordon. The approaching mob, which had now bunched up into a solid wall, was surging towards the first flimsy strands of tape slung across the road. They were no obstacle at all, and Winston could already see that the thin blue line of uniformed figures would be totally inadequate to hold the mob back. More to the point, he thought bitterly, he and his men would be equally powerless.

Suddenly Winston knew, with a cold certainty, why the gunman in the hotel had suddenly seemed so confident and why the mob was there. He felt almost physically sickened by the sheer cold-blooded cynicism of whoever had conceived the desperate plan. Second Holocaust were throwing the ultimate in cannon-fodder at them, knowing that they would be unable to fight back. They were using their own young men in a ruthless and reckless gamble, counting on the essential decency of the very system they wished to destroy to work in their favour.

Winston glanced down at the MP5K in his hand. He might as well be holding a peashooter, he thought, for all the use it was. For this was London, not Tiananmen Square. There was no way that any authority in the land would sanction firing into a crowd of unarmed civilians, no matter how threatening they were. The police and the SAS alike would have no choice but to fall back or be trampled underfoot by the sheer size of the rampaging mob, who had merely to swarm into the hotel and carry off their colleagues among their ranks.

And there was damn all any of them could do about it, Winston realized in a final moment of despair. His radiophone suddenly bleeped into life, announcing an incoming call. He tugged the instrument from his belt and switched it on. A wave of noise issued from the earpiece, along with bursts of crackling static. It took him a split second to identify the sound as the engine and rotors of a helicopter. Through it, he could faintly hear the sound of a familiar voice.

'Winston? This is Captain Blake. We'll be inserting in about one minute,' came the terse message. 'The hotel does appear to have a flat roof. Primary plan is to go in down the lift shafts, unless you have any better ideas.'

Winston glanced back up the road towards the police barrier. The first wave of rioters had broken through the tapes now, and were already engaged in vicious hand-to-hand fighting with the police officers. A second, and heavier wave hovered in the background, poised to sweep in behind their cronies and march directly to the hotel unopposed. They were two minutes away at the most, Winston calculated. It was cutting things too fine.

He returned his attention to Butch Blake and snapped out a curt message. 'Hold off. We have problems down here.'

The sound of the helicopter's engines were reaching his ears directly now. He glanced up, picking out the six-seater Agusta against the background of the night sky as it slipped in between a pair of towering office blocks perhaps half a mile in the distance.

Butch uttered a sudden and muffled curse as he caught a clear view of the hotel area, and the surging mob, for the first time. 'Oh Christ! I see what you mean.'

Winston thought quickly. 'Look, I've got an idea,'

he said. 'Can you drop just two or three troopers on that roof and get off again immediately?'

The answer was immediate, and affirmative. 'Can do. Then what?' In true SAS tradition, Captain Blake was ready and willing to take orders from a subordinate officer if that officer was on the spot and in a position to make a more informed judgement. It was all part of the unique flexibility and ability to adjust to changing circumstances which gave 22 SAS its edge.

'I assume you're carrying flash-bangs and tear-gas?' Winston asked, referring to the stun grenades and gas canisters which were standard armoury in Counter Revolutionary Warfare.

Winston didn't have to say any more. 'I'm way ahead of you, Sergeant,' Butch said. 'Close your eyes and put your earplugs in. It's going to get a bit unpleasant down there.'

Winston watched the chopper as it swept in towards the roof of the hotel and dropped out of sight. Seconds later it was rising again, wheeling in the sky to follow the line of the street towards the main mass of the rioters.

He moved quickly into action himself, calling over to the two Tweedles, Tremathon and Brennon. 'OK, pull back from that front door,' he told them. 'It's shake-out time.' He turned to the Lethal Leek. 'Leek, you take Miles with you and scoot round to cover the fire escape.'

'How's it going down, boss?' Tweedledee asked, as everyone moved to take up their new positions.

Winston smiled grimly. 'Just like Father Christmas,'

he muttered. 'We're going to drop our friends in there a few little presents down the chimney.'

In the thick of the second wave, Pretty Boy was almost at the broken lines of orange tape now. There were no policemen left on their feet, and the street was littered with bruised and bleeding bodies. It was time to break cover and choose sides, Pretty Boy decided, although he hadn't got the faintest idea what he could do which could possibly help the situation.

Mob violence was a frightening thing, even to a man like him, who had experienced all sorts of dangers and horrors. His ears were filled with the sounds of screaming, chanting people, and the crash of glass as the rioters smashed the windows of shops and parked cars. It was like being in the middle of a war zone – but this had an unreal, bewildering quality which threatened to swamp him. The mob seemed to have a life of its own – a raw, demonic and savage power which both fed and fed on the individuals within it. It was a mass psychosis, a form of possession which could take a man over, make him doubt his own sanity.

Cheryl and Johnny were a couple of yards ahead of him. The rest of the gang had been swallowed into the crowd. Pretty Boy forced his way through the surging mass of bodies between himself and them, planning his move.

A sharp kick in the back of Johnny's leg, right behind the knee joint, made the young man sag like a burst balloon. Discreetly, Pretty Boy delivered a short, jabbing punch to the back of his neck as he fell, rendering him unconscious. Johnny crumpled to the ground in a heap.

Cheryl was only vaguely aware of the action in her peripheral vision. She whirled on Pretty Boy, her eyes wide with question. 'What the fuck happened?' she demanded, looking down at Johnny's slumped form.

Pretty Boy shrugged. 'Something hit him. A stone, I think.'

There was no time to debate the matter, and nothing they could do about it anyway. The surging crowds behind them were already pushing them onward, with inexorable pressure. Pretty Boy stepped over Johnny's body, confident that he would be out for at least an hour. If he hadn't been trampled to death by the time this thing was all over, he'd still be around to answer a few questions. Now all he had to do was to get out of the mob to somewhere he could be more useful. It wasn't going to be easy. Then, suddenly, he heard the unmistakable sound of gunshots from somewhere behind them.

Paul Carney had come to the very same conclusions as Winston had some moments previously. There was no defence against the sheer mass of a solid mob. The SAS troopers would be swamped unless something could be done to break it up. There was only one thing he could think of. He reached inside his coat, tugged the Browning from its holster, pointed it into the air, and squeezed off six quick shots.

The sharp crack of the gunshots echoed out across the street above the general background din of rioting and destruction. Perhaps three dozen heads turned suddenly in Carney's direction, faces registering surprise, then fear. Nobody had said anything about guns. There were screams, confused shouts as individuals and small groups first froze in their tracks, their attention suddenly focused back on themselves rather than the mindless, shapeless mob. Then confusion turned to panic and began to sweep through the mob like ripples on a pond, pulsing through the seething crowd and dispersing it back into its component groups.

The reaction seemed out of all proportion to the stimulus, Carney thought, as the scattering crowd turned back in his direction. Then he heard the chattering roar of the helicopter as it swooped low over the heads of the panicking mob like a dive-bomber, pluming white, smoky trails behind it as CS gas canisters rained down into the street. A series of ear-splitting explosions rocked the air, accompanied by searing incandescent flashes which lit up the night.

The flash-bangs proved the final straw for the already confused and frightened mob. An SAS invention, they were virtually nothing more than gigantic fireworks, using grenade technology to place magnesium charges inside a non-fragmentation casing. They did little damage, but the loud bang and the fifty-thousand-candlepower flash they produced were enough to stun, temporarily blind and completely disorient those on the receiving end.

It was time to get the hell out, Carney thought, as a surging mass of humanity began to move back towards him. Jamming the Browning back into its holster, he turned and began to run back up the street as fast as his legs would carry him.

On the roof of the Courtland Hotel, Aberdeen Angus lifted off the inspection hatch of the lift shaft and peered down into its gloomy depths. Straightening, he turned to Jumbo Jackson with a satisfied grin on his face. 'All the way down to the ground floor,' he said cheerily. 'I'll bet the bastards have even put out a welcome mat.'

Roping up, the two troopers clambered through the hatch and began to abseil down the inside of the shaft. On reaching the top of the lift cage, they removed the service hatch cover and lowered themselves gently inside, dropping the last few inches on to their toes as quietly as possible.

There was now only the lift door itself between them and the lobby. Aberdeen Angus glanced at his companion, jerking his thumb towards the 'open' button. 'When I press that, dive out and hit the deck,' he whispered. 'We'll have a safer angle of fire from floor level.'

Jumbo nodded silently, understanding the man's reasoning. Firing upwards from floor level meant that the gunmen would be clear targets without any innocent hostages being in the line of fire behind them.

Both troopers set their MP5Ks for three-round bursts, tensing themselves for action. All they needed now was the sound of a diversion from Winston, and the trap would be sprung.

Winston's black face cracked into a broad grin as he

watched the last of the fleeing stragglers evaporate from the streets like mist in the morning sunlight. He glanced down at his watch, checking the time. He had allowed four minutes for his colleagues to descend the lift shaft and get into position. An additional safety margin of a further minute had already elapsed. It was time, he decided.

He nodded at the two Tweedles. 'You two might as well go back in by the way you came out,' he muttered, gesturing towards the shattered bar window. 'I'm just going to make a lot of noise by the front door to draw their attention.'

He turned towards the nearest communications van, where Ted Brennon was looking at him expectantly through the open door. Raising his hand, Winston jabbed his thumb into the air.

Nodding, Brennon ducked back inside the van. Seconds later the vehicle's loudspeakers began to blast out a solid wall of sound as the Rolling Stones launched into the drum-roll intro to 'Paint It Black'. A fitting choice, Winston thought.

He turned back towards the hotel. 'Right, let's do it,' he barked.

Only Jefferies had been unaffected by the sounds of the stun-grenade explosions in the street outside, assuming it to be part of Scott's master plan. Most of the hostages had reacted in blind panic, many of them throwing themselves to the floor instinctively, despite the threat of the guns. Dennings and McKinley had just panicked, anticipating a full-scale attack and being far too concerned about their own skins to worry about anything else. They had lost what small degree of control they had possessed and were now too far down the road of self-preservation to take orders or to be of any effective use.

So he was on his own, Jefferies thought to himself. Somehow, it didn't seem to matter. The drug was buzzing in his brain, filling him with a sense of invincibility. Almost casually, he picked up the red Samsonite suitcase and began to walk towards the bar area and the emergency escape door beyond it. The sudden blast of sound from the street outside seemed like nothing more than background music.

Even the sudden appearance of Tweedledum and Tweedledee through the shattered bar window failed to evoke any real sense of threat. Jefferies raised the Colt almost as a token gesture, pointing it vaguely in their direction without really taking aim.

Not that it would have made much difference. Two bursts from their Heckler & Koch sub-machine-guns took him in the chest before his finger had time to tighten on the trigger, spinning him round like a top in a spray of blood.

Dennings and McKinley turned towards the sound of gunfire just as the lift door sighed open. Caught off guard, they were both sitting targets as Aberdeen Angus and Jumbo dived across the floor in front of them, their own MP5Ks spitting a hail of death.

The chatter of gunfire ceased abruptly, leaving only the screaming of the hostages to fill the gap. Outside, Mick Jagger hadn't even finished the second verse.

It was over.

28

It was an informal meeting, in the bar of the Paludrine Club. The full debriefing would come later.

'Well, do you think we stopped them?' Major Anderson asked.

Lieutenant-Colonel Barney Davies shrugged. 'Probably not,' he admitted. 'We didn't stop the bastards in 1945 and there's no reason to feel any more optimistic now. How do you kill off a dream – even if that dream is completely bloody insane?'

Davies managed a wry smile. 'But at least we've slowed them down, damaged their command structure,' he added. 'It will probably be a few years before they can regroup sufficiently in this country to offer any concerted threat again.'

'And we've neutralized the drug menace, at least,' Anderson pointed out.

The raid on the farmhouse factory had given the green slime the information they needed to identify Nirvana's main chemical constituents and isolate the European pharmaceutical companies producing them. A rigid import embargo would now virtually ensure that no further bulk production of the drug would be possible within the UK.

'So that's it, then?' Winston put in. 'Until the next time?'

Davies sighed heavily. 'Yes, until the next time,' he echoed.

'And Carney?' Winston wanted to know. 'What happens to him now?'

Davies grinned. 'Oh, I don't think you should worry yourself about him,' he murmured. 'I think the Special Branch, or the green slime, are sorting out some sort of job for him right now.' He paused briefly. 'They can always find a use for a good man, even if we can't.'

SOLDIER U: SAS

BANDIT COUNTRY

Peter Corrigan

Prologue

South Armagh, 3 July 1989

The foot patrol moved quietly down the starlit street. There were four of them, forming a 'brick'. They made up a single fire team. The point man kept his SA-80 assault rifle in the crook of his shoulder, eyes glinting in his darkly camouflaged face as he scanned surrounding windows, doors and alleyways.

Behind the point came the fire team's commander, a corporal. Hung on the left side of his chest was a PRC 349 radio. It had a range of only a few kilometres, but the patrol was not far from home. The corporal had the 349 set on whisper mode. Its twin microphones were strapped to his throat and he edged a finger in between them, silently cursing the way they irritated his skin.

Behind the corporal came the gunner, armed with a Light Support Weapon. Similar to an SA-80, it had a longer barrel and a bipod to steady it.

The rear man was walking backwards, checking the street the patrol had just walked through. The men were in staggered file, two on each side of the road, covering each other as they made their way back to the safety of the Security Forces Base. It was pitch-dark, and they avoided the few street-lights that still worked in that part of the village. All of them had the needle in the sights of their weapons turned on so that it was a luminous line, helping them to pick out targets at night.

They were near the centre of the village now. The locals had whitewashed all the walls so that a patrolling soldier would stand out more clearly against them. That was the worst part.

A dog barked, and they all paused to listen, hunkering down in doorways. Nothing worse than a restless fucking dog; it told the locals they had visitors.

The barking stopped. The corporal waved a hand and they were on their way again.

The centre of Crossmaglen had a small, open square. Crossing it was the most dangerous part of any patrol. It had to be done quickly as the whitewashed house walls offered no concealment. As the brick paused on the edge of the square the point man looked back at his commander. The corporal nodded and took up a firing position, as did the other two men.

The point man set off across the square at

a sprint. He was halfway across when there was a sharp crack, startlingly loud in the still night air. The point man seemed to be knocked backwards. He fell heavily on to his back and then lay still.

For a second the rest of the fire team was frozen, disbelieving. Then the corporal began shouting.

'Sniper! Anyone see the flash?'

'Not a fucking thing, Corp.'

'Ian's out there – we've got to go and get him! Gunner, set up the LSW for suppressive fire. Mike, we're going to run out there and bring him in, OK?'

When the gunner was on the ground, with the LSW's stock in his shoulder, the other two soldiers dashed out into the open.

Immediately there was the sound of automatic fire. Tarmac was blown around their legs as the bullets thumped down around them. The point man lay in a pool of shining liquid. His chest looked as though someone had broken it open to have a look inside. Behind them, the LSW gunner opened up on automatic. Suddenly the little square was deafening with the sound of gunfire. Red streaks sped through the air and ricocheted off walls: the tracer in the LSW magazine. A series of flashes came from an alleyway opening off the square, and there was the unmistakable bark of an AK47, somehow lighter than the single shot that had felled the point man.

'Come on, Mike. Grab his legs.'

'He's dead, Corp!'

'Grab his fucking legs, like I tell you!'

They staggered back across the square with their comrade's body slung between them like a sack. The firing had stopped. All around, lights were flicking on at windows. There was the sound of doors banging.

'Get a fucking field-dressing on him, Mike. Gunner, did you see where that bastard is?'

'Saw the muzzle flash, Corp. But I think he's bugged out now. The locals will be all over us in a minute though.'

The corporal swore viciously, then thumbed the pressel-switch of the 349.

'Hello, Zero, this is Oscar One One Charlie. Contact, over.'

The far-away voice crackled back over the single earphone.

'Zero, send over.'

'One One Charlie, contact 0230, corner of . . .' – the corporal looked round wildly – 'corner of Hogan's Avenue and Cross square. One own casualty, at least two enemy with automatic weapons. I think they've bugged out. Request QRF and medic for casevac, over.'

'Roger, One One Charlie. QRF on its way, over.'

'Roger out.'

The corporal bent over his injured point man. 'How is he, Mike?'

The other soldier was ripping up field-dressings furiously and stuffing them into the huge chest wound.

'Fucking bullet went right through his trauma plate, Corp – right fucking through and went out the other side. What the hell kind of weapon was that?'

The soldiers all wore flak-jackets, and covering their hearts front and rear were two-inch-thick 'trauma plates' of solid Kevlar. These stopped most normal bullets, even those fired by a 7.62mm Kalashnikov AK47.

'It's that bastard sniper. He got us again.' The corporal was livid with fury. 'The bastard did it again,' he repeated.

There was a loud banging in the night, the metallic clatter of dustbin lids being smashed repeatedly on the ground. Crossmaglen's square was filling up with people.

The sound of engines roaring up other streets. A siren blaring. The flicker of blue lights. A Quick Reaction Force was on its way.

'He's gone, Corp. Poor bugger never had a chance.'

Armoured Landrovers, both green and slate-grey, powered into the square, scattering the approaching mob. The locals were shouting and cheering now – they had seen the little knot of men on the corner, the body on the ground. They knew what had happened.

'Nine-nil, nine-nil, nine-nil,' they chanted, laughing. Even when baton-wielding soldiers and RUC men poured out of the Landrovers to force them back, they continued jeering.

'Nineteen years old,' the corporal said. 'His first tour. Jesus Christ.'

He closed the blood-filled eyes of the boy on the ground.

The Border Fox had struck again.

1

HQNI Lisburn, 6 July 1989

'What do you have that I can use?' Lieutenant Colonel Blair asked, sipping his coffee.

Brigadier General Whelan, Commander of Land Forces in Northern Ireland, looked at his subordinate warily.

'I can give you an additional Special Support Unit from 39 Brigade's patch,' he replied.

'RUC cowboys? But sir, I've lost four men in four months, all to the same sniper. Morale is rock-bottom, and the local players know it. I've already had three complaints this week alone. The boys are taking it out on the population.'

Whelan held up a hand and said: 'This is a bad time of year, Martin. The marching season is almost upon us. We're overstretched, and Whitehall won't hear of us bringing in another battalion.'

'It's not another battalion we need. I was thinking of something more compact.'

'The Intelligence and Security Group?'

'Yes. To be frank, sir, we're getting nowhere. Our own Covert Observation Platoon has drawn a series of blanks. I don't have the resources within my own patch to tackle this problem. We need outside help – and I'm talking help from our own people, not the RUC.'

'Hasn't E4 come up with anything?'

'Special Branch guards its sources like an old maid her virginity. They're terrified of compromising the few touts they have. No – we need a new approach. This South Armagh Brigade is the tighest-knit we've ever encountered. It's better even than the Mid-Tyrone one was a few years back. The Provos seem to have taken the lessons of Loughgall to heart. They're very slick, and they've recovered amazingly quickly. This Border Fox now has up to three ASUs operating in close support. We need to take out not only him, but at least one of those back-up units.'

'Take out? You rule out more conventional methods of arrest, then?'

'I believe it would be too risky. No, this bastard is fighting his own little war down near the border. The South Armagh lot need to have the carpet pulled out from under them.'

'And your men need a kill.'

Lieutenant Colonel Blair, commanding officer of 1st Battalion the Royal Greenjackets, paused.

'Yes, they do.' He would not have been so open with any other senior officer, but Whelan was a member of the 'Black Mafia' himself – an ex-Greenjacket who had done his stint as CO of a battalion in South Armagh.

'This is irregular, Martin – you know that. You're asking me to initiate an operation in a vacuum. Usually it is the Tasking and Coordinating Group that comes to me . . .'

'More Special Branch,' said Blair with a wave of his hand. 'This is not an RUC problem. It is the Green Army that is taking the casualties, my men that are out there in the bogs day after day and night after night, while the RUC conduct vehicle checkpoints and collar drink-drivers.'

Whelan was silent. It was true that the uniformed 'Green Army' had been paying a heavy price lately for the patrolling of the border, or 'Bandit Country' as the men on the ground called it. And the Border Fox had made headlines both in the UK and America. He was a hero to the Nationalist population and their sympathizers across the Atlantic. Nine members of the Security Forces had been killed by him in the last eighteen months, the last only a few days ago. All of them had been killed by a single bullet from a high-calibre sniper rifle that had punched through the men's body armour as though it were cardboard. The capture of that weapon, more importantly, the termination of the Fox's activities, were obviously desirable.

But Whelan did not like authorizing what were in effect assassinations. He had no moral qualms about the issue – the Fox had to be stopped, and killing him was an effective way of doing that. But he hated giving the Republican Movement yet another martyr. Political consideration had to be taken into account also. If he authorized an op against the Fox he would have to inform the Secretary of State – in guarded terms of course – of what was about to happen.

More importantly, there was the feasibility of the operation. Intelligence in 3 Brigade's Tactical Area of Responsibility was poor. The IRA brigade in South Armagh seemed very tightly knit and so far all attempts to cultivate informers had failed. It was impossible to proceed without good intelligence, and seemingly impossible to obtain that intelligence. Hence the Security Forces were powerless, for all their helicopters and weapons. And so the Fox continued his killing unhindered, which was why he had Martin Blair in his office, seething with baffled anger.

'Damn it, Martin, don't you think I see your point? But how can we proceed with anything when we have nothing to go on? Special Branch has drawn a blank, and your own covert op has turned up nothing.'

'Then we must create our own intelligence,' Blair said doggedly.

'What do you mean?'

'Give me the Int and Sy Group. Let them loose in my patch. They may turn up something.'

'That's a hell of a vague notion.'

'They're doing bugger-all at the moment except interminable weapons training. I got that from James Cordwain himself. The rest of the Province is as quiet as the grave.'

Whelan winced at his subordinate's choice of words. Major Cordwain was OC of the combined Intelligence and Security Group and 14 Intelligence Company. 'Int and Sy', or more often just 'The Group', was another name for Ulster Troop, the only members of the SAS who were based permanently in the Province. Fourteen Intelligence Company was another pseudonym for a crack surveillance unit drawn from all units in the army and trained by the SAS themselves.

'Int and Sy's job description does not include charging in like the bloody cavalry, guns blazing.'

Colonel Blair smiled. 'Tell James Cordwain that.'

'Indeed.' Cordwain had taken over the Group less than a year ago. He and his young second in command, Lieutenant Charles Boyd, were a pair of fire-eaters. Cordwain had been with 22 SAS in the Falklands and was an expert in covert surveillance and the tricky business of so-called 'Reactive Observation Posts' – known to the rest of the army as Ambushes.

'You've spoken to Cordwain about this, then?' Whelan asked sharply. He did not like officers, even fellow Greenjackets, who flouted the chain of command.

Blair stiffened. 'Yes, sir, I did – informally of course.'

'And what was his reaction?'

'He thought he might have a way in.'

'What is it?'

'An operative of ours, based in Belfast at the moment. He used to be part of Int and Sy but MI5 have become his handlers. Been here for over a year, and has a perfect cover.'

'His name?'

'Cordwain wouldn't say. But he thinks it would be possible to relocate him, weasel him into the South Armagh lot.'

'He must be an exceptional man.'

'Actually, Cordwain says he's one of the best he's ever seen. Parents were from Ballymena, so he has the perfect accent for starters. They were in the South Atlantic together.'

Whelan got up, crossed the office to the sideboard and the decanter that stood there. He poured out two whiskies into Waterford-crystal tumblers and offered one to Blair.

'Bushmills – the Irish. Bloody good stuff.'

They drank. Whelan looked out of his office window, past the ranks of Landrovers and Saxon armoured personnel carriers, over to where the perimeter wall rose high with netting and razor-wire; it was supposed to intercept RPG 7 missiles or Mark 12 mortars, the Provos' current flavour of the month.

'We are skating on thin ice here, Martin,' Whelan said.

'Yes, sir, I know. But my men are dying.'

'Yes. But MI5, they're tighter with their operatives than E4 is with its information. They may not want to let us play with this man.'

'Cordwain thinks it may be possible to bypass MI5, sir.'

Whelan spun round. 'Does he now? And how would we do that?'

'This man, he has a personal reason for wanting to see the Border Fox brought in. One of my young subalterns was a relative of his.'

'Ah yes, I remember. That was tragic, Martin, tragic. So it's revenge this man wants. That may not make him totally reliable.'

'Cordwain seems to think he is, sir, and Boyd, his 2IC, is willing to provide back-up.'

Whelan set down his glass and leaned over the desk until his face was close to Blair's.

'You seem to have thought this out with

unusual thoroughness, Colonel.'

'Yes, sir.'

'I am not used to being given fully-fledged covert operational plans by my battalion commanders. Is that clear, Colonel?'

'Perfectly, sir.'

Whelan straightened.

'It may be we will be able to keep this under an army hat. I would certainly prefer it that way – and you say that Special Branch can give us nothing. But we must be even more discreet than usual – and I am not talking about the Paddies, Colonel. I will speak to Cordwain. I will give him the necessary authorization . . .' As Blair brightened, Whelan frowned thunderously and cut him off.

'But mark me, Martin, this conversation never took place. This man of Cordwain's will be disowned by every security agency in the Province if he so much as sniffs of controversy. And Cordwain's back-up will be on their own also. If the press – or God help us the Minister – ever find out about this we'll be crucified.'

'I understand, sir.'

'Be sure that you do, Martin.' The General tossed off the last of his Bushmills with practised ease. Now you'll have to go, I'm afraid. I have a bloody cocktail party to go to. I have to rub noses with the Unionists and win some hearts and minds.'

2

Belfast

The Crown Bar, opposite the much-bombed Europa Hotel, was quiet. It was two o'clock on a weekday afternoon and there seemed to be only a handful of men in there, seated in the walled-off snugs and nursing Guinness or whiskey, leafing through the *Belfast Telegraph*.

One of those men was Captain John Early of the SAS. He was a squat, powerful figure of medium height who appeared shorter because of the breadth of his shoulders. He could have – and frequently did – pass for a brickie on his lunch hour or whiling away the days of unemployment. His hands were blunt and calloused, the arms powerfully muscled. His face was square, the close-cropped hair sprinkled with premature grey at the temples and a badly broken nose making him look slightly thuggish. But the blue eyes were intelligent, belying the brutality of the face. Despite the haircut, he did not look like a soldier, certainly not a holder of the Queen's

Commission. And when he quietly asked the barman for another pint his accent bore the stamp of north-east Ulster.

There was no trace left of the clean-cut young officer who had joined the Queen's Regiment back in 1977, or even of the breezy subaltern who had agonized through SAS selection eight years previously. Turnover of officers among the SAS was much swifter than that of troopers; they rarely served more than five or six years with a Sabre Squadron. Early had come over with Ulster Troop in 1984 and gone undercover two years later. He was an 'independent', operating now under the aegis of MI5, but he never forgot where he had come from. If he died here, his name would be inscribed on the Clock Tower in Hereford, where all the dead of the SAS left their names.

Early sipped his whiskey patiently. He was waiting for a friend.

James Cordwain came through the door. Early recognized him instantly, though he hadn't seen him in years. The hair was longer of course – all the SAS seemed to believe that long hair was obligatory when serving in Northern Ireland. But he still had the aristocratic bearing, the finely chiselled jaw and flashing eyes. He looked every inch an officer. Early sighed, ordered another drink and took it into a snug.

It was ten minutes before Cordwain joined him, smiling.

'You're not an easy man to get hold of, John.'

'The name is Dominic, Dominic McAteer,' Early told him sharply. Cordwain winced.

'Why did we have to meet anyway? A phone call could have done it.'

Cordwain shook his head, regaining his self-assurance quickly. 'I had to talk to you in person.'

'Talk then.'

Cordwain looked at him, slightly offended. They had been good friends once, in the Falklands. Early seemed aged, irritable beyond his years. It was undercover work that did it, Cordwain decided.

'I have a Q car down the street. We can talk in there,' he said. A Q car was the army's name for an unmarked vehicle.

'Are you mad? Every dicker in the city knows a Q car when he sees one. We're safe enough here. I know the barman. He thinks I'm just another unemployed navvy and you're in here about a job.'

'Which, in a way, I am.'

'So tell me about it.'

Cordwain tried hard not to look smug. 'It's on.'

'When?'

17

'As soon as you can relocate. We have an opening down in Cross. Construction.'

'Not on a fucking army base, I trust.'

Cordwain grinned. 'Not likely. No, a local firm, Lavery's, has been given a contract – new bungalows.'

Early's eyes narrowed. 'It's a front, is it?'

'Yes and no. The contract is real enough, but our people are the ones behind it, buried three layers deep. Get yourself settled in, and then we'll start working on a channel of communication.'

'I take it Special Branch came up with fuck-all.'

'They don't even know you exist.'

Early nodded. He liked it that way.

'What about our friends the spooks?' he said, referring to his handlers in the Intelligence Service.

'You're on leave, seeing a sick auntie. They think you're back across the water. They'll be mightily pissed off when the truth comes out though.'

'Fuck them. This is my last caper, James. After this I'm getting out.'

'I'm sorry about Jeff. I take it he's the reason behind all this.'

Jeffrey Early had hero-worshipped John and gone into the army as soon as he could, following in his revered older brother's footsteps. But the Border Fox had killed Jeff three months ago. One bullet, taking off most of his head. Early had not even been able to go to the funeral.

'I want this bastard, James. I really want him.'

Cordwain nodded. 'Don't let hatred cloud your thinking, John. Remember, your job will be identification. I provide the Button Men.

'Who are they?'

'Charles Boyd for one. You don't know him, but he's a good man.'

'I don't want him tripping over my shadow, James. This South Armagh lot are the most formidable we've ever encountered. They sniff the colour green and I'm dead. Tell your man to keep his distance.'

Cordwain was not happy. 'They have to provide effective back-up.'

'So long as they don't compromise me.'

'They won't. I'll have a word. Boyd will want to meet you as soon as is practicable.'

'Why, for fuck's sake?'

'To get a feel of the thing. He wants you to draw him a few pictures.'

'Are you saying he's still wet behind the ears?'

Cordwain grinned. 'A little. He's out in west Tyrone at the minute, but that op should finish within a day at most.'

'Terrific.' Early finished his drink and stood up, glancing quickly over the wooden partition of the snug. The bar was still more or less deserted.

'I'll be in touch.'

Then he left, exchanging a farewell with the barman as he went. Cordwain lingered a while to leave a gap between them. This had to be the most hare-brained operation he had ever begun. But the men Upstairs had given the go-ahead, and besides, he did not like doing nothing while British soldiers were slaughtered with impunity. Talking once to an officer in the 'Green Army', he had been struck by a phase the man had used. 'We're just figure 11s, out standing on the streets,' the officer had said. A 'figure 11' was the standard target used on firing ranges. Cordwain did not like the image. It was time the terrorists took a turn at ducking bullets.

Lieutenant Charles Boyd shifted position minutely to try to get some blood circulating in his cramped and chilled legs. The rain had been pouring down for hours now, reducing visibility and soaking him to the marrow. There were streams of freezing water trickling down the neck of his combat smock and between his buttocks. He was lying in a rapidly deepening puddle with the stock of an Armalite M16 assault rifle close to his cheek. His belt-order dug into his slim waist and his elbows were sinking deeper into peat-black mud.

'July in Tyrone,' his companion whispered.

'Jesus fucking Christ. Why didn't I become a grocer?'

'Shut it, Haymaker.'

'Yes, boss,' the other man mumbled. The hissing downpour of the rain reduced the chances of their being heard but there was no point in taking risks.

It was getting on towards evening; the second evening they had spent in the observation post. They were screened by a tangle of alder and willow; behind them a stream gurgled, swollen by the rain. Their camouflaged bergens rested between their ankles.

They had not moved in thirty-six hours. Boyd began to wonder if the SB had been wrong. He had been tasked to provide a Reactive Observation Post to monitor an arms cache which was to have been visited last night, but no one had shown. The cache was at the base of a tree eighty metres away – they could see it plainly even with the rain. The local ASU, an IRA Active Service Unit of four men, was planning a 'spectacular' for the forthcoming Twelfth of July marches. Boyd and his team were to forestall them, and had been discreetly given the go-ahead to use all necessary means to achieve that aim. To Boyd that meant only one thing: any terrorist who approached this cache was going to die. It would give the Unionists something to crow about on their holiday and sweeten relations between them and the Northern Ireland Office. Boyd didn't give a shit about either, but he wanted to nail this ASU. They had been a thorn in 8 Brigade's flesh for some months now, though they were not as slick as their colleagues in Armagh.

Lying beside Boyd was Corporal Kevin 'Haymaker' Lewis, so called because of his awesome punch. It was rumoured he had killed an Argie in the Falklands with one blow of his fist. Haymaker was an amiable man, though built like a gorilla. He had the tremendous patience and stamina of the typical SAS trooper, but he loved grousing.

Hidden some distance to the rear of the pair were Taff Gilmore and Raymond Chandler. All troopers seemed to have some nickname or other. Taff was so called not because he was Welsh but because he had a fine baritone voice which he exercised at every opportunity. And Raymond – well, what else could the lads call someone with the surname Chandler? Some of them, though, called him 'The Big Sleep' because of his love of his sleeping bag.

It was unusual for an officer to accompany an op such as this. SAS officers had on the whole stopped accompanying the other ranks into the field since the death of Captain Richard Westmacott in 1980, gunned down by an M60 machine-gun in Belfast's Antrim Road. But Boyd loved working in the field – not for him the drudgery of the ops room in some security base. He knew that the men called him 'our young Rupert' behind his back, but he also knew that they respected him for his decision.

God, the bloody rain, the bloody mud, the bloody Provos. The players, as the Army termed the key terrorist figures, were probably warm and safe in their houses. Not for them the misery of this long wait in the rain, the pissing and shitting into plastic bags, the cold tinned food.

Boyd felt Haymaker tense beside him. His mind had been wandering. The big trooper looked his officer in the eye, then nodded out at the waterlogged meadow with its straggling hedgerows. There was movement out there in the rain, a dark flickering of shadow close to the hedge. Immediately Boyd's boredom and weariness disappeared. The evening was darkening but it was still too light to use Night Vision Goggles, which made the darkest night into daylight. He squinted, his fist tightening round the pistol-grip of the M16. One thumb gently levered off the safety-catch. The weapon had been cocked long ago, the magazine emptied and cleaned twice in the past thirty-six hours. The M16 was a good weapon for a nice heavy rate of fire, but it was notoriously prone to jamming when dirty.

Boyd's boot tapped Haymaker on the ankle. He gave the thumbs down, indicating that the enemy was in sight. Haymaker grinned, rain dripping off his massive, camouflaged face, and sighed down the barrel of his own Armalite. Boyd could hear his own heartbeat thumping in his ears.

Two men were walking warily up the line of the hedge. This had to be it – who else would be tramping the fields on such a shitty evening? Boyd forced himself to remember the mugshots of the key Tyrone players. Would it be Docherty? Or McElwaine?

The men had stopped. Boyd cursed silently. Had they been compromised? Besides him, Haymaker was like a great, wet statue. The pair of them hardly dared breathe.

They were moving again, thank Christ. Boyd could see them clearly now, buttoned up in parkas, their trousers soaked by the wet grass. McElwaine and the youngster, Conlan.

The two IRA men stopped at the tree which marked the cache, looked around again, and then bent to the ground and began rummaging in the grass. One of them produced a hand-gun with a wet glint of metal. They were pulling up turves, their fingers slipping on the wet earth.

Should he initiate the ambush now? No. Boyd

wanted a 'clean' kill – he wanted both terrorists to have weapons in their hands when he opened up. That way there would be no awkward questions asked afterwards. The 'yellow card', the little document all soldiers in the Province carried, specified that it was only permitted to open fire without warning if the terrorist was in a position to endanger life, either the firer's or someone else's.

They were hauling things out of the hole now: bin-liner-wrapped shapes.

'I'll take McElwaine,' Boyd whispered to Haymaker. He felt a slight tap from the trooper's boot in agreement.

There. It looked like a Heckler & Koch G3: a good weapon. McElwaine was cradling the rifle like a new toy, discarding the bin-liner it had been wrapped in.

Boyd tightened his fist, and the M16 exploded into life. A hot cartridge-case struck his left cheek as Haymaker opened up also, but he hardly felt it. They were both firing bursts of automatic, the heavy, sickly smell of cordite hanging in the air about their heads.

McElwaine was thrown backwards, the G3 flying from his hands. Boyd saw the parka being shredded, dark pieces of flesh and bone spraying out from the massive exit wounds. Then McElwaine was on the ground, moving feebly.

Boyd heard the 'dead man's click' from his weapon and changed magazines swiftly, then opened up again. McElwaine's body jumped and jerked as the 5.56mm rounds tore in and out of it.

He was aware that Conlan was down too. Haymaker changed mags also, then continued to fire. When they had emptied two mags each Boyd called a halt. They replenished their weapons and then lay breathing fast, their ears ringing and the adrenalin pumping through their veins like high-octane fuel. Haymaker was struggling not to laugh.

Boyd pressed the 'squash' button on the Landmaster radio to tell Taff and Raymond the mission had been a success. Then he and Haymaker lay motionless, rifles still in the shoulder, looking out on the meadow with its two shattered corpses.

Ten minutes they lay there, not moving – just watching. Then Boyd nudged Haymaker and the big man took off towards the bodies. Boyd pressed the squash button again, twice. Taff and Raymond would close in now.

Haymaker examined both bodies, then waved. Boyd grinned, then thumbed the switch on the radio once more.

'Zero, this is Mike One Alpha, message, over.'
'Mike One Alpha, send over.'

'Mike One Alpha, Ampleforth, over.'

'Zero, roger out.'

Boyd had given the code for a successful operation. In a few minutes a helicopter would arrive to spirit the SAS team away. The Green Army and the police would arrive to wrap up the more mundane details. Boyd ran over to Haymaker. The big trooper was kneeling by the bodies. It was hard to see the expression on his camouflaged face in the gathering twilight.

'Fucking weapons weren't loaded, boss. The magazines are still in the hole.'

Boyd shrugged, slipping on a pair of black Northern Ireland-issue gloves.

'That's not a problem.'

He reached into the hole and fetched the loaded magazines that the IRA men had not had time to fix to their weapons. Then he carefully loaded the G3 and an Armalite that was still in the cache, and placed them beside the two bodies.

'That's more fucking like it. No one will whinge about civil liberties now.'

The two men laughed. The adrenalin was still making them feel a little drunk. They turned at a noise and found Taff and Raymond approaching, grins all over their filthy faces.

'Scratch two more of the bad guys, eh boss?' Taff said.

'Damn straight.' Boyd lifted his head. He could

hear the thump of the chopper off in the rain-filled sky. They had timed it nicely – there was just enough light for a pick-up.

'Right, let's clean up this place. I don't want any kit left lying around for the RUC to sniff over.' He paused. 'Well done, lads. This was a good one.'

'Bit of a payback for those poor bastards in Armagh,' Haymaker said. He nudged one of the broken bodies with his foot.

'You're playing with the big boys now, Paddy.'

3

Armagh

It was good to be out of the city, Early thought.
Belfast was a depressing hole at times, as claustrophobic and as deadly as some Stone Age village
in a jungle. There were all the little invisible
boundaries. One street was safe, the one next to it
was not. This was Loyalist, that was Republican.
This was a safe pub, that was a death-trap. So
much depended on names and nuances, even the
way the people spoke, the things they said, the
football teams they supported, the sports they
played.

Not that Armagh was any different. He must
remember that. But it was good to see green
fields, cows grazing, tractors meandering along
the quiet roads. Hard to believe these places were
battlefields in a vicious little war.

He took the bus from Armagh city, through
Keady and Newtownhamilton, down to Cross-
maglen – 'Cross' to soldiers and locals alike.
Early preferred travelling by bus. It was less risky

than using a car, and fitted in with his identity as an unemployed bricklayer.

The bus was stopped at vehicle checkpoints three times in its journey south, and soldiers who seemed both tense and bored got on to walk up and down the aisle, looking at faces and luggage, and occasionally asking for ID. At two of the VCPs Early was asked his name, destination and the purpose of his journey. It amused and relieved him that the soldiers seemed to find him a suspicious-looking character. The other passengers stared stonily ahead when the bus was checked, but when the soldiers had left one or two of them smiled at him, commiserating. Early shrugged back at them, smiling in return. His false ID, his accent and his motives for travelling to Crossmaglen were impeccable. He was Dominic McAteer, a bricklayer looking for work with Lavery's Construction in the town.

Lavery's offices were in a small estate called Rathkeelan, to the north-west of Crossmaglen. Early got off the bus and stood looking around, hands in pockets, his duffle bag on his back. He bore no ID, but strapped to the inside of his right ankle was a compact Walther 9mm semi-automatic; not as effective as the Browning High Powers the SAS usually carried, but far more easily concealed. It could fit in his underpants if it had to.

Early passed beautifully painted murals on the whitewashed walls of the houses, the silhouettes of Balaclava-clad men bearing Armalites, and on one wall the recently repainted tally 'Provos 9 Brits 0' and below it the slogan 'One Shot, One Kill'.

His jaw tightened with anger for a second. His brother was one of those included in that score.

Then he recollected himself, and headed for the door of the nearest bar, whistling 'The Wild Colonial Boy'.

It was dark inside, as all Irish pubs were. He dumped his duffle bag with a sigh and rubbed the back of his thick neck. A cluster of men sitting and standing with pints in their hands paused in their conversation to look at him. He smiled and nodded. The barman approached, a large, florid man wiping a glass.

'What can I get you?'

'Ach, give us a Guinness and a wee Bush.'

The barman nodded. The conversations resumed. *Good Evening Ulster* had just started on the dusty TV that perched on a shelf near the ceiling. Early pretended to watch it, while discreetly clocking the faces of the other customers. No players present. He was glad.

The Guinness was good, as it always was nearer the border. Early drank it gratefully, and raised his glass to the barman.

'That's as good as the stuff in O'Connell Street.'

The barman smiled. 'It's all in the way it's kept.'

'Aye, but there's some pubs that don't know Guinness from dishwater. It's the head – should be thick as cream.'

'It's the pouring too,' the barman said.

'Aye. Ever get a pint across the water? They throw it out in five seconds flat and the head's full of bloody bubbles.'

The barman looked at him and then asked casually: 'You've been across the water, then?'

'Aye. But there's no work there now. I hear Lavery's has a job out here in Cross and needs some labourers. I'm a brickie meself, and sure there's bugger-all up in Belfast.'

'Ach, sure the city is gone to the dogs these days.'

'You're right.' Early raised his glass of Bushmills. '*Slainte*,' he said. He thought the barman relaxed a little.

'So you're down here for the work? This isn't your part of the world, then.' Early thought the other customers pricked up their ears at the barman's question. He was being cased. He doubted if any of these men were Provisionals, but they no doubt knew people who were, and in a small village like Crossmaglen, every outsider was both a novelty and a subject for scrutiny.

'Aye, I'm from Ballymena meself, up in Antrim.'

'Paisley's country.'

Early laughed. 'That big cunt. Oh aye, he's my MP. How's that for a joke?' Again, the slight relaxation of tension.

'If you're looking for work, you've come to the right place,' the barman said. 'The army never stops building in this neck of the woods. Their bases are as big as the town is. They're crying out for builders.'

Early scowled. 'I wouldn't fucking work for them if they paid me in sovereigns. No offence.'

The barman grinned.

'Would there be a B & B in the town? I need a place to stay — if these Lavery people take me on.'

The barman seemed to have relaxed completely, and was all bonhomie now. 'This is your lucky day. I've a couple of rooms upstairs I rent out in the summer.'

'Ah, right. What's the damage?'

'Fiver a night.'

Early thought, frowning. He had to appear short of cash. 'That's handy, living above a pub. Wee bit pricey though. How about knocking it down a bit, since I'd be here for a while, like. It's not like I'm some tourist, here today and gone tomorrow.'

'You get this job, and then we'll talk about it.'

'That'll do. I'm Dominic by the way.'

'McGlinchy?'

Early laughed. Dominic McGlinchy was the most wanted man in Ireland.

'McAteer.'

'Brendan Lavery,' the barman said, extending his hand. 'It's my brother you'll be working for.'

Early, blessing his luck, had been about to walk out to Rathkeelan to see about the job, but Brendan wouldn't hear of it. His brother, Eoin, would be in that night, he said. There was no problem about the job. Dominic could look the room over and have a bite to eat. Maggie, their younger sister, would be home from work in a minute, and she'd throw something together for them.

The room was small and simple but well kept, with a narrow bed, wardrobe, chair, dresser and little table. Through the single window Early could see the narrow back alleyways and tiny gardens at the rear of the street, and rising above the roofs of the farther buildings, the watch-towers of the security base with their anti-missile netting and cameras and infrared lights. He shook his head. It was hard to believe sometimes.

The door to the room had no lock, which was not surprising in this part of the world. Ulster had little crime worth speaking of that was not connected to terrorism, and this was, after all, Lavery's home he was staying in, not a hotel.

At the end of the long landing was the bathroom. Early ran his eyes over as much of the upstairs as he could, noting possible approach routes and escape routes. It had become second nature to him to view each place he stayed in as both a fortress and a trap. Satisfied, he went back downstairs.

The pub was filling up. Brendan Lavery was deep in conversation with a group of men at one end of the bar. Early immediately clocked two of them: Dermot McLaughlin and Eugene Finn, both players, and almost certainly members of the Provisional IRA's South Armagh brigade. Finn was an important figure. He had been a 'blanket man' in the Maze in the late seventies, before the Republican hunger strike that had resulted in eleven prisoners starving themselves to death. The Intelligence Corps believed that Finn might be the South Armagh Brigade Commander. McLaughlin was almost certainly the Brigade Quartermaster, in charge of weapons and explosives.

There was a woman at the bar: quite striking, dark-haired and green-eyed – a real Irish colleen.

She seemed to be selling newspapers. When she saw Early she immediately approached him.

'*An Phoblacht*?'

'Eh? Oh aye, sure.' He bought an edition of the IRA newspaper and she smiled warmly.

'Brendan says you'll be staying with us for a while.'

'Aye, looks that way, as long as the work appears.'

'It will. I'll have the dinner ready in an hour. Why don't you have a chat with the boys?'

'You're Maggie, right?'

'That's right. And you're Dominic, from Ballymena. We don't get many Antrim men down here.'

'Maybe it's the climate.'

'Or the Brits.' She laughed teasingly. She was disturbingly attractive, Early thought. He did not like that. He did not want any distractions.

'You know, I haven't bought this for ten years,' he said lightly, holding up the paper. 'I've been across the water, building and digging all the way from London to Glasgow.'

'Ach, I thought maybe there was something in your accent.'

Early's blood ran cold, but he smiled at her and said: 'You pick these things up. Now I'm home I'll get rid of it. It's nice not to have some bastard calling you "Paddy" all the time. If there's one thing gets up my nose, it's that. Bloody English never stop to think we've names of our own.'

'You're right there – sure, they haven't a clue. It's a roast for tea, and spuds and cauliflower. That suit you?'

'Depends on how it's cooked.'

She laughed. 'Ach, don't you worry about that, Dominic. I'll keep the flesh on you.' Then she left, exiting via the door behind the bar.

Early wondered if he had been wise with his remarks about England. He didn't want to lay it on too thick.

He leaned on the bar.

'How about a pint there, Brendan? And sure, have one yourself. I have to keep me landlord sweet,' he called.

The barman laughed but Finn and McLaughlin did not. They were appraising Early frankly. He buried his face in *An Phoblacht*. Two 'volunteers' had been killed on active service in Tyrone. The SAS were suspected. It was, the paper said, a typical SAS assassination. The men had been unarmed; the weapons they had been found with planted on them after death.

'Bastards,' Early said softly, shaking his head.

'Aye, those fuckers get away with murder,' said a voice at this elbow.

It was Finn, standing beside him.

Early remained sorrowful and angry. 'It never

stops, does it. Young boys dying in ditches. Will they ever leave us alone?'

Brendan Lavery set the brimming Guinness on the bar. 'Ach, sure, we're a good training ground for them. They don't give a damn. We're a nation of murderers to them.'

'Ireland unfree shall never be at peace,' Finn quoted, and drank from his own glass. Then he addressed Early again.

'You and me's going to be working together, Dominic.'

Early started. 'What?'

'Eoin – Brendan's brother – he's hit the big time, hasn't he, Brendan? He's taking on the world and his wife at the minute to build these bungalows they've contracted him for. Hiring all round him he is, like some Yank executive. Mind you' – Finn laid a finger against his nose – 'it's all on the $\overline{QT}$. Most of the men working for him will be doing the double.' He meant that they were also on the dole. Finn and Lavery laughed together, and Early forced himself to smile.

'If it comes to that, the taxman doesn't know *I* exist, either.'

'That's the way it's meant to be, Dominic. Take all you can off the bastards, and give nothing back. So how did a Ballymena man hear about a job in Cross?'

'Ach, a man in the Crown in Belfast told me,' Early said, quite truthfully.

Finn nodded. 'A black hole, Ballymena. You'd not get a job up there, if you're the wrong colour.'

'Bloody right,' Early agreed sincerely. North Antrim was a Unionist stronghold in the same way South Armagh was Republican. He sipped at his Guinness, realizing he was being cased again.

'But it's different down here. There's always a welcome here for the right sort of man. Isn't that right, Brendan?'

The barman's reply was lost in the growing hubbub. The evening crowd was gathering and the TV was blaring at what seemed like full volume. Early would have liked to scan the crowd for familiar faces, as he had studied the mugshots of all the South Armagh players before travelling down. But he did not dare with Finn standing next to him.

Finn was a tall, slim man, grey-haired but fit-looking. He had a narrow, ruddy face with deep-set eyes that seldom smiled, even if the mouth did. He was responsible for a spate of sectarian murders in the late seventies, but all that had been pinned on him in court was possession of arms and IRA membership. He had once been quartermaster of the Armagh bunch, but had been promoted on his release from the Maze. An experienced man, he had many years' practice in killing, extortion and gunrunning. He knew who the Border Fox was, without a doubt, but it was unlikely that the sniper was Finn himself. He had graduated into a leader, a planner. He was a survivor from the early days of the Troubles, and hence the object of much respect in the Republican community.

Early would have liked to take him out behind the pub and put a bullet in the back of his fucking head, but instead he offered him a drink.

'Na, thanks, Dominic. I'll take ye up on it some other time, but tonight I have to keep me wits about me.'

Was there an op on tonight? Early wondered.

Finn leaned close. 'You're new here. Let me give ye a wee bit of advice. Don't let the bastards provoke you, or you'll get hauled in the back of a pig. They're pissed off at the minute because things have been a wee bit hot for them down here, but believe me, that's just the beginning. Now just keep your cool.' Finn looked at his watch, and then winked at Early.

The door of the pub burst open, startling those sitting next to it. A glass crashed to the floor in an explosion of beer. Men got to their feet cursing.

British soldiers were shouldering in through the door. They were in full combat uniform, with helmets and flak-jackets and cammed-up faces. An English voice shouted: 'Don't you fucking move!'

Eight soldiers, a full section, were in the pub now. Lights from vehicles outside were illuminating the front of the building. The crowd had gone silent.

'Turn off that fucking TV!' the English voice yelled, and Brendan pressed a button on the remote control, muting the volume.

'What the fuck?' Early said, genuinely surprised. Finn gripped his arms tightly. 'Don't move. The fuckers are just trying to annoy us.'

While four soldiers remained by the door, rifles in the shoulder, two pairs were walking through the pub, looking at faces. One of them kicked a chair over, receiving murderous looks, but no one said a word.

A soldier stopped in front of Finn and Early. He had a corporal's stripes on his arm.

'Hello, Eugene, me old mucker,' he said brightly. 'How's things, then?'

Finn looked him in the eye. 'I'm fine, thanks, Brit.'

The corporal grinned, his teeth bright in his darkly camouflaged face. 'Who's your friend? Any ID, mate?'

He was addressing Early. The SAS man tensed,

then said clearly: 'Fuck off, you Brit bastard. Why can't you leave us alone?'

The soldier's grin vanished.

'That's not very polite, Paddy.'

'My name's not Paddy.'

'Give me some ID now, you fucking mick,' the corporal snarled.

Early produced his fake ID, a driver's licence issued in Coleraine. The corporal looked it over, then stared closely at him.

'You're a long way from home, Paddy.'

'So I've been told.'

The soldier nodded at Finn. 'I'd keep better company if I were you.'

'I'll keep the company I fucking well choose to. This is my country, not yours.'

'Have it your own way, arsehole. Outside now – and you too, Eugene. We don't want your friend getting lonely.'

Finn looked weary. 'Why don't you just drop it?'

The corporal gestured with the muzzle of his SA-80. 'Fucking outside – *now*. You can get there on your own two feet or you can be carried out – it's your choice.'

For once, Early was unsure what his reaction should be. He hesitated, but Finn gripped his arm again.

'Let's get it over with. Sure, all this wee shite

wants it to put the boot in, and there's no point in wrecking Brendan's bar.'

'Don't you worry about my bar, Eugene,' Brendan called out. 'I'll claim the fucking lot back in compensation.'

But Finn and Early trooped out unresisting into the night. Army vehicles were parked there, their headlights blindingly bright. A hand shoved Early in the small of his back.

'In the fucking wagon, mick.'

Someone tripped him and his palms went down on the tarmac. A boot collided with his backside, sending him sprawling again. He felt the first stirrings of real anger. These pricks would certainly win no hearts and minds in this town.

He was pushed and shoved into the dark interior of an armoured Landrover. He heard Finn shouting, the sound of blows, and was dimly aware that people were pouring out of the pub into the square. There was a ragged surf of shouting, the beginnings of a mob. Then the metal door of the Landrover was clanged shut behind him.

A light flicked on. Sitting in the vehicle grinning at him was Cordwain.

4

'Well well, John,' Cordwain said. 'We meet again.'

They were not alone in the back of the Landrover. A third man sat there on one of the narrow seats in an SAS-pattern combat smock. He looked young, pink-cheeked, and he stared at Early with obvious fascination.

Cordwain, as always, was breezy and confident. He helped Early off the floor. Outside there was the sound of people screaming and yelling. Stones rebounded off the armoured sides of the vehicle and it swayed at bodies pushed against it. Cordwain tapped the partition that divided the driver's section from the back, for all the world like a millionaire signalling to his chauffeur. The engine roared into life and the vehicle began reversing.

'Sounds as though we've stirred up a bit of trouble,' Cordwain said. 'But that's all for the best.'

'Who are this lot?' Early asked. 'Greenjackets?'

'Yes. They've been here for four months, and they've lost four men.'

'Well, they're fucking heavy-handed.'

'They were meant to be. I'm trying to give you a bit of street cred in the Republican community. Also, we need to talk.'

Early looked at the third occupant of the Landrover. The vehicle was lurching, starting and stopping. The shouting outside continued.

'Who is this, then?'

'Lieutenant Charles Boyd, Ulster Troop,' the young man said. He had a public-school accent and didn't look old enough to grow a beard, but his eyes were cold and eager. They reminded Early of Eugene Finn's. There was no humour in them.

'So you're my back-up,' Early said. 'Hooray.'

Boyd frowned but Cordwain cut short any riposte.

'Charles here is one of the best young officers we've got,' he said. 'You may have heard of the incident in Tyrone a few days ago. Textbook stuff. Now you and he are going to do the same thing to the South Armagh Brigade.'

'The Armagh lot is a different kettle of fish. Since that fiasco at Loughgall in '87 they're tighter-knit than ever.'

'Oh, we know. But you seem to have started

out on the right foot, becoming buddies with the biggest player in the area. My congratulations, John. You've been here less than a day and already you're rubbing shoulders with the head honcho.'

'Let's cut the crap, James. I can't sit in here in the middle of a riot all night. Give me the gen.'

'All right. The situation is as follows. I have most of the Group in Bessbrook at the moment, and 14 Company's people have covert OPs going in tonight. The riot is their cover. We'll search a few houses, insert the teams in the confusion – the usual thing.'

'How did you know I'd be in the bar?' Early interrupted.

'Hell, John, you should know better than that. You've been tailed ever since you got on the bus in Armagh.'

Early felt slightly annoyed with himself, for he had not noticed.

'We'll have the bar, Finn's house and McLaughlin's house all covered. Charles's boys will be looking after you. We'll use the old dead letterbox system for messages. Out beyond the centre beyond the town. You go out on the Castleblaney road, past the sports ground, and there will be an old milk churn in the ditch on the left-hand side. We site vehicle checkpoints there all the time. Leave your first comms there.

We'll get word to you where the second will be. You should be able to go for a walk now and again – it's only a ten-minute stroll. In a place this small, we can't have the stuff that works in Belfast. Do you want a panic button installed? We could get it in your room tonight.'

Early shook his head. 'I want you to keep your distance as much as possible. These guys are nervous as cats already.'

'Have it your way, then. We've fibre optics, laser microphones, the whole heap, but you've got bugger-all but your wits and that peashooter you carry.'

'Suits me. Now I think it's time I was on my way, don't you?'

Cordwain listened to the commotion outside. It showed no signs of abating. 'Yes. There is one more thing though: we have to make it all look convincing. Nothing personal, John.'

Early cursed. 'Get on with it, then.'

Boyd punched him on the eye once, twice, three times. Early remained still, though the third punch produced a stifled groan from his lips.

'Lie down on the floor,' Boyd said in that plummy accent of his.

Early did so, and Boyd went to work on him with his boots. After a particularly savage kick in the ribs, Early vomited helplessly. Boyd grimaced. He was out of breath.

'Sorry, old chap. Got a bit carried away.'

Early spat out blood. 'I'll bet you did. Now throw me the fuck out of here.'

The rear door of the Landrover swung open and Early was pitched out head first. He hit the tarmac of the square heavily, coloured lights dancing brightly in his head, and for a moment could do nothing but lie there in the reek of the vehicle's exhaust fumes. There were feet around him. The tarmac was covered with fragments of glass and broken stone, and the sound of the crowd yelling seemed to hurt his very brain.

Strong hands grabbed him and hauled him away from the Landrover.

'Look what the fuckers did to him! The rotten bastards! Sure, he's never hurt a fly – only got here this afternoon.'

Early looked up painfully. It was Brendan Lavery, and beside him, Maggie. Her eyes were full of concern.

'Jesus, my head hurts.'

'They've split your head. Here, hold that hanky there. We'll get you inside. They did the same to Eugene. What a fucking wonderful country!'

He was dragged back to the bar, through a milling crowd of shouting people. The riot was impromptu, not staged like so many were, but it seemed no less vicious for all that. Soldiers were swinging batons, and Early heard the hollow boom of a plastic bullet being fired. Then there was a flare and a hiss, and the crowd was scattering. They were using CS. It was a hell of a way to rig up a meeting. He suspected that Cordwain and Boyd enjoyed it – it was just their fucking style.

People were coming back inside now, coughing and spluttering. Several of the pub's windows had been smashed to smithereens. Early noted the thick, flesh-coloured cylinder of a plastic bullet rolling on the floor, but the noise from outside was lessening. The CS had done the trick. His own nose began to tingle and he realized that the gas was seeping into the pub. A last trio of figures staggered inside and then the doors were closed. People pulled the curtains across the shattered windows, coughing, eyes streaming.

'How's your head now? Jesus, Dominic, you're going to have a hell of a shiner in the morning.' Maggie was looking at Early solicitously. There was dirt on her cheek and her hair was all over the place.

'I hope the dinner's not burned,' Early said, which got a laugh from her.

Suddenly Finn was there too, squatting down beside Maggie. His face was a mass of rising bruises and his lip was split and still oozing. But he grinned at Early.

'Didn't I tell you not to provoke them now? And there we are – a babe in arms taken out by the big bad soldiers and given a wee kicking. That's life in Cross for you, McAteer. Still want to stay?'

'Those bastards aren't getting rid of me. I hope the fuckers get shot,' Early croaked. And thinking of Boyd, he almost meant it.

Finn had become very grave. He wiped his split lip. 'If wishes were horses, beggars would ride. Do you see now, Ballymena man, what we're up against down here? There's no law in Cross except what we make ourselves. Those thugs can't represent the law or the government. How can they? The law operates by the consent of the governed, and we withhold our consent. They're as good as criminals.'

'Now, Eugene, don't you start,' Maggie admonished him. 'The man's just after getting beaten up and you're talking to him about politics.'

Finn rose, smiling. The smile still did not reach his eyes.

'You and me will have a wee talk about this another time, Dominic, after you've seen Eion Lavery and got yourself that job. It's a desperate shame when the Brits pull in a man like yourself and give him the once-over; a man who's never been part of anything no doubt, a man as innocent as the day is long. You take care now, and watch this wee girl. I think she has an eye for you.'

Maggie swatted Finn with the cloth, and he laughed. Then he touched his bruised face tentatively.

'Have they made a right mess of me then, Maggie?'

'No more of a mess then there was before,' she retorted.

'And here's me going to be playing the bodhran down in Kilmurry this week, with me face looking like a potato. I doubt none of the local lassies will be giving me so much as a look.'

'Ach, Eugene, sure you know they'll be round you like flies on a jampot, just as usual, especially when you tell them how you got your bruises.'

He winked at her. 'You may be right there, wee girl. I must be going now. I've a feeling it's going to be a busy night. You look after Dominic now. The poor man looks a bit pale.'

Finn left them and went over to the door of the bar. He looked out, and signalled to two other men in the pub. One of them was McLaughlin. The trio exited silently.

Maggie was blushing, Early realized. But he noted it with only one portion of his mind. The rest was taken up with Finn's words. Had they been an echo of suspicion? It was too hard to say. And that reference to Kilmurry – it was in the Republic, and Cordwain would want to know about that. He would have to get a message through via the dead letterbox. He groaned. His body felt like one massive bruise. That bastard Boyd had enjoyed it, the smooth-chinned little shite.

'Let me help you up to your room,' Maggie said, helping him to his feet. 'I'll bring you up your tea later – there's a world of clearing up to do here. Never you worry about anything Eugene says. He's a passionate man, so he is, but he has reason to be.'

'I don't think he likes me,' Early said.

'Ach, that's just his way. He was born suspicious. What you need now is a bite to eat and then some sleep. It's bound to have been a long day.'

When he was finally alone in his room, Early found that someone had been through his things, discreetly, but not discreetly enough. He half hoped that it wasn't Maggie. He liked her, he realized. Not only that, she might be a way in. She seemed to know a lot about what was going on in the town, and her bed was as good a place to pump her for information as any. Early grinned to himself at the image that thought conjured up.

Just so long as Finn had been convinced by the evening's little charade. Early disliked the flamboyance of men like Cordwain and Boyd. He instinctively felt that it was counter-productive, fuelling the current enmity between soldiers and locals in the town. It certainly did not make his own job any easier.

His head and ribs throbbed. His eye was closing over rapidly. The 'kicking' had been convincing enough, anyway.

He padded out of his room and down the hallway to the bathroom, to wet a towel for his eye. The light was on inside and the door was ajar. He peeked round the doorway carefully. Maggie was in there, her back to him as she leaned out the window. She was wearing a short bathrobe and he had a wonderful view of her long, pale legs, a glimpse of her round buttocks. She was talking to someone outside, and leaned out until Early thought she would flip over the sill and out the window. Despite the splendid sight before him, Early tried to listen in on her conversation, but could make out little. He ducked back hurriedly as she backed in from the window carrying something in her hands, something long and heavy wrapped in plastic.

Early tiptoed back along the landing, cursing silently. She had been holding an AK47.

There was uproar in Crossmaglen that night. The streets were full of the roar of engines. Saracen armoured cars and Landrovers, police 'Hotspurs' and 'Simbas' went to and fro disgorging troops and heavily armed RUC officers.

Sledgehammers smashed down doors and soldiers piled into houses amid a chaos of cursing and shouting, breaking glass, screaming children. Households were reduced to shambles as the Security Forces searched house after house, the male occupants spread-eagled against the sides of the vehicles outside, the females shrieking abuse.

Carpets were lifted up, the backs of televisions wrenched off, the contents of dressers and wardrobes scattered and trampled. In the confusion, a covert surveillance team from the Group were inserted into the disused loft of a house in the heart of the town and set up an OP, peering out at the world from gaps in the roof tiles or minute holes in the brickwork. Finally, their work done, the army and police withdrew, leaving behind them a trail of domestic wreckage and huddles of people staring at the chaos of their homes. It had all gone like clockwork. From their concealed position up above, the SAS team watched silently the comings and goings of the town.

5

Bessbrook

'At last, we have intelligence,' Cordwain said, with an almost visible glow of satisfaction.

Lieutenant Boyd raised an eyebrow. 'Our man has turned something up already, has he?'

'Yes and no.' The roar of a Wessex helicopter landing on the helipad outside rendered conversation impossible for a moment. Bessbrook had one of the busiest heliports in Europe. There were Lynxes, fragile little Gazelles, sturdy troop-carrying Pumas, and the old Wessexes, the workhorse of the British Army. The base itself was surrounded by a four-metre-high fence, topped with anti-missile netting and bristling with watch-towers and sangars. In the Motor Transport yard were a motley collection of Saracens, hard-roofed four-ton trucks, Landrovers and Q cars. Bessbrook was a mix of high-tech fortress, busy bus station and airport. In truth, it was also something of a slum for the assorted British Forces personnel who had to live within its cramped confines in the ubiquitous Portakabins, reinforced with concrete and sandbags against mortar attack.

'No,' Cordwain went on when he could hear himself speak. 'You may find it hard to believe, but the initial info comes from across the border, from the Special Branch section of the Gardai.'

Boyd was incredulous. 'The micks have turned something up, and they're handing it to us?'

'They're afraid, Charles. They think they may have stumbled across something big and they want us to pull their potatoes out of the fire for them.'

Cordwain turned to the wall of his office, on which was pinned a large, garishly coloured map of South Armagh. He tapped the map.

'I Corps has been given information by them of an Irish music festival which is to be held in the hamlet of Kilmurry, County Louth, in two days' time. Kilmurry is approximately one kilometre from the River Fane, which, as you know, marks the border between north and south in that part of the world. An ideal jumping-off point for any operation. This morning our man Early in Cross utilized the DLB and left a message informing us that Eugene Finn will be at that festival. The Gardai have also informed us that they have identified at least eight major players from Louth or Monaghan ASUs heading north towards the border. Their routes all converge on Kilmurry.'

'A regular PIRA convention,' Boyd said. 'Have we anything else?'

'No. But I believe that this is not just a confab, Charles. We've hit Cross pretty hard in the past few days. It's my belief the Provos are going to stage some kind of spectacular, and Kilmurry will be their base of operations. This bash is their cover.'

'And because this place is in the Republic, there's not a damned thing we can do about it,' Boyd said bitterly.

'Just so. I cannot authorize an incursion into the Irish Republic, Charles, and there is no time to refer it to the CLF or to the Secretary of State. Our hands are tied.'

'So what can we do?' Boyd asked.

'Like you, I would dearly love to launch a pre-emptive strike, but the risk of adverse publicity is too high. There will be hordes of people in Kilmurry once this festival gets under way. There is no question of moving in there – the Provos have planned that part of it well. But I believe they will move north once they have been fully prepped, to launch a strike somewhere in the vicinity of Cross. That we *can* do something about. Look at the map.'

Boyd joined his superior at the wall and

together they stared at the complex pattern of small roads and hills, villages and hamlets, rivers and bogs.

'See here, this dismantled railway, that more or less follows the line of the Fane?'

Boyd nodded, and Cordwain went on.

'There are old cuttings all along its length, ideal places to conceal a group of men and form them up for a riving crossing. The Fane is broad, so they'll need a boat. It'll be a night operation of course. I think they'll get themselves ferried across where the cuttings, the river and the border all meet. Here.' Cordwain's finger stabbed at a point on the map.

'Now look north, only half a kilometre. There's a hill here, with an old ring-fort on top. Drumboy Fort, it's called; we've had OPs on it in the past. There is your ideal spot to wait and intercept them. Good fields of fire in all directions, no civvy houses close by, and a perfect view of the river, and thus the border.'

'You don't expect them to be picked up by car, then?' Boyd asked. Cordwain shook his head.

'The nearest road is half a kilometre away. They'll have to move across country to get to it. And we have all the roads down there sewn up tighter than a nun's knickers. No, my belief is that they'll yomp it, move across country to some prearranged RV and then perhaps meet up with a few friends north of the border before moving in on their objective.'

'Which will be?'

Cordwain shrugged. 'I have no idea, though I have my suspicions. If you extend a line from the Fane up past Drumboy Fort, where does it take you?'

Boyd peered at the map, then burst out: 'The base! Crossmaglen security base! But that can't be right.'

'That's what I thought. It would be foolhardy, to say the least. But you'll have to bear in mind, Charles, that these jokers are after something big. Not a mortar – they'll be travelling too light for that. But an ambush, certainly, perhaps of a foot patrol. I think they intend to wipe out an entire patrol, engage it face to face and then blow it away.'

Boyd whistled softly. 'What about their strength?'

'This will be a big operation in their terms, comparable to Loughgall perhaps. I think you can bank on at least ten or twelve of them.'

They turned away from the map and resumed their seats. Another helicopter took off, loaded to the gills with men and equipment. It was a Greenjacket fire team being airlifted out on rural patrol.

'Fuck,' Boyd said clearly. 'This is all surmise

though, isn't it? All we know for sure is that a bunch of players will be at a music festival close to the border.'

'Indeed, but I'll bet both our arses they aren't attending it to sit and fiddle. No, they'll be moving north – you can count on it.'

Boyd's eyes shone. If he pulled off a large-scale ambush on a sizeable PIRA force it would be an enormous coup for the Government, the army and the SAS. But also for Lieutenant Charles Boyd.

'I have four men tied up in the OP in Cross itself, but twelve men available here, a multiple of three bricks. That should do it.'

Cordwain was not so sure.

'I'd rather fly in some of the Special Projects team from G Squadron in Hereford.'

'But we haven't the time. And we don't have enough evidence to go on. We'll have egg all over our faces if we get G Squadron all the way over here and then nothing materializes.'

Cordwain paused, clearly uneasy. 'There is that, of course . . .'

'James, twelve SAS troopers will take out anything the Provos can throw at them.' Boyd appeared invincibly confident. Cordwain studied him for a moment. The young officer clearly still felt himself to be on a roll after the successful Tyrone operation, and wanted to add further lustre to his laurels. That was no bad thing, so long as it did not lead to overconfidence. But his brashness was appealing, and it was true that they had very little to go on. Cordwain did not put a lot of faith in Early's chances of infiltrating the South Armagh Brigade, but here on a platter was a chance to wipe them out wholesale; the ultimate 'clean kill'.

'All right,' he said at last. 'I'll make out the necessary orders. But what I'm giving you is a reactive OP, Charles. I'm not giving you licence to run amok through the countryside. I want you to keep that stretch of the Fane under observation and only to react under the most stringent circumstances. The last thing we need is twelve troopers staging a rerun of the OK corral in Armagh. And we will also liaise with Lieutenant Colonel Blair of the Greenjackets. His men will form your back-up – and Early's – until this op is over. Is that clear?'

'Perfectly. If you'll excuse me then, James, I'll go and give the boys a Warning Order. They'll be chuffed to fuck.'

Boyd left like a schoolboy let out for the holidays. Cordwain stared at the map thoughtfully for a long time. It was disquieting, to say the least, to be sanctioning an operation with so little intelligence to go on, but then intelligence was so thin on the ground in this part of the world. Not like Tyrone, or Belfast, where there were 'Freds', renegade Republicans, aplenty.

If this operation turned out as successfully as he hoped they might even be able to dispense with Early's services, and that would be another bonus. Early was a hot potato, with his MI5 handlers to be placated and his stubborn bloody-mindedness. Not a team player, but then undercover agents seldom were.

Cordwain shook his head as though a fly buzzed at it, trying to free himself of a sense of unease. He had the strangest feeling that Boyd did not quite know what he was up against, and he had an urge to cancel the whole operation, or at least scale it down. But it was on his plate alone. He could not involve the RUC, because they were not equipped to deal with a face-to-face confrontation with a heavily armed band of terrorists, nor with the covert surveillance that was needed to track them down. No, this was a job for the SAS alone, the sort of mission that they specialized in and relished.

Why then the uneasiness?

He bent over his desk, and began writing the orders that would take Boyd's command out into Bandit Country.

6

Kilmurry, County Louth

The bar was crowded with people, hot, noisy, hazy with tobacco smoke. In one corner a knot of musicians were playing a frantic, foot-tapping jig and most of the throng were clapping and stamping in time with the music. Pint glasses, empty and full, stood by the hundred on the bar and the tables or were clasped in sweaty hands.

In the upstairs room the hubbub below could be heard as a vague roar of sound echoing up through the floorboards. The long upper room had been booked in the name of Louth Gaelic Football Club. The irritating noise seeping up from the noisy bar below would nullify the effectiveness of any bugs planted in the place.

There were twenty-three men in the room, sitting round a long dining table or lounging against the walls. Heavy duffle bags littered the floor and on the table itself crouched two angular, blanket-draped shapes. The men were smoking rapidly, talking in low voices, chuckling or scowling as the mood took them. They comprised the bulk of two PIRA brigades. Some of them were elated at their numbers, some were nervous.

Eugene Finn entered the room rubbing his hands and smiling his cold smile.

'Don't worry, boys. The dickers are all in place and the landlord knows the form. This is a private room. The Gardai will need a warrant to enter it and we happen to know they don't have one.'

'Aye, but what about when we leave?' one of the men asked sourly.

'When we leave, Seamus, there's not a force in the whole of Ireland that'll be capable of stopping us.'

'It's bloody madness,' Seamus Lynagh, commander of the Monaghan Brigade, exclaimed. 'It might be all right for you boyos in the north, but the Gardai will tail us all the way to the border, and when we come back they'll slap the cuffs on us.'

'They won't be able to tail you,' Finn said firmly.

'What are you, Eugene – a fucking magician?'

Some of the men laughed. Eugene Finn grinned humourlessly. 'Maybe I am, Seamus, maybe I am. Or maybe I'm Santa Claus. I come bearing gifts.'

He leaned over the table and with a swift gesture whipped the blankets from the shrouded forms standing there. Everyone straightened, and one man gave a low whistle.

Lying supported on the table by their bipods were two American-made 7.62mm M60 machine-guns, their barrels gleaming in the dim light of the room.

'Jesus, Mary and Joseph,' Lynagh breathed. 'Where'd you get them?'

'Courtesy of the US National Guard,' Finn smirked. 'A trawler picked them up for us. Caught them in its nets, so it did.'

Lynagh was running his hands over one of the weapons as though it were the body of a woman.

'These fuckers chew through concrete like it's paper. They're as good as the GPMGs that the Brits use. Better, maybe.'

'Are you willing to listen to the plan now?' Finn asked.

'Aye, I'll listen, Eugene. I won't promise you a bloody thing though, not till I've heard it through.'

Finn produced a pair of rolled-up maps and began pinning them to one wall. All the men immediately recognized the familiar contours of the border. For them it was home turf, the countryside of their very backyards.

'Here we are, boys, our feet tapping to jigs in Kilmurry here. Now look up to the border. See the old railway . . .'

'Sure, I know that place well,' one man put in. 'It's all overgrown with brambles and stuff. You could hide an army in there.'

'Thanks, Sean,' Finn said icily, and the man looked away, red in the face.

'That is where we form up, boys, all twenty-four of us: two platoons of twelve men each. I will take one, and Seamus the other. Each platoon will have an M60. But we're not moving out all in a bunch – far too easy for the Brits to keep tabs on us that way. No, we'll split up once we're across the river, Seamus's men going to the west of Drumboy Fort, and my lot going to the east. We'll meet up again in Clonalig, and there'll be two transits waiting for us there, ready to take us to the objectives.'

A storm of voices broke out.

'How are we getting across the river?'

'Who'll have the M60s?'

'Who's meeting us in Clonalig?'

But the main question was voiced by Seamus Lynagh as he held up a hand for quiet.

'What the fuck are we going to hit, Eugene?' he asked softly.

Finn smiled coldly, and jabbed the map with a finger.

'That. Crossmaglen RUC station. We're going to wipe the peelers off the face of the earth.'

Another storm of noise. Lynagh shook his head angrily.

'You're fucking crazy, Finn. The army will be all over us in minutes.'

'No, Seamus. You see, while your platoon is taking out the RUC station – just like Ballygawley, lads, eh? – my platoon will be covering the approach roads, ready to take out any reinforcements the peelers call in.'

'You're fucking mad,' Lynagh said, amazed.

'Twelve men, armed to the teeth. We have medium machine-guns, RPGs, even a fucking two-inch mortar. We'll make sure that not so much as a mouse gets out of that base. And if a mobile patrol comes along, then we'll fucking destroy it. What do you say, Seamus? Are you ready to go to war?'

Men were clamouring, laughing in the room, their eyes shining. Lynagh looked troubled.

'All right, Eugene, we're in. But Christ help you if this turns out to be another Loughgall.'

'It won't, Seamus. We're about to hit the Brits harder than they've ever been hit in Ireland before.'

It was a bright, sunny morning. Early rolled out of bed, groaning at the pain of his bruises. Saturday morning. He had, thankfully, the weekend in front of him before he had to start work as a labourer at Lavery's building site. He had his job, now. In fact he seemed to be quickly becoming a member of the family. He smiled, remembering the sight of Maggie's long legs and taut buttocks in the bathroom, then frowned as he remembered what she had in her hands. They were all in it up to their necks, even the bloody women. Still, it meant that if he made any progress with her he would be furthering the cause of British intelligence as well as getting his end away. The thought made him grin again.

Automatically, he reached under the bed and checked the automatic and the spare mags, tucked into his shoe. A daft place to conceal a weapon, which is why no one ever looked there.

He wondered if the DLB had worked, if Cordwain had got the message about Finn. Early didn't like the system. It was old, prone to tampering, and somehow amateurish. But there was no chance they could use the 'live letterbox' here: a man in a Q car waiting to debrief and brief him at some prearranged spot. It was too risky. The whole bloody thing was too risky.

Maggie was cooking breakfast for her two brothers when Early came downstairs, yawning and scratching his head. There was a delicious smell of cooking bacon in the air.

'Jesus, Dominic, your face looks like a wee one's finger-painting,' Brendan said, pouring him a cup of tea.

'Feels like a bloody football, so it does,' Early said, touching his swollen eye gingerly. But then he turned to Eoin Lavery, his employer, who was munching on fried soda bread silently.

'Don't worry though. I'll be at work on Monday morning all right.'

Eoin waved a fork. 'Ach now, Dominic, Brendan here has been telling me what those bastards – excuse me, Maggie – did to you. There's no rush. We'll give it to Tuesday, and if you do a bit of overtime towards the end of the week, sure we'll say that makes up for it.'

'Thanks, Eoin,' Early said. Maggie set a heavily laden plate in front of him, smiling. 'There, get that down you, Dominic.' She was wearing a floral-print dress that seemed to emphasize the curves of her figure. Early's fork paused halfway to his mouth as he watched her walk back towards the kitchen, the morning light catching the reddish glints in her hair. When he remembered to eat again he found both the Lavery brothers grinning at him like clowns.

He lingered after breakfast, rehearsing in his mind the route to the second DLB point, speculating on what Finn was up to across the border, and thinking about how satisfying it would be to feel his fist impacting with Boyd's nose. Then he started as he realized that Maggie was talking to him.

'What? Sorry, I was a thousand miles away, so I am.'

'That's all right, Dominic. I was aking you if you'd like to go for a wee walk this afternoon. It's such a lovely day.'

'I'd love to, aye,' he said, and found that he meant it.

It was warm, and the sun was high and bright in a blue sky. Very un-Irish weather, Early thought, and almost said so to the girl walking beside him until he realized how odd it would sound, and cursed himself for his lack of concentration. He was effectively behind enemy lines here, even though he could see the watch-towers of Cross Security Forces base less than a mile away, and could make out a Lynx sinking down, distant as a dragonfly, bringing another brick back from rural patrol.

They sat down on the springy turf and Maggie opened the small bag she had brought with her. They were on a hillside to the south of Cross, and could look down to where the Fane meandered through the hills and faded into the distance. The Republic of Ireland lay on the far side of the river's sunlit bank. It was hard to believe in the savage little war which flickered to and fro over such beautiful country as this. It all looked too peaceful and quiet to harbour anything more sinister than the odd poacher.

Maggie produced a bottle of white wine, two glasses and a corkscrew. She asked Early to do the honours, and as he wrestled with the cork she produced a small pair of binoculars and began sweeping the land to the south with them.

'What are you looking for?' he asked her lightly, pouring the wine.

'Birds,' she said absently. 'You get some very odd birds about here at this time of year.'

'I'll bet.'

She lowered the binoculars and sipped her wine. 'Good stuff this, so it is. I hope Brendan won't miss it.'

'So you've brought me out birdwatching, then,' he said.

'Yes. I hope you don't mind, Dominic.'

'Ach, no.' He lay back in the grass and closed his eyes, letting the sun warm him, but despite his appearance his heart was beating fast. Maggie was checking the lie of the land south to the border and Kilmurry, where Finn was skulking. And what was more, she had the newcomer with her, so she could keep an eye on him. Early smiled to himself. She was a smart girl, killing two birds

with one stone. He would have to get another
message through to Cordwain, let him know that
there might be something happening down along
the Fane valley. Tonight perhaps.

The Lynx roared overhead, flattening the grass
and billowing Maggie's hair out behind her. She
watched its flight path intently, and nodded to
herself, no doubt noting it down as routine. Early
tried not to let his tension show. Here was his
chance to find out what was going down. Clearly
Finn's absence and Maggie's birdwatching were
connected.

'Tell me about yourself,' he said. 'How come
a pretty wee girl like you wasn't married off
years ago?'

She looked at him. 'I was married.'

'What happened?'

Again, the practised sweep with the binoculars.

'He was shot by the Brits. They said he
was in the IRA, and he was supposed to have
been caught in some ambush. When he died I
took back my old name. That was two years
ago.'

'What was your married name then?'

'Kelly.'

Early thought fast. Two years ago one Patrick
Kelly had died in the abortive attack on Loughgall
RUC station, along with seven other Provisionals.
It had been the SAS's biggest success in Northern

Ireland, and had effectively wiped out the East Tyrone Brigade. Kelly, a hot-head, had been an IRA quartermaster. He had been shot down, rifle in hand, in the road outside Loughgall.

He opened his eyes. This woman was very probably at the heart of the South Armagh Brigade. She probably knew who the Border Fox was.

'I'm sorry,' he said.

She smiled down at him. 'That's all right. He was an eejit, was Patrick; a lovely man, but like a wee boy sometimes. He made me feel like his mother.'

She looked like a young schoolteacher, or a young mother, not like the hardened activist Early now knew her to be. He reached up a hand and brushed her cheek gently. She did not pull away.

'Did you never think of leaving?'

'Never. My family is here, my life is here. One day I'll be here still and they' – she tossed her head at the frowning watch-towers of the base – 'they'll be gone, and Ireland will be at peace at last.'

Early felt the beginnings of irritation at hearing the old platitudes come so easily from such a young mouth. If British 'occupation' ended, then everything would be hunky-dory. Their minds all worked the same way. It was like hearing parrots mouth words they could not understand. But he did not let his irritation show. Instead he gently pulled her head towards him, and brushed her lips with his own. He felt an answering caress for a moment, then she pulled away. She was blushing, he realized, like some schoolgirl on a date.

'If ever you need any help, or anyone to turn to, Maggie, then I'd be happy if you thought of me,' he said softly.

She stared out over the lush green landscape that marked the border between two countries, a decades-old battlefield.

'Thanks, Dominic, but I hardly even know you.'

Then she took up the binoculars again, and began scanning the border as alertly and professionally as a soldier in an OP.

7

Drumboy Hill, South Armagh

Boyd stopped in the dark of the night and turned to Haymaker.

'What do you make that, then?'

'Four hundred, boss, give or take a metre.'

Boyd nodded. One more leg to go and they were at the final RV before the objective. Haymaker was pacer for the multiple, and was counting out the metres they logged on each bearing of the compass they navigated by.

Boyd looked at the tiny luminous arrows on the compass, lined them up, and found a reference point in that direction. It was not easy. It had clouded, and the night was as black as pitch. They were navigating by bearings and pacings alone, cross-checking when they came to a road or track, or a slope, which would be a huddle of brown contour lines on the tiny map. Most of the map Boyd had memorized, so as to avoid checking it during the 'tab', or Tactical Advance by Bounds. Once, however, he had had to get it

75

out, throw a poncho over his head to hide the glow of the minuscule red penlight, and then continue on his way.

He was that most dangerous of phenomena found on a battlefield, an officer with a map. The thought would have made him grin had he been less knackered.

Every man in the twelve-strong multiple was weighed down with over one hundred pounds of equipment, weaponry and ammunition. They were supposed to range over the ground in three four-man fire teams, their arcs of fire supporting each other, but it was so dark that they were in single file, every man occasionally touching the bergen on the back of the man in front to check he was still in the file. Navigation-wise, the pitch-darkness was a pain in the arse, but it was a blessing also. It meant that, barring disasters, they would make it to the objective completely unobserved.

They set off again. Boyd was his own point man – something tactically unsound, which he personally did not like, but as he was navigating, there was no alternative. Farther back in the stumbling, sweating and quietly cursing file the sergeant, Gorbals McFee, was check-navigating to make sure the young officer did not go astray. Gorbals was a tiny Glaswegian who was none-theless one of the most frightening men Boyd had ever known. Five foot six, with a shock of violently red hair and a temper to match, he had been in the SAS since before the Falklands, and when Boyd could decipher his accent, he found him to be a superb soldier and NCO.

The weaponry and equipment of the troopers were plentiful and varied. Boyd carried an Armalite AR15 rifle, as did most of the others. But there were two 7.62mm General Purpose Machine Guns in the team also, as well as three M79 grenade-launchers, which looked vaguely like huge, single-barrelled shotguns. In addition, each man had a 9mm Browning High Power pistol holstered at his thigh, for all the world, Boyd thought, like the Lone Ranger.

But that was what they were, he realized. The guys in white hats, the posse out to get the villains.

Every trooper carried, in addition to his own personal ammunition, a belt of two hundred rounds for the GPMGs, a pair of fragmentation and smoke grenades, and a claymore anti-personnel mine. A particularly ugly little weapon, the claymore was a shaped charge of P4 which would blow several hundred ball-bearings in the face of any attacker and could be set off manually or by a trip-wire. It was ideal for perimeter security, as the Americans had found in Vietnam.

Two men each carried in addition a 66mm

Light Anti-tank Weapon. A recoilless shoulder-fired missile, the '66' was light and easy to use, and was a single-shot throw-away item. It was very rarely carried in Northern Ireland, but Boyd had brought along a couple in case the opposition had RPG7 rocket-launchers. He believed in fighting fire with fire.

Other men in the multiple were weighed down with a variety of night-surveillance equipment and two of them were carrying 'Classic', a motion detector which was to be buried in the ground to detect the vibration of approaching footsteps. All in all, Boyd thought, they were equipped to fight a minor war all on their own.

He did not know it, but that was exactly what they would have to do.

They reached the objective. There was a faint wind blowing and the cloud was clearing somewhat. It was becoming a little lighter. There might even be a moon later on, though Boyd hoped not.

The multiple shrugged off their bergens within the earth banks of the old ring-fort on Drumboy Hill, and went into all-round defence. Individual Weapon Sights were switched on, NVGs swung down over their eyes. The SAS troopers waited for any sign that they had been followed or otherwise compromised. Thirty minutes they lay there, unmoving, and then Gorbals McFee went round the hollow ring, tapping each man's boot with his own.

The men worked in pairs. As one remained alert and on guard, the other got out an entrenching tool and began digging. Still others left the fort to sight the claymores so that they would blow laterally across every approach to the perimeter, and one fire team under Haymaker took 'Classic' out with them to seed the approaches from the south with the buried sensors. He would bury the sensors, leaving only the tiny whip-antennae above ground, and would map their locations for later retrieval. Each of the sensors, Gorbals had been careful to explain to him, was worth £5000, and if he lost any it would be docked out of his pay.

Haymaker was not sure if the little Glaswegian had been joking or not, but he didn't intend to take any chances. He had squared greaseproof paper folded in his pocket to make a foot-by-foot grid of the area where the sensors were to be buried.

The men remaining within the banks of the earth fort dug shell scrapes and began camouflaging them with scrim nets and local vegetation. They would have to lie up in the fort for a day at least, waiting for the Provos to make their move, and they could not afford to be discovered by any of the locals.

No light was allowed, and no one spoke. The PRC 351 man-portable radio was set on whisper, but radio silence was to be maintained until contact. Boyd also had a 'SARBE', a surface-to-air rescue beacon, which was only to be used as a last resort, if the multiple needed to leave in a hurry. He could not imagine needing it.

The troopers were all wearing 'goon boots': rubber overshoes that fitted their combat boots and left no distinctive army-boot tread-marks for the locals to find and examine later. But they made the feet uncomfortably hot. Conversely, the men's bodies were beginning to chill as the exertion of the night march wore off and the breeze hit the sweat that slicked their bodies and dampened their clothes. A few dug out thick Norwegian shirts from their bergens, but most were content to shiver and wait for the summer dawn, which was only a few hours off.

Haymaker made it back in, hands raised above his head so that the sentries would know who it was. The claymores were armed and the men retired to their camouflaged scrapes. Soon the old ring-fort was quiet as the men took turns at grabbing a few minutes' sleep. They were in position, ready for the show to begin.

8

Crossmaglen

Sunday morning. Early was at mass with the Laverys in St Patrick's, Cross's parish chapel. He was wearing a tie, something he hated, and Maggie was sitting beside him with her prayer-book in her lap and the sunshine was coming through the stained-glass windows setting her tawny hair aflame with colour and light. She was beautiful, Early thought, but also dangerous. And she had seemed tense all this morning, hardly speaking a word to him. He was sure that today, or tonight, Finn had something planned. He wondered if that gut feeling were worth a message via the DLB, and decided not.

He had hardly been out of Maggie's sight for a day and a half. Either she liked having him near her, or she was suspicious of him and was keeping him where she could keep an eye on him. Early did not like it. It had all been too easy, had happened too quickly, and his beating up at the hands of the 'Brits' could not completely explain her solicitude.

81

Suddenly he was glad of the often irritating weight of the pistol at his ankle.

The service went on and on. Early's mind wandered. He began thinking of Jeff, his younger brother, who had died in this very town, his head ripped off by a high-calibre bullet. There had been seven years between them, so they had never been as close as Early would have liked – sometimes more like uncle and nephew than anything else. Jeff would have tried for the SAS in time, and would have made it, Early thought. He had been more of a team player, who got along with everybody. Little Jeff, his brother, whose dying body the mobs had laughed over in Crossmaglen. Early wondered suddenly if Maggie had been there, jeering over the body with the rest. The thought made his face ugly with hatred, and he bowed his head so the priest might not see it.

Mass ended at last, and they trooped out into the July sunshine. Maggie took Early's arm.

'Come on, Dominic, I'll walk you home. The roast will take a wee while yet in the oven, so there's no hurry.'

They strolled arm in arm down the street towards the square. The kerbstones here were painted green, white and orange and Early could see the Irish tricolour flying from several flagpoles.

A four-man foot patrol passed them on both sides of the street, SA-80s held upwards in the 'Belfast Cradle'. The NCO gave Early's face a quick look, then moved on. Had Early been identified as a player, the soldier would have engaged him in conversation. It was both a subtle form of harassment and intelligence-gathering at its most basic level.

Maggie looked through the soldiers as though they didn't exist.

'Tell me about yourself, Dominic. You're a Ballymena Catholic, which is rare enough. Your family's still up in Antrim, then?'

Early's mind clicked through all his bogus background. It had been carefully researched for him, and the fact that his roots truly did lie in the north of the Province helped him with his falsehoods.

'Ach, I was a late child, so I was, and an only one. Me ma and da are both dead this five years. After me ma went I left the place, decided to chance me arm across the water, you know – building like, and bar work. I was all over the place. But I came back. We never fitted in over there, not really. They always see you as a thick mick when it comes to the crunch. And I swore I'd never let another Brit call me "Paddy" as long as I lived. I suppose that's what got me this.' He touched his black eye.

Maggie squeezed his arm. 'Just right. We don't mix, Dominic, the Brits and us. Ach, they're not all bad, but once the English and Irish get together, there's always trouble. There's too much water under the bridge, too many years of oppression.'

Too much claptrap talked, Early thought, but he only nodded to her words.

'We're fighting a war here in the North, Dominic. Ireland needs all her sons.' Suddenly she stopped. In a moment her arms were around him and she was kissing him lightly on his lips. He felt her palms flat against his back and thanked his lucky stars that he had never worn a shoulder-holster.

'What was that for?' he asked her when she released him.

'For standing up for yourself in the bar that night. For not just being polite or careful. I think you have a stubborn streak in you, Dominic. I don't think you like to take things lying down.'

Early laughed. 'You may be right there.'

They walked on, and finally came back to the bar. Brendan was in the lounge, wiping tables. He nodded and grunted as they came in. The place was full of the smell of roasting meat, potatoes and rich gravy.

'Come upstairs,' Maggie said to Early, and led him by the hand.

They went into her room, an airy, cushion-covered place with a wide bed and pastel-coloured walls. Early began to sweat. She shut the door.

They sat on the bed and she took him by the hands again.

'Listen, Dominic, you said that I could turn to you for help any time I needed it.'

'I did. And you said you hardly knew me, which is true.' His voice sounded hoarse. He was trying to discreetly note any other way out, wondering what kind of field of fire the window would give. The gun strapped to his ankle suddenly seemed huge, obtrusive.

'Aye, I did. But I have a feeling about you, Dominic. We need people like you. Men who aren't afraid to stand up for themselves, who have common sense, who share our views.'

'Who's we?' Early asked. Her hand loosened his tie and begun unbuttoning his shirt.

'I think you know, Dominic. The Volunteers. The men who are fighting to make Ireland free.'

She drew close. Her hand slipped inside his shirt and was caressing his chest. She kissed his neck. There was something clinical, determined about her that made Early tense.

She was looking for a concealed weapon.

'Shiner or no, you're a lovely-looking man, you know that? You're all muscle.'

'It's the work,' he said lamely. He was torn

between lust and fear. Her perfume rose in his nostrils. He kissed her lips, her ear, but was frantically trying to figure out how he could keep the ankle-holster concealed.

'You're just out of mass,' he said. 'Funny time to be doing a thing like this.'

Her hand had found his penis, and was carressing it gently. He could not help but respond.

'Oh, I know. It's a great sin, isn't it?'

'You'll let the roast burn in the oven, then?'

'To hell with the roast. What do you think, Dominic? Are you willing to help me? Are you willing to help your country?'

'Yes. Yes I am.'

She grinned at him, then bent her head and in a moment had taken his swollen member into her mouth. Early groaned as she worked on it, sucking and licking, her head moving up and down in his crotch. He buried his hands in her glorious hair, incredulous, but profoundly relieved.

Thank Christ, he thought. I managed to keep my trousers on.

Late that same Sunday, across the border, the room above the Kilmurry bar was humming with activity. Weapons, ammunition and other items of military equipment were scattered all over the floor. Men were oiling their rifles, loading magazines, or packing small rucksacks in preparation for the operation that night. In a quieter corner, Eugene Finn and Seamus Lynagh were going over the plan yet again.

'So this boat you have arranged will make two trips across the Fane, twelve men each time, and the drop-off points will be different,' Lynagh said.

'Aye,' Finn replied wearily. 'You'll be dropped off further to the west, about a mile south of Art Hamill's bridge. My ASUs will cross where the Fane sends out the fork to the north. We'll be almost a kilometre apart but we want to be sure we don't fire on each other by mistake. You have your radio. Only use it in an emergency. It's on an unused frequency, but if something happens the Brits may well start frequency-hopping on the off chance of listening in on us. We can't let them suspect our numbers – that's the key to the whole plan. We'll be the biggest and best-armed unit for miles around, so even if we run into something unexpected, there's no need to panic. We'll just blow it away.'

'I wasn't thinking of panicking,' Lynagh said coldly.

'I know, Seamus, but the instinct has always been to hit and run because up to now we've always been outnumbered and outgunned. This time we have the staying power to fight it out toe to toe with the bastards. If you hit something, bring up the M60 and level it.'

'And the escape routes?'

'The cars will be ready and waiting for us, six of them. Once the op is accomplished we pile in and put our foot down. The West Belfast Brigade is expecting us – they have three safe houses ready. We'll lie low for a few weeks before coming home.'

'I still think it would be a hell of a lot simpler to just duck back across the border, Eugene.'

'That's what the bastards will be expecting. And so will the Gardai. Remember they have this place under surveillance even as we speak. If we come running back across the Fane with guns in our hands then we'll be clapped in cuffs. No; we'll do what no one expects – head north. All the shit will be hitting the fan in Cross. They won't be expecting a move in the opposite direction.'

Lynagh nodded, and then said casually: 'What about the Fox? I take it he's in one of your ASUs?'

Finn laughed. 'No, Seamus, he is not. The Fox is a maverick. We give him back-up sometimes, but he doesn't like operating with a big bunch like this. No, he's in Cross at the minute, and he'll stay there.'

'We could do with him on this trip, so we could.'

'It's not his kind of show,' Finn said sharply.

Twenty-four men carrying duffle bags left the pub at irregular intervals through the late evening. They scattered, making their way to a dozen prearranged locations, where they changed into their overalls and Balaclavas, buckled on their webbing and rucksacks, and hefted their weapons. Then individually, in the dark, they made their separate ways to the banks of the Fane. The monitoring Gardai Special Branch officers were lost in the maze of fields and woods and streams that interlocked all along the border. They could not even be sure of the numbers of the men involved, for the IRA had recruited a score of other sympathizers as decoys. They knew that something big was in hand, but as a result of delays, misunderstandings, and plain distrust, this information would not reach British Intelligence until it was too late.

The boat was there, a long, open craft with a single, sputtering outboard, although tonight it was operating under muscle power. Lynagh's brigade rowed it out into the middle of the river, the light of the stars glinting off the rippled water. It was not as dark as the night before and the terrorists could see the shadowy tangle of alder and willow that grew along the banks.

The boat scraped against the northern bank, and the Monaghan Brigade of the IRA disembarked on the soil of Northern Ireland. The boat shoved off, and now the little outboard sputtered into life and put-put-putted away to pick up Finn's brigade. The Monaghan men sat tight, Lynagh peering at the luminous dial of his watch every so often. They had to wait and give Finn's men time to cross before starting out themselves.

Finally, after what seemed an interminable time, the radio uttered a single squash of static. Lynagh nodded to himself and then gestured to the heavily armed men in the trees all around him. The three ASUs shook out and began trekking north to their objective. A kilometre away, Finn's men were doing the same.

9

Lieutenant Boyd rubbed his tired eyes and stared yet again out into the starlit darkness of the summer night. He could see little but the vast dark expanse of Armagh and then Louth rolling out in a broad valley beneath him, now and then punctuated by the twin lights of a moving car. There were no other lights for miles. It was a lonely, God-forsaken place.

Tonight. They had to make their move tonight. His men were all on edge – he could feel their mood as clearly as he could feel his own tiredness. They lay in a rough circle within the banks of the ancient ring-fort, invisible in the darkness underneath their scrim nets and other camouflage.

Gorbals tapped him lightly on the shoulder and offered him an AB ration biscuit with some processed cheese on top. 'Cheese possessed' the men called it. They had eaten nothing but cold tinned food since leaving Bessbrook, and the 'compo' was already having an effect. Boyd's bowels would not move for days, and when they did, the result would be spectacular. He took the biscuit nonethless, nodding at his troop sergeant.

It was like being in a circle of wagons waiting for the Indians to ride up. Boyd did not like the formation he had chosen for the multiple, but since they could not be exactly sure of the IRA approach route, he had decided that all-round defence was the safest bet. If he had had more intelligence on the enemy approach he would have posted cut-offs to thwart any escape and a main 'killing group'. That way there would be no survivors. For the hundredth time, he wondered if he had been wise. They would look bloody fools if the Provos slid past them in the dark and hit their target while all of Ulster Troop were stuck up on a hill with their thumbs up their bums.

For some reason he thought of the undercover agent in Cross, Early. A dour character, no doubt nursing all kinds of chips on his shoulder. Boyd would not have had his job for all the world. It was one thing to be here, in uniform with a rifle in his shoulder and his men all about him, quite another to be alone and virtually defenceless in the enemy heartland. Yes, Early must be having a miserable time, he thought, having to play a role all the time for those Fenian bastards.

Gorbals dug him in the ribs. The little

Glaswegian was staring at the Classic monitor. Boyd tensed. The sensors had picked up movement on the lower slopes of the valley. The monitor told him that it was travelling south to north, and that it was more than one man. Then the monitor went still again. The moving men had passed by. That would mean they were on the lower approaches to the hill itself, on the westward side. He found himself grinning at his troop sergeant, and Gorbals grinned back, his white teeth shining in his darkened face.

'Looks like they're on their way, boss,' the Scot whispered.

Boyd nodded. 'Tell the boys. A southern approach, as we thought, but coming up on the western slope. Haymaker's team will hit them first, but wait for my signal.'

Gorbals slithered off to do the rounds of the little perimeter. He was as silent as a snake moving through the harsh upland grass. Boyd checked his Armalite, the familiar adrenalin flush doing away with his tiredness. He felt awake and alive now to his very fingertips, as though his body were hovering a fraction of an inch off the ground, charged with energy. This was it, a chance to wipe out the best brigade the Provos had.

He clicked on the infrared Individual Weapons Sight and peered into a green, brightly lit world. He could see the slopes of the hill clearly, the dark coldness of the trees down by the river – and there, moving up the long slope, tiny bright figures. Four, five, six, eight – at least ten of them. He pursed his lips in a soundless whistle. Cheeky bastards, strolling along as if they hadn't a care in the world.

He tried to make out what weapons they were carrying. He could definitely see an RPG on one man's back, but what was that heavy, stubby weapon another carried?

'Fuck,' he said in a whisper. Some kind of light machine-gun. GPMG or M60.

He crept over to where Haymaker's fire team were lying and whispered in the big trooper's ear.

'One RPG, one MG. Take them out first.'

Haymaker gave the thumbs up and Boyd crept back to his place in the line.

He heard a few faint clicks as safety-catches were set to 'Fire', and brought his own weapon with the infrared sight into his shoulder. He could hear his heartbeat rushing in his throat. Sweat was making his palm slippery on the grip of the rifle, though the night was cool.

The terrorists had fanned out into three bricks. Boyd could see that there were a dozen of them now. The numbers worried him – he doubted now if he could get a hundred per cent kill, and swore silently to himself. Bloody Gardai SB had got their information wrong.

Closer, let them walk closer, into the trap.

'Come on, Paddy,' Boyd found himself whispering. 'Come on – just a little more.'

The terrorists were within two hundred metres now, on the upper slopes of the hill itself. The ground was rocky there, with smaller boulders littering the slope. They could use these as cover, so Boyd wanted to open up at almost point-blank range and take them all out before they could go to ground. If any survived, and made it into cover, things could get messy. He didn't want that; he wanted an operation as antiseptic as the one he had led in Tyrone, as clear-cut as surgery.

That's what I am, Boyd thought: a surgeon, cutting the cancer out of this country.

The lead terrorist paused, and spoke into a walkie-talkie. Boyd sighted on him, and in the instant before he fired he realized something was very wrong.

Why have a radio unless it was to talk to another IRA unit? And the walkie-talkie was small, weak. They must be close by.

All this passed through his mind in a fraction of an instant, but in that instant he had tightened his fist and the Armalite had gone off in a ringing detonation of noise and light. He saw tracer streak out into the darkness. The lead terrorist was blasted off his feet.

All hell broke loose.

The old ring-fort erupted into a fury of automatic fire, tracer cutting criss-cross slashes through the night. Boyd shifted aim as one after another the targets were felled. He saw the RPG man fall along with half a dozen others, all lifted off their feet by the massive impact of the high-velocity rounds. But he also saw several shapes go to ground, as he had feared. Soon the SAS troopers were receiving return fire, and Boyd was sure he could hear the unfamiliar stutter of the M60.

Earth flew from the banks of the ring-fort as rounds began to go down on their position. Boyd cursed and left the perimeter, seeking out Taff Gilmore, the leader of the fire team farthest away from the enemy. He would get Taff's team to flank the bastards, flush them out into the open, where they would be destroyed.

He found Taff, and above the roar of the fire-fight he shouted instructions in the NCO's ear.

'Approach their position on the left flank. Fire a miniflare when you're in position yourself, and lay down fire. Make the bastards get up and run, Taff. We'll switch-fire as soon as we see your rounds going down.'

Taff nodded, smiling. 'No problems, boss. Lots of the bastards though, aren't there?'

'Too fucking right. Don't let them get away, Taff.'

Suddenly a section of the earth bank next to

them seemed to fly up in the air. Boyd was hurled away in a fountain of dirt and stones and landed heavily in the middle of the ring-fort. Groggily, he staggered to his knees, scrabbling for his Armalite.

'What the fuck?'

A second fire-fight had exploded into life on the eastern slopes of the hill. He could see Raymond there, firing short, savage bursts from the second GPMG. Another man was ripping up field-dressings. Two troopers lay inert on the ground, their limbs contorted. One of them was Taff, minus most of one leg. One of the three medics in Boyd's multiple was trying to apply a tourniquet to stem the dark jets of blood that were spurting from the stump of his thigh.

Boyd crawled forward on hands and knees, ears still ringing. It was a full-scale battle now, with the troop blasting away into the darkness and the surviving NCOs issuing fire control orders in hoarse shouts. Someone sent up a Schermuly rocket-flare, and then the night became as bright as day as it lit up the hill and came sailing lazily back down again under its tiny parachute.

Jesus, Boyd thought, still dazed. This is the United Kingdom.

He shook his head and found Gorbals. The Glaswegian was redistributing ammunition.

'The fuckers are on both sides of us, sir!' the little sergeant shouted. 'There's a fucking platoon of them out there, the cunts, and they've got an RPG and at least one MG still operating. Fuckers caught us napping. You all right? You're a right fucking mess.'

Boyd wiped blood out of his eyes.

'I'm fine. Where's the signaller?'

'Whitey's down, boss. Took one in the lungs and the round went right through the 351 too. It's fucked.'

'How are we for ammo?'

'Enough to fight a small war. The bastards aren't coming close – none of the claymores have been tripped.' Gorbals hesitated. 'Are you going to hit the SARBE?'

Boyd thought for a split second. With the 351 gone all they had were the 349s, useless at a range of more than three kilometres in these hills. They were cut off. But to activate the SARBE would be to admit defeat, which was unthinkable. And anyway, a chopper would never be able to land in the middle of a fire-fight. For the moment at least, Ulster Troop was on its own. Besides, this battle would not go unnoticed. There were probably several mobiles on their way even as they spoke.

'We'll fight it out – we don't have a choice.'

Gorbals nodded, satisfied. 'We've three

wounded, but the medics can stabilize them for a while. A platoon of them! Southern Special Branch really cocked it up this time.'

And so did I, Boyd thought, but he turned away without saying anything more.

What had been meant as a short, clinical ambush had turned into a messy, protracted battle against superior numbers. The terrorists were not doing a 'shoot and scoot'; they were fighting stubbornly, clearly intent on wiping out Boyd's troopers. It was bizarre. What was worse, it was perfectly feasible, given the fact that the SAS had for once been taken totally by surprise. Already a quarter of Boyd's small force was incapacitated and his perimeter, tiny though it was, was dangerously thin. Boyd hoped the enemy would rush his position; then the claymores would even the score.

He took his place in the line beside Haymaker. The barrel of the GPMG was already glowing a dull red and there was a pile of link and empty cases beside the big trooper. Boyd sighted down his own weapon, but the RPG had broken the infrared sight. He spent precious seconds sliding it off his rifle, and then began firing bursts at the muzzle flashes on the slopes below. The side of Drumboy Hill was stitched with the bright flares of enemy fire, and tracer was zooming up towards the summit of the hill in bright, graceful arcs. One of Taff's fire team was firing his M-79 grenade-launcher with a series of hollow booms, the recoil of the stubby weapon jerking his upper body back savagely. There were explosions, and screams on the hillside below. A ball of flame blossomed in the darkness and there was a whoosh as the RPG answered, kicking up a geyser of dirt and caving in another section of the earth bank behind which the SAS were fighting. Immediately, Haymaker sighted on the place where the RPG had been and fired burst after burst, the linked bullets disappearing into the breech of the GPMG like a rattling snake. Then the MG jammed, and the big man swore rabidly, snapping up the top cover of the weapon to prise free a piece of broken link. Three seconds later the weapon was barking again.

The fighting was furious and incessant. There were several stages to an infantry battle, Boyd remembered. The initial coming under fire, then locating the enemy, and then winning the fire-fight, which meant keeping the enemy's head down. The last stage was the assault. The Provos were intent on winning the fire-fight. When they thought they had suppressed the SAS return fire, they would attack the hill.

Or would they? Boyd didn't know. He was not sure what the men out in the darkness were thinking or planning. He was not even sure of their numbers, except that they were greater, probably twice as great, as his own. One thing was for sure: his men were not winning the battle. They were simply struggling to survive.

At Bessbrook the Greenjacket ops officer put down the telephone, puzzled. He sat and thought for a moment and then abruptly got up and walked out of the almost deserted ops room to find an orderly.

'Tell Lieutenant Grabham to put his men on alert, three minutes' notice to move,' he told the lance-corporal. The man nodded and strode off in the direction of the helipads where Grabham's men, doing their stint as Quick Reaction Force, were killing time in the cool July night. Then the ops officer went in search of his commanding officer.

Lieutenant Colonel Blair was awake at once when the ops officer entered his room. He sat up in bed, rubbing his eyes, his salt-and-pepper hair sticking up. He had been asleep for barely an hour and was still wearing his Norwegian shirt.

'Well, Robert, what is it? Have Boyd's men done their stuff?'

'We don't know, sir. The fact is, we've still no word from them. The RUC have just rung us though and say they've had a local phone in with a report of fireworks being let off in that area – rockets and things. It's hard to say what he saw since no one lives near there, and the locals are so reticent about talking to the RUC at the best of times. This man seems to think that there are some hooligans loose up there with some pyrotechnics, and he says they're frightening his cattle.

Blair was instantly wide awake.

'You haven't heard anything from Boyd? Nothing at all?'

'Not a cheep since he pressed the squash button to inform us he was in position, sir.'

Blair sucked his teeth, then pinched the bridge of his nose.

'I don't like it. We don't want to compromise Boyd, but if there are a few yobbos out there he may have been compromised already.'

'Surely then he would have contacted us, sir, or even hit the SARBE.'

'Yes, quite . . .'

Blair stood up. 'Fireworks,' he muttered. Then his face went white.

'Send the QRF out now, and warm up two more helis. I want another platoon at the ready within half an hour.'

'Yes sir, But . . .'

'Those aren't bloody fireworks, Robert – that's a fire-fight going on out there. Boyd's in trouble.'

'Sir, he has twelve men out with him.'

'Send the QRF *now*, and ready that other platoon. And alert the RUC in Armagh. We'll want their help in sealing off the area. Have you talked to Major Cordwain yet?'

'No, sir. I came straight to you.'

'Then get him up. He will want to go out with the second QRF. Go, Robert!'

The ops officer left hurriedly. Colonel Blair stood in his socks for a second, shaking his head.

'Christ,' he said. 'The young fool.'

They were running low on ammunition. It said a lot for the enemy's logistics that they were still laying down fire like there was no tomorrow, Boyd thought bitterly, while his own men were down now to two mags apiece and a hundred link for each of the GPMGs. They still had grenades and the 66s though, and the claymores lurked on the perimeter, undiscovered as yet.

He had three wounded on his hands. One was Taff Gilmore, his leg blown off above the knee. He was heavily sedated now, and lay unconscious among the multiple's bergens. Another was Boyd's signaller, Whitey Belsham, shot through the lung. He was sat up to keep the fluid in his chest from drowning him. Blood and mucus stained his face.

The third was Richard Shaw, who had taken a round through the hand. 'Rickshaw' was still on the perimeter, the wounded hand wrapped in field-dressings, his rifle held tightly in his good arm.

All the men still had their Brownings, and three mags each. If the worst came to the worst, they would resort to them.

Before that happened, Boyd had decided to hit the SARBE. Even if a chopper could not land, it would at least inform Bessbrook of what was happening.

The RPG roared again, and there was another explosion on the bank of the old fort. Haymaker staggered back from the perimeter, his hands held to his face, swearing. Boyd crawled over to him.

'Where is it?' he asked the trooper. He had to shout over the roar of the multiple's weapons and the rattle of the attackers' fire.

Haymaker's teeth were clenched tight. 'My eyes, boss. I can't see. I can't fucking see!'

Boyd eased the man's hand down from his torn face, but could see nothing but a mass of dirt and blood and ragged tissue. He handed him over to the medic and then took the trooper's place behind the GPMG. The barrel was white-hot and had set the grass below it on fire. Boyd beat out the flames with his hands, not feeling the burns.

Bullets sprayed up the earth around his head and he ducked.

Gorbals scrambled over, and said: 'I'm going to hit the SARBE now, boss.'

Boyd nodded numbly. He felt dazed again. He had failed utterly. All he had succeeded in doing tonight was to lead his men into a carefully crafted IRA ambush.

Gorbals thumped his arm. 'Cheer up, boss – worse things happen at sea!' Then he was gone again.

Responsibility seemed to weigh down Boyd's shoulders. He had been too cocky, too confident in his own and his men's ability. Well, he had paid, and so had Taff and Haymaker and the others.

The night lit up as one of the claymores went off in a flare of blinding light. There were screams that carried even above the gunfire. Then another went off. Both were on the eastern side of the hill. Had the Provos tried to rush the place? Boyd inched forward until he was in one of the battered breaches in the fort's wall.

There were bodies lying there, writhing. Boyd got out a pack of miniflares, fitting one of the little bulb-like objects to the striker and fired it out into the fire-studded night. It soared down the hillside like a missile, and in its light he could see the backs of figures running down the hill.

'Give it to them, boys!' he shouted, elated, and he fired flare after flare down at the retreating figures while his men blasted the last of their ammunition after them, viciously intent on knocking down every one.

The fire-fight sudsided with the dying of the last flare. There were a few random shots but it seemed almost silent after the tumult that had gone before. Boyd's hearing was uncertain, still buzzing with the din of the battle, but he cocked his head and heard a welcome sound borne on the night breeze.

Helicopters.

Gorbals was beside him, his face streaming with sweat.

'Looks like the cavalry have arrived, boss.'

'Too fucking right.'

It was over, Boyd realized. They had survived. He felt a wave of tiredness and relief, closely followed by utter dejection.

'I fucked up, didn't I, Gorbals?' he said to his troop sergeant.'

The Glaswegian smiled. 'I'll let you know that, boss, after we've had a body count. I wouldn't be a bit surprised if we topped a dozen of the wee fuckers tonight. And we're all still here, battered maybe, but alive. So buck up!'

Gorbals slapped him on the shoulder and then was off to do his job: counting remaining ammo, seeing to the wounded, checking the perimeter. The men were lying amid piles of glistening brass cartridge-cases. There was a heavy smell of cordite and blood and broken earth hanging over the hill like a fog. Down in the valley, the choppers were touching down, but up on Drumboy Hill the only sound for a while was the harsh liquid rattle of Belsham's breathing as he fought to get air into his ruptured lung. Boyd bent his head between his knees and was quietly sick.

10

It had been very good, Early thought. He had forgotten how good it could be.

It was not yet dawn, and Maggie lay asleep in his arms, her chestnut hair spilling on to his chest. She whimpered sometimes in her sleep, as though she were having bad dreams, and once she had wept silently, but now she was still.

Early was wide awake and alert. His compact Walther pistol was behind the cistern; he had stashed it there when he went to the loo. It was the only way he could do it without Maggie seeing – she had stuck to him all day like glue. And all night, he remembered, smiling into the still-dark room.

She was an eager lover. His lips still felt raw and he was sure her nails had carved red lines down his back. But for all that she had been almost totally silent. Necessary when living in her brother's house perhaps. It had not cramped her style, anyway.

Apart from the little matter of the pistol, Early was a shade less worried. No matter how consummate an actress she might be, he did not think she suspected him any longer of being a Fred. All to the good – perhaps now she could convince Finn and the South Armagh Brigade.

In fact, it sounded as though they were willing to let him in at the ground floor, from what she had said. Early smiled again. Yes, it was all going well.

There was a hammering downstairs at the back door. Early tensed and Maggie stirred sleepily. He heard Brendan's door open and then a step on the landing, creaking down the stairs. There was a commotion, a series of thumps, men's voices. Early shook Maggie gently by the shoulder.

'Maggie, something's up.'

She was awake in a second, her eyes round and staring.

'Go back to your room, Dominic.'

He looked at her hard face a second, then she smiled. 'Go on – Brendan's a bit protective of his wee sister.'

More voices downstairs. Then someone cried out in pain.

'What's going on? Do you know?'

She was out of bed and reaching for a dressing-gown, her superb breasts swinging as she bent.

'Maybe you'd better come down too.' She

looked suddenly haggard, tired, though when asleep her face had been wholly peaceful.

Early pulled on some clothes and followed her downstairs warily. There was no time to retrieve the gun – he would have to trust her. He hoped he was not walking into an IRA interrogation.

Though the sun was beginning to come up and there was a grey light outside, all the curtains in the public bar were tightly closed. There was a group of men in there, and a familiar smell which Early at once identified as cordite. Weapons lay all over the floor, among them a couple of G3s, an Armalite, an AK47, even a spent RPG.

'Jesus Christ,' he said to himself.

Brendan Lavery was in his dressing-gown, his eyes wide with fear. 'God love us, Eugene, you can't do this to me. You'll ruin me. The peelers'll be here any minute. Jesus, Mary and Joseph.'

'Shut your mouth, Lavery,' Finn said savagely. He was covered in earth and mud. His hands were red with blood and they clutched a G3 that stank of recent firing. He looked almost unhinged.

'My men are hurt. You'll fucking help them or I'll burn this place down round your ears. Seamus!'

Another battered-looking man who was peering out behind a curtain turned.

'It's all right, Eugene. The square's quiet, but

there's all sorts going on over at the base. Helicopters and everything.'

Finn laughed harshly. 'Stupid fuckers. We drove up the Cullaville road, right under their bloody noses. They've got troops galore pouring down to the south. They won't look in this direction for a while, so they won't.' He saw Early standing there beside Maggie and the muzzle of the G3 came up.

'What the fuck is he doing here?'

'He lives here,' Margaret snapped at him. 'He's all right, Eugene. He's on our side.'

'On our side,' Finn sneered. He looked round the crowded bar. The place looked like the aftermath of a battlefield, which in a way it was. There were fourteen IRA men there, three of whom were groaning on the floor while their comrades tried to staunch their wounds. The rest looked shocked, dull-eyed but dangerous. Early knew the look. These men had just come from a fire-fight. But where? South, Finn had said. Probably somewhere along the Fane valley, the area Maggie had been sweeping with her binoculars the day before. He cursed himself. While the IRA strike had been going on, he had been in bed with her. Had she planned it that way?'

'Brits coming into the square!' Lynagh hissed from the door.

'Lights off,' Finn barked, and Maggie obliged. The bar was silent but for the harsh breathing of the wounded. They heard the distinctive whine of army Landrovers outside.

Brendan Lavery was saying a whispered Hail Mary. Finn glared at him and he went quiet. Headlights swept the windows as the vehicles outside turned. Then the engine noise faded as they drove past the pub.

'They're heading down the Dundalk Road,' one of the terrorists said.

'Stupid fuckers are sealing off the border,' Finn told him, and he smiled, looking diabolical. Early had an urge to throw himself at the man's throat, but he stood stock-still.

The square was quiet again.

'What's the time?' Finn demanded.

'Just gone four,' Maggie told him, and he nodded grimly.

'Still quiet, then. Don't get your knickers twisted, Brendan. We just want to get these lads patched up a bit and then we'll be on our way.'

'Patched up!' Brendan was looking with despair at the bloodstains on his carpet. 'Jesus, Eugene, these boys need a hospital, not an Elastoplast.'

'Shut up, Brendan.' It was Maggie. 'Boil up some water and get out the first-aid kit. It's well stocked. And get some blankets and towels.' Then she turned to Early. 'What about you, Dominic – do you know anything about first aid?'

Early had been trying to work out a way to contact the Security Forces discreetly. Here was the bulk of two IRA brigades just waiting to be snapped up, the Border Fox among them perhaps. He raised his head.

'I . . . I did a course, a long time ago, for the building work, like.'

'Then give me a hand. For God's sake, Eugene, what happened?'

Finn sank down on a chair and set the G3 between his knees. Some of the tension seemed to leave him.

'They were waiting for us. The bastards were waiting for us, but we gave a good account of ourselves. I think we got half a dozen of them.'

Early was kneeling by one of the prone terrorists. The man had taken a bullet through the fleshy part of the thigh, leaving a huge exit wound. He could see the femoral artery laid bare in the torn flesh, pulsing delicately.

'What about you? How many of you were hit?' he asked.

Finn eyed him narrowly. The image of McLaughlin's corpse flashed across his mind. He said nothing.

Brendan was heading for the front door with a mop and bucket.

'Where the hell do you think you're going?' Lynagh asked him.

'To mop the step. There's blood all over it. Now that it's getting light the Brits'll see it.'

'Let him go, Seamus,' Finn ordered, and the stout publican slipped out the door to begin his work.

Maggie was splinting the shattered arm of another terrorist. The man groaned and wept as she straightened the limb.

'Brendan's right, Eugene. You have to get these fellas to a hospital.'

'We're taking them to the Royal.'

'That's bloody miles away!'

'We'll put it about that these are punishment shootings – they're all limb wounds anyway. Somebody shopped us, Maggie, and I intend to find out who.'

'Why Belfast for God's sake?'

'It's the last place they'll look. We'll give these boyos false Belfast ID, throw them into the Royal, and no one will be any the wiser. The Brits will be turning Armagh inside out and all the time we'll be lying low up in the city.'

Gingerly, Early bound up the ripped leg of his patient. He was a trained medic, like many SAS troopers, but he did not do too professional a job, both because he didn't want to arouse suspicion, and because he wanted the Fenian shit to suffer.

Inwardly though, he was jubilant. He would get word through to Cordwain then that Finn and his cohorts were in Belfast. It shouldn't prove too difficult to track them down. They were as good as behind bars already.

'I want you to get word to our mutual friend, Maggie,' Finn was saying. 'Tell him to step up his activity and keep the pot boiling down here. In fact, tell him to shoot the shite out of every mobile he sees. We've got to keep them on the hop.'

Maggie nodded without looking up from her work. Finn turned to Early.

'Sure, that's a great job you're doing there, Dominic, so it is. Anyone would think you were Florence Nightingale if you weren't such an ugly bastard.'

Early looked him in the eye.

'I didn't bargain on getting into this sort of thing, Eugene. It scares me, so it does – people running about with guns and all. And look at the state of these poor lads.'

'That's war,' Finn told him. He was regaining his smooth self-confidence.

'We've taken worse casualties tonight, I'll be honest with you, Dominic. There are good men lying dead out there in the fields that could have been safe at home now. But they died for Ireland. God have mercy on them, they died for freedom.'

Early had to bow his head to hide the contempt and hatred on his face.

'We stood up to those bastards and fought them face to face, man to man. And we beat them! Just as free men fighting for their liberty will always beat dictator-led mercenaries in the end.'

Some of the unwounded terrorists were nodding and smiling at Finn's words. Others were silent, taciturn, perhaps remembering the carnage of Drumboy Hill. Dupes, convinced by empty rhetoric, Early thought. He did not believe Finn's claims. If the IRA men had been so successful they would not be in here now, bleeding all over the floor.

'Hurry up there, Maggie,' Finn said, suddenly business-like again. 'We want out of here before the sun's too high. They'll be throwing road-blocks up everywhere. Seamus, what's the time?'

'Quarter past four.'

'Then the transits will be here in a minute. Give us a hand here, Dominic. Seamus, get a man to look out at the back. Come on, Rory, for fuck's sake – pick up your gun.'

The terrorists shuffled or were carried through to the back of the pub. The door was opened and grey early-morning light flooded in. The sun was still but a glint on the rooftops. They could hear helicopters.

An engine was turning over softly. There was a van parked in the backyard emitting blue smoke from its exhaust. The wounded men were loaded onto it, hands placed across their mouths to stifle screams from the rough handling. Another van backed into the yard, the driver puffing furiously on a cigarette, looking half mad with fear. The rest of the IRA men piled in, their weapons banging against the sides as they crowded the interior. Finn beckoned Maggie over for a word. Early could not catch what they were saying, but he saw her nod and then violently shake her head. Finn gave Early a quick, hard glance, and then ducked into the back of the van. Early and Maggie slammed shut the doors and then the vans were off, ticking away into the morning. Something clinked at Early's feet and he bent to pick up a bullet: 5.56mm.

Sloppy bastards, he thought.

Maggie leaned against him. He could smell the fresh shampoo fragrance of her hair. There was blood on her hands.

'Will they make it?' he asked lightly.

'If anyone will, he will. Eugene's a born survivor. Sometimes, Dominic, I think he's a wee bit mad, you know.'

Early laughed.

Brendan padded out into the yard, dressing-gown stretched tight around his ample middle.

'In the name of God, will you get in here? We have to try and clear up the mess. Jesus, Mary and Joseph, I'll end up in the Maze yet. And you, Dominic – I'm sorry you had to see all this. I don't know what you'll think of us – you with your work to go to this morning too.'

They went inside, where it still smelled of cordite and gun oil, fresh soil, sweat and blood.

'Maybe I'll just stay closed today,' Brendan said helplessly, surveying the wreckage of bandages and mud and bloodstains.

'You will not,' his sister told him sharply. 'You'll open up as bloody usual, and you'll have a smile on your face the whole day. Do you hear me, Brendan?'

The rotund landlord nodded numbly and then groped behind the bar for a brandy. Maggie led Early out into the kitchen.

'Thank you, Dominic. You're true blue, so you are.' She kissed him on the lips. 'There's many a man would have panicked or run off when he saw what you saw this morning, but you got stuck in.'

'So did you. I'd nearly think, Maggie, that this wasn't the first time.'

She looked at him but said nothing for a long moment.

'You're in it now, whether you like it or not,' she said in a harder voice at last. 'Eugene doesn't trust you yet, so you'll have to win him over. But I'll fight your corner, don't worry. And Dominic . . .' she paused. 'Don't you be going off anywhere for a while now, you hear me? You don't want to go getting people worried. There's a leak somewhere, you see, and we have to find out where it is.'

'Who it is, you mean.'

'Aye. I can't abide traitors. Whoever he is, he'll get what's coming to him in the end though. We have our own kind of justice down here.'

'I'm sure you do,' Early said, and hugged her lithe body close to him. He had seen the strange look in her eyes, and knew he was not out of the woods yet.

Maggie pulled away, laughing oddly. 'Oh, I'm sorry, Dominic. I forgot about my hands. Look at the mess — you're covered with blood. You'd think you had been shot yourself, so you would.'

11

The SAS troopers filed into their Portakabin
wearily. It had been a long night, and a longer
morning it seemed. The debrief had lasted for
hours, but now it was over at last. All they wanted
now was to wash and get some sleep.

Gorbals McFee strode into the cramped space
full of metal bunk-beds and piles of military
clothing and equipment. The men of the troop
were moving like sleepwalkers. They had been
keyed up and still raring to go when the helis
had brought them back to Bessbrook, but now
reaction and the strain of the past two days were
setting in. They would sleep for fourteen hours
apiece once they got their heads down.

'Listen in, lads,' the little Glaswegian NCO
told them. 'We've news from Dundonald on
our blokes.'

'How are they, Sarge?' Raymond asked. 'What
about Haymaker's eyes?'

'Och him, the big ponce. All it was was a bit of

120

gravel that mucked up his face. It was the blood that had blinded him.'

The SAS men laughed with relief. Haymaker was a popular figure in the troop.

'So he'll be back with us soon, then?'

'He'll be flown back tomorrow, but for tonight he's probably getting a blow-job from some wee nurse.'

'What about Taff and Whitey, Sarge?'

'And Rickshaw,' someone added.

'Taff's leg is gone above the knee. He'll be invalided out, but they can do great things with artificial limbs these days. Rickshaw's hand is a bit of a mess — tendons and everything blown to fuck — so it may not be much use to him. We'll have to wait out on that one. And Whitey, he'll be fine. Might even make it back to the Regiment in a few months, though I don't know what his wind will be like.'

'What was the body count in the end, Sarge?' a trooper asked. 'How many of the cunts did we nobble?'

Gorbals grinned. 'Seven blown away for good, and the Greenjackets picked up three more who were hiding in bushes and full of holes.'

There was an outburst of laughter and back-slapping among the six troopers.

Gorbals held up a hand. 'We hit more of the bastards — they picked up at least two blood trails leading to Clonalig, but the Greenjackets let them slip through their fingers.'

'Crap-hats,' someone said disgustedly.

'There were at least two dozen of them, Sarge. That means there's still a dozen or so of the fuckers at large, armed to the fucking teeth.'

'I know, Wilkie. The Green Machine is sealing off the border even as we stand here. A fucking mouse couldn't creep across to the Republic at the moment without being spotted. Once they try and cross, we'll get them.'

'If they haven't got across already. I'll bet the fuckers are in some pub in the South now with their feet up, having a pint and being treated like shagging heroes.'

'Clonalig,' said Robinson, one of the more thoughtful of the troopers. 'That's north of Drumboy. So they didn't try to head south straight away, anyway. Why's that, Sarge?'

Gorbals shrugged. 'My guess is they had transport arranged up there. Remember, they were on their way north to do a hit, maybe on Cross itself. They probably piled into a couple of cars and fucked off.'

'Well, we took out ten of them. Shit, that's better than Loughgall.'

'I think it's worth a few beers, lads, once we've had some gonk.'

'What do you reckon, Sarge? Can the NAAFI stretch to a few crates for us?'

Gorbals smiled. 'Aye, sure it can.'

'What's up, Sarge? You don't look so pleased. It's scratch ten of the bad guys!'

'That's right, lads, but there are those' – he jerked one thumb towards the ceiling – 'who think that the whole thing was a bit of a fuck-up.'

'You're kidding! Who?'

'The CO of the Greenjackets for one, and our own Major Cordwain.'

'What's their problem? We did the business, didn't we?' Wilkie protested.

'Aye, but there's some kind of argument over intelligence and sources and all that bullshit.'

'What, you mean the bod we have in Cross?'

'Aye. I think they're worried about him.'

Lieutenant Boyd sipped his tea. It was ludicrous, he thought. Here he was sipping tea from a china cup while still wearing torn and muddy combats. There was blood on his shoulder, from Haymaker's wound. It had dried into a thin black crust.

'I still can't see the problem,' he said.

Cordwain sighed. Outside, helicopters were coming and going like buses, ferrying troops all along the border. Bessbrook was a hive of activity; the resident battalion was pulling out all the stops in its effort to seal the border. But Cordwain knew that it was in vain. The birds had flown the nest.

'It's a stupid, inter-service thing. MI5 have finally cottoned on to the fact that we've poached one of their agents.'

'He's SAS too,' Boyd pointed out.

'Technically, he's been seconded to the Intelligence Service. He's theirs. And now they think we've compromised him, placed him at risk. They want him out.'

'How the hell have we compromised him?' Boyd asked angrily.

'We acted prematurely. Yes, it was a largely successful operation, but not completely so. We only got half of the players involved. The other half are still at large, and probably casting about for the tout who betrayed them. Early's life is in danger because our own action wasn't complete enough.'

'Christ, we took out ten of them, didn't we? It's not our fault that the Southern SB miscalculated their strength.'

'I know that, Charles, but you can see their point, surely. Early must be extracted. We've damaged the South Armagh Brigade, perhaps irreparably, and that's excellent. But the Border Fox is still at liberty, and he was our main target.

Intelligence believes that he will now step up activity to cover for the weakness of the Armagh bunch. He's a loner, so he needs no support from them.'

'Are you telling me we're back where we started?' Boyd asked, incredulous.

'In a way, yes.'

Boyd was bitter. It was true that the operation had been scrappy, a seat-of-the-pants job that could all too easily have ended in disaster, but by and large he had been beginning to see it as a great victory. His OC seemed to be treating it as a thing of little account.

'Don't get me wrong, Charles,' Cordwain went on. 'I think the men behaved magnificently. Their conduct throughout the operation was in the finest traditions of the Regiment. But it was also rather a half-baked affair, you have to admit. I take the blame too, for allowing it to go ahead.'

Boyd shook his head wonderingly.

'But we got *ten* of them.'

'I know, but MI5 believes that we were too gung-ho. They think that if we had given Early more time we could have bagged the whole bunch, and maybe the Fox to boot, and all without a messy fire-fight or friendly casualties.'

'That's bullshit. Those bastards weren't wandering around the countryside with M60s just for the exercise. They were going to hit something, and hit it hard. We put a stop to that.'

'I know, I know.'

'What about Early? Does he know yet he's to be extracted?'

'No. We're trying to think up a way to get word to him. The DLB system is far too dangerous now. It'll have to be live.'

Boyd paused with his teacup in mid-air.

'What if Early refuses to come out?'

'I don't know what you mean.'

'Isn't he in a better position to judge whether or not it's too dangerous for him to remain? I don't think we should throw away such a useful agent so quickly. He may not be suspected by the locals. The Cross OP says he's involved with one of the local women, a sympathizer herself. It could be he'll weather the storm.'

Cordwain looked doubtful.

'Don't you think, James, that this is just MI5's way of fucking us around for poaching in their preserve – and getting results by doing it?'

Cordwain chuckled. 'You may have a point there, Charles. What do you suggest, then?'

Boyd stood up and began striding back and forth across Cordwain's office. Mud dropped in clods from his boots.

'Let me set up a meeting with Early, meet him

face to face. We'll use the LLB method – I'll sign out a Q car.'

'Your accent isn't up to snuff,' Cordwain warned him.

'It'll do.'

'No, Charles, it won't. We can't afford a fuck-up at this stage. I'll do it. I'll call in at that bar where Early stays. It's about time the place was checked out anyway. And I want you to detail another fire team for possible OP duty. It's time the team in Cross was relieved; and if Early does stay in, then we'll want to keep an even closer eye on him.'

Boyd nodded reluctantly, and yawned.

'Christ, I'm tired.'

'You should get some rest. I'll see you're not disturbed for the next twelve hours. Leave everything to me.'

Boyd nodded, looking suddenly haggard. It was as if the last of the remaining adrenalin from the battle had finally leached out of him, leaving him limp and drained. Cordwain clapped the young officer on the shoulder.

'Chin up, Charles. You won a victory last night, and whatever the goons say, the troopers think you're Genghis Khan come again. And that's the most important thing. The men trust you with their lives.'

But Boyd, remembering the fire-fight on the

hill, could recall only his own bewilderment and despair. It had been luck, and the fighting quality of the SAS trooper, that had pulled them through. His own decisions had all been wrong. He wondered how many of the men knew or suspected that. Gorbals did, at any rate. The little Glaswegian had been distant ever since their return to Bessbrook.

Boyd's mind was going round in circles. He took his leave of Cordwain and shambled down the narrow corridor to the Officers' Mess: a grand name for a collection of tiny, windowless rooms.

He would not make the same mistakes again.

The vehicle checkpoint had slowed traffic on the Dundalk road to a crawl. The rain had started in, darkening the evening so that it seemed more like autumn than summer. The soldiers stood in the road or crouched in the bushes nearby with their SA-80s in the shoulder and the rain dripping from the brim of their helmets. Two RUC constables, armed with Heckler & Koch 9mm sub-machine-guns, and bulky body armour, stood with the soldiers and flagged down the advancing cars with a red torch. They had been there since mid-afternoon, checking every vehicle headed south.

There had been rumours all day of a fire-fight

down on the border, a real epic affair with a dozen players taken out. Some of the soldiers had been approached by journalists, but they had already been warned not to say anything by their OC. A statment would be issued soon, they were told.

There had been a lot of 'sneaky-beaky' stuff going on lately, and they, the Green Army, were excluded from it. Probably the SAS had been headhunting again, grabbing the headlines while they, the humbler foot-soldiers, did the donkey-work. Bloody typical.

One of the soldiers in the hedge stared darkly into the optic of his weapon's sight. Through the rain and gloom he could see the Irish Republic, not five hundred yards away. It was raining there, too – the weather did not take borders into account.

Despite his Gore-tex waterproof, just issued, he was wet and uncomfortable. Rain trickled down his neck and sleeves as he kept his rifle at the ready, and his boots were full of water from the ditch he crouched in. The bulky Kevlar armour he wore made his torso seem twice as bulky as it really was. He blew a droplet of water from the end of his nose and wondered how much longer there was to go. He was dying for a cup of tea.

Suddenly he was on his side, in the muddy water of the ditch. He found it hard to breathe.

What happened? he thought. Did I slip? His legs would not move.

There was shouting all around him, and now he could hear the sharp crack of gunshots, flashes illuminating the wet evening. Christ, he thought, we're under fire. But when he tried to get up his body would not respond. He was numb.

Someone splashed into the ditch beside him. Another soldier, breathing heavily. The barrel of his rifle was steaming in the rain.

'Jesus fuck . . . Corp! Kenny's hit!'

The second soldier yanked a first field-dressing from the pocket on his arm and applied it to his fallen comrade's chest.

'Get me some more fucking dressings here!'

Another soldier splashed over and ripped open a first-aid bag. The pair of them began working on the soldier named Kenny who lay motionless in the calf-deep water of the ditch.

'Kenny, look at me! Can you hear me? Hang in there, man – the heli's on the way. Fucking hang on, you bugger – don't you let me down.'

Kenny felt cold. It was the water, he decided.

So I was shot, the thought came. Bloody hell, I didn't feel a thing.

It had gotten very dark, he thought. He could hardly see his comrades' faces. And it was so cold. Why don't they get me out of this bloody ditch, on to the road? The answer came: cover. Bloody fire-fight going on, and I'm lying on my back. Just my luck.

It had become very dark. He could hear his friends speaking, shouting. Now they were dragging him on to the wet tarmac of the road at last. They were pummelling him with their fists, but it all seemed so far away. He drifted off, their voices fading into silence.

'We've lost him, Corp.'

The soldier knelt in the road with the body between his knees. He had taken off his helmet to give heart massage and the rain had plastered hair all over his face.

The RUC men were holding up the traffic. The three soldiers clustered round the body of their comrade. It lay in a pool of rain-pocked blood, the Kevlar body armour torn open and the shattered chest a mass of field-dressings and clotted gore.

The corporal shook his head, wiped his nose on the back of his hand and retrieved his helmet.

'Nobody got him?'

They all shook their heads.

'He was firing from the Republic, I'm sure of it. I thought I saw the flash. Just that one shot, and then he bugged out. The Fox, had to be.'

'Then there's fuck-all we can do about it, is there?'

The corporal wiped his eyes and then barked angrily: 'Well, don't just fucking stand around in a huddle! What about fire-positions? Jesus Christ. Thompson, where's that bastard helicopter?'

'ETA two minutes, Corp. It's having problems with the weather.'

'Fuck the weather. Fuck the rain. Fuck this whole shitty country! Pete, get a poncho out; cover Kenny up, for God's sake.'

One of the soldiers dug a waterproof sheet out of his webbing and spread it over the corpse lying open-eyed on the road.

The men looked up at the overcast sky. They could all hear it now: the thump of a helicopter negotiating the low cloud.

The corporal of the fire team joined one of the RUC constables in the road.

Will you look at them, the scum,' the policeman was saying, white with fury. He was looking at the line of cars. The occupants were grinning and laughing, and the driver of the first car stuck his arm out of his window and gave the V for victory sign. The corporal abruptly strode up to the car and leaned close to the driver's window.

'Something funny, mate?'

The occupant, a man in his twenties, looked at him scornfully and then stared straight ahead, whistling.

The soldier swung the butt of the SA-80 and smashed the driver's window with an explosion of glass. Then he leaned in, opened the door, and dragged the driver out of his car.

'Think it's funny, do you? Thinks it's something to laugh at, a man dying on the road? *Think it's fucking funny now?*

The corporal kicked the man in the stomach, and he collapsed on to the ground. He kicked him again, in the face; and again, and again. Then he leaned over the groaning, bloody civilian and put the muzzle of his rifle in the man's mouth. The eyes widened with terror and the man moaned around the barrel.

'Not so fucking hilarious now, is it, you piece of shit?'

There was a roar, and a high wind that drove the rain horizontally. The helicopter was landing in a field by the road. The corporal straightened and tucked his rifle back in his shoulder. He looked down at the bruised, terrified man on the ground, and smiled.

'The gloves are off now, Paddy. Tell your friends. We're throwing the book away because we've had enough. Now it's your turn.'

He kicked the man once more before turning back to where his fire team were loading the dead soldier's body on to the Wessex.

12

The bar was quiet when Cordwain walked in. It smelled strangely of bleach, he thought. He ordered a Bass from the plump man behind the bar and sipped it thoughtfully. Early should be back from work any minute. After that they'd have to play it by ear.

He was glad the fine July weather had broken; it gave him more of an excuse to wear the jacket which concealed the Browning in his armpit. It was raining outside, a fine drizzle wholly characteristic of South Armagh.

Things were hotting up. Three days had passed since Boyd's operation, and already another soldier had been killed by the Fox. There were signs that the Greenjackets were fed up with taking it lying down; there had been a spate of complaints about army brutality. The local RUC had given the complainants short shrift. In fact there was a rumour that one man, having gone to the local RUC station to complain about being beaten up by the army, had found himself beaten up again by the police. Cordwain smiled unwillingly. The Troop had loved that.

In two days' time a new covert OP would be set up in a derelict house in the square. Gorbals McFee would be handling it. That would make two covert OPs operating primarily to keep tabs on Early. Ulster Troop could not keep up the intensity of operations for long. Soon they would have to scale things down. One thing was for sure, Cordwain told himself: he was not letting a twelve-man multiple out headhunting in the countryside again.

He wondered if Early had any fresh intelligence for him. There had been no contact since the Drumboy op, to let things settle down a little. But Cordwain was seething with impatience. He wanted to know where Finn and the other surviving Armagh and Monaghan players had skedaddled to after their abortive mission. The Gardai reported that none of the Monaghan men had yet returned to their homes, and neither had the Armagh lot. They were lying low somewhere: Donegal maybe, or Mayo. They had slipped through his fingers when he had been on the verge of scooping the whole damn lot up.

But this Fox now – he was the main problem. He had taken out five Greenjackets in less than as many months. No wonder the squaddies on the ground had lost their sense of humour. And yet Cordwain had not one single clue about the formidable sniper, whether he was a Northerner or Southerner, old or young. Intelligence had come up with a great fat blank, which was unusual. Whoever he was, he was not a known player, in fact not even a familiar face. It was irritating.

'Desperate things going on in this part of the world lately,' he said to the barman in his Belfast accent. The man seemed nervous, jittery, and he sipped often at a tall glass of whiskey he had stashed behind the bar.

'Ach, Jesus, don't talk to me about it. It's terrible, so it is. All those young men dying, all this violence; and the soldiers going berserk around here too. I wish it would quieten down. All we want is to be left alone to get on with our lives.

He sounded sincere. Cordwain wondered if he had had some experience lately that had formed his views.

He ordered another pint, looking discreetly at his watch, and then unfolded his *Irish Times* and began reading. The headlines were still full of the news of the Drumboy killings. The paper speculated on whether this was confirmation of the British Government's 'shoot to kill' policy. Cordwain smiled at the absurdity of it. Army

Pamphlet No. 1 was actually entitled 'Shoot to Kill', and covered basic weapons handling. When a soldier fired his weapon, he was always intending to kill, never to wound. A wounded enemy could still kill a man. Journalists could be so fucking naive. They had to dance words on the head of a pin.

A girl walked into the bar laden down with shopping. She was highly attractive, Cordwain thought, her hair lank with the rain but still shining chestnut, her face pale as cream. Margaret Lavery, the sister of the landlord. She had been a Sinn Fein member a few years back and was still a sympathizer, but Intelligence said that she had not been actively involved since the death of her husband at Loughgall. The SAS OP observing the house had said that she and Early seemed to have a bit of a thing going.

Lucky Early, Cordwain thought, eyeing the way her wet dress clung to her slim body. He could see the imprint of her nipples through the thin material. The shower must have caught her by surprise.

The girl gave him a glance as she hauled her shopping away through the door at the back of the bar. She looked as haughty as a queen. Cordwain wondered what she saw in John Early, hard-faced, short and stocky. Women were funny things.

The door opened and a crowd of men burst into the bar, talking and laughing. They carried lunch-boxes and their overalls were covered in mud and plaster. They stood at the bar, shaking the rain out of their hair and calling loudly for beer. One of them prevailed upon the landlord to switch on the TV above the bar, and suddenly the racing from Sandown was blaring out at high volume. The men sank their pints with scarcely a pause and then ordered more. The girl came back into the bar, wearing dry clothes now but with her hair still damp, and began helping her brother pull pints. The lounge had been transformed in a twinkling from a quiet, empty room to a bustling, noise-filled place.

And there was Early, entering with a few more labourers. Cordwain saw him catch Margaret Lavery's eye and smile. She smiled back at him, looking not haughty now but girlish. Cordwain felt a twinge of envy, though he was happily married himself.

Early saw him. There was a flicker, almost like a twitch, and then he had turned away, elbowing his way to the bar and calling loudly for beer with the rest.

'You're dinner's nearly ready, Dominic,' the Lavery woman was telling Early. 'I'll fetch it out as soon as I get a minute.'

'Ach, there's no hurry,' Early said, and casually

propped himself up beside Cordwain but placed his back to the other SAS officer. He was laughing and joking with the other men in the bar. Cordwain was a little amazed. He had always known Early to be a taciturn, humourless type, but he seemed to have the locals eating out of his hand.

Time for business. Cordwain nudged Early slightly with his elbow and the shorter man turned, pouring the last of his beer down his throat. Cordwain got up as if to leave.

'Are you finished with your paper?' Early asked him. 'It's just I like to have a wee look at the horses, so I do.'

'Aye, no problem. It's yours,' Cordwain said casually, and he left the bar.

Still raining. He turned up his jacket collar and headed for the car park, where he had left the Q car. Written in the newspaper he had left with Early were the time and place for a live letterbox rendezvous that night. That was if Early could tear himself away from his flame-haired beauty.

The weather really had taken a turn for the worse. Cordwain switched on the windscreen wipers and peered out at the rain-swept evening. He looked at his watch. Forty minutes. Should be time enough.

He turned the car down a little side-road and saw a figure waiting at the bottom, hunched up against the rain. When he drew level with the man the door was opened and the wet figure leapt into the passenger seat. He sped up.

'I can't be long,' Early said, throwing back the hood of an old army surplus parka. 'They're keeping quite a close eye on me at the minute, I think.'

'The woman?' Cordwain asked.

'I don't know. Maybe.'

'All right,' Cordwain said. 'You first.'

Early paused, as if collecting his thoughts.

'Finn and the other PIRA members are in Belfast, in three safe houses. That's all I know about their location. They took their weaponry with them and they intend to lie low for several weeks, they said, before popping back south. I suppose you've nothing on them?'

'Not a damn thing,' Cordwain said. 'The wounded players we scooped up aren't talking.'

'Finn's a hard case – they're probably more scared of him than they are of you. Any luck with the weaponry?'

'One M60 has been traced to a theft from a National Guard arsenal in the States about eight months ago. The rest came up from bunkers in the South. The Gardai are working on it.'

'The Gardai,' Early scoffed.

'Anything else?'

'Yes. The Lavery woman is active. There is at

least one arms cache in the pub itself, but her brother doesn't know, I think. He seems a decent sort. I think he just wants to be left alone.'

'I got that impression.'

'The survivors of the operation came to the pub three – no, four nights ago. We patched them up before they went on their way. They were in two Ford Transits, one blue, one grey. Number-plates are as follows.' Early handed Cordwain a tiny scrap of paper. The SAS major nodded.

'Hijacked in Newry a week ago,' he said. 'One we've found, burnt out along the border near Omagh. That's what threw us off the scent. We thought they had headed west. So they're in Belfast! Cheeky buggers. Tell me about the crowd who made it to the pub.'

'There were fourteen of them. Some I couldn't place. Three of them were wounded: arm and leg injuries. They were to be admitted to the Royal in Belfast with false ID and passed off as punishment shootings.'

Cordwain smiled. 'Scratch three more of the bad guys. We'll leave them alone for the present. We don't want you coming under any more suspicion. The others?'

Early nodded at the piece of paper he had given Cordwain. 'Southern Special Branch will be able to confirm the names.'

'Excellent, John. I believe we have them cold.'

'What the hell happened the other night? You only bagged half of them, and the other half are thirsting for blood. You'll never get any Freds down in this part of the world if you keep coming up with operations like that.'

'It was Boyd. He's a good man, but a little . . . impulsive. Call it one of the follies of youth.'

'Fuck the follies of youth,' Early said savagely. 'He could have ruined the whole thing. I hadn't given you enough information to launch a pre-emptive strike. I thought you would just step up preventative measures, maybe catch them in the act. That young man is too much of a cowboy.'

'As I said,' Cordwain told him, his voice hardening, 'he's young, but he's very good. It was my fault if anybody's – I gave the go-ahead. Do you think you've been compromised by the operation?'

Early pondered the question as the car wound its way along the quiet roads of South Armagh.

'No,' he said at last. 'I patched up one of their wounded and helped them out the night of the fight. They are on their guard, certainly, but I don't think they suspect me any more than a few other locals that they've got their eye on.'

'And the Lavery woman?'

'What about her?'

'Damn it, John. Is she setting you up? We

142

know you're involved with her, and she's bloody attractive.'

'I won't let my prick rule my head, if that's what you're getting at, James.'

'Good. Now listen, John. Your handlers in the Intelligence Service have found out what we're up to and they're mightily pissed off at us intruding on their turf. They want you extracted. They're trying to portray the Drumboy op in the worst possible light.'

'They're full of shit. I've just given you the whole South Armagh Brigade on a platter.'

'Yes, but they want the Border Fox. The whole situation down here is being screwed up tighter every day, despite Drumboy. The resident battalion is causing trouble for itself, and questions are being asked in Parliament.'

Early laughed. 'How inconvenient for you all!'

'It could result in the Greenjackets being replaced early in their tour – their casualties alone almost warrant that. That would be a grave blow to us, politically as well as operationally.'

'What do you want me to do about it?'

'Find the Fox. He must be taken out before he strikes again. I am able to authorize any and every means to neutralize him once he has been identified. If the worst comes to the worst we'll drag the fucker over the border and top him ourselves. But he must go down.'

'The Fox is mine, Major.'

Cordwain sighed.

'This is not a personal vendetta. I'm sorry about your brother, John, but Christ, you've got to remember you're part of a team. We're establishing another covert OP in Cross square to keep an eye on you. The first one is being folded up – the risk of compromise is too great with two in the same town.'

'Fair enough. I'll tell you this though: we may be on to a loser with the Fox, precisely because he prefers to work alone. Not even the regular players in Cross know who he is – only Finn and the quartermaster, McLaughlin, one of whom is now dead and the other up in Belfast. Whoever he is, he's not in our files – he's an unknown, with no previous convictions. And he's a cool-headed bastard too, hitting that VCP the day after the Drumboy op.'

'We've figured out the weapon he uses,' Cordwain said. 'It's a Barratt-Browning .50-calibre rifle. Uses armour-piercing rounds. The fucker can punch through four inches of steel; it even pierces the trauma plates on body armour.'

Early whistled softly. 'Where the fuck did the Provisionals get a weapon like that?'

'The States, where else? It's American-made. But it's a fuck of a big weapon, John. A man wouldn't be able to run far with it, so this Fox depends on vehicular transport for every hit, if he uses no back-up. That means he operates near roads, tracks, lanes. He's not a cross-country man, unless he's in the Republic, where he can probably saunter around with his hands in his fucking pockets if he likes. Anyway, back to business.'

Cordwain handed Early one of the ubiquitous pieces of paper.

'Three times, dates and places for three LLBs. It's up to you whether or not you turn up at them; there will be a contact waiting for you at them but he will wait precisely five minutes and then bugger off. They're roughly every week for the next three weeks.'

'What if I get info that has to be delivered right away?'

The number at the bottom. Use a public phone box and let us know. If you're really in the shit, then hopefully the OP being established tonight will notice and call in the cavalry. That's the best we can do. Fibre optics and phone taps, they're all out at the moment, I'm afraid; things are too tense. We'll wait a while, and then see what we can do. I don't have to tell you to destroy that note, do I?'

Early shot him a withering look.

'Good. Here we are then, John – back where we started. What did you tell the girl?'

'That I was going for a walk.'

'On an evening like this? You'll have to think up better excuses than that.'

Early said nothing. The car stopped briefly and he got out.

'Good luck,' Cordwain said, and sped off. Looking in his rear-view mirror he saw the hooded figure hunched against the rain, walking back into Cross.

Maggie Lavery or no, he was glad he was not John Early.

13

The army foot patrol was a large one; twelve men in staggered file moving down both sides of the darkened street. It was three o'clock in the morning and the street-lights of Crossmaglen were an amber glow in the early hours. The village was silent and sleeping, but the soldiers checked every window and doorway as though they expected a face to appear at it, a rifle barrel to flash. They were tense, jumpy, and they eyed the death tally that graffiti artists had painted on one gable wall with hatred. Ten-nil, it said, seemingly forgetting the seven PIRA members killed at Drumboy Hill. The thought sweetened the mood of the patrol a little, though they were still burning with a desire for revenge, like all the members of their battalion. Scarcely three days had passed since the murder of rifleman Kenny Philips at the vehicle checkpoint outside the town.

Gorbals McFee and the three other members

of his team were at the rear of the patrol. Haymaker was there, the stitches removed from his face only that morning, Raymond Chandler, and Jimmy Wilkins: Wilkie. They were dressed and equipped identically to the Greenjacket soldiers that preceded them, except for the large bergens on their backs. The patrol was to cover their approach to the site of the OP.

On the northern side of Cross square was a line of three derelict houses, their windows boarded up and slates missing from their roofs. The local council had been promising for months to renovate them, but never seemed to get round to it. The patrol turned east on its approach to the square and moved down the narrow alley at the back of the houses. A head-high crumbling brick wall enclosed the tiny, overgrown back gardens. The doors in the wall were of wood, rotting and sagging on their hinges.

A cat darted across the alleyway, causing the point man to whip up his rifle, then breathe out softly and let the muzzle sink again. It was army policy to have weapons loaded but not cocked while patrolling in urban areas, so that there was no round 'up the spout' to cause a possible negligent discharge. But this moral nicety had gone to the wall a long time ago down in South Armagh. All the section's weapons had been cocked as soon as the patrol had left the base, and the trigger finger of each man rested on the little stud that was the SA-80's safety-catch, ready to flick it off and open up at the slightest hint of danger. The Greenjackets had lost too many men to worry much about infringements of Standard Operating Procedure now.

The patrol paused, the men seeking fire-positions. Gorbals nodded to Haymaker and the big man leaned against one of the doors in the alley, testing it. Letting his weapon hang from its sling, he produced a short crowbar from his thigh pocket and levered the door open. The hinges squeaked in protest, and then he had disappeared.

In a twinkling the other SAS men followed him, and the door was swung shut. The Greenjackets continued down the alley and then turned left to enter Cross's main square, on their way back to the base, which was off its southern end.

Gorbals, Raymond and Wilkie crouched in the tangled undergrowth that was the back garden of the deserted house. They were almost invisible in the darkness. Haymaker was working on the garden door, disguising the scar the crowbar had made.

The procedure was repeated for a window at the back of the house. Soon the team was inside, breathing dust and damp in the pitch-blackness.

They went up the stairs, Wilkie erasing their

footsteps behind them as they went. No one spoke. When they had reached the top floor they paused, listening. Then they slipped off their bergens and placed them in a pile, and swapped their boots for trainers.

The house had already been checked out by an Explosives Ordnance Disposal team, and the SAS men had clocked both the building and the surroundings on a previous patrol. The place was clean, in an operational sense, though as the SAS soldiers dug out their equipment they could feel rats scampering around their feet.

Each of the men had differing tasks to perform before the OP could begin to function. Haymaker went downstairs again and planted a series of trip-wires linked to stun grenades and flash initiators on the lower floor, so that if any of the locals came nosing around the team would have warning that they were compromised. Wilkie engineered a tiny hole in the brickwork under the eaves that would be their sole window on the world, and began setting up the surveillance equipment. Raymond got out two sleeping bags and unrolled them, and then set aside two sets of plastic bags, one pair for human waste and the other for empty food cans. The team would be in the OP for ten days, and in all that time they would not eat hot food, but only cold, tinned rations. They would not have hot drinks, except at first light, when there was the least chance of the little gas stove being heard. And they would drink tea, not coffee, which gives off an aroma.

Gorbals set up the radio, which would be used as little as possible, both to conserve batteries and cut down on noise. The procedure would be for two men to sleep while one monitored the radio and the fourth carried out the surveillance, logging everything he saw. Radio transmissions from the OP would be made at night only, since the VHF set had a habit of interfering with television transmissions. Every third night, an RGJ patrol would pass close to the OP and pick up a bergen full of waste and used camera films, and would leave behind a bergen full of food, film and radio batteries.

By first light that morning, the OP was up and running. Gorbals was sitting with his eye glued to the optic of the camera, while Raymond sat listening to the radio. Wilkie and Haymaker were asleep, wrapped in sleeping bags on the dust and filth of the floor.

As Maggie Lavery got out of bed and stretched her white arms towards the ceiling, Gorbals smiled and pressed the shutter on the camera. What a great pair of tits, he thought. Surveillance work has its perks, after all.

*　　*　　*

Eugene Finn lit another cigarette and stared down the rain-shiny roofs of the city. From this height he could even see the two huge yellow Harland and Wolff cranes, Samson and Goliath, over by the docks, as well as the green copper dome of the City Hall. A helicopter hovered, motionless, over Belfast city centre, keeping an eye on things.

He was in a high-rise in Divis, in west Belfast. The IRA safe house had turned out to be a grimy tenth-floor flat in the Republican heartland, the ghetto of the city. Belfast was a grim town, divided up into tribal territories, split by the Peace Line, patrolled by troops and controlled by paramilitaries. He had never liked the place. He was a countryman.

The door was knocked in a peculiar rhythm and the other man in the room, a big Falls Road native, got up to answer it. He was Seamus Toomigh, Finn's 'minder'. Or jailer, or executioner, Finn told himself. It all depends on how things go.

Six men came into the room, the last looking round the corridor before shutting the door behind him. Finn stubbed out his cigarette. The men sat down and Toomigh wandered off to the tiny kitchen to get drinks. Finn knew the names of two of the men. The other four he did not even recognize.

It was one of the beauties of the ASU system. The IRA Active Service Unit was a self-contained entity, and the foot-soldiers within it knew no one in the organization outside their own little cell. Only the commanders of the ASUs, and the brigade officers knew who the various quarter-masters and staff officers of their district were. And only a man who had been in the 'Ra' as long as Finn would know who the men on the Army Council were. This was the bulk of it: these six men. They dictated and co-ordinated the actions of all the IRA members on the island. It was rare to see them all together, especially up here in the North, for the Brits knew who at least a few of them were. Finn knew he would be moved again, to another place, as soon as the meeting was over. The Brits or the RUC would have these men under constant surveillance.

'Well, Eugene,' said one of them, a middle-aged, hard-faced character. He was Francis McIlroy, operations officer for the Belfast district.

'You've been having an exciting wee time to yourself down south, haven't you?'

'Have we now?'

'Seven Volunteers dead, three more in the Royal, some valuable weapons lost. I'd say you'd been busy enough,' another man said harshly. Finn did not know him.

'And for what? Four wounded SAS. You didn't

even manage to top any of them. The biggest operation we'd authorized in fifteen years and what have we to see for it? Fuck all. Now the South Armagh Brigade is out of action for the foreseeable future. You know what I think, Eugene? I think you just handed the Brits a victory on a platter, with nothing gained on our side but corpses.'

'What is this?' Finn asked heatedly. 'A trial?'

'Call it a court martial – we prefer that term. You lot in the South have always been a bunch of big-timers. Before you it was Kelly and the East Tyrone Brigade: and look where it got them – that disaster at Loughgall. Who the fuck do you think you are, Clint Eastwood?'

Finn leaned forward, his face white with anger. 'You authorized it. The Army Council backed the idea behind the operation.'

'We backed it before we knew there was a leak in your parish. Someone down there is singing, Eugene. Why else should the SAS be waiting for you?'

Finn was silent. The same thought had occurred to him.

'You Armagh boys have always been the tightest-knit bunch of us all, I'll make no bones about it. But now there's a screw loose, Eugene. Somebody in Cross is a tout.'

Finn shook his head. 'Even the other ASU

commanders only knew the details of the operation the night before. I can't see how it could happen.'

'Where are they now? Here?'

Finn smiled icily. 'They're six feet under, most of them. Lynagh is the only one that survived besides me. He's up here in the city. I don't know where you have him – you know that.'

'We'll talk to him too, then. But I don't think it was him or you, Eugene. Don't get us wrong – we don't suspect you yourself.'

Finn felt a cold wave of relief wash over him, but his face betrayed none of his feelings.

'No, it's someone in Cross, and they're good, whoever they are. My guess is they put together a whole lot of little pictures and came up with one big one.'

Finn nodded. 'I think the SAS were as surprised as us. There weren't more than a dozen of them. If they had known how many of us there were, they'd have brought in more. At Loughgall they had over thirty men. The East Tyrone bunch had nine.'

The senior IRA figures digested this for a few minutes while Toomigh came back in with glasses of beer and whiskey.

'Just how bad is the damage?' McIlroy asked at last.

'Bad enough. Two of the dead were mine, the

rest were Monaghan men under Lynagh. It was his platoon they hit first . . .'

'*Platoon!*' one of the older men guffawed in a mixture of wonder and admiration.

'Aye. They wiped out half of his men in the first minute, but they didn't seem to know my lot were there. We hit them in the rear, RPG and everything, and we were fucking winning, too, until that arsehole McLaughlin charged forward with a few of the hot-heads, and tripped a booby-trap. A claymore, I think it was. Well, he went down along with a few others, and after that I gave the order to pull out. Three of the wounded we managed to get on the vans, the others were picked up by the Brits. But the point is, we had them surrounded. I really think we could have beaten the cunts if only we'd had a little more time.'

'A dozen SAS – now wouldn't that have been something,' said one of the IRA men, eyes shining. The others were looking at Finn with something like respect.

McIlroy persisted, however.

'How many of your brigade are left, Eugene?'

'Eight. As I said, the Monaghan boys took the brunt of it. The Monaghan Brigade has more or less ceased to exist.'

McIlroy smiled strangely. 'I'll bet you a pound to a pinch of pigshit that the Brits think the South

Armagh Brigade is destroyed too. They think all they have to worry about now is the Fox.'

'If there's a tout in Cross they may know I'm here,' Finn warned.

'Sure they do. We'll have to get you and your boys out again as soon as we can.'

'What are you talking about? I thought the plan was that we'd lie low here for a while.'

'You're not safe here any more than you are in Cross, and you're more use to us down there. The Brits want the Fox now – desperately. And they'll not expect him to have any support with you lot up here. If we can use him as bait, then maybe we can get them into an ambush. Have your boys waiting for them – this time without any fuck-ups.'

'I'm not sure my boys will agree,' Finn said quietly.

'They'll obey orders, so they will.'

'I'm not sure the Fox will agree either. He's not a team player.'

'Then you'll convince him . . . Who the hell *is* he, Eugene? You know, don't you?'

'I know, but no one else does. We'll keep it that way, so we will.'

'Aye, it's better that way, I suppose. I'd like to shake his hand though. He's got the shits up every cunt on the border.' And McIlroy laughed.

'There is one thing though,' he added, serious

again. 'There will be no more operations down in your area until you weed out this fucking tout. That's your first priority. We'll send you back south first, and I want you to start looking around. The rest of the brigade will follow sometime in the next two weeks. Let the Brits think the Fox is on his own down there. And everything you find out is to be forwarded to the Army Council – no one else. We will handle the situation ourselves, and give you the go-ahead when we're satisfied it won't turn into another fucking shambles. Is that clear?'

'Perfectly,' Finn said, his voice cold as stone.

'Good. We've reached a turning point down in your part of the world, Eugene. The Brits think they have us on the run, so we have to prove them wrong. Tell the Fox to lay off for a while. No more hits until you get word from us. I want things to quieten down around Cross for a few weeks, lull the enemy into a false sense of security. Let them think that they have us beat down there, and then hit them hard, to show them we're still in business.'

Finn nodded wordlessly.

'You don't look too enthusiastic, Eugene.'

'I'm enthusiastic enough. It's the boys I'm thinking of. Half of them will end up in the Maze, if they come through it alive at all.'

'Negative thinking, Eugene, will get you

nowhere. Everyone does a stint in the Maze – it's part of the learning process. Thank your lucky stars they don't get sent to Castlereagh any more, and get the cigarette burns and the beatings we used to get, eh lads?'

There was a murmur of agreement from the older of the IRA men.

'And they don't have to smear their shit on the walls and live under a blanket for months on end. They have it easy nowadays, Eugene. No more Dirty Protest, no more hunger strikes. Hell, the Loyalists and us run the Maze between us. The screws don't do anything there without our say-so.'

'I know,' Finn said drily. He had done time in the Maze himself.

'Then what's the problem?'

'This tout. I have an idea who he might be. I just hope I'm wrong, that's all.'

'Why? Who is he?'

Finn smiled. 'A friend of mine is sweet on him. He's a Ballymena man. She's keeping an eye on him, don't worry. He's not going anywhere.'

14

The pub was crowded, hot, smoky. Early leaned against the bar with the cool glass of porter in his hand and surveyed the crowd. So many of the people here he knew, now. Not only from mugshots, but from working with them, drinking with them, even playing football with them at weekends. Gaelic football, that is. They had loved that; a Ballymena man who knew how to play Gaelic. He was a novelty.

His back ached. Eoin Lavery worked his men hard, but was not a bad employer. Early had begun to look forward to the weekends though. They were a respite from early mornings and hard physical labour, and they were a chance for Maggie and him to get away, into the fields. The good weather had returned, and South Armagh was peaceful for the moment. It amused and somehow saddened Early that he could walk this countryside freely now. He had patrolled it, heavily armed, before his transfer to the SAS, and had regarded it as a battlefield where every gate was booby-trapped, every road mined. Now he could enjoy it as a civilian. And the girl; he enjoyed her too.

He drank more of the cool beer, tapping one foot gently against his right ankle to check the automatic was still there in a gesture that had become instinctive. It wouldn't do to forget that he was an alien in this country. He was the enemy.

He had deliberately missed the first of the three LLBs that Cordwain had set up, because he had had nothing to say, and also because he had wanted to let things settle down for a while. At the second he had merely found out the next three locations and times. There was no intelligence forthcoming these days. The country seemed subdued after the battle at Drumboy Hill and the Fox's last killing. According to Cordwain, the three IRA men wounded in the Drumboy fight were doing well in hospital, under discreet surveillance. He doubted if they would be activated again. They would become Republican war heroes, but operationally they were hot potatoes for the IRA. They were out of the picture. That meant that Drumboy had actually taken out thirteen of the fuckers, but according to the Gardai, only four of the thirteen were Northerners. The rest were Monaghan boys.

Cordwain had therefore told Early to gather any information he could on those members of the South Armagh Brigade who returned to their old hunting grounds. The RUC had drawn a blank in Belfast, though it was known that there had been a meeting of the IRA Army Council at which at least one of them had been present.

Finn, Early thought. He would have been there. And he'll come back, too, looking for the tout who shopped him. Well, forewarned is forearmed, as they say.

Early's own enquiries, in the form of bar-room banter, had also come up with nothing. Most of the people of Cross preferred to forget about the Drumboy fiasco and concentrate on the continuing triumphs of the Border Fox. It made Early's gorge rise to see these outwardly placid, merry people cheering the murder of soldiers on their roads and in their fields, but he joined in with a will, singing along with the best of them. Damned if they weren't singing now – a bunch of them in the smoke-veiled warmth and crowd of the bar.

> Down on the Border, that's where I'd
> like to be,
> Down in the dark with me Provo
> company;
> With a comrade on me left and another
> one on me right,

And a bunch of ammunition just to feed
   me Armalite.

A brave RUC man came walking down
our street;
Six hundred British soldiers were
tripping round his feet.
He said: 'Come out, ye Fenian bastards,
come on out and fight.'
But he said he was only joking when he
heard me Armalite.

There was a roar of laughter and a torrent of
back-slapping as the song finished. Early stared
into his glass.

'*Tiocaigh ar la*!' someone shouted. 'Our day
will come.' Too fucking right it will, Early
thought darkly. If I have anything to do with it,
it'll come sooner than you think, you bastard.

Maggie leaned over the bar towards him, cleaning a glass. Her face was flushed with the heat and
perspiration beaded her forehead.

'This is a right crowd we have in tonight,
Dominic. They're great ones for the songs and the
slogans, this bunch, but that's about all they're
good for.'

He looked at her blankly, and she squeezed his
arm with a smile.

'We know there's more to it than that, don't we?'

163

He felt a sudden urge to confess all to her, to tell her everything and ask her to forgive him, to accept him, to run away from here with him. The classic dilemma of the undercover agent under pressure. Instead he leaned forward and kissed her lightly on the lips. Her brother Brendan saw the gesture and shouted across the bar: 'Hey, you two – none of that canoodling in here!' but he was grinning. Apparently he had come to consider Early a good egg, someone fit to court his sister.

One other drinker did not share in the general merriment. He was a well-dressed man in a suit, balding and overweight. He was holding on to a pint glass as though his life depended on it and looking at the people around him as though he were a rabbit surrounded by weasels. He drained his glass quickly and left, collecting an expensive overcoat from the hooks by the door and exiting into the July night. Early watched him go, intrigued. Then Jim Mullan, one of his workmates, nodded in the bald man's direction and nudged Early.

'See yon fella, Dominic? He's a Prod. Some of the boys have been watching him. He's nervous as a cat. He's one of them travelling salesmen, he says, but I don't believe a word of it.'

'What do you think, then?' Early asked, trying to sound unconcerned.

'We think he's a fucking spy. I've heard' —
and here his voice dropped to a whisper — 'that
those poor lads who were murdered at Drumboy
were set up by a fucking Brit spy. You know, a
secret agent.'

Early widened his eyes in horror. 'No!'

Mullan, a big, florid man with several inches
of gut bulging over his belt, closed one eye. 'But
don't worry — some of the boys is waiting outside
for him, the baldy-headed wee ponce. We're
going to have a wee word with him, so we are.'

'What are you going to do to him?'

Mullan winked again. 'Ach, nothing much,
maybe give him a wee tap or two and scratch
that expensive car of his. Now drink up, Dominic.
You're a broad sort of fella — we could do with
you out there as well.'

Early drained his pint and followed in Mullan's
wake as the bigger man left the bar.

It was a fine night, the stars ablaze in a clear
sky as he followed Mullan round to the car park
behind the pub. Already an ugly little drama was
being enacted there under the soft glow of the
street-lights. A tight knot of men were gathered
about something. Others were kicking a BMW
that sat nearby. There was a tinkle as a headlight
shattered. A man screamed in pain. Early's pace
quickened.

The salesman was being held by two of Early's

workmates while a third beat him about the head with a short iron bar. The man's head lolled from side to side with each blow. The flat, dull crack of the blows sickened Early. Without pause he stepped into the knot of men and snatched the weapon from the attacker.

'What the *fuck* do you think you're doing?' he demanded savagely.

The men looked at him in surprise. Behind him, the salesman slumped in their arms, glassy-eyed and barely conscious. There was a great wound in his head that trickled blood. His new suit was covered in it.

'We're interrogating him,' one of them said lamely.

'Aye – whose fucking side are you on anyway, Dominic?' There was a general growl at this, and suddenly Early knew that he had made a bad mistake. He had let his quick temper get the better of him.

'Now, lads,' big Jim Mullan said. 'Don't forget Dominic's a new boy here. He doesn't know our ways yet.'

'Fucking Ballymena,' one man said scornfully. 'Paisley's country. Well, we have a different way of doing things down here, son, and if you don't like it you don't have to stay.'

'Hang on just a wee minute,' Early said, marshalling his thought hurriedly and cursing his impulsiveness. 'I thought you were interrogating him. What's the use of beating him up so bad he can't talk if you want to ask him questions? That's cutting off your nose to spite your face, so it is.'

There was a pause, during which the salesman mumbled incoherently and his blood formed a small puddle on the tarmac.

'Maybe he has a point, boys,' one man said.

'And look at the blood. Don't get it on you – it's a bastard to get off. When this wee shite goes running to the peelers they'll be looking for bloodstained clothes, so they will.'

The two men holding the semi-conscious salesman immediately released their hold. He fell to the ground like a puppet with the strings cut, and lay there babbling.

'No . . . no trouble. Won't say anything. Won't say a word . . .' Then he passed out.

Early toed him over on to his side. 'Well, he's a lot of bloody use to you now, isn't he? You have to be more subtle about this kind of thing.'

'How would you know?' one man asked, still hostile.

'Sure, you see it on TV all the time. Good cop, bad cop. It's no good just beating the shit out of him.'

Mullan nodded, looking down at the crumpled form on the ground.

'You've a head on your shoulders, so you have, Dominic. Shit, he's a mess, isn't he? Doesn't look as though he'd harm a fly anyway.'

The men shifted uneasily.

'Maybe we should call an ambulance,' said one. 'Do it anonymously.'

'He's a fucking Prod!' another burst out. 'Let the bastard bleed!'

'No,' Early said. 'If you just leave him it'll be the police and the Brits and everything who find him. But if you just call an ambulance, we can keep it quiet.'

He knelt down beside the crumpled body and slapped the face lightly. One bloodshot eye opened.

'You won't say anything, will you, mister? You know what'll happen if you do. We'll find you, and then you'll get worse than a split head, so you will. Do you understand?'

The man nodded numbly through his mask of blood, and Early straightened, satisfied.

'I'll make the call meself. The rest of you might as well clear off.'

They hovered there, indecisive. Early despised them all.

'He's right, lads,' Mullan said. 'You might as well go home. We'll look after this.'

They trailed away, still discontented, muttering. Mullan turned to Early.

'You did the right thing there, Dominic. They've no brains, most of them, just bitterness and biceps, but you're not so slow yourself. Come on, let's see if we can clean the bugger up a bit.'

Charles Boyd slouched in his chair in the operations room at Bessbrook, bored and annoyed. The young Greenjacket subaltern who was acting as watchkeeper eyed him a little nervously. This was the gung-ho, fire-eating SAS officer who had led the Drumboy op and wiped out that ASU in Tyrone. So far, all the subaltern himself had had to brave this tour were a few bottles and the insults of the local harridans.

He had three units out on the ground at the moment, two of them on three-day rural patrols under other officers, the third a VCP on the Blaney road, operated in unison with the RUC. All around the room, operational maps of the area lined the walls and at one wall a bank of radios and their operators were an insistent interruption of static and low voices. The young officer sipped his dark brown tea and sighed, thinking of the West End, wondering if someone else was porking his girlfriend while he was away: one of the perennial worries of the soldier.

Boyd's thoughts were more complex. He was trying to think up some way to retrieve what he saw as his reputation. He wanted out on the ground again – he had wanted Gorbals's OP, but Cordwain had overruled him and given it to the Glaswegian NCO instead. The SAS major was in Cross now, overseeing the OP. Boyd was being put on a back burner for a while. He knew it and he didn't like it.

Sometimes he felt that the British Army was not in Northern Ireland to defeat the IRA or to wipe out terrorism, but to maintain a certain status quo. They knew who eighty per cent of the terrorists were, where they lived, what cars they drove, which football team they supported. But they could pin nothing on them. For Boyd that was a ridiculous situation. He believed the terrorists should be taken out – assassinated, for want of a better word. No one in Whitehall would cry for them except for a few tiny special-interest groups and some downright traitors. The judicial system was a farce, and when the army or RUC tried ways of circumventing or speeding it up – such as the use of supergrasses a few years back – then they always failed. Better to see the problem as the IRA saw it – as a purely military one. That would put the shits up the bastards and no mistake. They'd keep their heads well below the parapet after a few of the ringleaders had been found in ditches with bullets in the back of their heads.

But that, Cordwain had told him, would be to become terrorists themselves. Boyd could not see it. There was too much pussyfooting around, and all the while, soldiers and innocents died because of it. Sometimes when he thought about it he could hardly bottle up the fury.

A crackle of the radio. The Greenjacket second lieutenant leaned forward.

'Sir,' the operator said. 'Bravo Two One has stopped a major player on the Blaney road heading east into Cross. Eugene Finn, the name is. He wants to know if you'd like him held for a while.'

'Yes! Keep him there!' Boyd snapped before the other officer could speak. He was out of his chair. 'I want a heli to that VCP at once. We've been looking for this bastard.'

'Have we anything on him?' the Greenjacket asked, looking through his file.

'Nothing concrete – not yet. But it was probably him who masterminded the Drumboy operation. I want to talk to him. Now get me that fucking helicopter.'

The younger officer hesitated, then shrugged, and sent word to the helipad that a chopper was wanted: 'priority two, one passenger'.

It was a small, dragonfly-like gazelle that transported Boyd from the fortress of Bessbrook over the undulating, moonlit hills of Armagh. Ulster Troop was based in Bessbrook because of the fact that it was the best heliport along the border; the SAS needed the mobility it could provide, even though the Security Forces' base in Cross was adequate for most other purposes.

So Finn had come back south. It would be interesting to talk to him, this IRA hotshot. In a way, he and Boyd had already met, over gun barrels. It seemed though that he had survived Drumboy unscathed. A resourceful enemy indeed. The second IRA platoon that had caught them napping that night on the hill – that had been Finn's men, the South Armagh bunch. Intelligence now believed that the South Armagh Brigade had not suffered as badly as they had initially thought. Its members had been spirited away to Belfast. Did this mean that they were beginning to filter back south to their old stamping grounds?

Boyd would get no information out of Finn, he knew that; the man was too canny. And he had nothing to hold him on. Finn's wife, when questioned at her door by chatting British soldiers as to her husband's whereabouts, had merely said that he was away visiting relatives. Nothing to go on, then. But Boyd could at least make this a highly unpleasant evening for the bastard.

The gazelle landed in a field fifty yards from

the VCP on the Blaney road. Boyd leapt out. He had no weapon except for the Browning High Power, for form's sake in a webbing holster at his waist instead of in the armpit or on the thigh. He wore a Kevlar helmet and ordinary combats; there was nothing to suggest that he was SAS.

The helicopter took off again. Boyd would stay out and return to Bessbrook with the VCP members themselves. He sauntered over to the road where an old Ford Cortina was sitting to one side and an RUC constable was waving down cars with a red torch.

The corporal in command met him as he gained the road.

'Evening, boss.' The Greenjackets were almost as informal that way as the SAS. 'We've got him out of the car and given him the once-over; we were just going to start and search the vehicle.'

Boyd nodded. 'Go ahead. And Corporal . . .'

The man turned.

'To search it properly, you'll have to take out the seats and things – everything that's remotely movable. You get my meaning?'

The man grinned. 'Sure thing, boss.'

Boyd joined a small group of men in front of the Cortina. There was a soldier there, gripping his SA-80 as though he longed to use it, an RUC constable with his Heckler & Koch MP5K dangling across his armoured chest and his note-book out, and a lean, dark man in civvies who was smoking a cigarette and directing hate-filled glances at them both.

Boyd strode up. 'Evening, Eugene. Nice night for a drive, don't you think?'

Finn looked at him over the glowing tip of his cigarette, and blew out smoke silently.

'Well, constable?' Boyd asked the policeman. The RUC man was young, probably single, as all the police on the border were. He wore an army-style sweater under dark-green Gore-tex waterproofs, and his trousers were bloused into a pair of combat boots. In addition to the Heckler & Koch he carried a Ruger revolver in a holster at his waist. Apart from the green peaked cap with its harp badge, he looked like a soldier.

'Hello, sir,' the constable said cheerfully. Boyd's plummy accent had immediately marked him out as an officer.

'The gentleman here has come from Omagh, where he has been visiting relatives. Name, Eugene Finn, address 23 Conway Crescent, Dundalk Road, Crossmaglen. His driving licence seems to be in order, but unfortunately this is not his vehicle . . .'

'I told you, it's me cousin's,' Finn snarled suddenly.

'. . . and we are checking the ownership now.'

'Thanks, constable. I'll take it from here.'

The policeman nodded and moved away. Finn's eyes darted from Boyd's face to the car that the Greenjacket soldiers were now assiduously taking apart.

'You bastards,' Finn growled as both front seats were taken out and placed in the ditch.

'Now now, sir,' Boyd said with a smile. 'We're just doing our job.'

Finn stared at him closely, then flicked the half-finished cigarette at him so it bounced off Boyd's chest. The SAS officer stiffened.

'That's for your job. Now how long do you think your military sense of humour will keep me here at the side of the road, when me kids are waiting for me at home?'

'Maybe you should spend more time with your kids, Eugene, instead of tramping all over the countryside at all hours of the day and night.'

It was Finn's turn to pause. He regarded Boyd with keener interest.

'What regiment are you with, public school-boy?'

'Greenjackets, like the rest of them.'

'Is that a fact? You don't carry a rifle. Too heavy for you, is it?'

Boyd felt that he was losing the initiative.

'How are your friends in Belfast, Eugene? Coming along nicely, are they? Poor lads. A punishment shooting is an awful thing.'

'I don't know what you're talking about, Brit.'

'Sure you do, Eugene. Pity we managed to pick up that M60, off the field of battle, you might say. I bet those things don't grow on trees, eh?'

Finn did not reply, but lit another cigarette and blew the smoke into Boyd's face.

'Nasty habit that, Eugene. It'll kill you in the end.'

'Life's a lot more unhealthy for you lot, down here, than it is for me. Maybe Armagh should have a government health warning. "Patrolling here can be bad for your health." How many have you boys lost here in the last eighteen months? It's no wonder you're taking out your frustration on innocent men like me.'

The Greenjackets, eavesdropping on what Finn was saying, went at their work with added savagery. The steering wheel landed in the grass. Finn watched it dispassionately.

'You'll have to put it all back together again, you know.'

'Or what?'

'Or I might have to complain.'

'Who to – the police?'

Finn laughed. 'No – to the Border Fox. Him and his comrades. They're the only real authority in this part of the world. Time you understood that, soldier.'

The corporal joined them.

'Car's clean as a whistle, boss, and we did him before you arrived. Nothing. Omagh confirms that the car belongs to one Jimmy Finn. His story checks out.'

Boyd nodded. 'All right, Corporal. I suppose we had better let Mr Finn be on his way. Pack up the VCP and call in the heli.'

'OK, boss.' The Greenjacket strolled off.

'Going back to hide in your wee base, are you?' Finn sneered. 'I bet it's the only place you feel safe in this part of the world, Brit.'

Boyd smiled, and took Finn's arm in a grip of iron, pulling him closer.

'Listen, Eugene. You can take it from me, not from Parliament, or Whitehall or Lisburn: when we catch this Fox of yours – and we will – he's never going to see the inside of a court. He's going to get the same justice he's been meting out to us for the past eighteen months. That's a promise. And if we catch you stepping out of line, Finn, I swear to Christ, you'll get the same.'

Finn glared at him for a moment and then said: 'You're SAS, aren't you, schoolboy? You were on the hill that night.'

Boyd smiled again, but said nothing.

'Heli's on its way, boss,' the corporal said.

'Very good, Corporal. We'll leave Mr Finn here to his DIY. Have a pleasant evening, sir.' And he touched the brim of his helmet to Finn mockingly. The IRA man stood beside the wreckage of his car and said nothing, but Boyd could feel his eyes on his back all the way across the field where the other soldiers and the policeman were waiting, kneeling in the hedge. It made his skin crawl, as though the cross-hairs of a sight were resting on the back of his neck.

There was a roar, and the helicopter, a troop-carrying Puma, landed, flattening the grass. Boyd was last in the stick, and as he clambered on board he could see Finn still standing motionless in the road, watching them, the glow of his cigarette like a tiny window into hell.

15

Haymaker rubbed his eyes tiredly and peered once more through the powerful magnifying lens of the Nikon. Nothing doing. He stared at the tiny luminous hands of his watch. It was 2330 hours on a Wednesday night, and Lavery's bar was as quiet as a grave. From his position he could see the inside corner of the L-shaped building, covering both the bar itself – though not well, since the windows were frosted glass and the curtains were half drawn – and the private accommodation above and behind it. Gorbals had teased them all, in whispers, with the sight he said he had seen the previous morning. The Lavery woman in the noddy, tits out and ready for inspection. Haymaker thought privately it was a tall tale, designed to make them all look harder. If so, it had worked.

Wilkie was on the radio, his hand on the signals log. He was yawning. God, Haymaker hated OP duty. Lying in wait somewhere, waiting to do the business like they had in Tyrone – that was one thing. But this tedious logging of everyday occurrences was quite another. And if something did happen – if the shit actually hit the fan – then all they would do was inform Cross. And then they would just sit back and watch, like spectators at a football match. So much for the glamorous side of the SAS. He glued his eye to the camera again.

There he was: the undercover bloke, Early. Looked like a bit of a hard character. He was making himself tea in the kitchen. And there was the Lavery woman. Bit of all right, she was; nice hair. Oh, here we go, Haymaker thought, and he squeezed off a few shots of Early kissing her. Lucky bastard.

They went upstairs together, and Haymaker sighed. Wilkie looked at him questioningly and Haymaker made an unmistakable gesture. Wilkie scowled. Being in the SAS was like being a fucking monk sometimes.

Haymaker tensed. There were two cars coming into the square from his right. They were driving slowly, one an old, beaten-up Cortina, the other a Lada. He snapped them quickly, noting their number-plates in the log. One seemed familiar, and he flipped quickly through the P-file. It had been updated that evening. The Cortina – Finn had been driving it on the Blaney road less than two hours before.

Haymaker gave the thumbs down to Wilkie, who nodded. The big trooper squinted down his camera lens as though it were the sight on a weapon – which he often wished it was – and clicked off exposure after exposure. Five men in the two vehicles, all of them getting out at once. He recognised Finn right way: he was the tall, leery bastard smoking the cigarette. Others he found harder to place, but he had their mugs on film, no problem. It looked as though the South Armagh boys were back in town. He entered it all down in the log. They were heading towards Lavery's bar, for a late-night pint or a confab. Or to get Early maybe? Haymaker cursed softly, then showed the log to Wilkie and stabbed a finger at the last entry. Wilkie nodded and began sending the message back to Cordwain in Cross. Haymaker debated waking Gorbals and Raymond, but decided against it. Could be it was all a false alarm, and the other pair badly needed their sleep. No, he'd let them get a little more gonk. The shit hadn't hit the fan yet.

Maggie moaned under him as Early pushed into her. He felt her nails claw his back and her thighs grip his waist. Her face was a pale oval in the darkened room, the hair a shadowed tangle around it.

Then he froze. There were footsteps coming up the stair, several sets of them.

'Dominic, don't stop. What's wrong?' Maggie whispered.

He rolled off her. 'Somebody's coming.'

'Oh, never worry about Brendan. He doesn't mind now . . .'

'No, not him.'

They were on the landing. Early heard the door of his room being opened, and a voice he recognized.

Finn.

His Walther was behind the cistern, where he always put it when he slept with Maggie. He cursed himself now for his incompetence.

'Get dressed,' he told the naked girl, pulling on his trousers. She stared at him, her eyes shining in the dark.

'It's Eugene. What's he doing here?' she said.

'I don't know. Get dressed.'

She pulled on a dressing-gown hurriedly, just as the door to her room was knocked. Early's eyes met hers, and in that moment he knew that the game was up. She could see his fear.

Without taking her eyes off him, she called out: 'Who is it? I'm in bed.'

Early continued to stare at her, talking with his eyes.

'It's Eugene, Maggie. Sorry to bother you. Would Dominic be in there at all?'

She hesitated, her eyes never leaving his face. Then she laughed, bitterly, and said:

'He's here, Eugene. Come on in.'

The door opened, letting in a glare of light. At least three men stood in the doorway.

'Sorry to disturb you, Maggie,' Finn said. He was a shadow, silhouetted by the light behind him. 'We just want a wee word with Dominic here.'

Early straightened. 'Mind if I finish dressing?'

'Oh, go ahead, Dominic. We've all the time in the world.'

Then Finn turned to one of the men behind him. 'Rory, go and get the car started.'

'Going somewhere, are you?' Early asked, lacing up his shoes with trembling hands.

'Oh aye, Dominic. We're all going for a wee ride. You go back to bed, Maggie.'

'I'd like to come along,' she said.

'No, you'll stay here. It's just Dominic we want.'

Early stood up. 'I'm ready if you are, Eugene. Bit late for a drive though, isn't it?'

'Don't you worry – we're not going far. Come on.'

Early paused in his way out of the room to look at Maggie. Her head was bowed, and she did not say goodbye.

'All right, all right,' Early said soothingly as

he was shoved along the landing. Brendan stood at the head of the stairs, white-faced.

"What are you going to do to him, Eugene?"

'Nothing, Brendan. Just you shut up the pub as usual after we're gone.'

Early was hustled downstairs, and then out the door. It was cold outside, and under his shirtsleeves his flesh went into goose-pimples. He could still smell the fragrance of Maggie's hair on his skin.

'In you get, Dominic. Mind your head.'

He was pushed into a car, and then shoved down on the floor of the back seat. Finn got in after him and rested his feet on his chest. The IRA man produced a pistol and put it against Early's forehead.

'Now don't you make a sound, Dominic. I'd hate to mess up the floor of me cousin's car, so I would.'

He nodded at the driver, and they moved off. Early shut his eyes, knowing he was a dead man.

Gorbals woke at once to find Haymaker shaking him.

'What? What is it, you big cunt?'

'The undercover bloke, Early. They've taken him.'

The little Glaswegian was immediately alert. 'You've radioed Cross?'

'Yes. They're going to try and intercept them. Two cars, five players. I saw one pistol. If you ask me, our man's fucked.'

Gorbals inched out of his sleeping bag. Even now, they were aware of the need for silence. Their conversation had been in whispers.

'What road did they take?'

'The Monog. They're headed for the border, no doubt about it.'

'Fuck. I hope the QRF catches them before they reach it.'

'Shall we start packing up? Early knows there's an OP in Cross. If they work on him, they'll find out.'

Gorbals nodded. 'Don't pack up the surveillance kit, but get all the rest of the shit put away, ready for immediate evac. And comm Cross for instructions. We'll stay here as long as we can.'

In silence, two of the SAS troopers began packing up their gear and the rubbish they had accumulated over the past few days, while one remained monitoring the radio and the other peered out into the empty streets of Crossmaglen.

After a while the car's motion changed from smooth, fast travel to a slow bump and lurch. With his head down near the floor, Early could feel the vibrations of undergrowth clawing along the underside of the vehicle. Once, when a wheel hit a pothole, his head flew up to jar painfully with the muzzle of Finn's pistol, making the IRA man grin.

They stopped at last and cold air rushed in as the car doors were opened. Early felt vaguely sick from the ride on the floor. He was jerked out by two of his captors and stood, dizzy, trying to collect himself.

They seemed to be in the middle of nowhere. He was standing in tyre-churned mud. The night was still dark though there were stars overhead. Suddenly there was a tiny glow of light, and he could make out the humped shape of a derelict house some yards in front of him. Someone had lit a candle inside.

'Let's go, Dominic,' someone said, and he felt the barrel of a pistol in his back. He recognized the voice: it was Jim Mullan.

'I hadn't figured you out for this sort of caper, Jim,' he said casually over his shoulder.

'You hadn't figured out a lot of things. You're in the shite now, Dominic, if that's your name at all. I hope you're good at singing.'

Early said nothing, but let himself be bundled inside the derelict house. There was a small pool of candlelight there, and several men; and a chair, and rope.

He felt a moment of stark, incapacitating

terror, and froze. Mullan pushed him forward again. He shook himself.

'All right, Jim, all right.'

He was going to be tortured. His mind began working furiously The OP would have seen him being spirited away, so the QRF would have been sent out by now. Probably Cordwain had put the rest of Ulster Troop on alert too. Had they managed to follow him? These men seemed remarkably at ease considering half the border security forces were hot on their tail.

Unless they had made it over the border.

That thought chilled the blood in Early's veins.

'Search him,' Finn said curtly.

Early was shoved up against one damp wall and spread-eagled. Hands ran up and down his limbs, into his pockets. They even examined his shoes.

'Nothing,' Jim Mullan said.

Finn frowned. The house is clean too – Maggie checked it.' Then he shrugged. 'We'll soon find out the truth of it anyway. Take a seat, Dominic.' He was smoking a cigarette and smiling, gesturing to the stoutly built wooden chair. Early wanted to kill him, but he had to try to draw this out, to give his own people as long as possible to close in.

'If it's all the same to you, Eugene, I'll stand, thanks.'

Finn nodded to the other men. They advanced and took his arms. Then Finn brought up the pistol barrel.

'Fucking sit down, you cunt.'

Early was propelled to the chair and forced to sit in it. The men started tying his wrists, elbows, knees and ankles to the wood. When they had finished he was bound as rigidly to the chair as though he were part of it. He tried to breathe evenly, to contain his fear. These pieces of shit were not going to see him afraid.

Finn stubbed out his cigarette on the stone wall and lit another.

'Strange things have been happening lately, Dominic, so they have. The SAS are in town. Did you know that? Oh aye. They're in wee Crossmaglen, somewhere, and they have a tout who's doing their dirty work for them. Shocking, isn't it?'

Finn drew in smoke. The other men stirred.

'Work the bugger over now.'

'Fucking turncoat bastard.'

Finn held up his hand.

'We'll try this the easy way first, so we will. We're civilized people, after all.' He knelt down in front of Early.

'Now, Dominic, it looks like you're our number one suspect. You're a man without a past, you know that? You showed up here out of the blue, squirmed your way into Maggie Lavery's bed, and suddenly, you're one of us. Very easy. You're just too good to be true. So what's your real name then, eh?'

'Dominic McAteer. Jesus, Eugene, I don't know where you get your ideas from . . .'

Finn stubbed out his cigarette on Early's cheek.

The SAS officer cried out and twisted his head, but one of the other men grabbed it from behind and held it still. Finn ground out the glowing butt slowly, intently. The smell of burning flesh filled the room. Early clenched his teeth until blood started from the gums.

Finally, Finn straightened. Early's eyes were full of tears. His right cheek felt double its usual size, as though it were swollen with acid. He was breathing like a sprinter.

'You're a hard bastard, Dominic, you know that?' Finn said softly. 'I'll bet my arse you're no navvy from Ballymena. You're a Brit, so you are. Maybe you're even SAS.'

'You're out of your mind, so you are,' Early groaned. He could taste the blood in his mouth.

Finn said nothing, but nodded to the other men, and withdrew.

They began to work on him.

16

Cordwain slammed down the phone savagely.

'They've lost them!'

'How?' Boyd demanded.

'Fuck knows. They must have turned off the Monog road and avoided the VCP near Urcher Lodge. Then they simply disappeared. The check-point on the Foxfield road hasn't seen them, and neither has the watch-tower at Drummuckavall. They must have taken off across country.'

'In a car? It's boggy as hell down there.'

Cordwain turned to the operations map on the wall of his office.

'There are dozens of side-roads and tracks down in that area. It could be they went down the Alley road, south-west towards the border, through Moybane, and then turned off into Moybane Bog – there are tracks there, for the forestry workers. They could have taken the car all the way through the woods there, and hey presto! they're in the Republic.'

'Jesus,' Boyd said. 'That's it, then. Early's dead. Poor bastard.'

'They'll keep him alive a while, to try and find out whatever they can. Early's a tough nut. He knows the longer he holds out the more time it gives us.'

'What about the Gardai? Have they been informed?'

'Irish Army units are in the area. They're reacting with their customary lack of urgency. Fuck! What a mess.'

'The troop is ready to go, with the exception of Gorbals's men. They're being extracted now. The rest are all in plain clothes. We have three Q cars standing by in Cross.'

'Good. We're on our own with this one. If they are across the border, then the Regular Army's hands are tied.'

'You'll authorize a cross-border operation, then?'

'Fucking right I will. I'm not going to stand by and let them murder a member of the Regiment under our very noses.'

Cordwain stood staring at the map. Outside, helicopters were roaring as they landed and took off. It was still dark, but the choppers were helping to flood the area south of Crossmaglen with troops. They were more of a gesture than anything else. He was sure now that the enemy was across the border, perhaps only a few hundred metres into the Republic of Ireland, holed up in a house or hut somewhere, torturing Early.

'I want all three Q cars to head down for the Moybane area. That's where they've headed – the VCPs will have funnelled them in that direction. I want one down as far as the footbridge to the east of Moybane Lough, and two covering the forestry area of the bog. You're to continue on foot across the border – it's only two hundred metres away at that point. Sweep the area between the footbridge and the wood. They'll be in an abandoned house, a farmhouse or something.'

'And if we find them?'

'Take them out – as many as you can. And save Early, what's left of him.'

'There'll be an almighty stink – it has the makings of a proper diplomatic incident.'

'I know. I'll take the rap. It was me that got Early into this in the first place. They can have my head on a plate if they like, just so long as we get those fuckers and save our man. Is that clear, Charles?'

Boyd was smiling. 'Perfectly.'

'Then *go!*'

The men in the cars were heavily armed. There were three in each vehicle, one commanded by Boyd, another by Sergeant Hutton, a reliable Falklands veteran, the third by Corporal Little.

One man in each car had a Remington 870 pump-action shotgun – useful for blowing hinges off doors. The others carried Heckler & Koch MP5K sub-machine-guns, ugly, snub-nosed little weapons used by SAS hostage-rescue teams. Extra magazines were fastened to the weapons themselves with magnetic clips. As well as these, the men each had their Browning handguns in shoulder holsters and a variety of stun and smoke grenades. The team leaders carried small Landmaster radios with single earphones and wrist mikes.

They were dressed in nondescript civilian clothing: jeans, plaid shirts, bomber jackets. Every man there knew that they were going to undertake an illegal incursion into the Irish Republic, but it was to rescue a fellow soldier.

They were silent in the cars as they sped south, checking magazines, running through room-clearing drills in their heads. They were waved through army checkpoints, who had been told to expect them, and soon they were off the secondary roads and on to single-track roads, and finally unsurfaced tracks.

They split up on a signal from Boyd and headed for the three debussing points, from where they would continue on foot, sweeping a kilometre-wide area for their quarry.

The hunt was on.

*   *   *

A deluge of cold water brought Early round. His head slowly straightened and he tried to blink the droplets out of his eyes. His face was swollen to twice its normal size. It felt as though it belonged to someone else. His mouth felt as though it were full of fine gravel, but that was the remains of his teeth.

He found it hard to breathe, because they had thrust lighted cigarettes up his nostrils until the flesh had charred. He was locked within himself, withdrawn from the world except when the renewal of the agony brought it screaming back into sharp focus.

Two things kept him going, kept his mouth shut and stopped him from telling them everything, from begging for mercy. The first was the knowledge that the SAS would be looking for him. They were probably less than a mile away even now, combing the countryside. Border or no border, he believed that James Cordwain would do his utmost to rescue him.

That's what comes of going to a public school, he thought with dazed humour. A sense of honour. Cordwain will do the right thing, come hell or high water.

The second thing was quite simple. It was white, blinding hatred for the men who were doing this to him, and in particular for their ringleader. Early wanted to survive, because he wanted the satisfaction of killing Finn himself. He wanted to make the IRA man squirm as he was squirming now, wanted to wipe that fucking sneer off his face for eternity.

'Well, Mr X,' Finn said. 'You're no Dominic McAteer from Ballymena, so you're not. You know how I know?'

Early glared at him dumbly.

'Well, it's simple, you see. If you were some humble brickie, you'd be begging for mercy now, promising all sorts of things, and confessing to the murder of your own mother if you thought it would stop the pain for a while. But you're not, not you. You're just sitting there taking it and not saying a thing. Your eyes say it all though.

'You're a Brit, aren't you, me old son?'

Still Early said nothing.

'Well, we'll take that as a yes. Now, Mr X, since we've established that you're a Brit, and a bloody-minded one at that, we want you to talk to us even more. We just can't wait to hear what you have to say, can we, lads?'

There was a snigger from one of the other men. Jim Mullan, Early noted, looked a little green about the gills.

'This freedom fighting is a noble calling, eh Jim?' he managed to croak through his broken teeth. The big man looked away.

Finn slapped Early across his burnt cheek.

'Now now, me old son – no fraternization. You'll answer questions, but I don't want any of your bullshit.'

'Fuck off,' Early rasped.

'Stubborn cunt,' Finn said, not without admiration.

'Rory, go and bring that leather-covered box out of the car. Seamus, what's the time?'

'Just gone two.'

'Ach, sure we've loads of time, so we have.' Finn produced a hip-flask from his pocket and passed it around. The reek of whiskey was strong in the air.

'Want some?' he asked Early, and splashed some over his face.

It burned and seared Early's blistered and raw skin, but he shut his eyes against the pain and made no sound. The hatred mounted up and up in him like a steepening wave.

When he could open his eyes again Early saw that they had brought in a brown box from the car. They opened it and he saw the black, shining shape of a telephone. For a moment he was puzzled, until he realized, and the sweat broke out all over his body.

'You boys used these in Malaya,' Finn said, flicking away another cigarette butt. 'And the Yanks used them in Vietnam. And I'm not talking communications. Seamus, get his trousers down. Get the bastard's balls out.'

Early's trousers were torn down to his knees, then his boxer shorts. Finn came closer, with two crocodile clips attached to wires, and clipped them agonizingly on to Early's testicles.

'Now we'll have some fun,' Finn breathed. 'Your last chance. What regiment are you with?'

Early spat blood and fragments of teeth into his face. Finn straightened.

'Jim, turn that fucking handle.'

Early's world exploded in blinding pain. Involuntarily, he screamed aloud.

Boyd halted, his shoes sinking in the wet ooze of the bog.

'Did you hear that?'

'What, boss?'

'Somebody yelled, I'm sure of it.'

The three SAS men paused in the silent night, hearing an owl kee-wick, the squeak of hunting bats, their own feet sucking in the marsh that they had plunged into as soon as they had crossed the invisible border between Northern Ireland and Eire.

Then they all heard it, carrying over the fields in the silence of the summer night. A man screaming in agony.

'Jesus Christ,' one of the troopers said softly.

Boyd felt the hair on his neck rise up. He thumbed the wrist mike.

'Oscar One and Two, this is Zero. Objective to your front, estimate figures three zero zero metres, over.'

'Roger out,' came back the reply from the other two teams.

Boyd lifted a hand, and the three SAS men started forward again.

They were sinking ankle-deep in ooze at every step, their progress frustratingly slow as they hauled their feet out of the sucking mud as quietly as possible. At last one of the troopers tapped Boyd's arm.

'Off on the right, boss – there's a track going our way.'

Boyd nodded and they started towards it. The scream came again, louder now. Boyd felt an urge to run forward, guns blazing, and take out the torturing bastards, but he forced himself to slow down.

They reached the track and made better time. There was a wood ahead, gloomy and impenetrable-looking in the darkness.

Figures moving to their left. Boyd swung the muzzle of the Heckler & Koch.

'They're ours, boss.'

The figures were holding their hands in the air in the recognition signal. Boyd waved them over.

The two teams went to ground in the eaves of the wood, waiting for the third to join them. At last they did, announcing their arrival over the radio before appearing. Sergeant Hutton whispered in Boyd's ear.

'There's a little clearing in the wood ahead, some old derelict building with a light in it. Two doors at the front, one at the back. The screams are coming from there. That's the place, boss.'

Boyd digested this, and then made his plans accordingly.

Two teams would assault the place: his own and Corporal Little's. They would clear the house room by room in two pairs and flush the terrorists out into the open. The third man of each team would remain at the front of the house to provide possible fire support or catch any terrorists who slipped past the room-clearing teams. Sergeant Hutton's troopers would be the cut-off group and would station themselves at the rear of the building to catch any of the enemy leaving that way. There would be no escape for any of them.

The SAS men began moving into position.

17

They had drenched his lower body with water, to strengthen the shocks. Early's head hung over his naked knees. His genitals were scorched and discoloured from the hand-powered generator of the field telephone. There was an unpleasant smell in the air, of ozone and burning hair. He no longer cared. All he wanted was a release from the pain. He would almost have welcomed a bullet in the head, if it meant an end to the pain.

They were not coming for him; there would be no last-minute rescue. Cordwain had abandoned him.

Talk to them, a voice deep inside him urged. Tell them something – anything. Make them stop. It was tempting to believe that if he talked, they would stop. But they would never stop. He was their sport for the evening.

And besides, he thought: I am nothing if not a stubborn sonofabitch.

'Spin her round again, Jim,' Finn said. Even he sounded weary.

'No,' Mullan said. 'Sorry, Eugene. Let one of the other lads do it. I don't feel too well. I need a bit of fresh air.'

Finn stared at him closely, and then laughed.

'Right enough, Jim. You do look as though you're going to puke. Go on, then, go and clear your head. The night's not over yet. We'll have this cunt singing like a bird before dawn.'

Mullan left the room, shambling out into the night air. The other men were standing around, eyes bright, lapping it up.

'Seamus, go and give Jim your gun. Tell him to keep an eye out. And then you can have your turn.'

As the other man went out to do his bidding, Finn knelt in front of Early again.

'You know, Brit, I don't give much for your prospects of being a family man after this little escapade. Your balls are dark as a pair of plums.'

He grinned, but Early was too far gone to care. He could not see Finn's face in any detail – only a white blur.

'What regiment are you?' Finn asked for the thousandth time.

Seamus came in again and knelt beside the field telephone, his hand on the handle.

'Fuck me, Seamus, this bugger's as tight-lipped as a tinker's purse. Spin her again.'

The handle spun round, and it started once more.

Big Jim Mullan stood outside in the welcome fresh air of the night. That stink inside, it had made him sick to his stomach. He didn't like all this interrogation business. If Dominic was a spy, then they might as well shoot him and have done with it. This torturing stuff wasn't his cup of tea at all.

The pistol grip was cold in the palm of his hand. A Beretta Centurion, 9mm – a beautiful weapon. Mullan loved guns, always had, since the time his father had let him fire a shotgun as a boy. Or perhaps since the first time Finn had placed an AK47 in his hand.

He thought of Drumboy. He had been lucky or unlucky to miss that – he wasn't sure which. What a fight. But so many had died, because Dominic had somehow informed, Eugene had said. And that incident with the Prod salesman in Brendan's bar had confirmed Finn's suspicions about Dominic.

Mullan shook his head. Sometimes he wondered if the whole business was worth it at all.

Then he saw the shadows come rushing out of the trees like nightmares made real. The starlight glinted off the barrels of their weapons. He raised his pistol.

'Eugene!' he shrieked. 'They're here!'

A fusillade of bullets blasted him off his feet.

Boyd leapt forward. The big player at the door was on his back, eyes open and his pistol lying unfired at his side. He moved feebly, and Boyd put another two rounds in him – a 'double tap' to the head that blew away half his skull.

Trooper Quigley fired two shotgun blasts into the door of the house and Boyd kicked it off its mangled hinges. Then Quigley swiftly lobbed in a stun grenade. Corporal Little and his partner were at the other door, doing the same.

There was a flash and a bang within, and then Boyd rushed through the doorway.

The blast had blown out the candles. It was dark inside. There was a slumped, seated shape in the centre of the floor, other shapes moving at the back, leaving by a rear door. He opened up on them, the little sub-machine-gun bucking wildly in his hands. There were screams, and someone fell, but the others were still moving. He heard gunfire on the other side of the house as Little's team moved in.

'Room clear!' he shouted, and Quigley burst in. Boyd took a second to check that the figure tied to the chair was indeed Early, and then joined his partner at the far door. He pulled a pin on another stun grenade and threw it into the next room. After it had gone off, Quigley darted through the doorway, opening up on automatic as he went. Now that they had Early secured they could be less careful with letting off rounds, but they still had to be careful of ricochets. In a house this old and dilapidated there was a lot of bare stone visible that could send bullets bouncing back at their firer.

'Stoppage!' he heard Quigley shout, infuriated. More rounds were going down. He went through the doorway in pursuit and stood over Quigley firing two-round bursts as the trooper changed mags.

'OK!' Quigley yelled, and started firing again himself. Now it was Boyd's turn to change mags.

Another fucking doorway. This one was open, leading out into a kind of back kitchen. There were flashes in the darkness as the players fired back. Boyd was dimly aware that the cut-off team was firing too, out at the back of the house. He and Quigley put down rounds at the flashes and heard someone cry out. Then they moved forward again, as smoothly as a well-oiled machine.

Another stun grenade, then a burst of fire through the doorway. The room was empty but for a body lying in a shining pool at one wall. At the back a broken door was swinging on its hinges and letting in the night air.

'Room clear!' he heard Little shout, and then: 'We're at the back of the house, boss!'

'House clear!' Boyd shouted. There was firing out of the back. The trees were flashing and flickering with gunshots; clearly some of the players had made it to the trees.

A shot behind him. He turned to find that Quigley had put a bullet in the head of one of the downed players.

'Fucker was still wriggling, boss,' Quigley said, and Boyd nodded.

The job was done – there was nothing more for the two assault teams to do for the moment but wait. If they ran out into the woods there would be a danger of a blue-on-blue. Sergeant Hutton was there to see the players didn't escape.

Something moved at the edge of the trees. A man in civvies, crawling into the woods. He still had a pistol in one hand. Boyd put three rounds into him, and he jerked frantically, then lay still.

'I make that four of the fuckers,' he said.

'I think one got away,' Quigley told him. 'He ran out the back with the one you just shot, but I don't think Hutton's lads got him. That's who they're after now.'

'They'd better fucking get him,' Boyd growled, and then: 'I'm going to have a look at our man back there. Keep the backyard covered.'

He strode back through the house, stepping over two bodies on the way. Both of them were well and truly dead, finished off with head shots. Though the operation seemed to have been largely successful, Boyd was uneasy. The SAS were operating on the soil of the Irish Republic; technically, they had just carried out four murders. He wanted his men back in Northern Ireland ASAP, before the Gardai or the Irish Army picked them up.

More shots out the back, then silence. Boyd bent over Early, wincing as he made out what had been done to him. He felt for a neck pulse, got one, and sighed with relief. Then he began slicing through Early's ropes with a pocket knife.

The undercover officer's eyes opened and after a moment his burnt and battered face smiled as he said: 'You took your fucking time.' Then his head fell to one side again.

Quigley came running through the door.

'Boss, Hutton says one of them got away, and there's Southern police cars on their way up the track.'

'Shit! Grab Early. We've got to get the hell out of here.' He thumbed his wrist mike.

'Zero to all stations. Bug out, I repeat, bug out back to debus point, out.'

He and Quigley grabbed the semi-conscious Early's arms and trailed him out to the front of the house. Several other troopers were crouching in the deeper shadow of the trees. Boyd could see two sets of headlights advancing bumpily up the track less than half a mile away.

'Back across the bog,' he told Quigley. They set off. Two more troopers joined them and helped with Early so that each of them had a limb. They made good time until they hit the soft sections of the bog, when they began to sink into the muck up to their calves.

Boyd looked back. Two cars had stopped with their headlights trained on the house, and figures were moving around. It was farcical. Here they were, lugging an unconscious man whose trousers were down around his ankles through a bog in the middle of the night, on the run from the police. And he was a British Army officer on a top-secret mission. Jesus, what a world.

They saw the faint shine of water off to their right. Drummuckavall Lough. They were almost on the border now.

'We bleeding made it,' Quigley gasped. 'Back in the UK, thank fuck.'

When they were sure they were once more back in Northern Ireland they halted a moment while Boyd commed the other team. The troopers had merged into two groups: his four men, and Sergeant Hutton's five.

'Back in from the *ulu*, boss,' Hutton's reply

came back. 'All here. One target got away, legged it through the woods. No own casualties.'

Boyd felt suddenly exhausted. The exhilaration of the fire-fight had long since worn off. He was cold, wet and filthy. All he wanted was a bath and a bed.

'Let's get back to the cars,' he said, hauling on Early's arm again. 'We've got a story to get straight.'

Eugene Finn paused, chest heaving, and listened to the night sounds all around him. Nothing but the sound of a nearby stream and his own feet sucking slightly in the mud.

He bent over and grasped his knees. Christ, it had been close. The bastards had nearly caught him in the trees but he had lain under a tangle of brambles for half an hour, still as a stone, until they had all gone. Then he had heard the cars drawing up, and knew it was time to get away.

They were all dead: Jim, Seamus, Rory, Pat. Those SAS bastards had killed every one of them – in the Republic, too. And they had rescued Early. That shite had been SAS himself, all along.

He wondered how Maggie would feel when he told her she had been fucked by an SAS officer. He hoped she'd want revenge.

He straightened again. He was just north of the border, less than two miles from Crossmaglen.

It was too dangerous to go back there though; they had been keeping tabs on Early, that much was plain. There must be an OP with a view of Brendan's bar. No, he'd go elsewhere. He had friends all over this part of the world, including one known as the Border Fox.

18

The Commander of Land Forces in Northern Ireland, Brigadier General Brian Whelan, stared at the file on his desk and said nothing. His aide, Major Ben Hastings of the Intelligence Corps, fidgeted uneasily in front of the desk.

'Oh, sit down, Ben, for God's sake,' the CLF said irritably, not looking up.

There was a silence in the office, interrupted only by the sound of Landrovers humming past outside and the clicking of the secretary's keyboards next door.

Whelan straightened at last and produced a briar pipe from a drawer. He filled and lit it, the aromatic smoke making blue threads in the sunlit air of the office.

'I tell you, Ben,' he said absently around the stem of the pipe. 'That's the last time I ever go along with an out-of-channels suggestion. Martin Blair is washing his hands of it, of course.'

'Yes, sir,' the aide said uncertainly.

'So we must carry the can. And what a can of worms it is.' Whelan gestured to the pile of newspapers lying to one side on the desk.

He set down the pipe.

'They will have to go, of course, the whole damned lot of them. We'll ship them back to Hereford. And this Cordwain fellow ... well, heads will have to roll. The SAS will probably just RTU him, the bloody cowboy. Christ knows we'll have a time of it persuading the Irish Government the raid was without official sanction. This little episode has set back Anglo-Irish relations ten years. It's the last thing the PM needs at the moment.'

'Yes, sir.'

'What about the operative they rescued? Where do we have him at the moment?'

'In Dundonald, sir, strictly subfusc.'

'There's a guard on him I take it?'

'Yes, sir – RUC.'

Whelan barked with laughter. 'They don't trust us to keep an eye on him. What about the families of the dead?'

'They're pressing for a public inquiry. They want the SAS team put in the dock.'

'We can't have that. Our laundry is too dirty to be washed in public at present. I want you to get the Press Liaison Officer on line, get him to make placatory noises, but don't let slip a bloody thing.

The situation in Armagh is explosive enough without us admitting to murder.'

'Do you see it as murder, sir?'

'Heck no! I think it was a necessary operation. I'd have done the same thing in Cordwain's shoes.'

When he saw the sceptical look on the aide's face, Whelan laughed.

'All right, so I'd have covered my tracks rather better. This Cordwain fellow seems to be intent on shouldering all the blame. Rather noble of him, if rather naive. And bloody awkward for us. If anyone might end up going into the dock, it'll be him – he ordered the bloody operation. The Irish want his scalp.'

'I see, sir. I'll have the necessary orders issued then – for the removal of the SAS?'

The CLF sucked thoughtfully on his pipe.

'The damned thing is, we need them down there at the moment. Not for any more of this search and destroy stuff, but for surveillance. What feeble intelligence we now have suggests that the PIRA in Armagh – what's left of them – are planning a spectacular by way of revenge. Thanks to Cordwain's man in Cross, and the rest of Ulster Troop, seventeen players in the Armagh or Monaghan Brigades are dead or compromised. That's no mean achievement, despite the political fall-out. And despite the fact that one top-level player got away.' Whelan puffed away in silence for a few moments.

'Blair of 1 RGJ wants them out too. They've been stealing his thunder it seems . . .'

He came to a decision. 'Yes, Ben, issue those orders. Make sure everyone knows they're in the pipeline, and start flying back at least half the Troop. But I want the other half kept in the Province – we need them, blast it. And keep Cordwain here for the moment too – in an advisory capacity. He has a good grasp of the situation down there.'

'If the press finds out you'll be crucified, sir.'

'I know. And I'll have to convince the Secretary of State too. He's hopping mad at being kept in the dark over the whole affair. And the Chief Constable. But I think I can swing it. The Fox is still uncaught. If we can bag him quickly enough then that'll gloss over this episode. The public have a short memory.'

'And the relatives and their inquiry? The Irish will back them?'

'Possibly, but not once we let them know the whole story. I want all the facts filtered through to the NIO, and in turn to the Irish. Christ, were we supposed to stand by while one of our men was tortured to death? And make it clear that every terrorist shot was found to be armed.'

'Yes, sir.'

Whelan stared out of the window, smoking his pipe furiously.

'Rule number one in the army: Cover Your Arse. Well, there are a lot of arses hanging in the wind now – including mine. We'll give the SAS one last chance. If they can take out the Fox – which was their bloody mission to begin with, after all – then we may be able to salvage a little credibility . . .'

Early lay inert under the starched hospital sheets. He was in a private room but if he turned his head he could see the back of the plain-clothes policeman's head through the window in the door.

It was good to know he did not have to look over his shoulder any more. He was back among his own people. But he was burning to know the real details behind the Moybane killings, as the press was calling them. He wanted to know who had died and who had lived.

He touched his testicles gingerly under the sheet. They were almost back to normal size, though still tender. There would in all probability be no permanent damage, the doctors had told him, whereas the scars on his face were there for good, unless he submitted to plastic surgery.

Well, he had always been an ugly bastard anyway.

The door opened, and James Cordwain came

into the room, bearing a parcel under one arm. He was in civvies: a nondescript jacket and tie, the Browning making a slight bulge under one armpit.

'Hallo, John,' he said breezily, and took a chair by the bed. 'You look like three pounds of shit that's been squeezed into a two-pound bag.'

Early grinned, making his visitor start.

'Jesus, they didn't leave you much in the way of pearly whites, did they?'

'They're fitting me for crowns or dentures or something, the day after tomorrow,' Early said uncomfortably. He kept forgetting about the sight his shattered teeth must present.

'Well, I've something here that might speed your recovery.'

There was a clink, and Cordwain produced from the bulky parcel a bottle of Scottish malt whisky and two glasses. He twisted off the cap and began pouring.

'Up your arse,' he said, by way of a toast, and the two men savoured the flaming warmth of the Scotch. Early closed his eyes.

'Well, James, tell me what happened.'

Cordwain examined him closely. Early's face looked like one great purple bruise. One eye was still swollen shut and there were ugly burns on cheek and nose.

'How are your balls?' Cordwain asked.

'Still there, still working, just about. Tell me you got Finn, James. Tell me you shot the bastard.'

Cordwain poured them both another drink, darting a quick look over his shoulder at the door. 'You may as well know: we missed him. The bastard got away. The four other players were accounted for though; all South Armagh boys. That's two-thirds of the Brigade out of action now.'

'You missed him.' Early was stunned, disbelieving. 'How the hell did you miss him?'

'We lost him in the trees. We think he must have gone to ground until we bugged out. Anyway, I think even the Armagh boys know when they're licked. Maybe now there'll be some peace down there for a while.'

'You'll have no peace in Armagh while Finn and the Fox are still at large.

'Perhaps they're one and the same.'

Early shook his head. 'No. I thought that at the start, too, but now I'm sure the Fox is someone else, someone we don't have anything on. He's still out there somewhere, waiting to kill again.'

Cordwain stared into his glass.

'You've seen the papers, I suppose?'

'Which ones? The *Newsletter* is cock-a-hoop. It thinks that the Moybane operation is the sort of thing the British Army should be doing all the time. But the *Irish Times* sees it a little differently.'

'I can imagine. The long and the short of it is that we're in the shit up to our ears. There may be a public inquiry. The Irish Government is going berserk. Four murders on its sovereign soil perpetrated by a bunch of British-trained psychos. Hereford isn't too chuffed either.'

'You're going to get it in the neck, aren't you, James?'

The other man nodded ruefully. 'I'll be RTUd, without a doubt. I'll be named in the inquiry, too. My career is finished, John.'

'When do you leave?'

'That's the odd thing. I know the orders are in the pipeline, and half the Troop – as well as Charles Boyd – are packing up even as we speak. But the other half have been ordered to Cross to await further developments. And I've been ordered to stay put too. It's bloody peculiar.'

'Maybe they have a last piece of dirty work they want you to do.'

'Probably. I'm expendable now, and Blair of 1 RGJ has frozen me out, so I'm almost unemployed down there.'

They were both silent, savouring the Scotch and digesting the news.

'What about you?' Cordwain asked at last with forced cheerfulness.

'Me? Fuck knows. MI5 will want nothing more to do with me after this. I think I'm out of a job, James. We can sign on the dole together.'

'Well, you did a fine job in Armagh.'

'Did I? My brother's murderer is still walking around scot-free, as is the man who tortured me. I've left a lot of scores unsettled . . . Has Finn really disappeared?'

'Yes. And the border is entirely sealed off. We think he's in a safe house somewhere in Armagh, lying low.'

'Well, when he's caught, I can at least testify at his trial. He can't hide for ever.'

Cordwain looked uncomfortable. 'That's something I have to tell you about, John, although you never heard it, not from me or anyone.'

Early looked mystified. 'Go on.'

'Finn will never be brought to trial. I've heard from Rumour Control that the NIO will back off in Armagh in return for the Irish Government's co-operation in playing down the Moybane affair. The relatives may push for an inquiry, but the South won't back them up.'

'And in return, the army turns down the heat in Armagh,' Early said in a cold, bitter voice.

'Yes. So you see, Finn is to be left alone, at least for a few months, until this furore dies down.'

'Politics,' Early said, disgusted beyond measure. 'Jesus fucking Christ.'

'It may also be why I'm still here,' Cordwain said blackly. 'I'm being held in case they need to sacrifice me to grease the political wheels.'

Early stared into his empty glass.

'I'm going back in, James.'

'What?'

'I'm going back down there. I don't care if I serve twenty years, but I'm going to find Finn and the Fox and I'm going to kill them both.'

'You're in no condition to do anything.'

'Give me a few days, and I'll be out of here. Nobody knows what the hell to do with me. I'll slip through the official net, no problem.'

'John, don't be a fool.'

'Finn is hanging around the Cross somewhere. I'll need a Q car, and a weapon, of course. My Walther is behind the toilet in Lavery's bar.'

'You really think you can find him?'

'You forget that I lived in that community for a while. I've heard names mentioned. Finn will be in a safe house, the house of a sympathizer, and I know most of the candidates for his landlord. It shouldn't be too hard to figure out which of those locations he's staying at.'

'You're a dead man if you go anywhere near Cross, John. They know who you are, for God's sake.'

Early smiled his hideous smile.

'But not who you are.'

19

The car, an ageing Ford Escort, was parked in Slieve Gullion forest, nine kilometres east of Crossmaglen and a mere two north of the border. The two men inside it were dressed in sturdy hiking boots, cotton trousers and civilian waterproof jackets over thick shirts. One was studying a map, the other was looking intently at a piece of paper.

The evening was drawing in, and the woods around them were silent. They had driven off the Glendesha Road and bumped the car up through meandering forestry tracks for what seemed like miles, before finally parking the vehicle in the shadow of the pines and spruces of the plantation. The tracks had been wiped away, and all over the bonnet and roof of the car were laid old grey blankets, overlaid with a tangle of branches and foliage. The blankets cut out shine and disguised shape, the branches adding to the effect. The men in the car did not want a passing army helicopter to notice anything odd in the wood; they were only three kilometres from Forkhill Security Forces base, on the other side of Croslieve Mountain.

'There's quite a few names on this list,' Cordwain said doubtfully. 'You believe we can check them all out?'

Early shrugged. 'If we have to. But I'm hoping that I may be able to pick up info of one sort or another along the way – tonight especially.'

'And I see that Lavery's bar is down here. John, you can't seriously believe that Finn would go back there?'

'Why not? The place has been raided since Moybane, and found to be clean. He might think it's the last place we'd look – under our very noses. And besides, the twats in the search team weren't told to look for my Walther. It might still be where I left it – I want it back.'

'Christ,' Cordwain said. 'I must be out of my fucking mind.'

'Or out of options. We're both finished with the Regiment, James. You want to go out with a bang as much as I do.'

'But not with a court martial.'

'You've done nothing wrong. Nobody said you could no longer sign out weapons or a Q car. They're all too busy ignoring you to worry about what you might be up to.' Early laughed sourly.

Cordwain tucked away Early's list.

'First one tonight, then – Brian McMullan, Oliver Plunkett Park; less than two miles away. What's the route in?'

The pair of them pored over the map, agreeing on a route to the objective. They had driven past it earlier in the day; the last house in a row of semis in a small, isolated estate. There was a stream running along the front of the houses within a deep, overgrown ditch – that was their approach route.

Cordwain had signed out two Browning pistols and a pair of Heckler & Koch MP5Ks: sub-machine-guns small enough to be hung unobtrusively below one armpit. The Brownings they simply carried in the pockets of their waterproofs. They each had also a small day-sack with odds and ends of food, waterbottles, red-light torches and a small radio that could pick up army and police frequencies; they had no wish to run into a foot patrol.

Once it was fully dark they set off on foot across the fields and streams, and along the back roads, of South Armagh. Their presence was unsuspected by both the locals and the Green Army; Cordwain had logged in a false route and false timings with Operations. According to them he was up in Belfast, preparing his Freds for his imminent departure. It was another reason they could not afford to be stopped by a VCP.

Swiftly and silently, the two SAS men made their way to their objective, the last two hundred metres of the route being in the stream that fronted the house and its neighbours. They were soaked and scratched, and surprised skipping water-rats in the dark, but no observer could have marked their passing.

Early stopped. The gurgle of the knee-deep stream covered what noise they were making and the brambles concealed them as effectively as a curtain. A good position with regard to concealment, but crap for defence.

'We're here,' he whispered to Cordwain.

They leaned into the vegetation-choked bank and slipped out their surveillance gear. A pair of Night Vision Goggles, a small but powerful pair of infrared binos, and the Nikon.

Early stared through the NVGs intently. Nothing doing. Everyone was in bed, as they should be. No dogs, either, which was a bonus.

'All clear,' he whispered to Cordwain, and after the other officer had given him the thumbs up, he slithered off.

Brian McMullan, Sinn Fein activist, interned 1972, in 1974 jailed for seven years for possession of arms. Now a middle-aged family man with three daughters. He had worked at the same site as Early, or Dominic McAteer as he had been, and he had been drinking buddies with Eugene Finn and Dermot McLaughlin, the quartermaster. He topped Early's list of candidates for owners of safe houses. McMullan had kept his nose clean for eight years and was considered a dead letter by the Security Forces.

He was not especially bright, and had been merely an IRA foot-soldier, but he was revered as such by many of the young men of the area. They did not know perhaps how polite he was to the Security Forces when they stopped his car or patrolled through his back garden. His house had not been searched since the late seventies; it was a fairly safe bet for Finn.

Early crossed the road in a rush, the Heckler & Koch slapping the side of his ribs as he made it into the impenetrable shadow of a ditch on the far side. He twisted the dial on the NVGs until they were pouring out an invisible beam of infrared light and the night was clear as noon. Then he moved round to the back of the McMullan house.

No alarms, nothing. They were trusting people, these country folk, when they weren't murdering soldiers.

He plucked a handful of grass from the hedge at the back and wiped his boots with it meticulously.

Then he pulled on a pair of surgical gloves and moved up to the house.

He flicked out his lock-pick and began fiddling at the back door, looking round constantly. Thank God there was no moon.

There was a click. He inched back the last of the tumblers in the lock, felt them snick into place, and smiled. An SAS corporal had taught him how to do that years ago.

A small creak as he opened the door. He was in the kitchen. He paused, noting windows, doors, locks, and then unholstered the Heckler & Koch. It was already cocked. He held the stubby weapon in one hand and began checking the downstairs rooms one by one.

Empty. He began moving up the stairs step by step, the little SMG held out in front of him, the goggles covering the whole top of his face, making him look like a bug-eyed creature from another planet.

He would have preferred to move through the house without the NVGs and the weapon; then if he was discovered he might be mistaken for a common burglar. But if he did run into Finn, he wanted to be sure of his man.

He paused at the top of the stairs, turning things over in his head. He could hear quiet snoring from one bedroom. Four doors, two for the kids, one for the parents, one bathroom. He looked at the ceiling. No roof space, it seemed; no entry that he could see, anyway.

He checked, room by room.

Two little girls lying curled up in the same bed, teddies on their pillows. One girl alone, an adolescent with one forearm thrown above her head. And good old Brian and the missus. It was she who was snoring.

Early paused, checking the floor for snags, then he padded into the room. He would leave a trail of drips behind him from the stream but he hoped they would be dry by morning.

He thought for a second, staring down at the sleeping couple. Cordwain was right. The checking-off of his list was too vague. He needed concrete intelligence as to Finn's whereabouts. Perhaps the plan needed to be altered a little.

He bent down beside the bed and placed one gloved hand over McMullan's mouth at the same time as he gently touched the man's temple with the cold muzzle of the SMG.

The eyes opened, then widened. Early felt the man's mouth move under his hand and clamped down tighter. He pushed the weapon's muzzle into the corner of Mullan's eye and then spoke in a whisper, putting on the harsh, guttural accent of the Belfast ghetto.

'Not a word, Brian. Not a fucking sound. All right?'

McMullan nodded, terrified, and Early withdrew his hand but kept the gun pointed at his head.

'Don't you be worrying. The boys just want a wee word. Downstairs. Now.'

He backed away and McMullan clambered out of bed. His wife hitched up an octave higher in her snoring, turned over and then was still again. Poor bastard, Early found himself thinking, sleeping next to her every night.

He made McMullan precede him down the stairs, with the MP5K touching his back all the way. They both entered the kitchen at the bottom and Early stopped him from switching on the light, then gestured to a chair. The man huddled there in his pyjamas, shivering, obviously terrified.

'Don't worry, Brian,' Early said soothingly. 'You haven't done a thing. You don't know me, but I'm not from this part of the world. I'm with the boys up in the city.' He lowered the gun and stretched out a hand. 'We know you've done your bit for the cause in your time, so we do.'

McMullan shook the gloved hand gingerly. 'What do you want then?' he asked hoarsely.

'I'm here to warn you, so I am. We've word that the Brits are for searching this house tomorrow night, or maybe the night after. They're looking for Eugene, so they are; the bastards are turning over every stone in Armagh looking for him.'

'But he's not here,' McMullan protested.

'Ach, we know that, but we like to be sure of these things, you know, and we thought you'd like a wee warning, so you could get the kids out of the way and the china packed and suchlike.'

'Well . . . aye. Thanks, that's good of you. But what's a Belfast Volunteer doing down here?'

'Trying to get Eugene Finn the hell out of here and up to the city again in one piece. You know he was up there before, after Drumboy; well now – I can talk to you about these things, Brian, seeing as you're an ex-Volunteer yourself – now the Army Council have decided it's far too fucking risky for him to stay in Armagh. They have a place ready for him up in the city again. I have to get the bugger out of here in one piece.'

Early paused, waiting. He did not want to have to come out and ask McMullan where Finn was, but he would if he had to.

'What's that you're wearing on your head?'

'Night Vision Goggles. Good, aren't they? Like something out of *Star Wars*, so they are. We got them from America. Now Brian, about Eugene.'

'He's fucking mad,' Brian said, shaking his head. 'He's a fucking lunatic. You're going to have a hell of a time getting him out of there.

Right under their bloody noses. I tell ye, I think he's been too smart for his own good this time.'

'Have you seen him since that Moybane thing, then?'

'Seen him? I was out drinking with him last night.'

Early was startled into silence.

'All he can think about is revenge. It's a good job you boys are here to get him out to the city. He needs to get out of Armagh, like you said. And poor old Brendan Lavery – he's at his wits' end. He's not what you'd call a hard-core activist, you know. It's his sister. Now there's a marvellous woman.'

Early held up a hand. 'Brian, I must be on me way, or the boys'll be getting nervous. I hope those bastards don't make too big a mess of the house, and I'm sorry if I scared you there.

McMullan waved a hand. 'That's all right, so it is. Just you keep up the struggle, and say hello to Eugene for me.'

'Oh, I will,' said Early, and he slipped out the back door, into the moonless night.

'The cheeky bastard,' Cordwain said, shaking his head. He took a slug from the hip-flask and passed it to Early.

'Yes. Obviously, he's intent on staying – and on stirring up more mischief. So there he is, sitting maybe three hundred metres from Cross Security Forces base, drinking with the locals.'

'Balls of brass,' Cordwain said, then looked apologetically at Early.

They were back in the car, muddy and wet from their two trips across the fields. On the way back they had had to shelter in a ditch for a quarter of an hour while an army Gazelle with a searchlight ranged back and forth across the countryside like a wolf on the prowl. The forest had been as dark as pitch when they returned, and even Early had had some difficulty in locating the vehicle once again.

'We can't just go tearing into Lavery's bar with guns blazing,' Cordwain said. 'And what about McMullan? You told him his house would be raided within the next day or two. When that doesn't happen, he's going to start getting suspicious. I know he's not the smartest bloke in the world, but even he will have enough sense to warn Finn there's something in the air.'

'Never worry about it,' Early said imperturbably. 'McMullan's house will be raided all right – you'll see. Now it's time to get a bit of kip. The first stag is yours, James. Wake me up in a couple of hours.'

He reclined the passenger seat of the car, fished out a lightweight sleeping bag, and was soon asleep with his mouth open, his newly capped teeth gleaming slightly in the dark.

Cordwain cursed silently, then got out of the car and stood listening to the night noises. He looked at his watch. It was two-thirty. Another two hours until dawn.

He was uneasy. Though he had been known as a bit of a cowboy in his time, he had never gone so far off the rails before. Admittedly, the Moybane incursion had been a large black mark, but he knew that to all the lower and middle-ranking members of the SAS it had been a success. It was the upper echelons who were about to ruin him for it. He felt very bitter.

Early obviously did not care one jot for the consequences of his actions. He was as set on revenge as that bastard Eugene Finn was. The two were more similar than either of them might like to think; a couple of loose cannons.

So what was he doing here? He found it hard to answer his own question. Seeking some kind of justice perhaps, no matter how rough it might be. Or perhaps he was just getting even, like Early. Too many people had died to let the thing unravel now, just because some pen-pushers in Whitehall or Dublin said so. No, he was here to finish the job properly, to tie up the loose ends. And deep down he believed that if he and Early came up with the goods — if they could somehow take out both Finn and the Fox – then despite officialdom, they might somehow escape the heavy hand of disciplinary action. The waters in Northern Ireland were murky at the best of times, but at the moment they were damned-near opaque. It would be easy for the Regiment, or indeed the CLF to shield himself and Early one way or another.

But there was the rub: they had to come up with the goods. Finn they could manage, perhaps, but Cordwain still could see no clear way of nailing the Fox. He thought that Early might be concocting a way though, and he was not sure if he liked it.

They moved out just before sunrise, easing the car out of the forest and on to the deserted roads. They stopped at an isolated phone box at Early's insistence, and he made a long call without putting any money into the slot. When he got back into the car he was grinning broadly.

'Who was that, your mum?' Cordwain asked him as they moved off again.

'Better than that, my old son,' said Early. 'That was the Confidential Telephone. I've just been telling it that Finn is staying in the McMullan house – anonymously, of course. If the Greenjackets don't raid it in the next day or two then I'm an Irishman.' He laughed.

'So you've gained us time,' Cordwain said, refusing to share his high spirits. 'What now? Do we go after Finn?'

'Not just yet. I want to have a look at the place and do some thinking.'

'What are you going to do – walk in there and have a pint?'

'No, James, I'm not. You are.'

Lavery's bar was quiet as Cordwain walked in. A couple of old men were sitting in the corners reading the *Irish Times* and sipping pints of porter. Brendan Lavery was behind the bar, bottling up. He looked thinner, Cordwain thought, and tired. All the excitement must be getting to him.

'What can I do you for?' the care-worn landlord asked Cordwain, straightening with a grimace.

'Pint of Guinness, thanks. That's a fair day, so it is.'

Lavery looked out the sunlit windows as the black beer came trickling into a pint glass. 'Aye, it's not bad.' He was regarding Cordwain closely, and the SAS officer wondered if he could remember him from his last, brief visit to the pub. He hoped not, though it shouldn't make much difference if he did.

Taking out his own copy of the *Irish Times*, Cordwain retired to a corner table, nodding at the old men who watched him over the top of their papers. He felt as though everyone was on edge, and had a momentary urge to get the hell out of there. He forced himself to sit down, however, and shake out his newspaper. His job, Early had told him, was to act like a sponge, to notice everyone who came in and out, but to remain aloof.

Cordwain disliked taking orders, especially from someone who was nominally his subordinate, but Early was the one with all the ideas at the moment, so he had no choice. The other SAS officer was currently checking out the derelict houses at the other end of the square where Gorbals's team had had the OP. Why, he would not say, to Cordwain's immense irritation. He felt that Early was treating all this as some sort of game, and he didn't like it.

People came and went throughout the early afternoon. There was no sign of the Lavery woman, or of Finn, though that was hardly surprising. But there was a tenseness about the atmosphere in the bar and especially about the landlord, that was intriguing.

The afternoon drew on, and the men of Lavery's Construction came in after work, raising the noise level. Cordwain clocked their faces one by one, but could identify none as local players. He glanced at his watch and decided to give it another thirty minutes. If he sat there on his own for much longer he would begin to excite comment.

Then he hit paydirt. The Lavery woman came in, and with her was Patrick Mooney, a known player who was one of the few survivors of Drumboy. As they talked to Brendan at the bar Cordwain finished his pint and left the empty glass on the counter, his ears pricked. He folded his paper nonchalantly, and watched the two go behind the bar and through the door that led upstairs. The Lavery woman had been talking about the dinner. It looked as though Mooney was staying in the pub at the moment as well as Finn – perhaps as extra muscle. Cordwain turned and left.

'So you didn't see Finn,' Early said, wiping the Heckler & Koch with an oily cloth.

'Not a whisper. It looks like we'll have to take Mooney into account though. He's a youngster, but a vicious little bastard. He's probably there as a dicker of sorts, or maybe he's to provide a distraction if the army swoop on the place. I'll bet my bollocks there's a small arsenal concealed in that pub somewhere – as well as your bloody Walther.'

'As well as my bloody Walther,' Early echoed soberly.

'So what's the plan, and why were you sniffing

round those derelict houses to the north of the square?'

Early cocked and recocked the little SMG several times; then, satisfied, he set it down and took up the magazine, and began unloading it. The snub-nosed 9mm bullets fell into his lap as he eased them out one after the other. When the mag was empty he oiled it and tested the spring. Satisfied, he began reloading it again.

They had parked the car in yet another wood, this one near Silverbridge, some seven kilometres from Cross. The afternoon was waning, the sun going down behind the hills to the west, and Cordwain was restless. They were wasting time, he thought. The McMullan thing would not fool the local players for long. Soon they would contact the men in Belfast and put two and two together.

'The plan,' Early said at last. 'You'll love it. It involves tying up a lady.'

'The Lavery woman.'

'Maggie, yes. There are a few rolls of parcel tape in the back, as well as a couple of Balaclavas. We want to make this look as unmilitary an operation as possible.'

'Shouldn't be difficult,' Cordwain muttered.

'We incapacitate Mooney and the Laverys and spirit our friend Eugene away to a convenient location.'

'Where?'

'Under everybody's noses. I was checking out a few places around Cross today – discreetly, of course. The derelict houses in the square are too near to inhabited buildings, otherwise they'd be ideal. But there's a disused sewage works just on the outskirts, off the Dundalk road, and screened by trees, that's perfect. Very fitting, don't you think – a sewage works?'

'It's too close,' Cordwain said.

'No. Because as soon as we have the Fox's identity from Finn, we move in again. I'm sure the Fox is in Cross itself, so we don't want to have to drive over half the country to get him. This way, it'll be more of a lightning strike. It'll all be over by morning.'

'How do we persuade Finn?'

Early smiled evilly. 'The same way he tried to persuade me – only this time there will be no SAS riding to the rescue.'

'You mean kill him, of course, not hand him over to the RUC or the army.'

'Yes. Once we have the Fox as well we'll dump both of the bodies in the Republic. Eugene Finn will remain disappeared for good. If we handle it right, then we may be able to pass it off as an internal feud – the locals already think that the Belfast boys are in town. And I'm sure your Freds up there will be willing to give us alibis if we need them. No one will know what really happened.'

Cordwain thought it over. It seemed a harebrained plan, but he had to admire its pure brazenness.

'All right,' he said at last. 'When do we move in?'

'Tomorrow night.'

20

Finn flicked the cigarette butt away and drew out another. It was always cold down here, always damp. He was sick and tired of it. Tomorrow night he'd have another few pints in the bar after hours, to celebrate.

He was sitting on a pile of blankets and an old sleeping bag in the cellar of Brendan Lavery's bar. The air was heavy with the yeasty smell of beer and the sour reek of his cigarettes. Moisture ran down the walls. What a fucking dump. He lit his next cigarette, drawing the dry, sweet smoke deep into his lungs. Thank Christ for fags. They kept him going.

He only had himself to blame. He could have been across the border by now, living it up in Dublin, or drinking in some wee shebeen out in the Donegal mountains. But he had chosen to stay.

Finn lifted up the 9mm Walther pistol and studied it with narrowed eyes. He wiped some grit off the gleaming barrel, and smiled. Dominic had left his toy behind the cistern. What a shame. And two spare mags, too. Why, it was just like an early Christmas, so it was.

He stripped the weapon, familiarizing himself with it once again. It had been a windfall, finding that Brit's gun, since so many weapons had been lost at both Drumboy and Moybane. Fuck, but things had really messed up lately. Belfast would not be pleased, not at all. He would have some fast talking to do if he was to stay on here as ASU commander, and try to build up what was left of the Brigade again.

That Brit, McAteer, or whatever his real name was – it was all his fault. If it hadn't been for him neither of the two disasters which had struck the Volunteers in Armagh would have happened. God knows where those SAS bastards had spirited him away to. He was probably in England now, being treated like a hero. Maggie had been a bit strange after all that. She had wanted to know exactly what Finn had done to McAteer before the Brits showed up. If Finn hadn't known any better he would have said she was concerned for him, the cunt.

All that was past them now. He had to lie low while he planned this next strike – something to get the Brits running around like headless chickens, like they had been before Drumboy.

The papers were full of stories about how the SAS were being withdrawn from Ireland in the wake of the border incursion that had resulted in the deaths of four men. At least that was one good thing among all the bad. Maybe now things might return to normal. Or as normal as they ever were in this part of the world.

He threw aside part of the heap of blankets to disclose a bundle of wires and a digital clock-face; also a bulky package wrapped in greaseproof paper. Finn smiled again. It was a long time since he'd set up one of these fuckers. It would be good to get his hand in again. And Maggie, she would help him. She was a hell of a woman.

He'd slept with her once, back just after her husband had died, and that had been a night of fireworks, lingering in the memory.

He got to his feet, cigarette dangling from his mouth, and stepped deeper into the far corner of the cellar. Behind the beer-kegs was a blanket-shrouded shape. He drew off the covering and gazed at what was underneath with his eyes shining. They'd have to move everything, of course, before fresh deliveries were made down here on Thursday, but for the moment, he was looking down at a thing unique in Ireland: a Barratt-Browning .50-calibre rifle: the weapon of the Border Fox.

The SAS were going to get a going-away present.

For Charles Boyd, the past few days had been a hectic nightmare. It was midday on the day the first half of Ulster Troop was being hustled out of the Province, and though he had not been in the field since the Moybane operation, he was as exhausted as if he had just been out on rural patrol.

The twelve men who were leaving included Haymaker, Raymond and Wilkins. Gorbals McFee would be staying behind with the rest, though Rumour Control had it that they might be on their way out soon after. Cordwain, Boyd had not seen in three days. He was up in Belfast, tying up loose ends. And Early – he had checked himself out of Dundonald Hospital and then disappeared. Boyd had never liked him anyway, but he couldn't help wondering where Early was, and if Cordwain was somehow involved.

Anyway, it was not his problem any more. His kit was packed, and both he and the half-troop were ready to board the Puma helicopter that was waiting on the helipad to fly them to RAF Aldergrove, near Antrim. From there they would be put on a plane to Brize Norton, and his dealings with Northern Ireland would be over. He had mixed feelings about the whole thing.

Glad though he was to be going away, he knew that he and the men were being shuttled out in disgrace, scapegoats for the politicians in the wake of the Moybane operation. And there was also the unfinished business they had left behind them: Finn and the Fox still at large.

Haymaker came through the open door and jerked a thumb back up the corridor.

'The Crabs are ready when you are, boss; they're warming up the heli now. They want us on the pad in figures ten.'

Boyd waved a hand, and Haymaker left again.

He looked around him at the cramped little room he and Cordwain had shared. He would not miss it. Then he shouldered his kit and exited without a backward glance.

The Puma was roaring on the tarmac and the SAS troopers formed two sticks pointing towards its cockpit in an inverted V. At last the pilot gave the thumbs up, and they ran forward at a crouch, weapons in one hand, bergens in the other. Their equipment, including the weapons, would go back with them to Hereford.

They scrambled on board the helicopter, swearing loudly at one another as they packed the interior space as tightly as a sardine tin. Boyd boarded last, and tapped the pilot on the shoulder. The Puma rose slowly; it was carrying almost maximum load. He looked out through the doorway and saw the helipad recede, then shut the side door.

'Goodbye, fucking Armagh,' he said.

The Puma banked and began the turn that would take it up over the hills surrounding Bessbrook. Boyd looked back down the crowded interior of the helicopter. The men were seated on the flimsy canvas seats, their bergens on their knees, the muzzles of their weapons kept well away from the fuselage.

There was a sudden ticking noise that could be heard even over the roar of the engine. It was like someone punching a hammer on a sheet of tin. Boyd was about to ask the pilot about it when the Puma lurched crazily and he was thrown across the interior like a sack of potatoes. The crew were shouting to each other.

'What the fuck?' someone yelled.

The helicopter suddenly dropped. Boyd felt his stomach lift with the sudden descent. He laboured over to the pilot's shoulder.

'What's going on?' he shouted.

'We're taking ground fire. They've hit the tail rotor. I'll have to put her down. Get your men to brace themselves!'

'Jesus Christ.' Boyd turned to the tightly packed SAS troopers.

'Crash positions! We're going down!'

At that moment a hole the size of his fist

appeared in the fuselage. There was a smell of burning, and of spilled fuel. The Puma swooped and the SAS men hung on to whatever they could find. The bergens and weapons went flying around, and a loose rifle struck Boyd, laying open his forehead.

'We're going to hit!' the co-pilot yelled. 'Brace yourselves!'

There was an enormous impact, and then an explosion of flame.

Twenty seconds after the crash, the first mobiles were powering out of Bessbrook. A Lynx gunship with medics and a four-man brick was first on the scene, and the Landrovers of the mobiles roared along the quiet, sunlit country roads with more troops to cordon off the area.

The lead Landrover of the first mobile was passing over an old stone culvert when the bomb went off. It blew the vehicle off the road, crumpling in one armoured side as though it were cardboard. Lumps of stone from the shattered culvert were blown through the air like shrapnel, hitting the second Landrover and smashing its bulletproof windscreen. The second vehicle swerved to a halt. Soldiers poured out of the rear two vehicles and ran across the field to where the remains of the first Landrover were lying. The culvert was now a smoking crater. Bodies lay mangled in the grass. Someone was moaning. The soldiers knelt among the dead and dying and began to administer first aid while the report went back to Bessbrook that they had been ambushed.

Early was filling up at the petrol pump when Cordwain came walking back out of the little service station, white-faced, and got behind the wheel of the car without a word. Early settled the bill and then they pulled out. It was not until they had driven almost a mile in silence that Cordwain spoke.

'There was a television in there; I just caught the news. There's been a helicopter shot down just outside Bessbrook, fourteen on board. No word yet on a final casualty figure, but there are at least three dead.'

Early said nothing, and Cordwain went on.

'That was Ulster Troop. They were to fly out today at noon. Charles Boyd and eleven of my men were in that heli.'

'What shot them down?' Early asked harshly.

'They're not sure yet, but it looks like something heavy, using armour-piercing rounds. That's all they know.'

'The Fox,' Early said flatly.

'Yes. But that's not all of it, John. Bessbrook is short of choppers at the moment. That's why the troop went out in a Puma instead of in a Chinook.

So most of the troops sent out after the crash were in 'rovers. They were ambushed. A culvert bomb. Again, they haven't reached a final figure yet, but it looks like no one in the lead vehicle survived.

Early hung his head. Most Landrovers carried three to five men.

'How was it detonated?' he asked.

'No idea – it's just come up on the news. Probably a command wire.'

'Finn,' Early said softly.

'Yes. Finn and the Fox. You were right, you know. There will be no peace in this part of the world until they're both dead.'

'Does this mean that Finn may no longer be based in Lavery's, I wonder?' Early mused.

'Maybe. But we're going in tonight, as planned. It'll be my last chance – they'll want me down in Bessbrook to help sort out the mess. I must go back tomorrow.'

'Tonight, then,' Early agreed. 'Tonight we take out both of them, one way or another.'

'Yes. You see, John, it's personal for me now, as well as you. I don't care if I do twenty years, but tonight we're going to even the score.'

21

'It's quiet tonight,' Maggie said, cleaning a glass with rapid twists of the cloth in her hand.

'Aye,' Brendan said. He was leaning against the bar reading the paper with a half-full tumbler of whiskey in front of him.

'Where's that Mooney fella?' he asked his sister.

'Out the back, keeping an eye out.'

'And Eugene?'

'In the cellar, same as always. He wants to come out for a drink or two this evening.'

Brendan sipped at his whiskey. He looked as though he had sipped a lot of whiskey lately.

'Where'd you get to this morning anyway?'

'I told you, I went for a drive.'

He shook his head. 'That was desperate today, all those deaths. Jesus, Maggie, what a country.'

Maggie began cleaning a second glass, holding it up to the light to check for imperfections.

'Sure, they were all Brits, so they were – SAS most of them. They got what they deserved.'

'I'm sick of it, Maggie, sick of it all. I want Eugene out of here.'

'He won't be here much longer,' she said soothingly.

'It was him planted that bomb, wasn't it? I saw him come back in this afternoon, Mooney driving the car with a grin on his face as wide as a banana, the pair of them covered with muck. It was them did it, didn't they?'

Maggie laid a finger against her brother's lips. 'What you don't know can't harm you. Don't think about it, Brendan.'

'Don't think about it! Jesus, Mary and Joseph.'

'Turn on the news, there's a good fella. I want to hear what's going on.'

Brendan pressed the remote listlessly and the TV above the bar flicked into life. *Good Evening Ulster* had just started.

> '*There were two attacks today on the Security Forces in South Armagh. The first was on a helicopter which army sources say was transporting troops to RAF Aldergrove . . .*'

Eugene Finn and Patrick Mooney entered the bar through the interior door and wordlessly pulled themselves pints of Bass. Mooney winked at Brendan and Finn looked at Maggie. Then they sat and watched the news like children mesmerized by a Christmas tree.

'The helicopter was hit by heavy-calibre gunfire from the ground and was forced to make an emergency landing near its base. Eyewitnesses state that the aircraft was in flames as it descended and that it blew up as it hit the ground. Army sources have confirmed that three of the occupants were killed, one of whom is believed to be the pilot. At least eight others were seriously injured.'

Moony cheered and slapped hands with Finn. Margaret watched the news impassively.

'Army sources refuse to comment on press speculation that the attack was the work of the so-called "Border Fox", who for eighteen months has been carrying out attacks on both the police and the army using a high-calibre weapon. They also declined to confirm rumours that the Puma helicopter was carrying SAS soldiers when it was shot down.

'Minutes after the first, a second attack

was then carried out on army vehicles which went to the aid of the downed helicopter. It is believed a bomb was planted by a command wire when the lead army Landrover passed over it. All four occupants of the vehicle were killed, three of them dying at the scene, the fourth on the way to hospital. The army have yet to release their names but it is thought they were members of the 1st Battalion the Royal Greenjackets, who are stationed in the area.'

Finn and Mooney clinked glasses, beaming.

'Will you not join us, Maggie?' they chorused. 'Seven of the bastards in one day. It's another Warrenpoint, so it is.'

Maggie poured herself a brandy and sipped it calmly.

'Brendan, you go upstairs and have a lie-down – you don't look so well, so you don't. I'll look after the bar.'

Her brother left without protest. Maggie went to the front door of the bar and closed it firmly, locking it top and bottom. Then she rejoined the others.

'You've too big a mouth on you, Patrick,' she said coldly. 'And Eugene, you should know better than to be down here in the public bar at this time of day. Wait until after hours, that's the rule. And

Patrick, you're not being much of a lookout, are you? The bloody SAS could be at the back door for all you know.'

'They're not at the back door,' Mooney said gleefully. 'They're either back in England or splattered all over the hills of Armagh.'

He and Finn began laughing. They seemed a little drunk, intoxicated by the success of the joint operations.

'All right, we've had a success; but now there'll be hell to pay for it. It's time you were moving on, Eugene. Maybe you should go to Brian McMullan's house. It's too dangerous to stay in one place for so long.'

'McMullan's place was raided by the Brits yesterday,' Finn told her. 'Fuck knows why. But it's out.'

'Maybe you should head across the border,' Mooney suggested. 'Cavan, or Wicklow.'

'I'm not ready to leave yet,' Finn said. The humour had left him.

'For God's sake, Eugene,' Maggie exploded. 'You're the most wanted man in the North. You can't keep playing the lone hero for ever. It's time things were left to cool down a wee bit.'

'Oh, but I'm not the most wanted man,' Finn said quietly. 'Our friend the Fox is, far and away. It was him that brought that chopper down today, wasn't it? Maybe he should think about heading south too.'

'He can take care of himself,' Maggie said acidly. 'The Brits haven't even figured out who he is yet.'

'They will, Maggie, they will. They figure everything out in the end, the bastards.'

Seeing her look, Finn laughed.

'All right, Mammy, I'll do as you say. I'll head south in the morning. Patrick here can drive me up as far as Derry, and we'll cross the border there, head for Donegal. Maybe I'll do a spot of fishing.'

'And tonight?'

Finn raised his glass. 'Tonight I'm going to sit and have a few drinks to the success of our missions and the overthrow of British arms. *Slainte*.' And he drained his pint.

'And Maggie, open that door, love, will you? People will begin to think there's something wrong if Lavery's isn't open for the evening crowd.'

They checked the weapons again in the disused sewage works. The windows had been boarded up but Early had prised free one board with a crowbar, replacing it after they were inside. Now they were crouched in the musty darkness of the empty building, loading magazines by torchlight. The smell in the place, that damp, unused smell, was akin to the smell in the house where he had been tortured, Early realized. It was altogether fitting that Finn would receive the same treatment here.

But it all depended on speed. They had to snatch the player with a minimum of fuss, get him back there, work on him until he divulged the identity of the Fox, and then set out again to nail the other terrorist. And all this in one night. It could be done, Early was sure of it; but if they bungled the snatch, or if Finn was unexpectedly stubborn, then they could find themselves in a world of shit.

One good thing had come out of the two terrorist attacks that day: Cordwain was totally on board now. Early had felt that the SAS major had not been wholly committed to his plans before, but the news of the downing of the Puma and the subsequent ambush had changed all that.

They had been in contact with Bessbrook. Three had died in the chopper: the pilot, Chandler, and Boyd. Cordwain felt responsible. More importantly, he wanted revenge, and that was good.

'What's the time?' Cordwain asked.

'Eleven-thirty. Things should be calming down in the bar round about now. It's not a Saturday night or anything. At 0200 hours we move in.'

'I know,' Cordwain said testily. 'But what if there's still a customer or two in there, even at that time?'

'We truss them up and lock them in the cellar,' Early replied promptly. 'And remember – Ulster accents all the time. We're trying to suggest this is all part of a feud.'

Cardwain loaded his Heckler & Koch and hung it from his shoulder-sling. He and Early were both dressed in black boiler suits – the preferred dress of players out on a hit. They wore black caps which when pulled down over the face became Balaclavas, and surgical gloves. Their pockets bulged with parcel tape and a metal cosh dangled from a lanyard attached to Early's shoulder.

'How will we make Finn talk?' Cordwain asked. 'He's a hard bastard. We could kill him before he's said a word.'

Early reached in his day-sack and produced a gleaming metal object.

'What the . . . ?'

'It's a blowtorch. We'll fry his balls for him and see how he likes it.'

Cordwain was about to protest, but remembering the men who had died that day, he said nothing. Finn deserved whatever was coming to him.

'Grab some kip if you can,' Early advised him. 'I'll keep an eye open.'

Cordwain lay down on the hard floor, eyes open. Early flicked off the torch and they were in total darkness. And silence – they were well away from the road here, in a slight dip screened by trees. The car had been camouflaged and stashed in a small copse off the Monog road, some two hundred metres away, but Early didn't intend to use it. They were going in on foot, to avoid army foot patrols and VCPs as much as anything else, and if Finn caused too much trouble they'd carry him out bodily. They only had half a kilometre or less to travel.

It was a cowboy operation in the worst sense of the word, Cordwain knew that; but with time so short there was little else they could do. Seven men had died that day. If Early and he neutralized both Finn and the Fox, they could be sure that the Regiment, and the Northern Ireland Office, would pull out all the stops to see them out of trouble. That was the idea, anyway.

Cordwain looked at his watch. Midnight. Another two hours to lie there and think. He hated the slack time before the beginning of an op. It was the worst time – once the thing had begun he would feel better. He closed his eyes and tried to doze.

Early was wide awake, peering through a slit below the boards that covered the windows. He could see the odd car passing on the Dundalk road; a white, speeding light through the screening trees. For hours now he had been racking his brains, trying to remember anything he had learned in his time under cover, any seemingly worthless piece of information that might aid them tonight.

Noise was the thing. Everything would have to be carried out in near-silence, to buy time for Finn's interrogation. He and Cordwain would have to move swiftly. Now where in the pub would Finn be hiding? He might have to get that information out of Brendan or Maggie, and did not relish the prospect. Despite all he knew about her, he had to admit there was still a feeling there for Maggie, absurd though it might be. If things had been different . . .

'Fuck,' he growled, but not loud enough for Cordwain to hear him. He had to get that girl out of his mind.

The two hours crawled by. Early knew that Cordwain was awake, but neither spoke to the other. Both knew that tonight was their last chance to even the score, to wipe out their earlier mistakes, and neither intended to muff it.

Finally, Early checked his watch for the fiftieth time, and then crawled over to Cordwain and tapped him lightly on the shoulder.

'It's showtime.'

22

The sky was clouded, so there was no moon. Early and Cordwain made good time, travelling north-west along the triangle of open country between the Dundalk and the Monog roads. There was a farm ahead of them, which they bypassed, causing a restless dog to bark for a few moments. Soon they were in the outskirts of Crossmaglen, in the back of Carlingford Street. Their pace slowed. They pulled the Balaclavas down over their faces and unholstered their MP5Ks, cocking them simultaneously. Then they moved on, Early in the lead, Cordwain following five yards behind, turning every so often to check his rear.

They entered Carlingford Street. It seemed very bright after the darkness of the fields they had come across. The street-lights were glowing amber; the place was deserted. Early checked the time: 0215.

They moved forward more slowly now, taking

advantage of every shadow and every possible fire-position. There was no telling what state of alert the locals would be in – and Mooney, Finn's minder – it was likely he was detailed to keep an eye out through part of the night at least.

They halted in the yard at the rear of Lavery's bar. Early knew the place like the back of his hand. He ran to the back door while Cordwain covered the entrance to the yard. It was locked. There was no sound, no light from within, but that meant nothing. He would hear little from the public bar here, at the back, and the windows of the place were covered with heavy curtains.

He produced his lock-pick and knelt down by the back door. Then he began fiddling with the tumblers inside the lock, trying to gauge the pressure and the angle that would make each one click back.

Sweat trickled in his armpits, and the Balaclava seemed to stifle his breathing, but he forced himself to work patiently. There was no sign of Cordwain: the SAS major had chosen himself a concealed position to watch over the yard.

A click, and the tumblers had fallen. Early sighed with relief. He turned the door handle, keeping the SMG trained forward.

The door swung open.

He moved inside. It was darker than in the

yard, and he paused a moment to let his eyes adjust.

Cordwain was at the door with him, facing out into the yard. Early tapped him on the shoulder and then pointed wordlessly down the corridor that led from the kitchen. Cordwain nodded.

Early padded down the corridor or hallway that led to the back of the public bar. At the door to its rear he stopped and listened. He could hear it clearly now – several voices talking, someone laughing, glasses clinking.

Fuck! That made things vastly more complicated.

He gave Cordwain the thumbs-down sign for enemy, then held up five fingers – his guess at the number of people in the bar. Cordwain's eyes rolled behind the mask. He joined him at the door.

'After three,' Early whispered.

The door was kicked open with a crash and the two men burst into the room with guns levelled.

'Nobody move!' a harsh Belfast accent said. 'Anybody moves and they fucking die!'

Someone dropped a glass and it smashed on the floor. The rest stood or sat open-mouthed.

Finn was there. Early felt a surge of hatred and exultation that made him grin like a maniac behind his mask. They had him.

Brendan Lavery was sitting with his head in his hands; he looked tired rather than terrified, and obviously the worse for wear. Young Patrick Mooney looked absolutely blank; he'd have to be searched. There were two others, both locals; sympathizers but not active players Early recalled. No sign of Maggie though.

'On the floor, spread-eagled,' Cordwain was telling them. 'Come on – we haven't got all fucking night.'

'Who the hell are you?' Finn asked angrily.

Cordwain slammed the short butt of his weapon into Finn's face. The terrorist fell to the floor.

'You fuckers!' Mooney yelled. His hand reached under his jacket.

Early saw the glint of the pistol barrel and brought up his own weapon. He fired a three-round burst that tore out the man's chest and sent him careering across the room, ribbons of blood sprinkling the walls and floor as he hit the ground. An old Webley pistol was still clutched in his hand.

'Shit!' Early hissed. The gunfire had seemed shockingly loud in the confined space; it was too much to hope that the locals had not heard it – or the army for that matter.

'You bastards!' one of the men was saying. 'You murderers.'

'They're Brits,' Finn said thickly, blood marking his jaw. 'Fucking SAS out for revenge after their wee chopper had a bump. Isn't that right, boys?'

Early felt an urge to shoot him there and then but instead concentrated on trussing them up one by one in yards of parcel tape while Cordwain covered him. Mooney lay with his eyes open, staring sightlessly at the ceiling. The blood had stopped oozing out of his butchered chest with his heart no longer pumping.

'Where's Maggie?' Early demanded of Finn. He was the only one whose mouth he had not taped up.

'Fuck away off,' the IRA man said scornfully.

Early searched him roughly, feeling down his limbs. In the small of the terrorist's back he touched a hard shape, and pulled it out, smiling. A little Walther 9mm handgun, the one he had left behind. He tucked it in a thigh pocket.

'Time to go,' Cordwain said. He was looking out at the square from behind the curtains.

'There's people coming down the street. It won't be long before they're hammering at the door.'

'You pair are fucked,' Finn gloated.

Early lowered his face close to Finn's.

'So are you,' he said quietly.

They dragged Finn through the pub to the

back, having taped up his mouth at the last. When he dragged his feet he was beaten with Early's cosh. Finally they were at the back door. They paused before stepping into the yard.

'Listen,' Cordwain said.

They could hear the distinctive warbling sound of Landrover tyres from the square at the top of the street. The army were arriving.

'Time to go,' Cordwain went on.

'No, wait,' Early said. Something was wrong – they had missed something, he was sure of it.

'Come *on*!' Cordwain urged him.

'You go. Get Finn out of here. There's something I want to check.'

'For Christ's sake.'

'Go. I'll catch up with you.' Early turned and re-entered the pub.

He went back to the public bar and, kneeling over Brendan Lavery, ripped off the tape covering his mouth. Lavery yelled in pain.

'Brendan, where's your sister?'

'Leave me alone. Leave us all alone.' He was drunk and slurred his words.

Someone began hammering at the front door.

'Brendan! Are you all right in there? We heard shots.'

'Fuck.' Early began to sweat. 'Brendan, where's Maggie?'

'Toilet,' the man mumbled. He seemed almost comatose with a mixture of shock and alcohol.

The banging on the door began again. There were voices talking outside. One of the men on the floor began to struggle against the tape that bound his arms and legs. Early kicked him savagely until he was quiet.

He rose, and went down to the door at the end of the bar marked 'Ladies' and pushed it open.

A single stall, a hand-basin – nothing else.

He prodded open the door of the stall with the SMG. The toilet-seat was down, and the window above the cistern was open, letting in a draught of night air.

He cursed silently.

That hammering on the door of the bar again. Soon someone with sense would try the back door. It was time to go.

Early sped through the pub, turning out the lights as he left the public bar. He ran down the corridor and then out the back door.

Two men came pelting down the road after him, running out of the square at the top of the street.

'Hey, you!' they yelled.

Early spun, still running, and put a shot over their heads. They threw themselves to the ground and he ran on, into the darkness of the fields beyond the street-lights. He could hear sirens breaking the night quiet of Cross behind him. He kept running.

Finn's face was shining with blood from the blows Cordwain had dealt him in an effort to make him speed up. The IRA man was holding back, trying to delay them both. He knew, Cordwain thought, that he was being led to his death, and at this stage even capture by the British Army was preferable.

Farm buildings looked darkly ahead. If he looked back he could see downhill to where Cross was a tangle of lights. He could hear sirens.

The land ahead was rising gently, a river valley with trees scattered along its bottom. The Monog road was on the height to his left, the Dundalk road on the rise to his right.

He tugged Finn along brutally, wondering what had got into Early. The Lavery woman – was that it? She hadn't been there. In any case, the whole operation was fucked up now. They'd never get anywhere near Cross again tonight – it would be swarming with the Security Forces. They had failed to nail the Fox after all.

But they still had Finn. And Cordwain for one would be glad to put a bullet in the back of his head.

He tugged the IRA man along savagely. Finn was having trouble breathing because of the tape that covered his mouth. His nose was bleeding, and his eyes bulged like grapes, but Cordwain would not allow him to stop.

The trees were just up ahead. They were out of the town now, into the darkened countryside. Another hundred and fifty yards and they would be at the sewage works. Finn stumbled and Cordwain bent to haul him to his feet again.

A loud crack, startling in the night air. It sounded as though someone had let off a banger.

Cordwain threw himself to the ground beside Finn. A sniper. Christ – it might even be the Fox himself.

Another shot. This time a spray of earth exploded two feet from Cordwain's face. The SAS officer manhandled Finn round until he was lying behind the terrorist as though he were a sandbag. The firing stopped. Cordwain searched the darkness ahead but could make out nothing in the deeper shade under the trees. He cursed aloud, wishing they had brought the NVGs; but they had wanted to carry a minimum of equipment. He was blind, and had seen no muzzle flash. Doubtless, the sniper was now manoeuvring for a better fire-position.

He could hear the sirens wailing back down in Cross. Soon the army would start cordoning off the area. He had to move on.

'Come on, fucker,' he hissed to Finn, and dragged him to his feet. He pushed the IRA man in front of himself as cover and began shoving him forward, up the hill.

They made ten yards, and then Finn threw himself violently to one side, landing headlong in the grass. For a split second Cordwain stood alone.

A shot cracked out, and he was blasted off his feet.

23

Early heard the firing ahead and increased his pace to a fast, ground-eating run. He had heard three well-spaced shots: the mark of a sniper.

Something plucked at the air beside his ear. He felt a thump in his right shoulder and went down, rolling along the ground. Without a pause, he scrambled into a dip in the ground and lay there, panting.

He put up a hand to his shoulder and it came away wet, sticky. The bullet had given him the merest clip, like the slash of a blunt knife. He had not even heard the retort. Was there more than one sniper out there? If so, they were equipped with infrared sights, the bastards.

Cordwain was in trouble — he was sure of that at least. Ignoring the growing ache that ran down his right arm, he began crawling off to one flank, to try to get round the enemy.

*　　*　　*

Cordwain lay on the grass with the breath rattling in and out of his throat. There were dark shapes moving around him but he could not lift a finger. The high-calibre bullet had taken him squarely in the chest, exploding out his back and ripping his spinal cord to shreds. He coughed, bringing up blood and phlegm. At least one lung had been punctured.

A face bent over him, battered and savaged. It was Finn. Someone else crouched beside him, carrying the long shape of a heavy rifle. Cordwain could not speak.

'Here's a wee present for you, Brit,' Finn was saying, grinning, and Cordwain could feel the cold muzzle of his own weapon placed against his temple.

'Burn in hell, you fucker,' Finn said, and pulled the trigger.

There was a bright flare, like the flash of sunlight on water, and then nothing. The pain and the darkness of the night had gone. Cordwain was dead.

Finn straightened, rubbing his bleeding nose.

'There's another one round here somewhere. We'd better fuck off.'

His companion wore a Balaclava and carried a Barratt-Browning sniper rifle, the bipod extended. With a swift gesture, the mask was ripped off, and Maggie Lavery stood there, looking down on what was left of the dead SAS officer's face.

'I've seen him before. He came into the bar once, I think.'

'Aye, they've been creeping round our heels for weeks. Looks like we're rid of them now though. Come on, Maggie, let's move. We'll head east, and see if we can pick up a car in Monog.'

The pair of them started off, putting their backs to the lights of Cross, and leaving the corpse on the ground behind them.

Early heard the three-round burst of the MP5K, and then the silence. He forced himself not to hurry. At least Cordwain was still firing.

But there was something wrong – something he didn't like. Perhaps it was the sudden, heavy silence after that last burst. It made the firing sound too final – like a *coup de grâce*.

He began running at a crouch along the side of the valley, his eyes as wide as an animal's on the hunt. As soon as he saw the shape on the ground he knew what it was. His stomach turned over. He approached the body cautiously, checked it for signs of life even though the injuries were too massive for anyone to survive. Then he closed the blood-filled eyes and knelt in silence for a second. He had known James Cordwain in the Falklands, when they had both landed on the islands weeks before the Task Force. Now he lay dead on a South Armagh hillside, finished off by his own weapon. He had deserved better than to die in an ugly, petty little struggle like this.

Early rose, and examined the grass about the body. The dew was falling, wetting his legs. It was easy to pick up the trail running east along the floor of the valley; two people, walking abreast.

He started after them, his face filled with murder.

'Did you hear something?' Maggie asked Finn.

They paused. The lights of Cross were a distant glow now, half hidden by the slopes they had traversed.

'No,' Finn said. He was edgy, impatient.

'For fuck's sake, Maggie, that other bastard is still out there somewhere; we can't stand around all night.'

Maggie was stock-still, listening. Though the sniper rifle she bore was extremely heavy, she carried it as easily as if it were a broomstick.

'They were SAS, weren't they?'

'Too right. And they weren't going to get me into any court, either.'

'Lucky for you I had to have a pee, Eugene.'

'Maggie, come *on*!'

They started forward again.

*   *   *

Early stopped, breathing hard. He had heard the voices and had circled round them. Now he was upslope of the enemy, his back to the Monog road. The ground was broken here, covered with crags and boulders. He settled himself in behind one and peered out into the darkness, ears pricked for the slightest sound. His right arm was painful and clumsy, so he held the SMG in his left, steadying it on the rock in front of him.

Something about one of the voices had bothered him. Was it a boy's or a woman's? He couldn't tell – he had only heard them murmuring to each other. They must be close now.

A rattle of loose rock. They were very near, labouring up the rocky slope towards him.

A car came speeding up the road behind him. As it turned he glanced involuntarily at it and caught the glare of the headlights full in the face. The car sped off towards Cross.

Christ! His night vision was shot to shit. He blinked furiously, the after-images swimming before his eyes. The darkness of the night seemed impenetrable, like a blank wall, whereas a few moments before he had been able to distinguish shapes and objects. He had been too long out of the field; he shouldn't have been caught like that.

He closed his eyes, forced his breathing to slow, and listened as intently as a blind man.

Yes, they were closer now, maybe a hundred metres, maybe less. Slightly down to his left. He edged round the muzzle of the MP5K and clicked it on to automatic fire. His vision was not good enough to chance single shots.

Shapes were forming as he opened his eyes again. His eyes were recovering their night vision. He could see two figures walking towards him, one taller than the other. They were barely fifty metres away.

He squinted down the gun barrel and opened fire on the tall one.

The little weapon jumped like a live thing in his hands. Two quick bursts: the classic double tap. He thought he saw one figure go down and switched aim.

Shit! Too slow; the other terrorist had gone to ground. Early crawled out of his fire-position, just as a massively heavy round slammed into the boulder he had been hiding behind. He swore softly. So it was the Fox who was still in action.

He paused and changed mags, then listened. The night was silent again, dark and moonless. But the Fox was using a night-sight – he must remember that.

He began crawling off to the left, careful of every stone, trying to keep to lower dips in the ground.

The sharp retort of another shot. He heard the

thump of its impact, then the high whine of a ricochet as it rebounded off rock.

But he had seen the muzzle flash.

Now, you fucker, he thought. I've got you.

With infinite care, he edged over the rocky ground foot by foot, praying that the Fox would be either too afraid or too bloody-minded to bug out. His night vision was improving rapidly: he could see the individual boulders and rocks that littered the side of the hill.

Hoarse breathing, just in front.

He jumped up and fired at the shape he saw moving in front of him. There was a scream, and he threw himself down again, bruising his ribs on a stone. Relief flooded through him.

Got you . . . I got you.

He crawled forward, still cautious, and found a body lying draped over the rocks. He grabbed the hair and pulled the head round.

And found himself looking down at the shattered face of Eugene Finn.

The bullets had shot away his lower jaw; Early could see the tongue poking out into space like a fat worm. He released his grip in disgust and the head dropped to the stone with a sodden thud. Early dragged off his Balaclava and wiped his streaming face with it.

It must have been Finn he had hit the first time – his chest was riddled. He must have been trying to crawl to safety. So that meant . . . A rattle of falling rock off to his right. Early leapt up and sped off after it. He thought he saw a flicker of movement ahead, and grinned to himself. The Fox was running, panicked now.

Something smashed into Early's leg and knocked him off his feet. His weapon went flying and clattered off a rock a few feet away. He hit the ground heavily and screamed. The bullet had hit him squarely in the thigh. He could see broken splinters of bone glistening through his ripped flesh, and the torn material of his boiler suit.

Someone coming. He forced himself to ignore the agony, to draw the pistol and click back the hammer.

There was a roaring in the air, a great thudding noise. A helicopter wheeled over the hillside, its searchlight probing the shadows and lighting up the night unbearably. It was coming east, towards him. Early shielded his eyes.

A figure was silhouetted by the glare of the roving searchlight. It stood over him, rifle in shoulder.

'Dominic,' the voice said, shocked.

He squinted. The helicopter was almost overhead. Its light blinded him and the roar of its rotors blocked out all other noise. He raised his pistol at the silhouette that stood over him and fired. Even when the shape fell, he continued firing. The body hit the ground and twitched as the 9mm slugs ripped into it.

Early heard the 'dead man's click' of the empty magazine at the same time as he saw the face of his enemy, and the mane of chestnut hair that was fluttering in the backwash of the rotors.

He stared in horror at Maggie Lavery's dead face.

Epilogue

Brigadier General Whelan stared out of the window of his office at the rain that was coming down in sheets outside. He sucked on his pipe, but it had gone out. He turned back to his desk.

'Well?' the man in the suit said.

Whelan scowled at him.

'It's a bloody shambles, of course. The last of Ulster Troop left this morning; there are, as of noon today, no SAS operating in the Province.'

'I'm sure the Minister will be happy to hear that,' the man in the suit said, smiling. He was sitting with his briefcase on his lap. He held a manila folder in his hand.

'And this . . . Early chap. What about him?'

'He's in a bad way as I understand – may lose his leg. He's been flown back across the water to recover. The Regiment, funnily enough, is showing signs of standing by him. Usually they drop hooligans like him as though they were hot potatoes. He'll face charges, of course.'

'A sorry business.'

'Indeed. Eight men in one day, and three of them SAS. That's more than the Regiment has lost here in the past twenty years. It's a shame about James Cordwain. He was a good man, if a little flamboyant.'

'But the Border Fox is accounted for.'

'Yes, there is that, I suppose. This man Early shot her. The chopper caught it all on film. An absurdly pretty girl, too. Christ, what a country. Will you have a drink?'

'Thank you, no,' said the man in the suit.

Whelan regarded him suspiciously for a moment, then went over to the corner cabinet and poured himself a whiskey.

'So who is to be my replacement?' he asked sharply.

'General Joseph Waring, from NORTHAG.'

'Joe Waring, eh? Well, he'll do a good job.' Whelan went and stood at the window again, looking out at the grey day. He sipped his whiskey thoughtfully.

'They thought it was war, you see,' he said, without turning round. 'They thought they could make a difference all by themselves: the failing of all young men in all wars. But it's different here. We can go on shooting them and they can go on shooting us till doomsday because it won't make a blind bit of difference. There will always be more young men ready to step forward and fill the shoes of the dead.'

'That's hardly a very encouraging statement, coming from the Commander of Her Majesty's Land Forces, Northern Ireland.'

'Ex-Commander,' Whelan said wryly. He threw back the last of the whiskey and looked at the glass appreciatively.

'Bushmills, lovely stuff. Hard to believe that a country which can make this can have so much hatred in it.'

There was a knock at the door, and then Whelan's aide popped his head around it.

'The car's here, sir.'

Whelan nodded. 'Five minutes.'

He turned to his guest. 'Well, I wish you and the Select Committee well in your inquiry. You should have my official statement within days.'

'And your comments here were, of course, off the record.'

'Of course. Now, if you'll excuse me, I have a plane to catch.' The brigadier general took up his coat and hat, set down his glass, and left without another word.

The man in the suit remained in the room alone a few moments. He stared out the window into the streaming rain, and watched a column of armoured Landrovers file out of the gates of the base to begin their patrol. Just another day in Northern Ireland.

SOLDIER V: SAS

INTO VIETNAM

Shaun Clarke

Prelude

The Viet Cong guerrillas emerged from the forest at dawn, with the mist drifting eerily about their heads. There were nearly fifty men, most dressed like coolies in black, pyjama-style combat gear and black felt hats, with sandals or rubber-soled boots on their feet. Nearly all of them were small and frail from lack of nourishment and years of fighting. Their weapons were varied: Soviet-made Kalashnikov AK47 machine-fed 7.62mm assault rifles; 7.62mm RPD light machine-guns with hundred-round link-belt drum magazines; 7.62mm PPS43 sub-machine-guns with a folding metal butt stock and thirty-five-round magazine; Soviet RPG7V short-range, anti-armour, rocket-propelled grenade launchers; and, for the officers only, Soviet Tokarev T33 7.62mm pistols, recoil-operated, semi-automatic and with an eight-round magazine.

As the VC left the forest behind them and crossed the paddy-field, wading ankle deep in water, the officers quietly slid their Tokarevs from their holsters and cocked them.

The Vietnamese hamlet was spread over a broad expanse of dusty earth surrounded by trees and its edge was about fifty yards beyond the paddy-field. With thatched huts, communal latrines, some culti-vated plots, a regular supply of food from the nearby paddy-field, and a total of no more than fifty souls, it was exactly what the guerrillas were looking for.

Though this was an agricultural hamlet, the VC had been informed that the peasants had been trained by the CIA's Combined Studies Division and Australian Special Air Service (SAS) teams in hamlet defence, including weapon training, moat and palisade construction, ambushing and setting booby-traps. The peasants were being armed and trained by the Americans in the hope that they would protect themselves against guerrilla attacks. What had been happening in practice, however, is that the VC, more experienced and in much greater numbers, had been destroying such hamlets and using the captured American arms and supplies against American and South Vietnamese forces elsewhere.

This was about to happen again.

The first to spot the VC were two peasants working at the far edge of the paddy-field. One of them glanced up, saw the raiding party and hastily waded out of the paddy-field and ran back to the hamlet. The second man was just about to flee when one of the VC officers fired at the first with his Tokarev.

The sound of that single shot was shockingly loud in the morning's silence, making birds scatter from the trees to the sky, chickens squawk in panic, and dogs bark with the false courage of fear.

The 7.62mm bullet hit the man's lower body, just beside the spinal column, violently punching him forward. Even as the first man was splashing face down in the water, the other man was rushing past him to get to dry land and the villagers were looking up in surprise. He had just reached the dry earth at the edge of the paddy-field when several VC fired at him with their AK47s, making him shudder like a rag doll, tearing him to shreds, then hurling him to the ground as the dust billowed up all around him.

A woman in the hamlet let out a long, piercing scream as the wounded man managed to make it to his knees, coughing water and blood from his lungs. Even as he was waving his arms frantically to correct his balance, pistols and assault rifles roared together. When he plunged backwards into the paddy-field, his clothes lacerated, the bullet holes pumping blood, wails of dread and despair arose from the hamlet.

While the women gathered their children around them and ushered them into the thatched houses, the men trained by the Americans rushed to take up positions in the defensive slit trenches armed with 7.62mm M60 GPMGs – general-purpose machine-guns. Others rushed to their thatched huts and emerged carrying L1A1 SLR semi-automatic rifles of the same calibre as the machine-guns. They threw themselves on the ground overlooking the moat filled with lethal punji stakes and wooden palisades constructed by Australian SAS troops, taking aim at the attackers. The VC were now emerging from the paddy-field and marching directly towards the minefield that encircled the hamlet.

Abruptly, the VC, who knew that the village was part of the US Strategic Hamlet Program and therefore well protected, split into three groups, two of which circled around the village, weaving through the palm trees just beyond the minefield. As they were doing so, the third group were taking positions in a hollow at the far side of the moat, between the paddy-field and the hamlet, and there setting up two Chinese 60mm mortars.

Realizing with horror that the two VC groups could only be circling around the back of the hamlet because they knew the location of the patrol route exit through the minefield; and that they were also going to mortar-bomb a way through the minefield at the front – information they must have obtained from an informer – some of the villagers opened fire with their rifles and GPMGs as others raced back across the clearing to stop the guerrillas getting in.

This second group was, however, badly decimated when a third VC mortar fired half a dozen shells in quick succession, blowing the running men apart and then exploding in a broad arc that took in some of the surrounding thatched huts and set them ablaze.

As the flames burst ferociously from the thatched roofs and the wailing of women and children was heard from within, the first mortar shells aimed at the minefield exploded with a deafening roar. Soil, dust and smoke spewed skyward and then spread out to obscure the VC as some of them stood up and advanced at the crouch to the edge of the mined area. Kneeling there and checking where the mortars had exploded, the guerrillas saw that they nearly had a clear path and could complete the job with another few rounds.

Using hand signals, the leader of this group indicated a slightly lower elevation, then dropped to the ground as a hail of gunfire came from the frantic villagers at the other side of the minefield. When the second round of mortar shells had exploded, throwing up more billowing smoke and dust, the first of the VC advanced along the path of charred holes created by the explosions. That crudely cleared route led them safely through the minefield and up to the edge of the moat, where some of them were chopped down by the villagers' guns and the rest threw themselves to the ground to return fire.

By now the other two groups of VC had managed to circle around to the back of the hamlet and, using the map given to them by the informer, had located the patrol route exit and started moving carefully along it in single file. Almost instantly, the first of them were cut down by the few armed peasants who had managed to escape the mortars exploding in the centre of the hamlet. As the first of the VC fell, however, the rest opened fire with their AK47s, felling the few peasants who had managed to get this far. The rest of the guerrillas then raced along the patrol route exit, into the centre of the hamlet, where, with the screams and weeping of women and children in their ears, they were able to come up behind the villagers defending the moat to the front.

Some of the women kneeling in the clearing in front of their burning homes cried out warnings to their men, but it was too late. Caught in a withering crossfire from front and rear, the villagers firing across the moat, among them a few teenage girls, were chopped to pieces and died screaming and writhing in a convulsion of spewing soil and dust. Those who did not die immediately were put to death by the bayonet. When their mothers, wives or children tried to stop this, they too were dispatched in the same way. Within minutes the attack was over and the remaining VC were wading across the moat and clambering up to the clearing.

In a state of shock and grief, and surrounded by their dead relatives and friends, the rest of the villagers were easily subdued and forced to kneel in the middle of the clearing. The remaining thatched huts were then searched by the guerrillas and those inside prodded out at bayonet or gun point. After a rigorous interrogation – faces were slapped and lots of insults were shouted, though no other form of torture was used – the villagers considered to be 'traitors' to the communists were led away and made to kneel by the moat. There they were shot, each with a single bullet to the back of the head, then their bodies were kicked over the edge into the water.

When this grisly operation was over, the rest of the villagers, many in severe shock, were forced into separate work groups. One of these, composed only of men and teenage boys, was made to drag the dead bodies out of the moat with meat-hooks, then place them on ox carts and take them to a cleared area just outside the perimeter, where they were buried without ceremony in a shallow pit.

When, about three hours later, this work party, now exhausted and in an even worse state of shock, returned to the hamlet, they found their friends already at work clearing away the burnt-out dwellings and unwanted foliage with machetes, hoes, short-handled spades and buckets under the impassive but watchful gaze of armed VC guards. Assigned their individual tasks in this joint effort, they began with the others what would be weeks of hard, nightmarish, ingenious work: the construction of an elaborate tunnel system directly under the devastated hamlet.

First, a series of large, rectangular pits, each about fifteen feet deep, was dug on the sites of the destroyed huts. Over these pits were raised sloping thatched roofs of the type found on the other dwellings, though the newly built roofs were mere inches off the ground. Viewed from the air, they would suggest normal hamlet houses.

Once the thatched roofs had been raised, work began on digging a series of tunnels leading down from the floor of each pit. Most of these were so narrow that there was only enough space for a single, slim body to wriggle along them, and in places they descended vertically, like a well, before continuing at a gentler slope in one direction or another. The only tunnel not beginning in one of the pits and not making any kind of bend was a well, its water table about forty feet deep and its surface access, level with the ground, camouflaged with a web of bamboo covered with soil and shrubbery.

One of the pits served as a kitchen, complete with bamboo shelves and a stone-walled stove. Smoke was vented into a pipe that spewed it into a tunnel running about eight feet underground until it was 150 feet west of the kitchen, where it emerged through three vents hidden in the palm trees beyond the perimeter.

An escape tunnel descended from the floor of the kitchen, curving west and crossing two concealed trapdoors before dividing into two even narrower tunnels. One of these was a false tunnel that led to a dead end; the other, concealed, rose steeply until it reached an escape hole hidden in the trees beyond the smoke outlets. A third escape tunnel, hidden by a concealed trapdoor, led away from the tunnel complex but linked up with another under the next village to the west. Of the other two trapdoors in this escape route, one had to be skirted, as the weight of a human body would make it collapse and drop that person to a hideous death in a trap filled with poisoned punji stakes. The third concealed trapdoor ran down into a large cavern hacked out of the earth about thirty feet down, to be used as a storage area for weapons, explosives and rice.

A short tunnel running east from the entrance to the underground storage area led into the middle of the well, about halfway down. On the opposite side of the well, but slightly lower, where the man pulling water up with a bucket and rope could straddle both ledges with his feet, another tunnel curved up and levelled out. At that point there was another trapdoor, and this covered a tunnel that climbed vertically to the floor of a conical air-raid shelter, so shaped because it amplified the sound of approaching aircraft and therefore acted as a useful warning system.

Leading off the air-raid shelter was another tunnel curving vertically until it reached the conference chamber. Complete with long table, wooden chairs and blackboard, the conference chamber was located in another of the pits, under a thatched roof almost touching the ground.

A narrow airing tunnel led from the pyramidal roof of the air-raid shelter to the surface; another led down to where the tunnel below levelled out and ran on to a second dead end, but one with another trapdoor in the floor. This trapdoor, proof against blast, gas and water, covered a tunnel that dropped straight down before curving around and up again in a series of loops that formed a natural blast wall. The top of this tunnel was sealed off by a second, similarly protective trapdoor, located in another cavernous area hacked out of the earth about fifteen feet down.

Though this cavernous area was empty – its only purpose to allow gas to dissipate and water to drain away – a series of interlinking access and exit tunnels ran off it. One led even deeper, to a large, rectangular space that would be used as the forward aid station for the wounded. The escape tunnel leading from this chamber ran horizontally under the ground, about twenty-five feet down, parallel to the surface, until it reached the similar network of tunnels under the next hamlet to the east.

The tunnel ascending to the east of the empty cavern led to another concealed trapdoor and two paths running in opposite directions: one to a camouflaged escape hole, the other to another pit dug out of the ground, this one not covered with a decoy thatched roof, but camouflaged with foliage and used as a firing post for both personal and anti-aircraft weapons.

West of this firing post, and similarly camouflaged, was a ventilation shaft running obliquely down to the empty cavern over the tunnel trap used as a natural blast wall. West of this ventilation shaft was the first of a series of punji pits, all camouflaged. West of the first punji pit was another concealed, ground-level trapdoor entrance that led into another tunnel descending almost vertically to a further hidden trapdoor.

Anyone crawling on to this last trapdoor would find it giving way beneath them and pitching them to their death on the sharpened punji stakes below. However, anyone skirting the trapdoor and crawling on would reach the biggest chamber of them all – the VCs' sleeping and living quarters, with hammock beds, folding chairs and tables, stone chamber pots, bamboo shelves for weapons and other personal belongings, and all the other items that enable men to live for long periods like rats underground.

After weeks of hard labour by both South Vietnamese peasants and VC soldiers, this vast complex of underground tunnels was complete and some of the peasants were sent above ground to act as if the hamlet were running normally. Though still in a state of shock at the loss of friends, relatives and livelihood, the peasants knew that they were being watched all the time and would be shot if they made the slightest protest or tried to warn those defending South Vietnam.

Those peasants still slaving away in the tunnel complex would remain there to complete what would become in time four separate levels similar to the one they had just constructed. The levels would be connected by an intricate network of passages, some as narrow as eighty centimetres, with ventilation holes that ran obliquely to prevent monsoon rain flooding and were orientated so as to catch the morning light and bring in fresh air from the prevailing easterly winds.

The guerrillas not watching the peasants were living deep underground, existing on practically nothing, constantly smelling the stench of their own piss and shit, emerging from the fetid chambers and dank tunnels only when ordered to go out and strike down the enemy. Like trapdoor spiders, they saw the light of day only when they brought the darkness of death.

1

The swamp was dark, humid, foul-smelling and treacherous. Wading chest deep in the scum-covered water, Sergeant Sam 'Shagger' Bannerman and his sidekick, Corporal Tom 'Red' Swanson, both holding their jungle-camouflaged 7.62mm L1A1 self-loading rifles above their heads, were being assailed by mosquitoes, stinging hornets and countless other crazed insects. After slogging through the jungle for five days, they were both covered in bruises and puss-filled stings and cuts, all of which drove the blood lust of their attackers to an even greater pitch.

'You try to talk . . .' Red began, then, almost choking on an insect, coughed and spat noisily in an attempt to clear his throat. 'You try to talk and these bloody insects fly straight into your mouth. Jesus Christ, this is terrible!'

'No worse than Borneo,' Sergeant Bannerman replied. 'Well, maybe a little . . .'

In fact, it was worse. Shagger had served with

1 Squadron SAS (Australian Special Air Service) of Headquarters Far East Land Forces during the Malaya Emergency in 1963. In August of that year he had joined the Training Team in Vietnam, and from February to October 1964 had been with the first Australian team to operate with the US Special Forces at Nha Trang. Then, in February 1966, he was posted with 1 Squadron SAS to Sarawak, Borneo, and spent two months there before being recalled, along with a good half of 1 Squadron, to the SAS headquarters at Swanbourne, Perth, for subsequent transfer to 3 Squadron SAS, training especially for the new Task Force in Vietnam. They had not yet reached 'Nam, but would certainly be there soon, once they had completed this business in the hell of New Guinea. Shagger had indeed seen it all – and still he thought this was bad.

'Not much longer to go,' he said, still wading waist deep in the sludge and finding it difficult because the bed of the swamp was soft and yielding, being mainly a combination of mud and small stones but dangerously cluttered with larger stones, fallen branches and other debris. The task of wading on this soft bottom was not eased by the fact that Shagger and Red were both humping 90lb of bergen rucksack and 11lb of loaded SLR semi-automatic assault rifle. The problems were further compounded by the knowledge that the surface of the water was covered with a foul-smelling slime composed of rotted seeds, leaves and moss. It was also cluttered with obstructions that included giant razor-edged palm leaves and floating branches, the latter hard to distinguish from the highly venomous sea-snakes that infested the place. If these weren't bad enough, there were other snakes in the branches that overhung the swamp, brushing the men's heads, as well as poisonous spiders and bloodsucking leeches. So far, while neither soldier had been bitten by a venomous sea-snake or spider, both had lost a lot of blood to the many leeches that attached themselves to their skin under the water or after falling from the branches or palm leaves above them.

'My eyes are all swollen,' Red complained. 'I can hardly see a thing.'

'Your lips are all swollen as well,' Shagger replied, 'but you still manage to talk.'

'I'm just trying to keep your pecker up, Sarge.'

'With whinges and moans? Just belt up and keep wading. We'll get there any moment now and then you can do a bit of spine bashing' – he meant have a rest – 'and tend to your eyes and other swollen parts, including your balls – if you've got any, that is.'

'I don't remember,' Red said with feeling. 'My memory doesn't stretch back that far.' He had served with Shagger in Borneo, and formed a solid friendship that included a lot of banter. He felt easy with the man. But then, having a philosophical disposition, he rubbed along with most people. 'Actually,' he said, noticing with gratitude that the water was now below his waist, which meant they were moving up on to higher ground, 'I prefer this to Borneo, Sarge. I couldn't stand the bridges in that country. No head for heights, me.'

'You did all right,' Shagger said.

In fact, Red had been terrific. Of all the many terrifying aspects of the campaign in Borneo, the worst was crossing the swaying walkways that spanned the wide and deep gorges with rapids boiling through bottlenecks formed by rock outcroppings hundreds of feet below. Just as in New Guinea, the jungles of Borneo had been infested with snakes, lizards, leeches, wild pigs, all kinds of poisonous insects, and even head-hunters, making it a particularly nightmarish place to fight a war. And yet neither snakes nor head-hunters were a match for the dizzying aerial walkways when it came to striking terror into even the most courageous men.

The walkways were crude bridges consisting of three lengths of thick bamboo laid side by side and strapped together with rattan – hardly much wider than two human feet placed close together. The uprights angled out and in again overhead, and were strapped with rattan to the horizontal holds. You could slide your hands along the holds only as far as the next upright. Once there, you had to remove your hand for a moment and lift it over the upright before grabbing the horizontal hold. All the time you were doing this, inching forward perhaps 150 feet above a roaring torrent, the narrow walkway was creaking and swinging dangerously in the wind that swept along the gorge. It was like walking in thin air.

Even worse, the Australians often had to use the walkways when they were making their way back from a jungle patrol and being pursued by Indonesian troops. At such times the enemy could use the walkways as shooting galleries in which the Aussies made highly visible targets as they inched their way across.

This had been the experience of Shagger and Red during their last patrol before returning to Perth. Their patrol had been caught in the middle of an unusually high walkway, swaying over rapids 160 feet below, while the Indonesians unleashed small-arms fire on them, killing and wounding many men, until eventually they shot the rattan binding to pieces, making the walkway, with some unfortunates still on it, tear away from its moorings, sending the men still clinging to it screaming to their doom.

Shagger, though more experienced than Red, had suffered nightmares about that incident for weeks after the event, but Red, with his characteristic detachment, had only once expressed regret at the loss of his mates and then put the awful business behind him. And though, as he claimed, he had no head for heights, he had been very courageous on the walkways, often turning back to help more frightened men across, even in the face of enemy fire. He was a good man to have around.

'The ground's getting higher,' Shagger said, having noticed that the scummy water was now only as high as his knees. 'That means we're heading towards the islet marked on the map. That's our ambush position.'

'You think we'll get there before they do?' Red asked.

'Let us pray,' Shagger replied.

As he waded the last few hundred yards to the islet, now visible as a mound of firm ground covered with seedlings and brown leaves, with a couple of palm trees in the middle, Shagger felt the exhaustion of the past five days falling upon him. Three Squadron SAS had been sent to New Guinea to deploy patrols through forward airfields by helicopter and light aircraft; to patrol and navigate through tropical jungle and mountain terrain; to practise communications and resupply; and to liaise with the indigenous people.

For the past five days, therefore, the SAS men had sweated in the tropical heat; hacked their way through seemingly impassable secondary jungle with machetes; climbed incredibly steep, tree-covered hills; waded across rivers flowing at torrential speeds; oared themselves along slower rivers on 'gripper bar' rafts made from logs and four stakes; slept in shallow, water-filled scrapes under inadequate ponchos in fiercely driving, tropical rainstorms; suffered the constant buzzing, whining and biting of mosquitoes and hornets; frozen as poisonous snakes slithered across their booted feet; lost enormous amounts of blood to leeches; had some hair-raising confrontations with head-hunting natives – and all while reconnoitring the land, noting points of strategic value, and either pursuing, or being pursued by, the enemy.

Now, on the last day, Shagger and Red, having been separated accidentally from the rest of their troop during a shoot-out with an enemy column, were making their way to the location originally chosen for their own troop as an ambush position, where they hoped to have a final victory and then get back to base and ultimately Australia. After their long, arduous hike through the swamp they were both exhausted.

'I'm absolutely bloody shagged,' Red said, gasping. 'I can hardly move a muscle.'

'We can take a rest in a minute,' Shagger told him. 'Here's our home from home, mate. The ambush position.'

The islet was about fifty yards from the far edge of the swamp they had just crossed, almost directly facing a narrow track that snaked into the jungle, curving away out of sight. It was along that barely distinguishable track that the enemy would approach on their route across the swamp, but in the opposite direction as they searched for Shagger's divided patrol, which had undoubtedly been sighted by one of their many reconnaissance helicopters.

Wading up to the islet, pushing aside the gigantic, bright-green palm leaves that floated on its miasmal surface, Shagger and Red finally found firm ground beneath them and were able to lay down their SLRs and shrug off their heavy bergens. Relieved of that weight, they clambered up on to the islet's bed of brown leaves and seedlings, rolled on to their backs and gulped in lungfuls of air. Both men did a lot of deep breathing before talking again.

'Either I'm gonna flake out,' Red finally gasped, 'or I'm gonna have a good chunder. I feel sick with exhaustion.'

'You can't sleep and you can't chuck up,' Shagger told him. 'You can chunder when you get back to base and have a skinful of beer. You can sleep there as well. Right now, though, we have to dig in and set up, then spring our little surprise. Those dills, if they get here at all, will be here before last light, so we have to be ready.'

'Just let me have some water,' Red replied, 'and I'll be back on the ball.'

'Go on, mate. Then let's get rid of these bloody leeches and prepare the ambush. We'll win this one, Red.'

When they had quenched their thirst, surprising themselves by doing so without vomiting, they lit cigarettes, inhaled luxuriously for a few minutes, then proceeded to burn off, with their cigarettes, the leeches still clinging to their bruised and scarred skin. As they were both covered with fat, black leeches, all still sucking blood, this operation took several cigarettes. When they had got rid of the bloodsuckers they wiped their skins down with antiseptic cream and set about making a temporary hide.

The islet was an almost perfect circle hardly more than thirty feet in diameter. The thick trees soaring up from the carpet of seedlings and leaves were surrounded by a convenient mass of dense foliage over which the branches draped their gigantic palm leaves. As this natural camouflage would give good protection, Shagger chose this area for the location of the hide and he and Red then dug out two shallow lying-up positions, or LUPs, using the small spades clipped to their webbing.

This done, each man began to construct a simple shelter over his LUP by driving two V-shaped wooden uprights into the soft soil, placed about six feet apart. A length of nylon cord was tied between the uprights, then a waterproof poncho was draped over the cord with the long end facing the prevailing wind and the short, exposed, end facing the path at the far side of the swamp. The two corners of each end were jerked tight and held down with small wooden pegs and nylon cord. The LUP was then filled with a soft bed of leaves and seedlings, a sleeping-bag was rolled out on to it, and the triangular tent was carefully camouflaged with giant leaves and other foliage held down with fine netting.

Once the shelters had been completed, the hide blended in perfectly with the surrounding vegetation, making it practically invisible to anyone coming along the jungle track leading to the swamp.

'If they come out of there,' Shagger said with satisfaction, 'they won't have a prayer. Now let's check our kit.'

The afternoon sun was still high in the sky when each man checked his SLR, removing the mud, twigs, leaves and even cobwebs that had got into it; oiling the bolt, trigger mechanism and other moving parts; then rewrapping it in its jungle-coloured camouflage material. Satisfied that the weapons were in working order, they ate a cold meal of tinned sardines, biscuits and water, battling every second to keep off the attacking insects. Knowing that the enemy trying to find them would attempt to cross the swamp before the sun had set – which meant that if they came at all, they would be coming along the track quite soon – they lay on their bellies in their LUPs, sprinkled more loose foliage over themselves as best they could, and laid the SLRs on the lip of their shallow scrapes, barrels facing the swamp. Then they waited.

'It's been a long five days,' Shagger said.

'Too bloody long,' Red replied. 'And made no better by the fact that we're doing the whole thing on a shoestring. Piss-poor, if you ask me.'

Shagger grinned. 'The lower ranks' whinge. How do you, a no-hoper corporal, know this was done on a shoestring?'

'Well, no RAAF support, for a start. Just that bloody Ansett-MAL Caribou that was completely unreliable . . .'

'Serviceability problems,' Shagger interjected, still grinning. 'But the Trans Australian Airlines DC3s and the Crowley Airlines G13 choppers were reliable. They made up for the lack of RAAF support, didn't they?'

'You're joking. Those fucking G13s had no winch and little lift capability. They were as useless as lead balloons.'

'That's true,' Shagger murmured, recalling the cumbersome helicopters hovering over the canopy of the trees, whipping up dust and leaves, as they dropped supplies or lifted men out. He fell silent, never once removing his searching gaze from the darkening path that led from the jungle to the edge of the swamp. Then he said, 'They were piss-poor for resups and lift-offs – that's true enough. But the DC3s were OK.'

Red sighed loudly, as if short of breath. 'That's my whole point. This was supposed to be an important exercise, preparing us for 'Nam, and yet we didn't even get RAAF support. Those bastards in Canberra are playing silly buggers and wasting our time.'

'No,' Shagger replied firmly. 'We didn't waste our time. They might have fucked up, but we've learnt an awful lot in these five days and I think it'll stand us in good stead once we go in-country.'

'Let's hope so, Sarge.'

'Anyway, it's no good farting against thunder, so you might as well forget it. If we pull off this ambush we'll have won, then it's spine-bashing time. We can . . .'

Suddenly Shagger raised his right hand to silence Red. At first he thought he was mistaken, but then, when he listened more intently, he heard what he assumed was the distant snapping of twigs and large, hardened leaves as a body of men advanced along the jungle path, heading for the swamp.

Using a hand signal, Shagger indicated to Red that he should adapt the firing position. When Red had done so, Shagger signalled that they should aim their fire in opposite directions, forming a triangular arc that would put a line of bullets through the front and rear of the file of enemy troops when it extended into the swamp from its muddy edge at the end of the path.

As they lay there waiting, squinting along their rifle sights, their biggest problems were ignoring the sweat that dripped from their foreheads into their eyes, and the insects that whined and buzzed about them, driven into a feeding frenzy by the smell of the sweat. In short, the most difficult thing was remaining dead still to ensure that they were not detected by their quarry.

Luckily, just as both of them were thinking that they might be driven mad by the insects, the first of the enemy appeared around the bend in the darkening path. They were marching in the classic single-file formation, with one man out ahead on 'point' as the lead scout, covering an arc of fire immediately in front of the patrol, and the others strung out behind him, covering arcs to the left and right.

When all the members of the patrol had come into view around the bed in the path, with 'Tail-end Charlie' well behind the others, covering an arc of fire to the rear, Shagger counted a total of eight men: two four-man patrols combined. All of them were wearing olive-green, long-sleeved cotton shirts; matching trousers with a drawcord waist; soft jungle hats with a sweat-band around the forehead; and rubber-soled canvas boots. Like Shagger and Red, they were armed with 7.62mm L1A1 SLRs and had 9mm Browning High Power pistols and machetes strung from their waist belts.

In short, the 'enemy' was a patrol of Australian troops.

'Got the buggers!' Shagger whispered, then aimed at the head of the single file as Red was taking aim at its rear. When the last man had stepped into the water, Shagger and Red both opened fire with their SLRs.

Having switched to automatic they stitched lines of spurting water across the front and rear of the patrol. Shocked, but quickly realizing that they were boxed in, the men under attack bawled panicky, conflicting instructions at one another, then split into two groups. These started heading off in opposite directions: one directly towards the islet, the other away from it.

Instantly, Shagger and Red jumped up to lob American M26 hand-grenades, one out in front of the men wading away from the islet, the other in front of the men wading towards it. Both grenades exploded with a muffled roar that threw up spiralling columns of water and rotting vegetation which then rained back down on the fleeing soldiers. Turning back towards one another, the two groups hesitated, then tried to head back to the jungle. They had only managed a few steps when Shagger and Red riddled the shore with the awesome automatic fire of their combined SLRs, tearing the foliage to shreds and showering the fleeing troops with flying branches and dangerously sharp palm leaves.

When the 'enemy' bunched up again, hesitating, Shagger and Bannerman stopped firing.

'Drop your weapons and put your hands in the air!' Shagger bawled at them. 'We'll take that as surrender.'

The men in the water were silent for some time, glancing indecisively at one another; but eventually a sergeant, obviously the platoon leader, cried out: 'Bloody hell!' Then he dropped his SLR into the water and raised both hands. 'Got us fair and square,' he said to the rest of his men. 'We're all prisoners of war. So drop your weapons and put up your hands, you happy wankers. We've lost. Those bastards have won.'

'Too right, we have,' Shagger and Red said simultaneously, with big, cheesy grins.

They had other reasons for smiling. This was the final action in the month-long training exercise 'Traiim Nau', conducted by Australian troops in the jungles and swamps of New Guinea in the spring of 1966.

In June that year, after they had returned to their headquarters in Swanbourne, and enjoyed

two weeks' leave, the men of 3 Squadron SAS
embarked by boat and plane from Perth to help
set up a Forward Operating Base (FOB) in Phuoc
Tuy province, Vietnam.

2

In a small, relatively barren room in 'the Kremlin', the Operations Planning and Intelligence section, at Bradbury Lines, Hereford, the Commanding Officer of D Squadron, SAS, Lieutenant-Colonel Patrick 'Paddy' Callaghan, was conducting a most unusual briefing – unusual because there were only two other men present: Sergeants Jimmy 'Jimbo' Ashman and Richard 'Dead-eye Dick' Parker.

Ashman was an old hand who had served with the Regiment since it was formed in North Africa in 1941, fought with it as recently as 1964, in Aden, and now, in his mid-forties, was being given his next-to-last active role before being transferred to the Training Wing as a member of the Directing Staff. Parker had previously fought with the SAS in Malaya and Borneo and alongside Ashman in Aden. Jimbo was one of the most experienced and popular men in the Regiment, while Dead-eye, as he was usually known, was one of the most admired and feared. By his own choice, he had very few friends.

Lieutenant-Colonel Callaghan knew them both well, particularly Jimbo, with whom he went back as far as 1941 when they had both taken part in the Regiment's first forays against the Germans with the Long Range Desert Group. Under normal circumstances officers could remain with the Regiment for no more than three years at a time. However, they could return for a similar period after a break, and Callaghan, who was devoted to the SAS, had been tenacious in doing just that. For this reason, he had an illustrious reputation based on unparalleled experience with the Regiment. At the end of the war, when the SAS was disbanded, Callaghan had returned to his original regiment, 3 Commando. But when he heard that the SAS was being reformed to deal with the Emergency in Malaya, he applied immediately and was accepted, and soon found himself involved in intense jungle warfare.

After Malaya, Callaghan was returned to Bradbury Lines, then still located at Merebrook Camp, Malvern, where he had worked with his former Malayan Squadron Commander, Lieutenant-Colonel Pryce-Jones, on the structuring of the rigorous new Selection and Training Programme for the Regiment, based mostly on ideas devised and thoroughly tested in Malaya. Promoted to the rank of major in 1962, shortly after the SAS had transferred to Bradbury Lines, Callaghan was returned once again to his original unit, 3 Commando, but then wangled his way back into the SAS, where he had been offered the leadership of D Squadron just before its assignment to the Borneo campaign in 1964.

Shortly after the successful completion of that campaign, when he had returned with the rest of the squadron to Bradbury Lines, he was returned yet again to 3 Commando, promoted once more, then informed that he was now too old for active service and was therefore being assigned a desk job in the Kremlin. Realizing that the time had come to accept the inevitable, he had settled into his new position and was, as ever, working conscientiously when, to his surprise, he was offered the chance to transfer back to the SAS for what the Officer Commanding had emphasized would be his 'absolutely final three-year stint'. Unable to resist the call, Callaghan had turned up at Bradbury Lines to learn that he was being sent to Vietnam.

'This is not a combatant role,' the OC informed him, trying to keep a straight face. 'You'll be there purely in an advisory capacity and – may I make it clear from the outset – in an *unofficial* capacity. Is that understood?'

'Absolutely, sir.'

Though Callaghan was now officially too old to take part in combat, he had no intention of avoiding it should the opportunity to leap in present itself.

Also, he knew – and knew that his OC knew it as well – that if he was in Vietnam unofficially, his presence there would be denied and any actions undertaken by him likewise denied. Callaghan was happy.

'This is top-secret,' Callaghan now told Jimbo and Dead-eye from his hard wooden chair in front of a blackboard covered by a black cloth. 'We three – and we three alone – are off to advise the Aussie SAS in Phuoc Tuy province, Vietnam.'

Jimbo gave a low whistle, but otherwise kept his thoughts to himself for now.

'Where exactly is Phuoc Tuy?' Dead-eye asked.

'South-east of Saigon,' Callaghan informed him. 'A swampy hell of jungle and paddy-fields. The VC main forces units have a series of bases in the jungle and the political cadres have control of the villages. Where they don't have that kind of control, they ruthlessly eliminate those communities. The Aussies' job is to stop them.'

'I didn't even know the Aussies were there,' Jimbo said, voicing a common misconception.

'Oh, they're there, all right – and have been, in various guises, for some time. In the beginning, back in 1962, when they were known as the Australian Army Training Team Vietnam – 'the Team' for short – they were there solely to train South Vietnamese units in jungle warfare, village

32

security and related activities such as engineering and signals. Unlike the Yanks, they weren't even allowed to accompany the locals in action against the North Vietnamese, let alone engage in combat.

'Also, the Aussies and Americans reacted to the war in different ways. The Yanks were training the South Vietnamese to combat a massed invasion by North Vietnam across the Demilitarized Zone, established in 1954 under the Geneva Accords, which temporarily divided North Vietnam from South Vietnam along the 17th Parallel. The Americans stressed the rapid development of large forces and the concentration of artillery and air power to deliver a massive volume of fire over a wide area. The Aussies, on the other hand, having perfected small-scale, counter-insurgency tactics, had more faith in those and continued to use them in Vietnam, concentrating on map reading and navigation, marksmanship, stealth, constant patrolling, tracking the enemy and, of course, patience. Much of this they learnt from us back in Malaya during the fifties.'

'That's why they're bloody good,' Jimbo said.

'Don't let them hear you say that,' Dead-eye told him, offering one of his rare, bleak smiles. 'They might not be amused.'

'If they learnt from us, sir, they're good and that's all there is to it.'

'Let me give you some useful background,'

Callaghan said. 'Back in 1962, before heading off to Vietnam, the Aussie SAS followed a crash training programme. First, there was a two-week briefing on the war at the Intelligence Centre in Sydney. Then the unit spent five days undergoing intensive jungle-warfare training in Queensland. In early August of that year, with their training completed, twenty-nine SAS men took a regular commercial flight from Singapore to Saigon, all wearing civilian clothing. They changed into the jungle-green combat uniform of the Australian soldier during the flight.'

'In other words, they went secretly,' Dead-eye said.

'Correct. On arrival at Saigon's Tan Son Nhut airport, they were split up into two separate teams. A unit of ten men was sent to Vietnamese National Training Centre at Dong Da, just south of Hue, the old imperial capital. That camp was responsible for the training of recruits for the Army of the Republic of Vietnam, the ARVN, but the base was also used as a battalion training centre and could accommodate about a thousand men. There, though constantly handicapped by the almost total corruption of the ARVN officers, they managed to train recruits and replacements for the regular ARVN Ranger units.

'The second unit, consisting of a group of ten, was sent to the Civil Guard Training Centre at Hiep

Kanh, north-west of Hue. The function of the Civil Guard was to protect key points in the provinces – bridges, telephone exchanges, radio stations and various government buildings. Though they weren't nearly as corrupt and undisciplined as the troops of the ARVN, they were considered to be the poor relations, given clapped-out weapons and minimal supplies, then thrown repeatedly against the VC – invariably receiving a severe beating.

'However, shortly after the arrival of the Aussie SAS, most of the Yanks were withdrawn and the Aussies undertook the training of the Vietnamese – a job they carried out very well, it must be said. But as the general military situation in South Vietnam continued to deteriorate, VC pressure on the districts around Hiep Kanh began to increase and in November '63 the camp was closed and the remaining four Aussie advisers were transferred into the US Special Forces – the Ranger Training Centre at Duc My, to be precise – some thirty miles inland from Nha Trang.'

'They went there for further training?' Jimbo asked.

'Yes. I'm telling you all this to let you know just how good these guys are. At the Ranger Training Centre there were four training camps: the Base Camp and three specialized facilities – the Swamp Camp, the Mountain Camp and the Jungle Camp – for training in the techniques of fighting in those terrains. Reportedly, however, the men found this experience increasingly frustrating – mainly because they knew that a guerrilla war was being fought all around them, but they still weren't allowed to take part in it.'

'That would drive *me* barmy,' Jimbo said. 'It's the worst bind of all.'

Dead-eye nodded his agreement.

'Other team members,' Callaghan continued, 'were posted to Da Nang to join the CIA's Combined Studies Division, which was engaged in training village militia, border forces and trail-watchers. Two of those Aussie SAS officers had the unenviable task of teaching Vietnamese peasants the techniques of village defence – weapon training, ambushing and booby-traps, and moat and palisade construction. The peasants were transported from their own villages, equipped and trained at Hoa Cam, on the outskirts of Da Nang, then sent back to defend their own homes. Unfortunately, this failed to work and, indeed, inadvertently fed weapons and supplies to the enemy. By this I mean that once they heard what was going on, the VC, who vastly outnumbered the South Vietnamese villagers, simply marched in, took over the villages, and seized the American arms and supplies for use against US and South Vietnamese forces.'

'A bloody farce,' Jimbo said.

'And frustrating too. If the Aussies weren't being

driven mad by the corruption and incompetence of the ARVN officers, they were getting screwed by the South Vietnamese government, which bent according to the way the wind blew. For instance, one of the best men the Aussies had out there was Captain Barry Petersen, a veteran of the Malayan counter-insurgency campaigns. He was assigned to supervise paramilitary action teams of Montagnards in Darlac province in the Central Highlands . . .'

'Montagnards?' Dead-eye interrupted.

'Yes. Darker than the Vietnamese, the Montagnards are nomadic tribesmen who distrust their fellow South Vietnamese. But they were won over by the CIA, who directed a programme to help them defend themselves against the commies. When Petersen arrived, he was put to work with a couple of the Montagnard tribes, quickly learnt the language and eventually forged a close relationship with them. This enabled him to teach them a lot, including, apart from the standard forms of village defence, the disruption of enemy infiltration and supply routes, the destruction of enemy food crops, and various forms of raiding, ambushing and patrolling. With the subsequent help of Warrant Officer Bevan Stokes, the Montagnards were given training in weapons, demolitions, map reading and radio communications. The results were impressive, but . . .'

'Here it comes!' Jimbo put in sardonically.

'Indeed, it does ... Petersen's work with the Montagnards gained him the honour of a tribal chieftainship, success against the VC and recognition from his superiors. But the South Vietnamese government, alarmed that in two years Petersen had developed a highly skilled Montagnard army of over a thousand men who could be turned against them in a bid for independence, brought pressure to bear, forcing him to leave the country.'

'So it's tread with care,' Dead-eye said.

Callaghan nodded. 'Yes.'

'Are the Aussies now on aggressive patrolling?' Jimbo asked.

'Yes. The watershed was in '63 and '64, when the South Vietnamese government changed hands no less than six times in eighteen months and the country descended into political chaos. Seeing what was happening, the Yanks stepped in again to rescue the situation and asked Australia for more advisers, some of whom were to operate with regular ARVN field units. This was the springboard to lifting the ban on combat. In July '64 the Australian Army Training Team was strengthened to eighty-three men and the new recruits were assigned to the 1st ARVN Division in 1 Corps. Others were posted to military commands at province and district level, where their duties included accompanying Regional Force troops on operations, taking care of hamlet security, and liaising with ARVN troops operating in their area through the US advisory teams attached to the ARVN units. Officially, this was operations advising – the first step to actual combat.'

'And now they're in combat.'

'Yes. The original members of the Team were soon followed by the 1st Battalion of the Royal Australian Regiment – nearly eight hundred men, supported by an armoured personnel carrier troop, a signals detachment and a logistics support company. Those men were established in Vietnam by June 1965, under the operational control of the US 173rd Airborne Brigade at its HQ in Bien Hoa, north-east of Saigon, south of the Dong Nai river and the notorious VC base area known as War Zone D. Side by side with the Americans, they've been fighting the VC in that area for the past year and mopping them up. They've done a good job.'

'But we're not going there. We're going to Phuoc Tuy province,' said Dead-eye.

'Correct. Even as we talk, the first Australian conscripts are arriving there as part of the new Australian Task Force. They're based at Nui Dat and their task is to clear the VC from their base area in the Long Hai hills, known as the Minh Dam secret zone. They'll be supported by the Australian SAS and our task is to lend support to the latter.'

'They won't thank us for that,' Jimbo observed. 'Those Aussies are proud.'

'Too true,' Dead-eye said.

Callaghan tugged the cover from the blackboard behind him, raised the pointer in his hand and tapped it against the words 'PHUOC TUY', highlighed on the map with a yellow marking pen. 'The Phuoc Tuy provincial border is some fifty miles south-east of Saigon. As you can see, the province is bounded by the South China Sea, the Rung Sat swamps – a formidable obstacle to any advance – and Long Kanh and Binh Tuy provinces. The population of slightly over 100,000 is concentrated in the south central area and in towns, villages and hamlets close to the provincial capital, Baria. That area is rich in paddy-fields and market gardens. But the rest of the province, about three-quarters of it, is mostly flat, jungle-covered country, except for three large groups of mountains: the May Tao group in the north-east, the Long Hai on the southern coast, and the Dinh to the west. All these mountainous areas are VC strongholds.'

'Where's the Task Force located?' Dead-eye asked.

'Around Nui Dat. A steep hill covered in jungle and rising nearly 200 feet above the surrounding terrain. The area's big enough for an airfield and for the Task Force to move on if the new base comes under attack.'

'Major problems?' Dead-eye asked.

'The VC village fortifications of Long Phuoc and Long Tan, south-east of the base, were destroyed in a joint American and Vietnamese operation just before the Aussies moved in. The villages were laid waste and their inhabitants resettled in others nearby. While this effectively removed the VC from those two villages, it created a great deal of bitterness among the pro-VC inhabitants who are now even more busily spreading anti-government propaganda and helping to strengthen the local VC infrastructure. Meanwhile the major VC force is operating out of a chain of base areas in the northern jungles of the province, most with extensive bunker and tunnel complexes. Altogether there are seven battalions of VC in the area and they can be reinforced at short notice. Against that, the province has only one ARVN battalion permanently based there, supplemented by several Regional Force companies and the so-called Popular Forces – the PF – which are local militia platoons raised to defend the villages as well as bridges, communications facilities and so forth. They're poorly equipped, poorly trained, and repeatedly turned over by the VC.'

'Sounds wonderful,' Jimbo murmured.

'A real fairy tale,' Callaghan replied, then shrugged and continued: 'Right now the VC have the upper hand, both militarily and psychologically. They've isolated Xuyen Mock in the east and Duc Than in the north, both of which contained South Vietnamese district headquarters. They've heavily infiltrated all the other districts. They regularly cut all roads in the province and tax the loyal villagers who try to get out. Nevertheless, the area's of vital strategic importance to the US build-up, with Vung Tau earmarked to become a major port, supplying the delta, Saigon and Bien Hoa. This means that Route 15 on the western edge of Phuoc Tuy has to be kept clear as a prospective military supply route from Vung Tau to Saigon. In order to do this, the Task Force has to push the VC out of the central region of the province and provide a protective umbrella for the population there. The first step in this task is the clearing of the VC from the Nui Dat base area. This job will be given to the American 173rd Brigade, aided by the Australian 5th Battalion, which is being flown in right now. The latter will be supported by the Australian SAS and we're there to advise them.'

'Does our advisory role stretch to aggressive patrolling, boss?' Dead-eye asked slyly.

Callaghan grinned. 'Officially, we're not supposed to be there at all – officially, we don't exist – so once there, I suppose we just play it by ear and do what we have to do.'

'But if we fuck up, we get no support,' Jimbo said.

'Correct.'

'When do we fly out?'

'Tomorrow. On a normal commercial flight, wearing civilian clothing. We change into uniform when we get there.'

'Very good,' Dead-eye said.

Callaghan handed each of the two men a closed folder.

'These are your travel documents and bits and pieces of useful information. Report back here at six tomorrow morning. Before then, I'll expect you to have digested everything in these folders. Finally, may I remind you once more that our presence there might cause resentment from the Aussie troops. In other words, you may find that the hearts and minds you're trying to win aren't those of the South Vietnamese peasants, but those of the Aussie SAS. They're notoriously proud, so tread carefully. If there are no questions I'll bid you good evening, gentlemen.'

Dead-eye and Jimbo stood up and left the briefing room, carrying their top-secret folders. When they had gone, Callaghan turned to the map behind him and studied it thoughtfully. Eventually, nodding to himself, he unpinned and folded it, then went to prepare for his flight the next day.

3

Though it was still early in the morning, the sun was up and the light was brilliant, with the Long Hai hills clearly visible from the deck of the carrier HMAS *Sydney*, where the troops were waiting for the landing-craft. Most were National Servicemen, young and inexperienced, their suntans gained from three months of recruit training in the Australian heat. As the 5th Battalion advance party, they had come alone, with only a sprinkling of Australian SAS NCOs in their midst, but they would be joined by the remainder of their battalion in a few days, then by 6th Battalion, with whom they would form the 1st Australian Task Force in Vietnam. Right now, apart from being weary after the tedious twelve-day voyage from Australia, they were tense with expectation, wondering if they could manage to get to shore without either hurting themselves getting in and out of the landing-craft or, even worse, being shot at by the enemy.

'Minh Dam secret zone,' Shagger said to Red as

they stood together at the railing of the carrier. 'And there,' he continued, pointing north-west to the jungle-covered hills beyond the peninsula of Vung Tau, 'is the Rung Sat swamps. They're as bad as those swamps in Malaya, so let's hope we avoid them. We can do without that shit.'

Grinning, Red adjusted his soft cap and studied the conscript troops as they scrambled from the deck into the landing-craft, to be lowered to the sea. Hardly more than schoolboys, they were wearing jungle greens, rubber-soled canvas boots and soft jungle hats. Getting into the landing-craft was neither easy nor safe, as they had to scramble across from gates in the railing, then over the steel sides of the dangling boats. This necessitated a hair-raising few seconds in mid-air, high above the sea, while laden with a tightly packed bergen and personal weapons. These included the 7.62mm L1A1 SLR, the 5.56mm M16A1 automatic rifle with the 40mm M203 grenade launcher, the 9mm L9A1 Browning semi-automatic pistol and, for those unlucky few, the 7.62mm M60 GPMG with either a steel bipod or the even heavier tripod. Also, their webbing bulged with spare ammunition and M26 high-explosive hand-grenades. Thus burdened, they moved awkwardly and in most cases nervously from the swaying deck of the ship to the landing-craft dangling high above the water in the morning's fierce heat and dazzling light.

'Shitting their pants, most of them,' Red said as he watched the conscripts clambering into the vessel.

'It'll be diarrhoea as thin as water,' Shagger replied, leaning against the railing and spitting over the side, 'if the VC guns open up from those hills. They'll smell the stench back in Sydney.'

'I don't doubt it at all, Sarge. Still, I'm sure they'll do good when the time comes to kick ass for the Yanks. All the way with LBJ, eh?'

'I wouldn't trust LBJ with my grandmother's corpse,' Shagger replied. 'But if our PM says it's all the way with him, then that's where we'll go – once we get off this ship, that is.'

Shagger and Red were the only two Australian SAS men aboard HMAS *Sydney*, present to take charge of the stores and vehicles of 3 Squadron, which were being brought in on this ship. The rest of the squadron was to be flown in on one plane directly from the SAS base at Campbell Barracks, Swanbourne, once they'd completed their special training in New Guinea in a few days' time. Meanwhile Shagger had been placed temporarily in charge of this troop of regular army conscripts and was responsible for getting them from ship to shore. Once there, he and Red would split from them and go their own way.

'Whoops! Here she comes!'

The landing-craft for Shagger's men was released

from the davits and lowered to deck level, where it
hung in mid-air, bouncing lightly against the hull
with a dull, monotonous drumming sound. When
Red had opened the gate in the railing, Shagger
slapped the first man on the shoulder and said,
'Over you go, lad.'

The young trooper, eighteen at the most, glanced
down the dizzying depths to the sea and gulped,
but then, at a second slap on the shoulder, gripped
his SLR more firmly in his left hand and, with his
other, reached out to take hold of the rising, falling
side of the landing-craft, and pulled himself over
and into it. When he had done so, the other men,
relieved to see that it was possible, likewise began
dropping into the swaying, creaking vessel one after
the other. When everyone was in, Shagger and Red
followed suit.

'Hold on to your weapons,' the sergeant told the
men packed tightly together. 'This drop could be
rough.'

And it was. With the chains screeching against
the davits, the landing-craft was lowered in a
series of swooping drops and sudden stops, jerking
back up a little and swinging from side to side.
The drop did not take long, though to some
of the men it seemed like an eternity and they
were immensely relieved when, with a deafening roaring, pounding sound, the boat plunged
into the sea, drenching them in the waves that

poured in over the sides. The engine roared into life, water boiled up behind it, and it moved away from the towering side of the ship, heading for shore.

'Fix bayonets!' Shagger bawled above the combined roar of the many landing-craft now in the water.

As the bayonets were clicked into place, Shagger and Red grinned at each other, fully aware that as the VC guns had not already fired, they would not be firing; and that the men would be disembarking on to the concrete loading ramp in the middle of the busy Vung Tau port area rather than into a murderous hail of VC gunfire. In fact, the reason for making the men fix bayonets was not the possibility of attack as the landing-craft went in, but to instil in them the need to take thorough precautions in all circumstances from this point on. Nevertheless, when, a few minutes later, the landing-craft had ground to a halt, the ramp was lowered, and the men marched out on to the concrete loading ramp with fixed bayonets, the American and Vietnamese dock workers burst into mocking applause and wolf whistles.

'Eyes straight ahead!' Shagger bawled. 'Keep marching, men!'

Marching up ahead, Shagger and Red led the conscript troops to the reception area of the Task Force base, which had been set up on a deserted stretch of beach on the eastern side of the Vung Tau peninsula. The Task Force consisted of two battalions with supporting arms and logistic backup, a headquarters staff, an armoured personnel carrier squadron, an artillery regiment, an SAS squadron, plus signals, engineer and supply units, totalling 4500 men – so it was scattered across a broad expanse of beach.

'Sergeant Bannerman reporting, sir,' Shagger said to the 1st Australian Logistic Support Group (1 ALSG) warrant officer in charge of new arrivals. 'Three Squadron SAS. In temporary charge of this bunch of turnip-heads and now glad to get rid of them.'

'They all look seasick,' the warrant officer observed.

'That and a touch of nerves. They're National Servicemen, after all.'

'Not tough bastards like the SAS, right?'

'You said it.'

'Now piss off back to your SAS mates, Sarge, and let me deal with this lot. I'll soon knock them into shape.'

'Good on you, sir. Now where would the supplies for 3 Squadron be?'

'I'm regular army, not SAS. I look after my own. You've only been here five minutes and you're confessing that you've already lost your supplies? With friends like you, who needs enemies?'

'Thanks for that vote of confidence, sir. I think I'll be on my way.'

'As long as you're not in *my* way, Sarge. Now take to the hills.'

'Yes, sir!' Shagger snapped, then hurried away, grinning at Red, to look for his missing supplies. In the event, they had to be separated from the general mess of what appeared to be the whole ship's cargo, which had been thrown haphazardly on to the beach, with stores scattered carelessly among the many vehicles bogged down in the sand dunes. Luckily Shagger found that the quartermaster for 1 ALSG was his old mate Sergeant Rick McCoy, and with his help the supplies were gradually piled up near the landing zone for the helicopters.

'A nice little area,' McCoy informed Shagger and Red, waving his hand to indicate the sweeping beach, now covered with armoured cars, half-tracks, tents, piles of canvas-covered wooden crates and a great number of men, many stripped to the waist as they dug trenches, raised pup tents or marched in snaking lines through the dunes, heading for the jungle-covered hills beyond the beach. 'Between these beaches and the mangrove swamps to the west you have Cap St Jacques and the port and resort city of Vung Tau. Though Vung Tau isn't actually part of Phuoc Tuy province, it's where we all go for rest and convalescence. Apparently the

VC also use the town for R and C, so we'll all be nice and cosy there.'

'You're kidding!'

'No, I'm not. That place is never attacked by Charlie, so I think he uses it. How the hell would we know? One Vietnamese getting drunk or picking up a whore looks just like any other; so the place is probably filled with the VC. That thought should lend a little excitement to your next night of bliss.'

'Bloody hell!' said Red.

In fact, neither Red nor Shagger was given the opportunity to explore the dangerous delights of Vung Tau as they were moved out the following morning to take part in the establishment of an FOB, a forward operating base, some sixteen miles inland at Nui Dat. Lifted off in the grey light of dawn by an RAAF Caribou helicopter, they were flown over jungle wreathed in mist and criss-crossed with streams and rivers, then eventually set down on the flat ground of rubber plantations surrounding Nui Dat, a small but steep-sided hill just outside Baria.

The FOB was being constructed in the middle of the worst monsoon the country had experienced for years. Draped in ponchos, the men worked in relentless, torrential rain that had turned the ground into a mud-bath and filled their shelters and weapons pits with water. Not only did they work in that water – they slept and ate in it too.

To make matters worse, they were in an area still dominated by the enemy. Frequently, therefore, as they toiled in the pounding rain with thunder roaring in their ears and lightning flashing overhead, they were fired upon by VC snipers concealed in the paddy-fields or behind the trees of the rubber plantations. Though many Aussies were wounded or killed, the others kept working.

'This is bloody insane,' Shagger growled as he tried to scoop water out of his shallow scrape and found himself being covered in more mud. 'The floods of fucking Noah. I've heard that in other parts of the camp the water's so deep the fellas can only find their scrapes when they fall into them. Some place to fight a war!'

'I don't mind,' Red said. 'A bit of a change from bone-dry Aussie. A new experience, kind of. I mean, anything's better than being at home with the missus and kids. I feel as free as a bird out here.'

'We're belly down in the fucking mud,' Shagger said, 'and you feel as free as a bird! You're as mad as a hatter.'

'That some kind of bird, is it, Sarge?'

'Go stuff yourself!' said Shagger, returning to the thankless task of bailing out his scrape.

Amazingly, even in this hell, the camp was rapidly taking shape. Styled after a jungle FOB of the kind used in Malaya, it was roughly circular in shape with defensive trenches in the middle and sentry positions and hedgehogs: fortified sangars for twenty-five-pound guns and a nest of 7.62mm GPMGs. This circular base was surrounded by a perimeter of barbed wire and claymore mines. Shagger and Red knew the mines were in place because at least once a day one of them would explode, tripped by the VC probing the perimeter defences with reconnaissance patrols. Still the Aussies kept working.

'Now I know why the Yanks fucked off,' Shagger told Red as they huddled up in their ponchos, feet and backside in the water, trying vainly to smoke cigarettes as the rain drenched them. 'They couldn't stand this bloody place. Two minutes of rain, a single sniper shot, and those bastards would take to the hills, looking for all the comforts of home and a fortified concrete bunker to hide in. A bunch of soft twats, those Yanks are.'

'They have their virtues,' Red replied. 'They just appreciate the good things in life and know how to provide them. I mean, you take our camps: they're pretty basic, right? But their camps have air-conditioners, jukeboxes and even honky-tonk bars complete with Vietnamese waiters. Those bastards are organized, all right.'

'*We've* got jukeboxes,' Shagger reminded him.

'We had to buy them off the Yanks.'

'Those bastards make money out of everything.'

'I wish *I* could,' Red said.

'Well, we're not doing so badly,' said Shagger. 'This camp's coming on well.'

It was true. Already, the initial foxholes and pup tents had been replaced by an assortment of larger tents and timber huts with corrugated-iron roofs. Determined to enjoy themselves as best they could, even in the midst of this squalor, the Aussies, once having raised huts and tents for headquarters, administration, communications, first aid, accommodation, ablutions, transport, supplies, weapons and fuel, then turned others into bars, some of which boasted the jukeboxes they'd bought from the Yanks. There were also four helicopter landing zones and a single parking area for trucks, jeeps, armoured cars and tanks.

While they were waiting for the other members of 3 Squadron to arrive, Shagger and Red between them supervised the raising of a large tent to house the SAS supplies already there. The tent was erected in one day with the help of Vietnamese labourers stripped to the waist and soaked by the constant rain. When it was securely pegged down, the two SAS men used the same labourers to move in the supplies: PRC 64 and A510 radio sets, PRC 47 high-frequency radio transceivers, batteries, dehydrated ration packs, US-pattern jungle boots, mosquito nets and a variety of weapons, including SLRs, F1 Carbines and 7.62mm Armalite assault rifles with twenty-round box magazines. Shagger then inveigled 1 ALSG's warrant-officer into giving him a regular rotation of conscript guards to look after what was, in effect, 3 Squadron's SAS's quartermaster's store.

'I thought you bastards were supposed to be self-sufficient,' the warrant officer said.

'Bloody right,' Shagger replied.

'So how come you can't send enough men in advance to look after your own kit?'

'They're still mopping up in Borneo,' Shagger said, 'so they couldn't fly straight here.'

'And my name's Ned Kelly,' the warrant officer replied, then rolled his eyes and sighed. 'OK, you can have the guards.'

'I've got that prick in my pocket,' Shagger told Red when they were out of earshot of the warrant officer.

'You'll have him up your backside,' Red replied, 'if you ask for anything else.'

When construction of the camp had been completed, five days after Shagger and Red had arrived, the two men were called to a briefing in the large HQ tent. By this time the rest of 3 Squadron had arrived by plane from Perth and were crowding out the tent, which was humid after recent rain and filled with whining, buzzing flies and mosquitoes. As the men swotted the insects away, wiped sweat from their faces, and muttered a wide variety of oaths, 1 ALSG's CO filled them in on the details of the forthcoming campaign against the Viet Cong.

'The first step,' he said, 'is to dominate an area surrounding the base out to 4000 yards, putting the base beyond enemy mortar range. We will do this with aggressive patrolling. The new perimeter will be designated Line Alpha. The second step is to secure the area out to the field artillery range – a distance of about 11,000 yards. Part of this process . . .' – he paused uncomfortably before continuing – 'is the resettlement of Vietnamese living within the area.'

'You mean we torch or blow up their villages and then shift them elsewhere?' Shagger said with his customary bluntness.

The CO sighed. 'That, Sergeant, is substantially correct. I appreciate that some of you may find this kind of work rather tasteless. Unfortunately it can't be avoided.'

'Why? It seems unnecessarily brutal – and not exactly designed to win hearts and minds.'

The CO smiled bleakly, not being fond of the SAS's reputation for straight talking and the so-called 'Chinese parliament', an informal talk between officers, NCOs and other ranks in which all opinions were given equal consideration. 'The advantage of resettling the villagers is that whereas the VC aren't averse to using villagers as human shields, we can, in the event of an attack, deploy our considerable fire-power without endangering them – another way of winning their hearts and minds.'

'Good thinking,' Shagger admitted.

'I'm pleased that you're pleased,' the CO said, wishing the outspoken SAS sergeant would sink into the muddy earth and disappear, but unable to show his disapproval for fear that his own men would think him a fool. 'So one of our first tasks will be to finish the destruction of a previously fortified village located approximately a mile and a quarter south-east of this base. Huts and other buildings will be torched or blown up and crops destroyed. This we will do over a period of days. Unpleasant though this may seem to you, it's part of the vitally necessary process of reopening the province's north-south military supply route, and eventually driving the enemy back until they're isolated in their jungle bases.'

'So what's the SAS's role in all this?' Shagger asked him.

'Your task is to pass on the skills you picked up in Borneo to the ARVN troops and to engage in jungle bashing – patrolling after the VC who've turned this camp into their private firing range. Eventually, when Line Alpha has been pushed back to beyond the limits of field artillery, you'll be given the task of clearing out a VC stronghold in a bunker-and-tunnel complex. The location will be given to you when the time comes.'

'Why not give us the location now?' Red asked.

'Because the less you know the better,' the CO replied.

'You mean if we're captured by Charlie, we'll be tortured for information,' Red replied.

'Yes. And Charlie's good at that. Now, there's another important aspect to this operation. You'll be advised and assisted – though I should stress that the collaboration should be mutually beneficial – by a three-man team from Britain's 22 SAS. They'll be arriving from the old country in four days' time.'

A murmur of resentment filled the room and was only ended when Shagger asked bluntly: 'Why do we need advice from a bunch of Pommie SAS? We know as much about this business as they do. We can do it alone.'

'I'm inclined to agree, Sergeant, but the general feeling at HQ is that the British SAS, with their extensive experience in jungle warfare, counter-insurgency patrolling, and hearts-and-minds campaigning in places as different and as far apart as Malaya, Oman, Borneo and, more recently, Aden, have a distinct advantage when it comes to operations of this kind. So, whether you like it or not, those three men – a lieutenant-colonel and two sergeants – will soon be flying in to act as our advisers.'

'Bloody hell!' Red exclaimed in disgust.

The CO ignored the outburst. 'Are there any questions?' he asked.

As the men had none, the meeting broke up and they all hurried out of the humid tent, into the drying, steaming mud of the compound of the completed, now busy, FOB. The sky above the camp was filled with American Chinook helicopters and B52 bombers, all heading inland, towards the Long Hai hills.

4

When the USAF Huey descended over Nui Dat, having flown in from Saigon, Lieutenant-Colonel Callaghan, Jimbo and Dead-eye looked down at an FOB of the kind they had themselves constructed in Malaya: a roughly circular camp with defensive trenches in the middle and sentry positions and 'hedgehogs' – fortified sangars for twenty-five-pounders and a nest of 7.62mm GPMGs – located at regular intervals around the perimeter. This well-defended base was surrounded by another perimeter of barbed wire and – they assumed from the levelling of the ground – claymores. Surprisingly, instead of the foxholes and pup tents they had expected, they found large tents and timber huts with roofs of corrugated iron, plus four helicopter landing zones and a parking area for all the camp's vehicles.

'They've been busy,' Callaghan shouted over the roar of the helicopter. 'They only arrived here a few weeks ago. That's some job they've done.'

'Aussies work hard and play hard,' Jimbo said.

'Hard bastards,' Dead-eye said. 'You can't deny that.'

'Well, let's hope we can win their respect,' Callaghan replied.

'Good as done,' Jimbo assured him, while Dead-eye simply nodded.

As the Huey came down on one of the four LZs, its spinning rotors whipped up a cloud of dust and fine gravel that obscured the soldiers on the ground. Callaghan and his two men were out of the chopper even before the rotors had stopped spinning, stooped over and covering their eyes with their hands as they hurried out of the swirling dust. As they were straightening up again, a man wearing jungle greens with sergeant's stripes and a 9mm Browning holstered at his waist climbed down from his jeep and saluted Callaghan.

'Lieutenant-Colonel Callaghan?'

'Correct,' Callaghan replied, returning the salute. 'Two-two SAS.'

'Sergeant Bannerman, sir. Three Squadron SAS. I've been sent by the CO to collect you. Welcome to Nui Dat.'

'Thank you, Sergeant. This is Sergeant Ashman, commonly known as Jimbo, and Sergeant Parker, known to one and all as Dead-eye.'

Shagger nodded at both men, grinning slightly as he studied Dead-eye.

'I take it your nickname means you're pretty good with that SLR.'

Dead-eye nodded, and Jimbo said, 'That and everything else, mate. If it fires, Dead-eye's your man.'

'What about you, Sarge?'

'I get by,' Jimbo said.

Shagger grinned. 'Let's hope so.' He then nodded at Lieutenant-Colonel Callaghan and said, 'Right, boss, let's get to it. If you'd like to take a seat in the jeep I'll drive you straight to the boss. When you've had a chat with him, I'll show you to your quarters. By the way, they call me Shagger.'

They all laughed and piled into the jeep. The Australian drove them a short distance to a large wooden hut with a corrugated-iron roof and a sign at the top of the steps of the raised veranda, saying: 'Headquarters 3 Squadron SAS'. A second sign at the opposite side of the steps said: 'Abandon hope all ye who enter here.'

Grinning at each other, Callaghan, Jimbo and Dead-eye followed Shagger into the building. Inside was a spacious administration area sealed off behind a counter and ventilated by slowly spinning ceiling fans. Seated behind the desks were a mixture of 3 Squadron SAS and 5th Battalion male clerks, all of them looking busy. A proliferation of propaganda leaflets from the VC had been pinned to the notice-boards to entertain those waiting for their appointments, among them: 'Aussie go home: there is no resentment between the Vietnamese and the Australian people!' and 'Australian and New Zealand Armymen: Do not become Washington's mercenaries; urge your government to send you back home.'

'Someone obviously has a sense of irony,' Callaghan said.

'The VC drop them all the time,' Shagger told him. 'A wide variety. Troopers coming in here for appointments are generally amused by them. That's the favourite.' He pointed to an illustration of a handsome Australian soldier sharing drinks with a sexy lady. The caption said: 'The sensible man is home with his woman, or someone else will be. Is this war worth it?' 'Given the amount of Dear John letters that come from back home, that one's definitely ironic. This way, please.'

Shagger then led them to an office at the end of a short corridor. A sign on the open door said: 'Commanding Officer' but no name was given. They could see the CO at his desk, studying maps and charts, and when the sergeant coughed into his fist he looked up.

'Your visitors, boss,' Shagger said, ushering the three men from 22 SAS into the office. He introduced them to Lieutenant-Colonel Rex Durnford, who was blue-eyed, red-haired, suntanned and looked a lot younger than his thirty-nine years.

Tipping his chair back and stretching his legs, the CO waved a hand at the scattering of chairs in front of the desk and said, 'Please be seated, gentlemen.'

Durnford smiled brightly and said, 'Well, gentlemen, far be it from me to make you feel unwelcome – and I appreciate that you're only doing your jobs – but I *do* think I'm going to have trouble explaining to my men why they should need to be advised by the British SAS.'

'We're not so much advisers as observers,' Callaghan replied. 'It's therefore felt that the advice could flow both ways.'

'Not sure what you mean by that.'

'One of the reasons we've been sent here is that we have particularly good knowledge of counter-insurgency operations and jungle survival in particular.'

'We were in Malaya as well.'

'Not like us, as I'm sure you know.'

'Nothing you did that we didn't do,' Shagger put in, though with no trace of anger – more like a man just setting the record straight.

'Granted,' Callaghan said. 'But you didn't do it as much. Nor did you do it in such a wide variety of locations. The war here isn't like the war in Malaya. It's not like Borneo either. It's like a little bit of both – the VC live a nomadic life and know the jungle well – but apart from that it's not the same thing.

Therefore certain of your superiors in Canberra believe that no matter what your experiences in Malaya and Borneo, you can learn a lot from what we picked up, not only there, but also in places like Oman and the Yemen.'

'I dispute that,' Shagger said.

'You do. Canberra doesn't. And the orders to send us three here came all the way to Hereford from Canberra.'

'You're asking us to take advice regarding a war we're already involved in,' countered Shagger. 'You haven't been involved. You don't know what goes on here. With all due respect, sir, it's us who should be advising you. That's the root of the hard feelings.'

Callaghan smiled. He was pleased to note that although the Australian SAS were not related to the British, they certainly appeared to have adopted at least one of the lessons of Hereford. Sergeant Bannerman, whether he knew about Chinese parliaments or not, obviously felt at ease speaking his mind in front of his CO. Callaghan liked him for that and knew, from the expression on their faces, that Jimbo and Dead-eye felt the same.

'I understand the reason for resentment,' Callaghan said, 'but I think we can iron it out, Sergeant. As I said, this will be a two-way affair – a trade-off – and when your men see that, I believe their misgivings will fade away. We're here to offer advice in general small-team patrolling and other aspects of counter-insurgency warfare – at least as it relates to the particular way in which the VC fight. But I must repeat that we're also here to learn as much as we can from you.'

'So what can we teach you?' Lieutenant-Colonel Durnford asked.

Callaghan spread his hands in the air and said, 'We haven't been to Vietnam. We three are the first and possibly the last from 22 SAS to come here. We haven't fought people like the VC and we want to know how they think. This is a new kind of war, fought by men who can survive for extraordinary lengths of time without food, know the land intimately, are totally obedient, have little to lose, and can live for months, even years, underground. They're fighting a war of attrition, defeating vastly superior arms, particularly US air power, and we want to know what makes them tick. We also want to learn the lessons of engagement, particularly with regard to the tunnel complexes. We've never fought in such circumstances before; we want to learn what we can from it.'

'The tunnel complexes are a nightmare,' Durnford informed him. 'The men who go down into them in pursuit of the VC have the most dangerous job in Vietnam. We call them tunnel rats, and they're a very rare breed.'

'We still want that experience.'

'May I ask why you men in particular were picked for this task?'

'I was chosen because of my long-term experience with the Regiment, commencing with the LRDG in North Africa and including Malaya, Borneo and the Yemen. For the past year or so, I've been with Planning and Intelligence, in Hereford, and the information I pick up from this experience here in Vietnam will be used for future training and planning programmes. As for Sergeants Ashman and Parker, they have similar experience, though they were finally picked because of their exceptional proficiency at the double-tap – firing at close range with the Browning High Power – which we feel will come in handy when they go down into the tunnel complex.'

'Which particular complex?' Durnford asked. 'Do you have one in mind?'

'According to our intelligence, there's one located approximately five miles east of here, under a VC-held village. One of our purposes in coming here is to take part in the closing down of that complex when you secure the area out to the field artillery range.'

'I'd think twice about that if I were you,' Shagger said. 'Going down into those tunnels is a very specialized task. We may be new to this game, but we know more about it than you.'

'Good,' Jimbo said with a wicked grin. 'Then we'll go down with you.'

Shagger returned the grin, but his gaze was mocking.

'You must be scrub-happy if you think I'm going to take you down there. When I go down, I go down with my mate and no one else, thanks. I want no distractions.'

'What's scrub-happy mean?' Dead-eye asked.

'Mentally disturbed,' said Shagger.

'You have to be that way to apply for the SAS in the first place,' Jimbo informed him.

They all laughed, but the tone became serious again when Dead-eye asked, 'What's the problem? I mean, we're not exactly novices. We can react as quickly as anyone alive, so we could be useful to you and your mate, rather than distract you.'

'It's the knowledge,' Shagger said, concealing the fact, with his CO's prior agreement, that his experience of the tunnels was theoretical. For although his mate Red Swanson was a seasoned tunnel rat, he himself had never taken part in an operation to flush out VC guerrillas from an underground complex. The fact was that there were now so few survivors possessing those skills that first-rate soldiers like Shagger were having to undergo a crash training programme. 'You can't learn that until you go down. Those tunnel complexes are labyrinthine, filled with trapdoors and booby-traps. You're going into a maze – a vertical maze. It's dark, suffocating and absolutely unpredictable, with false tunnels that lead to dead-ends. As the tunnels are too narrow to turn around in, you have to get back out by crawling backwards on your hands and knees, which can cop you a VC bullet up the arsehole. Also, either VC assassins or booby-traps are waiting for you around the many sharp bends. No, to be a tunnel rat you need more experience than you can hope to learn on a single patrol.' Aware of his own complete lack of practical experience, Shagger decided to say no more.

'We're as quick with our eyes as we are with our nine-millies,' Dead-eye told him. 'We can learn what we need to know with one patrol and then do what's required.'

'I doubt that,' Shagger said.

'What Sergeant Bannerman's trying to tell you,' Lieutenant-Colonel Durnford put in, 'is that the only men presently acting as tunnel rats are the few survivors of the first forays down into the tunnels. Most men, when they go down without experience, don't came back up again. Only about twenty per cent have survived so far. That's how dangerous it is down there.'

'We've faced worse odds,' Jimbo told him.

'That's right,' Callaghan said, turning to Durnford. 'I say these men can go down with your men and come back up again. If they could survive the Keeni

Meeni operations in the crowded souks and bazaars of Aden, they can survive anything thrown at them in the tunnels. It's imperative that they have this experience and I know they can cope with it.'

Lieutenant-Colonel Durnford glanced at Shagger, who shrugged, then nodded his consent and said, 'Fair enough. When the time comes you can tackle the tunnel complex with me and my mate, Red Swanson. But it's not going to happen right away.'

'Because you have to clear this area first,' Callaghan said, 'and protect the camp.'

'Exactly.'

'So what are your first objectives?'

'The first,' Lieutenant-Colonel Durnford said, 'is to go on a bit of bush-bashing to route the VC snipers and reconnaissance patrols. Though they occasionally trip claymores and blow themselves to hell, they're still managing to kill too many of our men and hamper the proper running of the base. We have to go out there in small patrols and root them out of the area, gradually pushing back the perimeter.'

'And the second?'

'To finish the destruction of a previously fortified village a mile and a quarter south-east of the base. Huts and buildings will have to be torched and blown up – and crops destroyed.'

'We can certainly help you there,' Callaghan

told him. 'We'll deploy your men in four-man patrols and map out a strategy for covering the whole of the perimeter in criss-crossing elimination paths. As we clear Charlie out, we'll replace him with defensive gun emplacements, each manned by three troopers. By the time we finish, you'll have no problems with VC snipers or reconnaissance patrols.'

'Can you push that area out to at least 4000 yards?'

'Beyond mortar range?'

'Correct.'

'Yes, we can.'

'Good. That new perimeter will be designated Line Alpha. The second step, once you've completed the first, will be to secure the area out to the field artillery range. Once you've done so, we can finish off that village, which will leave us in total control of the area surrounding the base out to beyond Charlie's artillery range. Come back to me after you've accomplished that and we'll discuss the tunnels.'

Callaghan and Jimbo exchanged grins, but Deadeye remained stony-faced. Returning his attention to Durnford, Callaghan asked, 'Anything special to look out for?'

'Yes,' Shagger said before the CO could reply. 'Booby-traps. Lots of them. All deadly. That's what you watch out for.'

71

'We had lots of those in Borneo and Malaya. Are they similar here?'

'Bloody right! But they're even more diabolical.'

'In what way?'

Shagger walked over to the wall at one side of the CO's desk. There he pulled down a chart to reveal a variety of drawings of different VC booby-traps, most involving punji pits, spikes, arrows, nails or bullets.

'The cartridge trap,' he said, pointing to the first of the illustrations. 'A piece of bamboo is buried in the ground with the open end exposed. The other end rests on a solid wooden board with a nail hammered through it, the sharp end facing upwards. A bullet is set into the bamboo with the flat end resting on the sharp end of the nail and the tip sticking up out of the open end of the bamboo tube. This is then hidden in soil and grass or leaves. When a soldier steps on the upper end of the cartridge, he forces it down on the nail which then acts like a firing pin, sending the bullet through the man's foot and mangling it. In fact, the bullet sometimes goes right through the foot and ends up burying itself in the man's face, which can happen if he is bending forward at the time. Not a nice way to go.'

Bannerman pointed to another drawing and said, 'This one's known as the angled arrow trap. A length of bamboo about three feet long is fastened to a piece of solid wood. Inside the bamboo, a steel arrow is held ready to fire by means of a strong rubber band and a catch machanism fixed to a trip-wire. The whole contraption is then placed in a camouflaged pit and sloped at the angle required to send the arrow through the chest of an average-sized man when he trips the wire. Naturally, if he's smaller than that, he gets it through the throat or face; if taller, through the belly or balls.'

'Ouch!' groaned Jimbo.

Shagger grinned as he pointed to a third drawing. 'The whip,' he said. 'A strong piece of green bamboo with spikes as sharp as daggers attached to it. One end of the bamboo is tied to a tree trunk, the other end to another tree trunk or fixed post so as to bend the bamboo sharply backwards. This end is held by a catch in the firing position. The catch is released by a trip-wire that makes the pole spring round and propel the spikes into the body of the victim. The spikes are usually driven in so deep that the victim dies standing upright and is held in that position by the spikes. Not a pretty sight.'

'Welcome to Vietnam,' Jimbo whispered to Dead-eye. 'Land of smiling people and fun and games.'

'Of course, you're bound to know from Malaya about the various forms of punji pits. Here, they're pretty much the same, except the pits are sometimes filled with upward-pointing steel spikes, as well as sharpened bamboo sticks, and the bamboo lid pivots on an axle to tip the man in, rather than just caving in as they usually do in Malaya and Borneo. Otherwise they're just as deadly. Another common booby-trap is the min anti-personnel mine – that's m-i-n, not mini – which looks like a German stick grenade with a short handle. This handle contains a pull-friction delay fuse that's operated by a trip-wire hidden by foliage or grass and usually laid across a jungle path. So you have to watch what you step on at all times, which makes for pretty slow going through the bush. Then there are the usual natural dangers, such as wild boar, pig, poisonous snakes, stinging hornets, mosquitoes . . .'

'Right,' Jimbo said. 'I think we've got the picture, Sergeant.'

'Good,' Durnford said. 'Any more questions, gentlemen?'

When Callaghan glanced at Jimbo and Dead-eye, they both shook their heads. 'No questions,' Callaghan replied, 'except, where do we basha down?'

'Pardon?'

'Bunk up,' Dead-eye clarified.

'You got here just in time,' the CO replied. 'We've just moved out of trenches and pup tents into wooden barracks. You, Lieutenant-Colonel, will be in the officers' barracks with me and the other officers. You two men will be in the NCOs' barracks. Sergeant Bannerman will show you to your quarters. Have a good night's rest, gentlemen. You'll be moving out tomorrow.'

Shagger led them out of the building and across the central clearing of the camp, which included a flattened area used as a football pitch. Helicopters were taking off, aircraft rumbling overhead, troop trucks entering and leaving, twenty-five-pounders in hedgehogs firing the odd shell purely for the purposes of harassment, the GPMG gunners firing test bursts, and other troopers bawling at one another as they worked at various tasks. The new arrivals found their ceaseless activity familiar and reassuring.

They separated – Callaghan to enter the officers' barracks, Jimbo and Dead-eye the building beside it – and unpacked what kit they wouldn't need on their assignment. When they were ready, Jimbo and Dead-eye left and crossed to the mess tent with Shagger for a good nosh-up, washed down with beer. There they met Shagger's mate Corporal Red Swanson, the tunnel rat.

5

'Sergeants Ashman and Parker, from 22 SAS, Hereford, England,' Shagger said, indicating the two visitors with the pork sausage pronged by the fork he was holding as Red, carrying a plate and eating utensils, plopped down on the bench seat beside him. 'Jimbo and Dead-eye to you.'

They were in the large mess tent, which was filled with soldiers from the 5th and 6th Battalions of the 1st Australian Task Force in Vietnam, 1 and 3 Squadrons of the Australian Special Air Service (SAS), the 17th Construction Squadron, and a few members of the South Vietnamese Civil Guard and the regular ARVN reaction forces. Many of the men were stripped to the waist and pouring sweat; others were in uniform. Still others were wearing a bizarre mixture of civilian clothes, notably T-shirts emblazoned with cartoon figures and rude messages, baggy shorts, sandals and a wide variety of jungle hats. A lot of food was being eaten, washed down with pints of cold beer, and though the tent was open at both ends, it was rapidly filling up with the smoke from the cigarettes that nearly everyone was smoking. The conversation was loud and ebullient, shredded by raucous laughter.

'This is my mate, Red – Red Swanson,' Shagger continued. 'The tunnel expert I told you about. He's a bloody good man.'

Jimbo and Dead-eye nodded at Red as he settled into his seat, swallowed a mouthful of mashed potatoes, then said, 'The blokes from England, come to give us advice. Some bloody joke, that is!'

'We haven't come just to give you advice,' Jimbo answered diplomatically. 'We've come to exchange tactics and information; to learn from each other.'

Red shoved hot sausage and peas into his mouth, chewed, swallowed, then grinned at Shagger. 'They've come to give us advice,' he repeated.

'We can all use some advice now and then,' Dead-eye said solemnly. 'It's a two-way process.'

'Not for me, it ain't. I've taken all the advice I can stand from my own bloody officers. I don't need it from a couple of Pommie NCOs who've never even fought here.'

'We've fought everywhere else,' Jimbo said firmly. 'You name it, we've been there.'

'That counts for bollocks here, mate. What counts here is experience on the ground – and *under* the ground. That's something you don't have.'

'We can learn from each other,' Dead-eye insisted.

'Give support to each other. That's the point of us being here.'

Red glanced at Shagger and said, 'What do you think?'

Shagger studied Jimbo and Dead-eye in turn, then said: 'I think they'll have to prove themselves first. But why not give them a try?'

Red shrugged. In the end he preferred to get on with people. 'OK,' he said. 'Let's see how they shape up.'

'We'll shape up,' Dead-eye assured him. 'Anything you care to throw at us, we'll bounce it right back.'

'*We* won't be throwing anything at you,' Shagger told him. 'The VC will.'

'We can handle it,' Dead-eye said.

'Our visitors have spirit,' Shagger said. 'OK, gentlemen,' he added, raising his glass of beer. 'Let's have a truce for now.'

'I'll second that,' Jimbo said.

The four men raised and touched their beer glasses, then quenched their relentless thirst.

'Let me buy a round,' Jimbo said.

'Sure,' said Shagger, knowing exactly what Jimbo was doing and deciding to profit by it.

Jimbo went off to the bar and returned with four pint glasses balanced expertly between his hands. When he'd distributed the beers and they'd all had another drink, Dead-eye, always keen on military facts, said: 'I'm a little bit vague on how you blokes ended up here. Do you mind filling me in?'

'We first came in 1962,' Shagger replied.

'I believe it began with a crash training programme,' Dead-eye said.

'Bloody oath,' Red replied. 'With the Team – the Australian Army Training Team Vietnam. First, a two-week briefing on the war at the Intelligence Centre in Sydney; then an intensive five days at the Canungra Jungle Training Centre in Queensland.'

'What kind of training?'

'Jungle navigation, ambushing, patrolling and sharpshooting, finishing off with sneaker and shooting galleries.'

'What?'

Red sighed at the Pom's ignorance. 'We use a demonstration platoon to teach trainees the functions they'll have to perform in the field. Each man wears a coloured helmet identifying his role in the platoon, and trainees watch the actions of individuals as the group goes through field formations or ambush drills. What we call sneaker and shooting gallery exercises teach you to react instantly to enemy targets in the jungle or at night. It's a bit like your "Killing House" in Hereford, only outdoors.'

'How does it work?' Jimbo asked.

'Each man is ordered to sneak silently through a patch of pretend enemy-held jungle. As he does this, concealed targets in the shape of enemy soldiers suddenly pop up one after the other – in your face, to one side, sometimes to the rear. You only have a split second to blast the target with your weapon or be declared a casualty. Bloody good training.'

'What happened after that?' Dead-eye asked.

'We were flown in civvies on a regular commercial flight from Singapore to Saigon,' Shagger told him. 'That was in August '62. There were twenty-nine of us. When we arrived at Tan Son Nhut airport we were met by the Australian ambassador and senior Allied officers, given a golden handshake, then sent out to have a good time in Saigon – a last supper, so to speak.'

'It must've been some town then,' Jimbo said with genuine envy.

'Bloody oath!' Red exclaimed, taking up the story. 'I mean, the whole bloody war was going on just a few miles away, but you wouldn't have known it when you were in Saigon . . .'

'Biggest damn city in Vietnam,' Shagger cut in. 'Capital of South Vietnam, over a million people, primary objective of the communists, but in '62 you'd have thought you were in some French colonial paradise. Downtown you had hordes of bicycles, rickshaws, Honda scooters and Renault taxis – all doing terrific business – and a little farther out you had lush tropical gardens, tree-lined boulevards and the mansions of the rich. A beaut of a city.'

'Not now, though,' Red said. 'It was changing even when we were there. No sooner had we arrived – but particularly after the Yanks arrived – than the opportunists, crooks and pimps started opening cheap bars and seedy clubs between the old restaurants and pavement cafés. Suddenly those beautiful little Vietnamese dolls in black trousers, white *ao dais* and straw hats were replaced by a horde of tit-flashing whores – them and their pimps – and God knows how many pickpockets and con men. And there were plenty of beggars too. Then the clean atmosphere was fouled up by military vehicles, and what was a relatively peaceful place became a nightmare, with the constant noise of trucks, helicopters, aircraft, exploding VC mortar shells, and music and bawling from clubs. Almost overnight it turned into a real piss-hole.'

'It's still bloody exciting, though,' Shagger said quickly, lest they get the wrong impression.

'Too right,' Red agreed. 'Best place for R and C you can imagine, despite it all.'

'And after Saigon?' Dead-eye asked.

'We were split into two separate units,' Shagger told him. 'The first unit – ten of us – was sent to the Vietnamese National Training Centre at Dong Da, south of Hue. That camp was responsible for the training of recruits for the ARVN, but the base was also used as a battalion training centre and could accommodate about a thousand men. It was a bloody tip-heap. Our living quarters, the general hygiene, rations, even the training itself, were all bloody awful. We lived in long fibro huts that had no windows, just window spaces to let the breeze in. But they also let in the rain and, even worse, blood-thirsty mosquitoes and hornets. As for the open bogs and kitchens, they were filthy, swarming with rats and every imaginable kind of creepy-crawly. Practically all the ARVN officers were corrupt as buggery, including the commandant, and they pocketed most of the loot intended to feed us and the ARVN guys. Those same officers were crap as leaders. They'd been chosen for their social position rather than their abilities, and promoted because of their brown-nosing to those higher up, not because of their success at what they were doing. Because of this, discipline – and morale – were at rock bottom and most Vietnamese units were no more than uniformed rabble. Bloody savages, I tell you, mate!'

'And now, after the ARVN and the South Vietnamese, you think you're going to get fucked up by us,' Jimbo suggested boldly.

Shagger stared steadily, thoughtfully at him, then said, 'This is my second trip to 'Nam, and now I'm told I'm going to get advice on fighting here, courtesy of the revered SAS of Great Britain. How would *you* feel?'

'Pretty fucking miffed,' Jimbo admitted. 'But

believe me, we're not here to tell you what to do. Only to work alongside you, and maybe you'll benefit from our even broader experience, picked up in a lot of different countries over the past twenty-odd years. After all, no matter how good you boys are, the Australian SAS was only formed in 1957, which means you've had less experience than us.'

Shagger wasn't about to take this lying down. 'Just like you,' he said, 'we fought in Malaya and Borneo. We've got the experience, mate.'

'But we've fought in North Africa, Sicily, Italy and all over Europe in World War II,' Jimbo insisted, 'plus South Arabia, Aden and the Yemen. That gives us an awful lot more experience of different combat techniques. In fact, it was us who created hearts-and-minds, which you're using here to win over the South Vietnamese peasants. So, you know, you can learn from us.'

'We can't learn about Vietnam from you,' Red insisted. 'You'll have to learn that from *us*.'

'We're always keen to learn,' Dead-eye told him. 'So let's not work against each other, but *with* each other. Together we'll form an even stronger team. Nothing wrong with that, is there?'

Shagger glanced at Red, grinned slightly, then turned back to Dead-eye. 'You guys have a hell of a reputation, but I still have my doubts,' he said. 'Let's wait and see how you get on when we go on our bush-bash tomorrow. You'll get a fair crack of the whip and we'll see if you're as good as you're supposed to be. If you are, we'll play ball. If you're not, it'll have been a wasted journey for you, because you'll be going nowhere with us again. Fair enough?'

Dead-eye nodded his agreement.

'Fair enough,' Jimbo said. He polished off his beer, glanced down at his empty plate, then had a good look around the mess tent. Eating and drinking with gusto, the men were shouting to make themselves heard above the loud-speakers suspended from the canvas roof and blaring out Frank Sinatra's latest hit, 'Strangers in the Night'. 'It's like a fucking nightclub,' he said.

'Well, apart from the open-air movies,' Shagger replied, 'it's one of the only two places to go and relax – either here or the bar. Which is where me and Red are going right now. Fancy a beer?'

'I think we'll give it a miss,' Dead-eye said, after catching the look in Jimbo's eye. 'It's been a long flight out and we've got to finish sorting out our kit for our first taste of bush-bashing with you guys tomorrow. And I wouldn't mind catching up on some sleep.'

Shagger pulled a face at Red. 'These Pommies must be a bit on the soft side. What do you think?'

'I'm bound to agree, Shagger. What cobber worth

his salt would want to sleep when he could have a good piss-up? They must be as soft as a baby's bum.'

Jimbo grinned as he and the stony-faced Dead-eye, refusing to rise to the bait, pushed back their chairs and climbed to their feet. 'We'll see about that tomorrow,' he said, 'when we're out in the bush. For now, no matter what you hard men say, we're going to sort out our kit and get some shut-eye. We'll see you at first light.'

'We'll be ready and waiting,' Shagger said, 'with or without sleep.'

Jimbo nodded at Dead-eye and they left the mess tent, stepping into the faded light of the evening to see the palm trees sinking into silhouette against a rich, pink-hued sky. Walking side by side across the compound to their barracks, they passed the bar tent, where they heard drunken laughter, bawling and the sounds of the Walker Brothers. Glancing in, they saw a lot of red, sweaty faces illuminated in a gloom eerily coloured by the flickering lights of a Wurlitzer jukebox.

Tempted, they glanced at each other, but the puritanical Dead-eye shook his head, determined to be in tiptop condition the next morning. They walked on, passing the motor pool, which contained, in addition to jeeps and Bedford trucks, M113A1 armoured personnel carriers and fifty-ton Centurion Mark V tanks, each armed with an

83mm twenty-pound gun, a .50-calibre Browning machine-gun, and two .30-calibre Browning machine-guns. Each tank also had a 455-litre auxiliary fuel tank on its rear plate and infrared night-vision equipment.

'Very tasty,' Jimbo said.

As they neared the barracks, two Huey helicopters were coming in for the night, descending vertically and noisily through the billowing clouds of dust sucked up by their rotors. West of the landing zones, troopers dressed in jungle greens, with soft caps on their heads and their faces blackened with stick camouflage, entered the camp along the camouflaged patrol route entry, which enabled them to pass safely through the many claymores buried around the perimeter. They were armed with 7.62mm L1A1 SLRs, 5.56mm M16A1 gas-operated automatic rifles with M203 grenade launchers, 7.62mm Armalite assault rifles and M60 GPMGs. Some were carrying wounded men on stretchers; all looked extremely weary.

'Looks like they've had a hard day,' Jimbo said.

'Our turn tomorrow,' Dead-eye reminded him.

In the barracks, they found all the camp-beds empty and deduced that the Aussies, like Shagger and Red, were at the open-air movie or in the mess tent or pub. This gave them the first privacy they'd had since arriving, and they were grateful. Later, when they had sorted out their kit, they rested fully clothed on their beds, under their mosquito nets.

Propped up against his pillow, Dead-eye was studying maps of the terrain. Jimbo was stretched out on his back with his hands clasped behind his head, his gaze mesmerized by the fan spinning slowly above him.

'So what do you think of our Aussie friends, then?' he asked Dead-eye.

'Hard men. Know what they're doing. They're going to test us pretty rigorously and we'll have to match up to them.'

'I've never really thought about the Aussie SAS before. I mean, are they related to 22 Squadron?'

'No. They've nothing to do with the British regiment.' Dead-eye's hobby was reading military histories and he knew all about the Australian SAS. 'They came into being after their government agreed to send an infantry battalion to Malaya during the Emergency. That was in 1955, though it actually evolved out of the airborne platoon of the Royal Australian Regiment, which was formed in October 1951 and detached to the School of Land/Air Warfare at RAAF base Williamtown. By 1953 that platoon had become a separate unit on the army order of battle and began to take on an élite aspect, like us. In 1956, when Australia and New Zealand were asked to help with the Emergency, the Kiwis raised their own SAS squadron solely for service in Malaya and the Aussies raised a regular brigade group, 1 Australian Infantry Brigade. This consisted of two infantry battalions, one armoured regiment, a field artillery regiment, a field engineer squadron, and a special air service squadron.'

'Bob's your uncle!' Jimbo exclaimed.

'The Special Air Service squadron was a completely new unit whose members were culled mainly from the existing airborne platoon based at Williamtown. Now 1 Australian Infantry Brigade was located at Holsworthy, near Sydney, but as the emphasis with the Special Air Service squadron was naturally on air services, it was allotted to the Royal Australian Regiment as the 1st Special Air Service Company. It was located at Campbell Barracks, Swanbourne, near Perth, which is where it remains to this day.'

'So they've nothing to do with us at all.'

'No.'

'I noticed they wear a red beret, like our commandos.'

'Yes, because they're primarily an infantry-commando unit. Originally their beret badge was the crossed rifles of the Royal Australian Infantry Corps, but in 1960, when the regiment became a unit of the Royal Australian Regiment, its beret badge was changed from Infantry Corps to that of the RAR. About two years later, the link between

the 1st SAS Company and the RAR was broken
and it became the Special Air Service Regiment.
It was then expanded to provide a base squadron
and four SAS squadrons. Though not connected
to our SAS, in 1965 the Aussie SAS was invited
to help us out in Malaya, which they did, before
joining us in Borneo. Though they're an infantry-
commando-style unit, rather than an air service
squadron, their roles and tactics are similar to
ours, including reconnaissance through winning
hearts and minds. That may be why they resent
us. They probably think we look on them as pupils,
rather than equals. That's bound to rankle.'

'They'll get over it,' Jimbo said.

At that moment they were both distracted by a
deep, throbbing sound that had approached from
the west and was now growing louder directly
above the barracks. Rolling off their beds, they
went to the window and glanced up at the night
sky. Flying directly overhead, silhouetted by a star-
bright sky, were about twenty US B52 bombers,
heading inland to attack the enemy positions on the
Long Hai hills. Even as Jimbo and Dead-eye looked
up, amazed by the sheer number of aircraft, they
heard a distant pounding coming from the east side
of the barracks, directly behind them. They turned
away from the window and hurried to the other
side to look out of the windows.

The B52s' bombardment had already begun and

great balls of silvery-yellow and orange flames were rolling along the dark mass of hills to the east, obliterating the stars with a boiling black smoke that was illuminated from within by more darting fingers of flame, like millions of fireflies. The bombing raid went on and on, filling the air with distant thunder, turning the dark hills into an eerie, dreadful vision of rolling, spewing flames and boiling black smoke that eventually appeared to cover them completely, as if obliterating everything contained there with its awesome destructive power.

'That's our calling-card,' Dead-eye said. 'We're on our way, Jimbo.'

6

Lieutenant-Colonel Callaghan was understandably nervous the following morning when, just after dawn, he addressed the men of 1 and 3 Squadrons SAS, most of whom, as he well knew, were extremely sceptical of him and his two NCOs, Jimbo and Dead-eye. For this reason the latter pair had made a point of not being beside him when he commenced his lecture.

'They'll consider it grandstanding,' Dead-eye had told him. 'So Jimbo and I should take our places with 3 Squadron, beside Shagger and Red. We'll be more anonymous that way.'

'In the audience, he means,' Jimbo said sardonically. 'The best of luck, boss.'

Now, in the briefing tent, standing on a packing crate in order to let his audience see him, Callaghan felt that he was truly on the stage, and what was more, in a very bad play. He felt this because of the cynicism he saw in that sea of faces in front of him. Before speaking, he took a deep breath and let it out slowly.

'Before proceeding with the briefing proper,' he began, 'may I just say that I understand perfectly why some of you will undoubtedly resent the fact that three members of the British SAS have been sent here to accompany an Australian operation.'

'Hear, hear!' a voice in the crowd called out mockingly.

Callaghan nodded and smiled, acknowledging the jibe, then continued. 'Please let me emphasize, however, that we're not here to take you men over, but to exchange ideas and tactics in order to give more muscle to both regiments. We're not here to tell you what to do. We're here to take part in certain operations in order to learn from them. As for this morning's operation, please let me point out that while I'm nominally in charge of it, I'm really only here to learn and the actual planning of it was the responsibility of your own CO, Lieutenant-Colonel Durnford.'

That white lie received a smattering of applause and a few cheers. When they had died down, Callaghan said, 'So I hope that you can view me and my two men as honorary members of your Squadron, here to exchange ideas, and that you'll give us your fullest cooperation. And so to the briefing.'

He waited until the murmurs had subsided, then picked up a pointer and tapped the blackboard with it. A surprisingly detailed plan of the forward operating base had been drawn in chalk. He tapped the marked patrol route exit leading through the mined perimeter.

'The operation commencing today will be code-named Alpha. Its purpose is to secure this FOB and then push back the perimeter to at least 4000 yards, taking it beyond enemy mortar range.' He ran the pointer around the drawn perimeter, then lowered it to his side and turned to the listening men. 'I don't have to tell you that this camp is under constant threat from VC snipers and reconnaissance patrols. Indeed, too many of your friends have been killed by them for you not to know. So our primary objective for the next few days is to clear the present perimeter of VC, place our own men in their present sniper positions, and turn their patrol routes into ambush positions. This will prevent them getting within firing range of the camp and secure those same routes for our own supply purposes.'

'About bloody time!' someone called out.

When the murmurs of approval had died down, Callaghan said, 'Well, I'm glad you agree. Your CO will be pleased.' He let the subsequent laughter expend itself before continuing. 'In order to clear the perimeter we're going to break you up into four-man patrols, each with a selected area of the perimeter to cover. As you know, the perimeter beyond our own surrounding minefield consists mainly of paddy-fields, the forests of rubber plantations and stretches of dense jungle. For this reason, we'll be supported by the UH 1B Iroquois helicopters of No. 9 Squadron RAAF, located at Vung Tau. The Iroquois will be used for troop transfers, extractions and reconnaissance. We will keep in constant contact with each other and with the choppers by means of a combination of A510 radios, PRC 64 radio sets and some USAF PRC 47 high-frequency radio transceivers. Though we'll be eyeballing the enemy on the ground, the choppers will support us with aerial reconnaissance and direct the nearest groups by radio to any enemy sighted. In the event that an individual group, or number of groups, will be required to move out of their selected patrol area to another location, the choppers will extract them and insert them at the new DZ. The choppers will also be used for casevacs and resups. As each group's patrol area is cleared of VC snipers or patrols, the enemy sniper positions and patrol routes will be taken over by our own men and the remaining men from that cleared area will be moved to another location. In this manner we can gradually cover the whole outside perimeter, push it back to a minimum of 4000 yards, designated Line Alpha, and thus secure the camp from enemy snipers, patrols, mortars and, eventually, big guns. Any questions so far?'

'You say we're being broken up into groups of

four,' Shagger asked. 'We normally patrol in groups of ten. Why four-man patrols?'

'The four-man patrol is the fundamental operational unit of 22 SAS.' Grinning, Callaghan waved his free hand to silence the jeers and whistles. 'I know you don't want to hear this, but experience gained as far back as World War II has shown us that the four-man team is the most efficient and effective size for combining minimum manpower demands with maximum possibility of surprise. We've also learnt that in situations that produce great tension, the four-man team is the one most psychologically sound because the men can team up in pairs and look out for each other both domestically and tactically.'

'What do you mean by domestically?' someone called out.

'Building a hide or observation post, cooking, brewing up, washing utensils, and so forth,' Callaghan said over the wave of laughter and hooting.

'Four-man teams in bloody aprons!' someone else bawled. 'They'll soon have us in high heels!'

Callaghan patiently waited until the ribaldry had run its course before continuing. 'Each man in the four-man teams will have his specialist duty, while being able to use his cross-training for another duty, if required. Each team will therefore have a specialist in signalling, demolitions, medicine and, in case prisoners are taken, language – in this case Vietnamese. Also, for this particular operation, each four-man team will be matched to another and keep in close touch with it, ready to call in the other team, or to be called in by it, for assistance should contact be made with the enemy. In other words, in a conflict situation, the four-man team will be at least doubled in strength to turn it into an effective fighting patrol.'

'A four-man patrol doesn't allow for too much equipment, so what are we taking?' someone asked from the back of the tent.

'As I said, the four-man patrol combines minimum manpower with maximum potential for surprise. The patrol is therefore limited in its kit to what each individual can personally carry: personal weapons, bergen, hand-grenades and parts of the team's GPMG. What you lose in weapon power you gain with the possibility of surprise.'

'What about claymores or grenade launchers?'

'Neither.'

'Why not?'

'Though the individual groups will be spread all around the perimeter, they'll be in close proximity to one another, with some possibly overlapping into another's allotted patrolling area, even while being obscured from each other by rubber trees or dense forest. No weapons will therefore be fired until the enemy has been eyeballed on the ground, irrespective of locations given by the reconnaissance choppers. The resultant engagements will virtually be close-combat fire-fights, which places the enemy too close to you – and the patrols too close to each other – for the use of mines or grenade launchers. Any more questions?'

'Sir!' An Aussie raised his right hand and asked: 'So far, our patrols have been going out in the morning and returning to base at first light. Will this stay the same?'

'No. This is a long-term operation to clear the whole perimeter, push it back, and replace Charlie with our own men. For this reason you'll be required to stay out until the job is completed.'

'Full survival kit?'

'Correct. Any further questions?'

'Yeah,' said another Aussie. 'When do we move out?'

Callaghan checked his watch. 'Noon,' he said. 'As you already have your personal weapons, you can prepare fairly quickly and meet on the parade ground an hour from now. There you'll be allocated to your particular four-man team and each team given its backup team and grid references for its selected patrolling area. Stick make-up for yourselves, please, and jungle camouflage for your personal weapons. Once you're in separate teams, the teams will be sent individually to the armoury to collect a GPMG and radio and, in the case of the PC, a SARBE beacon for communication with the support-extraction choppers. You'll then gather together back at the parade ground, be marched out through the patrol route exit, and disperse to your allotted areas of patrol once outside the defensive perimeter. That's it, men. Get going.'

As the briefing broke up and the men dispersed to their barracks or tents, Callaghan indicated with his jabbing finger Jimbo, Dead-eye and the two Aussie SAS men, Shagger and Red. When these four had gathered around him, he said, 'Since you men have already met, you'll make up one team. That was my intention from the start, which is why you're in the same barracks.'

'I guessed that,' Dead-eye said.

'A little bit of bullshit is OK,' Callaghan said, 'but don't let it get out of hand when it comes to comparisons between the Brits and the Aussies. Bullshit can start as gentle banter and end up as a fist-fight. You lot have to work as two pairs of a four-man team – Dead-eye with Shagger, Jimbo with Red – and I expect you to be strongly supportive of each other, regardless of your differences of outlook. Is that understood?'

'Yes, boss,' Dead-eye said, while the other men nodded their reluctant agreement. 'I think we've all got the message.'

'Right, then, get to it.'

Following most of the others, the four men

marched across the parade ground, lowering their heads and shielding their eyes from the dust that was being blown up by the two Huey helicopters ascending from the LZ. Temporarily deafened by the noise, they said nothing until they were in the barracks, by the beds grouped together at the far end.

'Nice little ear-bashing from your boss,' Red said. 'I could tell he's concerned for our welfare. Or *your* welfare, at least.'

'Doesn't want us to get into a blue over bullshit flying out of control,' Shagger added, grinning. 'As if that could happen!'

'A blue?' Jimbo asked.

'A fight,' Red informed him.

'I always thought the Aussies spoke English,' Jimbo said. 'Now I'm beginning to wonder. We're going out to have a blue on a bush-bash after having an ear-bash. They might as well be speaking fucking Swahili!'

As Red started transferring unwanted kit from his bergen to the steel locker beside his bed, he looked up and said, 'You bastards cross-grain the buckets, take orders from your head shed and the other Ruperts, attack the enemy with mixed-fruit puddings, fire double-taps from nine-millies, get intelligence from the green slime in the Kremlin, go on the piss in the Sports and Social, then get some kip in the spider. If that's English, mate,

I've been speaking another language since the day I was born.'

'What did he just say?' Dead-eye asked deadpan.

'Don't know,' Jimbo replied. 'I didn't understand a fucking word. Maybe he was speaking Vietnamese. Let's make him the language specialist of our team.'

'*I'm* the language specialist,' Shagger informed him. 'And my speciality is Vietnamese, so you've no problem there.'

'It's your English that's the problem with me, mate. How about sign language?'

'The only sign I'll be giving you, cobber, is this,' said Red, giving him the two fingers.

'As long as it's purely visual,' Jimbo said, grinning broadly, 'we'll understand each other fine.'

As they were going out on a long-term mission, there wasn't much they could remove from their packed bergens and store in their lockers apart from a few personal items. Because of the demands of the patrol, the rucksacks still contained the heavier items, including survival kit, water bottle, waterproof poncho, survival bag and spare ammunition. When all of this had been packed in or strapped on, they proceeded to check and camouflage their personal weapons: 7.62mm L1A1 SLRs for Jimbo and Dead-eye, 5.56mm M16A1 automatic rifles for Shagger and Red, and Browning 9mm High Power handguns for all of them. Each man's Browning was holstered normally on his hip, but the recognizable outline of his rifle was disguised by wrapping the barrel with strips of cloth dyed to match the green and brown of the rubber trees and denser forest. The pistol grip, magazine and top cover were covered with pieces of disruptive-pattern material held on with masking tape.

'All joking aside,' Shagger said as he camouflaged his rifle, 'that Lieutenant-Colonel Callaghan seems pretty impressive to me. Not some upper-class Pommy ponce educated at Eton.'

'You're right to be impressed,' Dead-eye replied. 'Callaghan isn't upper class, he isn't a ponce and he was educated in the field rather than Eton. In fact, he's a former Irish rugby international and accomplished boxer. Originally with 3 Commando, he was in a military prison in Cairo for knocking out his CO, waiting to go on trial, when Stirling got him released to help in the formation of the first SAS squadron, way back in 1941.'

'He knocked out his CO?' Shagger asked, raising his eyebrows.

'That's right. Though Callaghan's normally good-natured and polite, he has a notorious temper. In fact, before knocking the bloke out, he ran him out of the officers' mess at the point of a bayonet.'

'I like the sound of that,' Shagger said.

'Me too,' Red agreed.

'So Stirling got him out of the cooler,' Shagger said, 'and then they started the SAS.'

Dead-eye nodded. 'Correct.'

'That was in 1941,' Jimbo said. 'I was there at the time. A twenty-year-old private. We trained at a hell-hole called Kabrit, in the Suez Canal Zone, and there was nothing that Callaghan asked us to do that he didn't do himself. Christ, he was tough! Once, after a murderous march, when one of my mates complained that we had to stop for a rest, Callaghan, who stopped for no one or nothing, grabbed the berk by the shoulders, picked him bodily off the ground, and held him over the edge of the cliff we were hiking along, threatening to drop him into the fucking sea. There were no more complaints after that.'

Shagger chuckled while Red looked on, wide-eyed.

'As for engaging with the enemy,' Jimbo continued, 'again he never asked you to do anything he wouldn't do himself. Of course, since he was so bloody fearless, he was constantly getting us to do things that we thought were either impossible or suicidal. But we did them. Pulled them off. He set a shining example.'

'I heard about you fellas in the desert,' Shagger told him. 'You inserted by parachute in the middle of bad storms. You raided German airfields in heavily armed jeeps, attacking on the move and roaring out again before they could catch you. You hiked halfway across the bloody desert. You worked with the Long Range Desert Group. Looks like you've done it all, mate.'

'We have,' Jimbo said proudly. 'And Daddy Callaghan was on practically every mission. He was out there in front.'

'Same in Malaya,' Dead-eye said. 'He spent months all alone in the jungle, living off the land and spying on the commies. He came out of it looking like a scarecrow, fed and exercised himself back to health, then led the whole bloody squadron right back in there. That man was amazing.'

Red gave a low whistle of admiration while Shagger just shook his head from side to side and said, 'Well, let's hope you guys are as good.'

'No one's as good as Callaghan,' Dead-eye admitted, 'but we're pretty damn close to it.'

'We'll soon see,' Shagger told him.

When the weapons had been disguised, each man camouflaged himself by using 'cam' cream to cover the exposed areas of his skin – face, neck, wrists and hands. The cream was applied in three stages: first, a thin base coating diluted with saliva to cover all exposed areas; second, the painting of diagonal lines of stick camouflage across the face, to break up the shape and outline of the features; finally, darkening highlighted areas such as forehead, nose, cheek-bones and chin. Then the men donned their green bush hats, which, along with their bergens, webbing, M26 high-explosive hand-grenades, and the separate components of the team's GPMG and the radio (the latter two items still to be obtained from the armoury tent), would be camouflaged with pieces of the vegetation to be found outside the perimeter.

When all was completed, the four men took turns at checking each other to ensure that nothing had been missed.

'I knew most Pommies were pansies,' Red said as he inspected the back of Jimbo's neck and behind his ears, 'but I didn't appreciate they were so good with make-up.'

'I've heard that Aussies are so hard,' Jimbo replied, 'because they're trying to hide the fact that they're really fairies. No wonder you managed to make up so quickly; you must do it all the time.'

'Ha, ha,' Red said touchily.

'All right, you two,' Shagger warned them. 'That's enough for now. Let's just finish this mutual inspection and get back outside. We're running late as it is.'

In silence the four men hauled on their bergens, picked up their personal weapons and headed back to the parade ground, which now was baking in the late-morning heat, even though the southern sky was darkening with clouds.

'Rain,' Shagger said, sounding grim.

'Shit,' Red replied with a weary shake of his head.

The parade ground was already filling up with most of the other men from 1 and 3 Squadrons, who were milling about in front of a notice-board placed at the edge of the field. Lieutenant-Colonels Callaghan and Durnford were standing beside Sergeant-Major Art Wheeler, looking on as the men, all now heavily laden, checked where their names were in the typed lists pinned to the board. When each man found his own name within a four-man group, he called out his group number and was sent by the sergeant-major to join that group. These groups were placed next to those who would give them backup and sarcastic jokes were being bawled back and forth between them.

'With a shower like you giving us support,' Corporal Dan Allen shouted at Shagger and Red, clearly meaning to include the two Pommies, Jimbo and Dead-eye, 'it's a case of God protect us from our friends!'

'God only protects the worthy,' Shagger bawled back, 'and that leaves you lot out!'

As the most experienced men there, Jimbo, Dead-eye, Shagger and Red were in Team 1, backed up by Team 2, consisting of Sergeants Don Ingrams and Giles Norton, plus two Corporals, Bob 'Blue' Butler and Michael 'Mad Mike' Dalton, all of whom had fought in Borneo just a few months ago.

'They really know their stuff,' Red told Jimbo and Dead-eye, after identifying them, 'but we can't admit that. We like to take the piss out of them. Keep their feet on solid ground. Hey, Blue!' he bawled. 'Is it true that every time you hear a shot fired, your hair turns grey? I mean, down below too?'

'My hair only turns grey, mate, when I'm given two Pommies and bludgers like you and Shagger as backup. Even God would turn grey at the thought of *that*, so don't come it, you drongo!'

'Seems to me . . .' Red was retorting until interrupted by Sergeant-Major Wheeler, who bawled, 'Pipe down, you grog-happy poofters. *I want silence this second!*' When the men had settled down, Wheeler held a pile of maps high in the air and said, 'As I call out the team number, I want the patrol commander of that team to come up and take his numbered map. Details of the team's area of patrol are given on each map. Once every PC has his map, the patrols will go one by one to the armoury and pick up their radio SARBE beacon and GPMG. I know you're just a bunch of bloody galahs, so I'll be calling out the team numbers in strict order, starting with . . . *Team 1!*'

As Shagger, the PC of Team 1, stepped forward to collect his map, Jimbo leaned sideways to whisper to Red, 'What the fuck's a galah?'

'A dumb cunt,' Red whispered back. 'Jesus, you Poms are pig-ignorant!'

The rest of the PCs were called out in strict order of teams to collect their maps from the sergeant-major. Once each PC had received his map, he led the other three members of his team to the armoury tent, where they collect a GPMG, a SARBE communications-rescue beacon, and either an A510 or PRC 64 radio, or a USAF PRC 47 high-frequency radio transceiver. When the man acting as signaller had humped his radio on to his back, on top of his bergen, the separate components of the GPMG, including barrel and tripod, were divided among the other three men. Then all four men returned to the parade ground for a final briefing from Callaghan.

'I want each PC to open his map and study it now. You'll be leaving the base via the patrol route exit and I want you to take your bearings from that – it's clearly marked on the map. The PC will carry the map on his person at all times, along with the SARBE, but we're allowing ten minutes for the other men to study it as well and get a rough idea of his allotted area of reconnaissance. Also marked on the map is the patrol area of your backup team. Memorize that as well. Bear in mind that once the patrol starts, you won't be coming back in until the whole perimeter has been cleared and Line Alpha established and secured. Bear in mind, also, that although you may at times feel isolated, our choppers will be right above you for reconnaissance, resups and casevacs, and you can contact them at any time by SARBE. Your PCs can also contact Operational Control back here on the base. Now if anyone wants to have a last cigarette while his PC studies the map, go ahead. You have ten minutes before you move out, so make the most of it.'

The PCs pored over their maps while the other men smoked or chewed gum. Then each gathered his men around him, laid the map on the ground, and let them study it for ten minutes. This done, and questions asked and answered, the PCs stood up and led their four-man teams, in strict numerical order, out of the base.

Moving out in file formation, as would all the rest, Team 1 was the first to depart. The sun was now high in the sky, but burning through gathering clouds as the teams dispersed into the paddy-fields, rubber plantations and dense jungle surrounding the camp.

7

Team 1, followed almost immediately by Team 2, marched carefully along the camouflaged, almost invisible patrol route exit, between the claymores buried on either side. Up ahead on point, Dead-eye held his SLR across his chest and kept his eyes on the ground, taking note from the flattened grass exactly where the patrol route exit lay. The mines, he knew, had been carefully concealed and came right up to both sides of the jungle path, so that one wrong step in either direction and a man could be blown to hell. Strung out in single file behind Dead-eye, the other three men were also on the alert, with Shagger second in line as PC, and Red behind him as signaller, both covering an arc of fire on both sides of the trail, and placing emphasis on studying the shadowy spaces between the rubber trees that came up to the very edge of the minefields. Last in line, as Tail-end Charlie, Jimbo also studied both sides of the path, though once out of the mined area and off the exit route, he would be compelled to constantly turn around and cover their rear.

Negotiating the mines was always a nerve-racking business, but luckily it didn't take long. A few minutes later the four men had reached the end of the exit and were able to breathe more easily as they knelt together in the shade of the rubber trees. There, as Team 2 could be seen making their way cautiously along the hidden pathway, Shagger checked his map again for the direction they would have to take to their selected patrol area, while the other three camouflaged the equipment they had picked up in the armoury, including the PRC 64 radio set and the separate parts of the GPMG. As they were moving off again, in a direction indicated silently by Shagger's hand signal, Team 2 was coming off the exit route. This time, the two groups of men did not shout jokes at one another, but remained totally silent. Shagger indicated with another hand signal the direction his team was to take. Then they moved off.

As they turned east into the nearest rubber plantation, they passed from fierce sunlight to deep gloom and appalling humidity. Instantly, they started sweating and the air around them filled up with clouds of mosquitoes and midges. Tormented by both the sweat dripping into their eyes and the attacking insects, they had to force themselves to study the shadows intently, Dead-eye concentrating on the front, Shagger and Red covering both sides, and Jimbo now in the stressful position of having to repeatedly turn around to cover their rear, as well as covering his two sides. Spaced well apart to prevent the whole team being hit by the same burst of enemy gunfire, they soon felt acutely aware of their isolation from one another and could not prevent the tension building up in them.

The deeper they went into the jungle, the gloomier and more humid it became, with the rubber trees often giving way to secondary vegetation that was a seemingly impenetrable tangle of shrubs, vines, and overhanging, intertwining branches bearing huge palm leaves that could slice open the skin without the victim feeling it. As both the ground beneath their feet and the overhanging branches could conceal snakes and poisonous spiders, they were compelled to inspect these carefully as they marched. They also had to check above and below for booby-traps. This need for caution slowed them down considerably and placed an even greater strain upon them. In addition, the jungle contained many narrow streams which had to be crossed and which, being exposed areas, were natural ambush positions for the enemy.

The jungle was not silent, for there was the ceaseless rustling of breeze-blown leaves, the scurrying of animals in the undergrowth, the flapping of birds, the chattering of monkeys and the babbling of streams. To make listening for the enemy even more difficult, these sounds, which the men were gradually becoming accustomed to filtering out, were repeatedly drowned by the deep rumble of bombers, the screeching of jets, or the whap-whapping of helicopters passing overhead. Their only consolation on hearing this din was the fact that some of those choppers were their own recon-naissance craft on the lookout for the enemy.

When they had passed through the rubber planta-tion and into the impenetrable foliage of secondary forest, their progress slowed even more as they had to hack their way through the undergrowth with machetes. This was sweat-inducing, back-breaking work, but, because it was so noisy, it was also dangerous. This combination of agonizing work, snail's-pace progress and constant awareness of danger was, even for experienced men, both draining and disheartening, and the wearier they grew the more demoralized they felt. They were therefore glad when, two hours later, yet only one mile on, they emerged from the jungle's gloom to the hotter, brighter and less humid open space of a broad paddy-field.

At the edge of the jungle Shagger dropped to one knee and hand-signalled that they should all do the same. When they had done so and were partially hidden by the stalks of bamboo and tall grass, Shagger studied the paddy-field through his green binoculars, seeing only the tall grass rippling like the waves of a bright-green sea, with shimmering heat waves rising eerily off it. He studied that expanse of grass for a long time, trying to see, in the constant, wave-like motion, a different kind of motion that would reveal the presence of the VC. Eventually, satisfied that the field was empty, he lowered the binoculars, used the PRC 64 to contact HQ and inform them of the team's whereabouts, then waved his hand in a forward motion.

The four men moved forward at the half crouch, weapons held at the ready, their eyes scanning the waving bamboo and grass on all sides of them. The sinking sun was obliterated by the dark clouds that still filled the sky, pregnant with rain. Occasionally, above the clouds, they could hear the reassuring beat of the Iroquois helicopters of No. 9 Squadron RAAF, flying in from Vung Tau to give them support with aerial reconnaissance and anything else required.

Then the rain came.

They were only halfway across the paddy-field when the clouds burst and, accompanied by thunder and lightning, unleashed on them a seemingly interminable downpour. Within seconds they were all drenched; within minutes they were forced to their knees and hiding under their ponchos as the water in the paddy-fields rose up to cover their thighs. The rain hammering on the ponchos over their heads sounded like deafening jungle drums.

Suddenly bullets stitched the field all around them, making the water spurt up in angry, jagged lines that formed arcs all around them and rapidly moved in closer.

'Down!' Shagger bellowed, dropping to one knee, which disappeared in the water, and raising his automatic rifle to the firing position and squinting along the sight.

'Where the fuck are they?' Red asked, looking ahead, then left and right, watching the water spitting up mere feet away, but inching closer to him.

'Shoot and scoot!' Dead-eye called out, then started wading away from the sizzling water while firing short bursts from his SLR in the direction of the enemy gunfire.

'Bug out!' Shagger bawled. '*Bug out!*'

Dead-eye, however, retreated only a short distance from where the enemy bullets were peppering the watery paddy-field and then, still firing his SLR, began circling around the field of fire, which was still directed at the other three men. Once out of its range, he slung the SLR over his shoulder, jerked an M26 hand-grenade from his webbing and hurled it with all his might. He was now in shallow water and even as the grenade was arcing down towards the enemy ambush position he ran towards it, firing his rifle from the hip. The grenade exploded with a thunderclap that created a fountain of water, bamboo, smouldering grass and smoke, followed by the high-pitched screams of wounded men.

It stopped the hail of enemy gunfire. As Dead-eye ran towards the VC position, still shooting from the hip, Shagger, Red and Jimbo followed suit, all pouring a relentless fusillade into the spiralling column of smoke. Dead-eye reached the position first, splashing out of the shallow water and running up on to muddy ground, firing into the guerrillas he saw in the remains of their hide, some dead, some still alive, the latter still dazed from the blast of the grenade and groping frantically, blindly, for their weapons.

Dead-eye poured a final burst into the man nearest to him just as the other three members of the team raced in from the other side, all firing at once. The VC hide turned into a convulsion of exploding bamboo and grass, flying tatters of bloody camouflaged cloth, geysering mud and soil, as the frail, dark-skinned men in black fatigues and black felt hats shuddered violently and were punched to the ground, soaked in their own blood.

While Shagger, Red and Jimbo were checking that the VC were all dead, Dead-eye was up and out of the hide to reconnoitre the area for other hides or individual guerrillas. He found none. Returning to the devastated hide, which was now a mess of blood-soaked bodies and charred vegetation, he found Red and Jimbo, who had inspected the bloody corpses, looking for maps or other valuable scraps of information, while Shagger was on the radio, calling for an OP team to be inserted and replace the dead VC. Receiving confirmation, he then called Team 2 to establish their whereabouts. Learning that they were in their allotted area of patrol, though had so far made no contact with the enemy, he gave details of his own position and then killed the communication. The rain was still pouring down.

'What a bloody mess,' he murmured, glancing about him at the low, sullen sky, the merciless rain, the pools of water clouded with orange mud, the dead Viet Cong, most of whom looked like adolescents, lying in pools of blood, their uniforms lacerated and their smashed ribs and other bones exposed. 'That's all we needed.'

'We didn't need it,' Dead-eye replied, 'but that's what we got. It's no big deal, Sarge.'

'There speaks the British SAS,' said Red. 'Let me bow down and kiss his boots.'

'Are we clear, Dead-eye?' Shagger asked, ignoring his mate's sarcasm.

'Yep.'

'Then we'll sit here and hold this position until the replacement team gets here.'

With no choice in the matter, the four men squatted around the devastated hide, their backs turned to the corpses inside, their eyes scanning the rain-drenched paddy-field in all directions. After about twenty minutes an Iroquois appeared through the murk and was soon roaring right above them, its rotors sweeping the rain around it in glistening sheets. First out when it landed were the 5th Battalion soldiers who would take over the VC hide and hold it as an Australian OP. Next out were the medics, who set about lifting the dead guerrillas on to stretchers and carrying them into the chopper for transfer to a burial site outside Vung Tau. Once the bodies had been removed, the men from the 5th Battalion began modifying the hide for their own purposes. As they were doing so, the chopper took off and Shagger's patrol waved goodbye, wished the soldiers good luck and marched on.

Heading east, eventually they left the paddy-field and started weaving between the soaring trees of another rubber plantation. The rain had now stopped and the heat of the sun returned, casting striations of light on the jungle floor and making steam rise from the soaked vegetation. Soon, the humidity was once again unbearable, making all the men drip sweat, while whining mosquitos and hordes of no less aggressive insects returned to assail them.

As usual, they were marching in single file and

it was Dead-eye, out on point, who saw a slight movement high in a tree up ahead and bawled a warning as the first shot rang out. He was already diving to the side of the narrow track when the bullet thudded into the ground where he had been walking.

Crashing through the undergrowth and rolling on to his belly, he aimed at where he had seen the movement and fired a short burst from his SLR, raking the barrel up and down, left to right, to ensure that he hit the unseen sniper. Leaves and branches were blown apart, raining to the ground. They were followed by a rifle, then the man fell screaming, smashing his way down through the branches to thud into the earth.

As Dead-eye jumped to his feet to advance again, more bullets whined past him and ricocheted off the nearby trees. Instantly, the combined weapons of Shagger, Jimbo and Red roared into action behind him, tearing the trees to shreds high up where the first sniper had been. Another guerrilla plunged to earth, his body breaking the branches as he fell.

Dead-eye was weaving through the trees, advancing, even before the VC hit the ground. In fact, the dead man thudded into the ground just as Dead-eye reached the trunk of the tree and raised his SLR to fire vertically, directly above him. The branches were torn to shreds, raining leaves and wood splinters, then another black-clad body crashed down, screaming, bouncing off the thick branches, smashing through the thin ones. Dead-eye stepped aside just in time, letting the bloody, mangled body thud into the earth where he had been standing. As he glanced up it was clear to him that no more snipers were hidden in that particular tree.

There was the sound of rushing feet, then Shagger and the other two were standing beside him, all breathless.

'Any more?' Shagger asked.

'Yes, I think so,' Dead-eye told him. 'I suspect there's a whole nest of them up in these trees. This bit of jungle is on high ground and they must have a wonderful view from the top of the trees to our base camp, so I think a lot of the sniping's been done from there.'

'Which means we have to get out of here and then get this area levelled completely.'

'Correct,' Dead-eye said. 'Bomb it all to hell, then take it over and use it as our own FOB.'

Shagger glanced at Red and grinned. 'A right little angel of mercy. I thought the English were soft, Red.'

'Not this bastard,' Red said. 'Just take a look at his fucking eyes: they're as dead as chopped liver.'

'Do we do it or not?' Dead-eye asked, neither amused nor offended by Red's remark.

'I say we do it,' Red told him.

'So do I,' Jimbo said.

'OK, let's do it, Shagger agreed. 'Every man for himself.'

'Then we need an RV at the other side of the jungle,' Dead-eye reminded him.

Shagger nodded and removed from his pocket the map, which he unfolded and held so that the other three, now bunched around him, could see it. After checking their present position, he jabbed at a point on the map some two hundred yards south of the far side of the jungle. 'There,' he said. 'Between the jungle and the next VC position, which is a bunker complex. If we get separated on our way through the jungle, we make our way to that location and from there call in air support to clear this lot out.' He folded the map and placed it back in his pocket, then said, 'So, let's do it.'

'Who goes first?' Red asked.

'Me,' Shagger said. 'If I draw their fire, you may be able to see them and take some of them out. When I get out of the trees, I'll give you covering fire and you'll each do the same in turn. Best of luck, piss-pots.'

Shagger carefully scanned the jungle around them, took a deep breath, then ran out from the cover of the immediate group of trees and raced away, crouched low and swerving left to right with his M16A1 automatic rifle at the ready. He had scarcely gone twenty yards when a sniper all in black rose from behind some bushes and took aim with an AK47 assault rifle. Instantly, Dead-eye leaned out of the side of his tree and fired a short, noisy burst that sent the man spinning back into the bushes. Other VC appeared, popping up from the foliage or craning out from behind the trees ahead of Shagger as he weaved left and right, always keeping a tree between him and the enemy.

Dead-eye, Jimbo and Red were now firing in turn, each picking a separate target, attempting to keep the VC pinned down until Shagger, who had veered around them to the right, was clear of their field of fire and heading for the far end of the jungle. When he reached the edge of the trees unhurt, he threw himself to the ground, rolled over on to his belly and fired at the backs of the VC, thus creating a withering crossfire.

Jimbo advanced next, following Shagger's course, firing his SLR from the hip as he darted from one tree to another, gradually making his way forward under the covering fire of his friends, front and rear. Though the VC were mostly pinned down, they still managed to fire a lot of shots, their bullets ricocheting noisily off tree trunks and branches, showering Jimbo in flying foliage as he ran.

Racing across a small clearing, through streaks of brilliant sunlight and pools of ink-black shadow, he was stopped in his tracks when a trapdoor suddenly popped open in the ground just in front of him. As grass and leaves slid off the trapdoor, which was made of bamboo, a yellow face came into view, one eye squinting along the sights of an AK47.

Not stopping for a second, though scarcely believing what he was seeing, Jimbo jumped over the man's head even as he fired his first shot. The combined guns of Dead-eye and Red resounded behind Jimbo as he ran on. Glancing back over his shoulder, he saw the bloody, shattered head of the VC sinking back down through the hole like a pomegranate smashed open with a hammer.

Still not too sure if he had seen right, Jimbo ran out, darting from tree to tree, firing from the hip at the shadowy figures he saw popping up from the undergrowth or leaning out from the trees. Then he hurled himself to the ground at the edge of the jungle, rolling on to his belly a few yards from Shagger.

'Bloody hell!' he exclaimed. 'That bastard came up out of the ground!'

'Like a trapdoor spider,' Shagger replied. 'They just raise the lid as you pass over and – whammo! – they've got you.'

'A tunnel complex?'

'Maybe. They're all over the bloody place. More likely, though, that was just an individual sniper in a camouflaged hide. Now shut up and start firing.'

Lying beside Shagger, Jimbo opened fire with his SLR, shredding the jungle ahead, where, in a dark-green sea of exploding foliage, he saw a group of VC, some facing Red and Dead-eye, the others frantically turning around to deal with this fresh gunfire from their rear.

'*Go!*' Dead-eye bawled at Red and the Australian hurled himself forward, heavily burdened with his bulky radio but still managing to weave left and right, dashing from one tree to another as bullets ricocheted off the trunks and branches, spitting lumps of bark and wood at him. Giving covering fire from the front, Dead-eye fired his SLR in short, savage, devastatingly accurate bursts, picking off a guerrilla the instant one exposed the slightest part of himself.

Red, meanwhile, was weaving through a hail of bullets and flying foliage, first left, then right, frequently hugging a tree trunk until Dead-eye's fire from his rear and the combined fusillade from his two friends in front had once more forced the enemy to lie low. Eventually, following the route taken by the others, he made it to the far side of the trees and knelt beside his two friends. After adjusting the cumbersome radio on his back, he lay belly down beside the others.

'There's more fucking VC than mosquitoes in there,' he said. 'A right fucking nest of them.'

'If Dead-eye makes it,' Shagger replied, 'we'll wipe out that whole stretch of jungle. Blow it all to hell. Here he comes. Start firing.'

Dead-eye moved with the speed and cunning he

had picked up in the jungles of Malaya and Borneo, running crouched as low as he could get, weaving from side to side, sometimes throwing himself to the ground and rolling behind a tree, while bullets from the guerrillas' AK47s thudded into the soil, bounced off tree trunks and showered him with shredded foliage and bark. As he advanced, his three friends kept up a barrage of gunfire from their combination of SLRs and M16A1s, eventually forcing most of the VC to turn away from Dead-eye and defend their rear. This enabled Dead-eye to make the last of his run around the enemy position, pass it and eventually reach a position parallel with his friends, though a good distance away.

'Bug out!' Shagger bawled.

Even as the others were rising to make their tactical retreat, Dead-eye was hurling an M26 hand-grenade at the VC who had dared to advance out of their hide. The grenade exploded in their midst, blowing some of them into the air, dazing others, and showering the living and the dead with raining debris as the branches of nearby trees caught fire and black smoke billowed up. Dead-eye hurled a second grenade as his three friends raced through the trees on the edge of the jungle, all heading off obliquely in different directions, firing on the run, intending to circle back and meet each other at the RV already agreed upon. As they were disappearing, Dead-eye raked the VC still moving in their devastated, smoke-obscured hide, then he too turned and raced away.

He did not have to run far. A couple of hundred yards beyond the trees, in a raised, dry stretch of monsoon drain that ran alongside another paddy-field, Shagger, Red and Jimbo were sprawled near each other, trying to get their breath back. When Dead-eye slithered down beside them, they continued breathing deeply for a while, soon started breathing normally, then at last sat up.

'That was a close one,' Jimbo said.

'Too close,' Shagger replied. 'And that bit of jungle is crawling with Charlie, so let's level the bastard. Red, get me HQ.' Red removed the radio from his back, placed it on the dry floor of the monsoon drain, contacted HQ, then handed Shagger the microphone. Checking his opened map, Shagger ordered gun support and an airstrike, followed by a body-removal team and troop insertion by chopper to enable the wooded hill to be held. He finished by giving the grid location, then cut the transmission and handed the microphone back to Red. 'Thirty minutes,' he said. 'If you drongos want a smoke or a brew-up, you can have it now. I'll get up on the rim of this monsoon drain and guide the aircraft in with the SARBE. Bring me a cuppa and a bar of chocolate, Red.'

'Will do,' Red said. He was already unpacking his stove from his bergen as Shagger unclipped his

SARBE beacon from his webbing and crawled up the sloping concrete side of the drain. After reaching the top, he remained on his belly while scanning the surrounding terrain with binoculars. He then surveyed the sky with his naked eye. Meanwhile, Red had set alight the hexamine blocks beneath his portable stove and was collecting a metal cup from each man. By now he had a cigarette between his lips, as had Jimbo, and both were puffing away with great pleasure. When the water had boiled, Red dropped a tea bag into each cup and poured on hot water. While the tea was brewing, each man, with the exception of Shagger, tucked into whatever cold, high-calorie rations took his fancy, which meant either chocolate or dried biscuits and cheese. Red handed up a mug of steaming tea to Shagger, followed by his requested bar of chocolate. All four men then settled back to wait for the gun bombardment, with Shagger eating his chocolate and sipping his tea while he scanned the western sky.

Exactly thirty minutes later, when all other Task Force teams had been ordered by radio to clear the area, the New Zealanders' battery of 105mm guns opened fire from Nui Dat. The distant thump-thump of the opening barrage was followed almost immediately by the ever louder whistling of the incoming shells, then the tree-covered hill to the west erupted in an inferno of soaring flames, billowing black smoke, and a rain of soil, stones, burning branches and shredded, smouldering foliage. This hellish devastation continued for what seemed like an eternity, though in fact it was only fifteen minutes. By the time it ended the summit of the hill – or what could be seen of it through the slowly spiralling smoke – was denuded of trees and seemed no more than a smouldering black crater.

When the smoke cleared there were in fact still trees left on the summit, though they were charred as black as the hilltop and completely stripped of branches. By contrast, the lower slopes were still dense with trees, and undoubtedly more VC were lurking there, either above or below ground. For this reason, the 105mm bombardment was followed by six USAF Phantom Jet F-4Cs which, guided in by Shagger's beacon, barrelled down from the sky to release a salvo of rockets. The exploding napalm formed vivid balls of fire that appeared to roll down the hill like boiling lava under billowing black smoke. The remaining trees burst into flames and these in turn torched more trees until the whole hill, beneath its charred summit, was a fearsome, dazzling furnace that resembled an overflowing volcano.

When the American jet fighters had departed, the flames burned for two more hours, covering the hills with a dreadful pall of oily black smoke. Eventually, when the smoke cleared away, the lower hill had been stripped of foliage and the remaining trees, bare of branches and charred black, were still smouldering.

Shortly afterwards, eight RAAF Iroquois helicopters emerged from the north and descended over the cratered summit of the hill, their noisy rotors whipping up great clouds of soil and black dust. Dangling on ropes below one of the choppers was a D6 bulldozer. Released before the other helicopters had landed, the bulldozer drifted down on eight parachutes and landed softly on one side of the devastated summit. The other choppers then landed one by one, great slugs in the swirling black dust, and disgorged the 6th Battalion troops who would arrange for the burial of the VC dead and then take over the hill, turning it into a forward operating base and defensive position that would give an invaluable view of the lowlands around it.

Even as Shagger and the other three SAS men clambered to their feet and prepared to march off, the bulldozer had begun the job of pushing up tons of scorched soil and the dead that littered it, to create a mass grave. By the time the SAS four-man team had scrambled out of the monsoon drain and continued their march south, the cratered hill, though still covered with what looked like coal dust, was a hive of activity, the many Australian soldiers resembling ghosts in the murk.

It was a vision from some terrible dream.

8

The smouldering hill had scarcely dropped out of sight when Red received a message from Team 2's PC, Sergeant Don Ingrams, informing him that he and his men were a mile further north-east and had just come up against a VC platoon ensconced in a camouflaged bunker complex. They needed urgent help. Ingrams had already called for air support and more men, but he was told that no fighters or helicopters would be available for at least another hour – ironically, many had been used to assist Team 1 at the hill they had just taken – and he needed Team 1 to help him out immediately. Ingrams gave Red the grid reference, warned him to watch out for minefields and booby-traps, then rang off even before saying, 'Over and out.'

'He must be pinned down,' Red suggested, replacing the radio's microphone on its hook. 'He sounded pretty desperate.'

'Let's get going,' Shagger said.

The first part of the march took them across the

open paddy-field, where they all felt particularly exposed. They marched in the usual single file, but spaced even farther apart than usual. Dead-eye, on point, advanced with extreme caution, keeping his SLR at the ready and carefully scanning the ground for the smallest sign of a booby-trap or mine. This task was rendered even more nerve-racking by the fact that the soft soil of the paddy-field was covered by shallow, muddy water that obscured what lay on the bottom. Also, the paddy-field was devoid of trees or any other kind of shelter, which meant they could only fall belly down should the VC open fire.

Troubled by this risk, after about thirty minutes of laborious wading Shagger momentarily stopped the advance and used the radio to call in a RAAF surveillance helicopter. Waiting for the chopper to arrive, the men were forced to kneel in the shallow water, each facing a point of the compass and each straining to see any unusual movement other than the gentle undulations of the tall grass blown by a warm wind. As usual, that warm wind provided scant relief from the humidity, which made them break out in sweat; nor were they spared the attentions of countless frantic insects.

'I can take anything but these fuckers,' Red informed the others, swotting desperately at the cloud of mosquitoes whining about his face. 'The

VC, their booby-traps, their bloody tunnels – anything but these bastards.'

'They don't bother me,' replied Jimbo, merely shaking his head to rid himself of the insects biting at him. 'But then I'm in the *British* SAS. I'm not a ball-and-chain migrant.'

'I'm no bloody immigrant,' Red snapped. 'I was born and raised in Australia, mate, and don't you forget it.'

'How can I forget it,' Jimbo retorted, 'when you talk like that?'

'Don't give me that kind of snobbery, you Pommie ponce. At least I speak. You just vomit . . .'

'Shut up, you pair of drongos,' Shagger broke in. 'I think I just heard the chopper.'

He was right. After what had seemed like an interminable ten minutes, when their legs had started aching from the strain of kneeling in shallow water, an RAAF Iroquois, converted to a gunship, appeared on the horizon, flying at low level across paddy-fields and jungle, clearly searching for Charlie as it approached. Framed by drifting clouds streaked with sunlight, it hovered above them, whipping up a wind, while Shagger transmitted the team's position with his SARBE. When the pilot dropped even lower to eyeball Shagger's position, the gunner sitting behind one of the heavy machine-guns waved at the team, letting them know he had seen them. The chopper ascended vertically to about 300 feet, hovered for a few seconds, then flew north-east at low level, reconnoitring the paddy-field ahead of the men on the ground.

Though the field looked absolutely empty, the pilot had obviously seen something below him, since he suddenly slowed down, circled back, then ascended low enough for the wind created by the rotors to violently whip the tall grass and bamboo stalks.

Suddenly bursts of AK47 automatic rifle fire were unleashed from the paddy-field, clearly aimed upward at the chopper, which ascended rapidly, vertically, with its heavy machine-guns roaring into action, returning the gunfire coming from the VC position directly below it.

'Charlie straight ahead!' Shagger bawled, jabbing his finger towards the VC ambush position.

Even as Shagger was shouting, the roar of a Soviet 7.6 mm RPD light machine-gun started up from the ambush position and a fusillade of bullets caused spitting water and mud to race in a snaking line towards the SAS team. Already scattering, the four men threw themselves to the watery ground and rolled away even farther as the line of bullets stitched its way between them and raced on. As the men rolled on to their bellies and took aim, they saw a black-clad guerrilla rising to his knees and squinting along the sights of the RPG7 rocket-propelled grenade launcher resting on his shoulder.

'*Grenade!*' Jimbo bawled.

Smoke belched from the rear of the Soviet-made grenade launcher, the rocket shot out on spitting flame and smoke, and the guerrilla was still recoiling from the backblast when the missile, completing its high arc, screeched down to explode with a deafening roar mere yards from the SAS men, tearing up the earth and showering them with soil and water.

Even as Shagger, Red and Jimbo were either slapping their ears to get their hearing back or wiping soil from their eyes, Dead-eye was rising to his knees, taking aim with his SLR, and firing a brief, savage burst that first made the earth spit and swirl around the VC, then threw him into convulsions and finally punched him back into the tall grass, with the grenade launcher spilling from his hands. Another guerrilla was crawling forward to pick up the grenade launcher when the RAAF helicopter descended to rake the VC position with a lethal combination of rockets and heavy machine-guns.

'*Advance!*' Shagger bawled.

The machine-guns of the Iroquois were pouring a hail of bullets into the mushrooming soil and smoke created by the helicopter's rockets when the other three SAS troopers jumped to their feet and ran forward at the crouch, spreading out in a broad arc that would enable them to encircle the ambush position ahead. Still in touch with the RAAF helicopter by means of his SARBE, Shagger learnt, just before the chopper ascended again out of range of the VC guns, that though the main ambush party had been decimated, one soldier had managed to get his hands on the grenade launcher and the few other VC were still in command of their RPD light machine-gun.

'We'll handle it,' Shagger said.

Using a hand signal, he indicated that the others should spread out and continue their advance on the area now clearly marked by burning brush and swirling clouds of smoke. The men did so, crouching low and moving slowly, keeping their eyes peeled for mines and booby-traps. This made their progress agonizingly slow.

Nevertheless, the smoke from the burning brush continued spiralling up ahead and eventually they found themselves entering that grey haze. Just before the haze thickened, Shagger used more hand signals to silently indicate that the men were to split up and operate as individuals until contact with the enemy had been made. Each man signalled back that he understood, then they spread out again and began their stealthy encirclement of the ambush position, from which not a sound could be heard.

It was eerie in the smoke. Because the wind had dropped, the smoke was both drifting and clearing very slowly. The ambush position had been located at the far edge of the paddy-field, close to the next stretch of jungle, where the VC bunker complex was dug in, and the stooped palm leaves and branches of the trees could be discerned slightly beyond the smoke, sometimes moving almost imperceptibly, like ghosts in a mist.

This was all the more disconcerting in that the smoke made it difficult to determine the difference between shapes created by the jungle foliage beyond the smoke and what may have been human figures trying to stay as still as possible in the ambush position at the edge of the paddy-field.

Now isolated from one another, advancing through the dense smoke, desperately trying to make no noise that would disturb the unnatural silence, each of the four SAS men had his personal moment of doubt, realizing that each second might be his last.

Though still concentrating hard on what he was doing, Shagger couldn't help thinking briefly of his wife and two children back in Woodvale, Western Australia, where they lived in a bungalow in a neat green suburb. His recollection of his home was unexpected and vivid, rushing into his head with memories of barbecues in the back garden, cycling with the kids, trips to the sea and the waterfront of Swanbourne, where Shagger kept a small boat for family trips into the Indian Ocean. All of that could end very soon if Charlie opened fire first.

The recollection of barbecues on long summer evenings had almost certainly been conjured up by the smell of the smoke through which Shagger was now so carefully making his way. When he realized that his thoughts were wandering, he jerked himself back to the present, focusing even more intently on what was happening around him.

Had something just moved up ahead?

Red, on the other hand, had no family to be concerned with, other than an ailing mother in Chatswood, Sydney, whom he tried to think about as little as possible because she was such a headache to him. But now she came back to his thoughts, as he felt himself tensing, waiting for the sudden roar of an AK47 and the bullet that would strike him down for good.

Red had been only twelve when his father had died. His main recollection of his life with his mother since then was of her being constantly ill and him looking after her. He'd had to do everything: clean the house, do the washing, go shopping, cook for her, feed her, make her bed, deal with her bedpan and sometimes, when she was particularly ill, bathe her. To make matters worse, she was cranky, endlessly demanding, and showed little appreciation of his efforts. By the time Red was eighteen he hated his mother with passion; not least because he had come to see clearly that looking after her had deprived him of a private life. In truth, he had joined the army just to get away from her, leaving her in the care of the social services. Then, once signed up, he had made up for all he had lost, boozing with his mates and screwing around while avoiding truly close relationships with women – until he had met Mildred. Red had only wanted his freedom.

Now, as he advanced at the crouch through the smoke, his weapon at the ready, he had a brief vision of his mother ill in bed, purple-faced, nagging him, and he found himself wondering, with a certain satisfaction, what she would do if he copped it from a VC bullet within the next few minutes.

He was brought abruptly back to reality when he saw something moving ahead . . .

Also advancing stealthily through the smoke, looking out simultaneously for mines, booby-traps and VC hiding at ground level, Jimbo found himself thinking that if he died in this action it would be particularly ironic. For this was, he had suddenly remembered, his penultimate operation in the field. After three decades of active service in North Africa, Europe, Oman, Malaya, Borneo, Aden and now here, age was taking its toll and his time was fast running out. Indeed, just before coming here he had been informed by Lieutenant-Colonel Callaghan that if he survived this tour in Vietnam he would be sent back to Aden and the Radfan for his final campaign – indeed, the final British campaign in that country. After that, he would be transferred to a teaching job in the Training Wing at Hereford.

Jimbo found it hard to believe that he was now that old, but the fact had to be faced. Yet even as he accepted it, he realized that he couldn't bear the thought of a teaching job, always being stuck in Hereford, and that he wanted to keep fighting for ever. Copping a bullet in the next minute or two might not be a bad thing, he decided. Go out with a bang, mate.

Then something or someone moved up ahead. A shadowy form in the still dense, drifting smoke, rising up from the ground.

Jimbo brought his SLR down from the cross position and raised it to take aim . . .

Dead-eye, being a lot younger than Jimbo, but still widely experienced and a born killing machine, was the one man in the team who had no thought for anything other than the instant. Concentrating like an animal only on what could be seen and heard in the dense smoke – including the ground, where booby-traps might be waiting to spike his foot or blow his legs off – all his senses were narrowly focused and ready to respond to any situation.

It was therefore probably no accident that in the instant the others either sensed or saw something ahead, Dead-eye was the first to realize that the almost imperceptible movement of a shadowy form in the smoke was not the trembling of a palm leaf or branch in the breeze, but the stealthy movement of an undernourished human being slowly standing upright.

No, that wasn't a shivering palm leaf or branch – it was a weapon, some kind of rifle, being lowered and aimed.

'*VC!*' Dead-eye bawled and then fired his SLR, raking the area straight ahead.

A Russian RPD light machine-gun roared in response.

Dead-eye was on the ground, on his belly, when the hail of bullets whistled and whined through the air. As the enemy machine-gun continued roaring, he saw a tiny yellow-blue flame in the murk, spitting out smoke that was blacker than the smoke still rising from the smouldering bamboo and grass. Glancing back over his shoulder, he saw that the other three had also gone to ground and were slithering backwards into a hollow that promised some protection. Once there, they began setting up the tripod for the GPMG.

Hoping to draw the VC fire and keep them distracted, Dead-eye opened up again with his SLR, firing at the slightest sign of movement.

Someone screamed in the murk, but his cry of pain was followed by the unmistakable thudding sound of the grenade launcher.

The ground erupted near Dead-eye, temporarily deafening him with its roaring, pummelling him with the blast, and showering him with loose soil, stones, bamboo and smouldering grass.

Shaking his head from side to side, trying to clear it of ringing sounds, he glanced ahead and saw the shadowy form of a man with something long and thin balanced on his shoulder – the RPG7. Dead-eye took aim and fired. The man screamed and convulsed, then dropped his weapon as he was punched to the ground and disappeared in smoke.

The GPMG roared into action behind Dead-eye as Jimbo raked the VC position with a savage, sustained burst. The instant he saw that chaos of spitting soil, stones, bamboo and shredded leaves around the shadowy forms of the VC in the smoke, Dead-eye was up and running, firing his SLR from the hip.

Within seconds Shagger and Red had done the same, racing out in opposite directions and circling around to come back in on the VC position from opposite sides, forming a triangular pincer movement with Dead-eye, who was coming up from the front. Imagining that they were surrounded by a superior force, the VC panicked and started turning every which way, firing blindly through the swirling smoke.

Just before reaching the lip of the VC hide, Dead-eye lobbed a hand grenade that fell between the man trying to adjust the elevation of the grenade launcher and the RPD light machine-gun crew, who had clearly just seen the advancing Shagger and were swinging the barrel of their weapon towards him. The explosion tore the VC position to shreds, obscuring them in smoke, and its roaring was followed by the dreadful cries of those still alive. Darting up on to the rim of the hide while the debris from the blast was still raining down, Dead-eye fired a series of short, precise bursts down into the position, at anyone he saw moving. Within seconds, Shagger and Red were doing the same, taking no chances, turning the smoky hide into a nightmare of spitting soil and stones, writhing limbs, screams, entreaties and dying moans. They stopped firing before their magazines were empty, then looked down at their handiwork.

'We got them all,' Dead-eye said with satisfaction, staring into that smoky hell. 'Not even a wounded man left. Not a twitch down there.'

'Bloody hell,' Red whispered, amazed at Dead-eye's icy remove and realizing, at last, that he wasn't dealing with a pair of soft Brits, but with at least one truly hard man and another, less cold but still tough and fearless.

Glancing at Shagger, he saw that he too was glancing from the dead men in the smouldering hide to Dead-eye, obviously thinking the same. Finally, letting his breath out in what sounded like a sigh, Shagger asked, 'Is the radio back there with Jimbo?'

'Yeah,' Red said. 'As he was manning the GPMG, I left the radio with him.'

'OK. Let's go back and join him,' Shagger said and turned to Dead-eye. 'I'm going to call HQ and ask for men to take over this hide. While I'm doing that, you check the area between here and the edge of that jungle.'

'Can do,' Dead-eye said. He strode off and melted into the thinning smoke, heading in the direction of the jungle where Team 2 were presently engaged in conflict with a VC bunker complex. Even before he had disappeared, Shagger had set off in the opposite direction to rejoin Jimbo. Knowing that the battle for the VC hide had ended, Jimbo was already dismantling the GPMG and tripod, in preparation for the march into the jungle in support of Team 2.

Kneeling beside him, Red switched on the radio, contacted HQ, then passed the microphone to Shagger, who asked for the usual burial detail and enough replacements to turn the captured VC hide into an OP and defensive position.

No sooner had Shagger handed the microphone back to Red than the latter received an incoming message from Ingrams, asking when Team 1 could be expected and sounding more desperate.

'We'll have to wait here for the replacements to arrive,' Shagger replied dispassionately, 'but we should be there in half an hour. You surrounded?'

'No. It's just that we can't get past them. There's what seems like a whole platoon of the bastards, dug into an extensive bunker complex. We can hardly lift our faces out of the dirt; we're well and truly pinned down. We urgently need your support.'

'Keep your faces in the dirt,' Shagger recommended laconically, 'and we'll be along as soon as possible.'

'Fair enough,' Ingrams said, sounding relieved. 'Over and out.'

Shagger cut the transmission and handed the receiver back to Red. Having just finished dismantling the GPMG, Jimbo glanced about him, wanting to know what was happening. 'Where's Dead-eye?' he asked.

Shagger jerked his thumb back over his shoulder. 'Checking that there are no more VC between here and the jungle.'

'If there are, God help them,' Jimbo replied.

'Too right. That's some animal.'

'He's no animal,' Jimbo told him. 'He's just a damn good soldier. He's been through things you couldn't even imagine, mate, that's why he's so quiet. He doesn't show his emotions.'

'What couldn't I imagine?' Shagger asked him.

'The Telok Anson swamp in Malaya,' Jimbo replied. 'That's something you couldn't imagine unless you've been through it.'

'When you've been in a tunnel complex,' Red butted in, 'you can imagine anything. You'll find that out soon enough.'

'It's that bad, eh?'

'It's that bad.'

'I'm having nightmares already.'

Saying no more, the three men sat there and waited for the helicopter to arrive from Vung Tau with the replacements. While they were waiting, Dead-eye returned from the edge of the paddy-field, clearly visible now that the smoke had cleared, and reported that there were no more VC between the hide and the edge of the jungle.

'Did you go into the jungle itself?' Shagger asked him.

'Yes. Just a few hundred yards. Far enough to hear the sounds of battle about a mile farther on.'

'Shouldn't take long to get to them,' Red said.

'It might take a lot longer than you expect,' Dead-eye told him. 'It turns into secondary jungle about a hundred yards in – and that's going to be hell to get through.'

Dead-eye was right, for land once cleared, then not used and allowed to revert to its original state, grows back even thicker and more tangled than it was before. Ahead of them was a dense sea of thorn, bracken, bamboo and tall grass with sharp blades.

Minutes later a USAF CH-47 Chinook helicopter appeared in the afternoon's grey sky, coming from the direction of Vung Tau. As it dropped vertically, its twin rotors created a whirlwind that sucked up water, pebbles and foliage, but its large, low-pressure tyres enabled it to land in the paddy-field without sinking into it. The ramp in the rear of its watertight fuselage was already open when it landed, so even before the rotors had stopped spinning, two-man teams bearing stretchers between them hurried out to pick up the dead VC soldiers. As they were rolling the bullet-riddled, bloody bodies on to stretchers, to be flown in the Chinook to a mass burial ground near Vung Tau, more members of the Australian 5th Battalion poured out, all heavily armed and humping pallets filled with equipment, to take up positions around the VC hide and begin the construction of what would be a long-term OP with defensive gun positions.

As the new arrivals toiled away, the Chinook roared back into life, its rotors whipping up another whirlwind that battered at them viciously. The helicopter ascended vertically, hovered about fifty feet above the ground, then headed back towards Vung Tau.

'Let's go and join Team 2,' Shagger said, 'and check out those bunkers.'

The four men wearily picked themselves up, splashed through the last fifty yards of the paddy-field, and entered the jungle in single file, then merged with the shadows and disappeared.

9

The first hundred yards or so were relatively easy, with the ground firm underfoot, the temperature lower because of the lack of sunlight, the foliage fairly light and the trees spaced well apart. Though still advancing at the crouch, weapons at the ready, and keeping their eyes peeled for booby-traps, the men were able to zigzag their way forward with little trouble.

But then, as Dead-eye had warned them, they came abruptly into secondary jungle, where the trees were much closer together and the undergrowth was an impenetrable tangle of thorny branches, gigantic, razor-sharp palm leaves, interwoven rattan, tall grass with vicious edges, and densely packed bamboo. Much of the overhanging foliage was covered in cobwebs that contained poisonous spiders and, as the men were uneasily aware, various kind of snake – some venomous, others not – were inclined to sleep curled around the branches and looked very much like them.

They could now hear the sounds of battle from up ahead, where the advance of Team 2 had been blocked by the VC bunker complex. That mile, they feared, would take several hours to traverse.

'We don't have any choice,' Dead-eye said. 'We'll have to hack our way through with the machetes, and look out for booby-traps at the same time, so it won't be easy.'

'One man at a time,' Shagger suggested. 'One man takes the lead and cuts his way through with his machete while the others follow, giving him cover should the need arise. We all take turns with the machete, fifteen minutes each. I don't think any of us could stick it for longer than that at one stretch. What do you think?'

Dead-eye and Jimbo nodded.

'I agree,' Red said.

'Since it's my bright idea,' Shagger said generously, 'I'll be the first to go out front.'

'Good on you,' Red said sardonically.

Shagger slung his assault rifle over his shoulder then untied the machete from his belt. Without another word, he stepped out ahead of the others and began hacking his way through the dense, tangled undergrowth. The other men fell back into single file behind him, spaced well apart, scanning the jungle to the front and both sides. As Tail-end Charlie, Jimbo also had to turn round repeatedly to cover their rear, though he knew it was unlikely that any VC would now come from that direction.

Progress was painfully slow. After chopping through the undergrowth with his machete, Shagger often had to tear the shredded foliage away with his bare hands, or push it to the side, in order to create a passage. Each blow of the machete would cause dust to rise in clouds from the branches and leaves, which would themselves shake violently, causing gigantic, sharp-edged palm leaves to whip into Shagger's face. Within minutes he was dripping with sweat, covered in bloody scratches, and being attacked by frenzied mosquitoes and midges. What slowed him down even more were the spiders and other insects that frequently fell on to him from the overhanging branches, making him stop to frantically slap them off his head, shoulders and arms. By the end of his first fifteen minutes he was exhausted and gratefully swapped places with Dead-eye.

Though one of the toughest men in 22 SAS, Dead-eye, like Shagger, was exhausted and soaked in his own sweat by the time his stint was over. He then swapped places with Red, who endured his quarter of an hour of hell, then swapped places with Jimbo. Fifteen minutes later, at the end of the first hour, it was Shagger's turn again. By that time they had only managed to cover less than a quarter of a mile.

As Shagger unslung the SLR from his shoulder

and prepared to attack the undergrowth once again, Jimbo nodded back over his shoulder.

'The gunfire certainly seems a lot closer,' he said, trying to sound as encouraging as he could.

'Bloody oath,' Shagger replied, then started hacking furiously with the machete as Jimbo headed back to the end of the line.

Again, Shagger had to suffer the hell of sweat, choking dust, noisy, bloodthirsty insects, rebounding branches and spiders and other creepy-crawlies dropping on to his head, shoulders and arms. Once he sprang back instinctively, cursing, when a startled snake hissed at him. He steadied himself, then lunged and chopped off its head. When the two pieces of the snake had fallen off the branch to the ground, he watched in amazement as the tongue of the severed head kept darting in and out and the rest of the body wriggled into the undergrowth, leaving a trail of blood and only stopping when the blood had drained out of it completely.

Shuddering, Shagger went back to work, slashing his way forward for another five minutes, until stopped suddenly by a warning cry from Dead-eye.

'Freeze!'

Shagger froze like a statue in the act of swinging the machete, and remained in that pose for several seconds, hardly breathing, sweat pouring down his face, before finally croaking: 'What . . . ?'

'Don't move anything but your head,' Dead-eye told him. 'Look down at your feet. Can you see something stretched across the ground, about ankle level?'

Shagger glanced gingerly down at the ground. 'No. Nothing. Just the undergrowth . . . No! There's something there. It looks like a camouflaged trip cord.'

'Is your leg touching it?'

'No. It's a couple of inches away from my shin, just above the ankle.'

'Anything at waist level?'

Shagger raised his gaze slightly, squinting into the foliage he had just been about to attack. 'Shit! A bow-shaped length of bamboo at waist level and covered in foliage. I can only see part of it.'

'OK,' Dead-eye said. 'Step away from it – slowly. Try not to shake anything. Take a couple of steps back, check that there's no trip cord right or left, then get well to the side of the area you've been trying to clear. Move very carefully now.'

Shagger blinked the sweat from his eyes, lowered the machete to his side, then very carefully took a couple of steps backward. When he was well away from the trip cord, he checked left and right, saw nothing, and stepped cautiously to his right. Without being told, Red and Jimbo did the same, taking up positions on either side of the passage hacked out by their team-mate. Finally Dead-eye did the same, positioning himself behind a tree and aiming down at the trip cord with his SLR. He switched to automatic and fired a sustained burst that sent leaves and soil leaping wildly in the air before tearing the trip cord to shreds.

Instantly, the length of bamboo was released and whipped forward with tremendous force, smashing noisily through the undergrowth and quivering like a bowstring when it reached its limit, with its vicious, razor-sharp spikes forming a line across the route at body level.

Those spikes would have impaled anyone in their path, leading to an excruciating death.

'Shit!' Jimbo whispered.

'Right through your cock and nuts,' Red said with a sly grin. 'You'd be singing a couple of octaves higher – and maybe sweating a little . . . Before bleeding to death, of course.'

'I've got to hand it to you,' Shagger said to Dead-eye. 'You've got the eyes of a hawk.'

'It's easier to see when you're not in the thick of it, swinging that machete.' Dead-eye raised his hand and studied his watch, then said dispassionately, 'You've still got five minutes to go, so get back to work, Sarge.'

'Fair enough,' Shagger said with a sigh, and then stepped carefully around the spiked length of bamboo and resumed his task as the others fell into single file behind him.

As the team's slow, back-breaking work continued, the outbreaks of gunfire from up ahead became louder, letting them know that they were at least making progress. Each of the four-man team had another stint of fifteen minutes with the machete, which took another hour and carried them beyond the half mile mark, or approximately halfway. Another reason why the going was so slow was that they had to stop frequently, either to enable chopped undergrowth to be dragged aside by hand or because of more booby-traps, including an angled-arrow trap. When Dead-eye had tripped the cord by blasting it apart with his SLR, the trap fired a steel arrow from a length of bamboo fixed to a piece of board covered with foliage. It was a deadly device.

Eventually, when they had covered about three-quarters of a mile, the secondary jungle gave way to normal jungle and the machete was no longer needed.

'Thank Christ for that,' Red whispered, wiping sweat from his forehead.

'Bit exhausting for you, was it?' Jimbo asked him.

'Bloody oath, mate.'

'Can you see *me* sweating?' Jimbo said, having already wiped his face dry with a cloth when Red wasn't looking. 'It's all down to good training.'

'Stop kidding yourself, mate. I can tell you're shagged by the sound of your breathing. I bet that handkerchief in your pocket's soaked with sweat. You must take me for a right fucking dill. Pah! Your training's no tougher than ours.'

Jimbo grinned and was about to retort when Shagger, who had been listening intently to the gunfire, turned back to them and used a hand signal to indicate that they should resume single file and press on. This they did, with Dead-eye again out on point and Jimbo bringing up the rear. The going was now much easier, though they still had to contend with the humidity, attacking insects and poisonous snakes, as well as remaining alert to the threat of mines or booby-traps.

After another half hour the noise of light machine-guns and AK47s was much louder, almost directly ahead, and being answered by Team 2's SLRs and single GPMG.

Even as they were advancing that last hundred yards, there was a particularly loud explosion, followed by a fountain of soil, uprooted foliage, leaves and billowing smoke.

'That was an 85mm missile,' Shagger said as he came up to stand beside Dead-eye, with the other two bunched up just behind them. 'Fired from a VC grenade launcher. Probably an RPG7V. Let's make sure we put *that* fucker out of action. Come on, cobbers, let's pick it up.'

The debris had stopped raining down and the smoke was drifting lazily when Shagger broke into a trot and the others followed suit, spreading out as they advanced and flitting from one tree to the other to avoid sniper fire. A few minutes later they arrived at what appeared to be a dried river-bed or gully, which Team 2 had taken over as a natural defensive position. The four of them were down there now. Just below the lip of the rise, Corporals Bob 'Blue' Butler and Michael 'Mad Mike' Dalton were manning the 7.72mm M60 GPMG, the former firing, the latter feeding the belt in. Sergeant Don Ingrams was kneeling beside the radio, bawling into the receiver while covering his left ear with his other hand to keep out the roaring of the guns. Beside him, but lying on his belly, Sergeant Giles Norton was methodically firing his combination 5.56mm M16A1 automatic rifle and M203 grenade launcher.

As Shagger and the others slid down into the river-bed, Norton fired a high-explosive round from his own M203. Dead-eye had already clambered up the other side of the gully and was peering over its lip when the round exploded with a harsh, bellowing sound, blowing enormous chunks of concrete off the bunker in the undergrowth two hundred yards away. When the smoke cleared, the bunker was still there, though great chunks of one corner had been blown off. It was a rectangular bunker with slit windows, through which the barrels of a machine-gun and other automatic weapons were poking out.

As if in retaliation for the grenade, the VC guns in the slit windows opened fire, turning the lip of the river-bed into a storm of spitting sand and flying stones which showered down on the men positioned on the slope.

'Shit!' Ingrams growled, wiping dirt from his eyes as he turned to face Shagger and Dead-eye. 'Good to see you, cobber.'

'You look knackered.'

'I am. We *all* are. Those bastards are well dug in and they're heavily armed.'

'You can stop shitting your pants now, mate,' Shagger said. 'We're here to give you support.'

'You won't be enough, but you'll do for now. I think we've got a whole regiment of VC out there, some in bunkers, others sniping at us from the jungle and constantly changing position. I've called for a couple of gunships to blow them to buggery, though we have to keep them occupied till the choppers get here. The airfield and village are a mile beyond that bunker complex, so no question: they have to be cleared. It's a fucking tough nut, though.'

'It won't break our teeth,' Shagger replied.

'Then let's do it,' Dead-eye said. 'How much space are they occupying over there?'

Ingrams indicated east and west with his left hand. 'The bunkers are spaced out to cover a front of about two hundred yards. Six bunkers evenly spread, but with more behind them, hidden by the trees. They also have what seems to be the rest of the regiment scattered through the trees, forming a protective cordon around the bunkers. Those bastards are the ones keeping us pinned down. They're the reason we can't encircle the bunkers. We have to remove them first.'

'No,' Shagger said. 'We have to deal with the bunkers first.' He checked his map, then looked up again. 'We'll call in Teams 5 and 9,' he said. 'They're patrolling right along this perimeter. They could all be here in thirty minutes, or an hour at most, to make up our strength. By that time the gunships should have been here to blow those bunkers to hell. When they've done that, our four teams combined can shoot their way through the complex, mopping up as we go.'

'That sounds rough to me,' Ingrams said.

'Bloody oath, it'll be rough,' Shagger replied, 'but it's all we can do. We have to take this place over by last light, then rest up and attack the village tomorrow. There's no other way.'

Shagger then called out to Red, 'Get on that radio and contact Teams 5 and 9. Give them this location and tell them to get here immediately. Remind them about the booby-traps and mines, but apart from those they're to make no detours. Tell them they were wanted here yesterday.'

'No problem, Sarge,' Red replied. 'Yesterday it is.'

'Bloody oath,' Shagger said. As Red fiddled with the radio, Shagger turned to Ingrams and asked, 'When you called up the gunships, did you . . . ?'

He was cut short when the GPMG operated by Blue and Mad Mike roared into action, sending a stream of purple tracer in a phosphorescent arc that sent bullets ricocheting off the partially concealed concrete bunkers. The tracer moved left and right to hit one bunker after the other, filling the air around them with flying pieces of concrete and cement and choking dust. The instant the GPMG fell silent, as Mad Mike was feeding in another belt of ammunition, the VC in the bunkers responded in kind, tearing the lip of the river-bed apart with a sustained, deafening burst from the RPD light machine-gun. This burst of fire was followed almost instantly by the muffled thudding sound of their grenade launcher. The missile exploded with a savage roaring near the gully, filling the air with boiling smoke and showering the men with soil and foliage.

'Bloody hell!' Shagger yelled, ducking low and shielding his eyes. He remained that way until the RPD had stopped firing, then straightened up again and continued the conversation he'd been having before with Ingrams. 'When you called up the gunships, did you also call up for replacements to take over that bunker complex?'

'Well, no, I . . .'

'Red! Shagger snapped, turning to his trust-worthy signaller. 'When you've finished with Teams 5 and 9, tell HQ we need a replacement detail – at least fifty men – to take over this bunker complex and hold it as a defensive position. We'll also need some APCs and a couple of Centurions. Got that?'

Red, who had earphones on and was speaking into the receiver, gave the thumbs up to indicate that he had understood the message to HQ.

'So,' Shagger said, turning to Dead-eye and Jimbo. 'Now we wait.'

'Can I smoke?' Jimbo asked.

'As Charlie obviously knows where we are, I don't see why not. Light up, cobber!'

Dead-eye didn't smoke, but Shagger, Jimbo and Red lit up and inhaled with pleasure as they awaited the arrival of the helicopter gunships. Sergeant Norton fired another missile from his combination 5.56mm M16A1 automatic rifle and M203 grenade launcher, then slid back down to the river-bed to enjoy a smoke with the others.

'Waste of my bloody time,' he told them. 'Might as well relax.' The GPMG roared into action above them, still being fired by Blue and Mad Mike.

'They fire at anything that moves,' Norton added, exhaling a thin stream of cigarette smoke. 'A pair of real enthusiasts.'

About thirty minutes later four helicopters appeared in the sky, coming from the direction of Vung Tau. Gradually they became recognizable as Cobra gunships armed with heavy machine-guns and rockets. Crawling back up to the lip of the gully, Shagger studied the VC bunkers, then guided the Cobra in with his SARBE. After clambering up beside him, Norton used his grenade launcher to drop a couple of coloured smoke bombs on to the enemy bunkers, clearly marking the target.

The VC had seen the helicopters as well and began firing from the bunkers with machine-guns and assault weapons. Ignoring this fusillade, the choppers descended one by one to attack the bunkers with simultaneous bursts of heavy machine-gun fire and rockets. The results were both spectacular and fearsome, with hundreds of bullets ricocheting noisily off the bunkers and the rockets exploding in silvery-yellow flames licking through vast clouds of black, oily smoke. The darting fingers of flame then set fire to the trees and turned the jungle immediately around the bunkers into an inferno.

As the trees blazed, black-shirted VC could be discerned running frantically to and fro, some of them on fire and screaming hideously. Instantly, the

SAS in the river-bed opened fire with their personal weapons and two GPMGs, picking off the guerrillas in the burning, smoking jungle.

Pinned down by the awesome might of the four Cobra gunships, the VC in the bunkers had stopped firing and could do little to retaliate as their positions were riddled by repeated bursts of heavy machine-gun fire, then systematically blown apart and scorched by the exploding rockets.

As this was going on, the eight men of Teams 5 and 9 emerged from the jungle behind and slipped down into the gully beside the others, their weapons clattering noisily as they settled in.

'Jesus!' Team 5's Sergeant Bloomfield said, glancing over the lip of the river-bed to where the bunkers were being blown apart by the gunships' rockets. 'That's some pounding they're getting.'

'They won't stop until all those bunkers have been smashed to hell,' Shagger informed him. 'That's the whole point.'

'Then we advance on the VC in the jungle?'

'You've hit the nail on the head, mate.'

By this time the four Cobras were hovering over the bunker complex, all firing their rockets and heavy machine-guns simultaneously, turning the area into a hell of flying concrete, pluming smoke, spiralling dust and blazing foliage. Behind and around the bunkers, the VC not in the bunkers were either running from the flames or firing up at the helicopters in futile gestures of defiance. Thus exposed, they were cut down by the SAS men in the gully, who picked them off with a combination of GPMGs and personal weapons.

The clash lasted for some twenty minutes, although it seemed much longer to all involved. When the Cobras ascended to return to Vung Tau, the remains of the bunkers could scarcely be discerned through dense clouds of smoke and dust. Some of the trees in the surrounding jungle were still burning, though most were charred and smouldering.

'Right,' Shagger said to the three PCs grouped around him, 'tell your men to move out and advance on the bunkers and the jungle surrounding them. Teams 1 and 2 will advance directly on the bunkers and clean them up. Team 5 will go round the left side of the bunker and advance into the jungle. Team 9 will do the same on the right side of the bunker. When Teams 1 and 2 have finished off those still alive in the bunker, they'll advance into the jungle. By that time the 6th Battalion replacements should have arrived to turn what's left of the bunker complex into one of our own defensive positions. OK, let's move out.'

When Shagger's instructions had been relayed to the rest of the men along the gully, they all clambered up the sloping side and began their cautious advance.

Immediately, sporadic rifle fire came from the

jungle on both sides of the bunkers, though none from the bunkers themselves. The SAS men ran from the cover of one tree to another, though they broke up into three separate teams, with two four-man teams, 5 and 9, moving around the side of the bunkers towards the burning jungle beyond and an eight-man team, composed of Teams 1 and 2, advancing right into the bunker complex. Once in the scorched, shattered remains of the sunken bunkers they were partially protected from sniper fire, though they had to make their way through the appalling tangle of scorched and broken bodies. Few of the VC were still alive and those few were in a bad way, scarcely able to move. In fact, there was not one man in the bunker in a condition to resist.

There was no threat left here, though the gunshots from the jungle on both sides of the bunker indicated that Teams 5 and 9 were engaging the enemy.

Even as the combined teams were examining the last of the bunkers, two USAF Chinooks from Nui Dat roared in over the complex, whipping up dust and the smoke from the smouldering trees. Guided in by a coloured smoke bomb put down by Jimbo, the helicopters settled on a path of cleared ground between the trees and the bunkers. The rear ramps were already down and while the rotors were still turning heavily armed soldiers of D Company, 6th

Battalion RAR/NZ hurried out and swarmed all over the bunker complex. The burial detail had already started collecting up the hideously burnt and broken VC dead for mass burial and the medics were carrying the VC wounded into the Chinooks as Shagger led Teams 1 and 2 away from the complex and into the jungle. There the other SAS men were engaged in close quarter battle (CQB) with the guerrillas who had survived the burning trees.

The fires had mostly gone out, but the trees were still smouldering and the jungle was filled with blinding, choking smoke. The CQB therefore became a cat-and-mouse game, with the SAS men advancing at the crouch, darting from one tree to the next, straining to see through the smoke, and firing at the black-shirted figures who suddenly leaned out from behind tree trunks or popped up from behind tangled undergrowth to fire their AK47s. It was like being in the Killing House in Hereford, except that the figures abruptly materializing in the smoke were not cardboard cut-outs with painted weapons, but flesh-and-blood men intent on revenge for the attack.

Realizing that the jungle was still thick with VC, the SAS men formed two-man teams, with one man giving covering fire to the other as he advanced, and vice versa. In this way they managed to advance slowly, and did so without taking any casualties.

Gradually they were reinforced by men from D Company, 6th Battalion, until nearly a hundred Australian and New Zealand troops were engaged in the CQB to clear the jungle that surrounded the bunkers and also led to the edge of the village that was to be their target the next day.

Four of them were killed and nearly a dozen were wounded before the last of the VC called it a day and came out from their hides with their hands raised. After being disarmed, they were blindfolded with 'sweat rags', bound with toggle ropes, and then marched at gunpoint back to the Chinooks, to be flown to the POW cage at Nui Dat.

By last light, when the trees had finally stopped smouldering and the smoke had cleared, the battle for the bunker complex had ended and the way was clear to make the assault on the VC-held airfield and village.

10

The light had gone completely when the Chinooks
which had taken the wounded Aussies and VC
back to Vung Tau returned one after another to
offload more equipment and vehicles, including
six armoured personnel carriers and two fifty-ton
Centurion Mark V tanks, which would be used in
the next day's advance against the VC stronghold.
They also dropped the two bulldozers requested
for the digging of a mass grave for the VC dead,
which would be done by simply shovelling up
the soil and corpses together, pushing them into
a great hole, and covering that hole up with earth.
The bulldozers were already doing this when a
second wave of Chinooks arrived with more men
and equipment.

The helicopters came down on an LZ located
close to the devastated bunker complex and illuminated with crude petrol flares. Whipped up by
the spinning rotors, the dust swirled violently across
the lights and bathed the men waiting below in a

flickering, strobe-like effect that made everyone feel unreal and disorientated. The helicopters kept coming and going until midnight, by which time the area was a hive of activity and the VC bunker complex was already well on the way to becoming a fortified defensive position for the Australians.

Lieutenant-Colonel Callaghan was one of those who walked down the ramp at the rear of the last Chinook. Crossing from the LZ to what had once been the VC stronghold, he was gratified to see that the construction of a circular FOB was already well under way, with one bulldozer interring a pile of VC corpses, a second clearing and flattening the ground for the eventual erection of tents to be used as headquarters, stores, armoury, communications, mess and a parking area for the APCs and tanks. Many of the other troops were already constructing sangars, placed equidistant in a circle to form a defensive ring around the camp. Eventually the sangars would become hedgehogs, bristling with machine-guns and other heavy weapons.

No one led Callaghan to the site selected for the HQ tent, but he recognized it instantly by the ranks of those gathered around it. Joining that group, he was introduced to Lieutenant-Colonel Ronald Fallow, CO of the replacement troops who would take over this captured site. After shaking hands, the two men cracked a couple of cans of beer and sat on wooden packing crates, facing each other over a third crate serving as a table. All around them, work on the construction of the camp was continuing in the pale light of the moon, under a vast, starry sky.

'A busy little place,' Callaghan said, nodding to indicate the many men still noisily working or raising pup tents in the moonlit darkness about him.

'Hard yacker,' Fallow said, meaning hard work, 'but they'll get it done on time.'

'By first light tomorrow.'

'Too right, Paddy. So here's to the mission.' They tapped their beer cans together then drank.

'You think you can hold this position?' Callaghan asked, lowering his can of beer.

'It's contained and will remain that way,' Fallow replied with confidence. 'Besides, all the VC have been cleared out from the base camp to here, so the only ones left are directly ahead, between here and the village. This camp won't be under threat of attack and we can only go one way – forward.'

'It promises to be one hell of a fight.'

'It will be,' Fallow said. 'But the SAS are going in first, so they'll take the brunt of it. A rough ride, I fear.'

'They'll manage,' Callaghan said.

'They're clearing the way for 5 and 6 Battalions?'

'Correct. Their job is to check for minefields, booby-traps and VC OPs or ambush positions and, if found, remove them. We'll be in constant touch with both battalions by radio and guide them in to the village.'

'Sounds sweet,' Fallow said. 'But there's an air-field by the village – that has to be taken care of first. And there's also a VC tunnel system right under the village.'

'I know. That's the last job to be done.'

'Hell on earth – or *under* the earth, to be more precise. Are you sending your men down?'

'Yes,' Callaghan said. 'My *only* two men.'

'They're going to have to be better than good,' Fallow told him, sounding grim. 'Those tunnel systems are a bloody nightmare.'

'So we've been told.'

'Have they ever been in a tunnel system before?'

'No, but they're going down with some experienced Aussie tunnel rats.'

'Shagger and Red.'

'That's the two.'

'Good men. You won't find much better.'

'So how are my two men getting on with the Aussies?' Callaghan asked.

'No problems that I know of, but you better ask them. Given the nature of Australians, there's bound to be a fair bit of bull, but I'm sure your men can give as good as they get.'

'We call it "bullshit", not "bull", and we can certainly dish it out.'

Fallow chuckled. 'I'll bet.' He drank some more beer, wiped his lips with the back of his hand, then glanced about him at the men working by moonlight and the eerie glow of spotlights as helicopters ascended and descended in billowing clouds of dust.

By now, just outside the main compound, the bloody, mangled VC dead had been bulldozed into an immense ditch and covered in soil and vegetation. Inside the compound, large and small tents had been erected. Stacks of wooden packing crates were being opened and their contents moved into the relevant tents. Where the ground had been flattened by bulldozers and men with hoes, 5th and 6th Battalion troops were digging shallow scrapes and defensive trenches or raising pup tents to be used as accommodation. In the stone-walled sangars, heavy machine-guns and twenty-five-pounders were being placed in position. The whole place was frantic.

'Impressive,' Callaghan said, suddenly filling up with a sense of loss, for this was almost certainly the last time he would serve overseas.

'Aussies work and play hard,' Fallow said. 'They've already got a bar over there, complete with juke-box, and the open-air movies will be running by tomorrow night. If they could open a brothel, they would, but they'll make do. And no matter how hung over they are tomorrow morning, they'll move out and fight like nobody's business. That's the Aussie way.'

'We Brits are a little more modest, but we're not far behind you.'

Fallow grinned and raised his glass in the air in a mocking toast. 'Better go and have a chat with your two men, so they won't feel so lonely. You'll find them in one of those pup tents, having their last night of rest. Early rise tomorrow.'

'For everyone,' Callaghan reminded him.

'That's the picture, Paddy.'

'Thanks,' Callaghan said. He finished off his beer, dropped the can into the rubbish bin beside Fallow's makeshift table, then stood up and walked across the compound to the row of tents. He had to be careful where he walked because the ground was now littered with opened crates, weapons, medical equipment, petrol cans, and boxes of food and drink, with men busily unpacking them and relaying their contents to the relevant tents. At the same time, helicopters continued to ascend and descend, making a hell of a din and whipping up the dust, while the Centurions and APCs were being tested, which added to the bedlam.

Eventually managing to wend his way through what appeared to be organized chaos, he reached the pup tents and followed the line until he came to two SAS-constructed lean-tos which were facing away from the wind. Dead-eye and Jimbo were in those, sitting side by side and checking their weapons.

'I don't think you'll need that Browning tomorrow,' Callaghan said. 'It'll be a straightforward rifle job.'

Both men glanced up, surprised to see their CO. They were sitting on their hollow-fill sleeping-bags, beside a rudimentary portable kitchen consisting of a hexamine stove, an aluminium mess tin, mugs and utensils; and a brew kit, including sachets of tea, powdered milk and sugar. Spread out on a rubber groundsheet were spare radio batteries, water bottles, extra ammunition, matches and flint; an emergency first-aid kit, signal flares, and various survival aids, such as compass, pencil torch and batteries; even surgical blades and butterfly sutures. Dead-eye smiled slightly, but Jimbo grinned in his customary broad, cocky manner.

'You know us, boss,' Jimbo said. 'Always prepared for any eventuality. Just doing our daily cleaning and check as we were taught back in Hereford.'

'I'm glad to see it,' Callaghan replied, kneeling on the ground between the two men. 'So where are your two Aussie mates?'

Dead-eye jerked his thumb toward a brightly lit tent from which rock 'n' roll was blaring. 'In the bar, having a few pints.'

'I'm surprised you're not with them. Loosen up a bit. Relax.'

'We will do,' Jimbo assured him, 'when these weapons are cleaned. So what's brought you here, boss?'

Callaghan shrugged. 'Just a visit. I wanted to see for myself what's happening here, and I must say it looks pretty impressive.'

'These Aussies know what they're doing,' Deadeye said. 'You've got to hand it to them.'

'So how are you getting on with them? Any problems?'

'Nope,' Jimbo said. 'They tend to be pretty sharp with their tongues, but otherwise they're OK. They don't seem to resent us any more and we get on just fine. I think we still have to prove ourselves in certain ways, but so far they seem pleased with us.'

'Good,' Callaghan said. 'What about Shagger and Red in particular? Do you get on with them?'

'Yes,' Jimbo said. 'They're no different from the others. They treat us the same way. They keep slinging the bullshit, but they get as good as they give and they're gradually coming round to accepting us as part of the team.'

'They'll be with you when you attack the airfield and village tomorrow?'

'Yep. Them and some other Aussie SAS teams.'

'Four-man patrols?'

'Mainly, though in certain situations we double up the teams for greater strike force.'

'But generally you're passing muster with them?' Callaghan asked.

'Generally speaking, yes.'

'The real test's still to come,' Dead-eye said. 'Down in the tunnel complex. Shagger and Red are really proud of their capabilities down there and are challenging us with it. If we go down there, and if we come up again in one piece, then we'll have won their respect.'

'And mine,' Callaghan said. He glanced around the busy base camp with what seemed like sadness.

'What are you thinking, boss?' Dead-eye asked him.

Callaghan sighed. 'My last active tour of duty, Dead-eye. After this, it's back to a boring desk job. Time certainly moves on.'

'You'll really miss it.'

'Yes.'

'You're not alone,' Jimbo said. 'My own time's running out and the next stop is the Training Wing. That isn't exactly a desk job, but it isn't active service either. It's the first step on the road to retirement and I can't bear to think about it.'

'You always were a bantam cock,' Callaghan told him. 'From the very earliest days in North Africa. You've been through a lot, Jimbo.'

'You survived even more, boss,' Jimbo replied. 'A legend in your own time.'

Callaghan flushed slightly. 'Now, now,' he said. 'Hopefully I'm old enough not to let that go to my head. But thanks for the thought.'

Then his face took on once more that distracted, rather sad look as he cast his gaze towards the LZs. There two Chinook helicopters were competing to see which could make the most noise and most dramatic dust storm as they descended side by side on to their respective landing pads. When they had touched down and were disgorging more troops, who emerged ghostlike from the billowing dust, Callaghan sighed again involuntarily, then picked up a fistful of dry soil and let it fall in a thin stream through his fingers.

'Oh, well,' he said softly.

Embarrassed himself now, Jimbo cleared his throat, then asked, 'Are you giving a briefing?'

'No. Lieutenant-Colonel Fallow is. At first light. The rest of the evening is free, gentlemen, so why not go and join the others? Enjoy yourselves.'

'Might just do that,' Jimbo said, completing the oiling of his SLR, which he slung over his shoulder just before Dead-eye did the same. 'Come on, Dead-eye, let's go.'

The three men stood together and Callaghan patted the shoulders of his two sergeants. 'Good luck,' he said, then walked off in the direction of Fallow's large tent, his spine as straight as a ramroad.

'The last of the best,' Dead-eye said.

'You're right,' Jimbo replied. 'Come on, let's go and get pissed.'

They crossed the compound to where the rock 'n' roll was pounding out from one of the larger tents. Stepping inside, they found the makeshift pub absolutely packed, with men sitting shoulder to shoulder on planks laid over beer barrels, resting elbows over beer glasses on other planks being used as tables. The jukebox was a flashing, brightly coloured Wurlitzer purchased from the Yanks. Smoke from numerous cigarettes filled the air and the conversation was loud.

Shagger and Red were sitting side by side on one of the benches, both ruddy and fairly drunk. Having earlier invited Dead-eye and Jimbo over for a drink, they had kept two spaces available on the bench directly facing them over the barrel-top table.

'It's the Poms!' Red said with a big grin, then indicated the places opposite him and Shagger. 'Have a seat, cobbers, and I'll fill up your glasses.'

When Dead-eye and Jimbo had squeezed themselves in, Shagger poured them a schooner of beer each from one of the many six-pint jugs on the table, then they all raised their glasses in a mock toast.

'To our poncey Pommy mates!' Shagger exclaimed.

'To our grog-happy Aussie no-hopers playing silly buggers,' Jimbo shot back.

Shagger laughed. 'Learning the language, I see,' he said. 'You'll soon be able to emigrate and communicate with the natives.

'I haven't been given my ball and chain yet,' Jimbo replied.

'Convicts are men of initiative who just got caught,' Red informed him. 'The criminal classes produce the real survivors, which is why we Aussies, with our ball-and-chain roots, are the bastards you just can't beat.'

'Bastards with big heads,' Dead-eye said. 'That's about as far as it goes, mate.'

'That's about as far as your sense of humour goes, more like,' said Shagger.

Dead-eye gave a wan smile. 'I've never seen much to joke about,' he said. 'It just doesn't come naturally, that's all.'

'I told you Dead-eye had seen some things in Malaya. You're not the same after experiences like that,' said Jimbo, anxious to defend his mate.

'So what happened there, cobber?' Red asked Dead-eye, who cast an angry glance at Jimbo and said in a monotone, 'Not much. Just the usual shit. I wouldn't . . .'

'Bullshit,' Jimbo interrupted. 'Sorry, Dead-eye. It must have been a fucking nightmare. Men spiked on punji stakes, crushed under spiked logs, heads chopped off with *parangs*, dead bodies floating in the swamps. Then on top of that, snakes, leeches, poisonous insects, vicious wild oxen and ravenous mosquitoes. And Dead-eye saw it all.'

'That's enough, Jimbo,' growled Dead-eye.

But Jimbo ignored his mate's plea and continued. 'In one instance, one of the men fell into a pit of punji stakes smeared with human shit as well as poison and had to be pulled off the fuckers. It was a nightmare . . .'

'Jimbo!' Dead-eye said threateningly.

'Another time,' Jimbo went on, oblivious, 'one of Dead-eye's best friends, Ralph Lorrimer, had his head chopped off by a commie bitch with a *parang*. Then, when his head fell on the ground, propped up on the severed neck and pumping blood, the eyes kept darting left and right, as if the poor bastard was desperately wondering what had happened to him. Dead-eye was there when it happened, which is why we nicknamed him . . .'

Very quietly, with wonderful economy of movement, Dead-eye leant sideways, grabbed the collar of Jimbo's tunic in his right fist and hauled him forward until they were eyeball to eyeball.

'I said that's enough!' Dead-eye whispered, his face icy with suppressed rage. 'And I mean it. I don't want to be reminded of that business, so let's change the subject.'

Choking, hardly able to speak, but brutally

reminded that Dead-eye had always refused to discuss the horrors of the Telok Anson swamp, Jimbo just nodded frantically until his friend released him. 'Sorry, Dead-eye,' he said. 'Forgot myself. Just running off at the mouth there. The drink went to my head.'

'OK,' Dead-eye said. He raised his glass to his lips, drained the remaining beer in one gulp, filled the glass again and then took another long pull at it. 'No problem.'

'What I want,' Red said, to calm the mood, 'is one night with my sheila.'

'Nice, is she?' Jimbo asked.

'Tits like cantaloups and built like a brick shithouse, that's my Mildred,' Red informed him.

'It's true love,' Shagger said. 'You can tell by the way he talks about her. Real romantic, Red is.'

'I was born in North Queensland,' Red explained. 'Not too much choice up there. You found someone who dropped her frilly knickers for you and you thought you were made. You put it in, you pulled it out, you wiped it dry and then you went to the altar and slipped on the gold ring. Jugs like cantaloups went a long way back home and they still do it for me.'

'The man's a poet,' Shagger said, trying to keep a straight face.

'I give her what she needs,' Red insisted, failing to see the joke. 'The old in-and-out. Two kids and another in the oven. And regular money. What more could a woman want?'

'You Aussies are so sensitive,' Jimbo said, 'I could cry in my beer.'

'I like a woman in her place,' Red informed him, 'which is flat on her back. What about you, Dead-eye?'

The question was not as casual as it sounded. In fact, Shagger and Red were both impressed by Dead-eye's calm, impassive nature and intrigued over what had made him that way. The truth was that Dead-eye had lost so many SAS friends in hideous circumstances that he no longer wanted the pain of any emotional involvement. The traumas he had suffering in and after the horrors of Telok Anson had scarred him for good, and in the end broke up his marriage. Dead-eye did not like to show his feelings and sex could make a man do that. For that reason, he never became romantically involved with women – he only used them for sexual relief – and he had found that life was easier that way.

'I don't want to discuss my private life,' he told Red.

Dead-eye was a man wrapped in total privacy and dedicated to soldiering. He was a fighting machine, a stone-cold killer, and not a man to mess with. A good man to have on your side when the going got tough.

Red, who was admiring though a little scared of Dead-eye, merely nodded, slugged down some more beer, then glanced about him. 'Right,' he murmured. 'No sweat, mate.'

'What's happening tomorrow?' Dead-eye asked. 'Anybody know yet?'

'The briefing's at first light,' Shagger told him, 'but I've already got the gist of it from the CO. The basic plan is for softening-up airstrikes throughout the night, covering the area between here and the airfield and village. We, the Aussie SAS – welcome aboard, Poms – will then advance by foot on the airfield, clearing out any VC we find on the way and radioing back info on minefields, booby-traps, sniper positions and anything else of strategic importance. When we reach the airfield, we recce it and decide whether or not we can take it alone. If we can, we call up 5th and 6th Battalions, then attack the target ourselves, clearing the way for them to take it over. But if we think it's too strongly defended, we wait for the two battalions to arrive and lend us support. Once the airfield's been taken, we all advance together on the village. And once the village is taken, we secure the ground with the help of both battalions, then us four will descend into the tunnel complex beneath the village and try clearing it out.'

'Sounds like an exciting day,' Dead-eye said.

'Let's drink to it,' Shagger said.

Just as they were touching glasses, five minutes after midnight, a familiar bass throbbing was heard from outside. Nearly all of the men in the smoky, noisy tent glanced up, then some of them left their tables to see what was happening.

Shagger, Red, Dead-eye and Jimbo followed them, stepping out from under the folding flaps of the tent into the cooler, fresher air outside. Gazing up at the night sky, they saw an enormous white moon surrounded by stars. As the throbbing grew louder, the silhouette of a giant Stratofortress crossed the moon, then a second, a third, and more, until they were many, all surrounded by a fleet of helicopter gunships. They crossed the pale moon, passed under the sea of stars, filled the sky directly above the base camp, deafening the men with their combined roaring. Shadowing the clouds, they flew on to the VC-held territory south of the camp, with each plane or helicopter crossing the moon being replaced by another.

'Jesus Christ!' Red whispered, awed by the sheer number of bombers and helicopter gunships.

Within minutes, the first explosions illuminated the distant sky as jagged patches of white and yellow, followed by crimson tipped with blue, then dazzling silver and gold. They looked like abstract paintings, but were in fact the colours of hell, and the flames and smoke – which is what the beautiful colours represented – were followed almost instantly by the distant whining and bellowing of rocket fire and explosions. Through the thickening smoke and multiplying colours, the silhouettes of the helicopters could be seen, ascending to low altitude, well below the Stratofortresses, to devastate the terrain with rockets and heavy machine-gun fire. Gradually, as if blood was seeping down out of the black, starry sky, the whole night took on a pale crimson hue streaked with yellow flames and billowing black smoke.

The bombers and gunships came and went, passing back and forth over the camp, engines roaring, jet engines whistling, props whipping up the air, making the clouds incandescent, blotting out whole swathes of stars, turning the night over the VC strongholds into spectacular webs of phosphorescent tracer, jagged sheets of flame, geysering sparks and tumbling smoke, until it looked as if the end of the world had come. It went on and on, for one hour, then two, and only at three in the morning did it finally cease. By then the land seemed to be on fire, with flames still flickering up in all directions as far as the eye could see, and the stars and the moon, which had formerly been so bright, obscured by the dense, drifting smoke.

Then, after what seemed like eternity, the last of the aircraft departed and a great silence descended.

'Four hours left for sleep,' Dead-eye said. 'I think we better get some.'

'Bloody oath!' Shagger agreed.

Slightly unsteady on their feet, the four men walked away from the still busy beer tent and then crawled into their separate lean-tos for a bit of shut-eye before the hell to come.

11

They left at first light, shortly after a hurried breakfast and the CO's briefing. Lieutenant-Colonel Fallow had told them little that they did not already know and most of them were glad when he finished and let them move out. Operating as a four-man advance party, Team 1 moved out an hour before 1 and 3 SAS.

The Englishmen were armed with 7.62mm L1A1 SLRs, the Aussies with 5.56mm M16A1 automatic rifles, and all four men had a 9mm L9A1 Browning semi-automatic pistol holstered on the hip, M26 high-explosive hand-grenades and ample spare ammunition.

As usual, Dead-eye was out on point, Shagger was second in line as PC, Red was behind him as signaller, heavily burdened with the radio, and Jimbo brought up the rear.

They were followed within minutes by Team 2, which had Ingrams as PC, with Blue and Mad Mike sharing the burden of the 7.62mm GPMG, and Norton, presently their Tail-end Charlie, armed with a combination 5.56mm M16A1 automatic rifle and M203 grenade launcher.

What they moved into, once they left the base camp, was a jungle landscape defoliated by the all-night air raids and bombardments from the twenty-five-pounders in Vung Tau. Normally the vegetation was a mixture of bamboo, head-high scrub and tall timber, but these had all been torn apart or scorched by the attacks and the blackened landscape was a scene of utter devastation.

At first the men advanced without trouble, using a standard operating procedure of ten minutes' movement, stop and listen for two or three minutes, ten minutes' movement, then finally a five-to-ten-minute break in all-round defence every hour. Eventually, however, as the temperature rose and the humidity increased, they approached the area devastated by the air raids and had to plough through swarms of fat, black flies that were buzzing noisily over the carcasses of the VC dead. These appeared to be as abundant as the flies, lying whole or in pieces – an arm here, a leg there, bloody intestines, exposed shattered bones – and were scattered broadly over the terrain, blending gruesomely into the charred and ravaged landscape.

It seemed inconceivable that anyone could have survived such carnage, but amazingly some had.

The evidence was to be found in the many abandoned gun-pits and trenches, where boot prints
were still visible in the scorched soil, heading
south-east towards the airfield and village.

'You've got to admire them,' Dead-eye said,
nodding at an abandoned gun-pit. 'Even in the
middle of that hellish bombing and bombardment,
they had the presence of mind to take everything
with them. They didn't leave us a bloody thing.'

'They're tough little buggers, all right,' Red
replied. 'They've all lived with this shit since childhood, practically being born and dying as soldiers.
They've got nothing else, mate.'

'Let's keep moving,' Shagger said.

Now that they were in open, defoliated country,
the two groups were advancing in the one, widely
spread diamond formation, allowing optimum fire-
power to be focused on the front, though it left
them more exposed in the smoky daylight. As
they neared the airfield outside the village, after
a two-mile hike, they came to the epicentre of
the bombing raid and were forced to wend their
way around enormous, charred bomb craters filled
with human remains and destroyed ordnance. Yet
even here, in this hideous devastation, the surviving
VC had managed to booby-trap weapons, pieces of
scorched, twisted equipment, and even the bodies
of their dead comrades.

With Dead-eye up ahead, and the members of

Team 2 covering both flanks, the men advanced at a snail's pace, stopping frequently to mark booby-traps for the sappers following to dismantle or defuse.

Amazingly, even before they reached the airfield, they were attacked by snipers who had survived the dreadful, night-long air raid. The first popped up from a camouflaged trapdoor in a shell hole filled with dead bodies. Not imagining for a second that even a VC could be fanatical enough to crawl back into that quagmire of scorched flesh and broken bones to dig himself a hide, the normally alert SAS men were caught completely off guard when the first short burst from a 7.62mm PPS43 sub-machine-gun shattered the silence.

Ingrams, out on the front of the left flank, took most of the burst. Shuddering violently, he was punched backwards and his rifle flew from his hands. Even as he was jerking epileptically on the ground amid spitting soil, dust and ash, those nearest to him flung themselves belly down and aimed a fusillade of bullets at the head and shoulders visible above the hole in the ground. The head exploded into a spray of blood and flying bone, and the weapon was dropped. Then the shoulders of the VC, supporting only the bloody stump of the neck, sank down into the hole and the trapdoor slammed back down over it.

Instantly, Dead-eye was up and running, weaving

erratically from left to right to avoid any other snipers, and soon he was at the hole. He raised the trapdoor and, without looking in, dropped in a hand-grenade, then threw himself backwards, well away from the imminent explosion.

As soil and smoke spewed upwards from the hole and rained back down over Dead-eye, the rest of the men raced forward, spread well apart, to check if any other guerrillas were in the vicinity.

There were.

All over this sea of black shell holes and scorched corpses, trapdoors was opening to allow snipers to pop up and unleash fire on the SAS men. Even worse, the savage roar of a 7.62mm RPD light machine-gun was suddenly added to the bedlam.

No sooner had Blue knelt beside his butchered sergeant, checking if he was still alive – he wasn't – than he was punched back by a hail of bullets from the machine-gun and slammed on to his back. Bleeding profusely from the belly, but still alive, he was groping for his automatic rifle as Dead-eye and Shagger, running side by side and clearly thinking alike, simultaneously threw a couple of hand-grenades towards where they could see the VC machine-gun winking, behind a natural barricade of upturned earth.

The grenades exploded at the same time with a mighty crash, sending loose soil spewing through clouds of smoke. Even before the smoke and dust had cleared, Shagger and Dead-eye were running towards the gun emplacement, Red was calling on the radio for the medics and reinforcements from 1 and 3 SAS Squadrons, the wounded Blue was crawling into the relative safety of a shell hole, leaving a trail of blood behind him, and the others were giving covering fire to Shagger and Dead-eye.

These two had reached the rim of the enemy gun position and were firing their automatic rifles into it without bothering to check that anyone was still alive. In fact, the gunner had been on his own and was now lying on his side beside his overturned machine-gun. Half of his jaw had been blown away and one hand had been mangled into a bloody mess. The flies were already swarming over him when Shagger and Dead-eye clambered up the other side of the trench, looked across a lunar landscape of shell holes, and saw more VC firing at them from holes in the ground, their heads and shoulders framed by raised trapdoors.

'We can't eliminate them on our own,' Dead-eye said.

'1 and 3 Squadrons are on their way,' Shagger answered.

'Even they'll get decimated,' Dead-eye said. 'We need the tanks to go ahead of us and take that lot out.'

'I agree,' Shagger said. Turning back, he used a

hand signal to indicate that Red should come up with the PRC 64. Red strapped the radio on to his back, picked up his automatic rifle, carefully studied the enemy positions, then jumped out of his shell hole and ran at the crouch, zigzagging from one shell hole to the next.

Instantly, the VC snipers opened fire, trying to hit him. They, in turn, received a barrage of fire from the combined weapons of the SAS men. Nevertheless, many of the guerrillas kept firing and bullets were still kicking up the soil around Red as he threw himself down beside Shagger and Dead-eye.

'Good enough for the Olympics,' Shagger said, grinning, to the breathless Red. 'You looked like you had a bee up the arse and were trying to fart it out.'

'Rather a bee up my arse than a bullet,' Red replied without rancour, unstrapping the radio.

At that moment another wave of semi-automatic fire came from the many VC hides, obviously aimed at somewhere behind the SAS men. Glancing back over their shoulders, they saw Jimbo zigzagging towards them, disappearing down into shell holes, then racing up and out again, desperately dodging the lines of soil and stones that whipped up on both sides of him. Miraculously, he managed to reach their position and threw himself down beside them, automatically tugging the peak of the slanting jungle hat from his eyes and gratefully gulping air into his lungs.

'Jesus Christ!' he gasped. 'Where did all those bastards come from? They must have stayed in those covered holes all night, through the air attacks and bombardments. Fucking unbelievable!'

'Right,' Red said. 'If they weren't completely deafened by the noise, they should have been driven crazy.'

'They don't seem very crazy to me,' Jimbo told him. 'Not the way they're firing those rifles. All those bastards are fighting fit.'

'Contact Callaghan,' Shagger told Red. 'Then give me the phone.' When Red had contacted the lieutenant-colonel and handed Shagger the phone, Shagger said, 'Sergeant Bannerman here, boss.'

'Yes, Sergeant. What's happening?'

'We're faced with a field filled with VC snipers in trapdoor hides. They've got us pinned down. To clear them out, we need those Centurions and reinforcements in APCs. We can't cross that field unprotected; it would just be a slaughter.'

'Tanks and APCs coming up immediately,' Callaghan confirmed. 'But I still need you men out front to recce the airfield. If you can't cross that field, can you go around it?'

Shagger studied the terrain ahead, then checked his map. 'Possibly,' he told Callaghan. 'We'll try and circle around it and close in on the airfield. If the tanks and APCs leave right now, they should arrive here just as we get to the other side.'

'Then advance on the airfield,' Callaghan said. 'Over and out.'

Handing the phone back to Red, Shagger picked up his M16A1 and said, 'OK, let's do it. Red, you stick with Dead-eye and me; I may need the radio again. We'll circle around to the south-west of the field. Jimbo, you join the remaining two men from Team 2 and circle around in the opposite direction. When we converge at the far side, we'll move in on the airfield together.'

'Right,' Jimbo said.

Suddenly the enemy snipers opened fire *en masse* and sent a hail of bullets whining over the heads of the four SAS men. Glancing back over their shoulders, they saw that an advance team from either 1 or 3 SAS Squadron, perhaps a mixture of both, was making its way between the shell holes, some of the men firing their personal weapons to give cover to the medical team carrying rolled-up stretchers. A smoke flare shot up from the shell hole where the badly wounded Blue had taken refuge, indicating that he was still alive and showing exactly where he was. Immediately, the medical team changed direction, zigzagging from one hole to another and gradually advancing on the one where the corporal lay. As they did so, the SAS men around them gave covering fire by jumping to their feet, firing a quick burst, then dropping behind what shelter they could find, all the time advancing slowly. To give them further support, Shagger and the others also opened fire on the enemy positions, pinning them down long enough for the SAS medical team to reach Blue's shell hole and roll down into it, beside him. The other SAS men followed suit, then crawled up to the lip of the hole to fire at the VC. At this point Shagger and his men stopped firing.

'Are you ready to go, Jimbo?' Dead-eye asked.

Jimbo glanced to his right and saw Norton and Mad Mike waving at him from a hole about thirty yards away. Turning back to Dead-eye, he nodded and jerked his thumb in the air.

'Right,' Dead-eye said. 'We'll give you covering fire. Get going the minute we open up.' He glanced at Shagger and received a curt nod.

'*Now!*' Shagger barked.

The three SAS men opened fire simultaneously, sending a hail of bullets into the VC positions, moving their weapons from left to right, up and down, to sweep across the whole target. Instantly, Jimbo jumped up and ran hell for leather towards Norton and Mad Mike, who had also opened fire to lend their support. Though many of the VC were forced to remain in their holes as bullets churned up the earth about them, the more foolhardy or courageous still threw their camouflaged trapdoors up and popped up to try to pick Jimbo off.

They almost succeeded. Bullets were stitching the ground ever nearer to Jimbo when he was only halfway through his run. Just before the spitting lines converged on the imagined track he was racing along, he threw himself down into the nearest shell hole. The guerrillas' bullets converged where he had been, turning the spot into a chaos of exploding soil and swirling dust as he rolled down to the bottom of the hole, scrambled up the other side and prepared to make the second half of the run.

The combined weapons of the SAS, including those of the men protecting the medical team, created a deafening bedlam as they poured a hail of bullets into the guerrillas. Many dropped out of sight, but others had their heads blown apart and the trapdoors shot to splinters before they, too, dropped down out of sight. Under that deadly covering fire, Jimbo jumped up and ran, crouching low and zigzagging again, this time making it all the way to Norton and Mad Mike without stopping. Soon he was lying belly down beside them.

'Nice one,' Mad Mike said with what seemed like a crazy leer. 'You ran like the wind, mate.'

'With good reason,' Jimbo replied.

'So what's the state of play?' Norton asked.

Jimbo jabbed his finger in the direction they were to take. 'We're going to circle around this lot and join up with Team 1 at the far side of the field, between the field and the airfield.'

'What about this bunch?' Norton asked, indicating the VC still popping up occasionally to take pot-shots at the SAS men. 'We just leave them to slaughter the men coming up after us?'

'No. That's been taken care of. The men directly behind us are staying put until the field is cleared by a couple of Centurions and some APCs. They'll only advance when that's done. By which time we should have reached the airfield and can guide them in there.'

'Fair enough,' Norton said. 'We go now?'

'Yeah,' Jimbo said. 'When I signal the others to give us covering fire, we get up and run. Once we get to the shelter of those trees at the side of the field, we should be OK.'

Norton scanned the line of badly burnt trees that ran alongside the devastated paddy-field. He nodded consent.

Jimbo used a hand signal to indicate that the other SAS men should open fire. The minute they did so, creating a dreadful racket, Jimbo and the two men from Team 2 jumped out and ran at the crouch, zigzagging towards the trees at the side of the field. VC bullets kicked up the earth all around them, but none of them was hit and soon they were crashing through what was left of the scorched undergrowth of the tree line, where they temporarily rested.

Seeing that they were safe, the rest of the SAS

men stopped firing and Shagger's team prepared to make a similar run in the opposite direction. Hearing the silence of the SAS guns, an occasional VC sniper would pop up and let off another shot, either at the SAS men in front or at the trees, sending the occasional bullet ricocheting off a tree trunk or scorched, leafless branch. However, Jimbo and the other two were well protected by the trees and, once they had got their breath back, were able to march on unmolested, circling around to the back of the field and the route that led to the airfield.

As Jimbo's team melted into the trees at the far side of the field, Shagger gave a hand signal and the SAS men protecting the medical team around Blue opened fire on the VC poking out of their hides, pinning enough of them down to enable Shagger and the others to jump up and race across the field as the bullets of the bolder guerrillas tore up the ground at their feet.

This time, however, a VC popped out of his hole, dragging the long stem of an RPG7V grenade launcher on to his shoulder. He managed to aim at the running men and fire just before a ferocious burst of SAS fire hammered into him, making him shudder dramatically, drop the grenade launcher and sink back into the hole as the raised trapdoor behind him disintegrated under the same hail of bullets. Simultaneously, the rocket-propelled grenade, leaving a stream of smoke behind it, exploded with a deafening roar just short of the running men. Almost bowled off their feet by the blast, they were then choked and temporarily blinded by the cloud of dust and gravel that swept over them. Burdened by his radio, Red staggered sideways and stopped, but immediately hurled himself forward again when a stream of bullets stitched a line towards him, almost clipping his boot heels.

Bursting out of the cloud of dust and fine gravel, the three men continued zigzagging until they reached the cover of the trees. Once there, they turned and circled the field in a north-easterly direction, well away from the VC hides, from where small arms could still be heard firing in a more sporadic manner. Eventually, after an uneventful ten minutes, they were able to turn right, now protected by another line of trees and the stunted remains of what had been a dense patch of jungle. Shagger called them to a halt with a hand signal, then drew them together for a whispered talk.

'It's not over yet,' he said. 'There could be more snipers or booby-traps in this stretch.'

'I doubt it,' Dead-eye replied, indicating the smashed, stunted, charred trees all around them. 'This bit of jungle has been practically flattened by the bombs and twenty-five-pounders. Our main problem is climbing over the fallen branches and foliage. There's an awful lot of it.'

That was true enough. The ground between

the destroyed trees was covered with mounds of smashed tree trunks, torn-off branches and burnt foliage, much of it little more than ash. When Red tentatively tapped some of this ash with the point of his boot, it rose up in a cloud.

'Bloody hell,' he said. 'We could choke to death getting through this shit.'

'We've got to do it,' Shagger said quietly. 'So come on, let's get going.'

They started their hike along the edge of the field, and immediately, as they clambered over the first pile of debris, the fine ash kicked up by their boots billowed all around them. As they continued to advance, it drifted around their faces, getting into their noses and lungs, making them choke and cough. But they had to keep going, scaling the mounds of debris, slipping and sliding down the other side, crossing a welcome stretch of relatively clear ground, then starting the whole process over again, all the while coughing and sneezing from the drifting ash.

They were halfway to the RV with Jimbo's team when they heard the pounding of heavy guns, followed instantly by the harsh chatter of machine-guns of various calibres. Glancing across the field, they saw two fifty-ton Centurion Mark Vs of the Australian 5th and 6th Battalions trundling towards the VC hides, each firing its single twenty-pounder gun, a .50-calibre Browning ranging machine-gun, and two .30-calibre Browning machine-guns while on the move.

When the first shells fell among the VC positions, the whole field appeared to erupt into flames and boiling smoke. Even so, some of the trapdoors remained open and the occupants of those hides continued recklessly to fire their weapons, though most of them were almost instantly shot to shreds by the Centurions' machine-guns.

By the time the tanks had reached the first of the hides, half a dozen M113A1 armoured personnel carriers, which looked similar to the tanks but lacked the high, revolving turret, came into view, following them into the field. The APCs had a crew of two, were capable of carrying up to eleven troops, and were also equipped with a .30-calibre and .50-calibre machine-gun combination mounted on the turret, as well as a 76mm machine-gun.

As the tanks rumbled over the hides, making the first of them cave in and crushing the occupants to death, other trapdoors flipped open and the black-clad snipers hurriedly scrambled out and tried to escape. This they did too late, however, for by the time they were out and running, the APCs had overtaken the Centurions and were spreading out to mow them down with their machine-guns. Those same weapons were also pumping a hail of bullets into every visible hide, whether opened or not, and turning the ground into a hell of swirling soil and dust.

Some of the VC desperately tried to roll hand-grenades under the steel treads of the tanks, but in most cases were shot down before they could do so, while some of them were blown up by their own grenades. Others tried to clamber up the rear of the tanks, but if they were not riddled by the machine-guns of the passing APCs, they lost their grip and fell off, to die screaming as they were crushed horribly under the treads.

Finally, when most of the visible VC were either dead or badly wounded, the men of 1 and 3 SAS Squadrons swarmed out of the APCs and began to check both the guerrillas on the ground and those in the remaining holes, to ensure that no survivors were still hidden down there. If they had the slightest reason to suspect that there were, they either fired their semi-automatic weapons down into the holes or dropped hand-grenades in and hared away.

This grim mopping-up procedure was still in progress as Shagger, Dead-eye and Red met Jimbo, Norton and Mad Mike at the RV.

'Christ,' Jimbo said, glancing back at that grim field of death. 'What an unholy slaughter!'

'Rather them than us,' Shagger said. 'Now let's get to that airfield.'

12

Even viewed from a distance of 500 yards through Shagger's binoculars, the VC airfield was clearly a makeshift affair hastily thrown up after they had captured the nearby village. The nominal perimeter was delineated by sandbagged gun emplacements manned by two-man teams armed with Chincom 57mm recoilless rifles, 7.62mm RPD light machine-guns and RPG7V rocket-propelled grenade launchers. But there was no fence of any kind – only barbed-wire entanglements spread along the ground – and the aircraft sat on a levelled field at the edge of the camp, which consisted of a thatched-roofed control tower raised on stilts, a similarly construc-ted water tower, and a wide variety of tents.

Fuel tankers were standing close by the aircraft, nearly a dozen troop trucks were parked near the tents, and dozens of VC soldiers, most wearing black fatigues, many armed with AK47s, were either resting by their tents, working at various tasks, or on guard outside the perimeter, between the gun emplacements. Beyond the airstrip, framed by the green of untouched jungle, lay the village, a cluster of concrete-and-tile houses inhabited by the Vietnamese who worked in the surrounding rubber plantations.

The SAS men were hiding behind a slight dip in the irrigated field that ran out to the edge of the airfield. Furrowed and muddy from recent heavy rain, the field contained many protective hollows, though most were filled with water.

'Judging by the number of trucks,' Shagger said, 'I'd say there were too many of them for us to take out alone.'

'I agree,' Dead-eye said. 'But we can still do a fair amount of damage – or at least harassment – with the help of 1 and 3 SAS, including those tanks and APCs, while the 5th and 6th Battalions are getting here. That way, we stand a chance of taking that village before last light.'

Shagger checked his watch. It was almost noon. 'I agree. Let's call up the SAS immediately and request that 5th and 6th Battalions be lifted in as soon as possible. Get HQ for me, Red.' When Red had given him the telephone, Shagger spoke to Callaghan, who agreed to order SAS reinforcements immediately and confirmed that he would contact HQ at Nui Dat and get 5th and 6th Battalions lifted out as soon as the helicopters could be prepared.

'Are you going to pave the way?' Callaghan asked.

'Yes, boss,' Shagger said.

'Good,' Callaghan said. 'Best of luck. Over and out.'

Handing the telephone back to Red, Shagger glanced across at the airfield and said, 'As 1 and 3 Squadrons are travelling in the APCs, they should make it here even quicker than we did. That means they should be here in about fifteen minutes. There's not much we can do until they get here except have a quick lunch – though it has to be cold. We don't want smoke from a brew-up. Not even cigarettes.'

The last comment drew exaggerated groans from the men gathered around Shagger.

'Shut up, you whinging drongos,' he said, 'and have something to eat while you can. Wash it down with cold water and be grateful to get it.'

'The way I feel, I'd be grateful to drink my own piss,' Jimbo said.

'Worked up a thirst, have you?' said Mad Mike.

'Throat's as dry as a camel's arse,' Jimbo informed him.

'Grew familiar in North Africa, did you?' Red asked. 'Got desperate out in the desert and explored forbidden territory, eh?'

'Up yours!' Jimbo exclaimed.

'We were talking about the camel's,' Mad Mike said.

'I never even rode a fucking camel. Couldn't stand the smell of them. Not my type at all, mate. Of course, the smell wouldn't have put you off. Your own smell would have smothered it.'

'I take a bath at least once a month, whether I need it or not,' Mad Mike said.

'Yeah,' Jimbo retorted. 'I've heard that the Aussie SAS demand a high standard of hygiene when they give each other their nightly blow-jobs.'

The Aussies burst out laughing, then Mad Mike placed his hand on Jimbo's shoulder and shook him affectionately. 'Good on you, mate.'

Each man had selected his own quick, dry lunch from his survival belt, which included enough food and equipment for two days. Their lunch consisted of high-calorie rations, including chocolate, dried biscuits and cheese, washed down with water from their bottles.

No sooner had they returned the remaining rations to their survival belts than the Centurions and APCs came into view over the crest of a slope and lumbered towards them. Instantly, the men around Shagger and Dead-eye checked their personal weapons, spread out along the incline, and prepared to follow the approaching vehicles into the airfield.

In fact, even before it had reached the men hidden

by the slight incline, the convoy was inevitably spotted by the VC and the dull pounding of three or four grenade launchers was heard as they were fired in quick succession. Within seconds, the smoke trails of four rocket-propelled grenades made languid arcs in the air and then looped down towards the tanks and APCs. Explosions tore up the ground between the vehicles, showering them with raining soil, but still they advanced. As more grenades started falling, the armoured vehicles were forced to weave wildly to make themselves more difficult targets, but eventually they reached the SAS team lying on the incline.

The captain of the leading tank, a 5th Battalion lieutenant, opened the turret to reveal himself from the shoulders up, and said to Shagger, 'We're going straight in, with the APCs behind us. I suggest you take cover behind them. When we reach the enemy forces in the airfield, your mates will dismount from the APCs and tackle the enemy forces on the ground while we blow the aircraft and transport to hell. Best of luck, lads.'

Just as the lieutenant dropped back down through the hatch, pulling the lid shut behind him, a series of grenades exploded short of the tanks and APCs, nearly deafening the men on the ground, pummelling them with the combined blasts, and raining soil and stones down on them. Hugging the earth, they watched as the steel treads of the armoured vehicles started turning, cutting deep grooves in the soil, until the vehicles were lurching away from the incline, towards the airfield – first the tanks, then the APCs. Once they were past, Shagger and the other men jumped to their feet and ran at the half crouch to take cover behind the latter.

As they were normally on their own, and usually well out in front of the main forces, this was an unusual position for the SAS to be in. But they stuck close to the rear of the advancing APCs as the enemy's grenades continued to explode all around them. These were followed immediately by the harsh chatter of their light machine-guns and recoilless rifles, which caused bullets to ricochet noisily off the vehicles.

Within seconds, however, when the tanks and APCs had spread well apart to form a long, well-spaced line, the tanks were returning the enemy fire with their twenty-pound guns and the combined ferocity of their .30-calibre, .50-calibre and 76mm machine-guns. In less than a second the enemy gun positions were obscured by showering soil and thick black smoke.

As was bound to happen, a VC grenade struck one of the tanks, exploding low on the front, blowing off both treads and shrouding it in smoke. The men inside were not hurt and as the tank shuddered to a standstill, with flames licking from its underside, they scrambled one after the other out of the turret, slid down the side and raced away. The other vehicles were already giving the flaming, smoking tank a wide berth when it exploded as a great ball of fire covered by an umbrella of black, oily smoke.

As if in instant reprisal, one of the shells from a Centurion's twenty-pounder blew a VC gun emplacement apart, hurling men into the air, along with exploding sandbags, soil and pebbles.

As the tanks neared the gun positions, with the APCs close behind them, Dead-eye started jumping out from behind the protection of his APC to fire short bursts at the black-shirted figures he saw running to and fro, carrying AK47s. Relieved to see many of them throw their arms up, drop their weapons, shudder or spin sideways and fall down, the other SAS men followed Dead-eye's example and started firing too.

One of the APCs was hit by a grenade, the explosion erupting beneath its front, lifting it briefly off the ground, then slewing it sideways in a cloud of oily smoke. As fierce yellow flames shot out from a punctured petrol can, the men inside, all from 3 SAS Squadron, clambered one after the other out of the turret and slid to the ground.

But before the last two could get out, a hail of VC bullets rattled off the APC with a horrible drumming sound and the first man was thrown back violently. He writhed spasmodically for a few seconds, screaming in agony as bullets punched into his body, then rolled down the front of the vehicle and fell to the ground with a thud.

The trooper behind him was just emerging when a second barrage of bullets ricocheted off the vehicle, some turning his head into a mess of blood and bone, and he fell back into the APC without a sound.

The men who had escaped the damaged APC were spreading out, holding their weapons at the ready, when it exploded with a muffled thump, shook violently and became a ball of bright-yellow flames and dense black smoke. The men were briefly obscured by the smoke, but when it cleared they could be seen still spreading out and now advancing on the enemy positions by running in short bursts, firing their semi-automatic weapons from the hip, then throwing themselves to the ground each time the enemy returned fire. Some were hit, but the others kept advancing.

The first of the Centurions passed over the perimeter created by the line of VC gun emplacements and were soon followed by the APCs. As the tanks continued rumbling towards the airstrip, the APCs stopped between the emplacements and poured a hail of machine-gun fire into them, enabling the men inside to clamber out through the turret and drop to the ground, where they engaged the enemy in close quarter battle.

'Let's go!' Shagger bawled.

He and the others raced towards the VC still remaining in the sunken gun positions, blasting away at them while on the move. The savage roar of the VC machine-gun was silenced when Jimbo threw a hand-grenade that landed right in the middle of the emplacement and blew the weapon to pieces, filling the air with the swirling sand from exploded sandbags and leaving the two gunners dead. Some of the VC continued firing from their gun positions until they were dispatched with automatic rifle fire at short range; others, in desperation, sprang out swinging machetes. As the SAS men had no bayonets on their weapons, they simply jumped back out of range and shot down their assailants at close range.

Dead-eye was running towards a VC gun position, firing from the hip, when he was deafened by a fearsome roar, hammered by an invisible force, then felt himself being picked up and hurled back down again. Hitting the ground hard, he blacked out for a few seconds. On regaining consciousness, he found himself lying on his back, covered with soil and still trying to recover his breath.

Just as he was gathering his senses, a guerrilla materialized directly above him, a youth of no more than sixteen, holding a machete on high, about to bring it down on his head. Rolling away just as the weapon thudded into the ground where his head had been, Dead-eye swiftly removed his 9mm Browning High Power handgun from its holster, came to rest on his back, steadied himself by bending his knees and pressing his feet on the ground, then fired up at the guerrilla before he could swing the machete again.

Though the first bullet hit the attacker in the chest and punched him back, Dead-eye kept firing until he had fallen and was making no movement; then he jumped back to his feet, picked up his SLR, and advanced on the nearest gun emplacement. He was now firing his SLR with his right hand, the stock tucked into his waist, while also firing single shots from the Browning in his left.

The VC in the emplacement annihilated, Dead-eye moved on.

By now the Centurions were blasting the parked aircraft with their twenty-five-pounders and explosions were ripping up the runway. First one, then another aircraft burst into sheets of flame and rolling clouds of smoke, with debris flying through the air in all directions to become yet another hazard to the VC on the ground.

As the aircraft were exploding, more guerrillas were racing out of the tents, many firing their weapons on the run. Two machine-guns located near the tents also opened fire, forcing the SAS men to throw themselves to the ground.

'We need air support,' Dead-eye told Shagger.

'Bloody oath, we do. *Red!* Get on to Callaghan and then give me the phone.' Red did as he was told, and Shagger told the CO exactly what he wanted.

'Pinned down, are you?' Callaghan asked.

'That's a mild way of putting it.'

Callaghan chuckled. 'Very good, Sergeant. The air support will be there in fifteen minutes, followed by 5th and 6th Battalions. Meanwhile, sit tight.'

'My very intention,' Shagger said.

He and the others sat tight by lying on their bellies and pouring a hail of bullets at the VC spreading over the flat ground between their tents and the SAS positions, most of them casting long shadows in the lights of the burning aircraft to the side. The tanks and APCs were now parked north of the SAS men and were concentrating on pounding the VC aircraft still untouched and the troop trucks nearby. Every so often one or the other would explode dramatically, while many were already ablaze and smoking. This, however, did not stop the relentless advance of around a hundred VC, all of whom were firing on the move and appeared not to care about their own losses.

However, well before the VC reached CQB positions, six USAF Phantom Jet F-4Cs appeared in the sky, coming from the directions of Nui Dat. One minute they were mere specks on the horizon, the next they were roaring in at low level to fire their rockets at the advancing VC and the enemy's remaining aircraft and vehicles. Within seconds, the oil tankers had been blown up and the airstrip had turned into a hell of searing yellow balls of fire, boiling black smoke, and running, screaming guerrillas, many of them on fire.

When the Phantoms circled around and returned to repeat the process, they targeted the raised control tower and water tower. The first rockets blasted through the control tower, blowing out its walls and setting fire to the collapsing roof, while the second pilot destroyed its base with deadly accuracy. His rockets blew the struts to pieces and caused the rest of the tower to first buckle, then break apart, with screaming men and navigation equipment raining down amid other flaming debris.

The third and fourth Phantoms concentrated on the tall water tower, blowing the tank to pieces, so that the water sprayed out in a silvery cascade that drenched the burning remains of the collapsed control tower and turned the flames into boiling clouds of steam. The fifth and sixth Phantoms then blew the struts of the water tower to pieces and left it collapsing as they banked for another run.

When the Phantoms circled around and returned for a third attack, creating even more hideous devastation, the VC who had been advancing on the SAS fled back towards the village, now barely visible through the smoke.

Shagger had just ordered his men to advance

across the smoke-covered airstrip when a flock of black birds appeared on the horizon. These soon became recognizable as USAF Chinooks, bringing in the men of the 5th and 6th Battalions. Pleased to see the approaching choppers, Shagger and Dead-eye advanced side by side, protected by the tanks and APCs, across an airstrip pock-marked with ugly, black shell holes, many of which were filled with VC dead. They were followed by Jimbo and Red, then by Norton and Mad Mike, each two-man team staying close behind a tank or an APC, and repeatedly leaning out from the rear to fire short bursts from their automatic rifles. By now their targets were mere shadows in the murk, all running the other way.

When the Phantoms banked for the final time and flew away, leaving an inferno of flame and smoke on the runway, the tanks and APCs accelerated, the former to weave through the blazing aircraft, firing their machine-guns, the latter to pursue the fleeing VC beyond their blazing tents and on to the village.

Left behind by the armoured vehicles, but no longer threatened by the VC, Shagger and the others stopped for a break, drinking water and lighting up cigarettes, squinting through the smoke as the Chinooks descended over the scarred ground, each pilot looking for a landing space between the shell holes.

As the Chinooks touched down one by one, their spinning rotors made the smoke swirl eerie patterns that changed shape constantly. Buffeted by the violent slipstreams, the men on the ground covered their eyes with their hands or used handkerchiefs to keep the flying dust out of their mouths and nostrils. Soon the men of 5th and 6th Battalions were marching down the rear ramps of the Chinooks, leaning into the beating wind being created by the still spinning rotors and likewise shielding their eyes from the swirling clouds of dust. Shadowy as ghosts, they spread out around the choppers, forming into long, loose lines, to begin mopping up any remaining VC, before marching on to the village.

'While they're doing that,' Shagger said to Dead-eye, Jimbo and the others, 'we'll go on ahead and see if we can give them any advance info. Let's get up and go, men.'

'No fucking rest for the wicked,' Mad Mike said, wearily shaking his head from side to side as he clambered to his feet and ground his cigarette with his boot.

'You're the man to know that,' Norton informed him. 'You're paying for your sins.'

'We're *all* paying for our sins,' Shagger said. 'Every day of our fucking lives. OK, men, move out.'

As the men headed off through the smoke,

following the tanks and APCs towards the village, two RAAF Iroquois arrived with D6 bulldozers slung from cables beneath them. At the same time American loadmasters were offloading crates of equipment from the Chinooks.

Some of the 5th and 6th Battalion troops spread out to take over the captured airstrip. The rest, along with 1 and 2 SAS Squadrons, prepared to follow Shagger's advance party on to the VC stronghold, which was just about visible in the gathering night, beyond the pall of smoke.

13

Great clouds of dust hung over the airfield like a shroud, blown there by all the choppers ferrying men and equipment in, as the SAS men left it behind. They had marched only about half the distance to the village when, to their surprise, the tanks and APCs up ahead stopped, some of the drivers popping up from the turrets and using hand signals to indicate that they had been ordered to halt.

'What the fuck are those drongos doing?' growled Shagger, studying the armoured vehicles and then squinting at the blood-red sun dipping towards the horizon. 'We've got to take that damn village by nightfall.'

'Incoming message,' Red informed him. 'Lieutenant-Colonel Callaghan. He must have left the bunker complex and come up here. There's an awful lot of static in the background, so I think he's calling from a moving vehicle – probably 5th or 6th Battalion. Anyway he's not far away.'

With Dead-eye and Jimbo looking thoughtfully at him, Shagger took the microphone from Red and said, 'Yes, boss. Sergeant Bannerman here.'

'I've ordered all the vehicles to stop their advance on the village. I want you to stop as well. Stick close to them, but don't move on the village until I get there. I'll be with you in ten minutes for a briefing.'

'Right, boss,' Shagger said. 'Over and out.' He handed the microphone back to Red, shook his head from side to side, spat on the ground, then stared sardonically first at Jimbo, then at the impassive Dead-eye. 'We're stopping,' he said.

'What for?' Dead-eye asked.

'Another bloody briefing from our Pommy CO,' Shagger said. 'What the fuck do we need a briefing for now? We're practically on top of the village.'

'If Callaghan calls a briefing, it's usually important,' Dead-eye said.

'Maybe,' Shagger replied, not convinced. 'Anyway, we're to join the vehicles and wait for him there, so let's move our arses.'

They reached the convoy just as the drivers and SAS troops were hoisting themselves up through the turrets and clambering down to the ground. A few minutes later Callaghan arrived in a jeep that had clearly been flown in by one of the choppers and contained, in the back seats, two Vietnamese in black uniforms. When the jeep screeched to a halt, leaving deep grooves in the soft soil on the paddy-field, Callaghan, aware that he was presently out of range of the VC guns in the village, stood on his seat and called the men around him.

'I know you're all anxious to take the village,' he said, 'but I thought you should know a few facts first.' This opening statement was greeted with a mixture of applause and sardonic comments. When the noise had died down Callaghan continued. 'Intelligence has estimated that the village was being controlled by a VC company of about a hundred men. That figure has now increased by approximately fifty per cent by the VC who've just fled the airfield.'

'No sweat, boss,' Jimbo said. 'We can still take them on.'

'I trust so. But you should know that this target was part of a US Strategic Hamlet Program, which removed people from their traditional villages and resettled them in fortified hamlets. For that very reason, it's surrounded by mines, booby-traps, a moat and a palisade of wooden stakes. The Yanks put them there for the protection of the village and now, ironically, they're going to be our biggest obstacle in recapturing it.'

'We can still do it, boss,' Shagger said with conviction.

Callaghan grinned and nodded. 'I like your attitude, Sarge, but it's not going to be as easy as you think.'

'What's the plan then, boss?'

'Well, it involves staging a noisy frontal feint along the road towards the main gate – that's the job of the SAS – while the 5th and 6th Battalions carry out the actual assault from the rear. The manoeuvre to get in position for the rear assault can only be carried out with great stealth, slowly and on foot, by following a wide arc around the village. It should take the 5th and 6th a few hours to complete this. Meanwhile the SAS, led by myself, will penetrate the palisade and secure a foothold while another platoon makes the first assault.'

'There's not a fence we can't get through,' Dead-eye said flatly.

'That may be true enough,' Callaghan replied, 'but we first have to find a safe way through the booby-trapped barrier that skirts the village. For this, I'm planning to use these two gentlemen' – he waved his hand at the two prisoners sitting solemnly in the back of the jeep – 'both of whom are VC defectors from the village. Guided by them, I think we can make it in.'

'When?' Dead-eye asked.

'Why wait?' Callaghan replied, to Dead-eye's obvious relief. 'We have the complete contingent of 1 and 3 SAS right here, backed up by the 5th and 6th. We move in right now, before last light, and clear the whole damn village. What say you, gentlemen?'

'I say yes,' said Dead-eye.

'I second that,' Jimbo said.

'Anything a Pom can do, we can do,' Shagger added.

'Then let's do it,' Callaghan said. He climbed down from the jeep and indicated that the VC defectors do the same. When they were on the ground beside him, he turned to Shagger and said, 'All right, Sergeant, we'll follow these gentlemen in. The rest of 1 and 3 Squadrons will be right there behind us. The 5th and 6th Battalions are already on their way here from the airstrip and I'll be keeping in touch with them by field phone. We'll make the frontal assault, breaching the palisade, while the 5th and 6th encircle the village and make the major assault from the rear.'

'Trust the regular army to choose the rear passage,' Jimbo whispered to Red. 'That says it all, don't it?'

'Just like the navy,' Red replied.

At that moment, a convoy of trucks came across the cleared path in the minefield, bringing the 5th and 6th Battalions from the captured airstrip. When the trucks had ground to a halt, the heavily armed soldiers of the two battalions poured out and formed into groups of a size that would form manageable single-file patrols through the rubber plantation, all the way round to the back of the village.

Callaghan walked over to have a word with the senior officers of the two battalions. Then, after what appeared to Shagger and Dead-eye to have been an extremely animated conversation, he returned to his own men.

'Right,' he said. 'The 5th and 6th are going to encircle the village and come up on its rear. However, we have to engage the enemy before they do, to cause a distraction. We've no time to waste, so let's move out immediately. The scouts will go first' – he paused and indicted the two Vietnamese – 'out on point, as it were, to guide us through the minefield and point out booby-traps, and the tanks and APCs will follow, with most of the men in the latter for protection.'

'*Most* of the men?' Shagger asked.

Callaghan looked steadily at him, then offered a tight smile. 'Yes, Sergeant,' he said. '*Most* of the men. The others – by which I mean you six – will go ahead with me and the VC scouts to ensure that they do what they should do and to relay back to the main forces anything we see while we're up at the front. Any problems, Sergeant?'

Shagger returned Callaghan's steady gaze for several seconds, then, accepting the challenge, even appreciating it, he said, 'No problem, boss. Where you lead, we will follow.'

'Good man.'

Turning to the VC guides, Callaghan nodded towards the village, and they loped away with the grace of deer. Callaghan then told Shagger and the other five men to fall in behind them. When they had done so, and were also heading towards the village, which was now sinking into an eerie, though less smoky twilight, Callaghan used a hand signal to order the tanks and APCs to follow the men on foot. The engines of the armoured vehicles rumbled into life and they advanced spread out in a long line, but moving slowly, keeping well behind the men on foot, to avoid mines and booby-traps.

In front, spread out in a well-spaced line just behind the sharp-eyed Vietnamese scouts, Shagger and the others had their automatic rifles at the ready and were likewise constantly alert for mines or booby-traps.

In Jimbo's mind this extra precaution was wholly justified. 'How the fuck can you trust them?' he asked. 'Those snaky little bastards could be leading us right on to the mines instead of guiding us through them.'

'Listen, mate,' Red replied. 'If you knew what would happen to those poor bastards if their VC friends caught them, you'd know just what kind of chance they've taken to come over to our side. They're not going to lead you on to any mines. No, they'll make sure we capture that village and wipe out the VC. That way they'll save their own arses. You can trust them, believe me.'

'*I* believe you,' Mad Mike said. 'But I still feel shit-scared of those mines. Can't help myself, fellas.'

'You're not worth a cuntful of cold water,' Red told him. 'All you'll lose if a mine goes off, mate, is your balls – and given your track record with the ladies, they're probably not worth worrying about.'

'Shut up, the lot of you,' Shagger whispered. 'This isn't a bloody exercise. It's the real thing. So zip your lips and keep your eyes to the front.'

'Right, Sarge,' both men whispered simultaneously.

They continued advancing behind the VC scouts and realized, with dread, that they were in the minefield when they saw them slowing down and casting their gazes to the ground.

'Christ!' Jimbo hissed.

'You've been through all this before, man,' Callaghan whispered.

'I'm OK, boss,' Jimbo replied. 'I'm just gulping some air in.'

'It helps,' Callaghan said.

They were crossing a broad, level paddy-field between the trees of rubber plantations and could see the village straight ahead, its brick-and-tile houses, surprisingly modern-looking, clearly outlined in the somnolent sunset, a slow and lazy dimming of air, deepening into darkness. Up ahead, the scouts were silhouetted in that changing light, repeatedly bending over to check the ground for mines and then straightening up to guide the armoured vehicles and SAS men forward with hand signals. The men walked gingerly, following the tracks of the armoured vehicles, but even the bravest of them could feel their hearts beating hard.

Twice they had to stop when the scouts pointed out booby-traps, planted right in the middle of the minefield: first a punji pit with a camouflaged tilting lid and then an angled arrow trap, concealed in a hole in the ground. They also stopped frequently to stick flagged markers into the ground on both sides of the tank and APC tracks, to show the way through the minefield to the 5th and 6th Battalion troops coming up behind them.

The hike across the minefield seemed to take for ever and was rendered even more nerve-racking by the failing light and the fact that they were now doing it in full view of the village, which was growing nearer all the time.

They came off the minefield just as darkness was falling. Knowing that his men couldn't attempt to cross the moat or breach the palisade in the darkness,

Callaghan ordered the vehicles to halt, then called the men together for a Chinese parliament.

'It's taken longer than I envisaged and we can't see a damn thing in this darkness,' he said. 'So I believe we should settle in for the night and attack at first light. What do you think, men?'

'I agree, boss,' Dead-eye said. 'Not even these two VC turncoats can see in the dark. We'd either get blown to hell by mines or nobbled by booby-traps. First light seems right to me.'

'I agree,' Shagger said, then glanced at the other men and received their nods of consent. Turning back to Callaghan, he said, 'We're all agreed, boss.'

'Good,' Callaghan said. 'Then let's bunk down right here. Shallow scrapes for sleeping and guards posted on all sides, two hours on, two hours off. No cigarettes, no fires, only cold rations. I'll get in touch with the 5th and 6th to let them know what we're doing.'

On making contact with the CO of the combined 5th and 6th, Callaghan informed him of what he and his men had decided. Lieutenant-Colonel Chambers, normally the CO of the 6th, now acting CO for both battalions, agreed that the idea was sound and said that he would position his men at the rear of the village, but keep them on hold until first light and, even then, not attack until he heard the sounds of engagement between Callaghan's men and the enemy.

Satisfied, Callaghan then ordered his demolitions men to lay a line of claymores along an invisible perimeter separating the makeshift camp from the route to the village. Activated by a trip-wire about 500 yards long, each mine would fire approximately 350 metal balls over a fan-shaped area up to a range of 100 yards, shredding anything in its path.

Callaghan went off to have tea with his fellow officers, all sitting on the ground near some rubber trees in the gathering darkness. His men, meanwhile, both English and Australian, were either digging their shallow scrape, covering it with a vacuum-compressed plastic sheet, or unrolling a sleeping-bag on to the sheet, depending upon how quick they were or how eager they were to bed down.

'I'm shagged,' Jimbo said, 'and I don't mind admitting it.'

'You always look shagged, mate,' said Red provocatively.

'You've only known me a few days.'

'It seems years to me, mate.'

'True love starts with the attraction of opposites, so there's hope for me yet.'

'Some Pommy nancy-boy, is he?' Mad Mike said to Red.

'I don't know, but I'm sleeping on my back tonight,' Red replied.

Chuckling, Jimbo pulled the sleeping-bag up to his chin and closed his eyes in the vain hope of sleep. In fact, he fell asleep quickly – as did the others around him – but none of them slept as long as they would have wished.

They were awakened just after midnight by the familiar, distant phut-phut of mortar fire, one mortar coming quickly after the other, like a growing drum roll. Even as they were opening their sleepy eyes, the first of the shells came hurtling down over their improvised camp and exploded all around them.

Pummelled by the blasts, stung by flying soil and stones, they hurriedly wriggled out of their sleeping-bags, picked up their rifles and rolled on to their bellies, trying to scan the night ahead.

The first waves of VC were charging directly at them in a surprise attack. Luckily, Callaghan's idea of laying claymores paid off when they ran straight on to them and the mines exploded, blowing some of the guerrillas apart and shredding the flesh of others with the hundreds of steel balls that flew upward at incredible speed.

Even as the mines were taking their terrible toll, the other VC were annihilated by withering sheets of automatic-rifle and machine-gun fire, backed by devastating blasts from the three different-calibre machine-guns on the APCs and Centurions, as well as canister rounds from the latter. Similar to the claymores, the canister shots contained hundreds of ball-bearings which spread out in a murderous arc, scything down everything in their path. The devastation wrought by this combined onslaught on the advancing VC was appalling.

And yet they kept coming.

Hardly believing what he was seeing, Callaghan used the radio to call for artillery support from the Australian 105mm battery located back in the captured VC bunker complex, three miles away. In less than a minute shells were raining down on the VC, exploding in silvery-white flashes that briefly illuminated the darkness and then obscured the emerging moon and stars with their intermingling streams of dense smoke. Under that umbrella of smoke, scattering to avoid the explosions, the advancing VC melted into the trees on either side of the open stretch of ground that led to the village.

'One Squadron to the right!' Callaghan bawled. 'Three Squadron to the left!'

Before most of the other men could react, Deadeye was running to the trees on the right, followed closely by Callaghan, Jimbo, then the startled Shagger, Norton, Red and Mad Mike, and finally by the rest of 1 Squadron. Once among the trees, where even the light of the stars was blotted out, they made their way forward, darting carefully from one tree to another, towards where they had seen the VC entering. To their surprise, since they had expected the VC to hide in the darkness, they had advanced only about four hundred yards when they saw a sea of flickering candles. These VC were carrying them as they made their way through the deepening darkness under the rubber trees.

Stunned by this surrealistic sight, most of the men looked on in disbelief. This collective trance was rudely broken by Dead-eye, who without a second thought, opened fire with his SLR, delivering a short, exploratory burst. He was gratified to see a couple of the tiny flickering flames whip through the air before blinking out, indicating that he had hit the men holding them.

Almost as one, the rest of the SAS men followed suit and many of the candles were dropped to the ground as those holding them were either killed or threw them down to return the fire, their bullets thudding into the trees and showering the SAS men below them with foliage.

One SAS man was killed, then another.

Unable to see the enemy because their candles were dimmed, Callaghan instructed some of his men to send up flares. These burst like purple flowers above the trees to shed an eerie blue-and-crimson glow over the enemy, revealing that they were already withdrawing with their casualties, dragging them like sacks along the ground.

Realizing that he could not expect his men to

advance through the dark jungle, prey to mines, booby-traps and VC snipers with infrared sights, Callaghan ordered a tactical withdrawal that would take them back to the two main battalions. This, however, was not as easy as it seemed because many of the VC had decided to stay in the jungle to harass the SAS with constant sniping.

One SAS man took a shot through the head and fell like a stone. Another was hit in the chest and punched backwards into a tree, then peppered with bullets even as he slid down the trunk, leaving a long smear of blood. A third kicked a trip-wire and was impaled on the half a dozen spikes of the booby-trap known as 'the whip'. Still standing upright, but quivering like a bowstring and pouring blood from his many wounds, he kept screaming dementedly until put out of his misery by a burst of VC machine-gun fire that practically tore him to shreds and actually punched him off the spikes and back down into the mud.

The slow, noisy, agonizing withdrawal took place in an eerie chiaroscuro: dark one instant, then brilliantly lit the next as flares were fired overhead to fall slowly, casting weird, distorted shadows on the trees. It took Callaghan's men two bloody hours, with substantial losses, to cover the 250 yards back through the perimeter.

At approximately four in the morning the battle tapered off as the surviving VC retreated to the village and Callaghan's team withdrew, knowing that they had to be well clear by first light and needed the time to look after their wounded and collect the dead.

Given that the medical team needed protection, Callaghan allotted his six best men – Shagger, Dead-eye, Norton, Jimbo, Red and Mad Mike – to accompany them. After making their way carefully back through the jungle, seeing only the odd glimmer of stars here and there through the canopy of trees, being acutely aware of the possible presence of mines and booby-traps, the men reached the area of the previous battle, where they formed a protective cordon around the medics as they went about their bloody business of picking up their wounded and dead.

Though no VC appeared in the jungle's enveloping darkness, the SAS men knew that they were nearby and engaged in exactly the same kind of grisly activity. This was confirmed when they heard what at first was a strange sound, but which became discernible as the creaking of wood. They realized at once that it was the sound of ox carts bearing away the VC casualties.

The medics, protected by the SAS men, remained in the jungle until just before dawn. As the sun's first pale rays fell on the jungle floor, they found the remains of about fifty guerrillas who had been missed in the darkness by their companions.

Scattered among the dead were the meat-hooks which the VC had used to drag the bodies to the ox carts. Also found was a ghastly litter of human remains, clothing, equipment and shattered rubber trees, oozing latex and splattered with blood.

As it was not possible for the medics to remove all the bodies, they called for a team of Australian engineers to be flown in by chopper to bulldoze the bodies and other human remains into a mass grave. When this grisly task was completed, the SAS men returned to their makeshift camp to prepare for the attack on the village.

With the 5th and 6th Battalions now in position at the rear of the village, the battle to clear the area could begin.

14

The men moved against the village about an hour after dawn, hiking behind the Centurions and APCs as they rolled towards the moat they would have to cross. The VC, armed with AK47s, light machine-guns, and rocket-propelled grenade launchers, had taken aim through the wooden stakes of the pali-sade at the far side of the moat, but were holding fire until the SAS were within range.

Within minutes of the advance, the attacking vehicles had churned up clouds of red dust that both choked and obscured the men behind them, most of whom had wrapped scarves around their faces to keep out the dust. Even so, it blinded them, forcing them to stick close to the rear of the armoured vehicles. Therefore it came as a great relief to the men on foot when the vehicles suddenly roared louder and raced ahead and the tanks opened fire with their twenty-pounders and the APCs with their machine-guns.

The first of the shells from the tanks' big guns

exploded, blowing whole sections out of the palisade, with broken stakes flying in all directions through the smoke and dead or wounded VC rolling down into the moat. Instantly, the other defenders opened fire with everything they had, including their Soviet-made grenade launchers.

As a hail of bullets was stitching the ground on both sides of the men marching behind the tanks and APCs, with other bullets clanging off the armoured bodies of the vehicles, a couple of grenades exploded between two of them, hurling up great columns of soil and dust, hammering the men behind the first vehicle with the blast. The tanks and APCs replied in kind, blowing more chunks out of the palisade and raking the rest of it with their machine-guns, tearing the stakes to shreds and filling the air with flying debris and dust.

By the time the vehicles had reached the edge of the moat, whole sections of the palisade had been blown open and the VC were edging away from it, shooting on the move as they were forced back into the village. There, as shells from the tanks' twenty-pounders exploded in the clearing between the houses, the inhabitants were cowering in their doorways or packing their belongings, before fleeing out the rear of the village.

At that moment, the tanks and APCs of 5th and 6th Battalion opened fire, raining a hail of shells on to the village which blew the walls out of some of the houses and caused more eruptions of soil and smoke in the clearing between them.

Shocked to find themselves being attacked from behind, some of the VC at the palisade turned away and hurried to the rear of the village, to take up defensive positions there. Even as they were doing so, the tanks and APCs of the 5th and 6th Battalions came into view, trundling towards the village with a mass of soldiers bunched up behind them, many already firing their assault rifles.

'Advance!' Callaghan bawled while using a hand signal to confirm the order for those out of earshot.

Unable to cross the water-filled moat, the vehicles kept up a continuous, murderous barrage of shells and machine-gun fire at the palisade, forcing the remaining VC back towards the village clearing while the SAS men slithered down the muddy bank and into the chest-high water.

Not all of them made it. The VC bold enough to stay at the palisade fired their last, defiant burst of gunfire and two or three of the SAS men were peppered with bullets, dropped their weapons and slithered into the water. As the medics slid down after them to check if they were dead or alive and, in the latter case, to prevent them from drowning, Callaghan and the other men waded across the moat, holding their weapons above their heads, then began the climb up the slippery slope on the other side.

Another shell exploded against what was left of the palisade, blowing it to pieces, and the attackers pressed themselves into the mud as the debris, including sharpened stakes, flew over their heads. Picking themselves up and wiping the mud from their faces, they resumed their climb and eventually made it to the top.

The Centurions and APCs stopped firing for fear of hitting their own men. Noting that the VC were retreating back into the centre of the village and that the tanks, APCs and men of 5th and 6th Battalions were advancing from the rear, Callaghan led his men in a charge against the village, firing their rifles and lobbing M26 high-explosive grenades.

The rest of 1 and 3 Squadron SAS came pounding after them.

Caught between the two advancing Australian forces, the VC began taking cover in the houses on either side of the clearing. As Callaghan, keen to fight his last battle to the utmost of his ability, rushed into one of the houses, firing his SLR from the hip, holding it in his left hand, and withdrawing his Browning handgun from his holster with the other, Shagger and Dead-eye, seeing VC snipers in the top windows of the same house, dropped to their knees and sent a hail of bullets into it. Plaster and powdered concrete exploded from around the window frame, someone screamed in agony, then the sniper's AK47 dropped to the street.

Jumping up again, Shagger and Dead-eye followed Callaghan into the house just as the latter kicked open the door of the downstairs living-room and fired a double-tap into the VC sniper he found lurking there. The man crashed backwards over a table, which collapsed beneath him, and fell on his back on the floor, where he lay still, his eyes open.

Callaghan was just backing out of the room when another VC sniper appeared at the top of the stairs. Even before Callaghan had seen him, Shagger and Dead-eye were firing simultaneously at him, the sound of their weapons shockingly loud in the small building, their bullets tearing the wooden stairs to shreds, splintering the unplastered brick walls, and turning the sniper into a shuddering, screaming mass of blood and exposed bone as he dropped his weapon and plunged headlong down the stairs to land at their feet.

'This house is cleared,' Callaghan said tersely. 'Let's move on to the next one.'

When they stepped back outside, they found the village centre filled with terrified, huddling peasants whom the VC were trying to use as human shields. This was not proving easy since the 5th and 6th Battalions were coming up on their rear even as 1 and 3 SAS Squadrons were advancing from the front, all of them firing on the move.

Leading off the square was a corrugated-iron

church, from where some VC were firing down on the SAS troops with a light machine-gun. Jimbo and Red on one side of the short street, and Norton and Mad Mike on the other, were hiding in opposite doorways and taking pot-shots up at the church, but with little success.

Impatient, Callaghan grabbed a 66mm M72 rocket launcher from a passing trooper, balanced the cumbersome weapon expertly on his right shoulder, took aim and fired a rocket at the target, some 250 yards away. The weapon almost knocked him off his feet as it belched flame and smoke, but the rocket, bearing a high-explosive anti-tank warhead, sailed right over the church. Instead it erupted right in the middle of a bunch of VC who were running up the road on the other side of the church, hurling men and weapons in all directions and putting an abrupt stop to their advance.

The VC machine-gun in the church tower roared again, spraying a line of bullets down the incline, between the two teams crouched in opposite doorways, and missing Callaghan by inches.

Cursing softly, Callaghan braced himself and fired another rocket at the church. This time he scored a direct hit, blowing away most of the roof of the bell-tower, with the machine-gunner thrown out and hurled to the ground, his weapon falling beside him in a shower of debris. When the gunner had thudded into the unsurfaced street, Callaghan handed the weapon back to the trooper, patted him on the shoulder, then hand-signalled to the other men to follow him up the slope to the church.

As they reached the top of the hill, machine-guns roared and a blizzard of bullets turned the earth in front of them into a hell of spitting soil and swirling dust.

'Take cover!' Callaghan bawled.

Throwing themselves against the wall of the church just as the angry line of soil and dust raced past them, they saw that they had run into a platoon of VC stationed in fighting trenches on the high ground at the side of the church.

'We're fully exposed!' Shagger bawled.

'Let's go round to the front,' Dead-eye suggested.

They had just run away from the side wall and around to the front of the church when the side wall, fully exposed to the VC guns, received a barrage of bullets that sent lumps of plaster and pulverized cement flying in all directions. The wind picked the dust up and blew it into the front courtyard, where the men were taking up positions behind the side wall and peering carefully over it, between ornate steel railings, at the VC trenches.

'How many?' Callaghan asked.

'I'd say about thirty men in all,' Dead-eye replied. 'With two machine-gun emplacements.'

'Too many for us six,' Shagger observed.

'I agree,' Jimbo said.

'We step out there,' Red added, 'and those machine-guns will chop us to ribbons.'

'Yeah, chop suey,' Norton said. 'Not to my taste at all.'

'We need a gun bombardment,' Shagger said.

'Precisely aimed,' Dead-eye told him. 'Those trenches are only 500 yards away. We could cop it as well.'

'Bloody oath,' Shagger said.

All the men looked at Callaghan. He pursed his lips, tapped his knuckles against his teeth, screwed up his eyes and studied the VC fighting trenches, then sighed and said, 'Right.' After carefully checking his map, he told Red to contact the CO of the makeshift FOB being raised by the Aussies around the captured VC bunker complex. When Red had done so, Callaghan asked for a twenty-five-pounder barrage to be laid down on the nearby VC trenches, and gave very precise calibrations. 'Plug your ears, gentlemen,' he said as he handed the phone back to Red.

He wasn't joking. In less than five minutes the first shells from the big guns came whistling down over the church and slammed into the ground about 200 yards in front of the VC trenches. The shells exploded with a catastrophic bellowing, hurling soil and dust into the air and briefly obscuring the trenches in streams of smoke. When the smoke had cleared, the trenches appeared to be untouched.

'Too short,' Shagger observed.

'I *know* that, Callaghan said rather testily. He grabbed the phone from Red and got back in touch with the gunners at the bunker complex, to slightly modify the calibrations.

'You'll get it right on the button this time, boss,' Jimbo said encouragingly.

Callaghan said nothing.

Moments later the second round of shells exploded with the same deafening noise and again created immense showers of soil, dust and smoke. This time, however, the shells fell among the VC trenches, some of them direct hits, sending scorched bodies somersaulting through the smoke in a rainfall of debris – wooden planks, exploding sandbags, strips of burning clothing, scorched, dismembered limbs – to smash with dreadful impact into the ground.

Given confirmation that they now had the correct calibration, the gunners back in the bunker complex began a relentless, non-stop barrage that turned the trenches into a hell of erupting earth, scorching flames, choking smoke, and fragments of flying metal and wood. Remarkably, some of the VC had survived and were trying to make their exit from the few remaining untouched trenches.

'Open fire!' Shagger bawled.

Aiming through the iron railings of the side

wall of the courtyard, the SAS opened fire with a murderous hail of bullets that cut down the guerrillas fleeing the trenches.

Suddenly, a shell from an Australian gun smashed through the remains of the bell-tower and exploded inside the church, blowing out part of the wall, deafening the SAS men, hitting them with flying bricks, cement and wood, and covering them with clouds of choking dust.

'Shit!' Red exclaimed.

Within seconds, more shells were exploding all around them, even one in the courtyard itself, and the men realized that one of the gun teams had for some reason changed its calibration and was now aiming at exactly where they were. With the church crumbling and explosions erupting about them, they had no choice but to move, so Callaghan, unable to make himself heard above the bedlam, used a hand signal to order an advance on the smoke-obscured enemy trenches. Already pummelled by the blast of the explosions, seared by the heat, showered with gravel and debris, and almost choked by the smoke, they were relieved to be able to leave the courtyard and, spreading out on the move to give themselves a broad arc of fire, zigzag towards what was left of the enemy positions.

What they found was a valley of death in which only a few human souls remained. Scorched though they were, covered with blisters, their bones broken, soaked in their own blood, some of the guerrillas still had the will to fight.

A single shot rang out.

Norton, who had been peering into the blackened remains of the trenches, not thinking for a moment that anyone could still be alive there, suddenly went into a spasm, jerking epileptically, dropped his weapon and let out a strangled moan before flopping face down in the dirt.

'Fuck!' Mad Mike bawled. 'Those bastards are still alive!'

Both enraged and shocked, he fired burst after burst of his M16A1 automatic rifle into the pitiful creatures still twitching in the shell holes, making sure that not a single one of them would ever fire his weapon or throw a grenade again. He was still firing, clearly out of control, when Shagger grabbed him by the shoulders and pulled him away.

'Enough!' Shagger snapped. 'All these bastards are dead.'

'Sergeant Norton!' Mad Mike exclaimed. 'Sergeant Norton! These bastards . . .'

'They're all dead,' Shagger repeated, again shaking Mad Mike furiously. 'There's no more we can do here. Get a grip on yourself, Corporal!'

Eventually, as if coming out of a trance, Mad Mike took half a dozen deep, even breaths and regained control of himself. But even then he looked back at the body of Sergeant Norton, lying face down in the dirt, and said, 'Come on, we've got to . . .'

'No!' Shagger snapped. 'We can't do anything for him. The burial detail will find him later. Let's get back to the village and join up with the others. OK?'

'Yeah. Sorry, Sarge.'

'Good on you! Let's go.'

As they hurried back to the centre of the village they could hear the sound of the battle still raging as fiercely as ever. Reaching the bottom of the hill, they soon saw what was happening.

'Bloody hell!' Red exclaimed.

By now, the VC using the peasants as hostages were ignoring them and were instead trying to flee into the houses on either side of the square. These, however, were already being cleared by the troopers of 1 and 3 Squadrons with a combination of rifles and hand-grenades. As the houses rang with the sound of automatic gunfire and roared with successive grenade explosions, and as whole chunks of wall and windows were blown out and VC bodies, occasionally SAS, fell into the street, the guerrillas hoping to get into the houses were forced to bunch up together in the middle of the square.

Now caught in a four-way crossfire and being brutally cut down, they nevertheless refused to give up and, forming into a rough circle, embarked on a seemingly suicidal fire-fight.

'Christ!' Jimbo exclaimed. 'You've got to admire the little bastards. They're going to slug it out to the last man.'

'And the last man it's going to be,' Dead-eye replied.

He didn't even wait for an order from Callaghan. As was his way, he raced out into the square, firing his SLR from the hip with deadly accuracy, taking out one VC after the other. Inspired by his performance, Shagger, Jimbo, Red and Mad Mike did the same, while Callaghan looked on, at first in amazement and then with a grim smile on his face. When he saw them in the midst of the turmoil, all weaving left and right, crouched low, firing on the move, he raced up to join them.

Within minutes, the fire-fight had become a CQB situation, with many of the SAS men using Browning pistols at close range and some even using their Fairburn-Skyes commando daggers to stab VC lunging at them with machetes. Meanwhile, as the bloody struggle was at its height, the rest of 1 and 3 Squadrons were completing the clearing of the houses on both sides of the square and the 5th and 6th Battalions, led by their tanks and APCs, were closing in to crush the guerrillas making their last-ditch stand.

Eventually, when they reached the VC, the latter,

recognizing their fate, threw up their hands. Within minutes, blindfolded and with their hands tied in front of them, they were roped together and led away at gunpoint to the APCs that would transport them back to the FOB. From there they would be flown by Chinooks to the immense POW camp at Nui Dat.

What happened next, in the darkness of night, was to no one's taste, though it was a job that had to be done. As the SAS got on with the dangerous task of checking every house in the village for any remaining VC snipers, the soldiers of 5th and 6th Battalions rounded up the frightened peasants and herded them into the APCs for transportation to a resettlement area. Once there, they would be fed, medically examined, given clothes and other necessaries, then be flown or driven to their allocated resettlement area, where they would help construct a new, fortified village, be trained to defend it themselves, and then helped with the planting of new crops to make them self-sufficient.

When the last of the peasants had been driven away, the captured village was put to the torch and, where necessary, blown up to ensure that it could not be used by the VC in the future. This was, for many of the soldiers and SAS men, an unpleasant and often deeply distressing task, but it could not be avoided. All through the night, as the check for remaining VC snipers continued, the destruction of the houses and other buildings was completed, by explosion or fire, with flames illuminating the darkness and a pall of smoke blotting out the moon and stars.

Adding a surrealistic, even nightmarish appearance to the scene were the USAF Chinooks and RAAF Iroquois which descended through the smoke with spotlights blazing. Having landed, they disgorged medics, stretchers and other basic medical equipment, more ammunition, food and water. Once these were delivered, the same choppers flew out the many wounded and dead, one of whom was SAS Sergeant Norton.

When first light came, it revealed a scene of black, smouldering devastation people by dozens of filthy, weary soldiers. Among them were Shagger, Dead-eye, Jimbo, Red and Mad Mike. Crouching together in a circle, they were sharing a welcome brew-up and a smoke.

They had barely taken the first sip when Callaghan approached them.

'There's only one job left to do,' he said.

The men nodded wearily.

15

Though the VC tunnel complex ran under the fake village, its entrances were all located in a cleared area of jungle just outside the settlement. The first task of the SAS was to investigate that area to ensure that none of the VC were still inhabiting the rectangular pits sunk into the ground. They also had to check the area for punji pits and other booby-traps.

The two VC defectors had given the SAS detailed maps of the tunnel system, and these enabled them to locate the sunken pits and punji traps at ground level. As each trooper was given his own copy of the maps, he was able to avoid the punji pits while moving stealthily through the village and checking that the rectangular pits were empty.

Crawling on his belly under one of the sloping thatched roofs raised only a few inches off the ground, Shagger found himself staring down into a complete kitchen, with a kiln-shaped stove covered with pots and pans and bamboo-and-plank shelves laden with eating and drinking utensils. Though the pots and pans were filled with soups or stews simmering on a low heat, there was no sign of anyone in the kitchen.

Shagger then saw, in one corner of the kitchen, beneath the shelves, a closed trapdoor.

Obviously the cook and his helpers had escaped down there, into the tunnel complex, when they realized that the village had been captured.

Turning away, Shagger indicated with a hand signal to those behind him that the pit was empty.

Meanwhile Dead-eye was also crawling on his belly under a low camouflaged roof. Glancing down and preparing to fire his SLR, he saw an empty rectangular pit that contained a scattering of plates, chicken bones and other scraps of food. Used cartridges littered the floor of the pit. Looking more carefully, Dead-eye made out the faint impressions made by guerrillas who had obviously been lying belly down on the sloping sides of the pit, ready to fire their weapons at the approach of an enemy. Realizing that he had come across a firing pit, he checked the defectors' map and noted that this pit also contained one of the concealed entrances to the tunnel complex. Pleased, he used a hand signal to indicate that the pit was empty.

Red had also crawled under one of the artificial roofs, to find himself looking down into a rectangular pit that contained a crude, hand-carved wooden table and chairs, the disconnected wires of what had been a field phone, and a wall of planks – the other walls were of compacted earth – that was covered with pins clearly used to pin up maps and graphs. Checking his map, he decided that he had found the conference chamber. Studying the floor again, he noticed a closed trapdoor exactly where it was indicated on his map. That trapdoor, he knew, led down into a conical air-raid shelter that also served to amplify the sound of approaching aircraft. Below that was the rest of the tunnel complex.

Like the others, Red indicated with his hand that the pit he had found was empty.

Meanwhile Jimbo and Mad Mike had both uncovered concealed trapdoors sunk a few inches into the soft earth and covered with grass and leaves so as to look like part of the flat ground.

When Mad Mike eased open his trapdoor and shone his torch in, the beam illuminated a narrow tunnel that curved away slightly about fifteen feet down. According to his map, it led to the VC sleeping chamber. There was no sign of anyone down there and Mike hand-signalled this fact to the others.

Jimbo, when he opened his trapdoor slightly and poked his torch in, found the beam reflecting off a dark pool of water some fifty feet below. Directing the beam left then right, he saw the circular walls of a well. Moving it upwards until it lit up an area about twenty-five feet higher, or halfway down the well, he saw what appeared to be two tunnels facing each other, one raised slightly higher than the other. Studying them more intently, he thought he could discern ridges cut out of the wall facing the lower tunnel. These, he surmised, could have been used as footholds for someone straddling the well – one foot on the floor of the passageway, the other on the ridge – to enable them to lower a bucket on a rope to the water-table. Admiring the cleverness of his enemy, Jimbo turned away from the trapdoor and used a hand signal to indicate that the well was clear and he was ready to go.

Callaghan was crouching with three SAS troopers under the trees beyond the perimeter of the village, by the three hidden smoke outlets from the kitchen, one trooper guarding each outlet to ensure that no VC tried escaping through them. Seeing his men's final hand signal, from Jimbo, Callaghan raised and sharply dropped his own hand, indicating that the attack was to commence.

Dead-eye was the first down. Like the others, he was armed only with a torch, his 9mm Browning High Power handgun, his dagger, M26 high-explosive hand-grenades, and an unusual amount of spare ammunition. After dragging the heavy, camouflaged covering slightly to the side, he jumped down into the sunken pit of the firing post, his boots cracking some of the plates left on the floor.

Kicking chicken bones and spent cartridges aside, he made his way to the trapdoor half hidden behind some packing crates. Kneeling down, and with his Browning in his right hand, the safety-catch already off, he carefully raised the trapdoor a little and glanced down.

The tunnel below was narrow, very dark and ran almost horizontally away from him. Gingerly sticking his head down the hole, Dead-eye thought he saw a few strands of pale light where the tunnel appeared to curve up again towards the surface.

Neither seeing nor hearing signs of movement, he carefully lowered himself into the tunnel until he was on his hands and knees. As in that position his back was still scraping the top of the tunnel, even he, who had bravely suffered every kind of horror and danger in the past, could not help but feel an overwhelming claustrophobia.

Frequently, he heard the soft scuffling of rats.

Taking a deep breath, then letting it out slowly, he turned on his torch, holding it in his left hand, gripped the Browning in his right, and began the slow crawl along the roughly horizontal tunnel. He had travelled only ten yards in as many minutes and was breaking out in a sweat, when he came to a spot where the tunnel started curving back up to the surface and rays of pale light beamed back down. Straining to see upwards, Dead-eye thought he could make out a square shape outlined by light. He was looking up at another trapdoor exit.

Realizing that the tunnel was unlikely to curve down and up from one trapdoor exit to another, but must surely go down deeper into the system, Dead-eye shone his torch on the floor directly in front of him. He saw what appeared to be a square-shaped portion of soil slightly raised above the rest of the floor of the tunnel. Wiping the sweat from his eyes, he inched forward to it, placed the torch on the floor, and very carefully groped around with his fingers, eventually finding what felt like the underside of a wooden trapdoor. Lifting it very slowly, fearful of booby-traps, he peered down and saw only another dark tunnel, this one curving away at a forty-five-degree angle.

There was no light of any kind, nor any sound of movement.

Aiming the torch down, Dead-eye saw the tunnel more clearly curving away out of sight. Pulling the trapdoor from the opening, he lowered himself in, found himself sliding dangerously down an almost vertical section, but came to rest when the tunnel started levelling out. He rolled over on to his belly, raised himself on to his hands and knees, then crawled forward as best he could, still holding the torch in his left hand, but keeping it aimed just a few feet in front of him in case the VC should see it, and holding the Browning in his right.

Gradually, as he inched forward, frequently tapping the ground ahead with the barrel of the gun to check for a trapdoor concealing a punji pit, the fetid air changed into something cleaner, cooler and he sensed, rather than saw, a similar, almost imperceptible brightening in the darkness ahead.

Crawling on, along a steep incline, he eventually reached a point where the tunnel levelled out and led into a large, empty space that looked like a natural cave but had, just like the tunnels, been hacked out by human hand.

Checking the ground directly in front of him, he noticed a pale, circular-shaped pool of light. Crawling forward to it, he saw that the light was beaming up along a particularly narrow tunnel – certainly too small for a human to pass through – which sloped down at forty-five degrees. When he squinted along it, he saw an even brighter light and thought he heard the murmur of many voices.

Straightening up as best he could, Dead-eye checked his copy of the defectors' map with his torch and concluded that he was almost certainly at the air vent leading up from the underground forward aid station for the wounded. About a yard further on from the vent was another trapdoor camouflaged with the same mud as on the tunnel floor. That, Dead-eye knew, was the entrance and exit to the forward aid station.

Shining his torch beyond that trapdoor, to the far

side of the empty cavern, he saw a raised portion of the floor which he assumed was another trapdoor. According to the map, it was one of the blast, gas and waterproof trapdoors sited at each end of a U-shaped tunnel drop that acted as a blast wall. Shining the torch to the left of that trapdoor, but much higher up, Dead-eye saw a tunnel heading upwards in the opposite direction and stopping at yet another trapdoor. This one, he knew, led up to the sleeping chamber, which, apart from containing many VC at all times, had a tunnel at its far end, leading up to the concealed trapdoor entrance that Red had been designated to enter.

Assuming that no VC were likely to emerge from the blast, gas and waterproof trapdoor nearby, but that a loud noise would almost certainly bring a horde of guerrillas along the tunnel leading down from the sleeping chamber into the cavern, Dead-eye realized he would have to be quick.

After crawling forward to the air vent, he un-clipped two hand-grenades, released the pins and dropped the grenades down the air vent, into the forward aid station. Even as they were rolling down, he crawled across the vent and went up to the entrance-exit trapdoor. He had just reached it when the grenades exploded with a muffled roar, followed by the terrible screaming of men scorched by heat, pummelled by the blast, and lacerated by flying, red-hot metal.

The screams were followed instantly by the high-pitched chattering and shouting of the surviving VC, then by the sounds of colliding weapons.

Lying flat out on his belly and holding his Browning in both hands, Dead-eye aimed at the entrance-exit trapdoor. When it opened, the head and shoulders of a VC appeared through the hole. Dead-eye fired once, putting a bullet right between the guerrilla's eyes. Even as the man was dropping back down through the hole, falling on top of those jabbering excitedly below him, Dead-eye crawled forward, dropped another grenade down through the hole, then slammed the trapdoor shut and rolled away from it.

This time the explosion was much louder and was again accompanied by terrible screaming. When Dead-eye opened the trapdoor again and looked down, he saw a pile of dead bodies at the bottom of the tunnel, illuminated eerily by a light beaming out of the smoking forward aid station.

Though he could hear the groans and occasional screams of the badly wounded, he knew that no one could have remained undamaged from that last grenade and that an attack from down there was now unlikely.

Slamming the trapdoor shut again to keep the smoke in, and aware that it would probably choke the wounded to death, Dead-eye turned away just as another muffled explosion rose from the far side of the empty cavern, up where the sleeping chamber was located. This was followed by a single, sustained scream so terrible that it blotted out the bawling of the men in the sleeping chamber.

With that chilling sound reverberating in his head, Dead-eye crawled through the darkness, lighting his way with the torch, until he reached the blast, gas and waterproof trapdoor. Lying there on his belly, still haunted by that terrible screaming, he switched off the torch, plunging the cavern into almost total darkness, and aimed his Browning at the tunnel leading down in a lazy curve from the sleeping chamber.

The agonized cries of the wounded man continued unabated.

It was Mad Mike who was screaming. Knowing from his map that the concealed trapdoor entrance to the sleeping chamber was almost perpendicular, sloping only slightly, and levelled out at the bottom over a camouflaged punji pit located between the tunnel and the sleeping chamber, Mike had raised the trapdoor and lowered himself down into the tunnel with extreme care, holding his thumb on the pin of the grenade in his left hand.

Though the tunnel was almost perpendicular, its circular wall had many man-made grooves which provided a tenuous hold for feet and hands; but holding the grenade, Mike had considerable difficulty in maintaining his balance and soon found himself sweating, not only from the suffocating heat and stench, but also from tension.

His intention was to climb down as closely as possible to the concealed trapdoor of the punji pit, then roll a couple of grenades over it, into the sleeping chamber. He would then dispatch the few survivors with his Browning, possibly following up with another grenade.

However, when he was only halfway down, the soil that formed the lip of one of the man-made grooves had come away in his hand and he felt himself falling backwards. Desperately using both hands to get a grip on something, he let the grenade go and it rolled down around the bend, where the tunnel levelled out, then across the trapdoor of the punji pit and on into the crowded sleeping chamber.

Mike had just managed to grab the lip of another groove and was desperately battling to regain his balance and position flat against the wall when the grenade exploded among the sleeping guerrillas.

Stunned by the noise, which reverberated dreadfully in the narrow tunnel, Mike lost first his grip, then his footing, fell backwards against the opposite wall, and slid down the tunnel.

Knowing exactly what was going to happen to him, he filled up with a blinding, heart-stopping fear and let out a strangled groan before falling on to the trapdoor, which tilted down under his weight and sent him plunging backwards on to the bed of poison and excrement-smeared, razor-sharp stakes in a pit of pitch darkness.

Pierced through his legs, arms and back, though his neck and head were missed, Mike spasmed relentlessly, helplessly, soaked in his own blood, blinded by it, choking on it, then released a long-drawn-out scream that blotted out the screaming of the VC in the sleeping chamber and seemed to him to reverberate for ever.

In fact, it was over quickly. Some of the surviving VC rushed out of the smoke-filled sleeping chamber and stopped at the lip of the booby-trap. Seeing that blood-soaked figure screaming in agony below them, and aware that he was the one who had killed or wounded so many of their comrades, they angrily emptied the magazines of their AK47s into him, making him spasm even more violently, blowing the stakes to pieces all around him, turning him into bloody flesh and bone, and finally – though they had not intended this – putting him out of his misery.

Unable to cross the punji pit, and having already heard the explosion from the direction of the forward aid station, the VC who had survived the grenade explosion in the sleeping chamber made their way back through the devastation, stepping over the groaning wounded and the bodies of their dead comrades, to raise the trapdoor and crawl one by one down the tunnel that led into the empty cavern containing the entrance to the forward aid station.

Waiting for them in the high-ceilinged cavern, Dead-eye saw them illuminated in the light pouring down the tunnel from the sleeping chamber. Knowing that if he shot the first man crawling out, the others might take another route to him, he waited until all five of them had crawled out before straightening up briefly and lobbing the grenade he had been holding in his hand. Even as it was arcing through the air, he dropped back down, stretched out on his belly and aimed his Browning two-handed at the guerrillas.

The sound of the exploding grenade was amplified tremendously in the large cavern and the group of VC were bowled over in all directions. Two remained where they had fallen, in the swirling smoke; one rolled on to his belly, badly wounded but still determined to fight; and the other two managed to get to their knees and aim their AK47s directly at Dead-eye.

They were too late. Dead-eye fired two shots, one at each man, and was already aiming at the wounded man before the other two fell. The wounded man managed to get off one shot, but weakened by loss of blood he couldn't hold the weapon steady and the bullet ricocheted off the wall high above Dead-eye's head. Dead-eye's third shot blew the man's brains out. All five men were dead.

Hearing another explosion, Dead-eye hurried over to the blast, gas and waterproof trapdoor, raised it, looked in, then carefully lowered himself down and began the arduous crawl along the narrow tunnel that led up to the conical air-raid shelter.

A whiff of smoke drifted down to him.

At the signal from Callaghan, Red lowered himself down into the rectangular pit shown on his map as the conference chamber. He had learnt from that same map that the trapdoor in the far-left-hand corner of that chamber led down, via a short, L-shaped tunnel, to the conical air-raid shelter.

Instead of going straight into the tunnel, Red spent some time examining the conference chamber and found some potentially useful maps and graphs curled up on the floor under the crude wooden table.

Satisfied that there was not much else of value, he went to the trapdoor and gently raised it with his left hand, holding his Browning in his right. There was enough light in the conference chamber to let him see most of the way down the unusually short tunnel before it curved out of sight to the right.

Leaning further forward, Red put his head sideways over the hole and listened with his left ear.

Convinced he could hear the murmuring of voices, therefore certain that the air-raid shelter was not only inhabited but was just around that bend about six feet down – too close for comfort – Red lowered the trapdoor again.

Aware from the map that there was a very narrow air vent running from the ground a few feet east of the conference chamber, down into the air-raid shelter, Red clambered out of the eastern side of the pit and went over to the concealed air vent. After removing the grass and leaves sprinkled over the flat, wooden cover, he removed the grille of the vent itself and stuck his ear to the hole. Again, but more distinctly, he heard the sound of murmuring from below.

Satisfied, he unclipped a grenade from his belt, released the pin, dropped the grenade into the vent, then rolled aside as fast as he could. He had just stopped rolling when he heard the muffled explosion from below, followed by screaming, then silence. He sprang to his feet, ran back to the rectangular pit, jumped down into the conference chamber and hurried back over to the trapdoor. Opening it, he smelt the smoke of the explosion drifting upwards, but heard no sound of movement from within.

Carefully lowering himself into the smoky darkness of the almost vertical tunnel, he practically slid down the rest of the way and almost became jammed in the sharp bend at the bottom. Realizing that it was wide enough for only the smallest of men, which he wasn't, he almost panicked, but eventually he managed to wriggle free and, having no other option, crawled backwards, his rectum tightening with the expectation of a bullet, into the smoke-filled air-raid shelter.

It was indeed conical and claustrophobically small. It also contained the bodies of two VC soldiers, both of whom had been badly scorched and slashed to ribbons.

Choking on the smoke, Red hurriedly raised the trapdoor in the floor, glanced in, saw nothing but the smoke that was escaping from the shelter, and carefully lowered himself down.

Again, it was an almost vertical tunnel, but it dropped only about six feet before turning right. Aware that even on hands and knees his back was scraping the top of the tunnel, and slightly unnerved by the almost total darkness, Red started sweating and then remembered to turn on his torch. Holding it awkwardly in one hand, tapping the ground ahead with the barrel of his Browning to check for booby-traps, and still sweating profusely, he made his way slowly along the tunnel until he came to a trapdoor located just before a dead-end.

With no other choice but to continue down even deeper into the tunnel complex – particularly since the smoke from the air-raid shelter was following him and starting to blind and choke him – Red tentatively raised the trapdoor and peered into the tunnel below.

He saw a pair of eyes staring up at him from behind the barrel of an automatic rifle.

It was Dead-eye.

'What the hell are you doing here?' Dead-eye whispered.

'I was going to make my way down as far as I could go,' Red replied, beginning to shake with the release of tension.

'I've cleared it all out down there,' Dead-eye told him, studying the tunnel Red had just come along. 'According to my map, if we go back in that direction, passing the vertical tunnel you just came down, we'll end up at the well. Let's see what's down there.'

Pouring sweat, breathing too deeply for comfort, Red nodded.

'OK,' he said. 'Only problem is, there's no room to turn in this tunnel, so I'll have to crawl backwards the whole way.'

'That way you might get a bullet up the arse,' Dead-eye told him. 'Look, I'm going to lower myself back down into this vertical tunnel – it's only six feet down to where it turns. When I'm at the bottom, you crawl across the trapdoor opening to the dead-end, then lower your legs into this hole. When you've done that, you can turn around and crawl out facing the way you've just come.'

'You beaut!' Red exclaimed.

They did just that: Dead-eye dropped to the bottom of his hole; Red crawled across it, lay belly down with his legs dangling down into it, turned around laboriously by clinging to the rim of the hole, and finally pulled himself back up on to the floor of the tunnel, back on to his hands and knees, but now facing in the right direction. When he moved off, shining his torch straight ahead, Dead-eye pulled himself up out of the vertical tunnel and followed him, also on hands and knees.

The two men advanced painfully along the tunnel, heading for the well. When they reached it, they found that the tunnel ended in the middle of the well, above twenty-five feet above the water-table, with another twenty-five up to the surface.

The bodies of two dead VC soldiers were sinking, one on top of the other, into the bloodied water below.

A rope had been slung from a rotating pole mounted between two Y-shaped uprights placed on two sides of the mouth of the well. The rope was now dangling free. At the opposite side of the well, but slightly higher than they were, was another tunnel.

From its dark mouth, a pair of eyes were staring at them.

They were Jimbo's.

After waving at them, Jimbo silently pointed directly below him with his index finger, indicating a deep groove that had been hacked out of the wall opposite the tunnel where Dead-eye and Red were kneeling. It was clear to both men that he meant they were to use it as a foothold.

'You mean we've got to straddle the two sides with both feet,' Red whispered, being out in front of Dead-eye, 'and then somehow swing around, grab the rope, pull ourselves up that couple of feet, and then swing ourselves into your tunnel?'

'That's right,' Jimbo replied. 'When you reach me, I'll grab you and haul you in.'

'I can't do that, mate,' Red said. 'I'm not claustrophobic – I've been down enough tunnels – but I've no head for heights.'

'Bullshit!' Jimbo retorted. 'I did it. And if I did it, you can.'

In fact, Jimbo was lying. He had not been forced to straddle the opposite sides of the circular wall. Instead, having been lowered into the top half of the well by rope, he had simply swung himself sideways and then thrown himself into the tunnel. But he knew that he would not help Red by telling him this.

'Turn towards me,' Jimbo whispered. 'Then

stretch out your right leg until your foot's resting in that groove. Keep your other foot on the floor of the tunnel. Without any delay or hesitation, you then swing your left foot off the floor of the tunnel, twist your body towards this wall, and reach up and grab hold of the rope. When you've done that, haul yourself up three feet, then kick the opposite wall to make yourself swing in my direction. Don't worry, I'll grab you.'

As the mouths of both tunnels widened enough to enable an average-sized man to stand upright, it was obvious that the fearless VC had done something similar to cross from one tunnel to the next. Knowing this, Red had no choice but to clip his torch back on to his belt, holster his Browning, stand upright, straddle the narrow well directly above the two dead bodies in the water twenty-five feet blow, then swing his left foot off the edge of the tunnel and grab for the rope.

He made it.

Dangling there, all that distance above the two dead VC, he almost blacked out with panic, but somehow managed to stay in control and gradually, painfully, hauled himself up until he was level with the floor of Jimbo's tunnel. Once there, he twisted around until his back was to Jimbo, raised his legs, pressed his feet against the wall, then pushed hard until he was swinging backwards. Flying into the wide mouth of the tunnel, into that dreadful darkness, he felt Jimbo's hands grabbing him and hauling him down to the ground. He was lying there, sprawled on top of Jimbo, when the rope sailed back out into the narrow well.

Breathing deeply, but immensely relieved, Red sat upright, then wriggled away to enable Jimbo to take up his original position at the mouth of the tunnel. When he did so, Dead-eye repeated Red's dangerous, acrobatic performance and was soon swinging backwards into Jimbo's embrace. Hauled in, he fell between the two men, then let the rope go.

Crawling to the edge of the tunnel, Dead-eye glanced down at the two guerrillas floating in the water, then turned back to Jimbo and asked, 'What happened?'

Jimbo shrugged. 'We rigged up this bucket-lowering contraption – like the well originally had – to lower me down, using the coiled rope as a stirrup for one foot. I was just above this tunnel – which, as you now know, is higher than the other – when one of those bastards came out of your tunnel, luckily with his back turned towards me. Stripped to the waist, he straddled the two sides of the wall and started lowering a bucket on a rope, obviously intending to collect water for his mates. So dangling there, directly above him, with my foot in the stirrup and holding the rope with one hand, I unholstered my nine-milly with the other and shot him through the top of the head. His head turned into a fucking pomegranate and he fell down through the well, into the water below.'

Jimbo grinned, clearly relishing his feat, before continuing. 'Two seconds later, his mate stuck his head out, looking up, not believing his bleeding eyes, and I got in a neat double-tap, popping him in the head, and he staggered about a bit, wondering where his head had gone, then fell off the edge of the tunnel and plunged into the water, right on top of his mate. I hung there a bit longer, waiting for more of the fuckers to materialize, and when they didn't, I swung myself on to here. I was just about to head off along this tunnel when I heard you two coming. Of course, I didn't know it was you – I thought it was Charlie – so you don't know how close you came to taking your last breath.'

Red grinned and shook his head from side to side. 'Jesus H. Christ!' he whispered.

'Where's Shagger?' Dead-eye asked.

'He went down through the kitchen,' Red told him, 'to try to find the connecting tunnel to the rest of the system. Apparently this system runs for miles – not just under this village, but under a hell of a lot more. Shagger wants to locate that connecting tunnel and block it, to stop the VC linking up again. We were hoping to meet up.'

'Where's the tunnel lead to?' Dead-eye asked.

'According to the map, down to a storage cache for weapons, explosives and rice. It's not on the map, but the defectors had reason to suspect that a passage leads from there to the connecting passage, which is used as a kind of supply route.'

'Then let's go,' Dead-eye said.

With Dead-eye in the lead, shining his dipped torch, they all crawled on their hands and knees along the dark, dank tunnel. After about ten minutes, when Red and even Jimbo were beginning to imagine fearfully that they were in a dead-end and might be trapped there for ever – buried alive, as it were, in this foul-smelling, pitch-black hole – they came to another trapdoor.

After giving a hand signal to indicate that the others should stay still and remain silent, Dead-eye switched off his torch, plunging them all into a terrifying, total darkness, then raised the trapdoor an inch. As he did so, light beamed up out of the tunnel. Peering through the slit between the trapdoor and the ground, Dead-eye saw a vertical tunnel of about five feet dropping down to a pile of packing crates, racks of weapons and boxes of rice. Raising the trapdoor a little higher, he heard the sound of boxes being moved about and of high-pitched Vietnamese conversation. It then dawned on him that they were now so far away from the rest of the complex that the VC down there probably still didn't know about the battle that had been fought in the other tunnels.

Not knowing exactly what was down there other than the supplies and the workers in charge of them, Dead-eye realized it would be foolish to just drop in and decided instead to throw in two grenades, then go in with the other men at the height of the commotion.

He had just unclipped two grenades from his belt and was releasing the pins when four loud explosions – almost certainly hand-grenades – occurred one after the other in quick succession, followed by much screaming and shouting.

Instantly, Dead-eye released the pins from his own two grenades and dropped them into the tunnel, right on top of the wooden crates directly below.

'Get down!' he bawled.

Although he and the other men were already on hands and knees, they dropped to their bellies, pressed their faces to the earth, and covered their ears with their hands.

The explosion was so noisy, so fierce, with flames even spitting up through the trapdoor near where Dead-eye was lying, that it could not possibly have been caused by two grenades alone. Then, when Dead-eye heard another explosion, then another, he realized that the grenades had set off the crates of explosive and ammunition, each explosion triggering another with devastating results.

Dead-eye lay near the trapdoor, pressing his face in the dirt, covering his ears with his hands, but still feeling the fierce heat coming up out of the tunnel and hearing the noise, despite blocking his ears. Eventually, however, the explosions tapered away and, when Dead-eye removed his hands, all he could hear were the moans and groans of the wounded.

'Let's go!' he snapped.

Crawling to the edge of the hole, he pulled himself to the other side until he was able to bend from the stomach down, with his legs dangling into the hole. When he was in that position, he unholstered his Browning, took the torch in his other hand, and let himself drop down through the tunnel.

Landing in the scorched debris of the exploded ammunition crates, sending expended shells clattering with each step he took, he turned around, saw only pitch-darkness, heard the moaning and groaning of the wounded on the floor, then finally switched on his torch, tensing himself for a VC bullet.

No bullet came. Instead, while the others dropped down through the tunnel behind him, also making a metallic racket as they trampled on expended shells, he saw in the beam of his torch the awesome devastation caused by the many explosions, with blistered, lacerated, bloody VC writhing and moaning amid pieces of blackened wood, bent nails, smashed weapons, piles of rice, lazily drifting dust, and a general stench of scorched human flesh, urine, excrement, cordite, burning wood and acrid smoke. Here and there, in the darkness, blue and yellow flames flickered eerily.

Suddenly, from that ghastly darkness filled with cries of human pain, Dead-eye's torch picked out a pair of human eyes staring along the barrel of an automatic rifle.

When the barrel was lowered, Dead-eye recognized Shagger.

In search of the connecting tunnel to the rest of the system, Shagger had gone down into the tunnel of the kitchen in its rectangular pit at ground level, followed it around for a good twenty minutes to a false tunnel with a dead-end, then was forced to go all the way back, backwards on his hands and knees. After checking his obviously outdated map, he had taken another tunnel which offered more hope because it was lined with camouflaged trapdoors and – as Shagger found out more than once when he tapped the ground ahead with the barrel of his Browning – more than one deadly punji pit.

Knowing that he could not place any weight on

either end of the punji pits' tilting lids, he had only been able to cross those he came to by throwing himself from his hands-and-knees posture directly on to the lid with his weight spread equidistant across it, midriff on the lid, hands on one side, feet on the other, and then inching slowly across to prevent the lid from tilting. Though this was effective, it took a tremendous amount of time and was extremely exhausting.

Eventually reaching another trapdoor that led into a descending tunnel, Shagger had slithered down into it, crawled along it, and finally came to another tunnel that linked it up with what – as he knew from his study of the VC map – could only have been the storage cache for weapons, explosives and rice.

Aware of this fact, he accepted that the tunnel he had found was the supply route to the other villages – the underground route he had been seeking.

Determined to destroy the storage cache and then arrange for another SAS sapper team to come down and block the connecting tunnel by laying delayed-timer explosives that would fill it with rubble, Shagger had rolled four hand-grenades, one after the other, down the tunnel, into the storage cache.

It was those explosions that Dead-eye had heard just before he sent down his own.

Now all of them, with the exception of the

unfortunate Mad Mike, had met up in the destroyed storage cache.

They had put the VC tunnel complex out of action.

After emotionally shaking hands, they crawled into one of the tunnels and made their way back to the surface, glad to see the light of day.

16

Shortly after the SAS men emerged from the tunnel complex, the remote smoke outlets from the kitchen were filled in with cement, to prevent smoke from escaping, then air blowers were used to force smoke through the trapdoors in the rectangular pits down into the tunnels, filling them with smoke and forcing out the last of the VC.

That other wounded VC may have been choked to death was an issue not widely discussed.

For the next three days, when the last of the VC had emerged and the smoke had cleared, the SAS men continued to search the complex and gradually discovered that it had contained a major VC headquarters hidden underground in a multi-level labyrinth covering a total area of approximately two square miles. The artificial village on top had been used as the living quarters and recreation area for the huge command post below, with the underground sleeping chamber used only for those on duty at any given time. Many weapons, including six 12.7mm anti-aircraft machine-guns, and more than 100,000 pages of invaluable documents, were uncovered during the next few days.

When it had been confirmed by the tunnel rats that every last VC had either been captured or killed, the connecting tunnel to the other tunnel complexes was filled with high explosive, which, when detonated by a timer device from the surface, filled the tunnel with densely packed rubble that would have been almost impossible to remove. The tunnel – and the VC supply route to the other underground tunnel complexes – was therefore blocked for good.

With this major job completed, as much as possible of the complex was destroyed and what was left was contaminated with crystallized CS tear-gas.

According to figures calculated from the actions taken at both the nearby village and the tunnel complex, 130 Viet Cong were killed, ninety-five were taken prisoner, and 509 suspects were rounded up for questioning. The Australian casualties were seven dead and twenty-three wounded.

By the time the operation had been completed, Lieutenant-Colonel Callaghan, Dead-eye and Jimbo had forged a strong friendship with the Australian 1 and 3 SAS Squadrons, based on mutual admiration and respect. The three men from 22 SAS stayed on in Vietnam for another month, taking part in other actions against the VC, including reconnaissance and more 'tunnel rat' operations. By the end of that month, they had learnt a lot about the enemy, about the Australian SAS, and about counter-insurgency operations in general.

Shortly after coming home, Lieutenant-Colonel Callaghan was returned to his original unit, 3 Commando, retired from active service, and assigned to a desk job in 3 Commando's Intelligence and Planning Department, where he put what he had learnt in Vietnam and elsewhere to good use.

Back in Hereford, Dead-eye and Jimbo kept in touch with Shagger and Red, swapping tall tales, insults and some more serious thoughts in regular letters. This correspondence ended abruptly seven months later. Dead-eye and Jimbo learnt that the two Aussies had been killed in the notorious multi-layered labyrinth of tunnels that centred on Cu Chi near Saigon and stretched as far as the Cambodian border.

Jimbo was sent back to the Radfan in 1967 to help cover the British withdrawal from Aden. On his return he was retired from active duty and transferred to the Training Wing, Hereford, as a reluctant member of the Directing Staff of 22 SAS.

Dead-eye, the youngest of the three SAS men, went on to serve in Belfast in 1976, then he too became a member of the Directing Staff. By that time, his old friend Jimbo, a victim of the passing years, had been retired completely from the service.

An era had ended.